# TO GREEN ANGEL TOWER:
# STORM

## Memory, Sorrow and Thorn
## Book Four

## Tad Williams

www.orbitbooks.co.uk

An *Orbit* Book

First published in Great Britain by Legend Books 1993
Reprinted by Orbit 1997, 1999, 2000, 2001, 2003, 2004, 2005

Copyright © Tad Williams 1993

A CIP catalogue record for this book
is available from the British Library.

ISBN 1 85723 583 5

Printed and bound in Great Britain by
Mackays of Chatham plc, Chatham, Kent

Orbit
A Imprint of
Time Warner Book Group UK
Brettenham House
Lancaster Place
London WC2E 7EN

This series is dedicated to my mother,
Barbara Jean Evans,
who taught me to search for other worlds,
and to share the things I find in them.


This final volume, *To Green Angel Tower*,
in itself a little world of heartbreak and joy,
I dedicate to Nancy Deming-Williams,
with much, much love.

# Author's Note

*And death shall have no dominion.*
*Dead men naked they shall be one*
*With the man in the wind and the west moon;*
*When their bones are picked clean and the clean bones*
  *gone*
*They shall have stars at elbow and foot;*
*Though they go mad they shall be sane,*
*Though they sink through the sea they shall rise again;*
*Though lovers be lost love shall not;*
*And death shall have no dominion . . .*

> ——DYLAN THOMAS
>    (from *"And Death Shall Have No*
>       *Dominion"*)

*Tell all the truth but tell it slant,*
*Success in circuit lies,*
*Too bright for our infirm delight*
*The truth's superb surprise;*

*As lightning to the children eased*
*With explanation kind,*
*The truth must dazzle gradually*
*Or every man be blind.*

> ——EMILY DICKINSON

*Tad Williams*

Many people gave me a great deal of help with these books, ranging from suggestions and moral support to crucial logistical aid. Eva Cumming, Nancy Deming-Williams, Arthur Ross Evans, Andrew Harris, Paul Hudspeth, Peter Stampfel, Doug Werner, Michael Whelan, the lovely folks at DAW Books, and all my friends on GEnie® make up only a small (but significant) sampling of those who helped me finish The Story That Ate My Life.

Particular thanks for assistance on this final volume of the Bloated Epic goes to Mary Frey, who put a bogglesome amount of energy and time into reading and—for lack of a better word—analyzing a monstrous manuscript. She gave me an incredible boost when I really needed it.

And, of course, the contributions of my editors, Sheila Gilbert and Betsy Wollheim, are incalculable. Caring a lot is their crime, and here at last is their well-deserved punishment.

To all of the above, and to all the other friends and supporters unmentioned but by no means unremembered, I give my most heartfelt thanks.

NOTE: There is a cast of characters, a glossary of terms, and a guide to pronunciation at the back of this book.

# Synopsis of
# The Dragonbone Chair

For eons the Hayholt belonged to the immortal Sithi, but they had fled the great castle before the onslaught of Mankind. Men have long ruled this greatest of strongholds, and the rest of Osten Ard as well. *Prester John,* High King of all the nations of men, is its most recent master; after an early life of triumph and glory, he has presided over decades of peace from his skeletal throne, the Dragonbone Chair.

*Simon,* an awkward fourteen year old, is one of the Hayholt's scullions. His parents are dead, his only real family the chambermaids and their stern mistress, *Rachel the Dragon.* When Simon can escape his kitchen-work he steals away to the cluttered chambers of *Doctor Morgenes,* the castle's eccentric scholar. When the old man invites Simon to be his apprentice, the youth is overjoyed—until he discovers that Morgenes prefers teaching reading and writing to magic.

Soon ancient King John will die, so *Elias,* the older of his two sons, prepares to take the throne. *Josua,* Elias' somber brother, nicknamed Lackhand because of a disfiguring wound, argues harshly with the king-to-be about *Pryrates,* the ill-reputed priest who is one of Elias' closest advisers. The brothers' feud is a cloud of foreboding over castle and country.

Elias' reign as king starts well, but a drought comes and plague strikes several of the nations of Osten Ard.

Soon outlaws roam the roads and people begin to vanish from isolated villages. The order of things is breaking down, and the king's subjects are losing confidence in his rule, but nothing seems to bother the monarch or his friends. As rumblings of discontent begin to be heard throughout the kingdom, Elias' brother Josua disappears—to plot rebellion, some say.

Elias' misrule upsets many, including *Duke Isgrimnur* of Rimmersgard and *Count Eolair,* an emissary from the western country of Hernystir. Even King Elias' own daughter *Miriamele* is uneasy, especially about the scarlet-robed Pryrates, her father's trusted adviser.

Meanwhile Simon is muddling along as Morgenes' helper. The two become fast friends despite Simon's mooncalf nature and the doctor's refusal to teach him anything resembling magic. During one of his meanderings through the secret byways of the labyrinthine Hayholt, Simon discovers a secret passage and is almost captured there by Pryrates. Eluding the priest, he enters a hidden underground chamber and finds Josua, who is being held captive for use in some terrible ritual planned by Pryrates. Simon fetches Doctor Morgenes and the two of them free Josua and take him to the doctor's chambers, where Josua is sent to freedom down a tunnel that leads beneath the ancient castle. Then, as Morgenes is sending off messenger birds to mysterious friends, bearing news of what has happened, Pryrates and the king's guard come to arrest the doctor and Simon. Morgenes is killed fighting Pryrates, but his sacrifice allows Simon to escape into the tunnel.

Half-maddened, Simon makes his way through the midnight corridors beneath the castle, which contain the ruins of the old Sithi palace. He surfaces in the graveyard beyond the town wall, then is lured by the light of a bonfire. He witnesses a weird scene: Pryrates and King Elias engaged in a ritual with black-robed, white-faced creatures. The pale things give Elias a strange gray sword of disturbing power, named *Sorrow.* Simon flees.

Life in the wilderness on the edge of the great forest Aldheorte is miserable, and weeks later Simon is nearly dead from hunger and exhaustion, but still far away from his destination, Josua's northern keep at Naglimund. Going to a forest cot to beg, he finds a strange being caught in a trap—one of the Sithi, a race thought to be mythical, or at least long-vanished. The cotsman returns, but before he can kill the helpless Sitha, Simon strikes him down. The Sitha, once freed, stops only long enough to fire a white arrow at Simon, then disappears. A new voice tells Simon to take the white arrow, that it is a Sithi gift.

The dwarfish newcomer is a troll named *Binabik,* who rides a great gray wolf. He tells Simon he was only passing by, but now he will accompany the boy to Naglimund. Simon and Binabik endure many adventures and strange events on the way to Naglimund: they come to realize that they have fallen afoul of a threat greater than merely a king and his counselor deprived of their prisoner. At last, when they find themselves pursued by unearthly white hounds who wear the brand of Stormspike, a mountain of evil reputation in the far north, they are forced to head for the shelter of *Geloë*'s forest house, taking with them a pair of travelers they have rescued from the hounds. Geloë, a blunt-spoken forest woman with a reputation as a witch, confers with them and agrees that somehow the ancient Norns, embittered relatives of the Sithi, have become embroiled in the fate of Prester John's kingdom.

Pursuers human and otherwise threaten them on their journey to Naglimund. After Binabik is shot with an arrow, Simon and one of the rescued travelers, a servant girl, must struggle on through the forest. They are attacked by a shaggy giant and saved only by the appearance of Josua's hunting party.

The prince brings them to Naglimund, where Binabik's wounds are cared for, and where it is confirmed that Simon has stumbled into a terrifying swirl of events. Elias is coming soon to besiege Josua's castle. Simon's serving-girl companion was Princess Miriamele traveling in disguise, fleeing her father, whom she fears has gone mad under Pryrates' influence. From all over the north and elsewhere, frightened people are flocking to Naglimund and Josua, their last protection against a mad king.

Then, as the prince and others discuss the coming battle, a strange old Rimmersman named *Jarnauga* appears in the council's meeting hall. He is a member of the *League of the Scroll,* a circle of scholars and initiates of which Morgenes and Binabik's master were both part, and he brings more grim news. Their enemy, he says, is not just Elias: the king is receiving aid from *Ineluki the Storm King,* who had once been a prince of the Sithi—but who has been dead for five centuries, and whose bodiless spirit now rules the Norns of Stormspike Mountain, pale relatives of the banished Sithi.

It was the terrible magic of the gray sword Sorrow that caused Ineluki's death—that, and mankind's attack on the Sithi. The League of the Scroll believes that Sorrow has been given to Elias as the first step in some incomprehensible plan of revenge, a plan that will bring the earth beneath the heel of the undead Storm King. The only hope comes from a prophetic poem that seems to suggest that "three swords" might help turn back Ineluki's powerful magic.

One of the swords is the Storm King's Sorrow, already in the hands of their enemy, King Elias. Another is the Rimmersgard blade *Minneyar,* which was also once at the Hayholt, but whose whereabouts are now unknown. The third is *Thorn,* black sword of King John's greatest knight, *Sir Camaris.* Jarnauga and others think they have traced it to a location in the frozen north. On this slim hope, Josua sends Binabik, Simon, and several soldiers off in search of Thorn, even as Naglimund prepares for siege.

Others are affected by the growing crisis. Princess Miriamele, frustrated by her uncle Josua's attempts to protect her, escapes Naglimund in disguise, accompanied by the mysterious monk *Cadrach.* She hopes to make her way to southern Nabban and plead with her relatives there to aid Josua. Old Duke Isgrimnur, at Josua's urging, disguises his own very recognizable features and follows after to rescue her. *Tiamak,* a swamp-dwelling

Wrannaman scholar, receives a strange message from his old mentor Morgenes that tells of bad times coming and hints that Tiamak has a part to play. *Maegwin,* daughter of the king of Hernystir, watches helplessly as her own family and country are drawn into a whirlpool of war by the treachery of High King Elias.

Simon and Binabik and their company are ambushed by *Ingen Jegger,* huntsman of Stormspike, and his servants. They are saved only by the reappearance of the Sitha *Jiriki,* whom Simon had saved from the cotsman's trap. When he learns of their quest, Jiriki decides to accompany them to Urmsheim Mountain, legendary abode of one of the great dragons, in search of Thorn.

By the time Simon and the others reach the mountain, King Elias has brought his besieging army to Josua's castle at Naglimund, and though the first attacks are repulsed, the defenders suffer great losses. At last Elias' forces seem to retreat and give up the siege, but before the stronghold's inhabitants can celebrate, a weird storm appears on the northern horizon, bearing down on Naglimund. The storm is the cloak under which Ineluki's own horrifying army of Norns and giants travels, and when the *Red Hand,* the Storm King's chief servants, throw down Naglimund's gates, a terrible slaughter begins. Josua and a few others manage to flee the ruin of the castle. Before escaping into the great forest, Prince Josua curses Elias for his conscienceless bargain with the Storm King and swears that he will take their father's crown back.

Simon and his companions climb Urmsheim, coming through great dangers to discover the Uduntree, a titanic frozen waterfall. There they find Thorn in a tomblike cave. Before they can take the sword and make their escape, Ingen Jegger appears once more and attacks with his troop of soldiers. The battle awakens *Igjarjuk,* the white dragon, who has been slumbering for years beneath the ice. Many on both sides are killed. Simon alone is left standing, trapped on the edge of a cliff; as the ice-worm bears down upon him, he lifts Thorn and swings it. The dragon's scalding black blood spurts over him as he is struck senseless.

Simon awakens in a cave on the troll mountain of Yiqanuc. Jiriki and *Haestan,* an Erkynlandish soldier, nurse him to health. Thorn has been rescued from Urmsheim, but Binabik is being held prisoner by his own people, along with *Sludig* the Rimmersman, under sentence of death. Simon himself has been scarred by the dragon's blood and a wide swath of his hair has turned white. Jiriki names him "Snowlock" and tells Simon that, for good or for evil, he has been irrevocably marked.

# Synopsis of
# Stone of Farewell

*Simon*, the Sitha *Jiriki*, and soldier *Haestan* are honored
guests in the mountaintop city of the diminutive Qanuc
trolls. But *Sludig*—whose Rimmersgard folk are the
Qanuc's ancient enemies—and Simon's troll friend
*Binabik* are not so well treated; Binabik's people hold
them both captive, under sentence of death. An audience
with the *Herder* and *Huntress*, rulers of the Qanuc,
reveals that Binabik is being blamed not only for desert-
ing his tribe, but for failing to fulfill his vow of marriage
to *Sisqi*, youngest daughter of the reigning family. Simon
begs Jiriki to intercede, but the Sitha has obligations to
his own family, and will not in any case interfere with
trollish justice. Shortly before the executions, Jiriki departs for his home.

Although Sisqi is bitter about Binabik's seeming fickle-
ness, she cannot stand to see him killed. With Simon and
Haestan, she arranges a rescue of the two prisoners, but
as they seek a scroll from Binabik's master's cave which
will give them the information necessary to find a place
named the Stone of Farewell—which Simon has learned
of in a vision—they are recaptured by the angry Qanuc
leaders. But Binabik's master's death-testament confirms
the troll's story of his absence, and its warnings finally
convince the Herder and Huntress that there are indeed
dangers to all the land which they have not understood.
After some discussion, the prisoners are pardoned and Si-

mon and his companions are given permission to leave Yiqanuc and take the powerful sword *Thorn* to exiled *Prince Josua*. Sisqi and other trolls will accompany them as far as the base of the mountains.

Meanwhile, Josua and a small band of followers have escaped the destruction of Naglimund and are wandering through the Aldheorte Forest, chased by the *Storm King's* Norns. They must defend themselves against not only arrows and spears but dark magic, but at last they are met by *Geloë*, the forest woman, and *Leleth*, the mute child Simon had rescued from the terrible hounds of Stormspike. The strange pair lead Josua's party through the forest to a place that once belonged to the Sithi, where the Norns dare not pursue them for fear of breaking the ancient Pact between the sundered kin. Geloë then tells them they should travel on to another place even more sacred to the Sithi, the same Stone of Farewell to which she had directed Simon in the vision she sent him.

*Miriamele*, daughter of *High King Elias* and niece of Josua, is traveling south in hope of finding allies for Josua among her relatives in the courts of Nabban; she is accompanied by the dissolute monk *Cadrach*. They are captured by *Count Streáwe* of Perdruin, a cunning and mercenary man, who tells Miriamele he is going to deliver her to an unnamed person to whom he owes a debt. To Miriamele's joy, this mysterious personage turns out to be a friend, the priest *Dinivan*, who is secretary to *Lector Ranessin*, leader of Mother Church. Dinivan is secretly a member of the League of the Scroll, and hopes that Miriamele can convince the lector to denounce Elias and his counselor, the renegade priest *Pryrates*. Mother Church is under siege, not only from Elias, who demands the church not interfere with him, but from the *Fire Dancers*, religious fanatics who claim the Storm King comes to them in dreams. Ranessin listens to what Miriamele has to say and is very troubled.

Simon and his companions are attacked by snow-giants on their way down from the high mountains, and the soldier Haestan and many trolls are killed. Later, as he broods on the injustice of life and death, Simon inadvertently awakens the Sitha mirror Jiriki had given him as a summoning charm, and travels on the Dream Road to encounter first the Sitha matriarch *Amerasu,* then the terrible Norn Queen *Utuk'ku.* Amerasu is trying to understand the schemes of Utuk'ku and the Storm King, and is traveling the Dream Road in search of both wisdom and allies.

Josua and the remainder of his company at last emerge from the forest onto the grasslands of the High Thrithing, where they are almost immediately captured by the nomadic clan led by March-Thane *Fikolmij,* who is the father of Josua's lover *Vorzheva.* Fikolmij begrudges the loss of his daughter, and after beating the prince severely, arranges a duel in which he intends that Josua should be killed; Fikolmij's plan fails and Josua survives. Fikolmij is then forced to pay off a bet by giving the prince's company horses. Josua, strongly affected by the shame Vorzheva feels at seeing her people again, marries her in front of Fikolmij and the assembled clan. When Vorzheva's father gleefully announces that soldiers of King Elias are coming across the grasslands to capture them, the prince and his followers ride away east toward the Stone of Farewell.

In far off Hernystir, *Maegwin* is the last of her line. Her father the king and her brother have both been killed fighting Elias' pawn *Skali,* and she and her people have taken refuge in caves in the Grianspog Mountains. Maegwin has been troubled by strange dreams, and finds herself drawn down into the old mines and caverns beneath the Grianspog. *Count Eolair,* her father's most trusted liege-man, goes in search of her, and together he and Maegwin enter the great underground city of Mezutu'a. Maegwin is convinced that the Sithi live there, and that they will come to the rescue of the Hernystiri as they did in the old days, but the only inhabitants they discover in the crumbling city are the *dwarrows,* a strange, timid group of delvers distantly related to the immortals. The dwarrows, who are metalwrights as well as stonecrafters, reveal that the sword *Minneyar* that Josua's people seek is actually the blade known as *Bright-Nail,* which was buried with *Prester John*, father of Josua and Elias. This news means little to Maegwin, who is shattered to find that her dreams have brought her people no real assistance. She is also at least as troubled by what she considers her foolish love for Eolair, so she invents an errand for him—taking news of Minneyar and maps of the dwarrows' diggings, which include tunnels below Elias' castle, the Hayholt, to Josua and his band of survivors. Eolair is puzzled and angry at being sent away, but goes.

Simon and Binabik and Sludig leave Sisqi and the other trolls at the base of the mountain and continue across the icy vastness of the White Waste. Just at the northern edge of the great forest, they find an old abbey inhabited by children and their caretaker, an older girl named *Skodi*. They stay the night, glad to be out of the cold, but Skodi proves to be more than she seems: in the darkness, she traps the three of them by witchcraft, then begins a ceremony in which she intends to invoke the Storm King and show him that she has captured the sword Thorn. One of the undead *Red Hand* appears because of Skodi's spell, but a child disrupts the ritual and brings up a monstrous swarm of *diggers*. Skodi and the children are killed, but Simon and the others escape, thanks largely to Binabik's fierce wolf *Qantaqa*. But Simon is almost mad from the mind-touch of the Red Hand, and rides away from his companions, crashing into a tree at last and striking himself senseless. He falls down a gulley, and Binabik and Sludig are unable to find him. At last, full of remorse, they take the sword Thorn and continue on toward the Stone of Farewell without him.

Several people besides Miriamele and Cadrach have arrived at the lector's palace in Nabban. One of them is Josua's ally *Duke Isgrimnur*, who is searching for Miriamele. Another is Pryrates, who has come to bring Lector Ranessin an ultimatum from the king. The lector angrily denounces both Pryrates and Elias; the king's emissary walks out of the banquet, threatening revenge.

That night, Pryrates metamorphoses himself with a spell he has been given by the Storm King's servitors, and becomes a shadowy *thing*. He kills Dinivan and then brutally murders the lector. Afterward, he sets the halls aflame to cast suspicion on the Fire Dancers. Cadrach, who greatly fears Pryrates and has spent the night urging Miriamele to flee the lector's palace with him, finally knocks her senseless and drags her away. Isgrimnur finds the dying Dinivan, and is given a Scroll League token for the Wrannaman *Tiamak* and instructions to go to the inn named *Pelippa's Bowl* in Kwanitupul, a city on the edge of the marshes south of Nabban.

Tiamak, meanwhile, has received an earlier message from Dinivan and is on his way to Kwanitupul, although his journey almost ends when he is attacked by a crocodile. Wounded and feverish, he arrives at *Pelippa's Bowl* at last and gets an unsympathetic welcome from the new landlady.

Miriamele awakens to find that Cadrach has smuggled her into the hold of a ship. While the monk has lain in drunken sleep, the ship has set sail. They are quickly found by *Gan Itai*, a Niskie, whose job is to keep the ship safe from the menacing aquatic creatures called *kilpa*. Although Gan Itai takes a liking to the stowaways, she nevertheless turns them over to the ship's master, *Aspitis Preves*, a young Nabbanai nobleman.

Far to the north, Simon has awakened from a dream in which he again heard the Sitha-woman Amerasu, and in which he has discovered that Ineluki the Storm King is her son. Simon is now lost and alone in the trackless, snow-covered Aldheorte Forest. He tries to use Jiriki's mirror to summon help, but no one answers his plea. At last he sets out in what he hopes is the right direction, although he knows he has little chance of crossing the scores of leagues of winterbound woods alive. He ekes out a meager living on bugs and grass, but it seems only a question of whether he will first go completely mad or starve to death. He is finally saved by the appearance of Jiriki's sister *Aditu*, who has come in response to the mirror-summoning. She works a kind of traveling-magic that appears to turn winter into summer, and when it is finished, she and Simon enter the hidden Sithi stronghold of Jao é-Tinukai'i. It is a place of magical beauty and timelessness. When Jiriki welcomes him, Simon's joy is great; moments later, when he is taken to see *Likimeya* and *Shima'onari,* parents of Jiriki and Aditu, that joy turns to horror. The leaders of the Sithi say that since no mortal has ever been permitted in secret Jao é-Tinukai'i, Simon must stay there forever.

Josua and his company are pursued into the northern grasslands, but when they turn at last in desperate resistance, it is to find that these latest pursuers are not Elias' soldiers, but Thrithings-folk who have deserted Fikolmij's clan to throw in their lot with the prince. Together, and with Geloë leading the way, they at last reach Sesuad'ra, the Stone of Farewell, a great stone hill in the middle of a wide valley. Sesuad'ra was the place in which the Pact between the Sithi and Norns was made, and where the parting of the two kin took place. Josua's long-suffering company rejoices at finally possessing what will be, for a little while, a safe haven. They also hope they can now discover what property of the three Great Swords will allow them to defeat Elias and the Storm King, as promised in the ancient rhyme of *Nisses.*

Back at the Hayholt, Elias' madness seems to grow ever deeper, and *Earl Guthwulf,* once the king's favorite, begins to doubt the king's fitness to rule. When Elias forces him to touch the gray sword *Sorrow,* Guthwulf is almost consumed by the sword's strange inner power, and is never after the same. *Rachel the Dragon,* the Mistress of Chambermaids, is another Hayholt denizen dismayed by what she sees happening around her. She learns that the priest Pryrates was responsible for what she thinks was Simon's death, and decides something must be done. When Pryrates returns from Nabban, she stabs him. The priest has become so powerful that he is only slightly injured, but when he turns to blast Rachel with withering magics, Guthwulf interferes and is blinded. Rachel escapes in the confusion.

Miriamele and Cadrach, having told the ship's master Aspitis that she is the daughter of a minor nobleman, are treated with hospitality; Miriamele in particular comes in for much attention. Cadrach becomes increasingly morose, and when he tries to escape the ship, Aspitis has him put in irons. Miriamele, feeling trapped and helpless and alone, allows Aspitis to seduce her.

Meanwhile, Isgrimnur has laboriously made his way south to Kwanitupul. He finds Tiamak staying at the inn, but no sign of Miriamele. His disappointment is quickly overwhelmed by astonishment when he discovers that the old simpleton who works as the inn's doorkeeper is *Sir Camaris*, the greatest knight of Prester John's era, the man who once wielded Thorn. Camaris was thought to have died forty years earlier, but what truly happened remains a mystery, because the old knight is as witless as a very young child.

Still carrying the sword Thorn, Binabik and Sludig escape pursuing snow-giants by building a raft and floating across the great storm-filled lake that was once the valley around the Stone of Farewell.

In Jao é-Tinukai'i, Simon's imprisonment is more boring than frightening, but his fears for his embattled friends are great. The Sitha First Grandmother Amerasu calls for him, and Jiriki brings him to her strange house. She probes Simon's memories for anything that might help her to discern the Storm King's plans, then sends him away.

Several days later Simon is summoned to a gathering of all the Sithi. Amerasu announces she will tell them what she has learned of Ineluki, but first she berates her people for their unwillingness to fight and their unhealthy obsession with memory and, ultimately, with death. She brings out one of the Witnesses, an object which, like Jiriki's mirror, allows access to the Road of Dreams. Amerasu is about to show Simon and the assembled Sithi what the Storm King and Norn Queen are doing, but instead Utuk'ku herself appears in the Witness and denounces Amerasu as a lover of mortals and a meddler. One of the Red Hand is then manifested, and while Jiriki and the other Sithi battle the flaming spirit, *Ingen Jegger*, the Norn Queen's mortal huntsman, forces his way into

Jao é-Tinukai'i and murders Amerasu, silencing her before she can share her discoveries.

Ingen is killed and the Red Hand is driven away, but the damage has been done. With all the Sithi plunged into mourning, Jiriki's parents rescind their sentence and send Simon, with Aditu for a guide, out of Jao é-Tinukai'i. As he departs, he notices that the perpetual summer of the Sithi haven has become a little colder.

At the forest's edge Aditu puts him in a boat and gives him a parcel from Amerasu that is to be taken to Josua. Simon then makes his way across the rainwater lake to the Stone of Farewell, where he is met by his friends. For a little while, Simon and the rest will be safe from the growing storm.

# Synopsis of
# *To Green Angel Tower*
# (Part One)

*Simon* and most of his companions have taken refuge with *Prince Josua* on Sesuad'ra—the great hill famous in Sithi history as the Stone of Farewell. There they wait and hope for some break in the storm clouds of war and fear that Josua's brother, *King Elias,* and his undead ally, *Ineluki the Storm King,* have set into swirling motion.

Simon is knighted for his services to Josua and his aid in the recovery of the sword Thorn. As he spends his vigil night in the old Sithi ruins, he sees a vision of The Parting, the day in the dim past when the Sithi and the Norns sundered the links between their two families. Soon after Simon is knighted, the Hernystirman *Eolair* arrives at Sesuad'ra with news he has gained from the subterranean *dwarrows: King John*'s sword, Bright-Nail, was actually the older sword Minneyar, one of three blades that an ancient rhyme suggests might be the only help against Ineluki and his dark sorceries. But Bright-Nail is buried in John's barrow, only a short distance from the Hayholt, Elias' castle fortress; there seems little chance of capturing it.

Far to the south, King Elias' daughter *Miriamele* has become the lover and increasingly unwilling guest of a Nabbanai lord, *Aspitis Preves.* When Aspitis reveals his plans to marry her she rebels, but he reveals that he knows her true identity and that one way or another, he will have her as his bride, to use as a political tool, Miriamele's companion, the monk *Cadrach,* has already been imprisoned; her only ally is the Niskie, *Gan Itai.*

At Sesuad'ra, Prince Josua decides to send *Duke Isgrimnur's* son *Isorn* to accompany Eolair back to Hernystir, hoping that along the way he can recruit some of the Rimmersmen scattered by war, aid Eolair's people, and then return to help Josua and the others. But soon after the mission departs, Josua, Simon and the others discover that King Elias has sent an army led by *Duke Fengbald* to bring his brother to heel. Simon, the witch-woman *Geloë,* and others use the power of the old Sithi ruins to walk the Dream-Road in an effort to summon to Sesuad'ra anyone who might help them.

In Hernystir, *Maegwin,* the king's daughter, is searching frantically for a way to save her defeated people, now living in caves in the mountains. She climbs a high peak and falls into a prophetic dream where she unwittingly encounters Simon, who is searching the Dream-Road for Miriamele. Maegwin experiences the dream-meeting between Simon and his Sitha friend *Jiriki* as a colloquy between the gods and heroes of her people, and interprets it as a sign from Heaven.

In the marsh-city of Kwanitupul, *Tiamak* the Wrannaman, Duke Isgrimnur, and the apparently senile great hero, *Camaris,* all wait at an inn for Miriamele. Tiamak is attacked by *Fire Dancers,* members of a human cult who worship the Storm King, but is saved by Camaris.

Deep beneath the Hayholt, Elias' mighty castle, *Guthwulf,* the king's onetime friend and general, wanders in darkness. He has been blinded by a spell from the alchemist *Pryrates,* and except for the companionship of a cat, is alone and nearly mad with grief and regret. Elsewhere in the castle's depths, *Rachel the Dragon,* former Mistress of Chambermaids, hides from the king and Pryrates, determined to survive until better days return.

Sesuad'ra prepares for war. Newly-knighted Simon leads a sortie to spy on Fengbald's camp. On the way back, he and his company see mysterious lights on the banks of the freezing lake that surrounds the Stone of

Farewell. Later, Simon's friend *Binabik* takes him to the source of the lights—a camp of the little man's troll kin, brought by Binabik's beloved *Sisqi* to fight for Josua. The reunion brings a moment of joy in a dark time.

On Aspitis' ship, Miriamele is helped by Gan Itai, first to talk to imprisoned Cadrach, then to plan an escape. Gan Itai is angered by Miriamele's discovery that Aspitis is aiding the Fire Dancers, who have persecuted the Niskies, and so instead of using her magical song to keep the demonic *kilpa* at bay, she brings the sea-creatures up to attack the ship. During the bloodletting and confusion, Miriamele gravely wounds Aspitis and she and Cadrach escape in a small boat. As they float on the empty ocean the next day, Cadrach tells her of his life, how he had been recruited by *Doctor Morgenes* into the League of the Scroll, but how his own dissolute ways and the discovery of a terrible old book, *Du Svardenvyrd,* had caused him to despair and fall away from the other Scrollbearers. Later, he had been captured by Pryrates—once a Scrollbearer himself, before the others found out his true nature—and tortured into revealing where he had disposed of the forbidden volume.

In the depths of Aldheorte forest the Sithi are mustering, for the first time in centuries, but whether they will come to the aid of Prince Josua and Simon, even Jiriki cannot say.

Duke Fengbald brings his army to the base of Sesuad'ra, camping on the shore of the frozen lake around the great hill. Josua's ragtag army prepares its resistance, and in a day of fierce fighting manages to hold its own against a superior force. Still, Simon and his friends are outnumbered, and they have little hope that they will be victorious in the end. But Fengbald, in an attempt to take Sesuad'ra by treachery, is himself caught in a trap, and drowns in the black water and crumbling ice floes of the lake.

In the west, Maegwin and the other Hernystiri, driven by the mistaken vision she has had during her vigil, emerge from the mountain caves to confront those who have driven them out of their homes, the army of *Skali* of Rimmersgard, King Elias' ally. At first it seems that they have merely hastened their doom, but the sudden appearance of the Sithi, come to repay their old debt to Hernystir, puts Skali and his men to flight. Maegwin, convinced that she has seen the gods themselves come down to earth to save her people, tips over into madness. When Eolair returns to Hernystir, it is to find the strange Sithi in full occupation and Maegwin convinced that she herself was killed in the battle—and that therefore Eolair too must be dead, her companion in the afterlife.

In the south, Miriamele and Cadrach at last reach Kwanitupul where they meet Isgrimnur and Tiamak, as well as the even more suprising spectacle of a resurrected Camaris. Before they can do more than exchange hurried news they learn that Aspitis, anxious for vengeance, has discovered their whereabouts. They escape the city just ahead of Miriamele's spurned lover and his soldiers, taking a small boat into the Wran, the vast and dangerous swamp that is Tiamak's home.

Things have changed in the Wran. The discovery that the people of Tiamak's village have vanished is followed rapidly by Tiamak's own disappearance. Helpless without a guide, Miriamele and her companions struggle to find their way out. They find another Wrannaman floating dazed and feverish in Tiamak's boat, and from him learn that Tiamak has been taken by the subhuman *ghants* and is being held prisoner—if he still lives—in their sprawling mud nest.

Cadrach is terrified of the nest, but Miriamele, Isgrimnur and Camaris enter it in search of Tiamak, and find him being used by the ghants as the centerpiece of a strange ritual. They rescue the little Wrannaman and bring him out into the light once more.

Back on Sesuad'ra, Simon and the others bury their dead, among whom is Josua's most stalwart companion, *Sir Deornoth*. The cost of defeating Fengbald has been very high, and their greater enemies, Elias and the Storm King, have not even begun to exert themselves. At a somewhat muted victory celebration, Simon's romantic encounter with a local girl is interrupted by the sudden appearance of *Aditu,* Jiriki's sister, who has come as an envoy. The Sithi are going to take a part in mortal wars for the first time in five centuries.

In the Hayholt, the High King is troubled. His soldiers have been defeated by Josua's peasant army, and now the immortals themselves have entered the fray. Pryrates tries to reassure him, but it is clear that he and Elias are pursuing separate strategies. Beneath the castle, Rachel the Dragon has a frightening encounter with the king's demented cupbearer, *Hengfisk,* and Guthwulf finds himself increasingly drawn by the magical pull of the king's sword, Sorrow, and its yearning for its brother swords.

Under the icy mountain Stormspike, the Norn Queen *Utuk'ku* is also troubled by events, and dispatches a team of assassins southward.

Miriamele and the others make their way out of the Wran. Relations are strained within the company—Tiamak thinks Cadrach is trying to steal his precious scroll, and Isgrimnur and Cadrach's arguments have also caused a smoldering distrust. After Aspitis Preves catches them at last on the fringes of the marsh, but is defeated by an unwilling Camaris, Cadrach steals a horse and disappears. Miriamele and the others push on toward Sesuad'ra and Josua. They reach Sesuad'ra at last, reviving hopes and bringing important news about Nabban and the Fire Dancers.

Simon is more than a little overwhelmed by Miriamele's return, and she in turn is suprised to see that the kitchen-boy she remembered is almost a grown man. Their friendship has an edge of attraction with which neither is quite comfortable. When she rejects his attempt to gift her with the White Arrow, he insists she let him become her knightly Protector. Pleased but troubled, Miriamele agrees.

Prince Josua mourns Deornoth and the other lost lives and tries to decide what to do next. Sesuad'ra's growing population and the Storm King's terrible winter have combined to reduce their resources almost to nothing. The prince's companions seem evenly split between pursuing the war against Elias into Erkynland or forging southward into Nabban in hopes of toppling the High King's more vulnerable ally, *Benigaris,* and using the Nabbani forces to bring them closer to parity with the king's power. Josua decides on this latter course, despite fierce opposition from Miriamele, who will not explain all her reasons, and from Simon, who wants a chance to reclaim the sword Bright-Nail from King John's barrow near the Hayholt.

Tiamak and *Father Strangyeard* become Scrollbearers, and with Binabik and Geloë they struggle to interpret Tiamak's scroll. It seems to speak of Camaris, whose wits are still clouded, and when they realize that the gift *Amerasu* of the Sithi sent to Josua with Simon is Camaris' old battle-horn, they resolve to try to bring him back to his senses. After the horn and the blade Thorn are put into his hands, and Josua implores him not to let Deornoth have died in vain, Camaris re-awakens, full of secret sorrow, but willing to do what he can to stem the encroaching tide of darkness. Josua's company prepare to move south.

In Hernystir, Eolair leads Jiriki down into the mountain fastnesses where he and Maegwin had encountered the shy dwarrows, but the cave-dwellers have fled, and only their magical Witness, the Shard, is left behind. Jiriki tries to turn it to his own purposes, but a more powerful force takes hold of it and he is almost killed, saved only by Eolair's intervention. Afterward, Jiriki and his mother *Likimeya* proclaim that they will lead the Sithi toward Josua's old stronghold Naglimund, which is now in the posession of the Norns. Eolair and some Hernystiri volunteer to go with them. Maegwin insists on coming along, and Eolair, despite his worries about her continuing delusions, has no choice but to accede.

Josua and company make camp, unaware that they are being stalked by Utuk'ku's Norn assassins. Geloë and Aditu discuss the mystery of Camaris, sharing fears that it may have something to do with the current conflict. Simon searches the camp for Miriamele and discovers her trying to escape the camp and set out on her own. She begs him not to stop her. Torn between his duty to Josua and his fears for Miriamele's safety, he at last decides to accompany her—he is, after all, her Protector. Together they ride out, leaving nothing behind but Simon's hasty note. As they depart, they see fire and smoke behind them. The camp has been attacked.

End of SIEGE

# PART ONE

❧

# The
# Turning Wheel

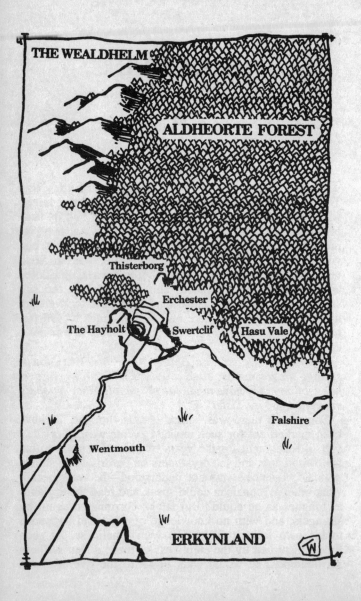

# 1

# Tears and Smoke

✵

**Tiamak found** the empty treelessness of the High Thrithing oppressive. Kwanitupul was strange, too, but he had been visiting that place since childhood, and its tumbledown buildings and ubiquitous waterways at least reminded him a little of his marshy home. Even Perdruin, where he had spent time in lonely exile, was so filled with close-leaning walls and narrow pathways, so riddled with shadowy hiding places and blanketed in the salt smell of the sea, that Tiamak had been able to live with his homesickness. But here on the grasslands he felt tremendously exposed and utterly out of place. It was not a comforting feeling.

*They Who Watch and Shape have indeed made a strange life for me,* he often reflected. *The strangest, perhaps, of any they have made for my people since Nuobdig married the Fire Sister.*

Sometimes there was solace in this thought. To have been marked out for such unusual events was, after all, a sort of repayment for the years of misunderstanding that his own people and the drylanders on Perdruin had shown him. Of course he was not understood—he was special: what other Wrannaman could speak and read the drylander tongues as he could? But lately, surrounded again by strangers, and with no knowledge of what had happened to his own folk, it filled him with loneliness. At such times, disturbed by the emptiness of these queer northern surroundings, he would walk down to the river that ran through the middle of the camp to sit and listen to the calming, familiar sounds of the water-world.

He had been doing just that, dangling his brown feet in the Stefflod despite the chill of water and wind, and was returning to camp a little heartened, when a shape flashed past him. It was someone running, pale hair streaming, but whoever it was seemed to move as swiftly as a dragonfly, far faster than anyone human should travel. Tiamak had only a moment to stare after the fleeing form before another dark shape swept past. It was a bird, a large one, flying low to the ground as though the first figure was its prey.

As both shapes vanished up the slope toward the heart of the prince's encampment, Tiamak stood in stunned amazement. It took some moments for him to realize who the first shape had been.

*The Sitha-woman!* he thought. *Chased by a hawk or an owl?*

It made no sense, but then she—Aditu was her name—made little sense to Tiamak either. She was like nothing he had ever seen and, in fact, frightened him a little. But what could be chasing her? From the look on her face she had been running from something dreadful.

Or *to* something dreadful, he realized, and felt his stomach clench. She had been heading toward the camp.

*He Who Always Steps on Sand,* Tiamak prayed as he set out, *protect me—protect us all from evil.* His heart was beating swiftly now, faster than the pace of his running feet. *This is an ill-omened year!*

For a moment, as he reached the nearest edge of the vast field of tents, he was reassured. It was quiet, and few campfires burned. But there was *too much* quiet, he decided a moment later. It was not early, but still well before midnight. People should be about, or at least there should be some noise from those not yet asleep. What could be wrong?

It had been long moments since he had caught his most recent glimpse of the swooping bird—he was certain now it was an owl—and he hobbled on in the direction he had last seen it, his breath now coming in harsh gasps. His injured leg was not used to running, and it burned him, throbbed. He did his best to ignore it.

Quiet, quiet—it was still as a stagnant pond here. The tents stood, dark and lifeless as the stones drylanders set in fields where they buried their dead.

But there! Tiamak felt his stomach turn again. There was movement! One of the tents not far away shook as though in a wind, and some light inside it threw strange moving shadows onto the walls.

Even as he saw it he felt a tickling in his nostrils, a sort of burning, and with it came a sweet, musky scent. He sneezed convulsively and almost tripped, but caught himself before falling to the ground. He limped toward the tent, which pulsed with light and shadow as though some monstrous thing was being born inside. He tried to raise his voice to cry out that he was coming and to raise an alarm, for his fear was rising higher and higher—but he could not make a sound. Even the painful rasp of his breathing had become faint and whispery.

The tent, too, was strangely silent. Pushing down his fright, he caught at the flap and threw it back.

At first he could see nothing more than dark shapes and bright light, almost an exact reflection of the shadow puppets on the outside walls of the tent. Within a few instants, the moving images began to come clear.

At the tent's far wall stood Camaris. He seemed to have been struck, for blood rilled from some cut on his head, staining his cheek and hair black, and he reeled as though his wits had been addled. Still, bowed and leaning against the fabric for support, he was yet fierce, like a bear beset by hounds. He had no blade, but held a piece of firewood clenched in one fist and waved it back and forth, holding off a menacing shape that was almost all black but for a flash of white hands and something that glinted in one of those hands.

Kicking near Camaris' feet was an even less decipherable muddle, although Tiamak thought he saw more black-clothed limbs, as well as the pale nimbus of Aditu's hair. A third dark-clad attacker huddled in the corner, warding off a swooping, fluttering shadow.

Terrified, Tiamak tried to raise his voice to call for help, but could make no sound. Indeed, despite what seemed to be life-or-death struggles, the entire tent was silent but for the muffled sounds of the two combatants on the floor and the hectic flapping of wings.

*Why can't I hear?* Tiamak thought desperately. *Why can't I make a sound?*

Frantic, he searched the floor for something to use as a weapon, cursing himself that he had carelessly left his knife behind in the sleeping-place he shared with Strangyeard. No knife, no sling-stones, no blow-darts— nothing! She Who Waits to Take All Back had surely sung his song tonight.

Something vast and soft seemed to strike him in the head, sending Tiamak to his knees, but when he looked up, the several battles still raged, none of them near him. His skull was throbbing even more painfully than his leg and the sweet smell was chokingly strong. Dizzy, Tiamak crawled forward and his hand encountered something hard. It was the knight's sword, black Thorn, still sheathed. Tiamak knew it was far too heavy for him to use, but he dragged it out from beneath the tangle of bedding and stood, as unsteady now on his feet as Camaris. What was in the air?

The sword, unexpectedly, seemed light in his hands, despite the heavy scabbard and dangling belt. He raised it high and took a few steps forward, then swung it as hard as he could at what he thought was the head of Camaris' attacker. The impact shivered up his arm, but the thing did not fall. Instead, the head turned slowly. Two eyes, shining black, stared out of the corpse-white face. Tiamak's throat moved convulsively. Even had his voice remained, he could not have made a sound. He lifted his shaking arms, holding the sword up to strike again, but the thing's white hand flashed out and Tiamak was knocked backward. The room whirled away from him; the sword flew from his nerveless fingers and tumbled to the grass that was the tent's only floor.

Tiamak's head was as heavy as stone, but he could not otherwise feel the pain of the blow. What he could feel were his wits slipping away. He tried to lift himself to his feet once more but only got as far as his knees. He crouched, shaking like a sick dog.

He could not speak but, cursedly, could still see. Camaris was stumbling, wagging his head—as damaged, seemingly, as Tiamak. The old man was trying to hold off his attacker long enough to reach something on the ground—the sword, the Wrannaman realized groggily, the black sword. Camaris was prevented from reaching it as much by the dark, contorted forms of Aditu and her enemy rolling on the ground beneath him as by the foe he was trying to keep at bay with his firelog club.

In the other corner, something glittered in the hand of one of the pale-faced things, a shining something red as a crescent of firelight. The scarlet gleam moved, swift as a striking snake, and a tiny cloud of dark shapes exploded outward, then drifted to the ground, slower than snow-flakes. Tiamak squinted helplessly as one settled on his hand. It was a feather. An owl's feather.

*Help.* Tiamak's skull felt as though it had been staved in. *We need help. We will die if no one helps us.*

Camaris at last bent and caught up the sword, almost over-balancing, then managed to lift Thorn in time to hold off a strike by his enemy. The two of them circled each other, Camaris stumbling, the black-clad attacker moving with cautious grace. They fell together once more, and one of the old knight's hands shot out and pushed away a dagger blow, but the blade left a trail of blood down his arm. Camaris fell back clumsily, trying to find room to swing his sword. His eyes were half-closed with pain or fatigue.

*He is hurt,* Tiamak thought desperately. The throbbing in his head grew stronger. *Maybe dying. Why does no one come?*

The Wrannaman dragged himself toward the wide bra-zier of coals that provided the only light. His dimming senses were beginning to wink out like the lamps of Kwanitupul at dawn. Only a dim fragment of an idea was in his mind, but it was enough to lift his hand toward the iron brazier. When he felt—as dimly as a distant echo—the heat of the thing against his fingers, he pushed. The brazier tumbled over, scattering coals like a waterfall of rubies.

As Tiamak collapsed, choking, the last things he saw were his own soot-blackened hand curled like a spider and, beyond it, an army of tiny flames licking at the bottom of the tent wall.

❦

"We don't *need* any more damnable questions," Isgrimnur grumbled. "We have enough to last three lifetimes. What we need are answers."

Binabik made an uncomfortable gesture. "I am agreeing with you, Duke Isgrimnur. But answers are not like a sheep that is coming when a person calls."

Josua sighed and leaned back against the wall of Isgrimnur's tent. Outside, the wind rose for a moment, moaning faintly as it vibrated the tent ropes. "I know how difficult it is, Binabik. But Isgrimnur is right—we need answers. The things you told us about this Conqueror Star have only added to the confusion. What we need to know is how to use the three Great Swords. All that the star tells us—if you are right—is that our time to wield them is running out."

"That is what we are giving the largest attention to, Prince Josua," said the troll. "And we think we may perhaps be learning something soon, for Strangyeard has found something that is of importantness."

"What is that?" Josua asked, leaning forward. "Anything, man, anything would be heartening."

Father Strangyeard, who had been sitting quietly, squirmed a little. "I am not as sure as Binabik, Highness, that it is of any use. I found the first of it some time ago, while we were still traveling to Sesuad'ra."

"Strangyeard was finding a passage that is written in Morgenes' book," Binabik amplified, "something about the three swords that are so much concerning us."

"And?" Isgrimnur tapped his fingers on his muddy knee. He had spent a long time trying to secure his tentstakes in the loose, damp ground.

"What Morgenes seems to suggest," the archivist said, "is that what makes the three swords special—no, more than special, *powerful*—is that they are not of Osten Ard. Each of them, in some way, goes against the laws of God and Nature."

"How so?" The prince was listening intently. Isgrimnur saw a little ruefully that these sorts of inquiries would always interest Josua more than the less exotic business of being a ruler, such as grain prices and taxes and the laws of freeholding.

Strangyeard was hesitant. "Geloë could explain better than I. She knows more of these things."

"She should have been coming here by now," Binabik said. "I wonder if we should be waiting for her."

"Tell me what you can," said Josua. "It has been a very long day and I am growing weary. Also, my wife is ill and I do not like being away from her."

"Of course, Prince Josua. I'm sorry. Of course." Strangyeard gathered himself. "Morgenes tells that there is something in each sword that is not of Osten Ard—not of our earth. Thorn is made from a stone that fell from the sky. Bright-Nail, which was once Minneyar, was forged from the iron keel of Elvrit's ship that came over the sea from the West. Those are lands that our ships can no longer find." He cleared his throat. "And Sorrow is of both iron and the Sithi witchwood, two things that are inimical. The witchwood itself, Aditu tells me, came over as seedlings from the place that her people call the Garden. None of these things should be here, and also, none of them should be workable . . . except perhaps the pure iron of Elvrit's keel."

"So how were these swords made, then?" asked Josua. "Or is that the answer you still seek?"

"There is something that Morgenes is mentioning," Binabik offered. "It is also written in one of Ookekuq's scrolls. It is called a Word of Making—a magic spell is what we might be naming it, although those who are knowing the Art do not use those words."

"A Word of Making?" Isgrimnur frowned. "Just a word?"

"Yes ... and no," Strangyeard said unhappily. "In truth, we are not sure. But Minneyar we know was made by the dwarrows—the *dvernings* as you would call them in your own tongue, Duke Isgrimnur—and Sorrow was made by Ineluki in the dwarrow forges beneath Asu'a. The dwarrows alone had the lore to make such mighty things, although Ineluki learned it. Perhaps they had a hand in Thorn's forging as well, or their lore was used somehow. In any case, it is possible that if we knew the way in which the swords were created, how the binding of forces was accomplished, it might teach us something about how we can use them against the Storm King."

"I wish I had thought to question Count Eolair more carefully when he was here," said Josua, frowning. "He had met the dwarrows."

"Yes, and they told him of their part in the history of Bright-Nail," Father Strangyeard added. "It is also possible, however, that it is *not* the making of them that is important for our purpose, but just the fact that they exist. Still, if we have some chance in the future to send word to the dwarrows, and if they will speak with us, I for one would have many questions."

Josua looked at the archivist speculatively. "This chore suits you, Strangyeard. I always thought you were wasted dusting books and searching out the most obscure points of canon law."

The priest reddened. "Thank you, Prince Josua. Whatever I can do is because of your kindness."

The prince waved his hand, dismissing the compliment. "Still, as much as you and Binabik and the rest have accomplished, there is still far more to do. We remain afloat in deep waters, praying for a sight of land ..." He paused. "What is that noise?"

Isgrimnur had noticed it, too, a rising murmur that had slowly grown louder than the wind. "It sounds like an argument," he said, then waited for a moment, listening.

"No, it is more than that—there are too many voices." He stood. "Dror's Hammer, I hope that someone has not started a rebellion." He reached for Kvalnir and was calmed by its reassuring heft. "I had hoped for a quiet day tomorrow before we are to ride again."

Josua clambered to his feet. "Let us not sit here and wonder."

As Isgrimnur stepped out of the door flap, his eyes were abruptly drawn across the vast camp. It was plain in an instant what was happening.

"Fire!" he called to the others as they spilled out after him. "At least one tent burning badly, but it looks like a few more have caught, too." People were now rushing about between the tents, shadowy figures that shouted and gesticulated. Men dragged on their sword belts, cursing in confusion. Mothers dragged screaming children out of their blankets and carried them into the open air. All the pathways were full of terrified, milling campfolk. Isgrimnur saw one old woman fall to her knees, crying, although she was only a few paces from where he stood, a long distance from the nearest flames.

"Aedon save us!" said Josua. "Binabik, Strangyeard, call for buckets and waterskins, then take some of these mad-wandering folk and head for the river—we need water! Better yet, pull down some of the oiled tents and see how much water you can carry in them!" He sprang away toward the conflagration; Isgrimnur hastened after him.

The flames were leaping high now, filling the night sky with a hellish orange light. As he and Josua approached the fire, a flurry of dancing sparks sailed out, hissing as they caught in Isgrimnur's beard. He beat them out, cursing.

❦

Tiamak awakened and promptly threw up, then struggled to catch his breath. His head was hammering like a Perdruinese church bell.

There were flames all around him, beating hot against his skin, sucking away the air. In a blind panic, he dragged himself across the crisping grass of the tent floor toward what looked like a patch of cool darkness, only to find his face pushed up against some black, slippery fabric. He struggled with it for a moment, dimly noting its strange resistance; then it flopped aside, exposing a white face buried in the black hood. The eyes were turned up, and blood slicked the lips. Tiamak tried to scream, but his mouth was full of burning smoke and his own bile. He rolled away, choking.

Suddenly, something grabbed at his arm and he was yanked forward violently, dragged across the pale-skinned corpse and through a wall of flame. For a moment he thought he was dead. Something was thrown over him, and he was rolled and pummeled with the same swift violence that had carried him away, then whatever covered him was lifted and he found himself lying on wet grass. Flames licked at the sky close beside him, but he was safe. Safe!

"The Wrannaman is alive," someone said near him. He thought he recognized the Sitha-woman's lilting tones, although her voice was now almost sharp with fear and worry. "Camaris dragged him out. How the knight managed to stay awake after he had been poisoned I will never know, but he killed two of the Hikeda'ya." There was an unintelligible response.

After he had lain in place for a few long moments, just breathing the clean air into his painful lungs, Tiamak rolled over. Aditu stood a few paces away, her white hair blackened and her golden face streaked with grime. Beneath her on the ground lay the forest woman Geloë, partially wrapped in a cloak, but obviously naked beneath it, her muscular legs shiny with dew or sweat. As Tiamak watched, she struggled to sit up.

"No, you must not," Aditu said to her, then took a step backward. "By the Grove, Geloë, you are wounded."

With a trembling effort, Geloë lifted her head. "No," she said. Tiamak could barely hear her voice, a throaty whisper. "I am dying."

Aditu leaned forward, reaching out to her. "Let me help you. . . ."

"No!" Geloë's voice grew stronger. "No, Aditu, it is ... too late. I have been stabbed ... a dozen times." She coughed and a thin trickle of something dark ran down her chin, glinting in the light of the burning tents. Tiamak stared. He saw what he took to be Camaris' feet and legs behind her, the rest of the knight's long form stretched out in the grass hidden by her shadow. "I must go." Geloë tried to clamber to her feet but could not do so.

"There might be something ..." Aditu began.

Geloë laughed weakly, then coughed again and spat out a gobbet of blood. "Do you think I ... do not ... know?" she said. "I have been a healer for ... a long time." She held out a shaking hand. "Help me. Help me up."

Aditu's face, which for a moment had seemed as stricken as any mortal's, grew solemn. She took Geloë's hand, then leaned forward and clasped her other arm as well. The wise woman slowly rose to her feet; she swayed, but Aditu supported her.

"I must ... go. I do not wish to die here." Geloë pushed away from Aditu and took a few staggering steps. The cloak fell away, exposing her nakedness to the leaping firelight. Her skin was slick with sweat and great smears of blood. "I will go back to my forest. Let me go while I still can."

Aditu hesitated a moment longer, then stepped back and lowered her head. "As you wish, Valada Geloë. Farewell, Ruyan's Own. Farewell ... my friend. *Sinya'a dun'sha é-d'treyesa inro.*"

Trembling, Geloë raised her arms, then took another step. The heat from the flames seemed to grow more intense, for Tiamak, where he lay, saw Geloë begin to shimmer. Her outline grew insubstantial, then a cloud of shadow or smoke seemed to appear where she stood. For a moment, the very night seemed to surge inward toward the spot, as though a stitch had been taken in the fabric of the Wrannaman's vision. Then the night was whole again.

The owl circled slowly for a moment where Geloë had been, then flew off, close above the wind-tossed grasses. Its movements were stiff and awkward, and several times it seemed that it must lose the wind and fall tumbling to the earth, but its lurching flight continued until the night sky had swallowed it.

His head still full of murk and painful clangor, Tiamak slumped back. He was not sure what he had seen, but he knew that something terrible had happened. A great sadness lurked just out of his reach. He was in no hurry to bring it closer.

What had been the thin sound of voices in the distance became a raucous shouting. Legs moved past him; the night seemed suddenly full of movement. There was a rush and sizzle of steam as someone threw a pail of water into the flames of what had been Camaris' tent.

A few moments later he felt Aditu's strong hands under his arms. "You will be trampled, brave marsh man," she said into his ear, then pulled him farther away from the conflagration, into the cool darkness beside some tents untouched by the blaze. She left him there, then returned shortly with a water skin. The Sitha pressed it against his cracked lips until he understood what it was, then left him to drink—which he did, greedily.

A dark shadow loomed, then abruptly sank down beside him. It was Camaris. His silvery hair, like Aditu's, was scorched and blackened. Haunted eyes stared from his ash-smeared face. Tiamak handed him the water skin, then prodded him until he lifted it to his lips.

"God have mercy on us . . ." Camaris croaked. He stared dazedly at the spreading fires and the shouting mob that was trying to douse them.

Aditu returned and sat down beside them. When Camaris offered her the water skin, she took it from him and downed a single swallow before handing it back.

"Geloë. . . ?" Tiamak asked.

Aditu shook her head. "Dying. She has gone away."

"Who . . ." It was still hard to speak. Tiamak almost did not want to, but he suddenly felt a desire to *know,* to have some reasons with which to balance off the terrible events. He also needed something—words if nothing else—to fill the emptiness inside of him. He took the skin bag from Camaris and moistened his throat. "Who was it. . . ?"

"The Hikeda'ya," she said, watching the efforts to quell the flames. "The Norns. That was Utuk'ku's long arm that reached out tonight."

"I . . . I tried to . . . to call for help. But I couldn't."

Aditu nodded. "Kei-vishaa. It is a sort of poison that floats on the wind. It kills the voice for a time, and also brings sleep." She looked at Camaris, who had leaned back against the tent wall that sheltered them. His head was thrown back, his eyes closed. "I do not know how he stood against it for the time he did. If he had not, we would have been too late. Geloë's sacrifice would have been for nothing." She turned to the Wrannaman. "You, too, Tiamak. Things would have been different without your aid: you found Camaris' sword. Also, the fire frightened them. They knew they did not have much time, and that made them careless. Otherwise, I think we would all be there still." She indicated the burning tent.

*Geloë's sacrifice.* Tiamak found his eyes filling with tears. They stung.

*She Who Waits to Take All Back,* he prayed desperately, *do not let her drift by!*

He covered his face with his hands. He did not want to think any more.

Josua ran faster. When Isgrimnur caught him at last, the prince had already stopped to make sure that the fires were being mastered. The original blaze had spread only a little way, catching perhaps a half-dozen other tents at most, and all but some in the first tent had escaped. Sangfugol was one of them. He stood, clothed only in a long shirt, and blearily watched the proceedings.

After assuring himself that everything possible was being done, Isgrimnur followed Josua to Camaris and the other two survivors, the Sitha-woman and little Tiamak, who were resting nearby. They were all bloodied and singed, but Isgrimnur felt sure after looking them over quickly that they would all live.

"Ah, praise merciful Aedon that you escaped, Sir

Camaris," said Josua, kneeling at the side of the old knight. "I feared rightly that it might be your tent when we first saw the blaze." He turned to Aditu, who seemed to have her wits about her, which could not quite be said of Camaris and the marsh man. "Who have we lost? I am told there are bodies inside the tent still."

Aditu looked up. "Geloë, I fear. She was badly wounded. Dying."

"God curse it!" Josua's voice cracked. "Cursed day!" He pulled a handful of grass and flung it down angrily. With an effort, he calmed himself. "Is she still in there? And who are the others?"

"They are none of them Geloë," she said. "The three inside the tent are those you call Norns. Geloë has gone to the forest."

"What!" Josua sat back, stunned. "What do you mean, gone to the forest? You said she was dead."

"Dying." Aditu spread her fingers. "She did not want us to see her last moments, I think. She was strange, Josua—stranger than you know. She went away."

"Gone?"

The Sitha nodded slowly. "Gone."

The prince made the sign of the Tree and bowed his head. When he looked up, there were tears running on his cheek; Isgrimnur did not think they were caused by the smoke. He, too, felt a shadow move over him as he thought of the loss of Geloë. With so many pressing tasks he could not dwell on it now, but the duke knew from long experience in battle that it would strike him hard later.

"We have been attacked in our very heart," the prince said bitterly. "How did they get past the sentries?"

"The one I fought was dripping wet," said Aditu. "They may have come down the river."

Josua swore. "We have been dangerously lax, and I am the worst miscreant. I had thought it strange we had escaped the Norns' attentions so long, but my precautions were inadequate. Were there more than those three?"

"I think there were no more," Aditu replied. "And they would have been more than enough, but that we were lucky. If Geloë and I had not guessed something was amiss, and if Tiamak had not somehow known and arrived when he did, this tale would have had a different ending. I think they meant to kill Camaris, or at least to take him."

"But why?" Josua looked at the old knight, then back to Aditu.

"I do not know. But let us carry him, and Tiamak, too, to some warm place, Prince Josua. Camaris has at least one wound, perhaps more, and Tiamak is burned, I think."

"Aedon's mercy, you are right," said Josua. "Thoughtless, thoughtless. One moment." He turned and called some of his soldiers together, then sent them off with orders for the sentries to search the camp. "We cannot be sure there were not more Norns or other attackers," Josua said. "At the very least, we may find something to tell us how these came into our camp without being seen."

"None of the Gardenborn are easily seen by mortals—if they do not wish to be seen," said Aditu. "May we take Camaris and Tiamak away now?"

"Of course." Josua called two of the bucket carriers. "You men! Come and help us!" He turned to Isgrimnur. "Four should be enough to carry them, even though Camaris is large." He shook his head. "Aditu is right—we have made these brave ones wait too long."

The duke had been in such situations before, and knew that too much haste was as bad as too little. "I think we would be better to find something to carry them on," he said. "If one of those outer tents has been saved from the fire, we might use it to make a litter or two."

"Good." Josua stood. "Aditu, I did not ask if *you* had wounds that needed tending."

"Nothing I cannot care for myself, Prince Josua. When these two have been seen to, we should gather those that you trust and talk."

"I agree. There is much to talk about. We will meet at Isgrimnur's tent within the hour. Does that suit you, Isgrimnur?" The prince turned aside for a moment, then turned back. His face was haggard with grief. "I was

thinking that we should find Geloë to come nurse them
. . . then I remembered."

Aditu made a gesture, fingers touching fingers before
her. "This is not the last time we shall miss her, I think."

"It is Josua," the prince called from outside the tent.
When he stepped inside, Gutrun still had the knife held
before her. The duchess looked fierce as an undenned
badger, ready to protect herself and Vorzheva from whatever danger might show itself. She lowered the dagger as
Josua entered, relieved but still full of worry.

"What is it? We heard the shouting. Is my husband
with you?"

"He is safe, Gutrun." Josua walked to the bed, then
leaned forward and pulled Vorzheva to him in a swift embrace. He kissed her brow as he released her. "But we
have been attacked by the Storm King's minions. We
have lost only one, but that is a great loss."

"Who?" Vorzheva caught his arm as he tried to
straighten.

"Geloë."

She cried out in grief.

"Three Norns attacked Camaris," Josua explained.
"Aditu, Geloë, and the Wrannaman Tiamak came to his
aid. The Norns were killed, but Aditu says that Geloë
took a fatal wound." He shook his head. "I think she was
the wisest of us all. Now she is gone and we cannot replace her."

Vorzheva fell back. "But she was just here, Josua. She
came with Aditu to see me. Now she is dead?" Tears
filled her eyes.

Josua nodded sadly. "I came to see that you were safe.
Now I must go meet with Isgrimnur and the others to decide what this means, what we will do." He stood, then
bent and kissed his wife again. "Do not sleep—and keep
your knife, Gutrun—until I can send someone here to
guard you."

"No one else was hurt? Gutrun said that she saw fires."

"Camaris' tent. He seems to have been the only one attacked." He began to move toward the door.

"But Josua," Vorzheva said, "are you sure? Our camp is so big."

The prince shook his head. "I am sure of nothing, but we have not heard of any other attacks. I will have someone here to guard you soon. Now I must hurry, Vorzheva."

"Let him go, Lady," Gutrun told her. "Lie back and try to sleep. Think of your child."

Vorzheva sighed. Josua squeezed her hand, then turned and hastened from the tent.

Isgrimnur looked up as the prince strode into the light of the campfire. The cluster of men waiting for the prince stepped back respectfully, letting him pass. "Josua ..." the duke began, but the prince did not let him finish.

"I have been foolish, Isgrimnur. It is not enough to have sentries running through the camp looking for signs of invading Norns. Aedon's Blood, it took me long enough to realize it—Sludig!" he shouted. "Is Sludig somewhere nearby?"

The Rimmersman stepped forward. "Here, Prince Josua."

"Send soldiers through the camp to see if everyone is accounted for, especially those of our party who might be at risk. Binabik and Strangyeard were with me until the fire started, but that does not mean they are safe still. It is late in the day for me to realize this might have been a diversion. And my niece, Miriamele—send someone to her tent immediately. And Simon, too, although he may be with Binabik." Josua frowned. "If they wanted Camaris, it seems likely it was about the sword. Simon carried it for a while, so perhaps there is some danger to him as well. Damn me for my slow wits."

Isgrimnur made a throat-clearing noise. "I already sent Freosel to look after Miriamele, Josua. I knew you would

want to see Lady Vorzheva as soon as you could and I
thought it should not wait."

"Thank you, Isgrimnur. I did go to her. She and Gutrun
are fine." Josua scowled. "But I am shamed you have had
to do my thinking."

Isgrimnur shook his head. "Let's just hope the princess
is safe."

"Freosel has been sent after Miriamele," Josua told
Sludig. "That is one less to hunt for. Go and see to the
rest now. And post two guards at my tent, if you would.
I will think better knowing that someone is watching over
Vorzheva."

The Rimmersman nodded. He commandeered a large
portion of the soldiers who were milling aimlessly around
Isgrimnur's camp and went off to do as he had been bid.

"And now," Josua said to Isgrimnur, "we wait. And
think."

Before the hour was too much older, Aditu reappeared;
Father Strangyeard and Binabik were with her. They had
gone with the Sitha to make sure Camaris and Tiamak
were resting comfortably in the care of one of New
Gadrinsett's healing-women—and also, apparently, to
talk, for they were all three deep in conversation when
they reached Isgrimnur's tent.

Aditu told Josua and the rest all the details of the
night's events. She spoke calmly, but Isgrimnur could not
help noticing that, although she chose her words with as
much care as ever, the Sitha seemed profoundly troubled.
She and Geloë had been friends, he knew: apparently the
Sithi felt grief just as mortals did. He liked her better for
it, then dismissed the thought as unworthy. Why should
immortals *not* take hurt like humans? From what
Isgrimnur knew, they had certainly suffered at least as
much.

"So." Josua sat back and looked around the circle. "We
have found no trace of anyone else being attacked. The
question is, why did they single out Camaris?"

"There *must* be something to this Three Swords rhyme
after all," said Isgrimnur. He didn't like such things: they

made him feel as though the ground beneath his feet was unsolid, but that seemed to be the kind of world he found himself in. It was hard not to yearn for the clean edge that things had when he was younger. Even the worst of matters, like war, terrible as it was, had not been so shot through with strange sorceries and mysterious enemies. "They must have been after Camaris because of Thorn."

"Or perhaps it was Thorn alone they were seeking for," Binabik said soberly. "And Camaris was not of the most importance."

"I still do not understand how they were able almost to overcome him," Strangyeard said. "What is that poison you spoke of, Aditu?"

"Kei-vishaa. In truth, it is not just a poison: we Gardenborn use it in the Grove when it is time to dance the year's end. But it can also be wielded to bring a long, heavy sleep. It was brought from Venyha Do'sae; my people used it when they first came here, to remove dangerous animals—some of them huge creatures whose like have long passed from Osten Ard—from the places where we wished to build our cities. When I smelled it, I knew that something was wrong. We Zida'ya have never used it for anything except the year-dancing ceremonies."

"How is it used there?" the archivist asked, fascinated.

Aditu only lowered her eyes. "I am sorry, good Strangyeard, but that is not for me to say. I perhaps should not have mentioned it at all. I am tired."

"We have no need to pry into your people's rituals," said Josua. "And we have more important things to speak of, in any case." He turned an irritated look on Strangyeard, who hung his head. "It is enough that we know how they were able to attack Camaris without his raising an alarm. We are lucky that Tiamak had the presence of mind to set the tent ablaze. From now on, we will be absolutely rigid in the arrangement of our camp. All who are in any way at risk will set their tents close together in the very center, so we all sleep within sight of each other. I blame myself for indulging Camaris' wish for solitude. I have taken my responsibilities too lightly."

Isgrimnur frowned. "We must all be more careful."

As the council turned to talk of what other precautions should be taken, Freosel appeared at the fireside. "Sorry, Highness, but the princess be not anywhere 'round her tent, nor did anyone see her since early."

Josua was clearly upset. "Not there? Aedon preserve us, was Vorzheva right? Did they come for the princess after all?" He stood up. "I cannot sit here while she may be in danger. We must search the entire camp."

"Sludig is doing that already," said Isgrimnur gently. "We will only confuse things."

The prince slumped down again. "You are right. But it will be hard to wait."

They had barely resumed the discussion when Sludig returned, his face grim. He handed Josua a piece of parchment. "This was in young Simon's tent."

The prince read it quickly, then flung it down on the ground in disgust. A moment later he stooped for it, then handed it to the troll, his face stiff and angry. "I am sorry, Binabik, I should not have done that. It seems to be for you." He stood. "Hotvig?"

"Yes, Prince Josua." The Thrithings-man also stood.

"Miriamele has gone. Take as many of your riders as you can quickly find. The chances are good that she has headed toward Erkynland, so do most of your searching west of the camp. But do not ignore the possibility that she might go some other way to throw us off before she turns back to the west."

"What?" Isgrimnur looked up in surprise. "What do you mean, gone?"

Binabik looked up from the parchment. "This was written by Simon. It is seeming that he has gone with her, but he also says he will try to bring her back." The troll's smile was thin and obviously forced. "There is some question in my head about who is leading who. I am doubting Simon will convince her for coming back very soon."

Josua gestured impatiently. "Go, Hotvig. God only knows how long they have been gone. As a matter of fact, since you and your riders are the fastest horsemen we have here, go west; leave the other part of the search to the rest of us." He turned to Sludig. "We will ride around the camp, making our circle wider each time. I will saddle Vinyafod. Meet me there." He turned to the duke. "Are you coming?"

"Of course." Silently, Isgrimnur cursed himself. *I should have known something was coming,* he thought. *She has been so quiet, so sad, so distant since we came here. Josua hasn't seen the change as I have. But even if she thinks we should have marched on Erkynland, why would she go on her own? Fool of a headstrong child. And Simon. I thought better of that boy.*

Already unhappy at the thought of a night in the saddle and what it would do to his sore back, Isgrimnur grunted and rose to his feet.

♣

"Why won't she wake up!?" Jeremias demanded. "Can't you do something?"

"Hush, boy, I'm doing what I can." Duchess Gutrun bent and felt Leleth's face again. "She is cool, not feverish."

"Then what's wrong with her?" Jeremias seemed almost frantic. "I tried to wake her for a long time, but she just lay there."

"Let me give another cover for her," Vorzheva said. She had made room in the bed for the girl to lie beside her, but Gutrun had disallowed it, frightened that Leleth had some sickness which Vorzheva might catch. Instead, Jeremias had carefully set the girl's limp form on a blanket upon the ground.

"You just lie still and I'll worry about the child," the duchess told her. "This is altogether too much noise and fretting."

Prince Josua stepped through the door, unhappiness etched on his face. "Is there not enough gone wrong? The guard said someone was sick. Vorzheva? Are you well?"

"It is not me, Josua. The little girl Leleth, she cannot be wakened."

Duke Isgrimnur stumped in. "A damned long ride and

no sign of Miriamele," he growled. "We can only hope that Hotvig and his Thrithings-men have better luck than we did."

"Miriamele?" Vorzheva asked. "Has something happened to her, also?"

"She has ridden off with young Simon," Josua said grimly.

"This is a cursed night," Vorzheva groaned. "Why does this all happen?"

"To be fair, I don't think it was the lad's idea." Isgrimnur bent and put his arm about his wife's shoulders, then kissed her neck. "He left a letter which said he would try to bring her back." The duke's eyes narrowed. "Why is the girl here? Was she hurt in the fire?"

"I brought her," Jeremias said miserably. "Duchess Gutrun asked me to look after her tonight."

"I didn't want her underfoot with Vorzheva so sick." Gutrun could not entirely hide her own discomfort. "And it was just for a while, when Geloë was going to meet with you men."

"I was with her all evening," Jeremias explained. "After she was asleep, I fell asleep, too. I didn't mean to. I was just tired."

Josua turned and looked at the young man kindly. "You did nothing wrong to fall asleep. Go on."

"I woke up when everyone was shouting about the fire. I thought Leleth would be frightened, so I went over to let her know I was still there. She was sitting up with her eyes open, but I don't think she heard a word I said. Then she fell back and her eyes closed, like she was sleeping. But I couldn't wake her up! I tried for a long time. Then I brought her here to see if Duchess Gutrun could help." As Jeremias finished, he was on the verge of tears.

"You did nothing wrong, Jeremias," the prince repeated. "Now, I need you to do something for me."

The young man caught his breath on the verge of a sob. "W–What, your Highness?"

"Go to Isgrimnur's tent and see if Binabik has returned. The troll knows something of healing. We will have him look at young Leleth."

Jeremias, only too glad to have something useful to do, hurried out.

"In truth," Josua said, "I no longer know what to think of all that has happened tonight—but I must admit that I am very fearful for Miriamele. Damn her frowardness." He clutched Vorzheva's blanket in his fingers and twisted it in frustration.

There had been no change in Leleth's condition when Jeremias returned with Binabik and Aditu. The little man inspected the girl closely.

"I have seen her being like this before," he said. "She is gone away somewhere, to the Road of Dreams or some other place."

"But surely she has never been like this for so long," Josua said. "I cannot help but think it has something to do with the night's happenings. Could the Norn poison have made her this way, Aditu?"

The Sitha kneeled beside Binabik and lifted the little girl's eyelids, then laid her slim fingers below Leleth's ear to feel how swiftly her heart beat. "I do not think so. Surely this one," she indicated Jeremias, "would also have been struck if the Kei-vishaa had spread so far."

"Her lips are moving!" Jeremias said excitedly. "Look!"

Although she still lay as if deeply asleep, Leleth's mouth was indeed opening and closing as though she would speak.

"Silence." Josua leaned closer, as did most of the others in the room.

Leleth's lips worked. A whisper of sound crept out. *". . . hear me . . ."*

"She said something!" Jeremias exulted, but was stilled by a look from the prince.

*". . . I will speak anyway. I am fading. I have only a short time left."* The voice that issued from the little girl's mouth, though thin and breathy, had a familiar cadence.

*". . . There is more to the Norns than we suspect, I think. They play some double game . . . Tonight was not a feint, but something even more subtle . . ."*

"What's wrong with the child?" Gutrun said nervously. "She's never spoken before—and she sounds wrong."

"That is Geloë speaking." Aditu spoke calmly, as though she identified a familiar figure coming up the road.

"What?" The duchess made the Tree sign, her eyes wide with fear. "What witchcraft is this?"

The Sitha leaned close to Leleth's ear. "Geloë?" she said. "Can you hear me?"

If it was the wise woman, she did not seem to hear her friend's voice. "*. . . Remember what Simon dreamed . . . the false messenger.*" There was a pause. When the voice resumed it was quieter, so that all in the room held their breath in an effort not to obscure a word. "*. . . I am dying. Leleth is here with me somehow, in this . . . dark place. I have never understood her completely, and this is strangest of all. I think I can speak through her mouth, but I do not know if anyone is listening. My time is short. Remember: beware a false messenger. . . .*"

There was another long, silent interval. When everyone was certain that they had heard the last, Leleth's lips moved again. "*I am going now. Do not mourn me. I have had a long life and did what I wished to do. If you would remember me, remember that the forest was my home. See that it is respected. I will try to send Leleth back, although she does not want to leave me. Farewell. Remember . . .*"

The voice faded. The little girl again lay like one dead.

Josua looked up. His eyes were bright with tears. "To the last," he said, almost in anger, "she tried to help us. Oh, God the Merciful, she was a brave soul."

"An old soul," Aditu said quietly, but did not elaborate. She seemed shaken.

Though they sat around the bedside in heavy, mournful silence for some time, Leleth did not stir any more. Geloë's absence seemed even more powerful, more devastating than it had earlier in the evening. Other eyes besides Josua's filled with tears of sorrow and fear as the realization of the company's loss settled in. The prince began to speak quietly of the forest woman, praising her bravery, wit, and kindness, but no one else seemed to have the heart to join in. At last he sent them all off to rest. Aditu, saying that she felt no need to sleep, stayed to watch over the child in case she awakened in the night. Josua lay down fully dressed beside his wife, ready for whatever calamity might befall next. Within moments, he had fallen into a deep, exhausted slumber.

In the morning, the prince awakened to discover Aditu still watching over Leleth. Wherever the child's spirit had journeyed with Geloë, it had not yet returned.

Not long afterward, Hotvig and his men rode into camp, weary and empty-handed.

# 2

# Ghost Moon

✦

**Simon and Miriamele** rode in near-silence, the princess leading as they made their way down into the valley on the far side of the hills. After they had gone a league or more, Miriamele turned them north so that they were riding back along the same track the company had taken on its way to Gadrinsett.

Simon asked her why.

"Because there are already a thousand fresh hoofprints here," Miriamele explained. "And because Josua knows where I'm going, so it would be stupid to head straight that way in case they find out we've left tonight."

"Josua knows where we're going?" Simon was disgruntled. "That's more than I do."

"I'll tell you about it when we're far enough that you can't ride back in one night," she said coolly. "When I'm too far away for them to catch me and bring me back."

She would not answer any more questions.

Simon squinted at the bits of refuse that lined the wide, muddy track. A great army of people had crossed this way twice now, along with several other smaller parties that had made their way to Sesuad'ra and New Gadrinsett; Simon thought it would be a long time before the grass grew on this desolated swath again.

*I suppose that's where roads come from,* he thought, and grinned despite his weariness. *I never thought about it before. Maybe someday it will be a real king's road, with set stones and inns and way stations ... and I saw it when it was nothing but a hoof-gouged track.*

Of course, that was presuming that whatever happened in the days to come, there would *be* a king who cared about roads. From what Jeremias and others had told him about the state of affairs at the Hayholt, it didn't seem very likely that Elias was worrying about such things.

They rode on beside the Stefflod, which glowed silver in the moon's ghostly light. Miriamele remained uncommunicative, and it seemed to Simon that they rode for days on end, although the moon had not yet moved much past the midpoint of the sky. Bored, he watched Miriamele, admiring how her fair skin took the moonlight, until she, irritated, told him to stop staring at her. Desperate for diversion, he then considered the Canon of Knighthood and Camaris' teachings; when that failed to hold his interest for more than half a league, he quietly sang all the Jack Mundwode songs he knew. Later, after Miriamele had rebuffed several more attempts at conversation, Simon began counting the stars that dotted the sky, numerous as grains of salt spilled on an ebony tabletop.

At last, when Simon was certain that he would soon go mad—and equally certain that a full week must have passed during this one long night—Miriamele reined up and pointed to a copse of trees standing on a low hill some three or four furlongs from the wide rut of the infant road.

"There," she said. "We'll stop there and sleep."

"I don't need to sleep yet." Simon lied. "We can ride longer if you want to."

"There's no point. I don't want to be out in the open in daylight tomorrow. Later, when we're farther away, we can ride when it's light."

Simon shrugged. "If you say so." He had wanted this adventure, if that was what it was, so he might as well endure it as cheerfully as possible. In the first moments of their escape he had imagined—during those few brief instants in which he had allowed himself to think at all—that Miriamele would be more pleasant once the immediate worry of discovery had lessened. Instead, she had seemed to grow even more morose as the night wore on.

The trees at the top of the hill grew close together, making an almost seamless wall between their makeshift camp and the road. They did not light a fire—Simon had to admit he could see the wisdom of that—but instead shared some water and a little wine by moonlight, and gnawed on a bit of Miriamele's bread.

When they had wrapped themselves in their cloaks and were lying side by side on their bedrolls, Simon suddenly found that his weariness had fled—in fact, he did not feel the least bit sleepy. He listened, but although Miriamele's breathing was quiet and regular, she did not sound like she was sleeping either. Somewhere in the trees, a lone cricket was gently sawing away.

"Miriamele?"

"What?"

"You really should tell me where we're going. I would do better as your protector. I could think about it and make plans."

She laughed quietly. "I'm certain that's true. I will tell you, Simon. But not tonight."

He frowned as he stared up at the stars peeping through the branches. "Very well."

"You should go to sleep now. It will be harder to do once the sun is up."

Did all women have a little Rachel the Dragon in them? They certainly seemed to enjoy telling him what he should do. He opened his mouth to tell her he didn't need any rest just yet, but yawned instead.

He was trying to remember what he had meant to say even as he passed over into sleep.

In the dream Simon stood on the edge of a great sea. Extending from the beach before him was a thin causeway of land that extended out right through the teeth of the waves, leading to an island some long distance offshore. The island was bare except for three tall white towers which shimmered in the late afternoon sun, but the towers were not what interested Simon. Walking on the island before them, passing in and out of their threefold shadow, was a tiny figure with white hair and a blue robe. Simon was certain it was Doctor Morgenes.

. He was considering the causeway—it would be easy enough to walk across, but the tide was growing higher, and soon might cover the thin spit of land entirely—when he heard a distant voice. Out on the ocean, midway between the island and the rocky shoal where Simon stood, a small boat was rocking and bobbing in the grip of strong waves. Two figures stood in the boat, one tall and solid, the other small and slender. It took a few moments to recognize Geloë and Leleth. The woman was calling something to him, but her voice was lost in the roar of the sea.

*What are they doing out in a boat?* Simon thought. *It will be night soon.*

He moved a few steps out onto the slender causeway. Geloë's voice wafted to him across the waves, barely audible.

"*. . . False!*" she cried. "*It's false. . . !*"

*What is false?* he wondered. The spit of land? It seemed solid enough. The island itself? He squinted, but although the sun had now dropped low on the horizon, turning the towers into black fingers and the shape of Morgenes into something small and dark as an ant, the island seemed indisputably substantial. He took another few steps forward.

"*False!*" Geloë cried again.

The sky abruptly turned dark, and the roar of the waves was overwhelmed by the cry of rising wind. In an instant the ocean turned blue and then blue-white; suddenly, all the waves stiffened, freezing into hard, sharp points of ice. Geloë waved her arms desperately, but the sea around her boat surged and cracked. Then with a roar and an outwash of black water as alive as blood, Geloë, Leleth, and the boat disappeared beneath the frozen waves, sucked down into darkness.

Ice was creeping up over the causeway. Simon turned, but it was now as far back to the beach as it was toward the island, and both points seemed to be receding from him, leaving him stranded in the middle of an ever-lengthening spit of rock. The ice mounted higher, crawling up to his boots. . . .

Simon jerked awake, shivering. Thin dawn light filled the copse and the trees swayed to a chill breeze. His cloak was curled in a hopeless tangle around his knees, leaving the rest of him uncovered.

He straightened the cloak and lay back. Miriamele was still asleep beside him, her mouth partially open, her golden hair pushed out of shape. He felt a wave of longing pass over and through him, and at the same time a sense of shame. She was so defenseless, lying here in the wilderness, and he was her protector—what sort of knight was he, to have such feelings? But he longed to pull her close to him, to warm her, to kiss her on that open mouth and feel her breath on his cheek. Uncomfortable, he rolled over and faced the other direction.

The horses stood quietly where they had been tied, their harnesses wrapped around a low-hanging tree branch. The sight of the saddlebags in the flat morning light suddenly filled him with a hollow kind of sadness. Last night this had seemed a wild adventure. Now, it seemed foolish. Whatever Miriamele's reasons might be, they were not his own. He owed many, many debts—to Prince Josua, who had lifted him up and knighted him; to Aditu, who had saved him; to Binabik, who had been a better friend than he deserved. And there were also those who looked up to Simon as well, like Jeremias. But he had deserted them all on a moment's whim. And for what? To force himself on Miriamele, who had some sad purpose of her own in leaving her uncle's camp. He had left the few people who wanted him to tag along after someone who did not.

He squinted at his horse and felt his sadness deepen. Homefinder. That was a pretty name, wasn't it? Simon had just run away from another home, and this time there was no good reason for it.

He sighed and sat up. He was here and there was little to be done about it, at least right now. He would try again to talk Miriamele into going back when she woke up.

Simon pulled his cloak about him and got to his feet. He untied the horses, then stood at the edge of the copse and peered cautiously around before leading them down the hill to the river to drink. When he brought them back, he tied them to a different tree where they could easily reach the long shoots of new-grown grass. As he watched Homefinder and Miriamele's unnamed steed contentedly break their fast, he felt his mood lighten for the first time since awakening from his frightening dream.

He gathered up deadwood from around the copse, taking only what seemed dry enough to burn with little smoke, and set about making a small fire. He was pleased to see that he had brought his flint and striking-steel, but wondered how long it would be until he discovered something he needed just as much but had forgotten in the hurry to leave camp. He sat before the fire for a while, warming his hands and watching Miriamele sleep.

A bit later, as he was looking through the saddlebags to see what there might be to eat, Miriamele began to toss in her sleep and cry out.

"No!" she mumbled. "No, I won't . . ." She half-raised her arms, as though to fight something off. After watching in consternation for a moment, Simon went and kneeled beside her, taking her hand.

"Miriamele. Princess. Wake up. You're having a bad dream."

She tugged against his grip, but strengthlessly. At last her eyes opened. She stared at him, and briefly seemed to see someone else, for she brought her free hand up as though to protect herself. Then she recognized him and let the hand fall. Her other hand remained clutched in his.

"It was just a bad dream." He squeezed her fingers gently, surprised and gratified by how much larger his hand was than hers.

"I'm well," she muttered at last, and drew herself up into a sitting position, pulling the cloak tightly about her shoulders. She glared around at the clearing as though the presence of daylight was some silly prank of Simon's. "What time of day is it?"

"The sun's not over the treetops yet. Down there, I mean. I walked down to the river."

She didn't reply, but clambered to her feet and walked unsteadily out of the copse. Simon shrugged and went back to his search for something on which they could break their fast.

When Miriamele returned a short time later, he had turned up a lump of soft cheese and round loaf of bread; he had split the latter open and was toasting it on a stick over the small fire. "Good morning," she said. She looked tousled, but she had washed the dirt from her face and her expression was almost cheerful. "I'm sorry I was so cross. I had a . . . a terrible dream."

He looked at her with interest, but she did not elaborate. "There's food here," he said.

"A fire, too." She came and sat near, holding out her hands. "I hope the smoke doesn't show."

"It doesn't. I went out a little way and looked."

Simon gave Miriamele half the bread and a hunk of the cheese. She ate greedily, then smiled with her mouth full. After swallowing, she said: "I was hungry. I was so worried last night that I didn't eat."

"There's more if you want it."

She shook her head. "We have to save it. I don't know how long we'll be traveling and we may have trouble getting more." Miriamele looked up. "Can you shoot? I brought a bow and a quiver of arrows." She pointed to the unstrung bow hanging beside her saddle.

Simon shrugged. "I've shot one, but I'm no Mundwode. I could probably hit a cow from a dozen paces or so."

Miriamele giggled. "I was thinking of rabbits or squirrels or birds, Simon. I don't think there will be many cows standing around."

He nodded sagely. "Then we'd better do as you say and save our food."

Miriamele sat back and placed her hands on her stomach. "As long as the fire's going . . ." She stood and went to her saddlebags. She brought out a pair of bowls and a small drawstring sack and returned to the fire, then placed two small stones in the embers to heat. "I brought some calamint tea."

"You don't put salt and butter in it, do you?" Simon asked, remembering the Qanuc and their odd additions.

"Elysia's mercy, no!" she said, laughing. "But I wish we had some honey."

While they drank the tea—Simon thought it a great improvement on Mintahoq *aka*—Miriamele talked about what they would do that day. She did not want to resume riding until sundown, but there were other things to be accomplished.

"You can teach me something about swordplay, for one thing."

"What?" Simon stared at her as though she had asked him to show her how to fly.

Miriamele gave him a scornful glance, then got up and walked to her saddlebag. From the bottom she drew out a short sword in a tooled scabbard. "I had Freosel make it for me before we left. He cut it down from a man's sword." Her disdainful look gave way to a wry, strangely self-mocking grin. "I said I wanted it to protect my virtue when we marched on Nabban." She looked hard at Simon. "So teach me."

"You want me to show you how to use a sword," he said slowly.

"Of course. And in turn, I will show you how to use a bow." She raised her chin slightly. "I can hit a cow at a great deal more than a few paces—not that I have," she said hurriedly. "But old Sir Fluiren taught me how to shoot a bow when I was a little girl. He thought it was amusing."

Simon was nonplussed. "So you are going to shoot squirrels for the dinner pot?"

Her expression turned cool again. "I didn't bring the bow for hunting, Simon—the sword, either. We are going somewhere dangerous. A young woman traveling these days would be a fool to go unarmed."

Her calm explanation made him suddenly cold. "But you won't tell me where."

"Tomorrow morning. Now come—we're wasting

time." She picked up the sword and drew it from the scabbard, letting the leather slide to the wet ground. Her eyes were bright, challenging.

Simon stared. "First, you don't treat your scabbard that way." He picked it up and handed it to her. "Put the blade away, then buckle on the sword belt."

Miriamele scowled. "I already know how to buckle a belt."

"First things first," Simon said calmly. "Do you want to learn or not?"

The morning passed, and Simon's irritation at having to teach swordsmanship to a girl passed with it. Miriamele was fiercely eager to learn. She asked question after question, many of which Simon had no answer to, no matter how much he wracked his memory for all the things Haestan, Sludig, and Camaris had tried to teach him. It was hard to admit to her that he, a knight, did not know something, but after a few short but unpleasant exchanges he swallowed his pride and said frankly that he did not know why a sword's hilt only stuck out on two sides and not all around, it just did. Miriamele seemed happier with that answer than she had been with his previous attempts at mystification, and the rest of the lesson passed more swiftly and pleasantly.

Miriamele was surprisingly strong for her size, although when Simon thought about what she had been through his surprise was less. She was quick as well, with good balance, although she tended to lean too far forward, a habit that could quickly prove fatal in an actual fight, since almost any opponent would be larger than she was and have a longer reach. All in all, he was impressed. He sensed that he would quickly run out of new things to tell her, and then it would just be practice and more practice. He was more than a little glad they were sparring with long sticks instead of blades; she had managed during the course of the morning to give him a few nasty swipes.

After they took a long pause for water and a rest, they changed places: Miriamele instructed Simon in the care of the bow, paying special attention to keeping the bow-string warm and dry. He smiled at his own impatience. As Miriamele had been unwilling to sit through his explanations of swordsmanship—much of it taken in whole cloth from Camaris' teachings to him—he himself was itching to show her what he could do with a bow in his hand. But she was having none of it, and so the remainder of the afternoon was spent learning the proper draw. By the time shadows grew long, Simon's fingers were red and raw. He would have to think of some way to acquire finger-leathers like Miriamele's if he was going to be shooting in earnest.

They made a meal for themselves with bread and an onion and a little jerked meat, then saddled the horses.

"Your horse needs a name," Simon told her as he fastened Homefinder's belly strap. "Camaris says your horse is part of you, but it's also one of God's creatures."

"I'll think about it," she said.

They looked one last time around the camp to make sure they had left no trace of their presence—they had buried the fire ashes and raked the bent grass with a long branch—then rode out into the disappearing day.

"There's the old forest," Simon said, pleased. He squinted against the first dawn light. "That dark line, there."

"I see it." She headed her horse off the road, aiming due north. "We will go as far toward it as we can today instead of stopping—I am going to break my own rule and ride in daylight. I'll feel safer when we're there."

"We aren't going back to Sesuad'ra?" Simon asked.

"No. We're going to Aldheorte—for a while."

"We're going to the forest? Why?"

Miriamele was looking straight ahead. She had thrown her hood back, and the sun was in her hair. "Because my uncle may send people after me. They won't be able to find us if we're in the woods."

Simon remembered all too well his experiences in the great forest. Very few of them had been pleasant. "But it takes forever to travel through there."

"We won't be in the woods long. Just enough to be sure that no one finds us."

Simon shrugged. He had no idea where exactly she wanted to go, or why, but she had obviously been planning.

They rode on toward the distant line of the forest.

They reached the outskirts of the Aldheorte late in the afternoon. The sun had sunk toward the horizon; the grassy hills were painted with slanting light.

Simon supposed they would stop and make camp in the thin vegetation of the forest's outer edge—after all, they had now been riding steadily since the evening before, almost a day straight, with only a few short naps stolen along the way—but Miriamele was determined to get well in, safe from accidental discovery. They rode through the increasingly close-leaning trees until riding was no longer practical, then led the horses another quarter of a league. When the princess at last found a site that was to her liking, the forest was in the last glow of twilight; beneath the thick tree canopy the world was all muted shades of blue.

Simon dismounted and hurriedly started a fire. When that was crackling healthily, they made camp. Miriamele had picked the site in part because of a small streamlet that trickled nearby. As she searched for the makings of a meal, he walked the horses over to the water to drink.

Simon, after a full day spent almost entirely in the saddle, found himself strangely wakeful, as though he had forgotten what sleep was. After he and Miriamele had fed themselves, they sat beside the fire and talked about everyday matters, although more by Miriamele's choice than Simon's. He had other things on his mind, and thought it strange that she should so earnestly discuss Josua and Vorzheva's coming child and ask for more stories about the battle with Fengbald when there were so many questions still unanswered about their present journey. At last, frustrated, he held up his hand.

"Enough of this. You said you would tell me where we are going, Miriamele."

She looked into the flames for a while before speaking. "That's true, Simon. I have not been fair, I suppose, to bring you so far on trust alone. But I didn't ask you to come with me."

He was hurt, but tried not to show it. "I'm here, though. So tell me—where are we going?"

She took a deep breath, then let it out. "To Erkynland."

He nodded. "I guessed that. It wasn't hard, listening to you at the Raed. But where in Erkynland? And what are we going to do there?"

"We're going to the Hayholt." She looked at him intently, as if daring him to disagree.

*Aedon have mercy on us,* Simon thought. Out loud, he said: "To get Bright-Nail?" Although it was madness even to consider it, there was a certain excitement to the thought. He—with help, admittedly—had found and secured Thorn, hadn't he? Perhaps if he brought back Bright-Nail as well, he would be . . . He didn't even dare to think the words, but a sudden picture came to him—he, Simon, a sort of knight-of-knights, one who could even court princesses. . . .

He pushed the picture back into the depths. There was no such thing, not really. And he and Miriamele would never come back from such a foolhardy venture in any case. "To try to save Bright-Nail?" he asked again.

Miriamele was still looking at him intently. "Perhaps."

"Perhaps?" He scowled. "What does that mean?"

"I said I would tell you where we were going," she responded. "I didn't say I would tell you everything in my head."

Simon irritatedly picked up a stick and broke it in half, then dumped the pieces into the firepit. " 'S Bloody Tree, Miriamele," he growled, "why are you doing this? You said I was your friend, but then you treat me like a child."

"I am not treating you like a child," she said hotly. "You insisted on coming with me. Good. But my errand is my own, whether I am going to get the sword or heading back to the castle to get a pair of shoes that I left behind by mistake."

Simon was still angry, but he couldn't suppress a bark

of laughter. "You probably *are* going back for shoes or a
dress or something. That would be just my luck—to get
killed by the Erkynguard in the middle of a war for trying
to steal shoes."

A little of Miriamele's annoyance had dissipated. "You
probably stole enough things and got away with it when
you were living at the Hayholt. It will only be fair."

"Stole? Me?"

"From the kitchens, constantly. You told me yourself,
although I knew it already. And who was it who stole the
sexton's shovel and put it in the gauntlet of that armor in
the Lesser Hall, so that it looked like Sir Whoever was
going out to dig a privy pit?"

Surprised she had remembered, Simon let out a quiet,
pleased chortle. "Jeremias did that with me."

"You dragged him into it, you mean. Jeremias would
never have done something like that without you."

"How did you know about that?"

Miriamele gave him a disgusted look. "I told you, you
idiot, I followed you around for weeks."

"You did, didn't you." Simon was impressed. "What
else did you see me do?"

"Mostly sneak off and sit around mooning when you
were supposed to be working," she snapped. "No wonder
Rachel had to pinch your ears blue."

Offended, Simon straightened his back. "I only
sneaked off to have some time to myself. You don't know
what it's like living in the servants' quarters."

Miriamele looked at him. Her expression was suddenly
serious, even sad. "You're right. But you don't know
what it was like being me, either. There certainly wasn't
much chance to be off by myself."

"Maybe," Simon said stubbornly. "But I'll bet the food
was better in your part of the Hayholt."

"It was the same food," she shot back. "We just ate it
with clean hands." She looked pointedly at his ash-
blackened fingers.

Simon laughed aloud. "Ah! So the difference between
a scullion and a princess is clean hands. I hate to disap-

point you, Miriamele, but after spending a day up to my elbows in the washing tub, my hands were *very* clean."

She looked at him mockingly. "So then I suppose there is no difference between the two at all."

"I don't know." Simon grew suddenly uncomfortable with the discussion; it was moving into painful territory. "I don't know, Miriamele."

Sensing that something had changed, she fell silent.

Insects were creaking musically all around, and the shadowy trees loomed like eavesdroppers. It was strange to be in the forest again, Simon thought. He had grown used to the vast distances to be seen from atop Sesuad'ra and the unending openness of the High Thrithing. After that, Aldheorte seemed confining. Still, a castle was confining, too, but it was the best defense against enemies. Perhaps Miriamele was right: for a while, anyway, the forest might be the best place for them.

"I'm going to sleep," she said suddenly. She stood up and walked to the spot where she had unrolled her bed. Simon noted that she had placed his bedroll on the far side of the campfire from her own.

"If you wish." He couldn't tell if she was mad at him again. Perhaps she'd just run short of things to say. He felt like that around her sometimes, once all the talk of small things was finished. The big things were too hard to speak of, too embarrassing ... and too frightening. "I think I'll sit here for a while."

Miriamele rolled herself in her cloak and lay back. Simon watched her through the shimmer of the fire. One of the horses made a soft, contented-sounding noise.

"Miriamele?"

"Yes?"

"I meant what I said the night we left. I will be your protector, even if you don't tell me exactly what I'm protecting you *from*."

"I know, Simon. Thank you."

There was another gap of silence. After a while, Simon heard a thin sound, quietly melodious. He had a moment of apprehension before he realized it was Miriamele humming softly to herself.

"What song is that?"

She stirred and turned toward him. "What?"

"What song is that you were humming?"

She smiled. "I didn't know I was humming. It's been running through my head all this evening. It's one my mother used to sing to me when I was little. I think it's a Hernystiri song that came from my grandmother, but the words are Westerling."

Simon stood and walked to his bedroll. "Would you sing it?"

Miriamele hesitated. "I don't know. I'm tired, and I'm not sure I can remember the words. Anyway, it's a sad song."

He lay down and pulled his cloak over him, abruptly shivering. The night was growing cold. The wind lightly rattled the leaves. "I don't care if you get the words right. It would just be nice to have a song."

"Very well. I'll try." She thought for a moment, then began to sing. Her voice was husky but sweet.

*"In Cathyn Dair there lived a maid,"*

she began. Although she sang quietly, the slow melody ran all through the darkened forest clearing.

*"In Cathyn Dair, by Silversea,*
*The fairest girl was ever born*
*And I loved her and she loved me.*

*"By Silversea the wind is cold*
*The grass is long, the stones are old*
*And hearts are bought, and love is sold*
*And time and time the same tale told*
*In cruel Cathyn Dair.*

*"We met when autumn moon was high*
*In Cathyn Dair, by Silversea,*
*In silver dress and golden shoon*
*She danced and gave her smile to me.*

*"When winter's ice was on the roof*
*In Cathyn Dair, by Silversea,*
*We sang beside the fiery hearth*
*She smiled and gave her lips to me.*

*"By Silversea the wind is cold*
*The grass is long, the stones are old*
*And hearts are bought, and love is sold*
*And time and time the same tale told*
*In cruel Cathyn Dair.*

*"When spring was dreaming in the fields*
*In Cathyn Dair, by Silversea,*
*In Mircha's shrine where candles burned*
*She stood and pledged her troth to me.*

*"When summer burned upon the hills*
*In Cathyn Dair, by Silversea,*
*The banns were posted in the town*
*But she came not to marry me.*

*"By Silversea the wind is cold*
*The grass is long, the stones are old*
*And hearts are bought, and love is sold*
*And time and time the same tale told*
*In cruel Cathyn Dair.*

*"When Autumn's moon had come again*
*In Cathyn Dair, by Silversea,*
*I saw her dance in silver dress*
*The man she danced for was not me.*

*"When winter showed its cruel claws*
*In Cathyn Dair, by Silversea,*
*I walked out from the city walls*
*No more will that place torment me.*

*"By Silversea the wind is cold*
*The grass is long, the stones are old*
*And hearts are bought, and love is sold*
*And time and time the same tale told*
*In cruel Cathyn Dair . . ."*

"That's a pretty song," Simon said when she had finished. "A sad song." The haunting tune still floated through his head; he understood why Miriamele had been humming it all unawares.

"My mother used to sing it to me in the garden at Meremund. She always sang. Everyone said she had the prettiest voice they'd ever heard."

There was silence for a while. Both Simon and Miriamele lay wrapped in their cloaks, nursing their secret thoughts.

"I never knew my mother," Simon said at last. "She died when I was born. I never knew either of my parents."

"Neither did I."

By the time the oddness of this remark sifted down through Simon's own distracted thoughts, Miriamele had rolled over, placing her back toward the fire—and toward Simon. He wanted to ask her what she meant, but sensed that she did not want to talk anymore.

Instead, he watched the fire burning low and the last few sparks fluttering upward into the darkness.

# 3

# Windows Like Eyes

❧

The rams stood so close together that there was scarcely room to move between them. Binabik sang a quiet sheep-soothing song as he threaded his way in and out among the woolly obstacles.

"Sisqi," he called. "I need to speak to you."

She was sitting cross-legged, retying the knots of her ram's harness. Around her several of the other troll men and women were seeing to final tasks before the prince's company resumed its march into Nabban. "I am here," she said.

Binabik looked around. "Would you come with me somewhere more quiet?"

She nodded and set the harness down on the ground. "I will."

They snaked their way back out through the herd of jostling rams and climbed up the knoll. When they sat down in the grass the milling camp lay spread below them. The tents had been dismantled early that morning, and all that remained of what had been a small city for three days was a formless, moving mass of people and animals.

"You are fretful," Sisqi said abruptly. "Tell me what is wrong, beloved—although we have certainly seen enough bad fortune in the last few days to make anyone sad for a long time."

Binabik sighed and nodded. "That is true. The loss of Geloë is a hard one, and not only because of her wisdom.

I miss *her*, too, Sisqi. We will not see anyone like her again."

"But there is more," Sisqi prompted him gently. "I know you well, Binbiniqegabenik. Is it Simon and the princess?"

"That is the root of it. Look—I will show you something." He pulled apart the sections of his walking stick. A long white shaft tipped with blue-gray stone slid out.

"That is Simon's arrow." Sisqi's eyes were wide. "The gift of the Sithi. Did he leave it behind?"

"Not on purpose, I think. I found it tangled in one of the shirts Gutrun made for him. He took with him little but the clothes he wore on his back, but he did take the sack that held his most treasured possessions—Jiriki's mirror, a piece of stone he brought from Haestan's cairn, other things. I believe the White Arrow must have been left by mistake. Perhaps he had taken it out for some other purpose and forgot to return it to the sack." Binabik lifted the arrow until it caught the morning sun and gleamed. "It reminds me of things," he said slowly. "It is the mark of Jiriki's debt to Simon. A debt which is no less than the one *I* owe, on my master Ookequk's behalf, to Doctor Morgenes."

A sudden look of fear came to Sisqi's face, although she did her best to hide it. "What do you mean, Binabik?"

He stared at the arrow miserably. "Ookequk promised help to Morgenes. I took on that oath. I swore to help protect young Simon, Sisqi."

She took his hand in hers. "You have done that and more, Binabik. Surely you are not to guard him day and night for the rest of your life."

"This is different." He carefully slid the arrow back into his walking stick. "And there is more than my debt, Sisqi. Both Simon and Miriamele are already in danger traveling alone in the wilderness, even more so if they go where I fear they do. But they are also a risk to the rest of us."

"What do you mean?" She was having trouble keeping the pain from her words.

"If they are caught, they will eventually be taken to

Pryrates, King Elias' advisor. You do not know him, Sisqi, but I do, at least from tales. He is powerful, and reckless in his use of that power. And he is cruel. He will learn from them whatever they know about us, and Simon and Miriamele both know a great deal—about our plans, about the swords, everything. And Pryrates will kill them, or at least Simon, in the getting of that knowledge."

"So you are going to find them?" she asked slowly.

He hung his head. "I feel I must."

"But why you? Josua has an entire army!"

"There are reasons, my beloved. Come with me when I speak to Josua and you will hear the reasons. You should be there, in any case."

She looked at him defiantly. "If you go after them, then I will go with you."

"And who will keep our people safe in a strange land?" He gestured at the trolls moving below. "You at least speak some of the Westerling speech now. We cannot both go and leave our fellow Qanuc altogether deaf and mute."

Tears were forming in Sisqi's eyes. "Is there no other way?"

"I cannot think of one," he said slowly "I wish I could." His own eyes were damp as well.

"Chukku's Stones!" she swore. "Are we to suffer everything we have suffered to be together, only to be separated again?" She squeezed his fingers tightly. "Why are you so straight-backed and honorable, Binabik of Mintahoq? I have cursed you for it before, but never so bitterly."

"I will come back to you. I swear, Sisqinanamook. No matter what befalls, I will come back to you."

She leaned forward, pushing her forehead against his chest, and wept. Binabik wrapped his arms around her and held tightly; tears rolled down his cheeks as well.

"If you do not come back," she moaned, "may you never have a moment's peace until Time is gone."

"I will come back," he repeated, then fell silent. They stayed that way for a long time, locked in a miserable embrace.

"I cannot say I like this idea, Binabik," said Prince Josua. "We can ill-afford to lose your wisdom—especially now, after Geloë's death." The prince looked morose. "Aedon knows what a blow that has been to us. I feel sick inside. And we have not even a body to weep over."

"And that is as she was wishing it," Binabik said gently. "But, speaking about your first worry, it is my thinking that we can even less be suffering the loss of your niece and Simon. I have made you know my fears about that."

"Perhaps. But what about discovering the use of the swords? We still have much to learn."

"I have little help left for giving to Strangyeard and Tiamak," said the little man. "Nearly all of Ookequk's scrolls I have already made into Westerling. Those few of them that are remaining still, Sisqi can be helping with them." He indicated his betrothed, who sat silently beside him, her eyes red. "And then, I must also be saying with regret, when that task is being finished she will take the remaining Qanuc and return to our people."

Josua looked at Sisqi. "This is another great loss."

She bowed her head.

"But you are many now," Binabik pointed out. "Our people suffer, too, and these herdsmen and huntresses will be needed at Blue Mud Lake."

"Of course," said the prince. "We will always be grateful that your people came to our aid. We will never forget, Binabik." He frowned. "So you are determined to go?"

The troll nodded. "There are many reasons it is seeming the best course to me. It is also my fear that Miriamele hopes to get the sword Bright-Nail—perhaps with thinking she can hurry the end of this struggle. That is frightening to me, since if Count Eolair's story was true, the dwarrows have already confessed to the minions of the Storm King that Minneyar is the sword that is resting now in your father's grave."

"Which is likely the end of our hopes, in any case,"

Josua said gloomily. "For if he knows that, why would Elias leave it there?"

"The Storm King's knowing and the knowing of your brother may not be the same thing," Binabik observed. "It is not an unheard-of strangeness for allies to be hiding things from each other. The Storm King may not be knowing that *we* also have this knowledge." He smiled a yellow smile. "It is a thing of great complication, is it not? Also, from the story that the old man Towser was so often telling—the story of how your brother acted when Towser was giving him the blade—it is possible that those who have the taint of Stormspike cannot bear its nearness."

"It is a great deal to hope for," Josua said. "Isgrimnur? What do you make of all this?"

The duke shifted on the low stool. "About which? The swords, or the troll's going off after Miri and the boy?"

"Either. Both." Josua waved his hand wearily.

"I can't say much about the swords, but what Binabik has to say makes a kind of sense. As to the other . . ." Isgrimnur shrugged. "Someone should go, that's clear. I brought her back once, so I'll go again if you want, Josua."

"No." The prince shook his head firmly. "I need you here. And I would not separate you from Gutrun yet again for the sake of my headstrong niece." He turned to the troll. "How many men would you take, Binabik?"

"None, Prince Josua."

"None?" The prince was astonished. "But what do you mean? Surely it would be safer to take at least a few good men, as you did on the journey to Urmsheim?"

Binabik shook his head. "I am thinking that Miriamele and Simon will not hide from me, but they would be hiding with certainness from mounted soldiers pursuing them. Also, there are places Qantaqa and I can go that even riders of great skill, like Hotvig's Thrithings-men, cannot. I can be more silent, too. No, it is a better thing if I go by myself."

"I do not like it," Josua said, "and I can see that your Sisqi does not like it either. But I will consider it, at least.

Perhaps it *would* be best—there is more of me than just an uncle's love that fears what might happen if Miriamele and Simon fall into my brother's hands. Certainly something must be done." He lifted his hand and rubbed at his temples. "Let me think on it a while."

"With certainty, Prince Josua." Binabik stood. "But remember that even Qantaqa's wonderful nose cannot be tracking a scent that has been too long on the ground." He bowed, as did Sisqi, then they turned and went out.

"He is small—they both are," Josua said reflectively. "But not only do I wish the trolls were not leaving, I wish I had a thousand more like them."

"He's a brave one, that Binabik, right enough," said Isgrimnur. "Seems sometimes as if that's all we have left."

Eolair watched the fly buzzing near his horse's head for some time. The horse, but for an occasional ear-flick, seemed little bothered, but Eolair continued to stare. There was not much else to look at while riding through this westernmost part of Hernystir on the fringes of the Frostmarch, and the fly also reminded him of something he could not quite summon to mind, but which was nevertheless bidding for his attention. The Count of Nad Mullach watched the tiny black speck for some time before he finally realized why it seemed significant.

*This is the first fly I've seen in a while—the first since the winter came down, I think. It must be getting warmer.*

This rather ordinary thought gave rise to a host of other, less usual speculations.

*Could it be that somehow the tide has turned?* he wondered. *Could Josua and his people have accomplished something that has diminished the Storm King's power and pushed back his magical winter?* He looked around at the small, tattered troop of Hernystiri that rode behind him, and at the great company of Sithi who led them, their banners and armor ablaze with color. *Could the fact that Jiriki's folk have entered the battle somehow have tipped the scale in our favor? Or am I making too much out of the tiniest of signs?*

He laughed to himself, but grimly. This last year and its attendant horrors seemed to have made him as omen-drunk as his ancestors of Hern's day.

His ancestors had been on Eolair's mind more than a little in the last few days. The army of Sithi and men riding toward Naglimund had recently stopped at Eolair's castle at Nad Mullach on the River Baraillean. In the two days the army was quartered there, the count had found another three score men from the surrounding area who were willing to join the war party—most of them more for the wonder of riding with the fabled Peaceful Ones, Eolair suspected, than out of any sense of duty or thirst for revenge. The young men who agreed to join the company were mostly those whose families had been lost or scattered during the recent conflict. Those who still had land or loved ones to protect had no desire to ride off to another war, no matter how noble or all-encompassing the cause—nor could Eolair have commanded them to do so: the landholders of Hernystir had not possessed that right since King Tethtain's day.

Nad Mullach had been less harshly treated than Hernysadharc, but it had still suffered during Skali's conquest. In the short time he had, Eolair rounded up those few of his retainers who remained and did his best to set things on the right course again. If he did manage somehow to return from this mad war that was growing madder by the day, he wanted nothing more than to put down the reins of responsibility as soon as possible and live once more in his beloved Nad Mullach.

His liege-folk had held out long against the small portion of Skali's army that had been left to besiege them, but when those prisoned within the castle's walls began to starve, Eolair's cousin and castellaine Gwynna, a stern, capable woman, opened the gates to the Rimmersmen. Many of the fine things that had been in Eolair's line since not long after Sinnach's alliance with the Erl-king were destroyed or stolen, and so were many objects that Eolair himself had brought back from his travels through-

out Osten Ard. Still, he had consoled himself, the walls
still stood, the fields—under a blanket of snow—were
still fertile, and the wide Baraillean, unhindered by war or
winter, still rushed past Nad Mullach on its way to
Abaingeat and the sea.

The count had commended Gwynna for her decision,
telling her that had he been in residence he would have
done the same. She, to whom the sight of Skali's outlanders in her great house had been the most galling thing
imaginable, was a little comforted, but not much.

Those outlanders, perhaps because their master was far
away in Hernysadharc, or perhaps because they were not
themselves of Skali's savage Kaldskryke clan, had been
less hateful in their occupation than the invaders in other
parts of Hernystir. They had treated their conquered prisoners poorly, and had plundered and smashed to their
hearts' content, but had not indulged in the kind of rape,
torture, and senseless killing that had marked Skali's
main army as it drove on Hernysadharc.

Still, despite the comparative lightness of the damage
to his ancestral home, as he rode out of Nad Mullach
Eolair was nevertheless filled with a sense of violation
and shame. His forebears had built the castle to watch
over their bit of the river valley. Now it had been attacked
and defeated, and the current count had not even been at
home. His servants and kin had been forced to make their
way alone.

*I served my king,* he told himself. *What else could I
do?*

There was no answer, but that did not make it any
easier to live with the memories of shattered stone,
scorched tapestries, and frightened, hollow-eyed people. Even should both war and spirit-winter end tomorrow, that harm had already been done.

"Would you like something more to eat, my´lady?"
Eolair asked.

He could not help wondering what Maegwin in her
madness made of the rather poor fare that had been their
lot so far on the trip toward Naglimund. Nothing much

could be expected of a war-ravaged countryside, of course, but the count was curious how hard bread and leathery onions could be considered food fit for gods.

"No, Eolair, thank you." Maegwin shook her head and smiled gently. "Even in a land of unending pleasure, we must rest from pleasure occasionally."

Unending pleasure! The count smiled back despite himself. It might not be bad to be as touched as Maegwin, at least during meals.

A moment later he chided himself for the uncharitable thought. *Look at her. She's like a child. It's not her fault—perhaps it was the blow Skali struck her. It may not have killed her, as she thinks, but it might have disordered her brains.*

He stared at her. Maegwin was watching the sunset with evident pleasure. Her face seemed almost to glow.

*What is that term they use in Nabban? "Holy fools." That's what she looks like—someone who is no longer of the earth.*

"The sky of heaven is more beautiful than I would have imagined," she said dreamily. "I wonder if perhaps it is our own sky, but we see it now from the other side."

*And even were there some cure,* Eolair wondered suddenly, *what right have I to take this away from her?* The thought was shocking, like cold water dashed in his face. *She is happy—happy for the first time since her father went off to war and his death. She eats, she sleeps, she talks to me and others . . . even if most of it is arrant nonsense. How would she be better off if she came back to her senses in this dreadful time?*

There was no answer to that, of course. Eolair took a deep breath, fighting off the weariness that assailed him when he was with Maegwin. He stood and walked to a patch of melting snow nearby, washed his bowl, then returned to the tree where Maegwin sat, staring out across the rolling fields of grass and gray snow toward the ruddy western sky.

"I am going to talk to Jiriki," he told her. "Will you be well here?"

She nodded, a half smile tilting her lips. "Certainly, Count Eolair."

He bowed his head and left her.

The Sithi were seated upon the ground around Likimeya's fire. Eolair stopped some distance away, marveling at the strangeness of the sight. Although close to a dozen of them sat in a wide circle, no one spoke: they merely looked at each other as though they carried on some wordless conversation. Not for the first time, the Count of Nad Mullach felt the hairs on the back of his neck rise in superstitious wonder. What strange allies!

Likimeya still wore her mask of ashes. Heavy rains had swept down on the traveling army the day before, but her strange face-painting seemed just as it had been, which made the count suspect that she renewed it each day. Seated across from her was a tall, narrow-featured Sitha-woman, thin as a priest's staff, with pale sky-blue hair drawn up atop her head in a birdlike crest. It was only because Jiriki had told him that Eolair knew that this stern woman, Zinjadu, was even older than Likimeya.

Also seated at the fire was Jiriki's red-haired, green-garbed uncle Khendraja'aro, and Chekai'so Amber-Locks, whose shaggy hair and surprisingly open face—Eolair had even seen this Sitha smile and laugh—made him seem almost human. On either side of Jiriki sat Yizashi, whose long gray witchwood spear was twined about with sun-golden ribbons, and Kuroyi, who was taller than anyone else in the entire company, Sithi or Hernystiri, and so pale and cold-featured that but for his tar-black hair he might have been a Norn. There were others, too, three females and a pair of males that Eolair had seen before, but whose names he did not know.

He stood uncomfortably for some time, uncertain of whether to stay or go. At last, Jiriki looked up. "Count Eolair," he said. "We are just thinking about Naglimund."

Eolair nodded, then bowed toward Likimeya, who lowered her chin briefly in acknowledgment. None of the other Sithi gave him much more attention than a flick of feline eyes. "We will be there soon," he said.

"A few days," agreed Jiriki. "We Zida'ya are not used to fighting against a castle held by enemies—I do not think we have done it since the last evil days back in Venyha Do'sae. Are there any among your folk who know Josua's stronghold well, or about such fighting? We have many questions."

"Siege warfare. . . ?" said Eolair uncertainly. He had thought that the frighteningly competent Sithi would have prepared for this long before. "There are a few of my men who have fought as mercenaries in the Southern Islands and the Lakeland wars, but not many. Hernystir itself has been peaceful during most of our lifetimes. As to Naglimund . . . I suppose that *I* know it best of any Hernystirman still living. I have spent much time there."

"Come and sit with us." Jiriki gestured to an open place near Chekai'so.

Black-haired Kuroyi said something in the liquid Sithi tongue as Eolair seated himself on the ground. Jiriki showed a hint of a smile. "Kuroyi says that surely the Norns will come out and fight us before the walls. He believes that the Hikeda'ya would never hide behind stone laid by mortals when the Zida'ya have come to resolve things at last."

"I know nothing of the . . . of those we call Norns," Eolair said carefully. "But I cannot imagine that if their purpose is as deadly earnest as it seems, they will give up the advantage of a stronghold like Naglimund."

"I believe you are correct," said Jiriki. "But it is hard to convince many of my people that. It is hard enough for most of us to believe that we go to war with the Hikeda'ya, let alone that they might hide within a fortress and drop stones on us as mortal armies do." He said something in the Sithi speech to Kuroyi, who replied briefly, then fell silent, his eyes cold as bronze plates. Jiriki next turned to the others.

"It is impolite for us to speak in a language Count Eolair does not know. If anyone does not feel comfortable speaking Hernystiri or Westerling, I will be happy to render your words for the count's understanding."

"Mortal tongues and mortal strategies. We will all have

to learn," Likimeya said abruptly. "It is a different age. If the rules of mortals now make the world spin, then we must learn those rules."

"Or decide whether it is possible to live in such a world." Zinjadu's voice was deep yet strangely uninflected, as though she had learned Westerling without ever having heard it spoken. "Perhaps we should let the Hikeda'ya have this world of mortals that they seem to desire."

"The Hikeda'ya would destroy the mortals even more readily than they would destroy us," Jiriki said calmly.

"It is one thing," spoke up Yizashi Grayspear, "to fulfill an ancient debt, as we have just done at M'yin Azoshai. Besides, those were mortals we routed, and the descendants of bloody Fingil's ship-men besides. It is another thing to go to war with other Gardenborn to aid mortals to whom we owe no such debt—including those who hunted us long after we lost Asu'a. This Josua's father was our enemy!"

"Then does the hatred never end?" Jiriki replied with surprising heat. "Mortals have short lives. These are not the ones who warred on our scattered folk."

"Yes, the lives of mortals are short," said Yizashi dispassionately. "But their hatreds run deep, and are passed from parents to children."

Eolair was beginning to feel distinctly uncomfortable but did not think the time was right for him to speak up.

"It is possible that you forget, noble Yizashi," said Jiriki, "that it was the Hikeda'ya themselves who brought this war to us. It was they who invaded the sanctity of the Yásira. It was truly Utuk'ku's hand—not that of the mortal catspaw who wielded the dagger—which slew First Grandmother."

Yizashi did not reply.

"There is little point in this," Likimeya said. Eolair could not help noticing how the depths of Likimeya's eyes cast the light back, glowing orange as the stare of a torchlit wolf. "Yizashi, I asked you and these others, the House of Contemplation, the House of Gathering, all the houses, to honor your debts to the Grove. You agreed.

And we are set upon our course because we need to thwart Utuk'ku Seyt-Hamakha's plans, not just repay an old debt or avenge Amerasu's murder."

Black-browed Kuroyi spoke up. "The mortals have a saying, I am told." His voice was measured and eerily musical, his Hernystiri somehow over-precise. " *'The enemy of my enemy is my friend ... for a little while.'* Silvermask and her kin have chosen one set of mortals to be their allies, so we will choose those mortals' enemies to be *our* allies. Utuk'ku and her minions have also broken the Pact of Sesuad'ra. I find no shame in fighting beside Sudhoda'ya until the issue is settled." He raised his hand as though to ward off questions, but the circle was completely still. "No one has said I must love these mortal allies: I do not, and feel sure that I will not, whatever happens. And if I live until these days end, I will return to my high house in hidden Anvi'janya, for I have long been surfeited with the company of others, whether mortal or Gardenborn. But until then, I will do as I have promised to Likimeya."

There was a long pause after Kuroyi had finished. The Sithi again sat in silence, but Eolair had the feeling that some issue was in the air, some tension that sought resolution. When the quiet had gone on so long that he was beginning to wonder again whether he should leave, Likimeya lifted her hands and spread them flat in the air before her.

"So," she said. "Now we must think about this Naglimund. We must consider what we will do if the Hikeda'ya do not come out to fight."

The Sithi began to discuss the upcoming siege as though there had been no dispute over the honorability of fighting beside mortals. Eolair was puzzled but impressed by their civility. Each person was allowed to speak as long as he wished and no one interrupted. Whatever dissension there had been—and although Eolair found the immortals difficult to fathom, he had no doubt there had been true disagreement—now seemed vanished: the debate over Naglimund, although spirited, was calm and apparently free of resentment.

*Perhaps when you live so long,* Eolair thought, *you learn to exist by such rules—learn you must exist by such rules. Forever is a long time to carry grudges, after all.*

More at ease now, he entered the discussion—hesitantly at first, but when he saw that his opinion was to be given due weight he spoke openly and confidently about Naglimund, a place he knew almost as well as he knew the Taig in Hernysadharc. He had been there many times: Eolair had often found that Josua's was a useful ear for introducing things into the court of his father, King John Presbyter. The prince was one of the few people the Count of Nad Mullach knew who would listen to an idea on its own merits, then support it if he found it good, regardless of whether it benefited him.

They talked long; eventually the fire burned down to glowing coals. Likimeya produced one of the crystal globes from her cloak and set it on the ground before her where it gradually grew bright; soon it cast its cool lunar glow all around the circle.

Eolair met Isorn on his way back from the council of the Sithi.

"Ho, Count," the young Rimmersman said. "Out for a stroll? I have a skin of wine here—from your own Nad Mullach cellars, I think. Let's find Ule and share it."

"Gladly. I have had a strange evening. Our allies ... Isorn, they are like nothing and no one I have ever seen."

"They are the Old Ones, and heathen on top of it," Isorn said blithely, then laughed. "Apologies, Count. I sometimes forget that you Hernystiri are ..."

"Also heathens?" Eolair smiled faintly. "No offense was taken. I have grown used to being the outsider, the odd one, during my years in Aedonite courts. But I have never felt so much the odd man as I did tonight."

"The Sithi may be different from us, Eolair, but they are bold as thunder."

"Yes, and clever. I did not understand all that was spoken of tonight, but I think that we have neither of us ever seen a battle like the one that will take place at Naglimund."

Isorn lifted an eyebrow, intrigued. "That is something to save and tell over that wine, but I am glad to hear it. If we live, we will have stories to amaze our grandchildren."

"If we live," Eolair said.

"Come, let us walk a little faster." Isorn's voice was light. "I am getting thirsty."

They rode across the Inniscrich the next day. The battlefield where Skali had triumphed and King Lluth had received his death-wound was still partially blanketed in snow, but that snow was full of irregular hummocks, and here and there a bit of rusted metal or a weathered spearhaft stuck up through the shrouding white. Although many prayers and curses were quietly spoken, none of the Hernystiri had any great interest in lingering at the site where they had been so soundly defeated and so many of their people had died, and for the Sithi it had no significance at all, so the great company passed by swiftly as they rode north along the river.

The Baraillean marked the boundary between Hernystir and Erkynland: the people of Utanyeat on the river's eastern side called it the Greenwade. These days, there were few living near either bank, although there were still fish to catch. The weather might have grown warmer, but Eolair could see that the land was almost lifeless. Those few survivors of the various struggles who still scratched out their lives here on the southern edge of the Frostmarch now fled before the approaching army of Sithi and men, unable to imagine any good that yet one more troop of armored invaders might bring.

At last, a week's journeying north of Nad Mullach— even when they were not in full charge the Sithi moved swiftly—the host crossed the river and moved into Utanyeat, the westernmost tip of Erkynland. Here the land seemed to grow more gray. The thick morning mists that had blanketed the ground during the ride across Hernystir no longer dispersed with the sun's ascension, so that the army rode from dawn to dusk in a cold, damp haze, like souls in some cloudy afterlife. In fact, a deathly pall seemed to hang over all the plains. The air was cold and seemed to reach directly into the bones of Eolair and his fellows. But for the wind and the muffled hoofbeats of their own horses, the wide countryside was silent, devoid even of birdsong. At night, as the count huddled with Maegwin and Isorn before the fire, a heavy stillness lay over everything. It felt, Isorn remarked one night, as though they were passing through a vast graveyard.

As each day brought them deeper into this colorless, cheerless country, Isorn's Rimmersmen prayed and made the Tree-sign frequently, and argued almost to bloodletting over insignificant things. Eolair's Hernystiri were no less affected. Even the Sithi seemed more reserved than usual. The ever-present mists and forbidding silence made all endeavor seem shallow and pointless.

Eolair found himself hoping that there would be some sign of their foes soon. The sense of foreboding that hung over these empty lands was a more insidious enemy, the count felt sure, than anything composed of flesh and blood could ever be. Even the frighteningly alien Norns were preferable to this journey through the netherworld.

"I feel something," said Isorn. "Something pricks at my neck."

Eolair nodded, then realized the duke's son probably could not see him through the mist, although he rode only a short distance away. "I feel it, too."

They were nine days out of Nad Mullach. Either the weather had again gone bad, or in this small part of the world the winter had never abated. The ground was carpeted in snow, and great uneven drifts lay humped on either side as they rode up the low hill. The failing sun was somewhere out of sight, the afternoon so gray there might never have been such a thing as a sun at all.

There was a clatter of armor and a flurry of words in the liquid Sithi speech from up ahead. Eolair squinted through the murk. "We are stopping." He spurred his horse forward. Isorn followed him, with Maegwin, who had ridden silently all day, close behind.

The Sithi had indeed reined up, and now sat silently on

their horses as if waiting for something, their bright-colored armor and proud banners dimmed by the mist. Eolair rode through their ranks until he found Jiriki and Likimeya. They were staring ahead, but he saw nothing in the shifting fog that seemed worth their attention.

"We have halted," said the count.

Likimeya turned to him. "We have found what we sought." Her features seemed stony, as though her whole face had now become a mask.

"But I see nothing." Eolair turned to Isorn, who shrugged to show that he was no different.

"You will," said Likimeya. "Wait."

Puzzled, Eolair patted his horse's neck and wondered. There was a stirring as the wind rose again, fluttering his cloak. The mists swirled, and suddenly something dark appeared as the murk before them thinned.

The great curtain wall of Naglimund was ragged, many of its stones tumbled out like the scales of a rotting fish. In the midst of its great, gray length was a rubble-filled gap where the gate had stood, a sagging, toothless mouth. Beyond, showing even more faintly through the tendrils of mist, Naglimund's square stone towers loomed up beyond the walls, the dark windows glaring like the empty, bone-socket eyes of a skull.

"Brynioch," Eolair gasped.

"By the Ransomer," said Isorn, just as chilled.

"You see?" Likimeya asked. Eolair thought he detected a dreadful sort of humor in her voice. "We have arrived."

"It is Scadach." Maegwin sounded terrified. "The Hole in Heaven. Now I have seen it."

"But where is Naglimund-town?" Eolair asked. "There was a whole city at the castle's foot!"

"We have passed it, or at least its ruins," Jiriki said. "What little remains of it is now beneath the snows."

"Brynioch!" Eolair felt quite stupefied as he stared first at the insignificant-seeming lumps of earth and snow behind them, then turned back to the huge pile of crumbling stone just ahead. It seemed dead, yet as he gazed at it his nerves felt tight as lute strings and his heart was pounding. "Do we just ride in?" he asked no one in particular.

Just thinking about it was like contemplating a headfirst crawl into a dark tunnel full of spiders.

"I will not go in that place," Maegwin said harshly. She was pale. For the first time since her madness had descended, she looked truly and completely fearful. "If you enter Scadach, you leave Heaven and its protection. It is a place from which nothing returns."

Eolair did not even have the heart to say anything soothing, but he reached out and took her gloved hand. Their horses stood quietly side by side, vaporous breath mingling.

"We will not ride into that place, no," Jiriki said solemnly. "Not yet."

Even as he spoke, flickering yellow lights bloomed in the depths of the black tower windows, as though whatever owned those empty eyes had just awakened.

Rachel the Dragon slept uneasily in her tiny room deep in the Hayholt's underground warrens.

She dreamed that she was again in her old room, the chambermaids' room that she knew so well. She was alone, and in her dream she was angry: her foolish girls were always so hard to find.

Something was scratching at the door; Rachel had a sudden certainty that it was Simon. Even in the midst of the dream, though, she remembered that she had been fooled once before by such a noise. She went carefully and quietly to the doorway and stood beside it for a moment, listening to the furtive noises outside.

"Simon?" she said. "Is that you?"

The voice that came back was indeed that of her long-lost ward, but it seemed stretched and thin, as though it traveled a long distance to reach her ear.

"*Rachel, I want to come back. Please help me. I want to come back.*" The scratching resumed, insistent, strangely loud. . . .

The onetime Mistress of Chambermaids jerked awake,

shivering with cold and fear. Her heart was beating very fast.

There. There was that noise again, just as she had heard it in the dream—but now she was awake. It was a strange sound, not so much a scratching as a hollow scraping, distant but regular. Rachel sat up.

This was no dream, she knew. She thought she had heard something like it as she was falling off to sleep, but had dismissed it. Could it be rats in the walls? Or something worse? Rachel sat up on her straw pallet. The small brazier with its few coals did no more than give the room a faint red sheen.

Rats in stone walls as thick as these? It was possible, but it didn't seem likely.

*What else would it be, you old fool? Something is making that noise.*

Rachel sat up and moved stealthily toward the brazier. She took a handful of rushes from her carefully collected pile and dipped one end into the coals. After they had caught, she lifted the makeshift torch high.

The room, so familiar after all these weeks, was empty but for her stores. She bent low to look into the shadowy corners, but saw nothing moving. The scraping noise was a little fainter now but still unmistakable. It seemed to be coming from the far wall. Rachel took a step toward it and smacked her bare foot against her wooden keepsake chest, which she had neglected to push back against the wall after examining its sparse contents the night before. She let out a muffled shriek of pain and dropped a few of the flaming rushes, then quickly hobbled to her jug for a handful of water to put them out. When this was done, she stood on one foot while she rubbed her smarting toes.

When the pain subsided, she realized that the noise had also stopped. Either her surprised cry had frightened the noise-maker away—likely if it were a rat or mouse—or merely warned the thing that someone was listening. The thought of something sitting quietly within the walls, aware now that someone was on the other side of the stone, was not one that Rachel wished to pursue.

*Rats, she told herself. Of course it's rats. They smell the food I've got in here, little demon imps.*

Whatever the cause had been, the noise was gone now. Rachel sat down on her stool and began to pull on her shoes. There was no point trying to sleep now.

*What a strange dream about Simon,* she thought. *Could it be his spirit is restless? I know that monster murdered him. There are tales that the dead can't rest till their murderers are punished. But I already did my best to punish Pryrates, and look where it got me. No good to anyone.*

Thinking of Simon condemned to some lonely darkness was both sad and frightening.

*Get up, woman. Do something useful.*

She decided that she would set out more food for poor blind Guthwulf.

A brief sojourn to the room with a slit of window upstairs confirmed that it was almost dawn. Rachel stared at the dark blue of the sky and the faded stars and felt a little reassured.

*I'm still waking up regular, even if I live in the dark most days like a mole. That's something.*

She descended to her hidden room, pausing in the doorway to listen for the scraping noises. The room was silent. After she had found suitable fare for both the earl and his feline familiar, she donned her heavy cloak and made her way down the stairwell to the secret passageway behind the tapestry on the landing.

When she arrived at the spot where she customarily left Guthwulf's meal, she found to her distress that the previous morning's food had not been touched: neither man nor cat had come.

*He's never missed two days running since we started,* she thought worriedly. *Blessed Rhiap, has the poor man fallen down somewhere?*

Rachel collected the untouched food and put out more, as though somehow a slightly different arrangement of what was really the same dried fruit and dried meat could tempt back her wandering earl.

*If he doesn't come today,* she decided, *I'll have to go*

*and look for him. He has no one else to see to him, after
all. It's the Aedonite thing to do.*

Full of worry, Rachel made her way back to her room.

♣

The sight of Binabik seated on a gray wolf as though it
were a war-horse, his walking-stick couched like a lance,
might have been comical in other circumstances, but
Isgrimnur felt no urge even to smile.

"Still I am not sure this is the best thing," Josua said.
"I fear we will miss your wisdom, Binabik of Yiqanuc."

"Then that is being all the larger reason for me to begin
my journey now, since it will be ended so much more
soon." The troll scratched behind Qantaqa's ears.

"Where is your lady?" Isgrimnur asked, looking
around. Dawn was creeping into the sky overhead, but the
hillside was deserted except for the three men and the
wolf. "I would think she'd want to come and say farewell."

Binabik did not meet his eye, but rather stared at
Qantaqa's shaggy neck. "We were saying our farewells in
the earliness of the morning, Sisqi and I," he said quietly.
"It is a hard thing for her to see me riding away."

Isgrimnur felt a great wash of regret for all the unwise,
unthinking remarks he had ever made about trolls. They
were small and strange, but they were certainly as bold-
hearted as bigger men. He extended his hand for Binabik
to clasp.

"Ride safely," the duke said. "Come back to us."

Josua did the same. "I hope you find Miriamele and Si-
mon. But if you do not, there is no shame in it. As
Isgrimnur said, come back to us as soon as you can,
Binabik."

"And I am hoping that things will be going well for
you in Nabban."

"But how will you find us?" Josua asked suddenly, his
long face worried.

Binabik stared at him for a moment, then, surprisingly,
let out a loud laugh. "How can I be finding an army of

grasslanders and stone-dwellers mixed together, led by a dead hero of great famousness and a one-handed prince? I am thinking that it will not be difficult obtaining word of you."

Josua's face relaxed into a smile. "I suppose you are right. Farewell, Binabik." He raised his hand, exposing for a moment the dulled manacle he wore as a reminder of his imprisonment and the debt he owed his brother for it.

"Farewell, Josua and Isgrimnur," said the troll. "Please be saying that for me to the others as well. I could not bear to be making good-byes to all at once." He leaned forward to whisper something to the patiently waiting wolf, then turned back toward them. "In the mountains, we are saying this: *'Inij koku na siqqasa min taq'*— 'When we meet again, that will be a good day.' " He sunk both his hands into the wolf's hackles. *"Hinik,* Qantaqa. Find Simon. *Hinik ummu!"*

The wolf leaped forward up the wet hillside. Binabik swayed on her broad back but kept his seat. Isgrimnur and Josua watched until the strange rider and his stranger mount topped the hill's crest and vanished from sight.

"I fear I will never see them again," said Josua. "I am cold, Isgrimnur."

The duke put his hand on the prince's shoulder. He was not himself feeling either very warm or very happy. "Let's go back. We have near a thousand people we need to get moving by the time the sun is above the hilltops."

Josua nodded. "So we do. Come, then."

They turned and retraced their own footsteps in the sodden grass.

# 4

# A Thousand Leaves,
# A Thousand Shadows

&#x2663;

**Miriamele and Simon** spent the first week of their flight in the forest. The traveling was slow and painfully laborious, but Miriamele had decided long before her escape that it would be far better to lose time than to be captured. The daylight hours were spent struggling through the dense trees and matted, tangling undergrowth, all to the tune of Simon's grumbling. They led their horses more often than they rode them.

"Be happy," she told him once as they rested in a clearing, leaning against the trunk of an old oak. "At least we are getting to see the sun for a few days. When we leave the forest again, we'll be riding by night."

"At least if we ride at night I won't have to look at the things that are tearing all the skin off my body," Simon said crossly, rubbing at his tattered breeches and the bruised flesh underneath.

It was heartening, Miriamele discovered, to have something to do. The feeling of helpless dread that had gripped her for weeks faded away, leaving her able to think clearly, to see everything around her as if with new eyes . . . and even to enjoy being with Simon.

She did enjoy his company. Sometimes she wished she didn't enjoy it quite so much. It was hard not to feel as though she were tricking him somehow. It was more than just not telling him all her reasons for leaving Uncle Josua and setting out for the Hayholt. She also felt as though she were not wholly clean, not wholly fit to be with someone else.

*It is Aspitis,* she thought. *He did this to me. Before him, I was as pure as anyone could want to be.*

But was that really true? He had not forced himself upon her. She had let him do what he wished—in some ways she had welcomed it. In the end, Aspitis had proved to be a monster, but the way in which he came to her bed was no different than that in which most men came to their sweethearts. He had not savaged her. If what they had done was wrong and sinful, she bore equal blame.

And what, then, of Simon? She had very mixed feelings. He was not a boy any more but a man, and a part of her feared the man he had become, as it would fear any man. But, she thought, there was also something about him that had remained strangely innocent. In his earnest attempts to do right, in the poorly-hidden hurt that he showed when she was short with him, he was still almost childlike. This made her feel even worse, that in his transparent regard for her he had no clue as to what she was truly like. It was precisely when he was kindest to her, when he most admired and complimented her, that she felt most angry with him. It seemed he was being willfully blind.

It was a dreadful way to feel. Luckily, Simon seemed to understand that his sincere affection was somehow painful to her, so he fell back on the jesting, mocking friendship with which she was more comfortable. When she could be around him without thinking about herself, she found him good company.

Despite growing up in the courts of her grandfather and father, Miriamele had found little opportunity to be with boys. King John's knights were mostly dead or long since retired to their estates scattered about Erkynland and elsewhere, and in her grandfather's later years the king's court had become empty of almost any but those who had to live near the king for the sake of their day-to-day livelihoods. Later, when her mother had died, her father had frowned on her spending time even with the few boys and girls of her age. He had not filled the void with his own presence, but had instead mewed her up with unpleasant old men and women who lectured her about the rituals and responsibilities of her position and found fault with everything she did. By the time her father had become king, Miriamele's solitary childhood was over.

Leleth, her handmaiden, had been almost her only young companion. The little girl had idolized Miriamele, hanging on the princess' every word. In turn, Leleth had told long stories about growing up with brothers and sisters—she was the youngest of a large baronial family—while her mistress listened in fascination, trying not to be jealous of the family she had never had.

That was why it had been so difficult to see Leleth again upon reaching Sesuad'ra. The lively little girl she remembered had vanished. Before they had fled the castle together, Leleth had been quiet sometimes, and many things frightened her, but it was as though some completely different creature now lived behind the little girl's eyes. Miriamele had tried to remember if there had ever been any sign of the sort of things that Geloë had discovered in the child, but could think of little, except that Leleth had been prone to vivid, intricate, and sometimes frightening dreams. Some of them had seemed so detailed and unusual in Leleth's retelling that Miriamele had been more than half certain the little girl had invented them.

When Miriamele's father had ascended to his own father's throne, she found herself both surrounded by people and yet terribly lonely. Everyone at the Hayholt had seemed obsessed with the empty ritual of power, something Miriamele had lived with for so long that it held no interest for her. It was like watching a confusing game played by bad-tempered children. Even the few young men who paid court to her—or rather to her father, for most of them had been interested in little more than the riches and power that would fall to the one who received her marriage-pledge—had seemed to her like some other type of animal than she, boring old men in the bodies of youths, sullen boys masquerading as adults.

The only ones in all of Meremund or the Hayholt who seemed to enjoy life for what it was rather than what gain could be coaxed from it were the servants. In the Hayholt especially, with its army of maids and grooms and scullions, it was as though an entirely different race of people lived side by side with her own bleak peers. Once, in a moment of terrible sadness, she had suddenly seen the great castle as a kind of inverted lich-yard, with the creaking dead walking around on top while the living sang and laughed below.

Thus Simon and a few others had first come to her attention—boys who seemed to want nothing much more than to be boys. Unlike the children of her father's nobles, they were in no hurry to take on the clacking, droning, mannered speech of their elders. She watched them dawdling through their chores, laughing behind their hands at each others' foolish pranks, or playing hoodman blind on the commons grass, and she ached to be like them. Their lives seemed so simple. Even when a more mature wisdom taught her that the lives of the serving-folk were hard and wearisome, she still dreamed sometimes that she could put off her royalty as easily as a cloak and become one of their number. Hard work had never frightened her, but she was terrified of solitude.

"No," Simon said firmly. "You should never let me get this close to you."

He moved his foot slightly and twisted the hilt of his sword so that its cloth-wrapped blade pushed hers away. Suddenly, he was pressing against her. His smell, compounded of sweat and leather jerkin and the sodden fragments of a thousand leaves, was very strong. He was so tall! She forgot that sometimes. The sudden impact of his presence made it hard for Miriamele to think clearly.

"You've left yourself open now," he said. "If I used my dagger, you wouldn't have a chance. Remember, you'll almost always be fighting someone with more reach."

Instead of trying to bring her sword back where it would do some good, she let it drop, then put both hands against Simon's chest and pushed. He fell back, stumbling, before he regained his balance.

"Leave me alone." Miriamele turned and walked a few

steps away, then stooped to pick up a few branches for
the fire so her shaking hands would have something to
do.

"What's wrong?" Simon asked, taken aback. "Did I
hurt you?"

"No, you didn't hurt me." She took her armful of wood
and dumped it into the circle they had cleared on the forest floor. "I'm just done with that game for a while."

Simon shook his head, then sat to undo the rags wound
about his sword.

They had made camp early today, the sun still high
above the treetops. Miriamele had decided that tomorrow they would follow the little streamlet that had long
been their companion down to the River Road; the course
of the stream had been bending in that direction for most
of this day's journey. The River Road wound beside the
Ymstrecca, past Stanshire and on to Hasu Vale. It would
be best, she had reasoned, for them to take to the road at
midnight and still have some walking time before dawn,
rather than spend all of this night in the forest and then
wait through daylight again so they could travel the road
in darkness.

This had been her first opportunity to use her sword in
several days, except for the inglorious purpose of clearing
brush. It had even been she who had suggested an hour of
practice before they ate their evening meal—which was
one of the reasons her abrupt change of heart obviously
puzzled Simon. Miriamele felt torn between a desire to
tell him it wasn't his fault, and an obscure feeling that
somehow it *was* his fault—his fault for being male, his
fault for liking her, his fault for coming with her when
she would have been happier being miserably alone.

"Don't mind me, Simon," she said at last, and felt
weak for doing so. "I'm just tired."

Mollified, he finished his careful rewinding of the
cloth, then dropped the ball of dusty fabric into his saddlebag before coming to join her beside the unlit fire. "I
just wanted you to be careful. I told you that you lean too
far."

"I know, Simon. You did tell me."

"You can't let someone bigger than you get that close."

Miriamele found herself wishing silently that he would stop talking about it. "I know, Simon. I'm just tired."

He seemed to sense that he had annoyed her again. "But you're good, Miriamele. You're strong."

She nodded, absorbed now with the flint. A spark fell into the curls of tinder, but failed to produce a flame. Miriamele wrinkled her nose and tried again.

"Do you want me to try?"

"No, I don't want you to try." She struck again without result. Her arms were getting weary.

Simon looked at the wood shavings, then up at Miriamele's face, then quickly back down again. "Remember Binabik's yellow powder? He could start a fire in a rainstorm with that. I saw him make one catch when we were on Sikkihoq, and there was snow, and the wind was blowing. . . ."

"Here." Miriamele stood, letting the flint and the steel bar tumble to the dirt beside the tinder. "You do it." She walked to her horse and began hunting through the saddlebags.

Simon seemed about to say something, but instead applied himself to the task of fire-lighting. He had no better luck than Miriamele for a long time. At last, when she had returned with a kerchief full of the things she had found, he finally caught a small spark and provoked it into flame. As she stood over him she saw that his hair was getting quite long, hanging down onto his shoulders in reddish curls.

He looked up at her shyly. His eyes were full of concern for her. "What's wrong?"

She ignored his question. "Your hair wants cutting. I'll do it after we eat." She undid the kerchief. "These are our last two apples. They're getting a little old, in any case—I don't know where Fengbald found them." She had been told about the source of much of Josua's confiscated foodstuffs. There was an obscure pleasure in eating what had once been destined for that strutting braggart. "There's still some dried mutton, too, but we're almost through with it. We may have to try out the bow some-time soon."

Simon opened his mouth, then shut it. He took a breath. "We'll wrap the apples in leaves and bury them in the coals. Shem Horsegroom used to do that all the time. Then it doesn't matter if they're a little old."

"If you say so," Miriamele replied.

Miriamele leaned back and licked her fingers. They still smarted a little from the hot apple skin, but it had been worth it. "Shem Horsegroom," she said, "is a man of astonishing wisdom."

Simon smiled. His beard was sticky with juice. "It was good. But now we don't have any more."

"I couldn't eat any more tonight, anyway. And tomor-row we'll be on the road to Stanshire. I'm sure we can find something almost as good along the way."

Simon shrugged. "I wonder where old Shem is," he asked after a few moments had passed. The fire popped and spat as the leaves in which the apples had cooked be-gan to blacken. "And Ruben. And Rachel. Do you think they're all still living at the Hayholt?"

"Why shouldn't they be? The king still needs grooms and blacksmiths. And there must *always* be a Mistress of Chambermaids." She offered a faint smile.

Simon chortled. "That's true. I can't imagine anyone getting Rachel to leave unless she wanted to. You might as well try to drag a porcupine out of a hollow stump. Even the king—your father, I mean—couldn't make her leave until she was ready."

"Sit up." Miriamele felt the sudden need to do some-thing. "I said I was going to cut your hair."

Simon felt at the back of his head. "Do you think it needs it?"

Miriamele's look was stern. "Even sheep get sheared once a season."

She got out her whetstone and sharpened her knife. The noise of the blade on the stone was like a louder echo of the crickets that chirped beyond the light of the small fire.

Simon peered over his shoulder. "I feel like I'm about to be carved for the Aedonmansa feast."

"You never know what may happen when the dried meat runs out. Now look straight ahead and be quiet." She stood behind him, but there was not enough light to see. When she sat, his head was too far above her. "Stay there," she said.

She dragged over a large stone, digging a rut in the moist earth; when she sat on it, she was just the right height. Miriamele lifted Simon's hair in her hands and stared at it judiciously. Just a little off the bottom . . . No. Quite a bit off the bottom.

His hair was finer than it looked. Although it was thick, it was quite soft. Nevertheless, it was grimed with the days of travel. She thought of how her own must look and frowned. "When is the last time you bathed yourself?" she asked.

"What?" He was surprised. "What do you mean?"

"What do you think I mean? Your hair is full of bits of sticks and dirt."

Simon made a noise of disgust. "And what do you expect when I've been crawling through this stupid forest for days and days?"

"Well, I can't cut it like this." She thought for a moment. "I'm going to wash it."

"Are you mad? What do I want it washed for?" He drew up his shoulders protectively, as though she had threatened to stick the knife into him.

"I told you. So I can cut it." She stood and went to fetch the water skin.

"That's drinking water," Simon protested.

"I'll fill it again before we set out," she said calmly. "Now lean your head back."

She had thought momentarily of trying to warm the water, but she was just cross enough at his complaining to enjoy the spluttering noises he made as she disgorged the chilly contents of the water skin on his head. She then took her sturdy bone comb, which Vorzheva had given her back at Naglimund, and combed out the snarls as best she could, ignoring Simon's indignant protests. Some of the twigs were so entangled she had to unbind them with her fingernails, difficult work which made her lean close. The scent of wet hair added to his pungent Simon-smell was somehow quite pleasant, and Miriamele found herself humming quietly.

When she had done the best she could with the knots, she took up her knife again and began to trim his hair. As she had suspected, merely taking off the ragged ends was not entirely satisfying. Moving quickly in case Simon should begin to complain again, she began to cut in earnest. Soon the back of his neck came into view, pale from the long months hidden from the sun.

As she stared at Simon's neck, at the way it broadened at its base, at the line of red-gold hairs gradually thickening toward the hairline, she was suddenly moved.

*There is something magical about everyone,* she thought dreamily. *Everyone.*

She ran her fingers lightly up his neck and Simon jumped.

"Hoy! What are you doing? That tickles."

"Oh, shut your mouth." She smiled behind his back where he could not see.

She trimmed the hair up over his ears as well, leaving just a little bit to hang down in front where the beard began. She lifted the front and shortened that as well, then stepped to the side to make sure it would not fall down into his eyes. The snowy streak was as vivid as lightning.

"This is where the dragon's blood splashed you." The white hair felt no different than the red as it trailed across her fingertips. "Tell me again what it was like."

Simon seemed about to make some flippant remark, but paused instead, then spoke softly. "It was . . . it was not like anything, Miriamele. It just happened. I was frightened, and it was like someone was blowing a horn inside my head. It burned when it touched me. I don't remember much more until I woke up in the cave with Jiriki and Haestan." He shook his head. "There was more to it than that. Some things are hard to explain."

"I know." She let the strands of damp hair fall, then took a breath. "I'm finished."

Simon raised his hands to pat at the back and sides. "It feels short," he said. "I wish I could see it."

"Wait until morning, then have a look in the stream." She felt herself smiling again, stupidly, for no reason. "If I had known you were so vain, I would have brought one of my mirrors."

He turned a look of mock contempt upon her, then sat up straight. "I *do* have a mirror," he crowed. "Jiriki's! It's in my sack."

"But I thought that it was dangerous!"

"Not just to look at." Simon rose and headed for his saddlebags, in which he began to rummage energetically, like a bear seeking honey in a hollow tree. "Found it," he said. A frown crossed his face. He withdrew the hand that held the mirror, then reached back into the saddlebags with the other and continued to search.

"What is it?"

Simon withdrew his drawstring bag and brought it over to the fire. He handed her the Sithi mirror, which she held carefully, almost fearfully, while he scrabbled with increasing desperation in the large sack. At last he stopped and looked up at her, his eyes wide, his face a picture of loss. "It's gone."

"What's gone?"

"The White Arrow. It's not in here." He took his hands out of the sack. "Aedon's Blood! I must have left it in the tent. I must have forgotten to put it back that time." His face then registered a deeper shock. "I hope I didn't leave it up on Sesuad'ra!"

"You took it back to your tent, didn't you? That day you wanted to give it to me?"

He nodded slowly. "That's right. It must have been in there somewhere. At least that means it's probably not lost." He looked down at his empty hands. "But I don't have it." He laughed. "I tried to give it away. It didn't like that, I guess. Sithi gifts, Binabik told me, don't take them lightly. Remember on the river, when we were first traveling together? I was showing off with it and I fell out of the boat."

Miriamele smiled sadly. "I remember."

"I've done it this time, though, haven't I?" he said morosely, and sighed. "Still, it can't be helped. If Binabik finds it, he'll take care of it. And it's not like I need to have it to prove something to Jiriki. If I ever see him again." He shrugged and tried to smile. "May I have the mirror back?"

He held it up and carefully examined his hair. "It's good," he said. "It's short in the back. Like Josua's or someone like that." He looked up at her. "Like Camaris."

"Like a knight."

Simon looked down at his hand for a moment, then reached out and took Miriamele's, enfolding her fingers in his warm grasp. He did not quite meet her eyes. "Thank you. You did it very handsomely."

She nodded, desperately wanting to pull her hand free, to be not so close, but at the same time happy to feel his touch. "You are welcome, Simon."

At last, almost reluctantly, he let her go. "I suppose we should try to sleep if we're going to get up at midnight," he said.

"We should," she agreed.

They packed away their few goods and unfurled their bedrolls in friendly, if slightly uneasy, silence.

Miriamele was awakened in the middle of the night by a hand over her mouth. She tried to scream, but the hand clamped even more tightly.

"No! It's me!" The hand lifted.

"Simon?" she hissed. "You idiot! What are you doing?"

"Quiet. There's someone out there."

"What?" Miriamele sat up, staring uselessly into the darkness. "Are you sure?"

"I was just falling asleep when I heard it," he said into her ear, "but it wasn't a dream. I listened after I was wide awake and I heard it again."

"It's an animal—a deer."

Simon bared his teeth to the moonlight. "I don't know any animals that talk to themselves, do you?"

"What?"

"Quiet!" he whispered. "Just listen."

They sat in silence. It was hard for Miriamele to hear anything over the pounding of her own heart. She sneaked a glance at the fire. A few embers still glowed: if there was a person out there, they had demonstrated their presence quite thoroughly. She wondered if it would do any good now to throw dirt on the coals.

Then she heard it, a crackling noise that seemed a good hundred paces away. Her skin tingled. Simon looked at her significantly. The sound came again, a little more distant this time.

"Whatever it is," she said quietly, "it sounds like it's leaving."

"We were going to try to make our way down to the road in a few hours. I don't think we should risk it."

Miriamele wanted to argue—this was her journey, after all, her plan—but found that she could not. The idea of trying to make their way along the tangled riverbank by moonlight, while something followed along after them . . . "I agree," she said. "We'll wait until light."

"I'll stay up for a while and keep watch. Then I'll wake you and you can let me sleep for a while." Simon sat himself cross-legged with his back against a stump. His sword was across his knees. "Go on, sleep." He seemed tense, almost angry.

Miriamele felt her heart slowing a little. "You said it was talking to itself?"

"Well, it could be more than one person," he said, "but it didn't seem to make enough noise for two. And I only heard one voice."

"What was it saying?"

She could dimly see Simon shake his head. "I couldn't tell. It was too quiet. Just . . . words."

Miriamele settled back onto her bedroll. "It might just be some cotsman. People do live in the forest."

"Might be." Simon's voice was flat. Miriamele suddenly realized that he sounded that way because he was frightened. "There are all kinds of things in these woods," he added.

She let her head fall back until she could see a few

stars peeping through holes in the forest roof. "If you start to feel sleepy, don't be a hero, Simon. Wake me up."

"I will. But I don't think I'll be sleepy for a while."

*Neither will I,* she thought.

The idea of being stalked was a dreadful one. But if someone was following them, someone her uncle had sent, why would the stalker go away again without doing anything? Perhaps it had been forest outlaws who would have slaughtered them in their sleep if Simon had not awakened. Or perhaps it had only been an animal after all, and Simon had imagined the words.

Miriamele at last drifted into an uneasy sleep, a sleep haunted by dreams of antler-headed, two-legged figures moving through the forest shadows.

It took them a good part of the morning to make their way out of the forest. The reaching branches and foot-snagging undergrowth almost seemed to be trying to hold them back; the mist rising from the forest floor was so treacherously dense that if they had not had the sound of the stream to keep them on track, Miriamele felt sure they might just as easily have gone in the wrong direction. At last, sore and sweaty and even more tattered than they had been at dawn, they emerged onto the sodden downs.

After a short ride across the uneven meadowland they reached the River Road late in the morning. There was no snow here, but the sky was dark and threatening, and the thick forest mist seemed to have followed them—the land was shrouded in fog as far as they could see.

The River Road itself was almost empty: as they rode along they met only one wagon, which bore an entire family and its belongings. The driver, a careworn man who looked older than he probably was, seemed almost overwhelmed by the effort of nodding to Simon and Miriamele as they passed. She turned to watch the wagon wheeling slowly eastward behind a thin-shanked ox, and wondered if they were going to Sesuad'ra to cast their fortunes with Josua. The man, his scrawny wife, and their silent children had looked so sad, so tired, that it was painful to think that they might be traveling toward a place she knew to be deserted. Miriamele was tempted to warn them that the prince was already marching south, but she hardened her heart and turned around. Such a favor would be dangerous foolishness: appearing in Erkynland with knowledge of Josua would attract far more attention than was healthy.

The few small settlements they passed as morning wore into afternoon seemed almost deserted; only a few plumes of gray wafting from the smoke holes of houses, a gray just a little darker than the surrounding mist, suggested that people still went about their lives in this depressing place. If these had been farming communities, there was little sign of it now: the fields were full of dark weeds and there were no animals to be seen. Miriamele guessed that if the times were as bad here as she had heard reported of other parts of Erkynland, the few cows and sheep and pigs not yet eaten were being jealously guarded.

"I'm not sure we should stay on this road too much longer." Miriamele squinted up from the broad, muddy causeway into the reddening western sky.

"We've barely seen a dozen people all day," Simon replied. "And if we're being followed, we're best out in the open, where we can see anyone behind us."

"But we'll be coming to the outskirts of Stanshire soon." Miriamele had traveled in this area a few times with her father, and had a fairly good idea of where they were. "That's a much bigger town than any of these little places we've passed. There'll be people on the road there, that's certain. Maybe guardsmen, too."

Simon shrugged. "I suppose. What are we going to do, ride through the fields?"

"I don't think anyone will notice or care. Haven't you seen how all the houses are shuttered? It's too cold for people to be looking out the windows."

In answer, Simon exhaled a puff of foggy breath and smiled. "As you say. Just be careful we don't run the horses into a bog or something. It'll be dark soon."

They turned their mounts off the road and through a

hedge of loose brush. The sun was almost gone now, a thin slice of crimson on the horizon all that remained. The wind increased, whipping through the long grass.

Evening had settled in across the hilly landscape by the time they saw the first signs of Stanshire. The village lay on both sides of the river, joined by a central bridge, and on the northern bank the clutter of houses extended almost to the eaves of the forest. Simon and Miriamele stopped on a hilltop and looked down on the twinkling lights.

"It's smaller," Miriamele said. "It used to fill this entire valley."

Simon squinted. "I think it still does—see, there are houses all the way across. It's just that only half of them have fires, or lamps burning, or whatever." He pulled off his gloves to blow on his fingers. "So. Where shall we stay tonight? Did you bring any money for an inn?"

"We are not going to sleep indoors."

Simon raised an eyebrow. "No? Well, at least we can find a hot meal somewhere."

Miriamele turned to look at him. "You don't understand, do you? This is my father's country. I have been here before myself. And there are so few travelers on the road that even if we weren't recognized by anyone, people would want to ask us questions." She shook her head. "I can't take the chance. We can probably send you in somewhere to buy some food—I did bring some money— but stay in a hostel? We might as well hire a trumpeter to walk before us."

It was hard to tell in the dim light, but Simon seemed to be flushing. There was certainly an angry edge to his voice. "If you say so."

She calmed her own temper. "Please, Simon. Don't you think that I would love a chance to wash my face and sit down on a bench and eat a real supper? I'm trying to do what's best."

Simon looked at her for a moment, then nodded. "I'm sorry. That's good sense. I was just disappointed."

Miriamele felt a sudden gust of affection for him. "I know. You're a good friend."

He looked up sharply, but said nothing. They rode down the hillside into the Stanshire valley.

There was something wrong with Stanshire. Miriamele remembered it from her visit some half-dozen years before as a bustling, thriving town populated mostly by miners and their families, a place where even at night the narrow streets were full of lamplight—but now the few passersby seemed in a hurry to be inside once more, and even the town's inns were quiet as monasteries and nearly empty.

Miriamele waited in the shadows outside *The Wedge and Beetle* while Simon spent some of their cintis-pieces on bread and milk and onions.

"I asked the owner about some mutton and he just stared at me," Simon said. "I think it's been a very bad year."

"Did he ask you any questions?"

"He wanted to know where I came from." Simon was already nibbling on his bread. "I told him I was a chandler from Hasu Vale, looking for some work. He looked at me funny again, then said, 'Well, you've found there's no work to be had here, haven't you?' It's just as well *he* didn't need some work because I've forgotten everything Jeremias ever told me about how to make candles. But he asked me how long since I'd left Hasu Vale, and was it true what everyone said, that there's hauntings in the hills there."

"Hauntings?" Miriamele felt a thin line of ice along her spine. "I don't like the sound of that. What did you tell him?"

"That I'd been gone a long time, of course. That I'd been traveling in the south looking for work. Then, before he could start asking me about *that,* I told him my wife was waiting in the wagon up on the River Road and that I had to go."

"Your *wife?*"

Simon grinned. "Well, I had to tell him something, didn't I? Why else would a man take his food and hurry back out into the cold?"

Miriamele made a disgusted noise, then clambered up into the saddle. "We should find a place to sleep, at least for a while. I'm exhausted."

Simon looked around. "I don't know where we could go here—it's hard to tell which houses are empty, even if there's no smoke and no light. The people may have left, or they just might not have any firewood."

As he spoke, a light rain began to fall.

"We should move farther out," she said. "On the western edge of town we can probably find an empty barn or a shed. Also there's a quarry out there, a big one."

"Sounds splendid." Simon took a bite from one of the rather shriveled-looking onions. "You lead."

"Just don't eat my supper by mistake," she said darkly. "And don't spill any of that milk."

"No, my lady," he replied.


As they rode west on Soakwood Road, one of Stanshire's main thoroughfares, Miriamele found herself oddly disturbed by Simon's words. It was indeed impossible to tell if any of the darkened houses and shops were occupied, but she had a distinct sense of being watched, as though hidden eyes peered out through the cracks in the window shutters.

Soon enough they reached the farmland outside town. The rain had eased, and was now little more than a drizzle. Miriamele pointed out the quarry, which from their vantage point on Soakwood Road was a great black nothingness. When the road had climbed a little higher up the hill, they could see a flickering of reddish light on the lower walls of the quarry.

"Someone's got a fire there," said Simon. "A big one."

"Perhaps they're digging stone," Miriamele replied. "Whatever they're doing, though, we don't need to know about it. The fewer people who see us, the better." She turned them off the wide road and down one of the small lanes, away from the quarry and back toward the River Road. The path was muddy, and finally Miriamele decided that it would be better to light a torch than risk a broken leg for one of the horses. They dismounted, and

Simon did his best to hold off the misting rain with his cloak while Miriamele struggled with the flint. At last she managed to strike a spark that set the oily rag burning.

After riding a little farther they found a likely shelter, a large shed standing in a field that had gone mostly to weeds and bramble. The house to which it apparently belonged, several hundred paces away down the glen, looked deserted. Neither Miriamele nor Simon were certain that the house was truly empty, but the shed at least seemed relatively safe, and they would certainly be drier and happier than beneath open sky. They tethered their horses to a gnarled—and sadly barren—apple tree behind the shed, out of sight of the house below.

Inside, the torchlight revealed a heap of damp straw in the middle of the dirt floor, as well as a few rusting tools with splintered or missing handles leaned against the wall in anticipation of repair. A corroded scythe was depressing to Miriamele in its forgotten uselessness, but also heartening in that it suggested no one had used this shed for some time. Reassured, she and Simon went back out and fetched their saddlebags.

Miriamele kicked the straw into two even piles, then laid out her bedroll on one of them. She looked around critically. "I wish we could risk a real fire," she said, "but I do not even like the torch."

Simon had stuck the burning brand into the dirt of the floor, away from the straw. "I need to be able to see to eat," he said. "We'll put it out soon."

They devoured what remained of their meal hungrily, washing the dry bread down with draughts of cool milk. As they wiped fingers and lips clean on their sleeves, Simon looked up.

"So what do we do tomorrow?" he asked.

"Ride. If the weather stays like this, we might as well ride by day. In any case, we'll see no towns of any size until we reach the walls of Falshire, so there shouldn't be many people on the road."

"If the rest of the countryside around here is anything like Stanshire," Simon said, "we won't see half a dozen people all day."

"Perhaps. But if we hear anything greater than a few riders coming toward us, we should get off the road, just to be safe."

There was a silence as Miriamele took a last drink from the water skin, then crawled onto her bedroll and pulled her cloak over her.

"Are you going to tell me any more about where we're going?" Simon asked at last. She could hear from his voice that he was trying to be careful, that he didn't want to make her angry. She was touched by his cautiousness, but also felt more than a little cross at being treated like a child susceptible to tantrums.

"I don't want to talk about it now, Simon." She turned away, not liking herself, but unwilling to spill out her secret heart. She could hear him clamber onto his own bedroll, then a quiet curse as he realized he had not snuffed the torch. He crawled back across the shed.

"Don't soak it," she said. "It will make it easier to light the next time we need it."

"Indeed, my lady." Simon's voice was sour. There was a sizzle and the light was gone. After a few moments, she heard him return to his sleeping spot.

"Good night, Simon."

"Good night." He sounded angry.

Miriamele lay in darkness and thought about what Simon had asked. Could she even explain to him? It would sound so foolish to someone else, wouldn't it? Her father was the one who had started this war—or rather, she felt sure, he had started it at Pryrates' urging—so how could she explain to Simon that she needed to see him, to talk to him? It wouldn't just sound foolish, she decided, it would sound like the worst and most reckless sort of madness.

*And maybe that's true,* she thought gloomily. *What if I am just fooling myself? I could be captured by Pryrates and never see my father at all. Then what would happen? That red-robed monster would have every secret of Josua's that I know.*

She shuddered. Why didn't she tell Simon what she planned? And more importantly, why hadn't she told Uncle Josua instead of just running away? Just the little bit she *had* told him had made him angry and suspicious . . . but maybe he was right. Who was she, one young woman, to decide what was right and wrong for her uncle and all his followers? And wasn't that what she was doing, taking their lives into her hands to satisfy a whim?

*But it's not a whim.* She felt herself divided into warring factions, like her father and uncle, two halves in conflict. She was coming apart. *It's important. No one can stop this but my father, and only I know what started it. But I'm so frightened. . . .*

The magnitude of what she had done and what she planned to do came rising up, until she suddenly felt she might choke. And no one knew but her—no one!

Something inside her seemed about to break beyond mending. She took in a great gulp of breath.

"Miriamele? Miriamele, what's wrong?"

Fighting to control herself, she did not reply. She could hear Simon moving nearby, the straw rustling.

"Are you hurt? Are you having a bad dream?" His voice was closer, almost beside her ear.

"No," she gasped, then sobbing took her voice away.

Simon's hand touched her shoulder, then tentatively moved up to her face.

"You're crying!" he said, surprised.

"Oh . . ." She struggled to speak. "I'm so . . . I'm so . . . *lonely!* I want t–to go h–h–home!" She sat up and bent forward, pressing her face into the damp cloak over her knees. Another great storm of weeping overtook her. At the same time, a part of her stood as though separate, watching her own performance with disgust.

*Weak,* it told her spitefully. *No wonder you won't get what you want. You're weak.*

". . . Home?" Simon said, wondering. "Do you want to go back to Josua and the others?"

"No, you idiot!" Anger at her own stupidity momentarily cut through the sobs so that she could speak, "I want to go home! I want things to be the way they used to be!"

In the dark, Simon reached for her and pulled her close. Miriamele struggled for a moment, then let her head fall against his chest. Everything hurt. "I'll protect you," he said softly. There was a curious note in his voice, a sort of quiet exultation. "I'll take care of you, Miriamele."

She pushed herself away from him. In the sliver of moonlight that leaked through the shed's doorway, she could see his tousle-haired silhouette. "I don't want to be protected! I'm not a child. I just want things to be right again."

Simon sat unmoving for a long moment, then she felt his arm again around her shoulder. His voice was gentle when she expected to have her own anger returned.

"I'm sorry," he said. "I'm scared, too. I'm sorry."

And as he spoke, she realized suddenly that this was Simon beside her, that he was not her enemy. She let herself sag back against his chest, craving for a moment the warmth and solidity of him. A fresh torrent of tears came rushing up and spilled out of her.

"Please, Miri," he said helplessly. "Don't cry." He put his other arm around her and held her tightly.

After a while the storm of weeping subsided. Miriamele could only lean against Simon, without strength. She felt his fingers run along her jaw, tracing the path of her tears. She pushed in closer, burrowing like a frightened animal, until she felt her face rub against his neck, his hidden blood pulsing against her cheek.

"Oh, Simon," she said, her voice ragged. "I'm so sorry."

"Miriamele," he began, then fell silent. She felt his hand on her chin, cupping it gently. He turned her face up to his, to his warm breath. He seemed about to say something. She could feel the words suspended between them, trembling, unspoken. Then she felt his lips upon hers, the gentle scratch of his beard around her mouth.

For a moment, Miriamele felt herself floating in some unfixed place, in some unrecorded time. She sought a huddling place, somewhere to flee from the pain that seemed all around her like a storm. His mouth was soft, careful, but the hand that touched her face was shaking. She was shaking, too. She wanted to fall into him, to dive into him like a quiet pool.

Unbidden, a picture came to her like a shred of dream: Earl Aspitis, his fine golden hair gleaming in lamplight, bending above her. The arm around her was suddenly a confining claw.

"No," she said, pulling away. "No, Simon, I can't."

He let go of her quickly, like someone caught pilfering. "I didn't ..."

"Just leave me alone." She heard her own voice, flat and cold. It did not match the swirl of violent feelings inside her. "I'm ... I just ..." She, too, was at a loss for words.

In the silence, there was a sudden noise. A long moment passed before Miriamele realized that it came from outside the shed. It was the horses, whinnying nervously. An instant later, a twig crackled just beyond the door.

"There's someone out there!" she hissed. The confusion of the moment before fell away, replaced by the ice of fear.

Simon fumbled for his sword; finding it, he stood and moved to the door. Miriamele followed.

"Should I open it?" he asked.

"We don't want to be caught in here," she whispered sharply. "We don't want to be trapped."

Simon hesitated, then pushed the door outward. There was a flurry of movement outside. Someone was hurrying away, a shadow lurching toward the road through the misted moonlight.

Simon kicked free of the cloak tangled about his legs, then sprang out the door after the fleeing shape.

# 5

# Flamedance

❦

**Simon was filled** with anger, a high, wild fury that
pushed him on like a wind at his back. The figure running
before him faltered and he drew closer. He felt as he
thought Qantaqa must feel when she ran some small fleeing thing to ground.

*Spy on me! Spy on me, will you?!*

The shadowy form stumbled again. Simon lifted his
sword, ready to hew the sneaking creature down in its
tracks. Another few paces . . .

"*Simon!*" Something caught at his shirt, tugging him
off stride. "Don't!"

He lowered his hand to regain his balance and his
sword caught in the weedy grass and sprang from his fingers. He pawed at the ground, but could not find it in the
deep brush, in the dark. He hesitated for a moment, but
the dark shape before him had regained its stride and was
pulling away. With a curse, Simon abandoned the sword
and ran on. A dozen strong paces and he had caught up
again. He wrapped his arms around his quarry's midsection and tumbled them both to the ground.

"*Oh, sweet Usires!*" the thing beneath him shrieked.
"*Don't burn me! Don't burn me!*" Simon grabbed the
thrashing arms and held on.

"What are you doing?!" Simon hissed. "Why have you
been following us?"

"Don't burn me!" the man quavered, struggling to keep
his face turned away. He flailed his spindly limbs in
seeming terror. "Weren't following no one!"

Miriamele arrived, Simon's sword clutched in both hands. "Who is it?"

Still angry, although even he was not quite sure why, Simon took the man's ear in his hand—as Rachel the Dragon had oftentimes done with a certain recalcitrant scullion—and twisted it until the face swung toward him.

His prisoner was an old man; Simon did not know him. The man's eyes were wide and blinking rapidly. "Didn't mean no harm, old Heanwig didn't!" he said. "Don't burn me!"

"Burn you? What are you babbling about? Why were you following us?"

Miriamele looked up suddenly. "Simon, we can't stay here shouting. Let's take him back."

"Don't burn Heanwig!"

"Nobody's burning anybody," Simon grunted. He dragged the old man onto his feet less gently than he might have, then marched him toward the shed. The intruder sniffled and pleaded for his life.

Simon retained his hold on the old man while Miriamele tried to relight the torch. She eventually gave up and took another from her saddlebag. When it was burning, Simon let go of the prisoner and then sat with his back against the door so that the old man could not make another bolt for freedom.

"He doesn't have any weapons," Simon said. "I felt his pockets."

"No, masters, got no nothing." Heanwig seemed a little less frightened, but still pathetically eager not to offend. "Please, just let me go and I'll tell no one."

Simon looked him over. The old man had the reddened cheeks and nose of a veteran tosspot, and his eyes were bleary. He was staring worriedly at the torch, as though it were now the greatest danger in the room. He certainly didn't seem much of a threat, but Simon had learned long ago from Doctor Morgenes' small-outside, large-inside chambers that things could be other than they appeared. "Why were you following us?" he demanded. "And why do you think we'd burn you?"

"Don't need to burn no one," the old man said. "Old Heanwig means no harm. He won't tell nobody."

"Answer my question. What are you doing here?"

"Was just looking for place to sleep, masters." The old man chanced a quick survey of the shed. "Slept here before once or twice. Didn't want to be outside tonight, no, not tonight."

"Were you following us in the forest? Did you come to our camp last night?"

The old man looked at him with what seemed genuine surprise. "Forest? In Oldheart? Heanwig won't go there. Things and beasties and such—that's a bad place, masters. Don't you go to that Oldheart."

"I think he's telling the truth," said Miriamele. "I think he was just coming here to sleep." She fished the water skin out of her saddlebag and gave it to the old man. He looked at it for a moment with suspicion. Understanding, Miriamele lifted it to her own mouth and drank, then passed it to him. Reassured, the old man swallowed hungrily, then looked at her as accusingly as if his fear of poison had been confirmed.

"Water," he murmured sullenly.

Miriamele stared at him, but Simon slowly smiled. He leaned across and fished out the other skin bag, the one Miriamele had told him she was saving for cold nights or painful injuries. Simon squirted a little bit of the red Perdruin into a bowl and held it out where the old man could see. Heanwig's trembling fingers reached for it, but Simon pulled the bowl back.

"Answer our questions first. You swear you were not searching for us?"

Heanwig shook his head emphatically. "Never seen you before. Won't remember you when you're gone. That's a promise." His thin hands snaked out again.

"Not yet. Why did you think we'd burn you?"

The old man looked at him, then at the wine, plainly torn. "Thought you were those Fire Dancers," he said at last, with obvious reluctance. "Thought you meant to burn me like they burned old Wiclaf who used to be First Hammerman up to quarry."

Simon shook his head, puzzled, but Miriamele leaned closer, fear and distaste in her expression. "Fire Dancers? Are there Fire Dancers here?"

The old man looked at her as though she had asked whether fish could swim. "Town be full of them. They chased me, chased Heanwig. But I hid from them." He smiled a weak smile, but his eyes remained wary and calculating. "They be in quarry tonight, dancing and praying to their Storm Lord."

"The quarry!" Miriamele breathed. "That's what the lights were!"

Simon was still not sure he trusted the old man. Something was bothering him, like a fly buzzing beside his ear, but he could not decide what it was. "*If* he's telling the truth."

"I tell the truth," Heanwig said with sudden force. He tried to draw himself up straight, fixing Simon with his rheumy eyes. "I was coming here for a bit of sleep, then I heard you. Thought the Fire Dancers were here—they roam all through town at night. People with houses bar their doors, do you see, but Heanwig's got no house no more. So I ran."

"Give the wine to him, Simon," Miriamele said. "It's cruel. He's just a frightened old man."

Simon made a face and handed Heanwig the bowl. The old man sniffed it and a look of rapture crossed his age-spotted features. He tilted the bowl and drank thirstily.

"The Fire Dancers!" Miriamele hugged herself. "Mother of Mercy, Simon, we don't want to get caught by them. They're all mad. Tiamak was attacked by some in Kwanitupul, and I saw others light themselves on fire and burn to death."

Simon looked from Miriamele to the old man, who was licking his wrinkled lips with a tongue that looked like something which made its home in a seashell. He felt an unlikely urge to reach out and cuff the old tosspot, although the man had done little enough, really. Simon suddenly remembered how he had raised the sword, that moment of fury when he might have slain this poor wretch, and was horribly ashamed.

*What sort of knight would cut down a feeble drunkard?*

But what dreadful fate had sent the old man to frighten the horses and break twigs in the very moment when he was finally holding Miriamele in his arms? They had been kissing! She, the princess, the beautiful Miriamele, had been kissing Simon!

He turned his gaze from the old man to Miriamele once more. She, too, had been watching Heanwig drain his bowl, but now her eyes flicked up to Simon's for a moment. Even in the torchlight, he could see her blush. Fate was cruel . . . but a little earlier, it had been kind as well. Oh, sweet Fate, sweet Luck!

Simon abruptly laughed. The greater part of his anger dissipated like chaff before the wind. The loveliest girl in all of Aedondom, clever and quick—and she had kissed him. Called him by his name! He could still feel the shape of her face on his fingertips. What right had he to complain?

"So what do we do?" he asked.

Miriamele avoided his eye. "We will stay the night. Then in the morning we will get as far away from the Fire Dancers as we can."

Simon darted a glance at Heanwig, who was looking hopefully toward the saddlebags. "And him?"

"We will let him stay here for the night, too."

"And what if he drinks all the wine and takes it into his head to strangle us in our sleep?" Simon protested. Even he found it rather silly to say such things about the bony, shivering old man, but he desperately wanted to be alone with Miriamele once more.

As if she understood this and was equally determined *not* to see it happen, Miriamele said: "He'll do nothing of the sort. And we will take turns sleeping. Will that make you feel better, Simon? You can guard the wine."

The old man looked from one to the other, evidently trying to decide where the battle lines were drawn. "Old Heanwig won't be no bother. You don't need to stay up, young masters. You be tired. Old fellow like me doesn't need sleep. I'll stay up and watch for them Fire Dancers."

Simon snorted. "I'm certain you would. Let's toss him

out, Miriamele. If he isn't the one who followed us, there's no reason to keep him."

"There's a perfectly good reason. He's an old man and he's frightened. You forget, Simon, I've seen the Fire Dancers and you haven't. Don't be cruel just because you're in a bad mood." She gave him a stern look, but Simon thought he saw a tiny flash of knowing amusement in it.

"No, don't send me out to those Fire Dancers," Heanwig begged. "They burned Wiclaf, they did. I saw it. And him not harming nobody. They lit him on fire down Pulley Road, screaming *'Here's what's coming! Here's what's coming!'* " Heanwig trailed off, shuddering. What had started out as a self-serving justification had become real as the memory played out before his mind's eye. "Don't send me away, masters. I'll never speak no word." His abrupt sincerity was apparent.

Simon looked from Miriamele to the old man, then back to the princess. He had been neatly outflanked. "Oh, very well," he growled. "But I'm staying up on first watch, old man, and if you do anything the least bit suspicious, you'll be out that door and into the cold so fast your head will spin."

He gave Miriamele a last look compounded of annoyance and longing, then settled back against the shed door.

Simon awoke in the early morning to discover Miriamele and the old man both up and chatting amiably. Simon thought that Heanwig looked even worse in daylight, his seamed features smudged with dirt, his clothes so tattered and soiled that even poverty could not excuse it.

"You should come with us," Miriamele was saying. "You'll be safer than by yourself. At least join us until you're far away from the Fire Dancers."

The old man shook his head doubtfully. "Those mad folk be most everywhere, these days."

Simon sat up. His mouth was dry and his head hurt, as though *he* were the drunkard of the company. "What are you saying? You can't bring him with us."

"I certainly can," said Miriamele. "You may accompany me, Simon, but you may not tell me where I can go or who I can bring along."

Simon stared at her for a moment, sensing an argument that he had no hope of winning, no matter what he did. He was still weighing his next words when he was saved from the useless engagement by Heanwig.

"Are you bound for Nabban?" the old man asked. "I never have seen those parts."

"We're going to Falshire," Miriamele said. "Then on to Hasu Vale."

Simon was just about to upbraid her for telling this complete stranger their travel plans—what had happened to the need for caution she had lectured *him* about?— when the old man made a gasping noise. Simon turned, angry already at the thought that the old tosspot was now going to be sick right in front of them, but was startled by the look of horror on Heanwig's mottled face.

"Going to Hasu Vale!?" His voice rose. "What, be ye mad? That whole valley runs haunted." He scrambled a cubit toward the door, grasping fruitlessly for a handhold in the moldering straw beneath him, as though the two travelers had threatened to drag him to the hated place by force. "Sooner I'd crawl down into quarry with those Fire Dancers."

"What do you mean, haunted?" Miriamele demanded. "We've heard that before. What does it mean?"

The old man stared at her, eyes rolling to show the whites. "Haunted! Bad 'uns, bogies from out the lichyard. Witches and suchlike!"

Miriamele stared at him hard. After a year like the last one, she was not inclined to dismiss such talk as superstition. "We're going there," she said at last. "We have to. But you don't have to travel any farther than you want to."

Heanwig got shakily to his feet. "Don't want to go west'ard. Heanwig'll stay here'bouts. There's folk in Stanshire as still have a morsel to spare, or a drop, even in bad times." He shook his head. "Don't go there, young mistress. You been kind." He looked pointedly at Simon to make it clear who had not been.

*The old sot,* Simon thought grumpily. *Who gave him the wine, anyway? Who didn't break his head when he could have?*

"Go south—you'll be happy there," Heanwig continued, almost pleading. "Stay out the Vale."

"We must go," said Miriamele. "But we won't make you come."

Heanwig had been sidling toward the door. Now he stopped with his hand already on the wood and ducked his head. "I thank you, young mistress. Aedon's Light be on you." He paused, at a loss for words. "Hope you come back again safe."

"Thank you, too, Heanwig," Miriamele replied solemnly.

Simon suppressed a groan of irritation, reminding himself that a knight did not make faces and noises like a scullion did—especially a knight who wished to stay on the good side of his lady. And at least the old man apparently would not be traveling with them. That was an acceptable reward for a little forbearance.

As they rode out of Stanshire into the countryside, the rain began to fall once more. At first it was little more than a flurry of drops, but by the time mid-morning came, it was falling in great sheets. The wind rose, carrying the rain toward them in cold, cascading slaps of water.

"This is as bad as being on a ship in storm," Miriamele shouted.

"At least on a ship you have oars," Simon called back. "We're going to need some soon."

Miriamele laughed, pulling her hood down low over her eyes.

Simon felt warmer just knowing he had amused her. He had been feeling a little ashamed of the way he had treated the old man; almost as soon as Heanwig had gone shuffling away down the lane, heading back toward the center of Stanshire, Simon had felt his bad temper evaporate. It was hard to say now what it was about the old man that had so perturbed him—he hadn't really done anything.

They headed back toward the River Road along a succession of wagon-rutted lanes that now were little more than sluices of mud. The countryside began to look more wild. The farmlands around Stanshire, although mostly given over to weeds, still bore the mark of past human care in the fences and stone walls and an occasional cottage, but as the town and its outlying settlements fell away behind them, the wilderness reasserted itself.

It was a peculiarly bleak place. The nearly endless winter had stripped all of the trees but the evergreens, and even the pines and firs seemed to have suffered unkind handling. Simon thought the strange, twisted shape of the trunks and branches resembled the writhing human bodies in the mural of The Day of Weighing-Out which stretched across the wall of the Hayholt's chapel. He had spent many a boring hour in church staring in fascination at the scenes of torment, marveling at the invention of the anonymous artist. But here in the real, cold, wet world, the gnarled shapes were mostly disheartening. Leafless oaks and elms and ash trees loomed against the sky, skeletal hands that clenched and unclenched as the wind bent them. With the sky bruised almost black by clouds and the rain flung slantwise across the muddied hillsides, it made a much drearier picture than even the decorations in the chapel.

Simon and Miriamele rode on through the storm, mostly unspeaking. Simon was chagrined that the princess had not once mentioned, or even hinted at, their kiss of the night before. It was not a day conducive to flirtatious conversation, he knew, but she seemed to be pretending it had never even happened. Simon did not know what to do about this: several times he was on the verge of asking her, but he could not think of anything to say about it that would not sound stupid in the light of day. That kiss had been a bit like his arrival in Jao é-Tinukai'i, a moment in which he had stepped out of time. Perhaps, like a trip to a fairy-hill, what they had shared the night before had been something magical, something destined to fade as quickly from memory as an icicle melting in the sun.

*No. I won't let it fade. I'll remember it always . . . even if she doesn't.*

He stole a glance at Miriamele. Most of her face was hidden by the hood, but he could see her nose and part of her cheek and her sharp chin. She looked almost Sithalike, he thought, graceful and beautiful, yet not quite knowable. What was going on in her head? How could she cling to him as she had, then say nothing about it afterward, until he wondered if he had dreamed the whole thing or was going mad? Surely she had returned that kiss as eagerly as he had given it? Little as he knew of women and kissing, he could not believe that the way she had responded meant nothing.

*Why don't I just ask her? I'll go mad if I don't find out. But what if she laughs at me, or gets angry—or doesn't remember?*

The idea that Miriamele might have no strong emotions corresponding to the feelings that churned within him was chilling. His resolve to make her talk abruptly vanished. He would think about it more.

*But I want to kiss her again.*

He sighed. The sound was lost in the hissing tumult of the rain.

The River Road was muddy and almost entirely empty; as Simon had predicted, they passed fewer than a dozen other travelers all day. Only one man bothered to do more than nod, a short, bandy-legged fellow whose knob-kneed horse pulled a tented wagon full of tinker's goods. Hoping for information about what might lie ahead, Simon took courage at his pleasant greeting and asked the man to stop. The tinker stood in the downpour, apparently glad for someone to talk to, and told them that there was a way station ahead that they should reach not long after sundown. He said he was on his way out from Falshire, and described that city as quiet and the business he had done there as poor. After quietly making sure that Miriamele approved, Simon invited the man to come join them beneath a stand of pines that kept out most of the rain. They handed him the wineskin, and while their new acquaintance took a few healthy swallows, Simon repeated his story of being an itinerant chandler.

"Thank you kindly." The tinker handed back the wineskin. "Cuts the chill a bit, that does." He nodded. "You'll be hoping to do some trade for Saint Tunath's and Aedonmansa, then. Good luck to you. But if you'll pardon advice not asked for, I think you'd best go no farther west than Falshire."

Simon and Miriamele locked eyes briefly before turning back to the traveler.

"Why is that?" asked Simon.

"People just say it's bad there." The man's grin seemed forced. "You know the sort of tales. Bandits, the like. Some talk of odd happenings in the hills." He shrugged.

Simon pressed him for details, but the man did not seem inclined to elaborate. Simon had never heard of a traveling tinker who would not happily finish a proffered wineskin while regaling his listeners with tales of his journeying; whether this man was an exception to the rule, or whether there was something that had disturbed him enough to keep him quiet, Simon could not tell. He seemed a reasonable sort.

"We're looking for nothing but a roof over our heads and a few fithings worth of work here and there," said Simon.

The tinker cocked an eyebrow at the sword on Simon's belt and the metal hauberk protruding beyond his sleeves. "You're tolerable well-armed for candle-making, sirrah," he said gently. "But I suppose that shows what the roads are like these days." He nodded with a sort of careful approval, as if to suggest that whatever he thought of a chandler wearing the gear of a knight—albeit a tattered knight who had seen better times—he saw no reason to ask further questions.

Simon, catching the implicit message that he was expected to adopt the same courteous disinterest, offered the tinker a handclasp as they all walked back to the road.

"Anything you need?" the man asked as he once more

took the bridle of his horse, which had been standing patiently in the rain. "I get a few things in trade from them as has not a cintis piece to pay—some vegetables, little bits of metal clutter . . . shoeing-nails, the like."

Simon said that they had everything they needed until they reached Falshire: he was quite sure that the things they most needed would not be in the back of a rain-soaked wagon. But Miriamele asked to see the vegetables, and picked out a few spindly carrots and four brown onions, giving the tinker a coin in return. Afterward they waved him farewell as he took his horse and went squelching away east along the muddy road.

As the gray afternoon wore away, the rain continued to spatter down. Simon was growing tired of it pounding on his head.

*Wish I'd remembered to bring my battle-helm*, he thought. *But that'd probably be like sitting under a bucket and having someone throw stones at you—rattle, rattle, rattle till you go mad.*

To entertain Miriamele, he tried to sing a song called "Badulf and the Straying Heifer" that Shem Horsegroom had taught him, which had a rainstorm in it and seemed appropriate, but most of the words had slipped his memory, and when he sang the parts he remembered, the wind flung rain down his gullet until he thought he would strangle. He abandoned the experiment at last and they continued in silence.

The sun which had been invisible all day at last sank beneath the rim of the world, leaving behind a deeper darkness. They rode on as the rain turned even colder, until their teeth were chattering and their hands grew numb on the reins. Simon had begun to doubt that the tinker had spoken truly when at last they found the way station.

It was only a shed, four walls and a roof, with a smoke hole and a circle of stones dug into the floor for a fireplace. There was a covered spot outside at the back to tie the horses, but Simon, after unsaddling them, tethered them in a copse nearby where they would be almost as dry, and would be able to crop at the thin grass.

The last inhabitant of the station—Simon guessed it was the tinker himself, who had seemed a decent and conscientious fellow—had brought in fresh wood before leaving. It had to be new-gathered, because it was still wet and proved difficult to light: Simon had to restart it three times after the smoldering tinder fizzled out against the damp branches. He and the princess made themselves a stew with some carrots and one of the onions and a bit of flour and dried beef from Miriamele's stores.

"Hot food," proclaimed Simon, sucking his fingers, "is a wonderful thing." He held the bowl up and licked the last drops of gravy from the bottom.

"You're getting stew on your beard," Miriamele said sternly.

Simon pushed open the door of the way station, then leaned out and let his cupped palms fill with rainwater. He drank some and used the rest to rub the grease from his whiskers. "Better?"

"I suppose." Miriamele began arranging her bedroll.

Simon got up, patting his stomach contentedly. He went and dragged his own bedroll loose from the saddle, then came back and laid it out close to Miriamele's. She stared at it silently for a moment; then, without looking up, pulled hers around the fire, putting several cubits of straw-matted floor between them.

Simon pursed his lips. "Should we keep watch?" he said at last. "There's no bar on the door."

"That would be wise. Who first?"

"Me. I have a lot to think about."

His tone finally made Miriamele look up. She eyed him warily, as though he might do something sudden and frightening. "Very well. Wake me when you get tired."

"I'm tired now. But so are you. Sleep. I'll get you up after you've had a little time to rest."

Miriamele settled back without protest, wrapping her cloak tightly about her before she closed her eyes. The way station was silent but for the patter of rain on the roof. Simon sat motionless for a long time, watching the flickering firelight play across her pale, composed features.

\* \* \*

Sometime in the earliest hours after midnight, Simon caught himself nodding. He sat up, shaking his head, and listened. The rain had stopped, but water was still dripping from the way station roof and drizzling on the ground outside.

He crawled over to wake Miriamele, but paused by the bedroll to look at her in the red light of the dying embers. She had twisted in her sleep, dislodging the cloak she used as a blanket, and her shirt had pulled loose from the top of the men's breeches she wore, exposing a measure of white skin along her side and the shadowed curve of her lowest ribs. Simon felt his heart turn over in his chest. He longed to touch her.

His hand, seemingly of its own volition, stole out; his fingers, gentle as butterflies, lit upon her skin. It was cool and smooth. He could feel goosebumps rise beneath his touch.

Miriamele made a groggy noise of irritation and brushed at him, flicking as though the butterflies had become less pleasant insects a-crawling. Simon quickly withdrew his hand.

He sat for a moment trying to catch his breath, feeling like a thief who had been nearly surprised in his crime. At last he reached out again, but this time only clasped her shoulder and gave a careful shake.

"Miriamele. Wake up, Miriamele."

She grunted and rolled over, turning her back to him. Simon shook her again, a little more strongly this time. She made a sound of protest and her fingers groped for her cloak without success, as though she sought protection from whatever cruel spirit plagued her.

"Come, Miriamele, it's your turn to keep watch."

The princess was sleeping soundly indeed. Simon leaned closer and spoke into her ear. "Wake up. It's time." Her hair was against his cheek.

Miriamele only half-smiled, as though someone had made a small joke. Her eyes remained shut. Simon slid down until he was lying next to her and stared for a few long moments at the curve of her cheek glowing in the emberlight. He slid his hand down from her shoulder and let it fall across her waist, then moved forward until his chest touched her back. Now her hair was all along his cheek and his body wrapped hers. She made a noise that might have been contentment and pushed back against him ever so slightly, then fell silent once more. Simon held his breath, fearing she would wake, fearing that he himself would cough or sneeze and somehow spoil this achingly splendid moment. He felt her warmth all down the length of his body. She was smaller than he, much smaller: he could wrap around her and protect her like a suit of armor. He thought he would like to lie this way forever.

As the two lay like nestling kittens, Simon drifted into sleep. The need to keep a watch was forgotten, eased from his mind like a leaf carried away by a river current.

Simon woke up alone. Miriamele was outside the way station, using a leafless branch to groom her horse. When she came in, they broke their fast on bread and water. She said nothing of the night before, but Simon thought he detected a little less brittleness in her manner, as though some of her chill had melted away while they lay huddled in sleep.

They traveled six more days on the River Road, slowed by the monotonous rains that had turned the broad track into sloppy mud. The weather was so miserable and the road generally so empty that Miriamele's fear of discovery seemed to lessen, although she still kept her face covered when they passed through smallish towns like Bregshame and Garwynswold. Nights they slept in way stations or beneath the leaky roofs of roadside shrines. As they sat together each night in the hour between eating and sleeping, Miriamele told Simon stories of her childhood in Meremund. In return, he recounted his days among the scullions and chambermaids; but as the nights passed, he spoke more and more about his time with Doctor Morgenes, of the old man's good humor and occasionally fierce temper, of his contempt for those who did not ask questions and his delight in life's unexpected complexity.

The night after they passed through Garwynswold,
Simon abruptly found himself in tears as he related something Morgenes had once told him about the wonders of
beehives. Miriamele stared, surprised, as he struggled to
control himself; afterward she looked at him in a strange
way he had not seen before, but although his first impulse
was shame, he could not truthfully see anything contemptuous in her expression.

"I wish he had been my father or my grandfather," he
said later. They had retired to their respective bedrolls.
Although Miriamele was, as usual, an arm's length away,
he felt that she was in some way nearer to him than she
had been any night since they had kissed. He had held her
since then, of course, but she had been asleep. Now she
lay nearby in the darkness, and he almost thought he felt
some unspoken agreement growing between them. "He
was that kind to me. I wish he was still alive."

"He was a good man."

"He was more than that. He was . . . He was someone
who did things when they needed to be done." Simon felt
a tightening in his chest. "He died so that Josua and I
could escape. He treated me like . . . like I was his own.
It's all wrong. He shouldn't have had to die."

"Nobody should die," Miriamele said slowly. "Especially while they're still alive."

Simon lay in silence for a moment, confused. Before he
could ask her what she meant, he felt her cool fingers
touch his hand, then nestle into his palm.

"Sleep well," she murmured.

When his heart had slowed, her hand was still there. He
fell asleep at last, still cupping it as gently as if it were a
baby bird.

More than the rains and gray mist plagued them. The
land itself, under the pall of bad weather, was almost
completely lifeless, dreary as a landscape of stones and
bones and spiderwebs. In the towns, the citizens appeared
tired and frightened, unwilling even to regard Simon and
Miriamele with the curiosity and suspicion that were usually a stranger's due. At night the windows were shut-

tered, the mucky streets empty. Simon felt as though they passed through ghost villages, as though the actual inhabitants had long departed, leaving only the insubstantial shades of previous generations, all doomed to a weary, pointless haunting of their ancestral homes.

In dim afternoon on their seventh day out of Stanshire, Simon and Miriamele rounded a bend in the river road and saw the squat bulk of Falshire Castle looming on the western horizon before them. Green grazing land had once covered the castled hill like a king's train, but now, despite the heavy rains, the hillside fields were barren; near the hillcrest some were even patched with snow. At the base of the hill lay the walled city, bestriding the river that was its lifeblood. From docks along the shore Falshire's hides and wool were loaded on boats to travel to the Kynslagh and beyond, returning with the gold and other goods that had long made Falshire one of the richest cities in Osten Ard, second in importance in Erkynland only to Erchester.

"That castle used to be Fengbald's," said Miriamele. "And to think my father would have had me marry him! I wonder which of his family lords it there now." Her mouth tightened. "If the new master is anything like the old one, I hope the whole thing falls down on him."

Simon peered into the diffuse western light that made the castle seem only an oddly-shaped black crag, then pointed to the city below to distract her attention. "We can be in Falshire-town before nightfall. We can have a true meal tonight."

"Men always think of their stomachs."

Simon thought the assertion unfair, but was pleased enough to be called a man that he smiled. "How about a dry night in a warm inn, then?"

Miriamele shook her head. "We have been lucky, Simon, but we are getting closer to the Hayholt every day. I have been in Falshire many times. There is too good a chance someone might recognize me."

Simon sighed. "Very well. But you don't mind if I go in somewhere and get us something to eat like I did in Stanshire, do you?"

"As long as you don't leave me waiting all night. It's bad enough being a poor traveling chandler's wife without having to stand in the rain while the husband's inside slurruping down ale by a hot fire."

Simon's smile became a grin. "Poor chandler's wife."

Miriamele looked at him dourly. "Poor chandler if he makes her angry."

The inn called *The Tarbox* was brightly torchlit, as if for some festive holiday, but as Simon peered in through the doorway he thought the mood inside seemed far from merry. It was crowded enough, with perhaps two or three dozen people scattered around the wide common room, but the talk among them was so quiet that Simon could hear the rainwater dripping off the cloaks that hung beside the door.

Simon made his way between the crowded benches to the far side of the common room. He was aware of many heads turning to watch him pass, and a slight increase in the buzz of conversation, but he kept his eyes to himself. The landlord, a thin, tuft-haired fellow whose face sparkled with the sweat of the roasting oven, looked up as he approached.

"Yes? D'you need a room?" He looked at Simon's tattered clothes. "Two quinis the night."

"Just a few slices of that mutton and some bread. And perhaps some ale as well. My wife's waiting outside. We've far to go."

The landlord shouted at someone across the room to have patience, then glared at Simon suspiciously. "You'll need your own jug, for none of mine's walking out the door." Simon lifted his jug and the man nodded. "Six cintis for all. Pay now."

A little nettled, Simon dropped the coins on the table. The landlord picked them up and examined them, then pocketed the lot and scurried off.

Simon turned to survey the room. Most of the denizens seemed to be Falshire-folk, humble in garb and settled in their residence: there were very few who looked as though they might be travelers, despite the fact that this was one of the closest inns to the city gates and the River Road. A few returned his gaze, but he saw little malice or even curiosity. The people of Falshire, if this room was any indication, seemed to have much in common with the sheep they raised and sheared.

Simon had just turned back to look for the landlord when he sensed a sudden stirring in the room. He wondered if the Falshire-folk had indeed had more of a reaction to him than he'd realized. Then a chill breeze touched the back of his neck.

The door of the inn was open again. Standing before a curtain of water sluicing down from the roof outside, a trio of white-robed figures calmly surveyed the room. It was not Simon's imagination that all the other folk in the common room shrank back a little into themselves. Furtive glances were darted, conversations grew quieter or louder, and some of the patrons nearest the door sidled slowly away.

Simon felt a similar urge. *Those must be Fire Dancers,* he thought. His heartbeat had grown swifter. Had they seen Miriamele? But what would she have meant to them in any case?

Slowly Simon leaned back against the long table, putting on an air of mild interest as he watched the newcomers. Two of the three were large, as muscled as the dockers who worked the Hayholt's sea gate, and carried blunt-ended walking staves that looked more useful for skull-cracking than hiking. The third, the leader by his position in front, was small, thick, and bull-necked, and also carried one of the long cudgels. As he lowered his rain-soaked hood, his squarish, balding head glinted in the lamplight. He was older than the other two and had clever, piggy eyes.

The hum of conversation had now reached something like its normal level once more, but as the three Fire Dancers moved slowly into the common room they still received many covert stares. The robed men seemed to be openly searching the room for something or somebody; Simon had a moment of helpless fear as the leader's dark eyes lighted on him for a moment, but the man only lifted an amused eyebrow at Simon's sword, then shifted his attention to someone else.

Relief swept over Simon. Whatever they wanted, it was apparently not him. Sensing a presence at his shoulder, he turned quickly and found the inn's proprietor standing behind him with a pitted wooden platter. The man gave Simon the mutton and bread, which Simon wrapped in his kerchief, then poured an appropriate measure of ale into the jug. Despite the attention these tasks required, the landlord's eyes scarcely left the three newcomers, and his reply to Simon's courteous thanks was distracted and incomplete. Simon was glad to be going.

As he opened the door, he caught a quick glimpse of Miriamele's pale, worried face in the shadows across the street. A loud, mocking voice cut through the room behind him.

"You didn't *really* think that you could leave without our noticing, did you?"

Simon went rigid in the doorway, then slowly turned. He had a parcel in one hand and a jug in the other, his sword hand. Should he drop the ale and draw the blade, or make the jug useful somehow—perhaps he could throw it? Haestan had taught him a little about tavern brawls, although the guardsman's main recommendation had been to avoid them.

He completed his pivot, expecting to confront a sea of faces and the threatening Fire Dancers, but found to his astonishment that no one was even looking in his direction. Instead, the three robed men stood before a bench in the corner farthest from the fire. The two seated there, a man and woman of middle years, looked up at them helplessly, faces slack with terror.

The leader of the Fire Dancers leaned forward, bringing his catapult-stone of a head almost to the level of the tabletop, but though his position suggested discretion, his voice was pitched to carry through the room. "Come, now. You didn't really think that you could just walk away, did you?"

"M—Maefwaru," the man stuttered, "we, we could not . . . we thought that . . ."

The Fire Dancer laid a thick hand on the table, silencing him. "That is not the loyalty that the Storm King expects." He seemed to speak quietly, but Simon could hear every word from the doorway. The rest of the room watched in sickly fascinated silence. "We owe Him our lives, because He has graced us with a vision of how things will be and a chance to be part of it. You cannot turn your back on Him."

The man's mouth moved, but no words came out. His wife was equally silent, but tears ran down her face and her shoulders twitched. This was obviously a meeting much feared.

*"Simon!"*

He turned to look back out the inn's door. Miriamele was only a few paces away in the middle of the muddy road. "What are you doing?" she demanded in a loud whisper.

"Wait."

"Simon, there are Fire Dancers in there! Didn't you see them?!"

He raised his hand to stay her, then wheeled to face the interior. The two large Fire Dancers were forcing the man and woman up from their bench, dragging the woman across the rough wood when her legs would not support her. She was crying in earnest now; her companion, pinioned, could only stare at the ground and murmur miserably.

Simon felt anger flame within him. Why didn't anyone in this place help them? There must be two dozen seated here and only three Fire Dancers.

Miriamele tugged at his sleeve. "Is there trouble? Come, Simon, let's go!"

"I can't," he said, quietly but urgently. "They're taking those two people somewhere."

"We can't afford to be caught, Simon. This is not a time for heroes."

"I can't just let them take those people, Miriamele." He prayed that someone else in the crowded room would stand up, that some general movement of resistance would begin. Miriamele was right: they couldn't afford to do anything foolish. But no one did more than whisper and watch.

Cursing himself for his stupidity, and God or Fate for putting him in this position, Simon pulled his sleeve from Miriamele's grasp and took a step back into the common room. He carefully set the supper parcel and jug down beside the wall, then curled his hand around the hilt of the sword Josua had given him.

"Stop!" he said loudly.

"Simon!"

Now all heads *did* turn toward him. The last to swivel around was that of the leader. Although he was only a little shorter than an average man, there was something curiously dwarflike in his large, cleft-chinned head. His tiny eyes flicked Simon up and down. This time there was no amusement.

"What? Stop, you say? Stop what?"

"I don't think those people want to go with you." Simon addressed the male captive, who was struggling weakly in the grip of one of the large Fire Dancers. "Do you?"

The man's eyes flicked back and forth between Simon and his chief captor. At last, miserably, he shook his head. Simon knew then that what the man feared must be truly terrible, that he would risk making this situation worse in the desperate—and unlikely—hope that Simon could save him from it.

"You see?" Simon tried, with mixed results, to keep his voice firm and calm. "They do not wish to accompany you. Set them free." His heart was pounding. His own words sounded curiously formal, even deliberately high-flown, as if this were a Tallistro story or some other chronicle of imaginary heroism.

The bald man looked around the room as if to judge how many might be prepared to join Simon in resistance. No one else was moving; the entire room seemed to share a single held breath. The Fire Dancer turned back to Simon, a grin curling his thick lips. "These folk betrayed their oath to the Master. This is no concern of yours."

Simon felt an immense fury wash over him. He had

seen all the bullying he had the stomach for, from the countrywide misdeeds of the king to the precisely pointed cruelties of Pryrates. He tightened his grip on the hilt. "I am making it my concern. Take your hands from them and get out."

Without further argument, the leader spat out a word and the follower who held the woman let her go—she slumped against the table, knocking a bowl onto the floor—and leaped toward Simon, his blunt-headed staff swinging in a wide arc. A few people shouted in fear or excitement. Simon was frozen for an instant, his sword only halfway out of his scabbard.

*Idiot! Mooncalf!*

He dropped to the floor and the staff whistled over his head, knocking several cloaks from the wall and becoming entangled in one of them. Simon seized the moment and threw himself forward into the man's legs. They both fell, tumbling, and Simon's sword came free of the scabbard and thumped into the floor rushes. He had hurt his shoulder—his attacker was heavy and solidly-built—and as he disentangled himself and pulled free, the Fire Dancer managed to catch him with a cudgel blow to his leg which stung cold as a knife wound. Simon rolled toward his lost sword and was hugely grateful when he felt it beneath his fingers. His attacker was up and moving toward him, his cudgel darting out like a striking snake. From the corner of his eye, Simon could see that the second big man was coming toward him as well.

*First things first,* was the inane thought that ran through his head, the same thing Rachel had always told him about doing his chores when he wanted to go climb or play a game. He rose to a standing crouch, his sword held before him, and deflected a blow from his first attacker. It was impossible to remember all the things he had been taught in the muddle of noise and movement and panic, but he was relieved to find that as long as he could keep his sword between himself and the Fire Dancer, he could keep the man at bay. But what would he do when the second arrived?

He received an answer of sorts a moment later, when a

blur of movement at the edge of his vision warned him to duck. The second man's staff whickered past and clacked against the first man's. Simon took a step backward without turning and then whirled and swung his blade around as hard as he could. He caught the man behind him across the arm, drawing an angry shriek. The Fire Dancer dropped his staff and stumbled back toward the doorway, clutching his forearm. Simon returned his attention to the man in front of him, hoping that the second man was, if not defeated, at least out of the battle for a few desperately-needed moments. The first attacker had learned the lesson of not getting too close, and was now using the length of his club to keep Simon on the defensive.

There was a crash from behind; Simon, startled, almost lost sight of the foe before him. Seeing this, the man aimed another whirling blow at his head. Simon managed to get his blade up in time to deflect it; then, as the Fire Dancer raised the staff once more, Simon brought his sword up, sweeping the cudgel even farther upward so that it struck the low timbers of the roof and caught in the netting below the thatch. The Fire Dancer stared up for a moment in surprise; in that instant, Simon took a step forward, lodged the sword against the man's midsection and pushed it home. He struggled to pull the blade free, conscious that at any moment the other attacker, or even the leader, might be upon him.

Something struck him from the side, flinging him against a table. For a moment, he was staring into the alarmed face of one of the common-room drinkers. He whirled to see that the person who had shoved him, the bald man Maefwaru, was pushing his way between the tables, headed toward the door; he did not pause to look down at either of his minions, the one Simon had slain or the other, who lay in a curious position near the doorway.

"It will not be so easy," Maefwaru shouted as he vanished through the door and into the rainy night.

A moment later Miriamele stepped back into the room. She looked down at the Fire Dancer laying there, the one

Simon had wounded on the arm. "I've broken our jug on his head," she said, excited and breathless. "But I think the one who just ran out is going to come back with more of his friends. Curse my luck! I couldn't find anything to hit him with. We'll have to run."

"The horses," Simon panted. "Are they. . . ?"

"A few steps away," replied Miriamele. "Come."

Simon bent and snatched up the supper sack he had left on the floor. The kerchief was wet, soaked by the ale that had splashed from the jug which lay in pieces around the limp Fire Dancer. He looked around the room. The man and woman that Maefwaru and his henchmen had threatened were cringing against the far wall, staring as bewilderedly as any of the inn's other customers.

"You had better get out of here, too," he called to them. "That bald one will bring back more. Go on—run!"

Everyone was looking at him. Simon wanted to say something clever or brave—heroes usually did—but he couldn't think of anything. Also, there was real blood on his sword and his stomach seemed to have crawled up into his throat. He followed Miriamele out the door, leaving behind two bodies and a room full of wide eyes and open, speechless mouths.

# 6

# The Circle Narrows

✹

**The swirl** of snow had lessened, but the wind still moved angrily across the hillside beneath Naglimund, fluting in the teeth of the broken wall. Count Eolair nudged his horse toward Maegwin's mount, wishing he could shield her somehow, not just from the cold but also from the horror of the naked stone towers, the windows now flickering with light.

Yizashi Grayspear rode forward from the ranks of the Sithi, his lance couched beneath one arm. He lifted the other and waved something that looked like a silver baton. His hand flashed in a wide arc, making a loud musical noise which had something of the metallic in it; the silver thing in his hand opened like a lady's fan, spreading into a glittering, semicircular shield.

"*A y'ei g'eisu!*" he shouted up at the blankly staring keep. "*Yas'a pripurna jo-shoi!*"

The lights in Naglimund's windows seemed to waver like wind-fluttered candles as shadows moved in their depths. Eolair felt himself almost overwhelmed with the urge to turn and ride away. This was no longer a human place, and the poisonous terror he was feeling was nothing like the anticipatory fear before any human battle. He turned to Maegwin. Her eyes were closed and her mouth moved in silent speech. Isorn seemed similarly unnerved, and when Eolair turned in his saddle and looked back, the pale faces of his fellow Hernystiri were as gape-mouthed and hollow-eyed as a row of corpses.

*Brynioch preserve us*, the count thought desperately, *we*

*do not belong in this. They will bolt in a moment if I do
the wrong thing.*

Deliberately, he tugged his sword from its scabbard and
showed it to his men, then held it high over his head for
a moment before dropping it to his side. It was only a
small show of bravery, but it was something.

Now Jiriki and his mother Likimeya rode forward, halting on either side of Yizashi. After a moment's whispered
conversation, Likimeya spurred her horse a few paces
ahead. Then, startlingly, she began to sing.

Her voice, thin at first against the rude piping of the
wind, grew slowly stronger. The impenetrable Sithi
tongue flowed out, slurring and clicking yet somehow as
smooth as warm oil poured from a jar. The song rose and
fell, pulsed, then rose again, each time growing more
powerful. Although Eolair understood nothing of the
words, there was something clearly denunciatory to the
roll and swoop of it, something challenging in the cadence. Likimeya's voice chimed like a herald's brazen
horn, and as with the call of a horn, there was a ring of
cold metal beneath the music.

"What goes on here?" whispered Isorn.

Eolair gestured for silence.

The mist floating before the walls of Naglimund
seemed to thicken, as though one dream was ending and
another beginning. Something changed in Likimeya's
voice. It took a moment before Eolair recognized that the
mistress of the Sithi had not altered her song, but rather
that another voice had joined it. At first the new thread of
melody clung close to the challenge-song. The tone was
as strong as Likimeya's, but where hers was metal, this
new voice was stone and ice. After some long moments
the second voice began to sing around the original melody, weaving a strange pattern like a glass filigree over
Likimeya's belling tones. The sound of it made the Count
of Nad Mullach's skin stretch and tingle and his body hair
lift, even beneath the layers of clothing.

Eolair raised his eyes. His heart began to beat even
more swiftly.

Through the dimming fog, a thin black shadow ap-

peared atop the castle wall, rising into view as smoothly
as though lifted by an unseen hand. It was man-sized,
Eolair decided, but the mist subtly distorted its shape, so
that one moment it seemed larger, the next smaller and
thinner than any living thing. It looked down on them,
black-cloaked, face invisible beneath a large hood—but
Eolair did not need to see its face to know that it was the
source of the high, stone-edged voice. For long moments
it only stood in the swirling mist atop the wall, embroid-
ering upon Likimeya's song. Finally, as if by some prior
agreement, they both fell still at the same moment.

Likimeya broke the silence, calling out something in
the Sithi tongue. The black apparition answered, its words
ringing like shards of jagged flint, and yet Eolair could
hear that the words they spoke were much the same, the
differences mainly in rhythm and the greater harshness of
the robed creature's speech. The conversation seemed in-
terminable.

There was a movement behind him. Eolair flinched; his
horse startled, kicking snow. Sky-haired Zinjadu, the lore-
mistress, had brought her own mount to where the mortals stood.

"They speak of the Pact of Sesuad'ra." Her eyes were
fixed on Likimeya and her opposite. "They speak of old
heartbreaks and the mourning songs yet to be sung."

"Why so much talk?" asked Isorn raggedly. "The waiting is dreadful."

"It is our way." Zinjadu's lips tightened; her thin face
seemed carved in pale golden stone. "Although it was not
respected when Amerasu was slain."

She offered nothing more. Eolair could only wait in uneasy fear and, ultimately, a kind of horrible boredom as
challenge and response were offered.

Finally the thing on the wall turned its attention away
from Likimeya for a moment; its eyes lit on the count and
his few scores of Hernystirmen. With a movement almost
as broad as a traveling player's, the black-robed one flung
back its hood, revealing a sleet-white face and thin hair
just as colorless which rose in the wind, floating like the
strands of some sea-plant.

*"Shu'do-tkzayha!"* the Norn said in a tone almost of exultation. "Mortals! They will yet be the death of your family, Likimeya Moon-Eyes!" He, if it was a he, spoke the Westerling tongue with the harsh precision of a game-keeper imitating a rabbit's death squeal. "Are you so weak that you summoned this rabble to aid you? It is hardly Sinnach's great army!"

"You have usurped a mortal's castle," said Likimeya coldly. Beside her Jiriki still sat his horse stiffly, his sharp-boned face empty of any recognizable emotion; Eolair wondered again how anyone could ever feel they knew the Sithi. "And your master and mistress have entered into the disputes of mortals. You have little to crow about."

The Norn laughed, a noise like fingernails on slate. "We use them, yes. They are the rats that have dug into the walls of our house—we might skin them for gloves, but we do not invite them in to sup at our table! That is your weakness, as it was Amerasu Ship-Born's."

"Do not speak of her!" Jiriki cried. "Your mouth is too foul to hold her name, Akhenabi!"

The thing on the wall smiled, a folding of white. "Ah, little Jiriki. I have heard tales of you and *your* adventuring—or should I say meddling. You should have come to live in the north, in our cold land. Then you would have grown strong. This tolerance for mortals is a terrible weakness. It is one reason why your family has grown dissolute while mine has grown ever sterner, ever more capable of doing what needs to be done." The Norn turned and lifted his head, directing his words now to Eolair and the nervously whispering Hernystiri. "Mortal men! You risk more than your lives fighting beside these immortals. You risk your souls as well!"

Eolair could hear the rustle of frightened speech behind him. He spurred his horse forward a few paces and raised his sword. "Your threats are empty!" he shouted. "Do your worst! Our souls are our own!"

"Count Eolair!" Maegwin called. "No! It is Scadach, the Hole in Heaven! Go no closer!"

Akhenabi leaned down, fixing the count with blackbead eyes. "The captain of the mortals, are you? So, little man, if you do not fear for your sake, or for your troop, what of the mortals still prisoned within these walls?"

"What are you saying?!" Eolair shouted.

The creature in the black robe turned and lifted both arms. A moment later two more figures clambered up into view beside him. Although they also wore heavy cloaks, their clumsy movements marked them as something other than the spider-graceful Norns.

"Here are some of your brethren!" trumpeted Akhenabi. "They are our guests. Would you see *them* die for the sake of your immortal allies as well?" The two figures stood silently, slumped and hopeless. The faces in the wind-lashed hoods were clearly those of men, not Gardenborn.

Eolair felt himself fill with helpless rage. "Let them go!"

The Norn laughed again, pleased. "Oh, no, little mortal. Our guests are enjoying themselves too much. Would you like to see them show their joy? Perhaps they will dance." He lifted his hand and made a florid gesture. The two figures began slowly to revolve. Horribly, they lifted their arms in a parody of a courtly dance, swaying from side to side, stumbling together in front of the grinning Norn. They locked arms for a moment, teetering precariously along the edge of the high wall, then pulled apart and resumed their solitary posturing.

Through the tears of fury that misted his eyes, Eolair saw Jiriki spur his horse a few ells nearer the wall. The Sitha lifted a bow; then, in a movement so swift as to be almost invisible, he withdrew an arrow from the quiver on his saddle, nocked it, and drew the bow until it trembled in a wide arc. Atop the wall, the Norn Akhenabi's grin widened. He made a wriggling movement, almost a shiver; a moment later he had disappeared, leaving only the two shambling shapes in hideous lockstep.

Jiriki let his arrow fly. It struck one of the two dancers in the foot, jerking back the leg and overbalancing both the one struck and the one to whom he clung. They flailed briefly at the air, then toppled off the wall, dropping twenty ells to hit with a terrible smacking noise on the snow-covered rocks beneath. Several of the Hernystiri shouted and groaned.

"Blood of Rhynn!" Eolair screamed. "What have you done?!"

Jiriki rode forward, scanning the now empty wall cautiously. When he reached the huddled bodies, he dismounted and kneeled, then waved Eolair forward.

"Why did you do that, Jiriki?" the count demanded. His throat felt as tight as if someone's fingers were curled around it. "The Norn was gone." He stared down at the twisted, dark-robed figures. The hands and fingers protruding from their robes were splayed as though they still grabbed at a safety they would never find. "Did you think to spare them torture? What if we drove out the Norns—is there no chance we could rescue them?"

Jiriki said nothing, but reached down with surprising gentleness and turned over the nearest of the bodies, tugging a little to pull it free of the partner with which it was entwined. He folded back the hood.

"Brynioch!" Eolair choked. "Brynioch of the Skies preserve us!"

The face had no eyes, only black holes. The skin was waxy, and in places had burst from the force of the fall, but it was clear that this corpse was not fresh.

"Whoever he was, he has been dead since Naglimund's defeat," Jiriki said softly. "I do not think there are any living prisoners within the walls."

Count Eolair felt his gorge rising and turned away "But they . . . moved. . . !"

"One of the Red Hand is lord here," Jiriki said. "That is now confirmed, for no others have the strength to do this. Their power is a part of their master's."

"But why?" Eolair said. He looked at the humped corpses, then turned his gaze outward, toward the massing of men and Sithi in the snow. "Why would they do this?"

Jiriki shook his head, his own hair as white and fluttering as that of the creature that had mocked them from the wall "I cannot say. But Naglimund will not fall without a full tithing of horrors, that is certain."

Eolair looked at Maegwin and Isorn waiting fearfully for him to return. "And there is no turning back."

"No. I fear the final days have begun," said Jiriki. "For good or ill."

♦

Duke Isgrimnur knew that he should be paying close attention to everything that was going on around him, to the people of Metessa, to the arrangements and manpower in the baronial hall. Metessa was the easternmost of Nabban's major outer states, and might be the place where Josua's challenge stood or fell. Success here could hinge on the smallest detail, so Isgrimnur had plenty to occupy him—but it was difficult to attend to his duties while the little boy followed him around like a shadow.

"Here," the duke said after he had almost trod upon the child for the dozenth time, "what are you up to? Don't you have somewhere to be? Where's your mother?"

The pale-haired, thin-faced little boy looked up at him, showing no fear of the large, bearded stranger. "My mother told me to stay away from the prince and you other knights. I did not agree."

The child was unnervingly well-spoken for his years, the duke reflected, and his Westerling was almost as good as Isgrimnur's own. It was odd to see how Prester John's Warinsten language had spread so thoroughly in only a couple of generations. But if things fell apart, as they seemed to be doing, would not the common tongue, like everything else, soon slip away? Empires were like seawalls, he thought sadly, even those which embodied the best of hopes. The tide of chaos beat at them and beat at them, and as soon as no one was shoring up the stones any more . . .

Isgrimnur shook his head, then growled at the youngling a little more sternly than he intended. "Well, if your mother told you to stay away from the knights, what are you doing here? This is men's business tonight."

The boy deliberately raised himself until the top of his head reached the duke's bottom rib. "I will be a man some day. I am tired of living with the women. My mother is afraid I will run away to fight in war, but that is just what I will do."

There was something so unintentionally comic in his fierce determination that Isgrimnur smiled despite himself. "What's your name, lad?"

"Pasevalles, Sir Foreign Knight. My father is Brindalles, Baron Seriddan's brother."

"A knight is not the only thing in the world to be. And war is not a game. It is a terrible thing, little Pasevalles."

"I know that," said the boy readily. "But sometimes there is no choice, my father says, and there must be men who will fight."

The duke thought of Princess Miriamele in the ghant nest, and of his own beloved wife standing with an ax before Elvritshalla, ready to defend it to her death before Isorn persuaded her at last to let it go and flee with the rest of the family. "Women also fight."

"But women cannot be knights. And I am going to be a knight."

"Well, I suppose since I am not your father, I cannot send you back to your chambers. And I certainly can't seem to be rid of you. You might as well come with me and tell me a little about the place."

Pleased, Pasevalles bounced up and down a few times like a puppy. Then, just as suddenly, he stopped and fixed Isgrimnur with a suspicious glance. "Are you an enemy?" he asked sharply. "Because if you are, Sir Foreign Knight, I cannot show you things that might hurt my uncle."

Isgrimnur's grin was sour. "In these days, young fellow, it's hard to say who is enemy to who. But I can promise you that my liege-lord Prince Josua intends no harm to any who live in Metessa."

Pasevalles considered this for a moment. "I will trust you," he said at last. "I think you tell the truth. But if you do not, then you are no knight, who would lie to a young child."

Isgrimnur's grin widened. *Young child! This mannikin*

*could give Count Eolair lessons in politicking.* "Tell me nothing that would help your uncle's enemies, and I will try not to ask anything that would put your honor in danger."

"That is fair," said the boy gravely. "That is knightly."

Metessa was more than just another Nabbanai hedge-barony. Situated beside the outermost edges of the Thrithings, it was a wide and prosperous piece of country, hilly and wide-meadowed. Even after the unseasonal snows, the rolling terrain gleamed greenly. One of the Stefflod's branches wound through the grasslands, a ribbon of silver foil bright even beneath the dull gray skies. Sheep and a few cows dotted the hillsides.

Chasu Metessa, the baronial keep, had stood atop one of the highest hills since the days of the later Imperators, looking down on these valleys full of small farms and freeholdings just as Isgrimnur did now.

He turned from the window to find Pasevalles pacing impatiently. The boy said: "Come and see the armor."

"That sounds like the kind of thing I shouldn't see."

"No, it's *old* armor." He was disgusted by Isgrimnur's obtuseness. "Very old."

The Rimmersman allowed himself to be tugged along. The child's energy seemed without bound.

*If Isorn had been this demanding,* he thought wryly, *I would likely have taken him out to the Frostmarch and left him, like they did in the old days when they had one mouth too many to feed.*

Pasevalles led him through a warren of hallways, past more than a few of the keep's inhabitants, who looked at Isgrimnur with alarm, to a corner tower that seemed a fairly late addition to the ancient hill fortress. After they had climbed far more stairs than were good for Isgrimnur's aching back, they reached a cluttered room near the top. The ceiling had not been recently swept—a canopy of cobwebs hung down almost to head height—and a heavy patina of dust covered the floor and all the crude furnishings, but Isgrimnur was nevertheless impressed with what he saw.

A series of wooden armor-stands ranged the room like

silent guardsmen. Unlike the rest of the objects in the circular chamber, they were comparatively clean. On every stand hung a set of armor—but not modern armor, as Pasevalles had so crossly pointed out: the helmets and breastplates and curious metal-strip skirts were of a type that Isgrimnur had seen before only in very old paintings in the Sancellan Mahistrevis.

"This is armor from the Imperium!" he said, impressed. "Or damn clever copies."

Pasevalles drew himself up to his full height. "They are *not* copies! They are real. My father has been keeping them for years. My grandfather bought them in the great city."

"In Nabban," Isgrimnur mused. He walked along the rows, examining the various costumes, his warrior's eye seeing which were flawed in design, which simply missing pieces from the original arrangement. The metal the old Imperatorial craftsmen had used was heavier than that now used, but the armor was splendidly made. He leaned close to examine a helm with a twining sea-dragon crest. To get a better look, he puffed away a fine layer of dust.

"These have not been polished in some time," he said absently.

"My father has been ill." Little Pasevalles' voice was suddenly querulous. "I try to keep them clean, but they are too tall for me to reach and too heavy for me to lift down."

Isgrimnur looked around the room, thinking. The uninhabited armor suits seemed like watchers at a Raed, waiting for some decision. There were still many things for him to do. Surely he had spent enough time with this boy? He walked to the tower window and peered out into the gray western sky.

"We will not eat for some hour or so yet," he said at last, "and your uncle and Prince Josua will not be speaking of the other important things that must be discussed until afterward. Go and get your father's cleaning things—at least a whisking broom to get the dust off. You and I can make short work of this."

The boy looked up, eyes wide. "Truly?"

"Truly, I am in no hurry to go back down all those stairs, in any case." The boy was still staring. "Bless me, child, go on. And bring a lamp or two. It'll be dark soon."

The boy sped out of the room and down the narrow stairwell like a hare. Isgrimnur shook his head.

The banqueting hall of Chasu Metessa had a fireplace along each wall, and was warm and bright despite the chilliness of the season. The courtiers, landed folk from all over the valley, seemed to be dressed in their finest: many of the women wore long shimmery dresses and hats almost as weirdly inventive as those to be seen at the Sancellan Mahistrevis itself. Still, Isgrimnur noted the air of worry that hung like a fog in the huge, high-raftered chamber. The ladies talked swiftly and brightly and laughed at tiny things. The men were mostly quiet; what little they did say was spoken behind their hands.

A cask of Teligure wine had been breached at the start of things and its contents shared out around the room. Isgrimnur noticed that Josua, who was seated at the right of their host Baron Seriddan, had raised his goblet to his lips many times, but had not yet allowed the page beside him to refill it. The duke approved of Josua's forbearance. The prince was not much of a drinker at the best of times, but since the chance of dislodging Benigaris from the ducal throne might rest on the knife-edge of tonight's doings, it was doubly important that Josua's wits be sharp and his tongue cautious.

As he surveyed the room, the duke was stopped short by a pale glimmer in the doorway, far across the room. Squinting, Isgrimnur suddenly smiled deep in his beard. It was the boy Pasevalles, who had doubtless once more escaped from his mother and her ladies. He had come, Isgrimnur had no doubt, to watch Real Knights at table.

*He may just get an eyeful.*

Baron Seriddan Metessis rose from his seat at the head of the table and lifted his goblet. Behind him a blue crane, symbol of the Metessan House, spread its long wings across a wall banner.

"Let us salute our visitors," the baron said. He smiled

ironically, his sun-browned, bearded face wrinkling. "I am doubtless a traitor already, just for letting you inside the gates, Prince Josua—so it does no further harm to drink your health."

Isgrimnur found himself liking Seriddan, and respecting him more than a bit. He little resembled the duke's fondly-held image of an effete Nabbanai baron: his thick neck and seamed peasant face made Seriddan look more a genial rogue than the hereditary master of a great fiefdom, but his eyes were shrewd and his manner deceptively self-mocking. His command of Westerling was so good that little Pasevalles' fluency no longer seemed surprising.

After the glasses were drained, Josua rose and lifted his own cup to thank the folk of Chasu Metessa for their hospitality. This was greeted by polite smiles and murmurs of approval that seemed more than a little forced. When the prince sat down, the whisper of table talk began to grow once more, but Seriddan gestured for quiet.

"So," he said to Josua, loud enough for everyone at the table to hear. "We have fulfilled the obligations that good Aedonites owe to their fellows—and some would say we have done far more than that, considering you appeared in our lands unasked for, and with an army at your back." Above the smiling mouth, Seriddan's stare was cool. "Will we see your heels in the morning, Josua of Erkynland?"

Isgrimnur suppressed a noise of surprise. He had assumed that the baron would send the lesser folk of his household away so that he could talk to the prince in privacy, but apparently Seriddan had other ideas.

Josua, too, was taken aback, but quickly said: "If you hear me out and are unmoved, Baron, you will indeed see our heels soon after sunrise. My people are not camped outside your walls as a threat to you. You have done me no wrong, and I will do you none either."

The baron stared at him for a long moment, then turned to his brother. "Brindalles, what do you think? Does it not seem odd that an Erkynlandish prince would wish to pass through our lands? Where might he be going?"

The brother's thin face bore many similarities to the

baron's, but the features that looked roguishly dangerous on Seriddan seemed merely tired and a trifle unsettled on Brindalles.

"If he is not going to Nabban," came the mild reply, "he must be planning to walk straight to the sea." Brindalles' smile was wan. It was hard to think that such a diffident man could be the father of bright-burning Pasevalles.

"We *are* going on to Nabban," said Josua. "That is no secret."

"And what purpose could you have that is not dangerous to me and dangerous to my liege-lord, Duke Benigaris?" Seriddan demanded. "Why should I not make you a prisoner?"

Josua looked around the now-silent room. Chasu Metessa's most important residents all sat at the long table, watching with rapt attention. "Are you certain you wish me to speak so openly?"

Seriddan gestured impatiently. "I will not have it said that I misunderstood you, whether I let you pass through my lands or hold you here for Benigaris. Speak, and my people here will be my witnesses."

"Very well." Josua turned to Sludig, who despite having drained his wine cup several times was watching the proceedings with a wary eye. "May I have the scroll?"

As the yellow-bearded Rimmersman fumbled in the pocket of his cloak, Josua told Seriddan: "As I said, Baron: we go to Nabban. And we go in hopes of removing Benigaris from the Sancellan Mahistrevis. In part, that is because he is an ally of my brother, and his fall would weaken the High King's position. The fact that Elias and I are at war with each other is no secret, but the reasons why are less well-known."

"If you think they are important," Seriddan said equably, "tell them. We have plenty of wine, and we are at home. It is your little army that may or may not be leaving with the dawn."

"I will tell you, because I would not ask allies to fight unknowing," said Josua.

"*Héa!* Allies? Fight!?" The baron scowled and sat

straighter. "You are walking a dangerous road, Josua Lackhand. Benigaris is my liege-lord. It is mad even to contemplate letting your people pass, knowing what I know, but I show respect for your father by letting you speak. But to hear you talk of me fighting beside you—madness!" He waved his hand. Some two dozen armed men, who had been standing back against the shadowed walls all during the meal, came rustlingly to attention.

Josua did not flinch, but calmly held Seriddan's eye. "As I said," he resumed, "I will give you the reasons that Elias must be driven from the Dragonbone Chair. But not now. There are other things to tell you first." He reached and took the scroll from Sludig's hand. "My finest knight, Sir Deornoth of Hewenshire, was at the battle of Bullback Hill when Duke Leobardis, Benigaris' father, came to relieve my castle at Naglimund."

"Leobardis chose your side," Seriddan said shortly. "Benigaris has chosen your brother's. What the old duke decided does not affect my loyalty to his son." Despite his words, there was a certain veiled look in the baron's eyes; watching him, Isgrimnur suspected Seriddan might just wish that the old duke were still alive and that his loyalty could be more comfortable. "And what does this Sir What-may-be-his-name have to do with Metessa?"

"Perhaps more than you can know." For the first time there was an edge of impatience in Josua's tone.

*Careful, man.* Isgrimnur tugged anxiously at his beard. *Don't let your sorrow over Deornoth betray you. We're farther along than I had thought we'd be. Seriddan's listening, anyway.*

As if he heard his old friend's silent thought, Josua paused and took a breath. "Forgive me, Baron Seriddan. I understand your loyalty to the Kingfisher House. I only wish to tell you things you deserve to know, not tell you where your duties lie. I want to read you Deornoth's words about what happened near Bullback Hill. They were written down by Father Strangyeard . . ." the prince pointed to the archivist, who was trying to make himself unobtrusive down near the long table's far end, "and sworn to before that priest and God Himself."

"Why are you reading some piece of parchment?" Seriddan asked impatiently. "If this man has a story to tell, why does he not come here before us?"

"Because Sir Deornoth is dead," said Josua. "He died at the hands of Thrithings mercenaries King Elias sent against me."

At this there was a small stir in the room. The Thrithings-folk were objects of both contempt and fear to the outland baronies of Nabban—contempt because the Nabbanai thought them little more than savages, fear because when the Thrithings-men went into one of their periodic raiding frenzies, outland fiefdoms such as Metessa bore the greatest part of the suffering.

"Read." Seriddan was clearly angry. Isgrimnur thought that the canny baron might already sense the snare into which his own cleverness had delivered him. He had hoped to deal with the odd and difficult situation of the prince by forcing Josua to speak his treason in front of many witnesses. Now the baron must sense that Josua's words might not be so easily dismissed. It was an awkward spot. But even now, Metessa's master did not disperse the other folk sitting at table: he had made his gambit and he would live with it. The Duke of Elvritshalla found himself appreciating the man anew.

"I had Deornoth tell his story to our priest before the battle for New Gadrinsett," Josua said. "What he saw was important enough that I did not wish to chance it might die with him, as there seemed little likelihood we would survive that fight." He held up the scroll, unrolling it with the stump of his right wrist. "I will read only the part that I think you need to hear, but I will gladly give the whole thing to you, Baron, so that you may read it at your ease."

He paused for a moment, then began. The listeners along the table leaned forward, greedy for more strangeness on what was already a night that would be discussed in Metessa for a long time.

"*. . . When we came upon the field, the Nabbanai had ridden after Earl Guthwulf of Utanyeat and his men of the Boar and Spears,* *who were falling back with great swiftness to the slope of Bullback Hill. Duke Leobardis and three hundred knights came at them in such a wise as to pass between Utanyeat and the High King's army, which was still some way distant, as we thought.*

*"Prince Josua, fearing that Leobardis would be delayed too long and that thus the king could come against him in the unprotected open lands south of Naglimund, brought many knights out of the castle to save Nabban from the king, and also perhaps to capture Utanyeat, who was the greatest of King Elias' generals. Josua himself led us, and Isorn Isgrimnurson and a score of Rimmersmen were with us too.*

*"When we struck against the side of the Boar and Spears, we at first did bring them great woe, for they were outnumbered manyfold. But Guthwulf and the king had prepared a trap, and soon it was sprung. Earl Fengbald of Falshire and several hundred knights came down a-horse from the woods at the top of Bullback Hill.*

*"I saw Duke Leobardis and his son Benigaris at the outermost edge of the fighting, behind their men-at-arms. As Fengbald's falcon-crest came down the hill, I saw Benigaris draw his sword and stab his father in the neck, slaying him in the saddle so that Leobardis fell across his horse's withers, bleeding most piteously . . ."*

At this last sentence, the silence abruptly dissolved into shocked cries and rebukes. Several of Baron Seriddan's liege-men stood, shaking their fists in fury as though they would strike Josua down. The prince only looked at them, still holding the parchment before him, then turned to Seriddan. The baron had retained his seat, but his brown face had paled except for bright spots of color high on each cheek.

"Silence!" he shouted, and glared at his followers until they sank back onto their benches, full of angry muttering. Several of the women had to be helped from the room; they stumbled out as though they themselves had been stabbed, their intricate hats and veils suddenly as sad as the bright flags of a defeated army. "This is an old story," the baron said at last. His voice was tight, but Isgrimnur thought there was more than rage there.

*He feels the snare drawing closed.*

Seriddan drained his goblet, then banged it down on the tabletop, making more than a few people jump. "It is an old tale," he said again. "Often repeated, never proved. Why should I believe it now?"

"Because Sir Deornoth saw it happen," said Josua simply.

"He is not here. And I do not know that I would believe him if he were."

"Deornoth did not lie. He was a true knight."

Seriddan laughed harshly. "I have only *your* word on that, Prince. Men will do strange things for king and country." He turned to his brother. "Brindalles? Have you heard any reason here tonight that I should not throw the prince and his followers into one of the locked cells beneath Chasu Metessa to wait for Benigaris' mercy?"

The baron's brother sighed. He held his two hands close together, touching at the fingertips. "I do not like this story, Seriddan. It has an unpleasantly truthful ring, since those who prepared Leobardis for burial spoke wonderingly of the evenness of the wound. But the word of any one man, even Prince Josua's knight, is not enough to condemn the Lord of Nabban."

*Wit is not lacking in the family blood!* the Duke of Elvritshalla noted. *But on such hard-headed men must our luck ride. Or fail.*

"There are others who saw Benigaris' terrible deed," Josua said. "A few of them are still alive, although many died when Naglimund was conquered."

"A thousand men would not be enough," Seriddan spat. "*Héa!* What, should the flower of Nabbanai nobility follow you—an Erkynlander and enemy of the High King—against the rightful heir to the Kingfisher House, on the strength of the writings of a dead man?" A murmur of agreement rose from Chasu Metessa's other inhabitants. The situation was growing ugly.

"Very well," said Josua. "I understand, Baron. Now I will show you something that will convince you of the seriousness of my undertaking. And it may also answer your fears about following an Erkynlander anywhere." He turned and gestured. A hooded man seated near Strangyeard at the shadowy end of the table abruptly rose. He was very tall. Several of the men-at-arms drew their swords; the hiss of emerging blades seemed to make the room grow cold.

*Do not fail us,* Isgrimnur prayed.

"You said one thing that was not true, Baron," Josua said gently.

"Do you call me a liar?"

"No. But these are strange days, and even a man as learned and clever as you cannot know everything. Even were Benigaris not a patricide, he is *not* first claimant on his father's dukedom. Baron, people of Metessa, here is the true master of the Kingfisher House ... Camaris Benidrivis."

The tall figure at the end of the table pushed back his hood, revealing a snowfall of white hair and a face full of sadness and grace.

"What. . . ?" The baron was utterly confused.

"Heresy!" shouted a confused landowner, stumbling to his feet. "Camaris, he is dead!"

One of the remaining women screamed. The man beside her slumped forward onto the table in a drunken faint.

Camaris touched his hand to his breast. "I am not dead." He turned to Seriddan. "Grant me forgiveness, Baron, for abusing your hospitality in this manner."

Seriddan stared at the apparition, then rounded on Josua. "What madness is this?! Do you mock me, Erkynlander?"

The prince shook his head. "It is no mockery, Seriddan. This is indeed Camaris. I thought to reveal him to you in private, but the chance did not come."

"No." Seriddan slapped his hand on the table. "I cannot believe it. Camaris-sá-Vinitta is dead—lost years ago, drowned in the Bay of Firannos."

"I lost only my wits, not my life," the old knight said

gravely. "I lived for years with no memory of my name or my past." He drew a hand across his brow. His voice shook. "I sometimes wish I had never been given either back again. But I have. I am Camaris of Vinitta, son of Benidrivis. And if it is my last act, I will avenge my brother's death and see my murdering nephew removed from the throne in Nabban."

The baron was shaken, but still seemed unconvinced. His brother Brindalles said: "Send for Eneppa."

Seriddan looked up, his eyes bright, as though he had been reprieved from some awful sentence. "Yes." He turned to one of his men-at-arms. "Fetch Eneppa from the kitchen. And tell her *nothing*, on pain of your life."

The man went out. Watching his departure, Isgrimnur saw that little Pasevalles had disappeared from the doorway.

The folk remaining at table whispered excitedly, but Seriddan no longer seemed to care. While he waited for his man to return, he downed another goblet of wine. Even Josua, as if he had given something a starting push and could no longer control it, allowed himself to finish his own cup. Camaris remained standing at the foot of the table, a figure of imposing stolidity. No one in the room could keep their eyes off him for long.

The messenger returned with an old woman in tow. She was short and plump, her hair cut short, her simple dark dress stained with flour and other things. She stood anxiously before Seriddan, obviously fearing some punishment.

"Stand still, Eneppa," the baron said. "You have done nothing wrong. Do you see that old man?" He pointed. "Go and look at him and tell me if you know him."

The old woman sidled toward Camaris. She peered up at him, starting a little when he looked down and met her eyes. "No, my lord Baron," she said at last. Her Westerling was awkward.

"So." Seriddan crossed his arms before his chest and leaned back, an angry little smile on his face.

"Just a moment," Josua said. "Eneppa, if that is your name, this is no one you have seen in recent days. If you did know him, it was long ago."

She turned her frightened-rabbit face from the prince

back to Camaris. She appeared ready to turn from him just as quickly the second time, then something caught at her. She stared. Her eyes widened. Abruptly, her knees bent and she sagged. Swift as thought, Camaris caught her and kept her from falling.

*"Ulimor Camaris?"* she asked in Nabbanai, weeping. *"Veveis?"* There followed a torrent in the same language. Seriddan's angry smile vanished, replaced by an expression that was almost comically astonished.

"She says that they told her I had drowned," Camaris said. "Can you speak Westerling, good woman?" he asked her quietly. "There are some here who do not understand you."

Eneppa looked at him as he steadied her, then let her go. She was dazed, crumpling the skirt of her dress in her gnarled fingers. "He ... he is Camaris. *Duos preterate!* Have ... have the dead come back to us again?"

"Not the dead, Eneppa," said Josua. "Camaris lived, but lost his wits for many years."

"But although I know your face, my good woman," the old knight said wonderingly, "I do not recognize your name. Forgive me. It has been a long, long time."

Eneppa began to cry again in earnest, but she was laughing, too. "Because that is not my name in that time. When I work in your father's great house, they call me *Fuiri*—'flower.' "

"Fuiri." Camaris nodded. "Of course. I remember you. You were a lovely girl, with smiles in full measure for everyone." He lifted her wizened hand, then bent and kissed it. She stared open-mouthed as though God Himself had appeared in the room and offered her a chariot ride through the heavens. "Thank you, Fuiri. You have given me back a little of my past. Before I leave this place, you and I will sit by the fire and talk."

The sniffling cook was helped from the room.

Seriddan and Brindalles both looked stunned. The rest of the baron's followers were equally amazed, and for some time no one said anything. Josua, perhaps sensing the battering that the baron had taken this night, merely sat and waited. Camaris, his identity now confirmed, allowed himself to sit down once more; he, too, fell into silence. His half-lidded gaze seemed fixed on the leaping flames in the fireplace at the table's far side, but it was clear to Isgrimnur that he was looking at a time, not a place.

The stillness was interrupted by a sudden burst of whispering. Heads turned. Isgrimnur looked up to see Pasevalles walking straddle-legged into the room; something large and shiny was cradled against his small body. He stopped just inside the doorway, hesitated as he looked at Camaris, then moved awkwardly to stand before his uncle.

"I brought this for Sir Camaris," the boy said. His bold words were belied by his shaky voice. Seriddan stared at him for a moment, then his eyes widened.

"That is one of the helmets from your father's room!"

He nodded solemnly. "I want to give it to Sir Camaris."

Seriddan turned helplessly to his brother. Brindalles looked at his son, then briefly at Camaris, who still was lost in thought. At last, Brindalles shrugged. "He is who he says he is. There is no honor he has not earned, Seriddan." The thin-faced man told his son: "You were right to ask first." His smile was almost ghostly. "I suppose sometimes things must be taken down and dusted off and put to use. Go ahead, boy. Give it to him."

Isgrimnur watched in fascination as Pasevalles walked past clutching the heavy sea-dragon helm, his eyes as fearfully fixed as though he walked into an ogre's den. He stopped before the old knight and stood silently, although he looked as though any moment he might collapse beneath the weight of the helmet.

At last, Camaris looked up. "Yes?"

"My father and my uncle said I may give you this." Pasevalles struggled to lift the helm closer to Camaris, who even sitting down still towered above him. "It is very old."

A smile stretched across Camaris' face. "Like me, eh?" He reached out his large hands. "Let me see it, young sir." He turned the golden thing to the light. "This is a helm of the Imperium," he said wonderingly. "It *is* old."

"It belonged to Imperator Anitulles, or so I believe,"

said Brindalles from across the room. "It is yours if you wish it, my lord Camaris."

The old man examined it a moment more, then carefully put it on. His eyes disappeared into the shadows of the helm's depths, and the cheek-guards jutted past his jaw like blades. "It fits tolerably well," he said.

Pasevalles stared up at the old man, at the coiling, high-finned sea-worm molded along the helmet's crest. His mouth was open.

"Thank you, lad." Camaris lifted the helmet off and placed it on the table beside him. "What is your name?"

"P–Pasevalles."

"I will wear the helm, Pasevalles. It is an honor. My own armor has gone to rust years ago."

The boy seemed transported to another realm, his eyes bright as candleflame. Watching him, Isgrimnur felt a twinge of sorrow. After this moment, after this experience with knighthood, how could life hold much but disappointment for this eager child?

*Bless you, Pasevalles,* the duke thought. *I hope your life is a happy one, but for some reason I fear it won't be so.*

Prince Josua had been watching. Now, he spoke.

"There are other things you must know, Baron Seriddan. Some of them are frightening, others infuriating. Some of the things I must tell you are even more amazing than Camaris alive. Would you like to wait until the morning? Or do you still wish us locked up?"

Seriddan frowned. "Enough. Do not mock me, Josua. You will tell me what I need to know. I do not care if we are awake until cockcrow." He clapped his hands for more wine, then sent all but a few of his benumbed and astonished followers home.

*Ah, Baron,* Isgrimnur thought, *soon you'll find yourself down in the pit with the rest of us. I could have wished you better.*

The Duke of Elvritshalla pulled his chair closer as Josua began to speak.

# 7

# White Tree, Black Fruit

＊

**At first** it seemed a tower or a mountain—surely nothing so tall, so slender, so bleakly, flatly white could be anything alive. But as she approached it, she saw that what had seemed a vast cloud surrounding the central shaft, a diffuse milky paleness, was instead an incredible net of branches.

It was a tree that stood before her, a great, white tree that stretched so high that she could not see the top of it; it seemed tall enough to pierce the sky. She stared, overwhelmed by its fearsome majesty. Even though a part of her knew that she was dreaming, Miriamele also knew that this great stripe of white was a very important thing.

As she drew closer—she had no body: was she walking? Flying? It was impossible to tell—Miriamele saw that the tree thrust up from the featureless ground in one smooth shaft like a column of irregular but faultlessly polished marble. If this ivory giant had roots, they were set deep, deep underground, anchored in the very heart of the earth. The branches that surrounded the tree like a cloak of worn gossamer were already slender where they sprouted from the trunk, but grew even more attenuated as they reached outward. The tangled ends were so fine that at their tips they vanished into invisibility.

Miriamele was close to the great tree now. She began to rise, passing effortlessly upward. The trunk slipped past her like a stream of milk.

She floated up through the great cloud of branches. Out beyond the twining filaments of white, the sky was a *flat gray-blue. There was no horizon; there seemed nothing else in the world but the tree.*

*The web of branches thickened. Scattered here and there among the stems hung little kernels of darkness, clots of black like reversed stars. Rising as slowly as swansdown caught in a puff of wind, Miriamele reached out—suddenly she had hands, although the rest of her body still seemed curiously absent—and touched one of the black things. It was shaped like a pear, but was smooth and turgid as a ripe plum. She touched another and found it much the same. The next one that passed beneath her fingers felt slightly different. Miriamele's fingers tightened involuntarily and the thing came loose and fell into her grasp.*

*She looked down at the thing she had captured. It was as taut-skinned as the others, but for some reason it felt different. It might have been a little warmer. She knew, somehow, that it was ready—that it was ripe.*

*Even as she stared, and as the tendrils of the white tree fell endlessly past her on either side, the black fruit in her hands shuddered and split. Nestled in the heart of it, where a peach would have hidden its stone, lay an infant scarcely bigger than a finger. Eyelids tiny as snowflakes were closed in sleep. It kicked and yawned, but the eyes did not open.*

So every one of these fruits is a soul, *she thought.* Or are they just . . . possibilities? *She didn't quite know what these dream-thoughts meant, but a moment later she felt a wash of fear.* But I've pulled it loose! I've plucked it too soon! I have to put it back!

*Something was still drawing her upward, but now she was terrified. She had done something very wrong. She had to go back, to find that one branch in the net of manyfold thousands. Maybe it was not too late to return what she had unwittingly stolen.*

*Miriamele grabbed at the tangle of branches, trying to slow her ascent. Some of them, narrow and brittle as icicles, snapped in her hands; a few of the black fruits worked loose and went tumbling down into the gray-white distances below her.*

No! *She was frantic. She hadn't meant to cause this damage. She reached out her hand to catch one of the falling fruits and lost her grip on the tiny infant. She made a desperate grab, but it was out of her reach.*

*Miriamele let out a wail of despair and horror....*

It was dark. Someone was holding her, clutching her tightly.

"No!" she gasped. "I've dropped it!"

"You haven't dropped anything," the voice said. "You're having a bad dream."

She stared, but could not make out the face. The voice ... she knew the voice. "Simon...?"

"I'm here." He moved his mouth very close to her ear. "You're safe. But you probably shouldn't shout any more."

"Sorry. I'm sorry." She shivered, then began to disengage herself from his arms. There was a strong damp smell to the air and something scratchy beneath her fingers. "Where are we?"

"In a barn. About two hours' ride outside the walls of Falshire. Don't you remember?"

"A little. I don't feel very well." In fact, she felt dreadful. She was still shivering, yet at the same time she felt hot and even more bleary than she usually did when she woke up in the middle of the night. "How did we get here?"

"We had a fight with the Fire Dancers."

"I remember that. And I remember riding."

Simon made a sound in the darkness that might have been a laugh. "Well, after a while we stopped riding. You were the one who decided to stop here."

She shook her head. "I don't remember."

Simon let go of her—a little reluctantly, it was clear even to her dulled sensibilities. Now he crawled away over the thin layer of straw. A moment later something creaked and thumped and a little light leaked in. Simon's dark form was silhouetted in the square of a window. He was trying to find something to prop the shutter.

"It's stopped raining," he said.

"I'm cold." She tried to dig her way down into the straw.

"You kicked off your cloak." Simon crawled back across the loft to her side. He found her cloak and tucked it up beneath her chin. "You can have mine, too, if you want."

"I think I'll be happy with this," Miriamele said, although her teeth were still chattering.

"Do you want something to eat? I left your half of the supper—but you broke the ale jug on that big fellow's head."

"Just some water." The idea of putting food in her stomach was not a pleasant one.

Simon fussed with the saddlebags while Miriamele sat hugging her knees and staring out the open window at the night sky. The stars were invisible behind a veil of clouds. After Simon brought her the water skin and she drank, she felt weariness sweep over her again.

"I feel . . . bad," she said. "I think I need to sleep some more."

The disappointment was plain in Simon's voice. "Certainly, Miri."

"I'm sorry. I just feel so ill. . . ." She lay back and pulled the cloak tight beneath her chin. The darkness seemed to spin slowly around her. She saw Simon's shadowed silhouette against the window once more, then shadows came and took her back down.

By early morning Miriamele's fever was quite high. Simon could do little for her but put a damp cloth on her forehead and give her water to drink.

The dark day passed in a blur of images: gray clouds sweeping past the window, the lonely sound of a solitary dove, Simon's worried face rising above her as periodically as the moon. Miriamele discovered that she did not much care what happened to her. All the fear and concern that had driven her was leached away by the illness. If she could have chosen to fall asleep for a year, she would have; instead, she bobbed in and out of consciousness like a shipwrecked sailor clinging to a spar. Her dreams were full of white trees and drowned cities with seaweed waving in their streets.

In the hour before dawn of their second day in the barn, Miriamele awakened to find herself clear-headed again, but terribly, terribly weak. She had a sudden fear that she was alone, that her companion had left her behind.

"Simon?" she asked. There was no answer. *"Simon!?"*

"Humf?"

"Is that you?"

"What? Miriamele? Of course it's me." She could hear him roll over and crawl toward her. "Are you worse?"

"Better, I think." She stretched out a shaking hand until she found his arm, then finger-walked down it until she could clasp his hand. "But still not very well. Stay with me for a little while."

"Of course. Are you cold?"

"A bit."

Simon caught up his cloak and laid it atop her own. She felt so strengthless that the very gesture made her want to cry—indeed, a cold tear formed and trickled down her cheek.

"Thank you." She sat in silence for a while. Even this short conversation had tired her. The night, which had seemed so large and empty when she woke, now seemed a little less daunting.

"I think I'm ready to go back to sleep now." Her voice sounded fuzzy even in her own ears.

"Good night, then."

Miriamele felt herself slipping away. She wondered if Simon had ever had a dream as strange as the one about the white tree and the odd fruits it bore. It seemed unlikely. . . .

When she awoke to the uncertain light of a slate-gray dawn, Simon's cloak was still covering her. He was sleeping nearby, a few wisps of damp hay his only covering.

Miriamele slept a great deal during their second day in the barn, but when she was not sunk in slumber, she felt much healthier, almost her old self. By midday she was able to take some bread and a morsel of cheese. Simon had been out exploring the local countryside; while she ate he told her of his adventures.

"There are so few people! I saw a couple on the road out of Falshire—I didn't let them see me, I promise you—but almost no one else. There's a house down below that's almost falling apart. I think it belongs to the people who own this barn. There are holes in the roof in a few places, but most of the thatching is good. I don't think anyone's living there now. If we need to stay longer, that might be a drier place than this."

"We'll see," said Miriamele. "I may be able to ride tomorrow."

"Perhaps, but you'll have to be able to move around a bit first. This is the first time you've sat up since the night we left Falshire." He turned toward her suddenly. "And I almost got killed!"

"What?" Miriamele had to grab for the waterskin to keep herself from choking on the dry bread. "What do you mean?" she demanded when she had recovered. "Was it Fire Dancers?"

"No," Simon said, his eyes wide, his expression solemn. A moment later he grinned. "But it was a near thing, even so. I was coming back uphill from the field next to the house. I had been picking some . . . some flowers there."

Miriamele looked at him quizzically. "Flowers? What did you want with flowers?"

Simon went on as though the question had not been asked. "Something made a noise and I looked up. Standing there at the top of the rise behind me was a bull."

"Simon!"

"He didn't look very friendly, either. He was all bony, and his eyes were red, and he had bloody scratches along his sides." Simon dragged his fingers down his ribs, illustrating. "We stood there staring at each other for a moment, then he began to lower his head and make huffing noises. I started walking backward toward where I'd been. He came down the hill after me, making these little dancing steps, but going faster and faster."

"But Simon! What did you do?"

"Well, running downhill in front of a bull seemed fairly stupid, so I dropped the flowers and climbed the first good-sized tree that I reached. He stopped at the bottom—I got my feet up out of the way just as he got there—then all of a sudden he lowered his head, and . . . *thump!*" Simon brought his fist into his open palm, "he smacked up against the trunk. The whole tree shook and it almost knocked me off the branch I was hanging on, until I got my legs wrapped around good and tight. I pulled myself up until I was sitting on the branch, which was a good thing, because this idiot bull began butting his head against the tree, over and over until the skin began to peel off his head and there was blood running down his face."

"That's terrible. He must have been mad, poor animal."

"Poor animal! I like that!" Simon's voice rose in mock-despair. "He tries to kill your special protector and all you can say about him is 'poor animal.' "

Miriamele smiled. "I'm glad he didn't kill you. What happened?"

"Oh, he got tired at last and went away," Simon said airily. "Walked on down the dell, so that he wasn't between me and the fence anymore. Still, as I was running up the slope, I kept thinking I heard him coming up behind me."

"Well, you had a close call." Unable to help herself, Miriamele yawned; Simon made a face. "But I'm glad you didn't slay the monster," she continued, "even if you are a knight. He can't help being mad."

"Slay the monster? What, with my bare hands?" Simon laughed, but sounded pleased. "But maybe killing him would have been the kindest thing to do. He certainly seemed past saving. That's probably why whoever lived there left him behind."

"Or he may have gone mad *because* they left him behind," Miriamele said slowly. She looked at Simon and saw that he had heard something odd in her voice. "I'm tired, now. Thank you for the bread."

"There's one thing more." He reached into his cloak

and produced a small green apple. "The only one within walking distance."

Miriamele stared at it suspiciously for a moment, then sniffed it before taking a tentative bite. It was not sweet, but its tartness was very pleasant. She ate half, then handed the rest to Simon.

"It was good," she said. "Very good. But I still can't eat much."

Simon happily crunched up the rest. Miriamele found the hollow she had made for herself in the straw and stretched out. "I'm going to sleep a little more, Simon."

He nodded. He was looking at her so carefully, so thoroughly, that Miriamele had to turn away and pull her cloak up over her face. She was not strong enough to support such attention, not just now.

She awakened late in the afternoon. Something was making a strange noise—thump and swish, thump and swish. A little frightened and still very weak, Miriamele lay unmoving and tried to decide whether it might be someone looking for them, or Simon's bull, or something entirely different and possibly worse. At last she nerved herself and crawled silently across the loft, trying not to make any noise as she moved over the thin carpet of straw. When she reached the edge, she peered over.

Simon was on the ground floor of the barn practicing his sword strokes. Despite the coolness of the day, he had taken off his shirt; sweat gleamed on his pale skin. She watched him as he measured a distance before him, then lifted his sword with both hands, holding it perpendicular to the floor before gradually lowering its point. His freckled shoulders tensed. *Thump*—he took a step forward. *Thump, thump*—he pivoted to the side, moving around the almost stationary sword as though he held someone else's blade trapped against it. His face was earnest as a child's, and the tip of his tongue protruded pinkly from his mouth as he gripped it between his teeth in solemn concentration. Miriamele suppressed a giggle, but she could not help noticing how his skin slid over his lean muscles, how the fanlike shapes of his shoulder blades and the knobs of his backbone pushed against the milky skln. He stopped, the sword again held motionless before him. A drop of sweat slid from his nose and disappeared into his reddish beard. She suddenly wanted very much for him to hold her again, but despite her desire, the thought of it made her stomach clench in pain. There was so much that he did not know.

She pushed herself back from the edge of the loft as quietly as she could, retreating to her hollow in the straw. She tried to fall into sleep once more, but could not. For a long time she lay on her back, staring up at the shadows between the rafters as she listened to the tread of his feet, the hiss of the blade sliding through the air, and the muffled percussion of his breath.

Just before sunset Simon went down to look at the house again. He came back and reported that it was indeed empty, although he had seen what looked like fresh bootprints in the mud. But there was no other sign of anyone about, and Simon decided that the tracks most likely belonged to another harmless wanderer like the old drunkard Heanwig, so they gathered up their belongings and moved down. At first Miriamele was so light-headed that she had to lean on Simon to keep from falling, but after a few dozen steps she felt strong enough to walk unaided, although she was careful to keep a good grip on his arm. He went very slowly, showing her where the track was slippery with mud.

The cottage appeared to have been deserted for some time, and there were, as Simon had pointed out, some holes in the thatching, but the barn had been even draftier, and the cottage at least had a fireplace. As Simon carried in some split timbers he had found stacked against the wall outside and struggled to get a fire started, Miriamele huddled in her cloak and looked around at their home for the night.

Whoever had lived here had left few reminders of their residence, so she guessed that the circumstances which had driven the owners away had not come on suddenly. The only piece of furniture that remained was a stool with a splintered leg squatting off-kilter beside the hearth. A single bowl lay shattered on the stone beside it, every piece still in the spot where it had tumbled to a halt, as if the bowl had fallen only moments before. The hard clay of the floor was covered with rushes which had gone damp and brown. The only signs of recent life in the room were the innumerable cobwebs hanging in the thatches or stretching in the corners, but even these looked threadbare and forlorn, as if it had not been a good season even for spiders.

"There." Simon stood up. "That's got it. I'm going to fetch down the horses."

While he was gone, Miriamele sat before the fire and hunted through the saddlebags for food. For the first time in two days, she was hungry. She wished the house's owners had left their stew pot—the hook hung naked over the growing fire—but since it was gone she would make do with what she had. She pushed a couple of stones into the fire to heat, then rooted out the few remaining carrots and an onion. When the stones were hot enough, she would make some soup.

Miriamele scanned the ceiling critically, then unrolled her bedroll in a spot that looked like it was far enough from the nearest hole to stay dry in case the rains returned. After a moment's thought she unrolled Simon's nearby. She left what she considered to be a safe distance between them, but his bedroll was still closer than she would have preferred had there not been a leaky roof to deal with. When all was arranged, she found her knife in the saddlebag and got to work on the vegetables.

"It's blowing hard now," Simon said as he came back in. His hair was disarranged, standing out in strange tufts, but his cheeks were red and his smile was wide. "It will be a good night to be near a fire."

"I'm glad we moved down here," she said. "I feel much better tonight. I think I'll be able to ride tomorrow."

"If you're ready." As he walked past her to the fireplace, he put his hand on her shoulder for a moment, then trailed it gently across her hair. Miriamele said nothing, but went on chopping the carrots into a clay bowl.

*     *     *

The meal had not been anything either of them would remember fondly, but Miriamele felt better for having something hot in her stomach. When she had rinsed the bowls and scoured them with a dry twig, she put them away, then crawled onto her bedroll. Simon fussed with the fire for a bit, then laid himself down as well. They spent a silent interval staring at the flames.

"There was a fireplace in my bedroom at Meremund," Miriamele said quietly. "I used to watch the flames dancing at night when I couldn't sleep. I saw pictures in them. When I was very little, I thought I saw the face of Usires smiling at me once."

"Mmmm," Simon said. Then: "You had your *own* room to sleep in?"

"I was the only child of the prince and heir," she said a little crisply. "It is not unheard of."

Simon snorted. "It's unheard of by me. I slept with a dozen other scullions. One of them, Fat Zebediah, used to snore like a cooper cutting slats with a handsaw."

Miriamele giggled. "Later on, in the last twelvemonth when I lived in the Hayholt, Leleth used to sleep in my room. That was nice. But when I was in Meremund, I slept by myself, with a maid just on the other side of the door."

"That sounds . . . lonely."

"I don't know. I suppose it was." She sighed and laughed at the same time, a funny noise that made Simon lift his head beside her. "Once I was having trouble sleeping, so I went in to my father's room. I told him that there was a cockindrill under my bed, so that he would let me sleep with him. But that was after my mother died, so he only gave me one of his dogs to take back with me. 'He's a cockindrill-hound, Miri,' he said to me. 'By my faith, he is. He'll keep you safe.' He was always a bad liar. The dog just lay by the door and whimpered until I finally let him out again."

Simon waited for a while before speaking. The flames made jigging shadows in the thatching overhead. "How did your mother die?" he asked at last. "No one ever told me."

"She was shot by an arrow." Miriamele still hurt when she thought of it, but not as badly as she once had. "Uncle Josua was taking her to my father, who was fighting for Grandfather John along the edge of the Meadow Thrithing during the uprising there. Josua's troop was surprised in broad daylight by a much larger force of Thrithings-men. He lost his hand defending her, and did succeed in winning free, but she was struck down by a stray arrow. She was dead before sunset."

"I'm sorry, Miriamele."

She shrugged, even though he could not see her. "It was long ago. But losing her gave my father even more misery than it gave me. He loved her so much! Oh, Simon, you only know what my father has become, but he was a good man once. He loved my mother more than he loved anything else in the world."

And thinking of her father's gray, grief-stricken face, of the pall of anger that had descended on him and never lifted, she began to cry.

"And that's why I have to see him," she said finally, her voice unsteady. "That's why."

Simon rustled atop his bedroll. "What? What do you mean? See who?"

Miriamele took a deep breath. "My father, of course. That's why we're going to the Hayholt. Because I have to speak to my father."

"What nonsense are you talking?" Simon sat up. "We're going to the Hayholt to get your grandfather's sword, Bright-Nail."

"I never said that. You did." Despite the tears, she felt herself grow angry.

"I don't understand you, Miriamele. We are at war with your father. Are you going to go see him and tell him there's a cockindrill under your bed again? What are you saying?"

"Don't be cruel, Simon. Don't you dare." She could feel the tears threatening to become a torrent, but a small ember of fury was burning inside her as well.

"I'm sorry," he said, "but I just don't understand."

Miriamele pressed her hands together as tightly as she

could, and concentrated on that until she felt herself in control again. "And I have not explained to you, Simon. I'm sorry, too."

"Tell me. I'll listen."

Miriamele listened to the flames crackle and hiss for a while. "Cadrach showed me the truth, although I don't think he realized it. It was when we were traveling together, and he told me of Nisses' book. He had once owned it, or a copy of it."

"The magical book that Morgenes talked about?"

"Yes. And it is a powerful thing. Powerful enough that Pryrates learned that Cadrach had owned it and so Pryrates . . . sent for him." She fell silent momentarily, remembering Cadrach's description of the blood-red windows and the iron devices with the skin and hair of the tortured still on them. "He threatened him until Cadrach told him all the things he remembered. Cadrach said that Pryrates was particularly interested in talking with the dead—'Speaking through the Veil,' he called it."

"From what I know of Pryrates, that doesn't surprise me." Simon's voice was shaky, too. Obviously he had his own memories of the red priest.

"But that was what showed me what I needed to know," Miriamele said, unwilling to lose the thread of her idea now that she was finally talking about it out loud. "Oh, Simon, I had wondered so long why my father changed the way he did, why Pryrates was able to turn him to such evil tasks." She swallowed. There were still tears standing wet on her cheeks, but for the moment she had found a new strength. "My father loved my mother. He was never the same after she died. He did not marry, did not even consider it, despite all the wishes of my grandfather. They used to have terrible arguments about it. 'You need a son to be your heir,' Grandfather used to say, but my father always told him he would never marry again, that he had been given a wife and then God had taken her back." She paused, remembering.

"I still don't understand," said Simon quietly.

"Don't you see? Pryrates must have told my father that he could talk to the dead—that he could let my father speak with my mother again, perhaps even see her. You don't know him, Simon. He was heartsick with losing her. He would have done anything, I think, to have her back, even for a little while."

Simon drew in a long breath. "But that's . . . blasphemy. That's against God."

Miriamele laughed, a little shrilly. "As if that would have stopped him. I told you, he would have done *anything* to have her back. Pryrates must have lied to him and told him that they could reach her . . . beyond the Veil, or whatever that horrible book called it. Maybe the priest even thought that he could. And he used that promise to make my father first his patron, then his partner . . . then his slave."

Simon pondered this. "Perhaps Pryrates *did* try," he said finally. "Perhaps that is how they reached through to . . . to the other side. To the Storm King."

The sound of this name, even as quietly it had been spoken, was greeted with a skirl of wind in the thatches above, a rush of sound so abrupt that Miriamele flinched.

"Perhaps." The thought made her cold. To think of her father waiting eagerly to speak with his beloved wife and finding that *thing* instead. It was a little like the terrifying old story of what the fisherman Bulychlinn brought up in his nets. . . .

"But I still don't understand, Miriamele." Simon was gentle but stubborn. "Even if all that is true, what good will it do to speak to your father?"

"I'm not sure it will do any good." And that was true: it was hard to picture any happy result from their meeting after so much time and so much anger and sorrow. "But if there's even a small chance that I can show him sense, that I can remind him that this began out of love, and so convince him to stop . . . then I have to take that chance." She lifted a hand and wiped at her eyes: she was crying again. "He just wanted to see her. . . ." After a moment she steadied herself. "But you do not have to go, Simon. This is my burden."

He was silent. She could sense his discomfort.

"It is too great a risk," he said at last. "You might

never get to see your father, even if that would do any good. Pryrates might catch you first, and then no one would ever hear from you again." He said it with terrible conviction.

"I know, Simon. I just don't know what else to do. I have to speak to my father. I have to show him what's happened, and only I can do it."

"You're determined, then?"

"I am."

Simon sighed. "Aedon on the Tree, Miriamele, it's madness. I hope you change your mind by the time we get there."

Miriamele knew there would be no change. "I have been thinking about it for a long time."

Simon slumped back onto his bedroll. "If Josua knew, he'd tie you up and carry you a thousand leagues away."

"You're right. He would never allow it."

In the darkness, Simon sighed again. "I have to think, Miriamele. I don't know what to do."

"You can do anything but stop me," she said evenly. "Don't try to stop me, Simon."

But he did not reply. After a while, despite all the fear and furor, Miriamele felt the heaviness of sleep pulling her down.

She was startled awake by a loud roar. As she lay with her heart pounding, something flashed up in the ceiling, brighter than a torch. It took a moment for her to realize that the source had been a sky-spanning sheet of lightning glaring through the holes in the roof. There was another crash of thunder.

The room smelled even damper and closer than it had before. When the next lightning flash came, Miriamele saw in its momentary brilliance a torrent of raindrops pouring through the ragged thatching. She sat up and felt along the floor. The rain was falling well short of her, but it was splashing on Simon's boots and the bottoms of his breeches. He was still asleep, snoring quietly.

"Simon!" She shook him. "Get up!"

He grunted, but showed no other signs of wakefulness.

"Simon, you have to move. You're being rained on."

After a few more shakes, he rolled over. Complaining muzzily, he helped Miriamele pull his bedroll closer to hers, then flopped onto it with every sign of going immediately back to sleep.

As she lay listening to the rain patter on the straw, she felt Simon move closer. His face was very close to hers in the dark; she could feel his warm breath on her cheek. It was oddly peaceful, despite all the danger they had seen and still faced, to lie here and listen to the storm with this young man close beside her.

Simon stirred. "Miriamele? Are you cold?"

"A little."

He moved closer still, then reached out his arm and put it under her neck, tipping her in toward his chest so that she could feel him the whole length of her. She felt trapped but not frightened. His mouth was now pressed against her cheek.

"Miriamele . . ." he said softly.

"Sssshhh." She stayed huddled against him. "Don't say a word."

They remained that way for some time. Rain rattled in the thatch. From time to time thunder sounded in the distance like giants' drums.

Simon kissed her cheek. Miriamele felt his beard tickling along her jaw, but it seemed so strangely right that she did not squirm. He turned her head slightly, then his lips met hers. The thunder rumbled again from farther away, something happening in another place, another time.

*Why does there have to be more than this?* Miriamele wondered sadly. *Why should there be all the complications?* Simon had put his other arm around her, gentle but insistent, and now they were pressed together, body against body. She could feel his lean, muscled arms and his hard chest against her stomach, against her breasts. If only time could stop!

Simon's kisses were stronger now. He lifted his face and buried it in her hair.

"Miriamele," he whispered, hoarse-throated.

"Oh, Oh, Simon," she murmured back. She was not quite sure what she wanted, but she knew she would be happy just kissing him, just holding him.

His face was against her neck now, sending chills all through her. It felt wonderful, but also frightening. He was a boy, but he was a man as well. She stiffened, but he brought his face back to hers. Again he kissed her, clumsy but ardent, pushing a little too hard. She lifted her hand to his bearded face and gentled him, so that their lips could meet and touch—oh, so softly!

Even as they shared breath, his hand was moving across her face, across her neck. He touched her everywhere he could without losing the warmth pressed between them, running his fingers across the swell of her hip, letting his hand rest in the hollow beneath her arm. She tingled, yearning to rub hard against him, but she felt a strange softness, too, as though they were slowly drowning together, sinking down into dark ocean depths. She could hear her own heartbeat above the rustle of rain in the straw.

Simon rolled farther, until he was half above her, then drew back a little. He was only a shadow, which she found somehow frightening. She reached up until she could feel his cheek, the delicate rasp of his beard. His mouth moved.

"I love you, Miriamele."

Her breath caught. Suddenly there was a knot of coldness in her stomach. "No, Simon," she whispered. "Don't say that."

"But it's true! I think I've loved you since I first saw you, up in the tower with the sun in your hair."

"You can't love me." She wanted to push him off, but she had no strength. "You don't understand."

"What do you mean?"

"You . . . you *can't* love me. It's wrong."

"Wrong?" he said angrily. His body was now quivering against her, but it was the trembling of suppressed fury. "Because I'm a commoner. I'm not good enough for a princess, is that it?" He twisted away, kneeling in the straw beside her. "Damn your pride, Miriamele. I fought

a dragon! A dragon, a real dragon! Isn't that enough for
you!? Do you prefer somebody like Fengbald—a m–m–
murderer, but a m–murderer with a t–title?" He fought
against tears.

The rawness in his voice tore at her heart. "No, Simon,
that's not it! You don't understand!"

"Tell me, then!" he snapped. "Tell me what I don't understand!"

"It's not you. It's me."

There was a long silence. "What do you mean?"

"Nothing's wrong with you, Simon. I think you're
brave, and kind, and everything you should be. It's me,
Simon. I'm the one who doesn't deserve to be loved."

"What are you talking about?"

She gasped and shook her head violently. "I don't want
to talk any more. Leave me alone, Simon. Find someone
else to love. There will be plenty who would be happy to
have you." She rolled over, turning her back to him. Now,
when she most wanted the relief of tears, tears would not
come. She felt high and cold and strange.

His hand clutched her shoulder. "By the bloody Tree,
Miriamele, would you talk to me!? What are you saying?"

"I'm not pure, Simon. I'm not a maiden." There. It was
out.

It took him several moments to respond. "What?"

"I have been with a man." Now that she was talking, it
was easier than she had thought it would be. It was like
listening to someone else speak. "The nobleman from
Nabban I told you about, the one who took Cadrach and
me aboard his ship. Aspitis Preves."

"He raped you. . . ?" He sounded stunned, but anger
was growing. "That . . . that . . ."

Miriamele's laugh was short and bitter. "No, Simon, he
did not rape me. He held me prisoner, yes, but that was
later. He was a monster—but I let him come to my bed
and I did not resist." Then, to bolt the door for good, so
that Simon would leave her alone, so that she would bring
him no further suffering after this night: "I wanted him
to. I thought he was beautiful. I wanted him to."

Simon made an inarticulate noise, then stood up. His breath sawed in and out, in and out. For all she could see of him in the darkness, he could have been shape-changing: he seemed wordless and bedeviled as a trapped animal. He growled, then ran for the door of the cottage. It crashed open as he fled out into the dying storm.

After a few moments Miriamele went and pulled the door closed again. He would be back, she felt sure. Then he would leave her, or they would go on together, but things would be different. That was what she wanted. That was what she needed.

Her head felt empty. Those few thoughts almost seemed to echo, like stones rattled down a well.

She waited a long time for sleep. Just as she was beginning to slip away, she heard Simon come back in. He dragged his bedroll to the far corner and lay down. Neither of them spoke.

Outside, the storm had passed, but water still dripped from the ceiling. Miriamele counted the drops.

By midday the next day, Miriamele felt herself recovered enough to ride. They set out under dark clouds of more than one kind.

After all the pain and emotion of the night before they were both flat with each other, bruised and sullen like two swordfighters waiting for their final bout. They spoke no more than was necessary, but Miriamele saw signs of Simon's anger all day, from the over-brisk way he saddled and readied his horse to the way he rode ahead of her, just close enough to stay in sight.

For her part, Miriamele felt a sort of relief. The worst was out now and there was no turning back. Now Simon would know her for what she was, which could only be for the good, ultimately. It hurt to have him despise her, as he so obviously did at present, but it was better than leading him on falsely. Nevertheless, she could not shake the feeling of loss. It had been so warm, so nice, to kiss him and hold him without thinking. If only he had not talked of love. If only he had not forced her to consider her responsibilities. Deep down, she had known that anything more than friendship between them would mean living in a lie, but there had been moments, sweet moments, when she had allowed herself to pretend it could be different.

Making the best time they could on the terrible, muddy roads, they rode well beyond the reach of Falshire by evening time, out into the wildlands west of the city. When darkness came down—little more than a thickening of the already murky day—they found a wayside shrine to Elysia and made their beds on its floor. After a sparse meal and even sparser conversation, they retired to their bedrolls. This time it did not seem to bother Simon when Miriamele unfurled her pallet on the opposite side of the fire from his.

After her first day in the saddle following several days of illness, Miriamele felt ready to sink into sleep immediately, but sleep would not come. She moved several times, trying to find a comfortable position, but nothing seemed to help. She lay in darkness, staring up at nothing, listening as a light rain pattered the roof of the shrine.

Would Simon leave her, she wondered? It was an unexpectedly frightening thought. She had said several times that she was willing to make this journey by herself, as she had originally planned, but she realized now that she did not want to travel alone. Perhaps she had been wrong to tell him. Perhaps it would have been better to give him some more face-saving lie: if she had disgusted him too completely, he might simply go back to Josua.

And she did not want him to go, she realized. It was more than the idea of traveling these gloomy lands by herself that disturbed her. She would miss him.

It was odd to think about, now that she had probably thrown up an unbreachable wall between them, but she did not want to lose him. Simon had worked his way into her heart in a way no other friend ever had. His boyish silliness had always charmed her when it didn't irritate her, but now it was counterbalanced by a serious air that was very handsome. Several times she had caught herself watching him in surprise, amazed he had become a man in such a short time.

And there were other qualities that had become dear to her as well, his kindness, his loyalty, his open-mindedness. She doubted that the most traveled of her father's courtiers faced life with the same unprejudiced interest as Simon did.

It was frightening even to contemplate losing all those things if he left her.

But she *had* lost him now—or at least, there would always be a shadow over their friendship. He had seen the stain that was at the core of her; she had made it as visible and unpleasant as she could. She was not willing to suffer for lies any more, and seeing the way he felt about her was more suffering than she could stand. He was in love with her.

And she had been falling in love with him.

The thought hit her with unexpected force. Was that true? Wasn't love supposed to come like a bolt of sky-fire, to blind and stun? Or at the least, like a sweet perfume that rose and filled the air until one could think of nothing else? Surely her feelings for Simon had been different. She thought of him, of the laughable way his hair looked in the morning, of his earnest glances when he was worried for her.

*Elysia, Mother of God,* she prayed, *take this pain away. Did I love him? Do I love him?*

It didn't matter now, in any case. She had taken steps of her own to remove the hurt. Letting Simon continue to think of her as a chaste maiden worthy of his youthful ideals would be worse than anything—worse even than losing him completely, if that was the result.

So why, then, was the pain still so very strong?

"Simon. . . ?" she whispered. "Are you awake?"

If he was, he did not answer. She was alone with her thoughts.

The next day seemed even darker. The wind was sharp and biting. They rode swiftly, unspeaking, with Simon again keeping Homefinder a short distance ahead of Miriamele and her still-nameless steed.

By late morning they came to the fork where the River

Road joined the Old Forest Road. Two corpses hung in iron cages at the crossing, and had clearly done so for some time: It was impossible to tell from the wind-tossed rags of clothing or the grinning bones who these unfortunates had been. Miriamele and Simon both made the sign of the Tree as they crossed, passing as far from the clanking cages as they could. They took the Old Forest Road turning, and soon the River Road vanished from sight behind the low hills to the south.

The road began to dip downward. On the north side they could now see the edge of Aldheorte Forest, which flowed onto and over the foothills there. As they passed down through the outskirts of Hasu Vale and into the shelter of the hills the wind became less, but Miriamele did not feel comforted. Even at midday the valley was dark and almost silent except for the slow drip of the morning's rains from the leafless branches of oak and ash. Even the evergreens seemed full of shadow.

"I don't like this valley, Simon." She spurred forward. He slowed to allow her to catch up. "It was always a quiet, secretive place—but it feels different now."

He shrugged, looking away across the deep-shaded hillside. It was only when he stared so long at the unchanging landscape that she understood he did not want to meet her eyes. "I have not liked most of the places we've been." His voice was cold. "But we are not traveling for pleasure."

She felt a flare of anger. "That's not what I meant and you know it, Simon. I mean that this valley feels ... I don't know, dangerous."

Now he did turn. His smile was a smirk that hurt her to see. "Haunted, you mean? Like that old drunkard said?"

"I don't *know* exactly what I mean," she said furiously. "But I can see it was a waste of time talking about it with you."

"No doubt." He gently but deliberately touched his spurs to Homefinder's side and sent her trotting forward. Watching his straight back, Miriamele fought down the urge to shout at him. What had she expected? No, more to the point, what had she wanted, after all? Wasn't it best

he had been told the truth? Perhaps things would be easier
when some time had passed, when he realized they could
still be friends.

The road descended deeper into the valley, so that the
thick-mantled hills seemed to be growing even higher on
either side. The road was deserted, and the few rough cottages they saw perched on the hillsides seemed equally
uninhabited, but at least it seemed they would be able to
find shelter somewhere tonight—which was a reassuring
thought, since Miriamele did not in the least wish to
spend a night here out of doors. She had conceived a serious dislike of Hasu Vale, although nothing had actually
happened to make her feel that way. Still, the smothering quality of the stillness and the thick, overgrown
hillsides—and perhaps, just a little bit, her own sorrow—
conspired to make her look forward to the moment they
rode out of this valley again and saw the headlands of
Swertclif, even though that would mean that Asu'a and
her father were very, very close.

It was also disheartening to think of spending another
strained, silent night with Simon. Before their last unpleasant exchange, he had spoken to her only a few times
today, and then only about practical things. He had discovered what he claimed were new footprints near the
shrine where they had spent the night and had told her
about them soon after they set out, but he had seemed
quite offhand and uncaring about it. Miriamele secretly
thought it likely that the muddy footmarks were their
own, since they had tramped about a great deal while
searching for firewood. Other than that, Simon had con-
versed with her only about whether it was time to stop
and eat and rest the horses, and to issue curt thanks when
she had given him food or shared the water skin. It would
not be a pleasant night, she felt sure.

They were in the deeps of the valley when Simon abruptly stopped, pulling back on Homefinder's reins so
that the mare paced nervously from side to side for a long
moment after she halted.

"There's somebody on the road ahead," he said quietly.
"There. Just through the trees." He pointed to a spot

where the path hooked to one side and passed out of sight. "Do you see them?"

Miriamele squinted. The early twilight had turned the road before them into a dim streak of gray. If something was moving beyond the trees, she could not see it from her angle. "We're getting near the town."

"Come, then," he said. "It's probably just someone on their way home, but we haven't seen anyone else all day." He eased Homefinder ahead.

As they rounded the bend they came upon two figures hunching along in the middle of the road, both of them carrying buckets. When the noise of Simon and Miriamele's horses reached the pair, they flinched and looked over their shoulders as guiltily as thieves surprised. Miriamele felt sure that they were just as startled as Simon to find other travelers on the road.

The pair moved to the verge of the road as the riders approached. From what Miriamele could see of their dark, hooded cloaks, they were probably local people, hill-folk. Simon lifted his hand to his brow in salute.

"God give you good day," he said.

The nearest of the pair looked up at him and cautiously raised his own hand to return the greeting, but stopped abruptly, staring.

"By the Tree!" Simon reined up. "You're the ones from the tavern in Falshire."

*What is he doing?* Miriamele wondered fearfully. *Are they Fire Dancers? Ride on, Simon, you idiot!*

He turned toward her. "Miriamele. Look here."

Unexpectedly, the two hooded folk dropped to their knees. "You saved our lives," a woman's voice said.

Miriamele pulled up and stared. It was the woman and man that the Fire Dancers had threatened.

"That's true," the man said. His voice was unsteady. "May Usires bless you, good knight."

"Please, get up." Simon was clearly pleased yet embarrassed. "I'm sure someone else would have helped you if we hadn't."

The woman stood, unmindful of the mud on the knees of her long skirt. "None seemed in a hurry to help," she said. "That's the way. Those who are good are given the pain."

The man darted a glance at her. "That's enough, wife. These folk don't need your tellin' what's wrong with the world."

She looked back at him with poorly-hidden defiance. "It's a shame, that's all. A shame the world works thus."

The man turned his attention back to Simon and Miriamele. He was middle-aged, with a face reddened and wrinkled by years of harsh sun. "My wife has her ideas, mind, but the bottom of it's true enough. You saved our lives, that you did." He forced a smile. He seemed nervous; having his life saved must have been almost as frightening as not having it saved. "Have you a place to stay for tonight? My wife's Gullaighn and I am Roelstan, and we would be pleased to offer you what shelter we have."

"We cannot stop yet," Miriamele said, unsettled by the thought of staying with strangers.

Simon looked at her. "You have been ill," he said.

"I can ride farther."

"Yes, you probably can, but why turn down a roof over our heads, even for one night?" He turned to look at the man and woman, then moved his horse closer to Miriamele. "It may be the last chance to get out of the wind and rain," he murmured, "the last until . . ." He broke off, unwilling even to whisper any hint of their destination.

Miriamele was certainly weary. She hesitated a moment longer, then nodded her head.

"Good," said Simon, then turned to the man and woman. "We would be glad of shelter." He did not offer their own names to these strangers; Miriamele silently approved of that at least.

"But we have nothing worthy of such good folk, husband." Gullaighn had a face that might have been kindly, but fear and hard times had made the skin slack, the eyes sorrowful. "It is no favor to bring them to our rude place."

"Be quiet, woman," her husband said. "We will do what we can."

She appeared to have more to say, but instead closed her mouth in a grim line.

"It's settled, then," he said. "Come. It is not much farther."

After a moment's consideration, Simon and Miriamele dismounted so that they could walk beside their hosts. "Do you live here in Hasu Vale?" asked Simon.

Roelstan laughed shortly. "For a short time only. We lived once in Falshire."

Miriamele hesitated before speaking. "And . . . and were you Fire Dancers?"

"To our sorrow."

"They are a powerful evil." Gullaighn's voice was thick with emotion. "You should have nothing to do with them, my lady, nor anything they've touched."

"Why were those men after you?" Simon reflexively fingered the hilt of his sword.

"Because we left," Roelstan said. "We could stand it no longer. They are mad, but like dogs, even in their madness they can do harm."

"But it is not so easy to escape them," said Gullaighn. "They are fierce and they do not let go. And they are everywhere." She lowered her voice. "Everywhere!"

"By the Ransomer, woman," Roelstan growled, "what are you trying to do? You have seen this knight wield a sword. He has naught to fear from them."

Simon walked a little straighter. Miriamele smiled, but a look at Gullaighn's anxious face made the smile fade. Could she be right? Might there be more Fire Dancers about? Perhaps by tomorrow it would be time to leave the main road again and travel more secretively.

As if echoing her thoughts, Roelstan stopped and waved at a track climbing up from the Old Forest Road, winding away into the wooded hillside. "We have made our place up there," he said. "It is no good to be too close to the road, where the smoke of a fire might bring visitors less welcome than you two."

They followed Roelstan and Gullaighn up the narrow

path. After the first few turnings the road had disappeared behind them, hidden beneath a blanket of treetops. It was a long and steep climb through the close-leaning trees, and the dark cloaks of their guides became harder and harder to follow as twilight came on. Just as Miriamele began to think that they would see the moon before they saw a place to stop, Roelstan halted and pulled back the thick branch of a pine tree that had hung across their path.

"Here it is," he said.

Miriamele led her horse through after Simon, and found herself in a wide clearing on the hillside. In the center was a house made of split timbers, plain but surprisingly large. Smoke twined from a hole in the roof.

Miriamele was taken aback. She turned to Gullaighn, suddenly full of misgivings. "Who else lives here?"

The woman gave no answer.

Miriamele saw movement in the doorway of the house. A moment later, a man emerged onto the dark hard-packed earth before the door. He was short and thick-necked, clothed in a white robe.

"We meet again," said Maefwaru. "Our visit in the tavern was too short."

Miriamele heard Simon curse, then the scrape of his sword leaving the scabbard. He pulled at her bridle to turn her horse around.

"Don't," Maefwaru said. He whistled. A half-dozen more white-robed figures stepped from the shadows around the edge of the clearing. In the twilight, they seemed ghosts born from the secretive trees. Several of them had drawn their bows.

"Roelstan, you and your woman move away." The bald man sounded almost pleasant. "You have done what you were sent to do."

"Curse you, Maefwaru!" Gullaighn cried. "On the Day of Weighing-Out, you will eat your own guts for sausages!"

Maefwaru laughed, a deep rumble. "Is that so? Move, woman, before I have someone put an arrow in you."

As her husband dragged her away, Gullaighn turned to

Miriamele with eyes full of tears. "Forgive us, my lady. They caught us again. They made us!"

Miriamele's heart was cold as a stone.

"What do you want with us, you coward?" Simon demanded.

Maefwaru laughed again, wheezing a little. "It is not what *we* want of you, young master. It is what the Storm King wants of you. And we will find out tonight, when we give you to Him." He waved to the other white-robed figures. "Bind them. There is much to do before midnight."

As the first of the Fire Dancers seized his arms, Simon turned to Miriamele, his face full of anger and desperation. She knew that he wished to fight, to make them kill him instead of simply surrendering, but was afraid to for her sake.

Miriamele could give him nothing. She had nothing left inside of her but stifling dread.

# 8

# A Confession

✦

"*Unto her side he came, he came,*"

sang Maegwin,

"*A youth dressed all in sable black*
*With golden curls about his head*
*And silken cape upon his back.*

'*And what would you my lady fair?*'
*That golden youth did smile and say.*
'*What rare gift may I give to you,*
*So you will be my bride this day?*

*The maiden turned her face aside.*
'*There is no gift so rich, so fine,*
*That I would give you in return*
*That rare thing that is only mine.*'

*The youth he shook his golden head*
*And laughed and said, 'Oh, maiden sweet*
*You may turn me away today,*
*But soon find that you can't say no.*
*My name is Death, and all you have*
*Will come to me anyway . . .*' "

It was no use. Over the sound of her own melody, she
could still hear the odd wailing that seemed to portend so
much unhappiness.

Maegwin's song trailed off and she stared into the flames of the campfire. Her cold-cracked lips made it painful to sing. Her ears stung and her head hurt. Nothing was as it should be—nothing was as she had expected.

It had *seemed* at first that things were going the way they should. She had been a dutiful daughter to the gods: it was no surprise that after her death she should be raised up to live among them—not as an equal, of course, but as a trusted subordinate, a beloved servant. And in their strange way the gods had proved every bit as wondrous as she had imagined they would, with their inhuman, flashing eyes and their rainbow-hued armor and clothing. Even the land of the gods had been much as she had expected, like her own beloved Hernystir, but better, cleaner, brighter. The sky in the godlands seemed higher and more blue than a sky could be, the snow whiter, the grass so green that its verdancy was almost painful. Even Count Eolair, who had also died and come to this beautiful eternity, seemed more open, more approachable; she had been able to tell him without fear or shyness that she had always loved him. Eolair, relieved like her of the burden of mortality, had listened with kind concern—almost like a god himself!

But then things had begun to go wrong.

Maegwin had thought that when she and the other living Hernystiri had faced their enemies, and by doing so brought the gods out into the world, they had somehow tipped a balance. The gods themselves were at war, just as the Hernystiri—but the gods' war had not been won. The worst, it seemed, was yet to come.

And so the gods had ridden across the broad white fields of Heaven, searching for Scadach, the hole into outer darkness. And they had found it. Cold and black it was, bounded in stone quarried from eternity's darkest recesses, just as the lore-masters had taught her—and full of the gods' direst enemies.

She had never believed that such things could exist, creatures of pure evil, shining vessels of emptiness and despair. But she had seen one stand on the ageless wall of Scadach, heard its lifeless voice prophesy the destruction of gods and mortals alike. All that was wrong lay behind that wall ... and now the gods were trying to bring the wall tumbling down.

Maegwin would have guessed that the ways of gods were mysterious. What she would not have guessed was just how mysterious they could be.

She raised her voice in song again, still hoping that she could blot out the disturbing noise, but gave it up after a few moments. The gods themselves were singing, and their voices were much stronger than hers.

*Why don't they stop?* she thought desperately. *Why don't they leave it alone?!*

But it was useless to wonder. The gods had their reasons. They always did.

Eolair had long since given up trying to understand the Sithi. He knew they were not gods, whatever Maegwin's poor, fevered mind might see, but neither were they a great deal more comprehensible than the Lords of Heaven.

The count turned away from the fire, turned his back on Maegwin. She had been singing to herself, but had fallen silent. She had a sweet voice, but set against the chanting of the Peaceful Ones it sounded thin and discordant. It was not her fault. No mortal voice would sound like much when set against ... this.

The Count of Nad Mullach shivered. The chorus of Sithi voices rose again. Their music was as impossible to ignore as were their catlike eyes when they stared you in the face. The rhythmic song gained in volume, pulsing like the oar-master's call to his rowers.

The Sithi had been singing for three days, clustered before the bleak walls of Naglimund in the flurrying snow. Whatever they were doing, the Norns within the castle did not ignore them: several times the white-faced defenders had mounted to the tops of the walls and let fly a volley of arrows. A few of the Sithi had been killed in these attacks, but they had their own archers. Each time, the Norns were driven from the walls and the Sithi voices would rise once more.

"I don't know that I can stand this much longer, Eolair." Isorn appeared out of the whirl of mist, his beard jeweled with frost. "I had to go hunting just to get away, but the noise followed me as far as I went." He dropped a hare onto the ground near the fire. Red dribbled from the arrow-wound in its side, staining the snow. "Good day, Lady," the duke's son said to Maegwin. She had stopped singing, but did not look up at him. She seemed incapable of seeing anything but the wavering fire.

Eolair received Isorn's curious look and shrugged. "It is not really such a terrible sound."

The Rimmersman raised his eyebrows. "No, Eolair, it is beautiful in its way. But it is too beautiful for me, too strong, too strange. It is making me ill."

The count frowned. "I know. The rest of the men are unsettled, too. More than unsettled—frightened."

"But why are the Sithi doing this? They are risking their lives—two more were killed yesterday! If this is some fairy ceremony they must perform, can they not sing out of bowshot?"

Eolair shook his head helplessly. "I do not know. Bagba bite me, I do not know anything, Isorn."

As continual as the noise of the ocean, the voices of the Sithi washed across the camp.

Jiriki came in the dark before dawn. The slumbering coals picked out his sharp features in scarlet light.

"This morning," he said, then squatted, staring at the embers. "Before noon."

Eolair rubbed his eyes, trying to bring himself fully awake. He had been sleeping fitfully, but sleeping nonetheless. "This . . . this morning? What do you mean?"

"The battle will begin." Jiriki turned and gave Eolair a look that on a more familiar face might have betokened pity. "It will be dreadful."

"How do you know that the battle will start then?"

"Because that is what we have been working toward. We cannot fight a siege—we are too few. Those you call Norns are fewer than we are, but they sit inside a great shell of stone, and we do not have the engines mortals make for such battles nor the time to build them. So we will do it our way."

"Does it have something to do with the singing?"

Jiriki nodded in his oddly avian way. "Yes. Make your men ready. And tell them this: whatever they may think or see, they are fighting against living creatures. The Hikeda'ya are like you and like us—they bleed. They die." He fixed Eolair with an even, golden stare. "You will tell them that?"

"I will." Eolair shivered and leaned closer to the fire, warming his hands before the dreaming coals. "Tomorrow?"

Jiriki nodded again, then stood. "We will have our best chance while the sun is high. If we are lucky, it will be over before the darkness comes."

Eolair couldn't imagine rugged Naglimund being brought down in so short a time. "And if it's *not* over? What, then?"

"Things will be . . . difficult." Jiriki took a step backward and vanished into the mist.

Eolair sat before the coals for a little while, clenching his teeth to keep them from chattering. When he was sure he would not embarrass himself, he went to waken Isorn.

⚜

Buffeted by brisk winds, the gray and red tent rode the peak of the hill like a sailing ship breasting a high wave. A few other tents shared the hilltop; many more were scattered down the slope and clustered in the valley. Beyond them lay Lake Clodu, a vast blue-green mirror, still as a contented beast.

Tiamak stood outside the tent, lingering despite the chill breeze. So many people, so much movement, so much life! It was disturbing to look down on that great sea of people, frightening to know that he was so close to the grinding stones of History, but still it was somehow hard to turn away. His own little story had been quite swallowed up by the great tales that stalked through Osten Ard in these days. It sometimes seemed that a sack full of the mightiest dreams and nightmares had been emptied out. That Tiamak's own small accomplishments, fears, and desires seemed likely to be ignored was the best he could hope for. An equally strong possibility was that they might be trampled entirely.

Shivering a little, he finally lifted the tent flap and stepped through.

It was not, as he had feared when Jeremias brought him the prince's summons, a council of war. Such things made him feel completely useless. Only a few waited—Josua, Sir Camaris, Duke Isgrimnur, all seated on stools, Vorzheva propped up in her bed, and the Sitha-woman Aditu, cross-legged on the floor at Vorzheva's side. The only other person in the tent was young Jeremias, who had apparently been very busy this afternoon. Just now, he was standing before the prince, trying to look attentive while gasping slightly for air.

"Thank you for your haste, Jeremias," said Josua. "I understand completely. Please just go back and tell Strangyeard to come when he can. After that, you are released."

"Yes, your Highness." Jeremias bowed, then headed for the door.

Tiamak, who was still standing in the doorway, smiled at the approaching youth. "I did not have a chance to ask you before, Jeremias: how is Leleth? Is there any change?"

The youth shook his head. He tried to keep his voice even, but the pain was obvious. "Just the same. She never wakes up. She drinks a little water, but takes no food." He rubbed fiercely at his eye. "No one can do anything."

"I am sorry," said Tiamak gently.

"It's not your fault." Jeremias moved uncomfortably from one foot to the other. "I have to go take Josua's message back to Father Strangyeard."

"Of course." Tiamak stepped out of the way. Jeremias slipped past him and was gone.

"Tiamak," the prince called, "please come and join us." He pointed to an empty stool.

When the Wrannaman was seated, Josua looked around. "This is very difficult," he said at last. "I am going to do a terrible thing and I apologize for it now. Nothing can excuse it but the strength of our need." He turned to Camaris. "My friend, please forgive me. If I could do this some other way, I would. Aditu feels that we should know whether you went to the Sithi home of Jao é-Tinukai'i, and if you did, why."

Camaris raised his tired eyes to Josua's. "Is a man permitted no secrets?" he asked heavily. "I promise you, Prince Josua, that it is nothing to do with this struggle against the Storm King. On the honor of my knighthood."

"But someone who does not know all the history of our people—and Ineluki was one of us, once—may not know all the ties of blood and fable." Aditu spoke without Josua's reluctance, clearly and forcefully. "Everyone here knows you are an honorable man, Camaris, but you may not realize whether what you have seen or learned is useful."

"Will you not tell just me, Camaris?" Josua asked. "You know I hold your honor as high as my own. You certainly need not spill all your secrets to a room full of people, if that is what you fear, even though they are your friends and allies."

Camaris looked at him for a moment. His gaze seemed to soften; he struggled visibly with some impulse, but after a moment he shook his head violently. "*No.* A thousand pardons, Prince Josua, but to my shame I cannot. There are some things that even the Canon of Knighthood cannot drive me to."

Isgrimnur was wringing his large hands together, clearly pained by Camaris' discomfort. Tiamak had not seen the Rimmersman so unhappy since they had left Kwanitupul. "And me, Camaris?" the duke asked. "I have known you longer by far than anyone here. We both served the old king. If it is something to do with Prester John, you can share it with me."

Camaris sat straighter, but it seemed to be weak opposition to something that was bending him down inside. "I cannot, Isgrimnur. It would put too great a burden on our friendship. Please, ask me not."

Tiamak felt the tension in the room. The old knight seemed to be backed into a corner no one else could see.

"Can you not leave him alone?" Vorzheva's voice was raw. She draped her hands over her round belly as though to protect the child from so much unpleasantness and sorrow.

*Why am I here?* Tiamak wondered. *Because I traveled with him when he was witless? Because I am a Scrollbearer? With Geloë dead and Binabik gone, the League is a sorry collection just now. And where is Strangyeard?*

A thought suddenly came to him. "Prince Josua?"

The prince looked up. "Yes, Tiamak?"

"Forgive me. This is not my place, and I do not know all the customs . . ." he hesitated, "but you Aedonites have a tradition of confession, do you not?"

Josua nodded. "Yes."

*He Who Always Steps on Sand,* Tiamak prayed silently, *let me walk the right path now!*

The Wrannaman turned to Camaris. The old knight, for all his dignified bearing, looked back at him with the eyes of a hunted animal. "Could you not tell your story to a priest," Tiamak asked him, "—perhaps Father Strangyeard, if he is the proper kind of holy man? That way, if I understand things rightly, your story would be between you and God. But also, Strangyeard knows as much about the Great Swords and our struggle as any man living. He could at least tell the rest of us whether we should truly look elsewhere for answers."

Josua slapped his hand on his knee. "You are indeed a Scrollbearer, Tiamak. You have a subtle mind."

Tiamak stored Josua's compliment away to be appreciated later and kept his gaze on the old knight.

Camaris stared. "I do not know," he said slowly. His chest rose and fell as he took a long breath. "I have not told this story, even in the confessional. That is part of my shame—but not the greatest part."

"Everyone has shame, everyone has done wrong."

Isgrimnur was obviously growing a little impatient. "We do not want to drag this out of you, Camaris. We only wish to know whether any dealings you might have had with the Sithi can answer some of our questions. Damn it!" he added as an afterthought.

A wintry smile moved across Camaris' face. "You were always admirably forward, Isgrimnur." The smile fell away, revealing a terrible, trapped emptiness. "Very well. Send for the priest."

"Thank you, Camaris." Josua stood up. "Thank you. He is praying at young Leleth's bedside. I will fetch him myself."

Camaris and Strangyeard had walked far down the hill together. Tiamak stood in the doorway of Josua's tent and watched them, wondering despite the praise of his cleverness if he had done the right thing. Perhaps something he had heard Miriamele say was correct: they might have done Camaris no favor by waking him from his witless state. And forcing him to dredge up such obviously painful memories seemed no kinder.

The pair, the tall knight and the priest, stood for a long time on the windy hillside—long enough for a long bank of clouds to roll past and finally reveal the pale afternoon sun. At last Strangyeard turned and started back up the hill; Camaris remained, staring out across the valley to the gray mirror of Lake Clodu. The knight seemed carved in stone, something that might wear away to a featureless post but would still be standing in that spot a century from now.

Tiamak leaned into the tent. "Father Strangyeard is coming."

The priest struggled up the hill hunched over, whether against the cold or because he now bore the burden of Camaris' secrets, Tiamak could not guess. Certainly the look on his face as he made his way up the last few ells bespoke a man who had heard things he would have been happier not knowing.

"Everyone is waiting for you, Father Strangyeard," Tiamak told him.

The archivist nodded his head distractedly. His eye was cast down, as though he could not walk without watching where he set his feet. Tiamak let him pass, then followed him into the comparative warmth of the tent.

"Welcome back, Strangyeard," said Josua. "Before you begin, tell me: how is Camaris? Should we send someone to him?"

The priest looked up in startlement, as though it was a surprise to hear a human voice. The look he gave Josua was curiously fearful, even for the timid archivist. "I . . . I do not know, Prince Josua. I do not know much . . . much of anything at this moment."

"I'll go see to him," Isgrimnur grumbled, levering himself up off the stool.

Father Strangyeard raised his hand. "He . . . wishes to be alone, I think." He fidgeted with his eye-patch for a moment, then ran his fingers through his sparse hair. "Oh, merciful Usires. Poor souls."

"Poor *souls?*" said Josua. "What are you saying, Strangyeard? Can you tell us anything?"

The archivist wrung his hands. "Camaris *was* in Jao é-Tinukai'i. That much . . . oh, my . . . that much he told me before he asked for the seal of confession, knowing that I would tell you. But the reason, and what happened there, are locked behind the Door of the Ransomer." His stare wandered around the room as if it hurt him to look at anything too long. Then his eye fell on Vorzheva, and for some reason lingered there as he talked. "But this much I can say, I believe: I do not think that his experiences have aught to do with the present situation, nor is there anything to be learned from them about the Storm King, or the Three Great Swords, or any of the other things you need to know to fight this war. Oh, merciful Usires. Oh, dear." He patted at his thin red hair again. "Forgive me. Sometimes it is hard to remember that I am merely the doorkeeper of the Ransomer, and that the burden is not mine to bear, but God's. Ah, but it is hard right now."

Tiamak stared. His fellow Scrollbearer looked as

though he had been visited by vengeful spirits The Wrannaman moved closer to Strangyeard.

"Is that all?" Josua seemed disappointed. "Are you certain that the things he knows cannot help us?"

"I am not certain of anything but pain, Prince Josua," the archivist said quietly but with surprising firmness. "But I truly think it unlikely, and I know for certain that to force anything more from that man would be cruel beyond belief, and not just to him."

"Not just to him?" Isgrimnur said. "What does that mean?"

"Enough, please." Strangyeard seemed almost angry— something Tiamak had not imagined possible. "I have told you what you needed to know. Now I would like to leave."

Josua was taken aback. "Of course, Father Strangyeard."

The priest nodded. "May God watch over us all."

Tiamak followed Strangyeard out through the tent door. "Is there something I can do?" he asked. "Perhaps just walk with you?"

The archivist hesitated, then nodded. "Yes. That would be kind."

Camaris was gone from the spot where he had stood; Tiamak looked for him, but saw no sign.

When they had traveled some way down the hill, Strangyeard spoke in a musing voice. "I understand now . . . why a man would wish to drink himself into oblivion. I find it tempting myself at this moment."

Tiamak raised an eyebrow but said nothing.

"Perhaps drunkenness and sleep are the only ways God has given us to forget," Strangyeard continued. "And sometimes forgetting is the only cure for pain."

Tiamak considered. "In a way, Camaris was as one asleep for two score years."

"And we awakened him." Strangyeard smiled sadly. "Or, I should say, God allowed us to awaken him. Perhaps there is a reason for all this. Perhaps there will be some result beside sorrow after all."

He did not, the Wrannaman thought, sound as though he believed it.

✦

Guthwulf paused and let the air wash over him, trying to decide which of the passageways led upward—for it was upward that the sword-song was leading him. His nostrils twitched, sniffing for the faintest indication from the damp tunnel air as to which way he should go. His fingers traveled back and forth along the stone walls on either side, questing like eyeless crabs.

Disembodied, alien speech washed over him once more, words that he did not hear so much as feel. He shook his head, trying to drive them from his brain. They were ghosts, he knew, but he had learned that they could not harm him, could not touch him. The chittering voices only interfered with what he truly wanted to hear. They were not real. The sword was real, and it was calling.

He had first felt the pull return several days before.

As he awakened into the confusion of blind solitude, as he had so many times, a thread of compelling melody had followed him up out of sleep into his waking blackness. It was more than just another of his pitiful dreams: this was a powerful feeling, frightful and yet comfortably familiar, a song without words or melody that rang in his head and wrapped him with tendrils of longing. It tugged at him so strongly that he scrambled clumsily to his feet, eager as a young swain called by his beloved. The sword! It was back, it was near!

Only as the last clinging remnants of his slumbers left him did he remember that the sword was not alone.

It was never alone. It belonged to Elias, his once-friend, now bitter enemy. Much as Guthwulf ached to be near it, to bask in its song as he would the warmth of a fire, he knew he would have to approach cautiously. Miserable as his current life was, he preferred it to what Elias would do to him if he was captured—or worse, what Elias would let that serpent Pryrates do to him.

It never occurred to him that it would be even better simply to leave the sword alone. The song of it was like the splash of a stream to a traveler dying of thirst. It drew him, and he had no choice but to follow its call.

Still, some animal cunning remained. As he felt his way through the well-learned tunnels, he knew he needed not only to find Elias and the sword, but also to approach them in such a way so as to avoid discovery and capture, as he had managed once before to spy on the king from a shelf of rock above the foundry floor. To this end, he followed the sword's compelling summons but remained at as great a distance as he could, like a hawk circling its master on a long trace. But trying to resist the complete pull was maddening. The first day he followed the sword, Guthwulf forgot completely to go to the spot where the woman regularly left food for him. By the second day—which, to the blind Earl of Utanyeat, was whatever came between one sleep and the next—the sword's call beating within him like a second heartbeat had almost dissolved the memory that such a spot even existed. He ate what crawling things his groping hands encountered, and drank from any moving trickle of water he could find. He had learned in his first weeks in the tunnels what happened when he drank from standing pools.

Now, after three sleeps full of sword-dreams, he had wandered far beyond any of the passageways familiar to him. The stones he felt beneath his hands had never met his touch before; the tunnels themselves, but for the always-present phantom voices and the equally constant pull of the Great Sword, seemed completely alien.

He had some small idea of how long he had been searching for the sword this time, and, in a rare moment of clear thinking, he wondered what the king was doing down in the hidden places beneath the castle for such a long time.

A moment later, a wild, glorious thought came to him.

*He's lost the sword. He's lost it down here somewhere, and it's just sitting, waiting for whoever finds it! Waiting for me! Me!*

He did not even realize that he was slavering in his dusty beard. The thought of having the sword all to himself—to touch, to listen to, to love and to worship—

was so horrifyingly pleasurable that he took a few steps and then fell to the floor, where he lay quivering until darkness took his remaining senses.

After he had regained his wits, Guthwulf rose and wandered, then slept once more. Now he was awake again, and standing before the branching of two tunnels, trying to decide which one was most likely to lead him upward. He knew, somehow, that the sword was above him, just as a mole beneath the ground knows which way to dig to reach the surface. In other lucid moments he had worried that perhaps he was grown so sensitive to the sword's song that it was leading him upward to the king's very throne room, where he would be caught and slaughtered just as a mole would be if it dug its way up into the kennels.

But even though he had been moving steadily upward, he had started very deep. He felt sure the rise had not been anything so great as he feared. He was also certain that in his roundabout way he was moving ever outward, away from the core of the castle. No, the beautiful, terrifying thing that drew him, the living, singing blade, must be somewhere here beneath the earth, coffined in rock just as he was. And when he found it, he would not be lonely any more. He only had to decide which of these tunnels to follow. . . .

Guthwulf raised his hands and reflexively rubbed at his blind eyes. He felt very weak. When was the last time he had eaten? What if the woman gave up on him and stopped putting out food? It had been so nice to eat real food. . . .

*But if I find the sword, if I have it all to myself,* he gloated, *I won't care about any of that.*

He cocked his head. There was a scratching noise just beyond him somewhere, as though something were trapped inside the stone. He had heard that noise before—in fact, he heard it ever more frequently of late—but it was nothing to do with what he sought.

The scratching ended, and still he stood in painful indecision before the forking tunnels. Even when he put down stones for markers, it was so easy to become lost, but he was certain that one of these passages led upward to the heart of the song—the crooning, sucking, soul-drowning melody of the Great Sword. He did not want to go the wrong way and spend another endless time trying to find his way back. He was weak with hunger, numb with weariness.

He might have stood for an hour or a day. At last, beginning as gently as a dust devil, a wind came tugging at his hair, a puff of breeze from the right-hand turning. Then, a moment later, a flurry of *somethings* welled up out of the tunnel and floated past him—the spirits that haunted the dark nether-roads. Their voices echoed in his skull, dim and somehow hopeless.

*. . . The Pool. We must seek him at the Pool. He will know what to do . . .*

*Sorrow. They have called down the final sorrow . . .*

As the twittering things blew past, blind Guthwulf slowly smiled. Whatever they were, spirits of the dead or bleak products of his own madness, they always came to him out of the depths, from the deepest, oldest parts of the labyrinth. They came from below . . . and he wished to climb.

He turned and shuffled into the left-hand tunnel.

The remains of Naglimund's massive gate had been plugged with rubble, but since it was lower than the surrounding wall and the piles of broken stone offered purchase for climbing feet, it seemed to Count Eolair the logical place for an assault to begin. He had been surprised when the Sithi had concentrated themselves before a blank and undamaged stretch of wall.

He left Maegwin and the contingent of anxious mortal warriors under Isorn's command, then crept up the snowy hillside to join Jiriki and Likimeya in the shell of a broken building a few hundred ells from Naglimund's outwall. Likimeya gave him a cursory glance, but Jiriki nodded.

"It is almost time," the Sitha said. "We have called for the *m'yon rashí*—the strikers."

Eolair stared at the contingent of Sithi before the wall. They had stopped singing, but had not moved away. He wondered why they should risk the arrows of the Norns when whatever their singing was intended for seemed finished. "Strikers? Do you mean battering rams?"

Jiriki shook his head, smiling faintly. "We have no history of such things, Count Eolair. I imagine we could devise such an engine, but we decided to fall back on what we know instead." His look darkened. "Or rather, what we learned from the Tinukeda'ya." He gestured. "Look, the m'yon rashí come."

A quartet of Sithi were approaching the wall. Although he did not recognize them, Eolair thought they looked no different than the hundreds of other Peaceful Ones camped in Naglimund's shadow. All were slender and golden-skinned. Like most of their fellows, no two seemed quite alike in the color of either their armor or the hair that streamed from beneath their helms; the m'yon rashí gleamed against the snow like misplaced tropical birds. The only difference the count could see between these and any other of Jiriki's people was that each bore a dark staff long as a walking-stick. These staffs were of the same odd gray-black stuff as Jiriki's sword Indreju; each was knobbed with a globe of some blue crystalline stone.

Jiriki turned from the Hernystirman and called out an order. His mother rose from her crouch and added words of her own. A contingent of Sithi archers moved up until they surrounded the group near the walls. The bowmen nocked arrows and drew, then froze in place, eyes scanning the empty walls.

The leader of the m'yon rashí, a female Sitha with grass-green hair and armor of a slightly deeper green, lifted her stick and slowly swung it toward the wall as if she forced it against the flowing current of a river. When the blue gem struck, all the m'yon rashí chanted a single loud syllable. Eolair felt a tremor in his bones, as though a tremendous weight had struck the ground nearby. For a moment the earth seemed to shift beneath him.

"What. . . ?" he gasped, struggling to find his balance. Before him, Jiriki raised a hand for silence.

The other three Sithi stepped forward to join the woman in green. As they all chanted, each in turn brought his staff forward to strike in a rough triangle around the first; each syrup-slow impact reverberated through the earth and up through the feet of Eolair and the other observers.

The Count of Nad Mullach stared. For a dozen ells up and down the wall from where the m'yon rashí stood, the snow slid off the stones. Around the jeweled heads of the four staffs, Eolair saw that the stone had turned a lighter shade of gray, as though it had sickened somehow—or as though it were covered with a web of fine cracks.

Now the Sithi lifted their striking-rods away from the wall. Their chanting grew louder. The leader struck again, a little more swiftly this time. The silent thunder of her blow rolled through the icy ground. The rest followed suit, each strike emphasized by a loudly chanted word. As they struck for the third time, bits of stone began to shiver loose from the top of the high wall, falling down to vanish into the high snow.

The count could not contain his astonishment. "I have never seen the like!"

Jiriki turned, his high-boned face serene. "You should go back to your folk. It will be only a moment more and they should be ready."

Eolair could not take his eyes from the strange spectacle. He walked backward down the hill, steadying himself with his arms outstretched whenever the shifting ground threatened to topple him from his feet.

At the fourth impact, a great section of the wall crumbled and fell inward, leaving a hole at the top that looked as though some huge creature had taken a bite from it. Eolair at last realized the imminence of what Jiriki had told him and hurried the rest of the way down to Isorn and the waiting Hernystiri.

"Ready!" he cried. "Be ready!"

There was a fifth shuddering, the strongest yet. Eolair lost his balance and fell forward, tumbling down the hill until he rolled to a stop, his nose and mouth stinging and cold from the snow. He half-expected his troop to laugh, but they were staring wide-eyed up the hill past him.

Eolair looked back. Naglimund's great wall, as thick as the height of two men, was dissolving like a wave-struck sand castle. There was a loud rasping of stone on stone, but that was all. The wall fell down into the banks of white with an eerily muffled sound. Great gouts of snow were thrown up everywhere, so that a fog of white flakes filled the air, obscuring all.

When it cleared, the m'yon rashí had retreated. A hole a dozen ells across was opened into Naglimund and its shadows. Slowly, a sea of dark figures was filling that hole. Eyes gleamed. Spear-points glimmered.

Eolair struggled to his feet. "Men of Hernystir!" he cried. "To me! The hour has come!"

But the count's troops did not budge, and instead it was the horde within Naglimund that came surging out through the breach, swift and uncountable as termites swarming from a shattered nest.

There was a great clang of blade on shield from the Sithi ranks, then a flight of arrows hissed out, felling many of the first Norns rushing down the hillside. Some of the Norns carried bows as well, and clambered up onto the castle wall to shoot, but for the most part neither side seemed content to wait. With the eagerness of lovers, the ancient kindred rushed forward to meet each other.

The battle before Naglimund quickly became a scene of horrible confusion. Through the swirling snow, Eolair saw that more than the slender Norns had issued from the crack in the wall. There were giants, too, creatures tall as two men and covered with gray-white fur, yet armored like humans, each bearing a great club which crushed bones like dry sticks.

Before the count could even retreat toward his men, one of the Norns was upon him. Incredibly, though a helm hid most of his pale face and armor covered his torso, the black-eyed creature wore no shoes, his long feet carrying him across the powdery snow as though it were solid stone. He was swift as a lynx. As Eolair stared in amazement, he almost lost his head to the Norn's first sweeping blow.

Who could fathom such madness? Eolair pushed all thoughts but survival from his mind.

The Norn bore only a small arm shield, and with his light sword was far faster than the Count of Nad Mullach. Eolair found himself instantly plunged into a defensive struggle, wading backward down the hill, encumbered by his heavy armor and shield, almost betrayed several times by treacherous footing. He fended off several blows, but the Norn's exultant grimace told Eolair that it was only a matter of time before his sinewy opponent found a fatal opening.

Abruptly, the Norn stood straight, his jet eyes puzzled. A moment later he sagged forward and fell. A blue-fletched arrow quivered in the back of his neck.

"Keep your men together, Count Eolair!" Jiriki waved his bow as he shouted from up the slope. "If they are separated from each other, they will lose heart. And remember—these foes can bleed and die!" The Sitha turned his horse and spurred back into the thick of battle; in a moment he was obscured by snow and the twisting shapes of battle.

Eolair hurried downhill toward the Hernystiri. The hillside echoed with the shrieks of horses and men and even stranger creatures.

The confusion was almost complete. Eolair and Isorn had only just managed to rally their men for a charge up the hill when two of the white giants appeared at the top of the rise, carrying between them the trunk of a tree. With a choking roar, the giants came rushing down on Eolair's men, using the tree like a scythe to crush all who were caught between them. Bones shattered and red-soaked forms vanished beneath the churned snow. A terrified Hernystirman managed to put an arrow into one giant's eye, then a few more feathered the second until it was reeling. Still, two more men were smashed to death by the flailing tree trunk before the remaining Hernystiri dragged the giant down and killed him.

Eolair looked up to see that most of the Norns were engaged with the Sithi. Horrible as was the chaos of battle, the count was still compelled to stop and stare. Never since the dawn of time had such a thing been seen, the immortals at war. Those that were visible through the snow seemed to move with a ghastly, serpentine swiftness, feinting, leaping, swinging their dark swords like they were willow wands. Many contests seemed settled before the first blow was struck; indeed, in many of the single combats, after much dancelike movement, only one blow *was* struck—the blow that ended the fight.

There was a sour skirling of pipes from atop the hillside. Eolair looked up to see what seemed to be a line of trumpeters atop the stone, their long, tubelike instruments lifted to the gray sky. But the piping noise came from some musicians in the shadows of Naglimund below, for when the Norns atop the wall puffed their cheeks and blew, what came from their tubes was not sound but a cloud of dust as orange as sunset.

Eolair watched in sickened fascination. What could it be? Poison? Or just some other incomprehensible ritual of the immortals?

As the plume of orange floated down across the hillside, the tide of battle seemed to surge and writhe beneath it—but no one fell. If poison, the count thought, it was of a more subtle sort than he had heard of. Then Eolair felt a burning in his own throat and nostrils. He gasped for breath, and for a moment thought he would surely choke and die. A moment later he could breathe again. Then the sky dropped down upon him, the shadows began to stretch, and the snow seemed to catch fire.

Eolair was filled with a fear that blossomed like a great, black, ice-cold flower. Men were screaming all around him. He was screaming, too. And the Norns that now came surging forward out of the ruined shell of Naglimund were demons that even the priests had never dreamed. The count and his men turned to run, but the

Sithi behind them, merciless and golden eyed, were just as terrifying as their corpse-white cousins.

*Trapped!* Eolair thought, all else subsumed in panic. *Trapped! Trapped! Trapped!*

Something grabbed him and he lashed out, scratching with his nails to pull free of the horrible thing, a monster with a great yellow-tendriled face and shrieking mouth. He raised his sword to kill it, but something else struck him from behind and he fell sideways into the cold whiteness with the monstrous thing still clutching at him, still clawing at his arms and face. He was pushed face forward into the freezing snow, and though he struggled, he could not get free.

*What is happening?* he suddenly thought. There were monsters, yes, giants and Norns—but nothing so near. *And the Sithi*—he remembered how ghastly they had looked, how he had been certain that they intended to trap Eolair and the other Hernystiri between themselves and the Norns, then crush the mortals—*the Sithi are not our foes. . .!*

The weight on his back had lessened. He slipped free and sat up. There was no monster. Isorn crouched in the snow beside him, hanging his head like a sick calf. Although the madness of battle still raged around him, and his own men were snapping at each other and struggling brother against brother like crazed dogs, Eolair felt the terrible fear ebbing away. He reached up and pawed at his chilled face, then held out his gloved hand and stared at the orange-tinted snow.

"The snow washed it away," he said. "Isorn! It is some poison they have blown at us! The snow washes it away!"

Isorn retched and nodded weakly. "Mine has come off, too." He gasped and spat. "I tried . . . to kill you."

"Quickly," Eolair said, struggling to his feet. "We must try and get it off the others. Come!" He scooped up an armful of snow, scraping off the thin sprinkling of orange dust, and staggered to a small knot of squealing, struggling men nearby. They were all bleeding, but most only shallowly from wounds made by nails and teeth: although the poison had maddened them, it had made them clumsy and ineffectual as well. Eolair smashed clean snow into each face he could reach.

After he and Isorn had managed to bring some semblance of sanity back to the nearest men, they hurriedly explained and sent those they had rescued off to help others. One man did not get up. He had lost both eyes and was bleeding to death, staining all the ground around him. Eolair pulled the man's cloak over his ruined face and then stooped to gather more snow.

The Sithi did not seem to be anywhere near as badly stricken by the dusty poison as Eolair and his men. Some of the immortals closest to the walls seemed dazed and slowed, but none showed symptoms of the unrestrained madness that had swept the Hernystiri. Still, the hillside was full of dreadful sights.

Likimeya and a few Sithi were surrounded by a company of Norn foot soldiers, and though Jiriki's mother and her companions were mounted and able to deal deadly blows from above, one by one they were being pulled down into a mass of white hands that waved and swayed like some terrible plant.

Yizashi Grayspear faced a howling giant who already held a crushed Sithi body in each hand. The Sitha horseman, his face as sternly impassive as a hawk's, spurred forward.

Jiriki and two others had knocked another of the giants to his knees, and now hacked at the still-living monster as though they butchered an ox. Great jets of blood fountained up, covering Jiriki and his companions in a sticky mist.

The limp body of Zinjadu, her pale-blue hair clotted with red, had been hoisted on the spears of a group of Norns as they ran back toward Naglimund's walls in triumph. Chekai'so and dark Kuroyi rode them down before they could bear their prize to safety, and each killed three of their white-skinned brethren, although both took many wounds. When they had slaughtered the Norns, Chekai'so Amber-Locks draped Zinjadu's corpse across his saddle. His own streaming blood mixed with hers as he and Kuroyi bore her back toward the Sithi camp.

*    *    *

The day wore on, full of madness and misery. Behind
the mist and snow, the sun rose past noon and began to
fall. The broken west wall of Naglimund began to glow
with the light of a murky afternoon, and the snows grew
even more red.

Maegwin walked along the edge of the battle like a
ghost—as indeed she was. At first she had hidden behind
the trees, afraid to witness such horrible things, but eventually her better sense had led her out again.

*If I am dead, then what do I fear?*

But it was hard to look at the bloody forms that lay
scattered about the snowy hillside and not fear death.

*Gods do not die, and mortals die but once,* she reassured herself. *When this is settled, they will all rise again.*

But if they should all rise again, then what was the
point of this battle? And if the gods could not die, then
what did they fear from the demon hordes out of
Scadach? It was puzzling.

Pondering, Maegwin walked slowly beside slayers and
slain. Her cloak fluttered behind her, and her feet left
small, even prints in the froth of white and scarlet.

# 9

# The Third House

**Simon was furious.** They had walked into a trap, as sweetly and stupidly as spring lambs led to the killing block.

"Can you move your hands at all?" he whispered to Miriamele. His own wrists were bound very securely: the two Fire Dancers who had done the job had some experience with knots.

She shook her head. He could barely see her in the deepening night.

They were kneeling side by side at the center of the forest clearing. Their arms had been tied behind their backs and their ankles roped. Seeing Miriamele trussed and helpless, the idea of brute animals readied for slaughter returned and black anger rose inside Simon once more.

*I'm a knight! Doesn't that mean anything? How could I let this happen?*

He should have known. But he had been busy strutting like a mooncalf over the man Roelstan's compliments. "You have seen this knight wield a sword," the traitor had said. "He has naught to fear from Fire Dancers."

*And I believed him. I am not fit to be a knight. I am a disgrace to Josua and Morgenes and Binabik and everyone who's ever tried to teach me anything.*

Simon engaged in another futile struggle with his bonds, but the ropes held him in an unbreakable grip.

"You know something of these Fire Dancers, don't you?" he whispered to Miriamele. "What are they going to do with us? What do they mean when they say they're going to give us to the Storm King? Burn us?"

He felt Miriamele shudder against him. "I don't know." Her voice was flat, dead. "I suppose so."

Simon's terror and anger were for a moment overcome by a stab of regret. "I let you down, didn't I?" he said quietly. "Some protector."

"It's not your fault. We were tricked."

"I wish I could get my hands on that Roelstan's throat. His wife was trying to tell us something was wrong, but I was too stupid to listen. But he—*he. . .* !"

"He was frightened, too." Miriamele spoke as from a great and lofty height, as though the things of which she spoke were of little import. "I don't know if I could give my own life up to save the lives of strangers. Why should I hate those two for not being able to?"

" 'S Bloody Tree." Simon didn't have the strength to waste pity on treacherous Roelstan and Gullaighn. He had to save Miriamele somehow, had to burst these bonds and fight his way free. But he didn't have the slightest idea how to begin.

The business of the Fire Dancer camp went on around them. Several white-robed folk were tending the fire and preparing a meal; others were feeding the goats and chickens, while still others sat and talked quietly. There were even a few women and children among them. But for the two bound prisoners and the omnipresent gleam of white robes, it might have been the onset of evening in any rural steading.

Maefwaru, the Fire Dancers' leader, had taken a trio of his lieutenants into the large cottage. Simon did not much wish to think about what they might be discussing.

The evening grew deeper. The white-clad figures ate a frugal meal, none of which they offered to share with the prisoners. The fire danced and fluttered in the wind.

"Get them up." Maefwaru's eyes flicked across Simon and Miriamele, then rolled up to the blue-black sky. "It is nearing the time."

Two of his helpers dragged the prisoners to their feet.

Simon's feet were numb, and it was difficult to balance with his ankles tied together; he swayed and would have fallen if the Fire Dancer behind him had not grabbed his arms and jerked him upright once more. Beside him, Miriamele also teetered. Her captor wrapped an arm around her, handling her as casually as if she had been a log.

"Don't you touch her," Simon snarled.

Miriamele gave him a tired look. "It does no good, Simon. Let it go."

The Fire Dancer at her side grinned and pawed at her breasts for a moment, but a sharp sound from Maefwaru sobered him fast. As the robed man turned to face his chief, Miriamele hung in his grasp, her face devoid of feeling.

"Idiot," Maefwaru said harshly. "These are not children's toys. They are for Him—for the Master. Do you understand?"

Miriamele's captor swallowed and nodded rapidly.

"It is time to go." Maefwaru turned and headed for the edge of the clearing.

The Fire Dancer behind Simon gave him a rough shove. Simon toppled like a felled tree. His breath flew out in a great huff and the night swam with points of light.

"Their legs are tied," the Fire Dancer said slowly.

Maefwaru whirled. "I know that! Take the ropes off their legs."

"But . . . but what if they run?"

"Tie a rope to their arms," said the leader. "Tie the other end around your waist." He shook his bald head in thinly-concealed disgust.

Simon felt a flash of hope as the robed man produced a knife and bent to saw through the knots at his ankles. If Maefwaru was the only clever one, as seemed to be the case, perhaps there was some hope after all.

When he and Miriamele were both able to walk, the Fire Dancers tied ropes around both of them, then pushed them ahead as though they were balky oxen, prodding them with spear-points if they stumbled or lagged. The spears were oddly formed, short and yet slim hafted and very sharp, not quite like anything Simon had seen before.

Maefwaru stepped through the vegetation at the edge of the clearing and disappeared, evidently leading them somewhere out of the clearing. Simon was a little relieved. He had been watching the fire for a long time and having very bad thoughts about it. At least they would be taken to some other place; it might be that their chance of escape would improve. Perhaps there would even be an opportunity as they traveled. He looked back and was dismayed to see that what seemed like the entire enclave of Fire Dancers was following them, a line of white trailing off into the gloom.

What had appeared to be solid forest was instead a well-packed trail that switched back and forth as it wound uphill. It was hard to see its progress more than a few ells ahead: the ground was thick with mist, a grayish murk that seemed to absorb sound as thoroughly as it masked sight. But for the muffled tread of two-score feet, the woods were silent. Not a nightbird sang. Even the wind had quieted.

Simon's mind was racing, but as quickly as he thought of plans for escape, he had to abandon each in turn as impossible. He and Miriamele were vastly outnumbered and in an unfamiliar place. Even if they managed to jerk themselves free from the Fire Dancers who held their ropes, they would be unable to use their arms for balance or clearing a path, and would be caught within moments.

He looked back at the princess plodding along behind him. She looked cold and miserable and drearily resigned to whatever might come. At least they had let her keep her cloak. In her only moment of spirit, she had convinced one of their captors to allow her to wear it against the night breeze. Simon had not been so lucky. His cloak had gone, along with his sword and Qanuc knife. The horses and saddlebags had been taken somewhere, too. The only things left to him now were the clothes he wore and his life and soul.

*And Miriamele's life, too,* he thought. *I have sworn to protect it. That is still my responsibility.*

There was some comfort in that. While he had breath in him, he had a purpose.

He was slapped in the face by a hanging branch. He spat out wet fir needles. Maefwaru was a small ghostly shape in the murk before him, leading them ever higher.

*Where are we going? Perhaps it would be better if we never found out.*

They stumbled on through the gray mist like damned souls trying to walk out of Hell.

It seemed they had been walking for hours. The mists had thinned a little, but the silence was still heavy, the air thick and damp. Then as swiftly as the passing of winter twilight, they emerged from a tangle of trees and found themselves on the hilltop.

While they had passed through the shadows of the wooded hill a great wash of clouds had covered the sky overhead, extinguishing the moon and stars, so that now the only light came from a few torches and the leaping flames of a huge bonfire. The summit's sloping ground bulged with strange vast shapes, forms limned with flickering red light so that they seemed to move fitfully, like sleeping giants. Once these might have been pieces of some great wall or other large structure; now they lay scattered and broken, smothered beneath a matted carpet of vines and grass.

In the middle of the wide hilltop one piece of stone had been cut free from vegetation—a huge pale rock, angular as an ax head, that jutted to twice the height of a man. Between the high bonfire and this naked stone stood three motionless dark-robed shapes. They looked as though they had been waiting for a long time—perhaps as long as the rocks themselves had waited. As the Fire Dancers pushed the prisoners toward the center of the hill, the dark trio turned, almost in unison.

"Hail, Cloud Children!" Maefwaru shouted. "Hail to the Master's first Chosen. We have come as He wished."

The black-robed things regarded him silently.

"And we have brought more even than we promised," Maefwaru continued. "Praise to the Master!" He turned and waved to his underlings, who hurried Simon and Miriamele forward; but as they approached the bonfire and the silent watchers, the Fire Dancers slowed, then stopped and looked helplessly back to their leader.

"Tie them to that tree, there." Maefwaru gestured impatiently at the wind-gnarled corpse of a pine standing some twenty paces from the fire. "Hurry—it is almost midnight."

Simon grunted in pain as one of their captors pulled his arms behind his back to secure them to the tree. As soon as the Fire Dancers had finished and withdrawn, he edged toward Miriamele until their shoulders touched, in part because he was frightened, and hungry for a little of her warmth, but also so that they might more easily whisper without attracting attention.

"Who are those three dark ones?" he asked under his breath.

Miriamele shook her head.

The nearest of the black-robed figures slowly turned toward Maefwaru. "And these are for the Master?" it said. The words were as cold and sharp as the edge of a knife. Simon felt his legs weaken. There was an unmistakable sound to the voice, a sour yet melodic accent he had heard only in moments of terror . . . the hiss of Stormspike.

"They are," said Maefwaru, nodding his blunt head eagerly. "I dreamed of the red-haired one some moons ago. I know that the Master gave me that dream. He wants this one."

The robed thing seemed to regard Simon for a moment. "Perhaps," it said slowly. "But did you bring another as well, in case the Master has other plans for these? Did you bring blood for the Binding?"

"I did, oh, yes!" In the presence of these strange beings the cruel Fire Dancer chieftain had become as humble and ingratiating as an old courtier. "Two who tried to flee the Master's great promise!" He turned and gestured to the knot of other Fire Dancers still waiting nervously at the edge of the hilltop. There was shouting and a convulsion of activity, then a handful of the white-robed figures dragged two others forward. One of the captured pair had lost his hood in the struggle.

"God curse you!" shouted Roelstan, sobbing. "You promised that if we brought you those two we'd be forgiven!"

"You *have* been forgiven," Maefwaru said cheerfully. "I forgive you your foolishness. But you cannot escape punishment. No one flees the Master."

Roelstan collapsed, sagging to his knees while the men around him tried to tug him back onto his feet. His wife Gullaighn might have fainted; she hung limply in the arms of her captors.

Simon's heart seemed to rise into his throat; for a moment, he could not breathe. They were powerless, and there was no help to be expected this time. They would die here on this windswept hill—or the Storm King would take them, as Maefwaru had said, which would surely be unimaginably worse. He turned to look at Miriamele.

The princess seemed half-asleep, her eyes lidded, her lips moving. Was she praying?

"Miriamele! Those are Norns! The Storm King's servants!"

She ignored him, absorbed in her own thoughts.

"Damn you, Miriamele, don't do this! We have to think—we have to get free!"

"Shut your mouth, Simon!" she hissed.

He was thunderstruck. "What!?"

"I'm trying to get something." Miriamele pushed against the dead tree, her shoulders moving up and down as she fidgeted behind her back. "It's at the bottom of the pocket of my cloak."

"What is it?" Simon strained closer, until his hands could feel her fingers beneath the cloth. "A knife?"

"No, they took my knife. It's your mirror—the one Jiriki gave you. I've had it since I cut your hair." Even as she spoke, he felt the wooden frame slide free from the pocket and touch his fingers. "Can you take it?"

"What good will it do?" He gripped it as firmly as he

could. "Don't let go yet, not until I've got it. There." He tugged it loose, holding it tightly in his bound hands.

"You can call Jiriki!" she said triumphantly. "You said that it was to be used in direst need."

Simon's momentary elation ebbed. "But it doesn't work that way. He doesn't just appear. It's not that kind of magic."

Miriamele was silent for a moment. When she spoke, she, too, was more subdued. "But you said it brought Aditu when you were lost in the forest."

"It took her days to find me. We don't have days, Miri."

"Try it anyway," she said stubbornly. "It can't hurt. Maybe Jiriki is somewhere close by. It can't hurt!"

"But I can't even see it," Simon protested. "How can I make it work without being able to look into it?"

"Just try!"

Simon bit back further argument. He took a deep breath, then forced himself to think of his own face as it had looked the last time he had seen it in the Sithi glass. He could remember things generally, but suddenly could not remember details—what color were his eyes, exactly? And the scar on his cheek, the burning mark of dragon's blood—how long was it? Past the bottom of his nose?

For a brief moment, as the memory of the searing pain from Igjarjuk's black blood washed through him, he thought he felt the frame of the looking glass warm beneath his fingers. A moment later, it was cold again. He tried to summon the feeling back, but was unsuccessful. He kept on fruitlessly for long moments.

"It's no use," he said wearily. "I can't do it."

"You're not trying hard enough," Miriamele snapped.

Simon looked up. The Fire Dancers were paying no attention to Miriamele or him, their interest fixed instead on the weird scene beside the bonfire. The two renegades, Roelstan and Gullaighn, had been carried to the top of the large stone and forced onto their backs. Their four captors stood atop the rock holding their ankles, so that the prisoners' heads hung down, arms dangling helplessly. "Usires Aedon!" Simon swore. "Look at that!"

"Don't look," said Miriamele. "Just use the mirror."

"I told you, I can't. And it wouldn't do any good anyway." He paused for a moment, watching the contorted, upside-down mouth of Roelstan, who was shouting incoherently. The three Norns stood before him, looking up as if at some interesting bird sitting on a branch.

"Bloody Tree," Simon swore again, then dropped the mirror to the ground.

"Simon!" Miriamele said, horrified. "Have you gone mad? Pick it up!"

He lifted his foot and ground his heel into the looking glass. It was very strong, but he hooked it over so that it was tilted against the tree, then stepped down hard. The frame did not give, but the crystalline surface broke with a faint percussive sound; for a moment, the scent of violets rose around them. Simon kicked it again, scattering transparent shards.

"You *have* gone mad!" The princess was in despair.

Simon closed his eyes. *Forgive me, Jiriki,* he thought. *But Morgenes told me any gift that cannot be thrown away is not a gift but a trap.* He crouched as deeply as he could, but the rope that held him to the trunk would not allow his fingers to reach the shattered mirror.

"Can you get to that?" he asked Miriamele.

She stared at him for a moment, then slid herself as low as she could. She, too, was several handlengths short of the goal. "No. Why did you do it?"

"It was no good to us," Simon said impatiently. "Not in one piece, anyway." He caught at one of the larger shards with his foot and dragged it closer. "Help me."

Arduously, Simon got his toe beneath the piece of crystal and tried to lift it high enough for Miriamele's abbreviated reach, but the contortion was too difficult and it slid away, tumbling to the ground once more. Simon bit his lip and tried again.

Three times the shard fell free, forcing them to begin over. Fortunately, the Fire Dancers and the black-robed Norns seemed caught up in the preparations for their ritual, whatever it might be. When Simon sneaked a glance toward the center of the clearing, Maefwaru and his minions were on their knees before the stone. Roelstan had stopped shouting; he made weak sounds and thrashed, striking his head against the stone. Gullaighn hung motionless.

This time, as the jagged thing began to slide off his boot again, Simon lurched to the side and managed to trap it against the leg of Miriamele's breeches. He pushed his own leg against it to keep it from falling, then lowered his foot to the ground before he toppled.

"Now what?" he asked himself.

Miriamele pushed against him, then slowly moved up onto her toes, lifting the shard higher along Simon's leg. It sliced through the rough cloth with surprising ease, drawing blood, but Simon remained as still as he could, unwilling to let a little pain deter them. He was impressed by Miriamele's cleverness.

When she had lifted herself as high as she could, they moved again so that the crystal fragment rested primarily on Simon, then Miriamele eased herself back down. Next it was Simon's turn. The process was excruciatingly slow, and the crystal itself seemed sharper than any normal mirror-glass. By the time the shard was almost close enough for Simon to grasp in his hand, both prisoners had legs ribboned with blood.

As he strained his fingers toward it, and found it still just beyond reach, Simon felt the hackles on his neck rise. Across the hilltop, the Norns had begun to sing.

The melody rose like a serpent rearing above its coils. Simon found himself starting to slide away into a sort of dream. The voices were cold and fearsome, but also strangely beautiful. He thought he heard the hollow echo of measureless caverns, the musical drip of slow-melting ice. He could not understand the words, but the ageless magic of the song was unmistakable. It drew him along like a subterranean stream, down, down into darkness. . . .

Simon shook his head, trying to drive the grogginess away. Neither of the captives dangling across the top of the rock was struggling now. Beneath them, the Norns had spread out until they formed a rough triangle around the jut of stone.

Simon strained against the rope as hard as he could, wincing as the hemp bit into his wrists; it tormented his flesh as though he were bound in smoldering metal. Miriamele saw the tears form in his eyes and leaned against him, pushing her head against his shoulder as though she could somehow force the pain away. Simon strained, gasping for air. At last, his fingers touched the cold edge. Just the light contact sliced his skin, but the thin bright line of pain signaled victory. Simon sighed in relief.

The Norns' song ended. Maefwaru rose from his kneeling position and made his way forward to the stone. "Now is the time," he cried. "Now the Master shall see our loyalty! It is time to call forth His Third House!"

He turned and said something to the Norns in a voice too low for Simon to hear, but Simon was paying little attention in any case. He grasped the shard of crystal in his fingers, unmindful of shedding a little more of his own blood as long as it did not make his hold too slippery, then turned and began feeling blindly for Miriamele's bound wrists.

"Don't move," he said.

Maefwaru had been given a long knife that glinted in the wavering firelight like something from a nightmare. He stepped to the rock, then reached up and grabbed Roelstan's hair, pulling it so hard that the captive's ankles were almost tugged loose from the grip of the Fire Dancers atop the rock. Roelstan raised his hands as if to fight, but his movements were horribly slow: he might have been drowning in great depths. Maefwaru pulled the blade across Roelstan's neck and stepped back, but could not avoid all the blood that spurted free; darkness spattered his face and white robe.

Roelstan thrashed. Simon stared, sickened but fascinated, as streams of blood ran down the face of the pale rock. Gullaighn, hanging upside down beside her dying husband, began to shriek. Where the red liquid pooled at the base of the stone, the ground-hugging mist turned crimson, as though the blood itself had been rendered into fog.

"Simon!" Miriamele bumped against him. "Hurry!"

He reached out to find her fingers, then followed them up to the knots around her wrists. He placed the slick fragment of crystal against the bristling rope and began to saw.

They still faced the bonfire and the bloody stone. Miriamele's eyes were wide in her pale face. "Please hurry!"

Simon grunted. It was difficult enough just keeping the crystal in his lacerated, blood-dripping hand. And what was happening in the center of the hilltop was making him even more frightened than he had been.

The red mist had spread until it surrounded and partially obscured the great stone. The Fire Dancers were chanting now, cracked voices unpleasantly echoing the poison-sweet song of the Norns.

There was a movement in the mist, a pale bulky something that Simon at first thought was the stone itself given magical life. Then it strode forward out of the reddened darkness on four huge legs and the earth seemed to shudder beneath its tread. It was a great white bull, bigger than any Simon had ever seen, taller than a man at its shoulders. Despite its solidity, it seemed oddly translucent, as though it had been sculpted from fog. Its eyes burned like coals, and its bone-hued horns seemed to cradle the sky. On its back, riding like a knight on a horse, sat a massive black-robed figure. Terror beat out from this apparition like the heat of a summer sun. Simon felt first his fingers, then his hands go nerveless, so that he could not tell if he was still holding the precious shard. All he could think of was escaping from that terrible, empty black hood. He wanted only to throw himself against the weight of his ropes until they burst, or gnaw them until he was free to run and run and run. . . .

The chanting of the Fire Dancers grew ragged, shouts of awe and terror intermixed with the ritualistic words. Maefwaru stood before his congregation, waving his thick arms in horrified glee.

"*Veng'a Sutekh!*" he shouted. "Duke of the Black Wind! He is come to make the Master's Third House!"

The great figure atop the bull stared down at him, then the hood turned slowly, surveying the hilltop. Its invisible eyes passed across Simon like a freezing wind.

"Oh, Usires on the T–T–Tree!" Miriamele moaned. "W–What is it?"

Strangely, for a moment Simon's madness lessened, as though the fear had become too great to sustain any longer. He had never heard Miriamele so frightened, and her horrified voice pulled him back from the brink. He realized that he still held the bit of crystal clutched between his stiffened fingers.

"It is a bad ... a bad thing," he panted. "One of the Storm King's ..." He caught at her wrist and began sawing away once more. "Oh, Miri, hold still."

She was gulping air. "I'll ... try. ..."

The Norns had turned and were speaking to Maefwaru, who alone of his congregation seemed able to stand the sight of the bull and its rider: the rest of the Fire Dancers groveled in the tangled undergrowth, their chanting now entirely given way to sobs of almost ecstatic fear. Maefwaru turned and gesticulated toward the tree where Simon and Miriamele were tied.

"They're c–coming for us," Simon stuttered. As he spoke, the shard sliced through the last strands of Miriamele's ropes. "Cut mine, quick."

Miriamele half-turned, trying to use her fluttering cloak to hide what they were doing from their captors. He could feel her vigorous movements as she dragged the edge of the crystal fragment back and forth across the thick hemp. The Norns were making their way slowly across the hilltop toward them.

"Oh, Aedon, they're coming!" Simon said.

"I'm almost through!" she whispered. He felt something gouge into his wrist, then Miriamele cursed. "I dropped it!"

Simon hung his head. So it was hopeless, then. Beside him, he felt Miriamele hastily winding her own severed rope around her wrists once more so that it would appear she was still bound.

The Norns came on, their graceful walk and billowing

robes making them almost seem to float over the rough ground. Their faces were expressionless, their eyes black as the holes between stars. They converged around the tree and Simon felt his arm caught in a cold, unbreakable grip. One of the Norns severed the rope that had leashed the prisoners, then Simon and Miriamele were drawn stumbling across the hilltop toward the looming stone and the terrifying shape that had appeared from the red mist.

He felt his heart speeding as he neared the bull and its rider, racing faster with each step until he thought it would burst through the walls of his chest. The Norns who held him were frighteningly alien, implacably hostile, but the fear they inspired was as nothing before the all-crushing terror of the Storm King's Red Hand.

The Norns flung him to the ground. The bull's hooves, each wide as a barrel, were only a few cubits away. He did not want to look, wanted only to keep his face pressed against the shielding vegetation, but something drew his head inexorably upward until he was staring at what seemed a shimmer of flame in the depths of the black hood.

*"We have come to raise the Third House,"* the thing said. Its stony voice rumbled both without and within Simon, shaking the ground and his bones as well. *"What is . . . this?"*

Maefwaru was so frightened and excited that his voice was a squeal. "I had a dream! The Master wanted this one, great Veng'a Sutekh—I know that he did!"

An invisible something abruptly grasped Simon's mind as a falcon's claws might seize a rabbit. He felt his thoughts shaken and flung about with brutal abandon, so that he fell down onto his face, shrieking with pain and horror. He only dimly heard the thing speak again.

*"We remember this little fly—but it is no longer wanted. The Red Hand has other business now . . . and we need more blood before we are ready. Add this one's life to that of the others upon the Wailing Stone."*

Simon rolled over onto his back and stared up at the clouded, starless sky as the world reeled about him.

*No longer wanted . . .* The words spun crazily in his

head. Someone somewhere was calling his name. *No longer wanted . . .*

"Simon! *Get up!*"

He dimly recognized Miriamele's voice, heard its shrill terror. His head lolled. There was a form approaching him, a pale smear in his blurry sight. For an appalling moment he thought it might be the great bull, but his vision cleared. Maefwaru was stalking toward him, the long knife held up so that it glinted in the bonfire's wavering light.

"The Red Hand wants your blood," the Fire Dancer chieftain said. His eyes were completely mad. "You will help to build the Third House."

Simon struggled to free himself from the tangling grasses and clamber up onto his knees. Miriamele had thrown off her false bonds, and now flung herself toward Maefwaru. One of the Norns caught at her arm and tugged her to his black-cloaked breast, pulling her as close as a lover would—but to Simon's surprise, the immortal did no more than hold her helpless; the Norn's black eyes were intent on Maefwaru, who had continued toward Simon without sparing an instant's attention to the girl.

Everything seemed to pause; even the fire seemed to slow in its fluttering. The Red Hand, the Norns, Maefwaru's cowering followers, all stood or lay still, as if waiting. The blocky Fire Dancer chieftain raised his knife higher.

Simon tugged furiously at his restraints, straining until he thought he could feel his muscles pulling free from his bones. Miriamele had cut through part of the rope.

*If only . . . if only . . .*

The rope snapped. Simon's arms flew outward, and the coil slithered down his arm and dropped to the ground. Blood dribbled down his wrists and hands where the shard had cut him, the ropes had scored him.

"Come, then," he gasped, and lifted his hands before him. "Come and get me."

Maefwaru laughed. Beads of sweat stood out on his brow and bald scalp. The thick muscles of his neck jumped as he pulled another knife from inside his robe. For a moment Simon thought the Fire Dancer was going to throw it to him, to make it a fair fight, but Maefwaru had no such intentions. A blade in each hand, he took another step toward Simon. He stumbled, caught himself, then strode forward another pace.

A moment later Maefwaru straightened up, bringing his hands to his neck so suddenly that he gashed himself with his own knife. His furious joy turned to puzzlement, then his legs folded beneath him and he toppled forward into the undergrowth.

Before Simon could make sense of what was happening, a shadowy form flew past him and struck the Norn who prisoned Miriamele, knocking the white-skinned thing to the ground. The princess tumbled free.

*"Simon!"* someone shouted. *"Take the knife!"*

Dazed, Simon saw the long blade that still gleamed in Maefwaru's fist. He dropped to a knee—the night air was suddenly full of strange noises, growls and shouts and a strange rumbling hum—and tugged it loose from the Fire Dancer's death-grip, then stood up.

Even as his two fellows hurried to his aid, the Norn who had held Miriamele was rolling on the ground with a gray, snarling something. The princess had crawled away; now, as she saw Simon, she scrambled to her feet and ran toward him, tripping on clinging vines and leaf-hidden stones.

*"Here, come here!"* someone shouted from the edge of the hilltop. *"This is the way!"*

As Miriamele reached him, Simon grabbed her hand and ran toward the voice. A pair of Fire Dancers leaped up to stop them, but Simon slashed one with Maefwaru's knife, opening a red wound through the white robe; Miriamele escaped the other, scratching at the man's panicky face as she pulled free of his grasp. The rumbling roar of the thing atop the bull—it was speaking, Simon realized, but now he could no longer understand it—grew until Simon's head hammered.

"Over here!" A small figure had emerged from the

trees at the edge of the hilltop. The roiling bonfire painted the little man in flame-colored light.

"*Binabik!*"

"Run to me," the troll cried. "With swiftness, now!"

Simon could not help taking a look back. By the sacrificial stone, the great bull snorted and pawed at the ground, tearing great furrows in the damp earth. Ineluki's servitor was glowing, red light leaking through the black robes, but it made no move to pursue Simon and Miriamele, as though reluctant to leave the circle of blood-drenched ground. One of the Norns lay with its neck ragged and red; another was sprawled nearby, a victim of one of the troll's darts. The third black-robed figure was struggling with whatever had torn out its fellow's throat. But the Fire Dancers were finally gathering their wits, and as Simon watched, half a dozen of Maefwaru's followers turned to follow the escaping prisoners. An arrow flew past Simon's ear and vanished into the trees.

"Down here," Binabik said, hopping nimbly ahead of them down the hill. He gestured for Simon and Miriamele to move past him, then stopped and raised his hands to his mouth. "*Qantaqa!*" he shouted. "*Qantaqa sosa!*"

As they plunged down the hillside into the trees, the confusing roar grew slightly less behind them. Before they had taken a score of steps, two shapes loomed before them in the mist—two horses.

"They are tied with looseness," the troll called down to them. "Climb and ride!"

"Here, Binabik, ride with me," Simon panted.

"There is no need," he replied. Simon looked up to see a large gray shape appear on the foggy rise just above Binabik. "Brave Qantaqa!" Binabik grabbed the wolf's hackles and pulled himself up onto her back.

The noise of pursuit was rising again. Simon fumbled with the reins, pulling them free at last. Beside him, Miriamele dragged herself up by her saddle horn. Simon struggled onto his horse's back—it was Homefinder! After all the other mad things that had happened, Simon was so astonished to be reunited with his horse that he simply stopped thinking. Qantaqa leaped past with Binabik on hor back, loping rapidly down the hillside. Simon clutched Homefinder's neck and dug in his heels, following the wolf's bobbing tail through the clutching branches, down into darker shadows.

The night had become a sort of waking dream, a blur of twisted trees and damp murk; when Binabik finally stopped, Simon was not sure how long they had been traveling. They were still on the hill slope, but in deep trees, cut off from even a sight of the cloudy sky. The darkness had become so thick that they had been moving at a walk for some time, Simon and Miriamele straining to see Qantaqa's gray form though the wolf was only cubits ahead of them.

"Here," Binabik said quietly. "Here is shelter."

Simon dismounted and followed the sound of his voice, leading Homefinder by the reins.

"Be keeping your head low," the troll said. There was an echo behind his words.

The damp, spongy ground gave way to something drier and more firmly packed. The air was musty.

"Now, stop where you are standing." Binabik fell silent but for some rustling noises. Long moments passed. Simon stood and listened to his own heavy breathing. His heart was still pounding, his skin still damp with cold sweat. Could they really be safe? And Binabik! Where had he come from? How had he arrived, so improbably, so fortunately?

There was a hiss and a flicker, then a blossom of flame rose at the end of a torch clutched in the troll's small hand. The light revealed a long, low cavern, its farthest end out of sight around a bend in the rock.

"Deeper in we are going," he said. "But it would not be safe for traveling in here with no light."

"What is this place?" Miriamele asked. The sight of her bloodied legs and pale, frightened face made Simon's heart cinch in pain.

"A cave, only." Binabik smiled, a welcome and familiar baring of yellow teeth. "Trust it for a troll to be finding a cave." He turned and gestured for them to follow. "Soon you can rest."

The horses balked at first, but after a few moments' soothing they allowed themselves to be led on. The cave was strewn with dry branches and leaves. Here and there the bones of small animals winked up from the litter on the floor. Within a few hundred paces they had reached the innermost end, a grotto that was a little loftier and a great deal wider than the outer tunnel. At one end a sheet of water ran down a flat stone and drizzled into a small pool; Simon tethered Miriamele's steed and Homefinder to a stone beside it.

"Here we will make our home for the evening," said Binabik. "The wood I have left here is dry, and the smoke it is making will not be great." He pointed up to a dark crevice in the roof. "I was making a fire here last night. The smoke is carried up there, so breathing is possible."

Simon sank down onto the floor. The dry brush crackled beneath him. "What about the Norns and the others?" At this moment he didn't really much care. If they wanted him, they could come and get him. Every inch of his body seemed to throb painfully.

"I am doubting they will find this place, but I am doubting even more they will be searching long." The troll began piling wood atop the ashes in the circle of stones he had made the night before. "The Norns were at some great task, and seemed to need you only for your blood. I am thinking that there will be blood enough among those remaining mortals for the task to be completed."

"What did they want, Binabik?" Miriamele's eyes were fever-bright. "What were they saying about the Third House? And what was that . . . that thing?"

"That fearsome thing was one of the Red Hand," Binabik said, his matter-of-fact tone betrayed by the worried look on his face. "I have never seen with my eyes anything like it, although Simon was telling me stories." He shook his head, then took his flint to put a spark to the wood. "I do not know what its purpose was, although it seems clear to me that it was doing the Storm King's bidding. I will think on that more." As the fire caught, he lifted his pack and began to search in it. "Now, let me be cleaning those cut places you both have."

Simon sat quietly as the troll dabbed at Miriamele's various wounds with a damp rag and rubbed something from a small pot on each. By the time it was his turn, Simon felt his eyes drooping. He yawned.

"But how did *you* get here, Binabik?" He winced as the little man probed a painful spot. "What . . . what. . . ?"

The troll laughed. "There will be time enough for all telling soon. First, though, food and sleeping are needed." He eyed them both. "Perhaps first sleeping, then food?" He rose to his feet and dusted his hands off on his wide breeches. "There is something you will be pleased to see." He pointed to something lying in the darkness near where Homefinder and Miriamele's mount stood drinking from the pool.

"What?" Simon stared. "Our saddlebags!"

"Yes, and with your sleeping-beds still upon them. A luckiness it was for me that the Fire Dancers had not removed them. I left them here when I followed you up the hill. It was a risk, but I did not know what might be in them that would be bad for losing." He laughed. "Neither did I wish to make you ride laden horses in the dark."

Simon was already dragging loose his bedroll and examining the saddlebags. "My sword!" he said, delighted. Then his face fell. "I had to break Jiriki's mirror, Binabik."

The little man nodded. "That I was seeing. But I doubt I could have helped your escaping if you had not freed your hands. A sad but clever sacrifice, friend Simon."

"And my White Arrow," he mused. "I left that back at Sesuad'ra." He tossed Miriamele her bedroll, then found a relatively smooth place to unroll his own. "I have not taken very good care of my gifts. . . ."

Binabik smiled a tiny smile. "You are having too much worry. Sleep for a while now. I will wake you later with something warm to eat." He returned to the task of building the fire. The torchlight played on his round face.

Simon looked at Miriamele, who had already curled up

and closed her eyes. She did not seem too badly hurt, although she was clearly as exhausted as he. So they had survived, somehow, after all. He had not failed his pledge.

He sat up suddenly. "The horses! I have to unsaddle them!"

"I will be doing all," Binabik assured him. "It is time for your resting."

Simon lay back on the bedroll and watched the shadows playing along the cavern roof. Within moments he was asleep.

# 10

# A Wound in the World

✤

**Simon awakened** to the delicate patter of falling water.

He had been dreaming about being caught in a ring of fire, flames that seemed to grow closer and closer. Somewhere outside the fiery circle, Rachel the Dragon had been calling him to come and do his chores. He had tried to tell her that he was trapped, but smoke and ashes had filled his mouth.

The water sounded as lovely as morningsong in the Hayholt chapel. Simon crawled across the rustling cavern floor and dipped his hands in the pool, then stared at his palms for a moment, unable to tell by the light of the low fire whether the water looked safe. He smelled it and touched it briefly with his tongue, then drank. It was sweet and cold. If it was poisonous, then he was willing to die that way.

*Mooncalf. The horses drank from it, and Binabik used it to wash our cuts.*

Besides, even poisoning would be preferable to the doom that had almost been theirs . . . last night?

The cold water made the wounds on his wrists and hands sting. All his muscles ached, and his joints were stiff and sore. Still, he did not feel quite as dreadful as he might have expected to. Perhaps he had been asleep longer than a few hours—it was impossible to tell what time of day it might be. Simon looked around the cavern, searching for clues. How long had he slept? The horses still stood quietly nearby. On the far side of the campfire he could see Miriamele's golden hair peeping out from beneath her cloak.

"Ah, Simon-friend!"

He turned. Binabik was trotting up the tunnel toward the central chamber, his hands cupped before him. "Greetings," said Simon. "And good morning—if it *is* morning."

The troll smiled. "It is indeed that time, although the middle-day will be soon arriving. I have just been out in the cold and misted woods, stalking a most elusive game." He held up his hands. "Mushrooms." He walked to the fire and spilled his treasures out on a flat stone, then began sorting through them. "Gray-cap, here. And this is being a rabbit-nose—and tasting far better than any true rabbit's nose, I am thinking, as well as having much less messiness to prepare." He chortled. "I will cook these and we will break our fast with great enjoyment."

Simon grinned. "It's good to see you, Binabik. Even if you hadn't rescued us, it would be very good to see you."

The troll cocked an eyebrow. "You both did much to make your own rescuing, Simon—and that is a fortunate thing, since you seem to be flinging yourself constantly into odd troubles. You said once that your parents were being common folk. It is my thought that at least one of them was not a person at all, but a moth." He smiled wryly and gestured toward the fire. "You are always heading toward the nearest burning flame."

"It does seem that way." Simon found himself a seat on an outcropping of stone, shifting gingerly to find the least painful position. "So now what do we do? How did you find us?"

"As to what thing we should be doing," Binabik wrinkled his brow in concentration as he cut up mushrooms with his knife, " 'eat' is being my suggestion. I decided that it would be more kindness to let you sleep than to wake you. You must now be feeling great hungriness."

"*Great* hungriness," Simon affirmed.

"As to the other question, I think I will be waiting until Miriamele is also awake. Much as I enjoy talking, I do not want to be telling all my stories twice."

"If you wanted me awake," Miriamele said crossly from her bedroll, "then talking so loud is just the way to go about it."

Binabik was unperturbed. "We have made a favor for you, then, for I will soon have food for you both. There is clean water here for washing, and if you wish to go outside, I have looked around with care and there does not seem anyone about."

"Oh," Miriamele groaned. "I hurt." She dragged herself off her bedroll, wrapped her cloak about her, then staggered out of the cavern.

"She isn't very cheerful in the mornings," Simon offered with some satisfaction. "Not used to getting up early, I suppose." He had never liked getting out of bed much either, but a scullion was given little say over how early he would rise or when he would work, and Rachel had always made it quite clear that sloth was the greatest of all sins.

"Who would be having much cheer after what you went through last night?" said Binabik, frowning. He tossed the mushroom bits into a pot of water, added some powdery substance from a pouch, then set the pot on the outermost edge of the coals. "I am surprised that the things you have been seeing in this year gone past have not made you mad, Simon, or at least trembling and fearful always."

Simon thought about this for a moment. "I do get frightened sometimes. Sometimes it all seems so *big*—the Storm King, and the war with Elias. But all I can do is what is in front of me." He shrugged. "I'll never understand it all. And I can only die once."

Binabik looked at him shrewdly. "You have been talking to Camaris, my knightly friend. That sounds with great similarity to his Canon of Knighthood—although the words have true Simon-like humbleness." He peered into his pot and agitated the contents with a stick. "Just a few things to add, then I will be leaving it to itself for a time." He tossed in a few strips of dried meat, chopped a small and rather lopsided onion into pieces and added those as well, then gave the mixture another stir.

When he had finished this chore, the troll turned and pulled his hide bag close to him, rummaging through it with an air of great concentration. "There is something in here I thought might give you interest . . ." he said absently. After a few moments, he pulled a long parcel wrapped in leaves out of the sack. "Ah. Here."

Simon took it, knowing it by the feel even before it was unwrapped. "The White Arrow!" he breathed. "Oh, Binabik, thank you! I was sure I had lost it."

"You did lose it," said the troll dryly. "But since I was coming for visiting you in any case, it seemed that I might as well be carrying it along."

Miriamele reentered. Simon held up his prize. "Look, Miri, my White Arrow! Binabik brought it!"

She gave it barely a glance. "That was kind, Simon. I'm glad for you."

He stared at her as she made her way to her saddlebags and began searching for something. What had he done to make her mad now? The girl was more changeable than weather! And wasn't *he* supposed to be upset with *her?*

Simon snorted quietly and turned back to Binabik. "Are you going to tell us how you found us?"

"Patience!" Binabik waved a stubby paw. "Let us have our food and a little peace, first. Princess Miriamele has not even come for joining us yet. And there is other news as well, some of it not happy." He bent over his sack and rooted some more. "Ah. Here they are." The troll produced yet another parcel, a small drawstring bag. He up-ended it and his knucklebones tumbled out onto a flat rock. "While we are waiting, I will find what the bones may be telling me." The bones made a soft clicking noise as he gentled them in his hands then tipped them out onto the stone. He squinted.

"The Shadowed Path." The troll grinned sourly. "That is not the first time I have been seeing that." He rolled them out again. "The Black Crevice." Binabik shook his head. "Still we are having that, as well." He shook the bones for a final time and spilled them before him. *"Chukku's Stones!"* His voice was unsteady.

"Is Chukku's Stones a bad throw?" Simon asked.

"It is a cursing word," Binabik informed him. "I was using it because I have never been seeing this pattern of bones." He leaned closer to the pile of yellowed objects. "A little like Wingless Bird," he said. "But not." He lifted one of the bones, which was delicately perched on two of its fellows, then took a deep breath. "Could this be Mountains Dancing?" He looked up at Simon, eyes bright, but not in a way Simon liked. "I have never been seeing it, and have not known anyone who was seeing it. But I think I was hearing of it once, when Ookekuk my master talked to a wise old woman from Chugik Mountain."

Simon shrugged helplessly. "What does it mean?"

"Changing. Things changing. Large things." Binabik sighed. "If it is indeed Mountains Dancing. If I had my scrolls, I could perhaps be discovering with sureness." He swept up the bones and dropped them back into their pouch; he seemed more than a little frightened. "It is a throw that has only been appearing a few times ever since the Singing Men of Yiqanuc have written their lives and learning on hides."

"And what happened?"

Binabik put the pouch away. "Let me wait before more talking, Simon. I must be thinking on this."

Simon had never taken the troll's bone oracles too seriously—they had always seemed as general and unhelpful as a fortune-reader from a traveling fair—but he was shaken now by Binabik's obvious uneasiness.

Before he could press the troll for more information, Miriamele returned to the fire and sat down. "I'm not going back," she said without preamble. Binabik, like Simon, was taken by surprise.

"I am not understanding your meaning, Princess Miriamele."

"Yes, you do. My uncle sent you to bring me back. I'm not going." Her face was as hard and determined as Simon had ever seen it. Now he understood her preoccupation. He also felt more than a little anger. Why was she always so stubborn, so cross? It almost seemed she enjoyed pushing people away from her with words.

Binabik spread his palms in the air. "I could not make

you do anything that was not your wanting, Miriamele—and I would not try such doing." His brown eyes were full of concern. "But, yes, your uncle and many others worry for you. They worry about your safeness, and they worry about what you plan. I will *ask* you to be coming back ... but making I cannot do."

Miriamele looked slightly relieved, but her jaw was still set. "I'm sorry, Binabik, if you have traveled so far for nothing, but I am not returning. I have something to do."

"She wants to tell her father that this whole war is a mistake," Simon muttered sullenly.

Miriamele gave him a look of disgust. "That's not why I'm going, Simon. I told you the reason." She haltingly explained to Binabik her ideas about what might have led Elias to the clutches of the Storm King.

"I am thinking you may indeed have discovered his mistake," Binabik said when she had finished. "It is close to some of my own supposing—but that does not mean that there is any likeliness you will be succeeding." He frowned. "If your father has been brought close to the Storm King's power, whether by the trickiness of Pryrates or something else, he may be like a man who drinks too much *kangkang*—telling him that his family is starving and his sheep are wandering away may not be heard." He laid a hand on Miriamele's arm. She flinched, but did not pull away. "Also—and this is a hard thing for my heart to be saying—it is perhaps true that your father the king *cannot* anymore survive without the Storm King. The sword Sorrow is a thing of great power, a strong, strong thing. Perhaps if it is taken from him, he will go sliding into madness."

Miriamele's eyes welled with tears, but her expression remained grim. "I am not trying to take the sword from him, Binabik. Only to tell him that things have gone too far. My father—my *real* father—would not have wanted so much harm to come from his love for my mother. Everything that has happened since must be the work of others."

Binabik raised his hands again, this time in resignation.

"*If* you have guessed the reasons for his madness, for this war, for his pact with the Storm King. And if he can be hearing you. But as I told you, I cannot stop your journey. I can only accompany you to help keep you from harm."

"You're going to come with us?" Simon asked. He was very pleased and strangely relieved to think that someone else would share what felt like a heavy burden.

The troll nodded, but his smile was long gone. "Unless you are to be returning with me to Josua, Simon? That might be reason for not going on."

"I have to stay with Miriamele," he pronounced firmly. "I gave my oath as a knight."

"Even though I didn't ask for it," said Miriamele.

Simon felt a moment's angry pain, but remembered the Canon of Knighthood and mastered himself. "Even though you didn't ask for it," he repeated, glowering at her. Despite the terrible times they had shared, she seemed determined to hurt him. "I still have my duty. And," he said to Binabik, "if Miriamele is going to the Hayholt, *I'm* going to Swertclif. Bright-Nail is there, and Josua needs it. But I can't think of any way to get into the castle to get Sorrow," he added reflectively.

Binabik sat back and let loose a weary sigh. "So Miriamele is going to the Hayholt to plead with her father for stopping the war, and you are going there to be rescuing one of the Great Swords, just your single knightly self?" He leaned forward suddenly and dragged the stirring stick through the mixture simmering in the pot. "Are you hearing how like younglings you sound? I was thinking you were both wiser after your many dangers and almost-dyings than to take such things on yourselves."

"I'm a knight," said Simon. "I'm not a child any more, Binabik."

"That is just meaning that the damage you can be doing is greater," the troll said, but his tone was almost conciliatory, as though he knew he could not win the argument. "Come, let us be eating. This is still a happy meeting, even if the times are those of unhappiness."

Simon was relieved to have the argument end. "Yes, let's eat. And you still haven't told us how you found us."

Binabik gave the stew another stir. "That and other news when you have been eating your food," was all he said.

When the sound of contented chewing had slowed a little, Binabik licked his fingers and took a deep breath. "Now that your stomachs at least are full, and we are safe, there is grim news that needs telling."

As Simon and Miriamele sat in growing horror, the troll described the Norns' attack on the camp and its aftermath.

"Geloë dead?" Simon felt as though the earth was eroding beneath him; soon there would be nowhere safe left to stand. "Curse them! They are demons! I should have been there! A knight of the prince. . . !"

"It is perhaps true you should both have been there," Binabik said gently, "or at least that you two should not have left. But you could have done nothing, Simon. Everything was happening with great suddenness and silence, and only one target there was."

Simon shook his head, furious with himself.

"And Leleth." Miriamele rubbed away tears. "That poor child—she has had nothing but pain."

After they had sat in mournful silence for a while, Binabik spoke again. "Let me now be speaking of a less sad thing—how I was finding you. In truth, there is not a great deal for telling. Qantaqa it was who did the most of the tracking. She has a cunning nose. My only fear would be that we would fall too far behind—horses are traveling faster than wolves over long distances—and that the smells would grow too old. But our luck held.

"I was following you into the edge of Aldheorte Forest, and there things grew muddled for some time. I had the most worry that we would lose you in that place, since it was slow going, and then it was raining, too. But clever Qantaqa managed to keep your trail."

"Was it you, then?" Simon asked suddenly. 'Were you the one who was skulking around our camp in the forest?"

The troll looked puzzled. "I am not thinking it was. When did this thing happen?"

Simon described the mysterious lurker who had approached the camp and then retreated into darkness.

Binabik shook his head. "It was not me. I would not have been talking to myself, although perhaps I might have been saying words to Qantaqa. But I am promising you," he drew himself up proudly, "Qanuc do not make so much noise. Especially in the forest at night. Very concerned with not becoming a meal for something large, we Qanuc are." He paused. "And the time is wrong, also. We would have been a day or two days at least behind you then. No, it was doubtless one of the things you were guessing, a bandit or a forest cotsman." Still, he considered for a few moments before continuing with his tale.

"In any manner, Qantaqa and I followed you. We were forced to make our hunting secret—I had no wish for riding Qantaqa into a large town like Stanshire—so I could only have hope that you were coming out of these places again. We wandered about on the outskirts of the large settlements trying to find your track. Several times I thought that I had made it too difficult for Qantaqa's scenting, but always she found you again." He scratched his head, contemplating. "I suppose that if you had not emerged, I would have then been forced to go searching for you. I am glad I did not need to do that thing—I would have had to leave Qantaqa out in the wildlands, and I would have myself been an easy target for Fire Dancers or frightened villagers who had never been seeing a troll." He smiled slyly. "The people of Stanshire and Falshire have *still* not seen a troll."

"When did you find us?"

"If you think on it, Simon, you will be guessing very easily. I had no reason to hide from you, so I would have been greeting you as soon as I came upon you—unless some reason there was not to."

Simon considered. "Because we were with someone you didn't know?"

The troll nodded, satisfied. "Exactly. A young man and

woman may be traveling in Erkynland and speaking to strangers without too much attention. A troll may not."

"So it must have been when we were with that man and woman—the Fire Dancers. We met other people, but we were alone each time afterward."

"Yes. I came upon you here in Hasu Vale—I had been making camp in this very cave the night before—and followed you and that pair up into the hills. Qantaqa and I were watching all from the trees. We saw the Fire Dancers." He frowned. "They have become numerous and unafraid—by spying on other travelers along the road and listening to their gossip I was learning that. So I saw what these Fire Dancers did, and when they were taking you to the hilltop, I freed your horses and followed." He grinned, pleased with his own cleverness.

"Thank you, Binabik," Miriamele said. Some of her earlier frosty manner had disappeared. "I haven't said that yet."

He smiled and shrugged. "We all are doing what we can when we are able. As I was once before telling Simon, we three have saved each other's lives enough times that the tallying is no longer important." As he picked up a hank of moss and began to scrub his bowl, Qantaqa strode silently into the cavern. Her fur was wet; she shook herself, sending a fine spray of droplets everywhere.

"Ah." Binabik placed the bowl on the floor before the wolf. "*You* may be performing this task, then." As Qantaqa's pink tongue scoured out the last bits of stew, the troll stood up. "So, that is the telling. Now, if we are going carefully, I think we can leave this place today. We will stay away from the road until Hasu Vale is being safely behind."

"And the Fire Dancers won't find us?" Miriamele asked.

"After the last night's doings, I am doubting that there are many left, or that they are wishing to do much of anything but hide. I am thinking that the Storm King's servant gave them as much fright as it gave to you." He bent to begin picking up. "And now their chieftain is dead."

"That was one of your black-tipped darts," Simon said,

remembering Maefwaru's puzzled expression as he clutched at his throat.

"It was."

"I'm not sorry." Simon went to tie up his bedroll. "Not sorry at all. So you're really going to come with us."

Binabik thumped his chest with the heel of his hand. "I am not believing what you do is wise or good. But I cannot be letting you go off when I might be able to help you survive." He frowned, pondering. "I wish there was some way for sending a message back to the others."

Simon remembered the trolls in Josua's camp, and especially Sisqi, the loved one Binabik must have left behind to come here. The magnitude of the little man's sacrifice struck him and he was suddenly ashamed. Binabik was right: Simon and Miriamele were behaving like wayward children. But one look at the princess convinced him that she could no more be talked out of this than the waves could be argued out of crashing onto the beach—and he could not imagine himself leaving her to face her fate alone. Like Binabik, he was trapped. He sighed and picked up the bedroll.

Either Binabik was a good guide or the Fire Dancers had, in fact, given up looking for them. They saw nothing living during their afternoon's journey through the damp, thick-forested hills of Hasu Vale except for a few jays and a single black squirrel. The woods were densely crowded with trees and ground plants, and every trunk was blanketed in spongy moss, but the land still seemed strangely inactive, as though everything that lived there slept or waited silently for the intruders to pass.

An hour after sunset they made camp beneath a rocky overhang, but the accommodations were far less pleasant than the dry and secret cave. When the rains came and water ran streaming down the hillside, Simon and the others were forced to huddle as far back under the overhang as they could. The horses, appearing none too pleased, were tethered at the front where they were intermittently lashed by rain. Simon hoped that since horses often stood in fields during bad weather, they would not suffer too badly, but he felt obscurely guilty. Surely Homefinder, a knight's companion, deserved better treatment?

After she hunted, Qantaqa came and curled herself against all three of them as they huddled in a row, making up with the warmth she provided for the strong smell of damp wolf that filled the shelter. They fell asleep at last, then awakened at dawn, stiff and sore. Binabik did not want to light a fire in such an exposed place, so they ate a little dried meat and some berries the troll gathered, then set out again.

It was a difficult day's traveling, the hillsides and dales slippery with mud and wet moss, the rain blowing up in sudden squalls that lashed them with water and slapped branches into their faces; when the rain ceased, the mist crept back in, hiding treacherous pitfalls. Their progress was achingly slow. Still, Simon was impressed that his trollish friend could find a way at all with no sun visible and the road far away and out of sight.

Sometime after noon Binabik led them along the hillside past the outskirts of the town of Hasu Vale itself. It was difficult to make out much more through the close-knit trees than the shapes of some rough houses, and—when the mist was momentarily cleared by a stiff wind—the snaking course of the road, a dark streak some furlongs away. But the town seemed just as muted and lifeless as the forest: nothing but gray mists rose around the smoke holes of the cottages, and there was no sign of people or animals.

"Where has everyone gone?" Miriamele asked. "I have been here. It was a lively place."

"Those Fire Dancers," Simon said grimly. "They've scared everyone away."

"Or perhaps it is the things with which the Fire Dancers have been making celebration on the hilltops at night," Binabik pointed out. "It is not necessary, I am thinking, to *see* those things, as you two were seeing, to know that something is wrong. It is a feeling in the air."

Simon nodded. Binabik was right. This entire area felt much like Thisterborg, the haunted hill between the forest and Erchester, the place where the Anger Stones stood . . .

the place where the Norns had given Sorrow to King
Elias. . . .

He did not like thinking about that horrible night, but
for some reason the memory suddenly seemed important.
Something was pulling at him, scattered thoughts that
wanted to be fit together. The Norns. The Red Hand.
Thisterborg. . . .

"What's that?" Miriamele cried in alarm. Simon
jumped. Homefinder startled beneath him and slipped a
little in the mud before finding her footing.

A dark shape had appeared in the mist before them,
gesticulating wildly. Binabik leaned forward against
Qantaqa's neck and squinted. After a long, tense moment,
he smiled. "It is nothing. A rag caught by the wind.
Someone's lost shirt, I am thinking."

Simon squinted, too. The troll was correct. It was a tattered bit of clothing wrapped around a tree, the sleeves
fluttering in the wind like pennants.

Miriamele made the sign of the Tree, relieved.

They rode on. The town vanished into the thick green-
ery behind them as quickly and completely as if the wet,
silent woods had swallowed it.


They camped that evening in a sheltered gully at the
base of the valley's western slope. Binabik seemed preoccupied; Simon and Miriamele were both quiet. They ate
an unsatisfying meal and made some small talk, then everyone took refuge in the darkness and the need to sleep.

Simon again felt the awkward distance that existed now
between himself and Miriamele. He still did not quite
know what to feel about the things she had told him. She
was no maiden, and it was by her own choice. That was
painful enough, but the way she had told him, the manner
in which she had lashed out at him as though to punish,
was even more infuriatingly confusing. Why was she so
kind to him sometimes, so hateful at others? He would
have liked to believe that she was playing the come-
hither, go-away games that young court women were
taught to play with men, but he knew her too well:
Miriamele was not one for that kind of frippery. The only

solution that he could find to this puzzle was that she truly wanted him for a friend, but was afraid that Simon wanted more.

*I* do *want more,* he thought miserably. *Even if I won't ever have it.*

He did not fall asleep for a long time, but instead lay listening to the water pattering through the leaves to the forest floor. Huddled beneath his cloak, he probed at his unhappiness as he might at a wound, trying to find out how much pain came with it.

By the middle of the next afternoon they climbed out of the valley, leaving Hasu Vale behind. The forest still stretched out at their right hands like a great green blanket, vanishing only at the horizon. Before them was the hilly grass country that lay between the Old Forest Road and the headlands at Swertclif.

Simon could not help wishing that this journey with Binabik and Miriamele could be more like the first heady days they had traveled together after leaving Geloë's lake house, so many months ago. The troll had been full of songs and silliness during that journey; even the princess—pretending then to be the servant girl Marya— had seemed excited and happy to be alive. Now the three of them went forward like soldiers marching toward a battle they did not expect to win, each immersed in private thoughts and fears.

The empty, rolling country north of the Kynslagh did not inspire much cheer in any case. It was fully as dreary and lifeless as Hasu Vale, equally as wet, but did not afford the hiding places and security to be found in the densely forested valley. Simon felt that they were terribly exposed, and could not help marveling at the astonishing courage—or stupidity, or both—of walking virtually unarmed into the High King's gateyard. If there were left any scrap of the companions or their tale when these dark times had someday passed, surely it would make a wonderful, unbelievable song! Some future Shem Horsegroom, perhaps, might tell some wide-eyed scullion: *"Do ye listen, lad, whilst I tell ye of Brave Simon and his friends, them who rode open-eyed and empty-handed into the very Jaws of Darkness. . . ."*

Jaws of Darkness. Simon liked that. He had heard that in a song of Sangfugol's.

He suddenly thought of what that darkness really meant—the things he had seen and felt, the dreadful, clutching shadows waiting beyond the light and warmth of life—and his skin went shudderingly cold from head to foot.

It took them two days to ride across the hilly meadowlands, two days of mist and frequent cold rains. No matter which direction they traveled, the winds seemed always to be blowing into their faces. Simon sneezed the entirety of the first night and felt warm and unstable as melting candle wax. He was a bit recovered by morning.

In mid-afternoon of the second day, the headlands of Swertclif appeared before them, the raw edge of the high, rocky hill on whose summit the Hayholt perched. As he stared into the twilight, Simon thought he could see an impossibly slim white line looming beyond Swertclif's naked face.

It was Green Angel Tower, visible even though it stood the better part of a league beyond the nearest side of the hill.

Simon felt something tingle up his back, lifting the hairs on the nape of his neck. The tower, the great shining spike that the Sithi had built when the castle was theirs, the tower where Ineluki had lost his earthly life—it was waiting, still waiting. But it was also the site of Simon's own boyhood wanderings and imaginings. He had seen it, or something like it, in so many dreams since he had left his home that now it almost seemed like just another dream. And below it, out of sight beyond the cliff, lay the Hayholt itself. Tears welled up in Simon, but only dampened his eyes. How many times had he yearned for those mazy halls, the gardens and scullion hiding-holes, the warm corners and secret pleasures?

He turned to look at Miriamele. She, too, was staring fixedly into the west, but if she thought of the pleasures of home, her face did not show it. She looked like a hunter who had finally run a dangerous but long-sought quarry to ground. He blinked, ashamed that she might see him tearful.

"I wondered if I'd ever see it again," he said quietly. A flurry of rain struck his face and he wiped his eyes, grateful for the excuse. "It looks like a dream, doesn't it? A strange dream."

Miriamele nodded but said nothing.

Binabik did not hurry them away. He seemed content to wait and let Qantaqa nose the ground while Simon and Miriamele sat and silently gazed.

"Let us make camp," he said finally. "If we are riding another short time, we can find shelter at the base of the hills." He gestured toward Swertclif's massive face. "Then in the morning we will have better light for ... whatever we may be doing."

"We're going to John's barrow," Simon said, more firmly than he felt. "At least that's what I'm doing."

Binabik shrugged. "Let us be riding. When we have a fire and food will be time for making of plans."

The sun vanished behind Swertclif's broad hump long before evening. They rode forward in cold shadow. Even the horses seemed uneasy: Simon could feel Homefinder's unwillingness, and thought that if he allowed her she would turn and race in the opposite direction.

Swertclif waited like an infinitely patient ogre. As they drew closer, the great dark hill seemed to blot out the sky as well as the sun, spreading and swelling until it seemed they could not turn away from it even if they tried. From the slope of its outermost foothills, they saw a flash of gray-green to the south, just beyond the cliffs—the Kynslagh, visible for the first time. Simon felt a pang of joy and regret, as he remembered the familiar, soothing song of the gulls and thought of the fisherman-father he had never known.

At last, when the hill's almost perpendicular face stood above them like a vast wall, they made camp in a ravine.

The winds were less here, and Swertclif itself blocked much of the rain. Simon smiled grimly at the thought that the ogre's waiting was over: he and his companions were going to sleep in its lap tonight.

No one wanted to be first to speak of what they would do tomorrow. The making of the fire and the preparation of a modest supper were undertaken with a minimum of conversation and little of the fellowship that usually enlivened the evenings. Tonight Miriamele did not seem angry but preoccupied, and even Binabik was hesitant in his actions, as though his thoughts were elsewhere.

Simon felt surprisingly calm, almost cheerful, and was disappointed that his companions did not share his mood. This was a dangerous place, of course, and the next day's doings would be fearful—he was not letting himself think too much about where the sword was and what needed to be done to find it—but at least he was doing something. At least he was performing the kind of task for which he had been knighted. And if it worked—oh, glory! If it worked, surely Miriamele would see that taking the sword to Josua would be more important than trying to convince her mad father to halt a war that was doubtless already beyond his power to stop. Yes, surely when they had Bright-Nail—think of it, Bright-Nail! Prester John's famous sword!—in hand, Miriamele would realize that they had obtained the greatest prize they could hope for, and he and Binabik could coax her back to the comparative safety of her uncle's camp.

Simon was considering these ideas and letting his meal settle when Binabik finally began to speak.

"Once we are climbing this hill," the troll said slowly, "we will be having great difficulty to turn back. We are having no knowledge whether there are soldiers above— perhaps Elias has placed guards for protecting his father's sword and tomb. If we are going any farther westward, we will be coming to where people in that great castle can be seeing us. Do you have certainness—real, real true certainness!—that you both want this? Please think before you are speaking."

Simon did as his friend asked. After a while, he knew

what he wished to say. "We are here. The next time we are so close to Bright-Nail, there may be men fighting everywhere. We may never be able to get near it. So I think it would be foolish not to try to take it now. I'm going."

Binabik looked at Simon, then slowly nodded. "So we will go to take the sword." He turned to the princess. "Miriamele?"

"I have little to say about it. If we need to use the Three Swords, then that will mean I have failed." She smiled, but it was a smile Simon did not like at all. "And if I fail to convince my father, I doubt that whatever happens afterward will mean much to me."

The troll made a close-handed gesture. "There is never sure knowledge. I will help you as I can, and Simon will also, I am not doubting that—but you must not give up any chance of coming out again. Thinking of this sort will make you careless."

"I would be very happy to come out again," said Miriamele. "I want to help my father understand so that he will cease the killing, then I want to say farewell to him. I could never live with him after what he has done."

"I am hoping that you get the thing you are wishing for," Binabik replied. "So—first we are to go sword-searching, then we will decide what can be done for helping Miriamele. For such weighty efforts, I have need of sleep."

He lay down, curling against Qantaqa, and pulled his hood over his face. Miriamele continued to stare into the campfire. Simon watched her awkwardly for a short while, then pulled his own cloak tight around him and lay back. "Good night, Miriamele," he said. "I hope . . . I hope. . . ."

"So do I."

Simon threw his arm over his eyes and waited for sleep.

He dreamed that he sat atop Green Angel Tower, perched like a gargoyle. Someone was moving beside him.

It was the angel herself, who had apparently left her

spire and now seated herself beside him, laying a cool hand on his wrist. She looked strangely like the little girl Leleth, but made of rough bronze and green with verdigris.

"It is a long way down." The angel's voice was beautiful, soft but strong.

Simon stared at the tiny rooftops of the Hayholt below him. "It is."

"That is not what I mean." The angel's tone was gently chiding. "I mean down to where the Truth is. Down to the bottom, where things begin."

"I don't understand." He felt curiously light, as though the next puff of wind might send him sailing off the tower roof, whirling like a leaf. It seemed that the angel's grip on his arm was the only thing that held him where he sat.

"From up here, the matters of Earth look small," she said. "That is one way to see, and a good one. But it is not the only one. The farther down you go, the harder things are to understand—but the more important they are. You must go very deep."

"I don't know how to do that." He stared at her face, but despite its familiarity it was still lifeless, just a casting of rough metal. There was no hint of friendship or kindness in the stiff features. "Where should I go? Who will help me?"

"Deep. You." The angel suddenly stood; as her hand released him, Simon felt himself beginning to float free of the tower. He clutched a curving bit of the roof and clung. "It is hard for me to talk to you, Simon," she said. "I may not be able to again."

"Why can't you just tell me?" he cried. His feet were floating off the edge; his body fluttered like a sail, trying to follow. "Just tell me!"

"It is not so easy." The angel turned and slowly rose back to her plinth atop the tower roof. "If I can come again, I will. But it is only possible to talk clearly about less important things. The greatest truths lie within, always within. They cannot be given. They must be found."

Simon felt himself tugged free of his handhold. Slowly, like a cartwheel spun loose from its axle, he began to revolve as he floated out. Sky and earth moved alternately past him, as though the world were a child's ball in which he had been imprisoned, a ball now sent rolling by a vengeful kick. . . .

Simon awakened in faint moonlight, sweating despite the chill night air. The dark bulk of Swertclif hung above him like a warning.

The next day found Simon considerably less certain about things than he had been the night before. As they readied for the climb, he found himself worrying over the dream. If Amerasu had been right, if Simon had truly become more open to the Road of Dreams, could there be a meaning to what he had been told by the dream angel? How could he go deeper? He was about to climb a tall hill. And what answer was within? Some secret that even *he* didn't know? It just didn't make sense.

The company set out as the sun began to warm in the sky. For the first part of the morning they rode up through the foothills, mounting Swertclif's lower reaches. As the lower, gentler slopes fell away behind them, they were forced to dismount and lead the horses.

They stopped for a mid-morning meal—a little of the dried fruit and bread that Binabik had brought with him from Josua's camp stores.

"I am thinking it is time to leave the horses behind us," said the troll. "If Qantaqa is still wishing to come, she will climb on her own instead of carrying me upon her back."

Simon had not thought about having to leave Homefinder. He had hoped there would be a way to ride to the summit, but the only level path was the one on the far side of Swertclif, the funeral road that led across the top of the headland from Erchester and the Hayholt.

Binabik had brought a good quantity of rope in his saddlebag; he sacrificed enough of it for Simon and Miriamele to leave their mounts tied on long tethers to a low, wind-curled tree within reach of a natural rocky pool full of rainwater. The two horses had ample room to graze during the half a day or more they would be required to wait. Simon laid his face against Homefinder's neck and quietly promised her he would be back as soon as he could.

"Any other things there are that need doing?" asked Binabik; Simon stared up at the pinnacle of Swertclif and wished he could think of something that would forestall the climb a little longer. "Then let us be going," the troll said.

Swertclif's eastern face was not as sheerly vertical as it seemed from a distance. By traversing diagonally, the company, with Qantaqa trailing behind, were even able occasionally to walk upright, although more often than not they went crouching from handhold to cautious handhold. In only one spot, a narrow chink between the cliff face and a standing stone, did Simon feel any worry, but he and his two companions inched through while Qantaqa, who had found some private wolfish path, stood on the far side with her tongue dangling pinkly, watching their struggles with apparent amusement.

A few hours after noon the skies darkened and the air grew heavy. A light rain swept across the cliff face, wetting the climbers and worrying Simon. It was not so bad where they were, but it looked to get more difficult very soon, and there was nothing pleasant about the idea of trying to cross some of the steeply angled stones if they were slick with rain. But the small shower passed, and although the clouds remained threatening, no larger storm seemed imminent.

The climb did grow steeper, but it was better than Simon had feared. Binabik was leading, and the little man was as surefooted as one of his Qanuc sheep. They only used the rope once, tying themselves for safety as they leapt from one grassy shelf to another over a long, slanting scree of naked stones. Everyone made the jump safely, although Miriamele scratched her hands and Simon banged his knee hard when he landed. Qantaqa seemed to find this part laughably easy as well.

As they paused for breath on the far side of this crossing, Simon found that he was standing just a few cubits below a small patch of white flowers—starblooms—

whose petals gleamed like snowflakes in the dark green grass that surrounded them. He was heartened by the discovery: he'd seen very few flowers since he and Miriamele had first left Josua's camp. Even the Wintercap or Frayja's Fire that one might expect to see at this cold time of the year had been scarce.

The climb up Swertclif's face took longer than they had anticipated: as they toiled up the last long rise, the sun had sunk low in the sky, gleaming a handbreadth above the horizon behind the pall of clouds. They were all bent nearly double now and working hard for breath; they had been using their hands for balance and leverage so frequently in this last stage that Simon wondered what Qantaqa must think to see all her companions turned as four-footed as she. When they stepped up and could at last stand upright on the grassy verge of Swertclif's summit, a sliver of sun broke through, washing the rounded hill with pale light.

The mounds of the Hayholt's kings lay before them, some hundred ells from where they stood struggling to regain breath. All except one of the barrows were nothing more than grassy humps, so rounded by time as to seem part of the hill: that one, which was surely John's, was still only a pile of naked stones. At the hill's distant western edge lay the dim bulk of the Hayholt; the needle-thin spire of Green Angel Tower was brighter than anything else in sight.

Binabik cocked an eye up at the weak sun. "We are being later than my hope. We will not be able to go down again before we are in darkness." He shrugged. "There is nothing that will help that. The horses will be able to feed themselves until the morning when we can return to them."

"But what about . . ." Simon looked at Qantaqa, embarrassed; he had been about to say "wolves," ". . . what about wild animals? Are you sure they'll be all right?"

"Horses can be defending themselves very well. And I have seen few animals of any kind or name in these lands." Binabik patted Simon's arm. "And also there is nothing we can be doing otherwise except risking a bro-

ken neck or other unfortunate crunching or snapping of
bones."

Simon took a breath and started off toward the barrows.
"Come on, then."

The seven mounds were laid out in a partial circle.
Space had been left for others to share this place. Simon
felt a twinge of superstitious fear as he thought about
that. Who else would lie here someday? Elias? Josua?
Or neither? Perhaps the events that had been set in motion meant that nothing expected would ever happen
again.

They walked into the center of the incomplete circle
and stopped. The wind stirred and bent the grasses. The
hilltop was silent. Simon walked to the first barrow,
which had sunk into the waiting earth until it was scarcely
a man's height, though it stretched several times that in
length and was nearly equally wide. A verse floated into
Simon's head, a verse and a memory of black statues in
a dark, silent throne room.

*"Fingil first, named the Bloody King."*

he said quietly,

*"Flying out of the North on war's red wing."*

Now that he had spoken the initial verse, it seemed unlucky to stop. He moved to the next barrow, which was as
old and weatherworn as the first. A few stones glinted in
the grass, like teeth.

*"Hjeldin his son, the Mad King dire*
*Leaped to his death from the haunted spire."*

The third was set close to the second, as if the one
buried there still sought protection from his predeces-
sors.

*"Ikferdig next, the Burned King hight*
*He met the fire-drake by dark of night."*

Simon paused. There was a gap between this trio of mounds and the next, and there was also another verse prodding his memory. After a moment, it came.

*"Three northern kings, all dead and cold*
*The north rules no more in lofty Hayholt."*

He moved to the second group of three, the song swiftly coming back to him now, so that he did not have to search for words. Miriamele and Binabik stood in silence, watching and listening.

*"The Heron King Sulis, called Apostate*
*Fled Nabban, but in Hayholt he met his fate*

*"The Hernystir Holly King, old Tethtain*
*Came in at the gate, but not out again*

*"Last, Eahlstan Fisher King, in lore most high*
*The dragon he woke, and in Hayholt he died."*

Simon took a deep breath. It almost seemed that he was saying a magical spell, that a few more words might bring the barrows' inhabitants up from their centuried sleep, grave ornaments clinking as they broke through the earth.

*"Six kings have ruled in Hayholt's broad halls*
*Six masters have stridden her mighty stone walls*
*Six mounds on the cliff over deep Kynslagh-bay*
*Six kings will sleep there until Doom's final day . . ."*

When he finished, the wind grew stronger for a moment, flattening the grass and moaning as it whirled across the hilltop . . . but nothing else happened. The mounds remained silent and secretive. Their long shadows lay on the sward, stretching toward the east.

"Of course, there are seven kings here now," he said, breaking the silence. Now that the moment had come, he was tremendously unsettled. His heart was rattling in his ribs and he suddenly found it hard to speak without the wordo oatohing in hio throat. Ho turnod to faoo tho laot barrow. It was higher than the rest, and the grass had only partly covered the pile of stones. It looked like the shell of an immense sea-creature stranded by the waves of some ancient flood.

"King John Presbyter," said Simon.

"My *grandfather.*"

Struck by the sound of Miriamele's voice, Simon turned. She appeared positively haunted, her face colorless, her eyes hollow and frightened.

"I can't watch this," she said. "I'm going to wait over there." She turned and made her way around Fingil's barrow, sinking down out of sight at last as she sat, presumably to look out to the east and the hilly land they had just crossed.

"Let us be working, then," said Binabik. "I will not be enjoying this task, but you spoke rightly, Simon: we are here, and it would be foolishness not to take the sword."

"Prester John would want us to," he said with more confidence than he felt. "He would want us to do what we can to save his kingdom, his people."

"Who knows what the dead are wishing?" Binabik said darkly. "Come, let us work. Still we must be making at least some shelter for ourselves before night comes, for hiding the light of a fire if nothing else. Miriamele," he called, "can you look to see if some of those shrubs there along the hill could provide some wood for burning?"

She raised her hand in acknowledgment.

Simon bent to John's cairn and began tugging at one of the stones. It clung to the grassy earth so tenaciously that Simon had to put his boot on the stone beside it to help him pull it free. He stood up and wiped sweat from his face. His chain mail was too bulky and uncomfortable for this sort of work. He unlaced it and removed it, then took off the padded jerkin, too, and laid them both in the grass beside the mound. The wind clawed at him through his thin shirt.

"Halfway across Osten Ard we have been traveling," Binabik said as he dug his fingers into the earth, "and no one was thinking to find a shovel."

"I have my sword," said Simon.

"Save it until there is real need." A little of the troll's usual dryness had returned. "Gouging at stones has a dulling effect on blades, I am told. And we may be needing a sword with some sharpness. Especially if anyone notices us at our work digging up the High King's father."

Simon shut his eyes for a moment and said a brief prayer asking Aedon's forgiveness—and Prester John's, too, for good measure—for what they were about to do.

The sun was gone. The gray sky was beginning to turn pink at its western edge, a color that Simon usually found pleasant, but which now looked like something beginning to spoil. The last stone had been pulled out of the hole in the side of Prester John's grass-fringed cairn. The black nothingness that lay beyond looked like a wound in the flesh of the world.

Binabik fumbled with his flints. When at last he struck a spark, he lit the end of the torch and shielded it from the brisk wind until it caught. Unwilling to stare at the waiting blackness, Simon looked out instead across the dark green of the hilltop. Miriamele was a small figure in the distance, bending and rising as she scavenged for the makings of a campfire. Simon wished he could stop now, just turn and go. He wished he had never thought of such a foolish thing to do.

Binabik waved the flame inside the hole, pulled it out, then pushed the torch back inside again. He got down on his knees and took a cautious sniff. "The air, it is seeming, is at least good." He pushed more clods of earth from the edge of the hole before poking his head through. "I can see the wooden sides of something. A boat?"

"*Sea-Arrow.*" The gravity of what they were doing had begun to settle on Simon like a great weight. "Yes, Prester John's boat. He was buried in it."

Binabik edged in a little farther. "There is plenty of room for me to stand in here," he said. His voice was muffled. "And the timbers above are seeming to me quite sturdy."

"Binabik," said Simon. "Come out."

The little man backed up until he could turn to look. "What is wrong, Simon?"

"It was my idea. I should be the one to go in."

Binabik raised an eyebrow. "No one is wishing to take from you the glory of finding the sword. It is only that I am being smallest and best suited for cave-wandering."

"It's not the glory—it's in case anything happens. I don't want you hurt because of my stupid idea."

"Your idea? Simon, there is no blame here. I am doing what I think is being best. And I am thinking there is nothing inside here to hurt anyone." He paused. "But if you wish . . ." He stepped aside.

Simon lowered himself to his hands and knees, then took the torch from the troll's small hand and pushed it into the hole before him. In the flickering light he could see the great muddy sweep of *Sea-Arrow*'s hull; the boat was curved like a huge dead leaf, like a cocoon . . . as though something within it was waiting to be reborn.

Simon sat up and shook his head. His heart was hammering.

*Mooncalf! What are you afraid of? Prester John was a good man.*

Yes, but what if his ghost was angry about what had happened to his kingdom? And surely no spirit liked its grave being robbed.

Simon took in a gulp of air, then slowly eased himself through the hole in the side of the mound.

He slid down the crumbling slope of the pit until he touched the boat's hull. The dome of spars and mud and white root tendrils stretching overhead seemed a sky created by a feeble, half-blind god. When he finally took another breath, his nostrils filled with the smells of soil and pine sap and mildew, as well as stranger scents he could not identify, some of them as exotic as the contents of Judith the Kitchen Mistress' spice jars. The sweet strength took him by surprise and set him choking. Binabik popped his head through the hole.

"Are you well? Is there badness to the air?"

Simon regained his breath. "I'm well. I just . . ." He swallowed. "Don't worry."

Binabik hesitated, then withdrew.

Simon looked at the side of the hull for what seemed a very long time. Because of the way it was wedged in the pit, the wales rose higher than his head. Simon could not see a way to climb with one hand, and the torch was too thick to be carried comfortably in his mouth. After a moment in which he was strongly tempted to turn and clamber back out again and let Binabik solve the problem, he wedged the butt of the torch in beside one of the mound timbers, then threw his hands over the wale and pulled himself up, kicking his feet in search of a toehold. The wood of *Sea-Arrow*'s hull felt slimy beneath his fingers but held his weight.

Simon pulled the top half of his body over the wale and hung there for a moment, balanced, the edge of the boat pushing up against his stomach like a fist. The sweet, musty odor was very strong. Looking down, he almost cursed—biting back words that might be unlucky and were certainly disrespectful—when he realized that he had placed the torch too low for its light to reach into the boat's hull. All he could see beneath him were ill-defined lumps of shadow. Of course, he thought, it should be simple enough to find a single body and the sword it held, even in darkness: he could do it by touch alone. But there was not a chance in the world that Simon was going to try that.

"Binabik!" he shouted. "Can you come help me?" He was proud of how steady his voice sounded.

The troll clambered over the lip of the hole and slid down the incline. "Are you trapped somehow?"

"No, but I can't see anything without the torch. Can you get it for me?"

As Simon hung over the dark hull, the wooden wale trembled. Simon had a moment's fear that it might collapse beneath him, a fear that was not made less by a quiet creaking that drifted through the underground chamber. Simon was almost certain that the noise came from the tormented wood—the king's boat had been two years in the wet ground, after all—but it was hard not to imagine a hand . . . an ancient, withered hand . . . reaching up from the shadowed hull. . . .

*"Dinabik!?"*

"I am bringing it, Simon. It was higher than I could be reaching."

"Sorry. Just hurry, please."

The light on the roof of the barrow changed as the flame was moved. Simon felt a tapping on his foot. Balancing as carefully as he could, he swung his legs around, pivoting until he was lying with his stomach along the length of the wale and could reach down and take the torch from Binabik's upstretched hand. With another silent prayer— and his eyes half-shut for fear of what he might see— Simon turned and leaned over the void of the inner hull.

At first it was hard to see anything. He opened his eyes wider. Small stones and dirt had worked loose from the barrow ceiling and covered much of *Sea-Arrow*'s contents— but the detritus of the grave had not covered everything.

"Binabik!" Simon cried. "Look!"

"What!?" The troll, alarmed, rushed along the hull to a spot where the boat touched the wall of the barrow, then clambered up, nimble as on a high Mintahoq trail. Balancing lightly atop the wale, he worked his way over until he was near Simon.

"Look." Simon gestured with the shaking torch.

King John Presbyter lay in the bosom of *Sea-Arrow*, surrounded by his funeral gifts, clad still in the magnificent raiment in which he had been buried. On the High King's brow was a golden circlet; his hands were folded on his chest, resting on his long snowy beard. John's skin, but for a certain waxy translucency, looked as firm as the flesh of a living man. After several seasons in the corrupting earth, he seemed to be only sleeping.

But, terrifyingly strange as it was to see the king whole and uncorrupted, that was not all that had made Simon cry out.

*"Kikkasut!"* Binabik swore, no less surprised than Simon. A moment later he had clambered down into the hull of the boat.

A search of the grave and its effects confirmed it: Prester John still lay in his resting place on Swertclif—but Bright-Nail was gone.

# 11

# Heartbeats

⁂

"**Just because** Varellan is my brother does *not* mean I will suffer stupidity," Duke Benigaris snarled at the knight who kneeled before him. He smacked his open palm on the arm of his throne. "Tell him to hold firm until I arrive with the Kingfishers. If he does not, I will hang his head from the Sancellan's gate-wall!"

"Please, my lord," said his armorer, who was hovering just to one side, "I beg you, do not thrash about so. I am trying to measure."

"Yes, do sit still," added his mother. She occupied the same low but ornate chair she had when her husband ruled in Nabban. "If you had not been making such a pig of yourself, your old armor would still fit."

Benigaris stared at her, mustache twitching with fury. "Thank you, Mother."

"And do not be so cruel to Varellan. He is hardly more than a child."

"He is a dawdling, simpering halfwit—and it is you who spoiled him. Who talked me into letting him lead the troops at the Onestrine Pass, in any case?"

Dowager Duchess Nessalanta waved her hand in airy dismissal. "Anyone could hold that pass against a ragtag mob like Josua's. *I* could. And the experience will do him good."

The duke jerked his arm free of the armorer's grasp and slammed it on the chair arm once more. "By the Tree, Mother! He has given up two leagues in less than a fortnight, despite having several thousand foot soldiers and

half a thousand knights. He is falling back so fast that by
the time I ride out the front door, I will probably trip over
him."

"Xannasavin says there is nothing to fret about," she
replied, amused. "He has examined the skies carefully.
Benigaris, please calm yourself. Be a man."

The duke's stare was icy. His jaw worked for a moment
before he spoke. "One of these days, Mother, you will
push me too far."

"And what will you do—throw me into the cells? Cut
off my head?" Her look become fierce. "You need me.
Not to mention the respect you owe the one who bore
you."

Benigaris scowled, took a deep breath, then turned his
attention back to the knight who had delivered young
Varellan's message. "What do you wait for?" he demanded. "You heard what I had to say. Now go and tell
him."

The knight rose and made an elaborate bow, then
turned and walked from the throne room. The ladies in
colorful dresses who were talking quietly near the door
watched him go, then huddled and began discussing
something that caused them to giggle loudly.

Benigaris again tugged his wrist free of the armorer's
clutch, this time so he could snap his fingers at one of the
pages, who trotted over with a cup of wine.

The duke took a draught and wiped his mouth. "There
is more to Josua's army than we first thought. People say
that the High King's brother has found a mighty knight
who fights at the head of his army. They are claiming it
is Camaris. Seriddan of Metessa believes it, or at least he
has joined them." He grimaced. "Traitorous dog."

Nessalanta laughed sourly. "I didn't give Josua as
much credit as he deserved, I admit. It is a clever ploy.
Nothing arouses the common folk like the mention of
your uncle's name. But Seriddan? You ask me to worry
about him and a few other puny barons from the wilderness? The Metessan Crane hasn't flown from the palace
towers in five hundred years. They are nobodies."

"So you are quite sure that this talk of Sir Camaris is

just a ploy?" Benigaris' words, intended to be mocking, came out a little hollow.

"Of course it is! How could it be him? Camaris is forty years dead."

"But his body was never found. Father always agonized because he couldn't give his brother an Aedonite burial."

The duchess made a noise of dismissal but kept her eyes on her needlework. "I knew Camaris, my brave son. You did not. Even if he had joined a monastery or gone into hiding, word would have leaked out: he was so madly honest he could never have lied to anyone who asked him who he was. And he was so self-satisfied, such a meddler, that it is not possible he would have stood by while Prester John fought the second Thrithings War without leaping in to be Camaris the Magnificent, Camaris the Holy, Camaris the Great." Nessalanta pricked her finger and cursed under her breath. "No, this is no living Camaris that Josua has found—and it is certainly no ghost. It is some tall imposter, some oversized grassland mercenary with his hair whitened with powder. A trick. But it makes no difference in any case." She examined her stitchery for a moment, then put the hoop down with an air of satisfaction. "Even the real Camaris could not unseat us. We are too strong ... and his age is gone, gone, gone."

Benigaris looked at her appraisingly. "Unseat *us*. . . ?" he began, but was interrupted by a movement at the room's far end. A herald with the golden kingfisher sigil on his tabard had appeared in the throne room doorway.

"Your Highness," the man said in loud ceremonial tones. "Count Streáwe of Ansis Pellipé arrives at your summons."

The duke settled back, a smile tightening his lips. "Ah, yes. Send the count in."

Streáwe's litter was carried through the doors and set near the great high-arched windows that overlooked the sea, windows covered today in heavy draperies to keep out the cold air. The count's minions lifted out his chair and put it down before the dais that bore the ducal throne.

The count coughed, then caught his breath. "Greetings, Duke," he wheezed. "And Duchess Nessalanta, what a pleasure to see you! As usual, please forgive my sitting without your leave."

"Of course, of course," Benigaris said cheerfully. "And how is your catarrh, Streáwe? I cannot think that it is helped by our cold sea air. I know how warm you keep your house on Sta Mirore."

"As a matter of fact, Benigaris, I had wished to speak to you of just that . . ." the old man began, but the duke cut him short.

"First things first, I regret to say. Forgive me my impatience, but we are at war as you know. I am a blunt man."

Streáwe nodded. "Your straightforwardness is well-known, my friend."

"Yes. So, to the point, then. Where are my riverboats? Where are my Perdruinese troops?"

The count raised a white eyebrow ever so slightly, but his voice and manner remained unperturbed. "Oh, all are coming, Highness. Never fear. When has Perdruin not honored a debt to her elder sister Nabban?"

"But it has been two months," Benigaris said with mock sternness. "Streáwe, Streáwe, my old friend . . . I might almost think that you were putting me off—that for some reason you were trying to stall me."

This time the count's eyebrows betrayed no surprise, but nevertheless a subtle, indefinable change ran across his face. His eyes glittered in their net of wrinkled flesh. "I am disappointed that Nabban could think such a thing of Perdruin after our long and honorable partnership." Streáwe dipped his head. "But it is true that the boats you wish for river transport have been slow in coming—and for that I apologize most abjectly. You see, even with the many messages I have sent back home to Ansis Pellipé, detailing your needs with great care, there is no one who can get things accomplished in the way that I can when I take them in hand personally. I do not wish to malign my servitors, but, as we Perdruinese say, 'when the captain is below decks, there are many places to stretch a hammock.'" The count brought his long, gnarled fingers up to brush something from his upper lip. "I should go back to Ansis Pellipé, Benigaris. As sad as I should be to lose the company of you and your beloved mother—" he smiled at Nessalanta, "—I feel confident that I could send your riverboats and the troop of soldiers we agree on within a week after returning." He coughed again, a wracking spasm that went on for some moments before he regained his wind. "And for all the beauty of your palace, it is, as you said, a trifle airier than my own house. My health has worsened here, I fear."

"Just so," said Benigaris. "Just so. We all fear for your health, Count. It has been much on my mind of late. And the men and boats, too." He paused, regarding Streáwe with a smile that seemed increasingly smug. "That is why I could not allow you to leave just now. A sea voyage at this moment—why, your catarrh would certainly worsen. And let me be brutally honest, dear Count . . . but only because Nabban loves you so. If you were to grow more ill, not only would I hold myself responsible, but certainly it would also slow the arrival of boats and men even more. For if they are haphazard now, with your careful instructions, imagine how laggard they would become with you ill and unable to oversee them at all. There would be many hammocks stretched then, I'm sure!"

Streáwe's eyes narrowed. "Ah. So you are saying that you think it best I do not leave just now?"

"Oh, dear Count, I am *insisting* you remain." Benigaris, tiring at last of the ministrations of his armorer, waved the man away. "I could not forgive myself if I did anything less. Surely after the boats and your troop of soldiers arrive to help us defend against this madman Josua, the weather will have turned warm enough that you can safely travel again."

The count considered this for a moment, giving every impression of weighing Benigaris' arguments. "By Pellipa and her bowl," he said at last, "I can see the sense of what you are saying, Benigaris." His tight grin displayed surprisingly good teeth. "And I am touched at the concern you show for an old friend of your father's."

"I honor you just as I honored him."

"Indeed." Streáwe's smile now became almost gentle. "How lovely that is. Honor is in such short supply in these grim days." He waved a knobby hand, summoning his bearers. "I suspect that I should send another letter to Ansis Pellipé, urging my castellain and boatwrights to hasten their efforts even more."

"That sounds like a very good idea, Count. A very good idea." Benigaris sat back against the throne and finger-brushed his mustache. "Will we see you at table tonight?"

"Oh, I think you will. Where else would I find such kind and considerate friends?" He leaned forward on his chair, sketching a bow. "Duchess Nessalanta—a pleasure as always, gracious lady."

Nessalanta smiled and nodded. "Count Streáwe."

The old man was lifted back into his litter. After the curtain was drawn, his four servitors carried him from the throne room.

"I do not think you needed to be so ham-fisted," said Nessalanta when the count had gone. "He is no danger to us. Since when have sticky-fingered Perdruinese ever wanted more than to earn a little gold?"

"They have been known to accept coins from more than one pocket." Benigaris lifted his cup. "This way, Streáwe will have a much stronger wish to see *us* victorious. He is not a stupid man."

"No, he certainly is not. That is why I don't understand the need to use such a heavy hand."

"Everything I know, Mother," said Benigaris heartily, "I learned from you."

※

Isgrimnur was growing annoyed.

Josua could not seem to keep his attention on the matters at hand; instead, every few moments he went to the door of the tent and stared back up the valley at the monastery standing on the hillside, a humble collection of stone buildings that glowed golden-brown in the slanting sunlight.

"She is not dying, Josua," the duke finally growled. "She is only expecting a child."

The prince looked up guiltily. "What?"

"You have been staring at that place all afternoon." He levered his bulk off the stool and walked to Josua's side, then placed a hand on the prince's shoulder. "If you are so consumed, Josua, then go to her. But I assure you she is in good hands. What my wife doesn't know about babies isn't worth knowing."

"I know, I know." The prince returned to the map spread out on the tabletop. "I cannot stop my mind churning, old friend. Tell me what we were talking about."

Isgrimnur sighed. "Very well." He bent to the map. "Camaris says there is a shepherd's trail that runs above the valley. . . ."

Someone made a discreet noise in the doorway of the tent. Josua looked up. "Ah, Baron. Welcome back. Please come in."

Seriddan was accompanied by Sludig and Freosel. All exchanged greetings as Josua brought out a jug of Teligure wine. The baron and Josua's lieutenants bore the marks of a day's muddy riding.

"Young Varellan has dug in his heels just before Chasu Yarinna," the baron said, grinning. "He has more grit than I thought. I had expected him to fall back all the way to the Onestrine Pass."

"And why hasn't he?" Isgrimnur asked.

Seriddan shook his head. "Perhaps because he feels that once the battle for the pass begins, there is no turning back."

"That might mean that he is not so sure of our weakness as his brother Benigaris is," Josua mused. "Perhaps he may prove willing to talk."

"What is just as likely," said Sludig, "is that he is trying to keep us out of the pass until Duke Benigaris comes up with reinforcements. Whatever they might have thought of our strength to start with, Sir Camaris has changed their minds, I promise you."

"Where is Camaris?" Josua asked.

"With Hotvig and the rest up at the front." Sludig

shook his head in wonderment. "Merciful Aedon, I heard all the stories, but I thought they were just cradle songs. Prince Josua, I have never seen anything like him! When he and Hotvig's horsemen were caught between two wings of Varellan's knights two days ago, we were all sure that he was as good as dead or captured. But he broke the Nabbanai knights like they were kindling wood! One he cut nearly in half with a single stroke. Sheared right through him, armor and all! Surely that sword is magical!"

"Thorn is a powerful weapon," said Josua. "But with it or without it, there has never been a knight like Camaris."

"His horn Cellian has become a terror to the Nabbanmen," Sludig continued. "When it echoes down the valley, some of them turn and ride away. And out of every troop Camaris defeats, he takes one of the prisoners and sends him back to say: 'Prince Josua and the others wish to talk with your lord.' He has beaten down so many that he must have sent two dozen Nabbanai prisoners back by now, each one carrying the same message."

Seriddan raised his wine cup. "Here's to him. If he is a terror now, what must he have been like in the height of his powers? I was a boy when Camaris . . ." he laughed shortly, "—I almost said 'died.' When he disappeared. I never saw him."

"He was little different," Isgrimnur said thoughtfully. "That is what surprises me. His body has aged, but his skills and fighting heart have not. As though his powers have been preserved."

"As though for one final test," Josua said, measuring out the words. "God grant that it is so—and that he succeeds, for all our sakes."

"But I am puzzled." Seriddan took another sip. "You have told me that Camaris hates war, that he would rather do anything than fight. Yet I have never seen such a killing engine."

Josua's smile was sad, his look troubled. "Camaris at war is like a lady's maid swatting spiders."

"What?" Seriddan lowered his eyebrows and squinted, wondering if he was being mocked.

"If you tell a maid to go and kill the spiders in her lady's chamber," the prince explained, "she will think of a hundred excuses not to do anything. But when she is finally convinced that it must be done, no matter the horror she feels, she will dispatch every single spider with great thoroughness, just to make sure she does not have to take up the task again." His faint smile disappeared. "And that is Camaris. The only thing he hates worse than warfare is *unnecessary* warfare—especially killings which could have been avoided by making a clean ending the first time. So once he is committed, Camaris makes sure that he does not have to do the same thing twice." He raised his glass in salute to the absent knight. "Imagine how it must feel to do best in all the world what you least wish to do."

After that, they drank their wine in silence for a time.

Tiamak limped out across the terrace. He found a place on the low wall and hoisted himself up, then sat with his legs dangling and basked in the late afternoon light. The Frasilis Valley stretched before him, two rippling banks of dark soil and gray-green treetops with the Anitullean Road snaking between them. If he narrowed his eyes, Tiamak could make out the shapes of Josua's tents nestled in the purple shadows of the hillside to the southwest.

*My companions may think we Wrannamen live like savages,* he thought to himself, *but I am as happy as anyone to be in one place for a few days and to have a solid roof over my head.*

One of the monks walked by, hands folded in his sleeve. He gave Tiamak a look that lasted the length of several steps, but only nodded his head in formal greeting.

*The monks do not seem happy to have us here.* He felt himself smiling. *Unwilling as they are to be caught up in a war, how much more dubious must they be about having women and marsh men within the cloisters, too?*

Still, Tiamak was glad that Josua had chosen this spot

as a temporary refuge, and that he had allowed his wife and many others to remain here as the army moved farther down the gorge. The Wrannaman sighed as he felt the cool, dry breeze, the sunshine on his face. It was good to have shelter, even for just a little while. It was good that the rains had let up, that the sun had returned.

*But as Josua said,* he reminded himself, *it means nothing. A respite is all—the Storm King has not been slowed by anything we have done so far. If we cannot solve the riddles before us, if we cannot gain the swords and learn how to use them, this moment of peace will mean nothing. The deadly winter will return—and there will be no sunshine then. He Who Always Steps on Sand, let me not fail! Let Strangyeard and me find the answers we seek!*

But answers were becoming fewer and farther between. The search was a responsibility that had begun to feel more and more burdensome. Binabik was gone, Geloë was dead, and now only Tiamak and the diffident priest remained of all the Scrollbearers and other wise ones. Together they had pored over Morgenes' manuscript, searching it minutely from one end to the other in hope of finding some clues they had missed, some help with the riddle of the Great Swords. They had also scrutinized the translated scrolls of Binabik's master Ookequk, but so far these had provided nothing but a great deal of trollish wisdom, most of which seemed to concern predicting avalanches and singing away the spirits of frostbite.

*But if Strangyeard and I do not find more success soon,* Tiamak thought grimly, *we may have more need of Ookequk's wisdom than we will like.*

In the past few days, Tiamak had set Strangyeard to relate every bit of information that the archivist possessed about the Great Swords and their undead enemy—his own book-learning, the things old Jarnauga had taught him, the experiences of the youth Simon and his companions, everything that had happened in the last year that might contain some clue to their dilemma. Tiamak prayed that a pattern might show somewhere, as the ripples in a river demonstrated the presence of a rock beneath the surface. In all the lore of these wise men and women, these adventurers and accidental witnesses, *someone* must know something of how to use the Great Swords.

Tiamak sighed again and wiggled his toes. He longed to be just a little man with little problems again. How important those problems had seemed! And how he longed to have only those problems now. He held up his hand and looked at the play of light across his knuckles, a gnat that crept across the thin dark hairs on his wrist. The day was deceptively pleasant, just like the surface of a stream. But there was no question that rocks or worse lay hidden beneath.

"Please lie back, Vorzheva," said Aditu.

The Thrithings-woman made a face. "Now you talk like Josua. It is only a little pain."

"You see what she's like." Gutrun wore an air of grim satisfaction. "If I could tie her to that bed, I would."

"I do not think that she needs to be tied to anything," the Sitha woman replied. "But Vorzheva, neither is there any dishonor in lying down when you are in pain."

The prince's wife reluctantly slumped back against the cushions and allowed Gutrun to pull the blanket up. "I was not raised to be weak." In the light filtering down from the high small window she was very pale.

"You are not weak. But both your life and the child's life are precious," Aditu said gently. "When you feel well and strong, move around as you like. When you are hurting or weak, lie down and let Duchess Gutrun or me help you." She stood and took a few steps toward the door.

"You are not going to leave?" Vorzheva asked in dismay. "Stay and talk to me. Tell me what is happening outside. Gutrun and I have been in this room all day. Even the monks do not speak to us. I think they hate women."

Aditu smiled. "Very well. My other tasks can wait in such a good cause." The Sitha seated herself upon the bed once more, folding her legs beneath her. "Duchess

Gutrun, if you wish to stretch your legs, I will be here to sit with Vorzheva for a little while longer."

Gutrun sniffed dismissively. "I'm just where I should be." She turned back to her sewing.

Vorzheva reached out her hand and clasped Aditu's fingers. "Tell me what you have seen today. Did you go to Leleth?"

The Sitha nodded, her silver-white hair swinging. "Yes. She is just a few rooms away—but there is no change. And she is growing very thin. I mix nurturing herbs with the small draughts of water she will swallow, but even that is not enough, I fear. Something still tethers her to her body—to look at her she seems only to be sleeping—but I wonder how much longer that tie will hold." A troubled look seemed to pass over Aditu's alien face. "This is another way that Geloë's passing has lessened us. Surely the forest woman would know some root, some leafy thing that might draw Leleth's spirit back."

"I'm not sure," Gutrun said without looking up. "That child was never more than half here—I know, and I cared for her and held her as much as anyone. Whatever happened to her in the forest when she traveled with Miriamele, those dogs and merciful Usires only knows what else, it took a part of her away." She paused. "It's not your fault, Aditu. You've done all that anyone could, I'm sure."

Aditu turned to look at Gutrun, but betrayed no change of expression at the duchess' conciliatory tone. "But it is sad," was all she said.

"Sad, yes," Gutrun replied. "God's wishes often make His children sad. We just don't understand, I suppose, what He plans. Surely after all she suffered, He has something better in mind for little Leleth."

Aditu spoke carefully. "I hope that is so."

"And what else do you have to tell me?" Vorzheva asked. "I guessed about Leleth. You would have told me first if there was any new thing."

"There is not much else to relate. The Duke of Nabban's forces have fallen back a little farther, but soon they will stop and fight again. Josua and the others are trying to arrange a truce so that they can stop the fighting and talk."

"Will these Nabbanai talk to us?"

Aditu shrugged sinuously. "I sometimes wonder if I understand even the mortals I know best. As to those who are completely strange to me ... I certainly cannot offer any firm idea as to what these men may do. But the Nabbanai general is a brother of the ruling duke, I am told, so I doubt that he will be very sympathetic to anything your husband has to say."

Vorzheva's face contorted. She gasped, but then waved the solicitous Aditu back. "No, I am well. It was just a squeezing." After a moment she took a deep breath. "And Josua? How is he?"

The Sitha looked to Gutrun, who raised her eyebrows in a gesture of amused helplessness. "He was just here this morning, Vorzheva," the duchess said. "He is not in the fighting."

"He is well," Aditu added. "He asked me to send his regards."

"Regards?" Vorzheva sat up. "What sort of word is that from a man, from a husband? Regards?"

"Oh, Elysia, Mother of Mercy," Gutrun said in disgust. "You know that he cares for you, Vorzheva. Let it go."

The Thrithings-woman sank back, her hair spreading against the pillow like a shining dark cloth. "It is only because I cannot *do* anything. Tomorrow I will be stronger. Tomorrow I will walk to where I can see the battle."

"Only if you can drag *me* that far," said the duchess. "You should have seen her, Aditu—she couldn't stand this morning, the pains were so dreadful. If I had not caught her, she would have fallen down right on the stone floor."

"If she is strong enough," Aditu said, "then for her to walk is certainly good—but carefully, and not too great a distance." She paused, looking at the Thrithings-woman carefully. "I think perhaps you are too excitable to look at the battle, Vorzheva."

"Hah." Vorzheva's disgust was plain. "You said your

people hardly ever have children. Why are you now so wise about what I should do?"

"Since our birthings are so infrequent, we take them all the more seriously." Aditu smiled regretfully. "I would greatly love to bear a child one day. It has been a privilege to be with you while you carry yours." She leaned forward and pulled back the coverlet. "Let me listen."

"You will only say that the baby is too unhappy to go walking tomorrow," Vorzheva complained, but she did not prevent Aditu from laying a golden cheek against her tautly rounded stomach.

Aditu shut her upturned eyes as though she were falling asleep. For a long moment, her thin face seemed set in almost perfect repose. Then her eyes opened wide, a flashing of brilliant amber. *"Venyha s'ahn!"* she hissed in surprise. She lifted her head for a moment, then placed her ear back against Vorzheva's belly.

"What?" Gutrun was out of her chair in a heartbeat, stitchery tumbling to the floor. "The child! Is the child . . . is something wrong?"

"Tell me, Aditu." Vorzheva was lying perfectly still, but her voice cracked at the edges. "Do not spare me."

The Sitha began to laugh.

"Are you mad?" Gutrun demanded. "What is it?"

Aditu sat up. "I am sorry. I was marveling at the continuing astonishment I feel around you mortals. And when I think that my own people count themselves lucky if we birth a handful of children in a hundred years!"

"What are you talking about?" Gutrun snapped. Vorzheva looked too frightened to ask any more questions.

"I am talking about mortals, about the gifts you have that you do not know." She laughed again, but more quietly. "There are two heartbeats."

The duchess stared. "What. . . ?"

"Two heartbeats," Aditu said evenly. "Two children are growing inside of Vorzheva."

# 12

# Sleepless in Darkness

**Simon's disappointment** was an emptiness deep and hollow as the barrow in which they stood. "It's gone," he whispered. "Bright-Nail isn't here."

"Of that there is being little doubt." In the torchlight, Binabik's face was grim. "Qinkipa of the Snows! I almost am wishing we did not find out until we had come here with Prince Josua's army. I do not wish to take him such news."

"But what could have happened to it?" Simon stared down at the waxen face of Prester John as though the king might wake from his deathly sleep to give an answer.

"It seems plain to me that Elias knew its value and took it away. I am not doubting it is sitting in the Hayholt now." The troll shrugged; his voice was heavy. "Well, we knew always that we must be taking Sorrow from him. Two swords or one seems to me a small difference only."

"But Elias couldn't have taken it! There was no hole until we dug one!"

"Perhaps he was taking it out shortly after John was buried. The marks would be gone after such a time passing."

"That doesn't make any sense," Simon stubbornly insisted. "He could have kept it in the first place if he wanted it. Towser *said* that Elias hated it—that he couldn't wait to get rid of it."

"I have no certain answers, Simon. It is being possible that King Elias did not know its value then, but heard of it later. Perhaps Pryrates was discovering its power and so had it removed. There are many things possible." The troll passed his torch to Simon, then crawled off the wale of Prester John's boat and began to clamber back up toward the hole they had made. The twilit sky shone through, blue-gray and muddy with clouds.

"I don't believe it." Simon's hands, weary with digging, painfully sore still from the ordeal in Hasu Vale, hung limply in his lap. "I don't *want* to believe it."

"The second, I am afraid, is the truer thing," Binabik said kindly. "Come, friend Simon, we will see if Miriamele has made a fire. Some hot soup will be making the situation a little easier for thinking about." He climbed to the lip of the hole and wriggled out, then turned. "Hand the torches to me, then I will be helping you out."

Simon barely heard the troll's words. His attention abruptly caught by something, he held both torches higher, leaning out over the boat once more to stare at the base of the barrow's far wall.

"Simon, what are you seeking still?" Binabik called. "We have already nearly turned the poor king's body overside-up in searching."

"There's something on the other side of the mound. Something dark."

"Oh?" A trace of alarm crept into Binabik's tone. "What dark something are you seeing?" He leaned farther in through the entrance they had dug, blocking the view of the sky.

Simon took both torches in one hand, then slid along the wale of *Sea-Arrow* until he could get close enough to confirm his suspicions. "It's a hole!"

"That does not seem to me surprising," the troll said.

"But it's a big one—right into the side of the mound. Maybe it's the one they used to get in."

Binabik stared at the spot where he pointed, then suddenly vanished from the opening. Simon inched closer. The ragged hole in the side of the barrow was as wide as an ale cask.

The troll reappeared. "I see nothing on the outer side

that matches," he called. "If they were making their hole there they covered it with great care, or they were doing it long ago; the grass is untouched."

Simon made his way carefully around to the narrow stern. He let himself down from the wale into *Sea-Arrow* and moved as carefully as he could to the other railing, then clambered up. There was a space little more than a cubit wide between the outside of the hull and the barrow's wall of mud and timber. He slid down to the floor so that he could examine the hole more closely, bringing the torch close to the shadowed gap. Surprise set his neck tingling. "Aedon," he said quietly. "It goes *down*."

"What?" Binabik's voice reflected some impatience. "Simon, there are things to do before the darkness is becoming full."

"It goes down, Binabik! The tunnel beyond this hole goes down!" He thrust his torches into the opening and leaned as close as he dared. There was nothing to see but a few gleaming, hair-thin roots; beyond them the torchlight faded as the tunnel wound down and away into blackness.

After a moment, the troll said: "Then we will be examining it more tomorrow, after we have had a chance for thinking and sleeping. Come up, Simon."

"I will," said Simon. "Go ahead." He moved closer. He knew he should be more frightened than he was—anything that made a hole this large, animal or human, was nothing to sneer at—but he felt an unmistakable certainty that this gaping rent in the earth had something to do with Bright-Nail's disappearance. He stared into the empty hole, then lifted the torch out of the way and squinted.

There was a gleam down in the darkness—some object that reflected the torchlight.

"Something's in there," he called.

"Something of what sort?" Binabik said worriedly. "Some animal?"

"No, something like metal." He leaned into the hole. He smelled no animal spoor, only a faint acridity like sweat. The gleaming thing seemed to lie a short way down the tunnel, just where it bent out of sight. "I can't reach it without going in."

"We will be looking for it in the morning, then," Binabik said firmly. "Come now."

Simon edged a little way into the hole. Maybe it was closer than it looked—it was hard to tell by torchlight. He held the burning brands before him and moved forward on his elbows and knees until he was entirely into the tunnel. If he could just extend himself to full length, it should be almost within his grasp. . . .

The soil beneath him abruptly gave way and Simon was flailing in loose dirt. He grabbed at the tunnel wall, which crumbled but held for a moment as he braced himself with arms outstretched. His legs continued to slip downward through the oddly soft earth until he was buried waist-deep in the tunnel floor. One of the torches had fallen from his grip and lay sizzling against the damp soil just a few handbreadths from his ribs. The other was pinioned by his palm, rammed against the tunnel wall; he could not have dropped it even if he wished. He felt strangely empty, unafraid.

"Binabik!" he shouted. "I've fallen through!"

Even as he struggled to work himself free, he felt the soil shifting beneath him in a very strange way, unstable as sand beneath a retreating wave.

The troll stared, eyes so wide the whites gleamed. *"Kikkasut!"* he swore, then shouted: *"Miriamele! Come here quickly!"* Binabik scrambled down the incline into the barrow, working his way around the broad hull of the boat.

"Don't come too close," Simon cautioned him. "The dirt feels strange. You might fall through, too."

"Then do not be moving." The little man gripped the protruding edge of the boat's buried keel and stretched his arm toward Simon, but his reach was short by more than a cubit. "Miriamele will bring our rope." The troll's voice was quiet and calm, but Simon knew that Binabik was frightened.

"And there's something . . . something *moving* down there," Simon said anxiously. It was a dreadful sensation, a compression and relaxation of the soil that held him, as though some great serpent twisted its coils in the depths. Simon's dreamlike sense of calm evaporated, replaced by mounting horror. "B–Bin . . . *Binabik!*" He could not get his breath.

"Do not be moving!" his friend said urgently. "If you can but . . ."

Simon never heard the rest of what the troll meant to say. There was a sharp stinging around his ankles as though they had been suddenly wrapped in nettles, then the earth twitched again beneath him and he was swallowed. He barely had time to close his mouth before the clotted soil rose up and closed over his head like an angry sea.

Miriamele saw Binabik emerge from the hole. As she stacked the brambles and twigs she had gathered, she watched him hover beside the entrance they had dug into the mound, talking to Simon, who was still inside the barrow. She wondered dully what they had found. It seemed so pointless, somehow. How could all the swords in the world, magical or not, put a stop to the runaway wagon that her father's maddened grief had set in motion? Only Elias himself could cry halt, and no threat of magical weapons would make him do that. Miriamele knew her father only too well, knew the stubbornness that ran through him just as his blood did. And the Storm King, the shuddersome demon glimpsed in dreams, the master of the Norns? Well, her father had invited the undead thing into the land of mortals. Miriamele knew enough old stories to feel sure that only Elias could send Ineluki away again and bar the door behind him.

But she knew that her friends were set on their plan, just as she was on hers, and she would not stand in their way. Still, she had not for a moment wished to descend with them into the grave. These were strange days, yes, but not strange enough that she wished to discover what two years in the disrespectful earth had done to her grandfather John.

It had been difficult enough to go to the burial and watch his body lowered into the ground. She had never been close to him, but in his distant way, he had loved her and been kind to her. She had never been able to imagine him young, since he had already been ancient when she was a small girl, but she had once or twice seen a glint in his eye or a hint in his stooped posture that suggested the bold, world-conquering man he must have been. She did not want even those few memories to be sullied by . . .

"*Miriamele! Come here quickly!*"

She looked up, startled by the fearful urgency in Binabik's tone. Despite his call the little man did not look back to her, but slid into the gouge in the barrow's side and vanished, quick as a mole. Miriamele leaped to her feet, knocking over her pile of gathered brush, and hurried across the hilltop. The sun had died in the west; the sky was turning plum-red.

*Simon. Something has happened to Simon.*

It seemed to take forever to cross the intervening distance. She was out of breath when she reached the grave, and as she dropped to her knees dizziness swept over her. When she leaned into the hole, she could see nothing.

"Simon has . . ." Binabik shouted, "Simon has . . . *No!*"

"What is it? I can't see you!"

"*Qantaqa!*" the troll shrieked. "*Qantaqa sosa!*"

"What's wrong!?" Miriamele was frantic. "What is it!"

Binabik's words came in ragged bursts. "Get . . . torch! Rope! *Sosa, Qantaqa!*" The troll suddenly let out a cry of pain. Miriamele kneeled in the opening, terrified and confused. Something dreadful was happening—Binabik clearly needed her. But he had told her to get the torch and the rope, and every instant she delayed might help doom the troll and Simon both.

Something huge pushed her aside, bowling her over as though she were an infant. Qantaqa's gray hindquarters disappeared down the incline and into the shadows; a moment later the wolf's furious snarl rumbled up from the depths. Miriamele turned and ran back toward the place where she had begun her fire, then stopped, remembering that the rest of their belongings were somewhere closer to Prester John's mound. She looked around in desperation until she saw them lying on the far side of the half-circle of graves.

Panting, her hands shaking so badly that it was difficult even to hold the flint and steel in her hands, Miriamele worked frantically until the torch caught. She grabbed a second brand; as she searched in desperation for rope, she set this torch alight with the first.

The rope was not among their belongings. She let out a string of Meremund river-rider curses as she hurried back to the mound.

The coil of rope lay half-buried in the dirt Simon and the troll had excavated. Miriamele wrapped it loosely about her so she could keep her hands free, then scrambled down into the barrow.

The inside of the grave was as strange as a dream. Qantaqa's low growling filled the space like the hum of an angry beehive, but there was another sound, too—a strange, insistent piping. At first, as her eyes became used to the darkness, the flickering torchlight showed her only the long, broad curve of *Sea-Arrow* and the sagging timbers jutting through the barrow's earthen roof like ribs. Then she saw movement—Qantaqa's agitated tail and back legs, all that was visible of her past the stern of the boat. The earth around the wolf was aboil with small dark shapes—rats?

"Binabik!" she screamed. "Simon!"

The troll's voice, when it came, was hoarse and tattered with fright. "No, run away! This place is being . . . full of *boghanik!* Run!"

Terrified for her companions, Miriamele scrambled around the side of the boat. Something small and chittering leaped down from the wale above her head, raking her face with its claws. She shrieked and knocked it away, then pinned it to the ground with the torch. For a horrifying instant she saw a wizened little manlike thing writhing beneath the burning brand, matted hair sizzling, sharp-toothed mouth stretched in a shrill of agony.

Miriamele screamed again, pulling the torch away as she kicked the dying thing into the shadows.

Her pulse beating in her temples until she felt her head would burst, she forced her way forward. Several more of the spidery things swarmed toward her, but she swiped at them with the twin torches and they danced back. She was close enough now to touch Qantaqa, but felt no urge to do so: the wolf was hard at work, moving swiftly in the confined space, breaking necks and tearing small bodies.

"Binabik!" she cried. "Simon! I'm here! Come toward the light!"

Her call brought another cluster of the chittering terrors toward her. She hit two with her torch, but the second almost pulled the brand from her grasp before it fell to the earth, squealing. A moment later she saw a shadow above her and jumped back, raising the torch again.

"It is me, Princess," Binabik gasped. He had climbed up onto *Sea-Arrow*'s railing. He stooped for a moment and vanished, then reemerged, only his eyes clearly visible in the blood and earth that smeared his face. He thrust the butt of a long spear down for her to grasp. "Take this. Do not let them become close!"

She grasped the spear, then was forced to turn and sweep a half dozen of the things against the barrow wall. She dropped one of the torches. As she bent, another of the shriveled creatures pranced toward her; she speared it as a fisherman might. It wriggled on the spearhead, slow to die.

"Simon!" she shouted. "Where is he?" She picked up the second torch and held it toward Binabik, who had ducked down into the boat once more, and now stood with an ax clutched in his hands, a weapon nearly as long as the troll was tall.

"I cannot be holding the torch," Binabik said breathlessly. "Push it into the wall." He raised the ax over his head and then jumped down beside her.

Miriamele did as he said, jamming the butt of the torch into the crumbling earth.

"*Hinik Aia!*" Binabik shouted. Qantaqa backed up, but the wolf seemed reluctant to disengage; she made several snarling rushes back toward the chirping creatures. While she was engaged on one such sortie, another swarm of the things scurried around her. Binabik swept several into bloody ruin with the ax and Miriamele fended off others with jabs of the spear. Qantaqa finished her engagement and swept in to finish off the raiding party. The rest of the crowding creatures sputtered angrily, their white eyes gleaming like a hundred tiny moons, but they did not seem anxious to follow Miriamele and her companions as they backed toward the hole.

"Where is Simon?" she asked again. Even as she spoke, she knew she did not want to hear the answer. There was a kind of cold nothingness inside her. Binabik would not leave Simon behind if he still lived.

"I am not knowing," Binabik said harshly. "But he is beyond our power for helping. Lead us into the air."

Miriamele pulled herself up and through the hole in the mound. She emerged from the darkness into the violet of evening and a chilly wind. When she turned to extend the spear's haft down into the barrow for Binabik to clasp, she saw the creatures capering in impotent anger around the base of *Sea-Arrow,* their shadows made long and even more grotesque by torchlight. Just befor  Binabik's shoulders rose to block the hole, she caught a momentary glimpse of her grandfather's pale, serene face.

The troll huddled before the paltry fire, his face a soiled mask of loss. Miriamele tried to find her own pain and could not. She felt empty, scoured of feeling. Qantaqa, reclining nearby, cocked her head to one side as if puzzled by the silence. Her chops were sticky with gore.

"He was falling through," Binabik said slowly. "One moment he was before me, then he was gone. I was digging and digging, but there was only dirt." He shook his head. "Digging and digging. Then the *boghanik* came." He coughed and spat a glob of mud onto the fire. "So many they were, up from the dirt like worms. And more were coming always. More and more."

"You said it was a tunnel. Maybe there were other tunnels." Miriamele heard the unreal calmness of her voice with wonder. "Maybe he just fell through into another tunnel. When those things, those . . . diggers . . . go away, we can search."

"Yes, with certainty." Binabik's voice was flat.

"We'll find him. You'll see."

The troll ran his hand across his face and brought it away smeared with dirt and blood. He stared at it absently.

"There's water in the skin bag," she said. "Let me clean those cuts."

"You are also bleeding." Binabik pointed a stubby black finger at her face.

"I'll get the water." She stood on shaky legs. "We'll find Simon. You'll see."

Binabik did not reply. As Miriamele walked unsteadily toward their packs, she reached up to dab at her jaw, at the spot where the digger's claws had raked her. The blood was almost dry, but when she touched her cheeks, they were wet with tears—tears that she had not even known she was crying.

*He's gone,* she thought. *Gone.*

Her eyes blurred so that she almost stumbled.

Elias, High King of Osten Ard, stood at the window and stared up at the pale, looming finger of Green Angel Tower, silvered by moonlight. Wrapped in silence and secrecy, it seemed a specter sent from another world, a bearer of strange tidings. Elias watched it as a man who knows he will live and die a sailor watches the sea.

The king's chamber was as disorderly as an animal nest. The bed in the middle of the room was naked but for the sweat-stained pallet; the few blankets that remained lay tangled on the floor, unused, home now to whatever small creatures could bear the chilly air that Elias found more a necessity than a comfort.

The window at which the king stood, like all the other windows of the long chamber, was flung wide. Rainwater was puddled on the stone tiles beneath the casements; on some particularly cold nights it froze, making streaks of white across the floor. The wind had also carried in leaves and stems and even the stiffened corpse of a sparrow.

Elias watched the tower until the moon haloed the angel's silhouette atop the spire. At last he turned, pulling his tattered robe about him, his white skin showing through the gaps where the threads had rotted in their seams.

"Hengfisk," he whispered. "My cup."

What had seemed another clump of bedding wadded in the corner of the room now unfurled itself and stood. The silent monk scurried to a table just inside the chamber door and uncapped a stone ewer. He filled a goblet with dark, steaming liquid, then brought it to the king. The monk's ever-present smile, perhaps a little less wide than usual, glimmered faintly in the dark room.

"I shall not sleep again tonight," the king said. "It is the dreams, you know."

Hengfisk stood silently, but his bulging eyes offered complete attention.

"And there is something else. Something I can feel but cannot understand." He took his goblet and returned to the window. The hilt of the gray sword Sorrow scraped against the stone sill. Elias had not taken it off in a long time, even to sleep; the blade had pressed its own shape into the pallet beside the indentation of the king's form.

Elias raised his cup to his lips, swallowed, then sighed. "There is a change in the music," he said quietly. "The great music of the dark. Pryrates has said nothing, but I know. I do not need that eunuch to tell me everything. I can *see* things now, hear things . . . smell things." He wiped his mouth with the sleeve of his robe, leaving a new smear of black among the countless others already dried on the cloth. "Somebody has changed things." He paused for a long moment. "But perhaps Pryrates isn't merely hiding it from me." The king turned to regard his cupbearer with an expression that was almost sane. "Perhaps Pryrates himself doesn't know. It wouldn't be the only thing he doesn't know. I still have a few secrets of my own." Elias brooded. "But if Pryrates doesn't realize how ... how things have changed ... now what might *that* mean, I wonder?" He turned back to the window, watching the tower. "What might that mean?"

Hengfisk waited patiently. Finally, Elias finished his draught and held out the cup. The monk took it from the king's hand and returned it to the table beside the door, then moved back to his corner. He curled himself against the wall, but his head stayed up, as though he waited further instruction.

"The tower is waiting," Elias said quietly. "It has been waiting a long time."

As he leaned against the sill a wind arose and set his dark hair fluttering, then lifted some of the leaves from the floor and sent them whispering and rattling around the chamber.

"Oh, Father ..." the king said softly. "God of Mercy, I wish I could sleep."

For a horrifying time, Simon felt himself drowning in cold, damp earth. Every nightmare he had ever had of death and burial flooded through him as dirt filled his eyes, his nose, pinioned his arms and legs. He clawed until he could not feel his hands at the ends of his arms, but still the choking earth surrounded him.

Then, just as abruptly as the earth had swallowed him, it seemed to vomit him out once more. His legs, kicking like a drowning man's, were suddenly thrashing without resistance; an instant later he felt himself tumbling downward in a great avalanche of loose soil. He landed heavily, the breath he had held so long pushed out of him in a painful hiss. He gasped and swallowed dirt.

He was on his knees for long moments, choking and retching. When the flashes of light swarming before his eyes began to disperse, he lifted his head. There was light somewhere—not much, but enough to show him the vague outlines of a rounded space only a little wider than he was. Another tunnel? Or just a pit down in the depths, a grave of his very own where the air would soon give out?

A small flame seemed to have sprouted from the loose mound of soil upon which he crouched. That was the source of light. When he could force his trembling limbs to move, he crawled toward it and discovered that it was the tip of one of his torches, the only part of the burning brand that had not been buried in the great fall of earth. As carefully as he could, he worked his hand into the loamy earth and freed the torch, then flicked off the clinging dirt, cursing distractedly when he scorched his fingers. When it was as clean as he could get it, he turned it upside down so that the small flame could spread; soon the glow widened.

The first thing Simon saw was that he was indeed in another tunnel. In one direction it led downward, just like the one he had entered from the barrow, but *this* tunnel had no opening to the world above: the end was just beside him, a featureless spill of dirt, a great blunt nothingness of damp clods and loose soil. He could see no light or anything else beyond it; whatever gap he had fallen through was now choked with earth.

The second thing he saw was a dull glint of metal in the pile of dirt before him. He reached to pick it up, and was distractedly disappointed at how easily it came loose, how small an object it was. It was not Bright-Nail. It was a silver belt buckle.

Simon lifted the mud-smeared buckle up to catch the torchlight. When he wiped the dirt away with his fingers, he laughed, a harshly painful sound that died quickly in the narrow confines. So this was what he had risked his life for—*this* was the lure that had dropped him into the prisoning depths. The buckle was so scratched and worn that the markings were only faintly recognizable. Some kind of animal head was at the center of it, something square-snouted like a bear or pig; around it were a few slender things that might be sticks or arrows. It was old and meaningless. It was worthless.

Simon plunged his torch handle into the ground, then abruptly scrambled up the mound of soil. The sky *must* be

oomewhere above. His terror was growing strong Surely
Binabik was digging for him! But how would the troll
find him if Simon did not help!? He slid back a cubit for
every cubit he scrambled at first, until he found a way to
move without dislodging so much soil. At last he climbed
far enough that he could lay his hands against the loose
earth at the tunnel's end. He dug there frantically, freeing
a shower of dirt, but more dirt kept appearing to take its
place. As long moments passed his movements became
even more uncontrolled. He tore at the unresisting earth,
gouged it away in great handfuls, bringing down avalanches of soil from above, but all to no effect. Tears
streamed down his face, mixing with the beads of sweat
until his eyes stung. There was no end to it, no matter
how he dug.

He stopped at last, shuddering, covered in settling dirt
almost to his waist. His heart was racing so swiftly that it
took him a moment to realize that the tunnel had grown
darker. He turned to see that his heedless digging had almost buried the torch once more. Simon stared, suddenly
afraid that if he crawled back down the slope, down the
pile of loose earth, sliding soil would cover the flame
completely. Once extinguished, there would be no re-
lighting it. He would be in complete and utter blackness.

He carefully freed himself from the small landslide that
prisoned his legs, moving as delicately as he once had
while stalking frogs across the Hayholt's moat.

*Gently, gently,* he told himself. *Not the dark, no. Need
the light. There won't be anything left for them to find if
I lose the light.*

A tiny avalanche was stirred. Clods of dirt went tumbling down the pile and a small slide stopped just short of
the flame, which wavered. Simon's heart nearly stopped.

*Gently. Gently. Very gently.*

When his hands pushed into the crumbly soil beneath
the torch, he held his breath; when he had lifted it free, he
let the breath out again. There was such a narrow line—
really only a fraying edge of shadow—between the darkness and the light.

Simon went through the process of cleaning the torch

all over again, singeing the same fingers, cursing the
same curses, until he discovered that his sheathed Qanuc
knife was still strapped to his leg. After saying a prayer
in gratitude for this, what seemed his first piece of luck in
some time, he used the bone blade to finish the task. He
wondered briefly how long the torch would continue to
burn, but pushed the thought away. There was no chance
of clawing his way out, that seemed clear. So he would
move a little farther down the tunnel and wait for Binabik
and Miriamele to dig down from above. Surely they
would be doing so soon. And there was plenty of air,
when he stopped to think of it. . . .

As he tipped the torch over so that the whole head
caught fire once more, another patter of dirt came tumbling down the slope. Simon was so intent on what he
was doing that he did not look up until a second fall of
earth caught his attention. He held up the torch and
squinted at the plugged end of the tunnel. The dirt was
. . . *moving.*

Something like a tiny black tree pushed up from the
soil, flexing flat, slender branches. An instant later another sprouted next to it, then a small lump forced its way
up between them. It was a head. Blind white eyes turned
toward him and nostrils twitched. A mouth opened in a
terrible semblance of a human grin.

More hands and heads were pushing up through the
dirt. Simon, who had been staring in shocked terror,
lurched up onto his knees, holding his torch and knife before him.

*Bukken!* Diggers! His throat clenched.

There were perhaps half a dozen in all. As they freed
themselves from the loose earth they bunched together,
twittering quietly among themselves, their spindly, hairy
limbs so intertwined and their movements so twitchingly
sudden that he could not count them accurately. He
waved the torch at them and they shrank back, but not far.
They were being cautious, but they were certainly not
frightened.

*Usires Aedon,* he prayed silently. *I am in the earth with
the diggers. Save me now. Somebody please save me.*

They advanced in a clump, but then suddenly separated, skittering toward the walls. Simon shouted in fear and smacked the nearest with his torch. It shrilled in agony but leaped and wrapped its legs and arms about his wrist; sharp teeth sank into his hand so that he almost dropped the torch. His shout turning to a wordless rasp of pain, he smashed his arm against the wall of the tunnel, trying to dislodge the thing. Several more, heartened by the removal of the flame, pranced forward, piping eagerly.

Simon slashed at one and caught it with his knife, tearing at the moldy bits of rags the diggers wore like garments, cutting deeply into the meat beneath. He drove his other hand against the wall again, as hard as he could, and felt small bones break. The thing that had clutched his wrist dropped free, but Simon's hand was throbbing as though bitten by a venomous serpent.

He moved back, sliding awkwardly down the slope on his knees, struggling to keep his balance on the loosely-packed earth as the diggers ran at him. He swung his torch back and forth in a wide arc; the three creatures still standing stared back at him, shriveled little faces drawn tight, mouths open in hatred and fear. Three. And two small crumpled forms lying in the dirt where he had kneeled a moment before. So had there been only five. . . ?

Something dropped from the tunnel roof onto the top of his head. Ragged claws scraped at his face and a hand grabbed his upper lip. Simon shrieked and reached up, grabbed the squirming body as hard as he could, then pulled. After a moment's struggle it came free with several tufts of his hair clutched in its fists. Still screaming in disgust and terror, he smashed it down against the ground, then flung the broken body toward the others. He saw the remaining three tumble back into the shadows before he turned and crawled away down the tunnel as fast as he could, cursing and spluttering, spitting to rid his mouth of the vile taste of the digger's oily skin.

Simon expected any moment to feel something clutch at his legs; when he had crawled for some time he turned and raised the torch. He thought he saw a faint, pale gleam of eyes, but couldn't be sure. He turned and continued scrambling downward. Twice he dropped the torch, snatching it up as swiftly and fearfully as if it were his own heart tumbled from his breast.

The diggers did not seem to have pursued him. Simon felt some of the fear dropping away, but his heart still pounded. Beneath his hands and knees, the soil of the tunnel had become firmer.

After a while he stopped and sat back. The torchlight showed nothing following in the featureless tunnel behind him, but something was different. He looked up. The roof was much farther away—too far to touch while sitting down.

Simon took a deep breath, then another. He stayed where he was until he felt as though the air in his lungs was beginning to do him some good once more, then held up the torch and repeated his inspection. The tunnel had indeed grown wider, higher. He reached out to touch the wall and found that it was almost as solid as mud brick.

With a last look behind him, Simon struggled up onto his feet. The roof of the tunnel was a handsbreadth above his head.

Weary beyond belief, he raised the torch before him and began to walk. He knew now why Binabik and Miriamele had not been able to dig down to him. He hoped the diggers had not caught Binabik in the barrow. It was something he could not think about for more than a moment—his poor friend! The brave little man! But Simon had his own very immediate problems.

The tunnel was featureless as a rabbit warren, and led downward, ever deeper into the earth's black places. Simon desperately wanted to return to the light, to feel the wind—the last thing he wanted was to be in this place, this long, slender tomb. But there was nowhere else to go. He was alone again. He was utterly, utterly alone.

Aching in every joint, struggling to push away each dreadful thought before it could find a resting place in a mind which felt no less pained than his body, Simon plodded down into shadow.

# 13

# The Fallen Sun

✦

**Eolair stared** at the remnants of his Hernystiri troop. Of the hundred or so who had left their western land to accompany him, only a little more than two score remained. These survivors sat huddled around their fires at the base of the hillside below Naglimund, their faces gaunt, their eyes empty as dry wells.

*Look at these poor, brave men,* Eolair thought. *Who would ever know that we were winning?* The count felt as drained of blood and courage as any of them; he felt insubstantial as a ghost.

As Eolair walked from one fire to the next, a whisper of strange music came wafting down the hill. The count saw the men stiffen, then whisper unhappily among themselves. It was only the singing of the Sithi, who were walking sentry outside Naglimund's broken walls ... but even the Hernystirmen's Sithi allies were alien enough to make mortals anxious. And the Norns, the Sithi's immortal cousins, sang, too.

A fortnight of siege had razed Naglimund's walls, but the white-skinned defenders had only retreated to the inner castle, which had proved surprisingly resistant to defeat. There were forces at play that Eolair could not understand, things that even the mind of the shrewdest mortal general could not grasp—and Count Eolair, as he often reminded himself, was no general. He was a landowner, a somewhat unwilling courtier, and a skilled diplomat. Small surprise that he, like his men, felt that he was swimming in currents too powerful for his weak skills.

The Norns had established their defenses by the means of what sounded, when Jiriki described it to him, like pure magic. They had "sung a Hesitancy," Jiriki explained. There was "Shadow-mastery" at work. Until the music was understood and the shadows untangled, the castle would not fall. In the interim, clouds gathered overhead, stormed briefly, then retreated. At other times, when the skies were clear, lightning flashed and thunder boomed. The mists around Naglimund's keep sometimes seemed to become diamond hard, sparkling like glass; at other moments they turned blood red or ink black, and sent tendrils swirling high above the walls to claw at the sky. Eolair begged for explanation, but to Jiriki, what the Norns were doing—and what his own people were trying to do in retaliation—was no stranger than wooden hoardings or siege engines or any of the other machinery of humankind's wars: the Sitha terms meant little or nothing to Eolair, who could only shake his head in fearful wonder. He and his men were caught up in a battle of monsters and wizards out of bardic songs. This was no place for mortals—and the mortals knew it.

Pondering, walking in circles, the count had returned to his own fire.

"Eolair," Isorn greeted him, "I have saved the last swallows for you." He motioned the count toward the fire and held up a wineskin.

Eolair took a swallow, more out of comradeship than anything else. He had never been much of a drinker, especially when there was work to do: it was too hard to keep a cool head at a foreign court when one washed large dinners down with commensurate amounts of spirits. "Thank you." He brushed a thin skin of snow from the log and sat down, pushing his bootsoles near to the fire. "I am tired," he said quietly. "Where is Maegwin?"

"She was out walking earlier. But I am certain she has gone to sleep by now." He gestured to a tent a short distance away.

"She should not walk by herself," Eolair said.

"One of the men went with her. And she stays close by. You know I would not let her go far away, even under guard."

"I know." Eolair shook his head. "But she is so sick-spirited—it seems a criminal thing to bring her to a battlefield. *Especially* a battlefield like this." His hand swept out and gestured to the hillside and the snow, but Isorn certainly knew that it was not the terrain or weather that he meant.

The young Rimmersman shrugged. "She is mad, yes, but she seems to be more at ease than the men."

"Don't say that!" Eolair snapped. "She is not mad!" He took a shaky breath.

Isorn looked at him kindly. "If this is not madness, Eolair, what is? She speaks as though she is in the land of your gods."

"I sometimes wonder if she is not right."

Isorn lifted his arm, letting the firelight play across the jagged weal that ran from wrist to elbow. "If this is Heaven, then the priests at Elvritshalla misled me." He grinned. "But if we are dead already, then I suppose we have nothing left to fear."

Eolair shuddered. "That is just what worries me. She *does* think that she is dead, Isorn! At any moment she may walk out into the middle of the fighting again, as she did the first time she slipped away. . . ."

Isorn put a wide hand on his shoulder. "Her madness seems more clever to me than that. And she may not be as terrified as the men, but she is not unafraid. She doesn't like that damned windy castle or those damned, filthy white things any more than we do. She has been safe so far and we will keep her that way. Surely you do not need more things to worry about?"

The count smiled wearily. "So, Isorn Isgrimnurson, you are going to take up your father's job, I see."

"What do you mean?"

"I have seen what your father does for Josua. Picks the prince up when he wants to lie down, pokes his ribs and sings him songs when the prince wants to weep. So you will be my Isgrimnur?"

The Rimmersman's grin was wide. "My father and I are simple men. We do not have the brains to worry like you and Josua."

Eolair snorted and reached out for the wineskin.

For the third night running, the count dreamed of the most recent skirmish inside Naglimund's walls, a nightmare more vivid and terrifying than anything mere imagination could contrive.

It had been a particularly dreadful battle. The Hernystirmen, now wearing masks of cloth rubbed with fat or tree sap to keep off the Norn's madness-dust, had become as frightening to look at as the rest of the combatants; those mortals who had survived the first days of the siege now fought with terrified determination, knowing that nothing else would give them a chance of leaving this haunted place alive. The greatest part of the struggle had taken place in the narrow spaces between scorched, crumbling buildings and through winter-blasted gardens—places where Eolair had once walked on warm evenings with ladies of Josua's court.

The dwindling army of Norns defended the stolen citadel with a kind of heedless madness: Count Eolair had seen one of them shove forward against a sword rammed through his chest, working his way up the blade to kill the mortal that clutched the hilt before dying in a coughing spray of red.

Most of the giants had also died, but each one exacted a horrible toll of men and Sithi before it fell. Dreaming, remembering, Eolair was again forced to watch one of the huge brutes grab Ule Frekkeson, one of the few Rimmersmen who had accompanied the war party out of Hernysadharc, then swing him around and dash his brains out against a wall as easily as a man might kill a cat. As a trio of Sithi surrounded him, the Hunë contemptuously shook the almost headless corpse at them, showering them with gore. The hairy giant then used Ule's body as a club, killing one of the Sithi with it before the spears of the other two punched into the monster's heart.

Squirming in the dream's unshakable grasp, Eolair

helplessly watched dead Ule used as a weapon, smashed left and right until his body began to come apart. . . .

He woke quivering, head throbbing as though it might burst. He pressed his hands against his temples and squeezed, trying to relieve the pressure. How could a man see such things and keep his reason?

A hand touched his wrist.

Terrified, Eolair gasped and flung himself to one side, scrabbling for his sword. A tall shadow loomed in the doorway of his tent.

"Peace, Count Eolair," said Jiriki. "I am sorry I startled you. I called from outside the door, but I thought you must be asleep since you did not reply. Please forgive my intrusion."

Eolair was relieved, but angry and embarrassed. "What do you want?"

"Forgive me, please. I came because it is important and time is short."

The count shook his head and took a slow breath. "What is it? Is something wrong?"

"Likimeya asks that you come. All will be explained." He lifted the tent flap and stepped back outside. "Will you come? I will wait for you to dress."

"Yes . . . yes, certainly I will."

The count felt a sort of muted pride. Likimeya had sent her son for him, and since these days Jiriki seemed involved only in things of the first and most crucial order, the Sithi must indeed think it important that Eolair come. A moment later his pride turned to a gnawing of disquiet: could circumstances be so bad that they were searching for ideas or leadership from the master of two score terrified mortal warriors? He had been sure they were winning the siege.

It took only a few moments to secure his sword belt and pull on his boots and fur-lined cloak. He followed Jiriki across the foggy hillside, marveling that the footfalls of the Sitha, who was as tall as Eolair and almost as broad, should only dimple the snow while his own boots dug deep gouges in the white crust.

Eolair looked up to where Naglimund crouched on the

hilltop like a huddled, wounded beast. It was almost impossible to believe that it had once been a place where people danced and talked and loved. Prince Josua's court had been thought by some rather grim—but, oh, how those who had mocked the prince would feel their mouths dry and their hearts flutter if they saw what grim *truly* meant.

Jiriki led the count among the gossamer-thin tents of the Sithi, tents that gleamed against the snow as though they were half-soaked in moonlight. Despite the hour, halfway between midnight and dawn, many of the Fair Folk were out; they stood in solemn clusters and stared at the sky or sat on the ground singing quietly. None of them seemed at all bothered by the freezing wind that had Eolair clutching his hood close beneath his chin. He hoped that Likimeya had a fire burning, if only out of consideration for the frailties of a mortal visitor.

"We have questions to ask you about this place you call Naglimund, Count Eolair." There was more than a hint of command in Likimeya's voice.

Eolair turned from the blaze to face Jiriki, his mother, and tall, black-haired Kuroyi. "What can I tell you that I have not told you already?" The count felt a mild anger at the Sithi's confusing habits, but found it hard to hold that emotion in the presence of Likimeya's powerful, even gaze. "And is it not a little late to be asking, since the siege began a fortnight ago?"

"It is not such things as the height of walls and the depth of wells that we need to know." Jiriki sat down beside the count, the cloth of his thin shirt glinting. "You have already told us much that has helped us."

"You spent time in Naglimund when the mortal prince Josua ruled here." Likimeya spoke briskly, as though impatient with her son's attempts at diplomacy. "Does it have secrets?"

"Secrets?" Eolair shook his head. "Now I am completely confounded. What do you mean?"

"This is not fair to the mortal." Kuroyi spoke with an emotionless reserve that was extreme even for the Sithi.

"He deserves to know more. If Zinjadu had lived, she could tell him. Since I failed my old friend and she is now voyaging with the Ancestors, I will take her place as the lore-giver." He turned to Likimeya. "If Year-Dancing House approves, of course."

Likimeya made a wordless musical noise, then flicked her hand in permission.

"Jiriki i-Sa'onserei has told you something of the Road of Dreams, Count Eolair?" Kuroyi asked.

"Yes, he has told me a little. Also, we Hernystiri still have many stories of the past and of your people. There are those living among us who claim they can walk the Dream Road, just as you taught our ancestors to do." He thought sourly of Maegwin's would-be mentor, the scryer Diawen: if some Hernystiri did still have that power, it had little to do with good sense or responsibility.

"Then I am sure he has spoken of the Witnesses, too—those objects that we use to make the journeying easier." Kuroyi hesitated, then reached into his milk-white shirt and produced a round, translucent yellow object that caught the firelight like a globule of amber or a ball of melted glass. "This is one such—my own." He let Eolair look for a moment, then tucked the thing away again. "Like most others, it is of no use in these strange times— the Dream Road is as impassable as a road of this world might be in a terrible blizzard.

"But there are other Witnesses, too: larger, more powerful objects that are not moveable, and are linked to the place where they are found. Master Witnesses, they are called, for they can look upon many things and places. You have seen one such."

"The Shard?"

Kuroyi nodded his head once. "In Mezutu'a, yes. There were others, although most are now lost to time and earth-changes. One lies beneath the castle of your enemy King Elias."

"Beneath the Hayholt?"

"Yes. The Pool of Three Depths is its name. But it has been dry and voiceless for centuries."

"And this has something to do with Naglimund? Is there something of that sort here?"

Kuroyi smiled, a narrow, wintery smile. "We are not sure."

"I don't understand," the count said. "How can you not be sure?"

The Sitha lifted his long-fingered hand. "Peace, Eolair of Nad Mullach. Let me finish my tale. By the standards of the Gardenborn it is quite short."

Eolair shifted slightly; he was glad for the firelight, which disguised his flush of embarrassment. How was it that among these folk he was as easily cowed as a child—as if all his years of statecraft had been forgotten? "My apologies."

"There have always been in Osten Ard certain places," Kuroyi resumed, "which act much like Master Witnesses . . . but in which no Master Witness seems to be present. That is; many of the effects are there—in fact, sometimes these places exhibit more powerful results than *any* Witness—but no object can be found which is responsible. Since we first came to this land long ago, we have studied such places, thinking that they might answer questions we have about the Witnesses and why they do what they do, about Death itself, even about the Unbeing that made us flee our native land and come here."

"Forgive me for interrupting again," said Eolair, "but how many of these places exist? And where are they?"

"We know of only a handful between far Nascadu and the wastelands of the white north. *A-Genay'asu'e,* we call them—"Houses of Traveling Beyond" would be a crude rendering in your tongue. And we Gardenborn are not the only ones to sense the power of these places: they often draw mortals as well, some merely seekers-after-knowledge, some god-maddened and dangerous. What mortals call Thisterborg, the hill near Asu'a, is one such spot."

"I know it." Remembering a black sled and a team of misshapen white goats, Eolair felt his flesh tighten. "Your cousins the Norns also know about Thisterborg. I saw them there."

Kuroyi did not seem surprised. "We Gardenborn have been interested in these sites since long before the families parted. The Hikeda'ya, like us, have made many attempts to harness the might of such places. But their power is as wild and unpredictable as the wind."

Eolair pondered. "So there is not a Master Witness here at Naglimund, but rather one of these things, a ... Beyonding House? I cannot remember the words in your tongue."

Jiriki looked toward his mother, smiling and nodding with what almost looked like pride. Eolair felt a flash of annoyance; was a mortal who could listen and reason such a surprise to them?

"An *A-Genay'asu*. Yes, that is what we believe," said Kuroyi. "But it came to our attention late, and there was never a chance to find out before the mortals came."

"Before the mortals came with their iron spikes." Likimeya's soft voice was like the hiss that preceded a whip-crack. Surprised by her vehemence, Eolair looked up, then just as quickly turned his gaze back to Kuroyi's more placid face.

"Both Zida'ya and Hikeda'ya continued to come to this place after men built their castle here at Naglimund," the black-haired Sitha explained. "Our presence frightened the mortals, though they saw us only by moonlight, and even then only rarely. The man the Imperators had given to rule over the locality filled the fields all around with the iron that gave the place its name: Nail Fort."

"I knew that the nails were there to keep out the Peaceful Ones—what we Hernystiri call your folk," said Eolair, "but since it was built in the era when your people and ours were at peace, I could not understand why the place should have needed such defenses."

"The mortal named Aeswides who had it done may have felt a certain shame that he had trespassed on our lands in building this keep so close to our city Da'ai Chikiza, on the far side of those hills." Kuroyi gestured toward the east. "He may have feared that we would some day come and take the place back; he may also have thought that those of our folk who still made pilgrimage to this place were spies. Who knows? In fact, he traveled less and less out of the gates, and died at last a recluse—afraid, it was said, even to leave his own well-guarded chamber for terror of what the dreaded immortals might do." Kuroyi's cool smile returned. "Strangely, although the world is already full of fearful things, mortals seem always to hunt for new worries."

"Nor do we relinquish the old ones." Eolair returned the tall Sitha's smile. "For, like the cut of a man's cloak, we know that the tried and true is best in the long run. But I doubt you have brought me here only to tell about what some long-dead mortal did."

"No, we have not," Kuroyi agreed. "Since we were driven from the land at a time when we considered it better policy not to interfere, and to let the mortals build where they wished, we have unanswered questions still about this place."

"And we need those questions answered now, Count Eolair," Likimeya broke in. "So tell us: this place you call Naglimund—is it known among mortals for strangeness of any kind? Apparitions? Odd happenings? Is it reputed a haunt of spirits of the dead?"

The count frowned as he considered. "I must say that I have never heard anything like that. There are other places, many others, some within a league of my birth-place, of which I could tell you a whole night's worth of tales. But not Naglimund. And Prince Josua was always a lover of odd lore—I feel sure that if there were such stories, it would have been his pleasure to relate them." He shook his head. "I am sorry to force you to tell such a long tale yourself for so little result."

"We still think it likely that this place *is* an A-Genay'asu," Jiriki said. "We have thought so since long before Asu'a fell. Here, Count Eolair, you look thirsty. Let me pour for you."

The Hernystirman gratefully accepted another cup of mulled ... something; whatever it was, it tasted of flowers and warmed him very nicely. "In any case," he said after he had taken a few sips, "what does it mean if Naglimund *is* such a place?"

"We are not certain. That is one of the things that worries us." Jiriki sat down across from Eolair and raised a slim hand. "We had hoped that the Hikeda'ya came here only to pay their part of the bargain with Elias, and that they had remained here because it was a way station between Stormspike and the castle that stands on Asu'a's bones."

"But you do not think that any longer." It was a statement, not a question.

"No. Our cousins have fought too hard, long past the time when they could have gained anything from resisting. This is not the final confrontation. However much Utuk'ku has reason to hate us, it is not a blind anger: she would not throw away the lives of so many Cloud Children to hold a useless ruin."

Eolair had not heard much about the Norn Queen, Utuk'ku, but what he had was shuddersome. "So what does she want? What do *they* want?"

Jiriki shook his head. "They want to remain in Naglimund. That is all we know for certain. And it will be dreadful work to drive them out. I fear for you and your remaining soldiers, Count Eolair. I fear for all of us."

A horrible thought occurred to the Hernystirman. "Forgive me, since I know little of these things—although perhaps more now than I would have wished—but you said that these Beyonding places had something to do with the secrets of . . . of death?"

"All mysteries are one mystery until they are solved." said Kuroyi. "We have tried to learn more about Death and Unbeing from the A-Genay'asu'e, yes."

"These Norns we are fighting are living creatures—but their master is not. Could they be trying to bring the Storm King . . . back to life?"

Eolair's question brought neither derisive laughter nor shocked silence.

"We have thought on this." Likimeya was blunt. "It cannot happen."

"Ineluki is dead." Kuroyi spoke more softly, but with equal firmness. "There are some things we know about only little, but death we know very well." His lips twitched in a tiny, dry smile. "Very well, indeed. Ineluki is dead. He cannot return to this world."

"But you told me he was in Stormspike," Eolair said to Jiriki. "You said that the Norns do as he bids. Are we at war against something imaginary?"

"It is indeed confusing, Count Eolair," Jiriki replied. "Ineluki—although he is not truly Ineluki any more—has no more existence than a sort of dream. He is an evil and vengeful dream, one that possesses all the craftiness that the Storm King had in life, as well as knowledge of the ultimate darknesses no living thing has ever had ... but he is only a dream, for all of that. Trust that I speak truly. As we can travel on the Road of Dreams, and see and feel things there, so Ineluki can speak to his followers in Nakkiga through the Breathing Harp, which is one of the greatest of the Master Witnesses—although I would guess that Utuk'ku alone has the skill even to understand him. So he is not a thing, Eolair, with an existence in this world." He gestured to the walls of the tent. "He is not real, like this cloth is real, like the ground is real beneath our feet. But that does not mean he cannot do great evil ... and Utuk'ku and her servitors are more than real enough."

"Forgive me if I seem stubborn," Eolair said, "but I have heard much tonight that is still confused in my head. If Ineluki cannot return, then why are the Norns so eager to hold Naglimund?"

"That is the question we must answer," said Jiriki. "Perhaps they hope to use the A-Genay'asu to make their master's voice clearer. Perhaps they intend to tap its force in some other way. But it is clear that they want this place very much. One of the Red Hand is here."

"The Red Hand? The Storm King's servants?"

"His greatest servants, since like him they have passed through death and into the outer realms. But they cannot exist in this world without an immense expenditure of power by him every moment they are embodied, for they are almost as much of a deadly contradiction as he is. That is why when one of them attacked us in our fastness at Jao é Tinukai'i, we knew that the time had come to take up arms. Ineluki and Utuk'ku must have been desperate to expend so much force to silence Amerasu." He paused. Eolair stared, bewildered by the unfamiliar names. "I will explain this to you at a later time, Count Eolair." Jiriki stood. "I am sure you are weary, and we have talked much of your sleeping time away."

"But this Red Hand creature is here? Have you seen it?"

Jiriki pointed at the campfire. "Do you have to touch the flames to know that the fire is hot? He is here, and that is why we have not been able to overcome their most important defenses, why we must instead knock down stone walls and struggle with sword and spear. A large portion of Ineluki's power is burning down in the heart of Naglimund's keep. But for all his might, the Storm King has limits. He is spread thin . . . so there must be some reason he wishes this place to remain in the hands of the Hikeda'ya."

Eolair stood, too. The blur of strange ideas and names had begun to tell on him: he was indeed feeling the need for sleep. "Perhaps the Norns' task is something to do with the Red Hand, then," the count said. "Perhaps . . ."

Jiriki's smile was sad. "We have cursed you with our own plague of 'perhaps,' Count Eolair. We had hoped you would give us answers, but instead we have weighed you down with questions."

"I have not been free of them since old King John died." He stifled a yawn. "So this is nothing strange." He laughed. "What a thing to say! It is *maddeningly* strange. But not unusual. Not in these times."

"Not in these times," agreed Jiriki.

Eolair bowed to Likimeya, then nodded a farewell to stone-faced Kuroyi before walking out into the cold wind. Thoughts were buzzing in his head like flies, but he knew that nothing useful could be done about any of them. Sleep was what he needed. Perhaps, if he was lucky, he would sleep right through the remainder of this gods-cursed siege.

Maegwin had quietly left her tent while the weary guard—he seemed a sad and ragged sort to have received Heaven's favor, but who was she to question the gods?—gossiped by the fire with one of his fellows. Now she stood in the deep shadows of a copse of trees, not a hundred cubits downslope from the tumbled walls of Naglimund. Above her loomed the silhouette of the blocky stone keep. As she stared at it, wind sifted snow across her boots.

*Scadach,* she thought. *It is the Hole in Heaven. But what lies beyond?*

She had seen the demons that had come swarming through from the Outer Darkness—horrible corpse-white things and shaggy, monstrous ogres—and had watched the gods and a few dead mortal heroes fight with them. It was clear that the gods wished this wound in heaven's flesh healed so that no more evil could creep in. For a while it had seemed that the gods would win easily. Now she was not so sure.

There was . . . *something* inside Scadach. Something dark and hideously strong, something that was empty as a flame is empty, but that nevertheless had a kind of brooding life. She could feel it, could almost hear its dreadful ruminations; even the faint part of its brooding that licked against her mind cast her into despair. But at the same time, there was something oddly familiar about the thoughts of whatever lurked in Scadach, whatever godsbane burned so angrily in the deeps. She felt strangely drawn, as to a darkly fascinating sibling: that horrid something . . . was much like her.

But what could that mean? What a mad thought! What could there be in that gnawing, spiteful heat that was *anything* like her, a mortal woman, king's daughter, slain beloved of the gods now privileged to ride with them across the fields of heaven?

Maegwin stood in the snow, silent, motionless, and let the incomprehensible thoughts of the thing within Scadach wash over her. She felt its turmoil. Hatred, that was what it felt       and something more. A hatred of the living coupled with an agonized longing for quietude and death.

She shivered. How could heaven be so cold, even in this black outer fringe?

*But I don't long for death! Perhaps I did when I was alive, for a time. But now that is behind me. Because I died—I died—and the gods lifted me up to their country. Why should I still feel that so strongly? I am dead. I am no longer afraid, as I once was. I did my duty and brought the gods to save my people—no one can say I did not. I no longer mourn for my brother and father. I am dead, and nothing can harm me. I have nothing in common with that . . . thing out there in the darkness, beyond those walls of heaven-stone.*

A sudden thought came to her. *But where is my father? And where is Gwythinn? Didn't they both die heroes? Surely the gods have lifted them up and carried them away after their deaths, just as they did me. And surely they would have demanded to be allowed to fight here, at the side of the Masters of Heaven. Where are they?*

Maegwin stood, dumbfounded. She shivered again. It was wretchedly cold here. Were the gods playing some trick on her? Was there still some test she had yet to pass before she could be reunited with her father and brother, with her long-dead mother Penemhwye? How could that be?

Troubled, Maegwin turned and hurried back down the slope toward the lights of the other homeless souls.

♛

More than five hundred pikemen of Metessa stood shoulder to shoulder in the neck of the Onestrine Pass, shields lifted above their heads so that it seemed some great centipede had lodged in the narrows between the cliffs. The baron's men wore boiled leather cuirasses and iron helms, armor that was nicked and abraded from long use. The Crane banner of their House waved above the serried pikes.

Nabbanai bowmen along the canyon walls filled the sky with a swarm of arrows. Most bounced harmlessly from the shield roof, but some found their way through the locked shields. Wherever a Metessan fell, though, his fellows drew together.

"The bowmen cannot move them!" Sludig enthused. "Varellan must charge! By the Aedon, the baron's men are proud bastards!" He turned to Isgrimnur with a look of glee on his face. "Josua has chosen his allies well!"

The duke nodded, but could not match Sludig's excitement. As he stood with the elite of Josua's forces, what was now being called the prince's household guard—a curious phrase Isgrimnur thought, considering the prince had no house—the duke only wanted the fighting to end. He was tired of war.

As he stared out across the narrowing valley, he was struck by how the ridged hills on both sides resembled a cage of ribs, the Anitullean Road its breastbone. When Prester John had fought his way through to victory in this same Frasilis Valley more than fifty years before, it was said that so many had died that the bodies were not all buried for months. The pass and the open land to the north of the valley had been littered with bones, the sky black with carrion birds for days.

*And to what purpose?* Isgrimnur wondered. *Less than a man's lifetime has passed and here we are again, making more feasts for the vultures. Over and over and over. I am sick with it.*

He sat uncomfortably in the saddle, looking down the length of the pass. Below him stood the waiting ranks of the prince's newest allies, their house banners bright in the noon sun, an aviary of Goose, Pheasant, Tern, and Grouse. Seriddan's neighboring barons had not been slow to follow his lead: none seemed happy with Duke Benigaris, and the resurrected Camaris was difficult to ignore.

Isgrimnur was struck by the circularity of the situation. Josua's forces were led by a man thought long-dead, and they were fighting a crucial battle in the very place where Prester John, Josua's father and Camaris' closest friend, had won his greatest triumph. It should have been a good omen, Isgrimnur thought ... but instead he felt the past reaching up to squeeze the life out of the present, as though History was some great and jealous monster that wished to force all that followed after into unhappy mimicry.

*This is no life for an old man.* The duke sighed. Sludig, watching raptly as the battle developed, was oblivious. *To fight a war, you must believe it can accomplish something. We fight this one to save John's kingdom, or perhaps even to save all of mankind ... but isn't that what we always think? That all wars are useless—except the one we're fighting now?*

He fingered his reins. His back was stiff, sore already, and he had not even put it to any hard work. Kvalnir hung sheathed at his side, untouched since he had sharpened it and polished it in the sleepless hours last night.

*I'm just tired,* he thought. *I want Elvritshalla back. I want to see my grandchildren. I want to walk with my wife by the Gratuvask when the ice is breaking up. But I can have none of those things until this damnable fighting is over.*

*And that is why we do it,* he decided. *Because we hope it will bring us peace. But it never, never does....*

Sludig cried out. Isgrimnur looked up, startled, but his carl's shout had been one of glee.

"Look! Camaris and the horsemen are coming down on them!"

When it had become clear that bowshot would not dislodge Seriddan's Metessan shield wall from the center of the pass, Varellan of Nabban had ordered another charge by his knights. Now that Varellan's forces had committed themselves to pushing the prince's troops back down the valley, Camaris and Hotvig's Thrithings-men had come down from the hillroads and thrown themselves into the side of Varellan's larger force.

"Where is Camaris?" Sludig said. "Ah! There! I see his helm!"

Isgrimnur could see it, too. The sea-dragon was little more than a flaming smear of gold from this distance, but its wearer stood tall in his stirrups, a visible circle of dismay spreading around him as the Nabbanai knights struggled to stay out of Thorn's black reach.

Prince Josua, who had been watching the battle from a point about a hundred cubits downslope from Isgrimnur and Sludig, now turned Vinyafod toward them. "Sludig!" he called. "Tell Freosel I want his troop to wait until he counts his fingers ten times after I give the sign for the rest of us to charge."

"Yes, Highness." Sludig wheeled his steed around and jogged toward where Freosel and the rest of Josua's household troop stood in fretting anticipation.

The prince continued upslope until he was at Isgrimnur's side. "Varellan's youth is finally beginning to show. He has proved himself overeager."

"There are worse faults in a commander," Isgrimnur replied, "but you're right. He should have been content to hold the mouth of the pass."

"But he thought he saw a weakness when he threw us back yesterday." Josua squinted up at the sky. "Now he is committed to pushing us back. We are lucky. Benigaris, for all his rashness in other matters, would never have taken such a risk."

"Then why did he take the chance of sending little brother in the first place?"

Josua shrugged. "Who knows? Perhaps he underestimated us. Remember also that Benigaris does not rule alone in Nabban."

Isgrimnur grunted. "Poor Leobardis. What did he do to deserve such a wife and son?"

"Again, who knows? But perhaps there is some end that we cannot see to all this."

The duke shrugged.

The prince was watching the flow of the battle critically, eyes shadowed in the depths of his helm. He had drawn Naidel, which lay across his saddle and knee. "Almost time," he said. "Almost time."

"They are still many more than us, Josua." Isgrimnur pulled Kvalnir from its sheath. There remained a momentary pleasure in this: the blade had stood him well in many a contest, witnessed by the fact that he was still here, still alive, with aching back and chafing armor and doubts and all.

"But we have Camaris—and you, old friend." Josua grinned tightly. "We can ask for no better odds." His gaze had not left the neck of the pass. "May Usires the Ransomer preserve us." The prince solemnly made the sign of the Tree on his breast, then lifted his hand. Naidel caught the sunlight, and for a moment Isgrimnur found it hard to breathe. "To me, men!" Josua cried.

A horn sounded on the slopes above him. From the narrows of the pass, Cellian blared back an answer.

As the prince's troops and the rebel barons and their men charged up the road, Isgrimnur could not help marveling. They had become a real army at last, several thousand strong. When he remembered how it had begun, Josua and a dozen other bedraggled survivors slipping out of Naglimund through a back door, he felt heartened. Surely God the Merciful could not bring them so far only to dash their hopes!

The Metessans had held firm. Josua and his army swirled around and past them; the pikemen, freed from their deadly chore, dragged their wounded back down the road. The prince's forces flung themselves on Varellan's knights, whose superior numbers and heavy armor had been overwhelming even the ferocity of Camaris and the Thrithings-men.

Isgrimnur held back at first, lending aid where he could, but unwilling to throw himself into the thick, where lives seemed to be measured in instants. He spotted one of Hotvig's men unhorsed, standing over his dying steed and warding off the pike of a mounted knight. Isgrimnur rode forward, bellowing a challenge; when the Nabbanai knight heard him and turned, the Thrithings-man leapt forward and shoved his sword in beneath the man's arm where there was no shielding metal on his leather coat. As the knight toppled, bleeding, Isgrimnur felt a twitch of fury at his ally's dishonorable tactic, but when the rescued man shouted his thanks and legged down the slope, back into the heart of the struggle, the duke did not know any longer what to think. Should the Thrithings-man have died to preserve the lie that war could be honorable? But did another man deserve death because he believed that lie?

Slowly, as the afternoon turned, Isgrimnur found himself drawn deeper into the bloody conflict, slaying one man and driving several others back, bloodily wounded. He sustained only minor hurts himself, but only because luck was with him. He had stumbled once, and his opponent's swinging two-handed sword blow had glanced off the top of his helm; had he not fallen, it would likely have separated head from neck. Isgrimnur fought with none of his old battle rage, but fear brought out a strength he had forgotten he had. It was like the ghant nest all over again: everywhere he turned there were hard-shelled things that wanted to kill him.

Upslope, Josua and his knights had pushed Varellan's force back almost to the outer lip of the pass. Surely, thought Isgrimnur, some of those who fought in the front line must be able to see the broad valley below, green in the sunlight—except that to look at anything except the man in front of you and his weapon was to court swift death.

The knights of Nabban bent, but did not give. If they had made a mistake in trying to push their earlier advantage, they would make no mistake now. Whatever Prince Josua wanted, it was clear that he and his army would have to take it with their own hands.

As the sun began to dip down toward the horizon, Isgrimnur momentarily found himself in a backwater of the fighting, a spot in which the struggle had ended for a time; all around the bodies of murdered men lay sprawled like the leavings of a receding tide.

Just down the hill Isgrimnur saw a gleam of gold: it was Camaris. The duke watched him in amazement. Hours since the battle had begun, and although his movements seemed a little slower, still the old knight fought on with undiminished purpose. Camaris sat upright in his saddle, his movements as regular and unexcited as those of a farmer at work in his field. The battle horn swung at his side. Thorn whistled through the air like a black scythe, and where it touched, headless bodies fell like harvested wheat.

*He's not as fierce as he ever was,* Isgrimnur marveled, *he's fiercer. He fights like a damned soul. What is in that man's head? What gnaws at his heart?*

Isgrimnur suddenly felt shame that he stood watching as Camaris, twenty years his senior, fought and bled. The most important battle, perhaps, that had ever been fought, and it still hung in the balance, unclaimed. He was needed. Old and tired of war he might be, but he was still an experienced blade.

He lightly dug his spurs into his mount's side, heading toward the place where Sir Camaris now kept three foot soldiers at bay. It was a spot blocked from view by a web of low trees. Even though he had little doubt that Camaris could hold out until others reached him, it might be some while before they spotted him ... and in any case, Camaris in the saddle was an inspiration to the rest of Josua's troops that would be a shame to waste behind concealing shrubbery.

Before he had gone more than a dozen cubits, Isgrimnur saw an arrow suddenly sprout from his horse's chest, just before his leg; the horse reared, shrilling with agony. Isgrimnur felt a burning pain in his own side, then a moment later he was tumbling free of his saddle. The ground rose up and hit him like a club. His horse, struggling for balance on the rocky slope, wavered above him with front legs flailing, then its shadow descended.

The last thing Isgrimnur saw and felt was a tremendous concussion of light, as though the sun had dropped from the sky to land on top of him.

# 14

# Empires of Dust

✿

**It was maddening.** Simon was parched, his mouth dry as bone dust, and all around him echoed the sound of dripping water . . . but there was no water to be found. It was as though some demon had looked into his thoughts, then plucked out his fondest desire and turned it into a cruel trick.

He stopped, peering into the darkness. The tunnel had widened, but still led downward, and there had been no place to turn, no crossing corridors. Whatever made that dripping was now behind him, as though he had passed it somehow in the featureless shadows.

*But that can't be! The sound was before me, and now it's behind me—but it was never* beside *me.* Simon fought to keep down his fear, which felt like a living thing inside him, all tiny clicking scales and scrabbling claws.

He might be lost beneath the ground, he told himself, but he was not dead. He had been trapped in tunnels like these before and had come out into the sun again. And now he was older; he had seen things that few others had seen. Somehow, he would survive. And if he didn't? Then he would face the end without shame.

*Brave words, mooncalf,* an inner voice mocked him. *Brave words now. But when a sunless day and a moonless night pass with no water? When the torch burns out?*

*Be quiet,* he told the inner voice.

✿

*"King John went down the darksome hole."*

Simon sang quietly. His throat hurt, but he was growing tired of the monotony of his bootheels clumping against the stone. Not to mention the miserable, lonely way the sound made him feel.

*"To seek the fiery beast below,*
*Through caveish haunt of toad and troll,*
*Where none but he had dared to go ..."*

Simon frowned. If only this *were* the haunt of trolls. He would have given anything for Binabik's companionship—not to mention a skin full of water followed by a healthy swallow of *kangkang*. And if Prester John had brought nothing but a sword down into the earth—which he hadn't, come to think of it: wasn't that what the Hernystirman Eolair had come to Sesuad'ra to tell them? That John had found Minneyar somewhere down in the ground?—then what had he done for light? Simon had one torch, and its flame was beginning to look a little thin around the edges. It was all very well to go thumping and bumping about looking for dragons, but the songs never said much about food and water and trying to make fires.

Old cradle songs and missing swords and tunnels in the dark, fetid earth. How had his life ever come to revolve around such things? When Simon had prayed for knightly adventures, he had hoped for more noble things—battlefields and gleamingly polished armor, deeds of bravery, the love of the multitudes. He had found those, more or less, but they had not been what he had expected. And time and time again he was drawn back into this madness of swords and tunnels, as though he were being forced to play some childhood game long past the point where he had tired of it. ...

His shoulder bumped against the wall and he almost fell. The torch dropped from his grasp and lay on the tunnel floor. Simon stared at it stupidly for a moment before suddenly regaining his senses. He snatched it up and held it tightly, as though the torch itself had tried to escape.

*Mooncalf.*

He sat down heavily. He was tired of walking, tired of empty nothingness and solitude. The tunnel had become a winding hole through irregular slabs of rock, which likely meant he was now deep among the bones of Swertclif; he seemed to be bound for the center of the earth.

Something in his pocket chafed against his leg, catching his attention. What was he carrying? He had been stumbling down these passageways for what seemed like hours, and he had not even bothered to see what oddments he had brought with him when he fell through the crumbling earth.

Emptying out the pockets stitched on his breeches, wincing and making soft sounds at the stinging of his abraded fingers, he discovered that he had not missed much by postponing his inventory. There was a stone, a round smooth one that he had picked up because he liked the heft of it, and the almost featureless belt buckle, which he had thought he discarded. He decided to keep it, thinking vaguely that it could be used for scratching or digging.

The only significant find was a bit of dried meat from yesterday's mid-afternoon meal. He looked longingly at the wrinkled strip, which was about the length and width of his finger, then put it aside. He had a feeling that he would want it more later than he did even now.

That accounted for his pockets. The gold ring Morgenes had sent to him was still on his finger, almost invisible under a layer of dirt, but whatever use or significance it might have in the world of sunlight was meaningless here: he could not eat it, and it would not frighten an enemy. His Qanuc knife was still in the sheath tied to his leg. Other than that and the torch, he was truly defenseless. His sword was somewhere above the ground—with Binabik and Miriamele, if they had escaped the diggers—along with his White Arrow, his cloak, his armor, and the rest of his meager possessions. He was nearly as empty-handed as when he had fled the castle almost a year before. And he was back in the black earth again. In the smothering earth . . .

*Stop it*, he ordered himself. *What was it Morgenes said? "Not what's in your hands, but what's in your head." That's something, anyway. I have a lot more in my head than I did then.*

*But what good will it do me if I die of thirst?*

He struggled to his feet and began walking again. He had no idea where the tunnel might lead, but it must lead somewhere. It must. The possibility that this direction might finish as the other end had, in an impenetrable wall of fallen dirt or stone, was not something he could afford to consider.

*"Down pitch-black pit went young King John."*

Simon sang again, quieter than before,

*"Where Fire-Drake lurked on hoard of gold,*
*And no one knew that he had gone,*
*For not a person had he told . . ."*

It was strange. Simon did not *feel* mad, but he was hearing things that were not truly there. The sound of splashing water had returned, louder and more forceful than before, but now it seemed to come from all sides, as though he walked through the curtain of a waterfall. Mixed with it, just barely separable from the hiss and spatter, was the murmur of speech.

*Voices! Perhaps there are cross-tunnels somewhere nearby. Perhaps they lead to people. To real, living people . . .*

The voices and the water-sounds stayed with him for a time without revealing their source, then faded away, leaving him again with the noise of his footsteps as his only company.

Confused and weary, frightened by what the phantom sounds might mean, he almost stepped into a hole in the tunnel floor. He tripped and then caught himself, braced his hand against the wall, and stared down. The light of another torch seemed to gleam in the depths below, and for a moment he thought his heart would stop.

"Who . . . Who's th . . ." As he leaned down, the light below him seemed to rise.

A reflection. *Water.*

Simon dropped to his knees and pushed his face toward the tiny pool, then stopped as its smell came up to him, oily and unpleasant. He dipped his fingers in and brought them out. The water seemed oddly slippery on his skin. He brought the torch forward for a better look. A sheet of flame leapt up and slapped hotly against his face; he shouted in pain and surprise as he tumbled backward. For a moment it seemed the whole world had caught fire.

Sitting splay-legged on the ground, he lifted his hand to his cheek and felt gingerly across his features. The skin was as tender as if he had been too long in the sun, and he could feel the hairs of his beard turned crisp and curled, but everything seemed to be in its proper place. He looked down to see a flame dancing in the hole in the tunnel floor.

*Usires Aedon!* he cursed silently. *Mooncalf's luck. I find water and it's the kind that burns—whatever that is.*

A tear coursed down his hot cheek.

Whatever was in the pool was burning merrily. Simon stared at it, so disappointed to find his drinking water undrinkable that he could not for a long time make sense of what he was seeing. At last, something Morgenes had once said came back to him.

*Perdruinese Fire—that's what it is. The doctor said it's found in caves. The Perdruin-folk used to make catapult balls of it and throw it at their enemies and burn them to cracklings.* That was the kind of history lesson that Simon had paid close attention to—the sort where interesting things happened. *If I had more sticks and more rags, I could use it to make torches.*

Shaking his head, he clambered to his feet and started down the tunnel once more. After a few paces he stopped and shook his head again.

*Mooncalf. Stupid mooncalf.*

He returned to the burning pool and sat down, then took off his shirt and began to tear strips of cloth from the hem. The Perdruinese Fire was pleasantly warm.

*Rachel would skin me if she saw me ruining a perfectly good shirt.* He giggled too loudly. The echoes rolled down the corridor into empty darkness. *It would be good to see Rachel again,* he realized. The idea seemed strange but indisputable.

When he had a dozen strips—his shirt now ended not far beneath his armpits—he sat and stared at the flames for a moment, trying to decide how to dip the cloth without burning the skin off his hands. He considered using the torch but decided against it. He had no idea how deep this hole in the tunnel ran and he was afraid he might drop the brand. Then the only light he possessed would be one he could not move.

At last, after long moments of thought, he set the torch to one side, then began shoveling loose dirt from the cracks between slabs of stone into the hole. After he had poured in a score of handfuls, the flame flickered and died. He waited a little longer, having no idea of how long it might take to cool, then shoveled the sticky dirt away until there was an open space into which he could dip the rags. When he had soaked all the strips of cloth, he put one aside and then rolled each of the others tightly and set them all side by side on the last and largest piece he had torn from his shirt. He bundled up this makeshift sack and hung it on his belt. The remaining strip he carefully wrapped around the torch just below the flame, then turned the brand until the cloth soaked in Perdruinese Fire caught. It burned brightly, and Simon nodded. He still needed food and water, but if he managed carefully, he would not have to worry about losing his light for some while yet. Lost and alone he might be, but he was not just Simon Mooncalf—he was the fabled Seoman Snowlock as well.

But he would much rather have been just Simon, and free to walk upon the green world with his friends.

Choices, he thought unhappily, could be both a blessing and a curse.

Simon had already slept once, curled in a ball on the hard tunnel floor with a fresh rag of Perdruinese Fire wrapped around his torch. When he awakened from a panicky dream in which all light was gone and he crawled through muddy blackness, the torch's flame was still burning steadily.

Since then, he had walked for what seemed like several more hours. His thirst had grown greater and greater until every step seemed to leach moisture from his body, until he could think of almost nothing but finding water. The strip of meat was still in his pocket—just the thought of eating the dry, salty thing made his head ache, despite a hunger almost as great as his thirst.

Now, suddenly, the monotonous stone and earth walls of the tunnel had been breached. A cross tunnel, a ragged but substantial hole that was clearly not natural, opened out on either side. After a near-infinity of choiceless plodding, he had a decision to make: should he go forward, right, or left?

What he wanted, of course, was a path leading upward, but neither of the two branches seemed anything but level. He walked a little way down each in turn, sniffing the air, looking and listening for anything that might be a sign of open air or water, but to no avail: the cross tunnel seemed as devoid of interest as the one through which he had been trudging since Aedon only knew when.

He moved back to the main tunnel and stood for a moment, trying to decide where he might be. Surely he was somewhere far beneath Swertclif itself—he could not have walked downward at such a steady angle for so long without having descended to beneath the hill itself. But his way had wound so many times he could not possibly guess where he might stand in relation to the world above. He would just have to make a choice and see what happened.

*If I only ever turn one direction, I can at least find my way back to where I've been.*

Based on nothing definite, he resolved to take the left-hand tunnel, and to always take the left-hand turning from here on. Then, if he decided he had made a bad decision, he would just turn around and take all the turns back to the right.

He turned to the left and stumbled on

At first the tunnel seemed no different than the one he
had left, a tube of uneven stone and earth without any
sign of use or purpose. Who had made these grim holes?
It must have been men, or manlike beings, for in places
he felt sure he could see spots where rock been chipped
or broken away to open the meandering course.

His thirst and dreary loneliness were such that he did
not notice the soft voices again until they were all about
him once more. This time, though, there was a sensation
of movement as well—a plucking at his clothes like the
touch of the wind, a hurrying of shadows that made the
light in the tunnel seem to flicker. The voices were wailing softly in a language he could not understand. As they
passed around him or through him he felt a sad coldness.
These were memories . . . of a sort. These were lost
things, shapes and feelings that had come unstuck from
their own time. He was nothing to them, and they, disturbing as they might be, were really nothing to him.

*Unless I become one of these myself.* He felt bubbles of
fear rising within him. *Unless someday some other wandering mooncalf feels a Simon-shadow brushing past him
saying "Lost, lost, lost . . ."*

It was a horrible thought. Long after the flurry of
almost-shapes was gone and the voices were silent, it
stayed with him.

He had turned three more times, on each occasion
choosing the left-hand direction, when at last things began to change.

Simon was considering going back—his last turning
had led him into a tunnel that now sloped sharply
downward—when his eye was caught by a blotchiness
along the walls. He brought his torch close and saw that
the cracks of the stone were full of moss. Moss, he felt
sure, meant water somewhere nearby. He was so parched
that he pulled loose a matted handful and put it in his
mouth. After a few tentative chews he managed to swallow it. Bile rose in his throat, and for a moment he
thought he might be ill. It was dreadfully bitter, but there

*was* moisture in it. If he had to, he could eat it and probably stay alive for a while—but he prayed he could find some other alternative.

He was staring at the tiny fronds, trying to decide whether he could stomach a second helping, when he noticed pale marks in the gap where he had pulled loose the first handful. He squinted and held the torch closer. It was the remains of some kind of design, that was clear—great curving parallels and eroded shapes that might have been leaves or petals. Time had worn them away almost completely, but they seemed to have some of the looping grace of carvings he had seen in Da'ai Chikiza and Sesuad'ra. Sithi work? Had he gone so deep so quickly?

Simon looked around at the tunnel itself, at the crude, jagged-faced stones. He couldn't imagine the Sithi making such a place, even for the most basic of purposes. But if they had not dug these tunnels, why would there be Sithi carving on the walls?

He shook his head. Too many questions when the only ones that mattered were, where could he find some water—and which way was out?

Although he began to examine the walls carefully as he walked, his discovery of the moss was not immediately followed by anything more useful. The tunnel now began to widen, and the next two passageways he chose seemed more artfully constructed, the walls symmetrical, the floor even. Then, as he explored yet another branching, he put his foot down on nothing.

With a shout of horrified surprise, Simon caught at the entrance of the tunnel. His torch flew from his hand and tumbled down into the darkness where he had nearly gone himself. As he watched in fearful anticipation, it struck and then rolled; it stopped at last, flickering . . . but did not go out.

Stairs. His torch was lying on a flight of rough stairs leading downward. The first half-dozen steps had crumbled or been broken away, leaving nothing behind but a few rough edges.

He did not want to go down. He wanted to go up.

*But stairs! Maybe there's something real down there—*

*some place that makes sense. What could be worse than what's already happening?*

*Nothing. Everything.*

It was a left-hand turning, so he would not be completely lost if it proved a bad choice. But it would be much easier to drop down the gap comprised by the missing steps—a distance almost twice his height—than to climb back up again if he changed his mind. Perhaps he should take one of the other paths. . . .

*What nonsense are you thinking?* he berated himself. He would have to go down just to retrieve his torch.

Simon sat, dangling his legs over the stairless gap, and pulled the strip of dried meat from his pocket. He broke off a small piece and sucked on it meditatively as he looked down. The torchlight showed the steps had been chiseled square, but left unfinished: they were made to be useful, nothing else. Looking at them, there was no way to tell whether they led anywhere.

He chewed and stared. His mouth filled with saliva as he savored the salty, smoky taste. It was wonderful to have something solid between his teeth again!

Simon rose, then turned and went back up the corridor, feeling with his hand when the light grew dim, until he found more moss clinging to the wall. He pulled loose several handfuls, then shoved the sticky mass into his pocket. He returned to the stairwell and peered down until he felt he had located the best spot to land. He slid his legs over, then rolled onto his front and let himself down as carefully as he could, gritting his teeth as the stone scraped against his stomach and chest. When he was almost hanging full length, he let go.

A piece of loose stone, perhaps a fragment of the missing steps, was lying in wait for him like a viper. He felt one foot touch before the other, then the first foot rolled over at the ankle. A flash of pain shot through his leg.

Tears in his eyes, Simon lay on the topmost step for a moment, cursing his luck. He sat up, slid forward until he could reach the fallen torch, then set it down beside him and took off his boot to examine his injured ankle.

He could bend it reasonably well, although each

change of position was painful. He decided that it was not broken—but what could he have done about it if it were? He pulled off his shirt and tore loose yet another strip, then pulled the ever-shrinking garment back on. When he had bound the cloth around his ankle and foot as snugly as he could, he pulled the boot back on and tested himself. He could walk, he decided, but it would hurt.

*Walk, then. What else can you do?*

He began his limping descent.

Simon had hoped that the stairs would lead him down to some place more real than the endless, pointless tunnels. But the more real his surroundings became, the more they also became unreal.

After several score small but painful descents, the stairs ended and Simon hobbled out through a jagged hole into another corridor, a passage quite unlike the tunnels through which he had been traveling. Moss-festooned and almost black with the dirt of ages, it was nevertheless made of carefully-cut dressed stone; its walls were thick with carvings. But when he stared at these carvings for more than an instant, those that were just at the corners of his vision seemed to shimmer and move, as though they were not marks in stone at all, but rather some kind of parchment-thin creatures, slender as thread. The walls and floor seemed somehow unstable, too: when Simon looked away for a moment in his plodding progress, lured by yet another smear of movement at the edge of his eye, or was distracted by the flickering of the torch flame, they appeared to change. The long straight corridor suddenly had an upward slant, or seemed abruptly narrower. If he turned away and then looked back, everything was as it had been before.

Nor were these the only tricks this place played on him. The noises that he had heard before returned, voices and rushing water now joined by a strange, abstract music, all sourceless and ghostly. Unexpected scents washed over him, too, rushes of sweet flowery air one moment that quickly gave way to dank emptiness once more, only to be supplanted a moment later by the harsh smell of something burning.

It was too much. Simon wanted to lie down, to go to sleep and wake up with everything stable and unchanging. Even the monotony of the tunnels above was preferable to this. He might have been trudging at the bottom of the sea, where the currents and uneven light made everything sway and dance and shimmer.

*How long did you think you could walk in the empty earth before you went mad, Mooncalf?*

*I'm not going mad,* he told himself. *I'm just tired. Tired and thirsty. If only there weren't all these water-noises. They just make things worse.*

He pulled some of the moss from his pocket and chewed as he walked, forcing himself to swallow the hateful stuff.

There was no question that he was walking in a place in which people . . . in which *someone* . . . had once lived. The ceiling rose higher above him, the floor was level beneath the rubble and dust, and the crossing passages, almost all of them choked with stone and soil, were faced with carved arches, soiled and worn to pebble-smoothness but clearly the work of careful craft.

Simon paused for a moment before one of these entranceways. As he stood resting his throbbing ankle, staring at the jumble of rocks and dirt that plugged it, the mound of dirt seemed to darken, then turn black. A small light bloomed in that blackness, and Simon suddenly felt he was looking *through* the doorway. He took a step closer. In the darkness beyond he saw a single spot of luminance, an orb of light dimly glowing. Near it, bathed in faint radiance, was . . . a face.

Simon gasped. The face lifted, as though the person sitting in near-darkness had heard him, but the high-slanted eyes did not meet his, staring instead out past him. It was a Sitha face, or seemed so in the moment he could observe it, a world of pain and concern in the shining eyes. He saw the lips move in speech, the eyebrows rise in sad inquiry. Then the darkness blurred, the light vanished, and

Simon was standing with his nose a finger's breadth away from a doorway choked with rubble.

*Dry. Dry. Dead. Dead.*

A sob hitched in his throat. He turned back to the long corridor.

Simon didn't know how long he had been staring at the flame of his torch. It wavered before him, a universe of yellow light. It was a terrible effort to wrench his gaze away.

The walls on both sides had turned to water.

He stopped, staring in awe. Somehow the tunnel floor had become a narrow walkway over a great darkness and the walls had retreated: they no longer touched the floor on which he stood, and their stone facing was completely covered by flowing sheets of water. He could hear it rushing down into the emptiness below, see the uneven reflection of the torch as it played across the liquid expanse.

Simon moved to the edge of the walkway and stretched out his hand, but his fingers did not reach. He could feel a faint dew of mist on his fingertips, and when he drew the hand back and touched it to his mouth, there was a faint taste of wet sweetness. He leaned out again, swaying perilously over the darkness, but still could not touch even a fingertip to the sheeting water. He cursed in fury. If he only had a bowl, a cup, a spoon!

*Think, Mooncalf! Use your head!*

After a moment's consideration, he put his torch down on the walkway and shucked his tattered shirt over his head. He got down on his knees; then, clutching one sleeve, he flung the rest of it out as far as he could. It touched lightly against the cascade and was pulled downward. He yanked it back, his heart beating faster as he felt the shirt's new heaviness. He threw back his head, then pushed the sodden cloth against his mouth. The first drops were like honey on his tongue. . . .

The light flickered. Everything in the long chamber seemed to lurch to one side. The rush of the water grew louder, then hissed away into silence.

Simon's mouth was full of dust.

He gagged and spat, spat again, then fell to the floor in a panicked fury, growling and thrashing like a beast with a thorn in its side. When he looked up, he could still see the walls and the gap that stretched between them and the walkway on which he crouched—that much was real—but there was no sheeting water, only a lighter-colored smear on the stone wall where his shirt had flicked loose a few centuries' worth of grime.

Simon shook with tearless sobbing as he wiped the dirt from his face and rubbed the last of crumbs of soil from his swollen tongue. He tried to eat a little of the moss to take the taste of the dust away, but it was so foul he was almost sick again. He spat the leafy wad down into the abyss.

*What kind of cursed, haunted place is this? Where am I?*

*I'm alone, alone.*

Still shaking, he dragged himself to his feet, looking for a safer place to lie down for a while and sleep. He needed to get away. There was no water. There was no water anywhere. And no safety either.

Faint voices up in the shadows of the high ceiling sang words he could not understand. A wind he could not feel fluttered the torch flame.

*Am I alive?*

*Yes, I am. I am Simon, and I am alive, and I will not give up. I am not a ghost.*

He had slept twice more, and had chewed enough of the bitter moss to keep himself moving in between rests. He had used more than half of his treated rags to keep the torch burning. It was difficult to remember a time when he had not seen the world by wavering torchlight, or when the world itself had not consisted of unpeopled stone corridors and whispering, bodiless voices. He felt as though his own essence had begun to melt away, as though he were becoming a chittering shade.

*I am Simon,* he reminded himself. *I met the dragon and I won the White Arrow. I am* real.

As in a dream, he moved through the halls and corridors of a great castle. For illuminated moments swift as the whiteflash of lightning, he could see it in full life, the halls full of faint golden faces, the walls pale, shining stone that reflected the colors of the sky. It was a place unlike anything he had ever seen, with streams prisoned in stone banks that ran from room to room, and waterfalls that frothed down the walls of chambers. But for all the splashing, it was still dream-water. Each time he reached, the promise turned to grit in his hands; the walls darkened and slouched, the light dimmed, the beautiful fretwork withered away, and Simon found himself walking in ruined stone halls again, a homeless spirit in a vast tomb.

*The Sithi lived here,* he told himself. *This was Asu'a, shining Asu'a. And somehow they are* still *here ... as though the stones themselves are dreaming of the old days.*

A poisonously seductive idea began to make itself felt. Amerasu Ship-Born had said that somehow Simon lived closer to the Dream Road than others—he had seen the Parting of the Families during his vigil atop Sesuad'ra, hadn't he? Perhaps, then, if he could discover some way to do it, he could ... step across. He would go *into* the dream, he would live in beautiful Asu'a and plunge his face into the living streams that meandered through the palace—and this time they would not turn to dust. He would live in Asu'a, and never come back again to this dark, haunted world of crumbling shadows....

*Never come back to your friends? Never come back to your duty?*

But the dream-Asu'a was so beautiful. In the instants of its flickering existence, he could see roses and other startlingly bright flowers climbing up the walls to bask in the sun from the high windows. He could see the Sithi, the dream-people who lived here, graceful and strange as bright-plumed birds. The dream showed a time before Simon's kind had destroyed the Sithi's greatest house. Surely the immortals would welcome a lost traveler ... Oh, Mother of Mercy, might they welcome him in from the darkness...?

Weak and weary, Simon stumbled on a loose paving

stone and fell to his hands and knees. His heart felt like
an anvil in his chest. He could not move, could not go another step. Anything was better than this mad loneliness!

The wide room before him pulsed, but did not disappear. Out of the nebulous cloud of moving forms, one of
the figures became clearer. It was a Sitha woman, skin
golden as sunlight, hair a cloud of nightblack. She stood
between two twining trees laden with silvery fruit, and
her eyes slowly turned to Simon. She paused. A strange
look came over her face, as though she had heard a voice
calling her name in a lonely place.

"Can . . . can you see me?" Simon gasped. He scrabbled toward her across the floor. She continued to stare at
the spot where he had been.

Terror rushed through him. He had lost her! His limbs
turned boneless and he slumped forward onto his belly.
Behind the black-haired woman a fountain of water sparkled, the drops that flew through the slanting light of the
windows glowing like gems. She closed her eyes, and Simon felt a questing touch at the farthest edge of his mind.
She seemed only a few short steps away, but at the same
moment as distant as a star in the sky. "Can't you see
me!?" he howled. "I want to come inside! Let me in!"

She stood as immobile as a statue, her hands folded before her. The high-windowed chamber grew dark, until
she alone stood in a column of radiance. Something
brushed against Simon's thoughts, light as a spider's step,
soft as a butterfly's breath.

*Go back, little one. Go back and live.*

Then she opened her eyes and looked at him again. Her
eyes were full of a wisdom so vast and kind that Simon
felt himself lifted and held and known. But her words
were bitter for him.

*This is not for you.*

She began to fade. For a moment, she was only another
shadowy figure in the ancient parade of shapes. Then the
beautiful airy room itself flickered and vanished. Simon
was sprawled in the dirt. His torch burned fitfully on the
ground, half a pace from his outstretched fingers.

*Gone. Left me behind.*

Simon cried until he could not cry any more, until he was hoarse with weeping and his face hurt. He dragged himself to his feet and went on.

He had almost forgotten his name—he had certainly forgotten how many times he had slept, and how many times he had sucked at the diminishing wad of moss crammed in his pocket—when he found the great stairs.

There were only a few rags left to replace the one that burned on his torch. Simon was thinking about what that meant, and realizing that he had gone too far to find his way back to the pool of Perdruinese Fire before he was plunged into darkness, when he walked through one of the sweeping portals of the labyrinthine castle and found himself on a vast landing. Above and below this open place stretched a flight of wide stairs circling around emptiness, an uncountable sweep of steps that curled up into shadow and down into darkness.

*The stairs!* A memory, dim as a fish in a muddy pond, came floating up. *The ... Tan'ja Stairs? Doctor Morgenes said ... said ...*

Long ago, in another life, another Simon had been told to look for stairs like these—and they had led him upward to night air and moonlight and damp green grass.

*Then that means ... if I go up ...*

A shockingly ragged laugh burst out and echoed in the stairwell. Something, bats or sad little memories, fluttered away into the darkness above, rustling like a handful of parchments. Simon began climbing the stairs, his throbbing ankle, his terrible thirst, his utter, utter loneliness almost forgotten.

*I'll breathe the air. I'll see the sky. I'm ... I'm ... I'm Simon. I won't be a ghost.*

Before he had gone half a hundred steps upward, he found that a section of the wall had tumbled down, smashing the outermost edge of the steps so that a ragged gap faced out into the empty darkness. The rest of the staircase was blocked by fallen stone.

"*Bloody Tree!*" he screamed in rage. "Bloody, Bloody Tree!"

"... *roo* ..." the echo repeated, "... *ee* ..."

He waved the torch over his head in a furious challenge to the empty air; the flame billowed and streaked across the black. At last, defeated, he hobbled back down the wide stairs.

He remembered little of his first journey up the Tan'ja Stairs almost a year before, a journey that had taken place through both outer and inner darknesses ... but surely there had not been so many of these damnable steps! It was almost impossible to believe that he could descend so far without finding himself in the pits of Hell.

His plodding descent seemed to take at least a day. There was no way off: the arches that led from the landings were blocked by rubble, and the only other escape would be over the baluster and a plummet down into ... who knew what? By the time he stopped at last to sleep on one of the dusty landings, he wished he had never stepped onto the stairs at all, but the thought of dragging himself all the way back up that near-infinitude of steps to the spot where he had entered was horrifying. No, down was the only direction left to him. Surely even these monstrous stairs must come to an end somewhere! Simon curled up and fell into a thick slumber.

His dreams were powerful but confusing. Three almost painfully vivid images haunted him—a young fair-haired man bearing a torch and a spear down a steeply-sloping tunnel; an older man, robed and crowned, with a sword lying across his knees and a heavy book opened on top of it; a tall figure, hidden in shadow, who stood straight-backed in the middle of a strangely mobile floor. Again and again the same three visions appeared, changing slightly, showing more while revealing nothing. The spearman cocked his head as though he heard voices. The gray-haired man looked up from his reading as though disturbed by a sudden noise, and a bloom of red light filled the darkness, painting the man's strong features scarlet. The shadow-shape turned; a sword was in his hand, and something like antlers lifted from his brow. . . .

Simon awakened with a gasp, sweat cooling on his

forehead, limbs a-tremble. This had not been the stuff of ordinary sleep: he had fallen into some rushing river of dream and been carried along like a piece of bark, helplessly careening. He sat up and rubbed his eyes, but he was still on the broad landing, still adrift on the ocean of stairs.

*Dreams and voices,* he thought desperately. *I need to get away from them. If they don't leave me alone, I'll die.*

His second-to-last rag was now on the torch. Time was running out. If he did not find his way soon, if he did not find the air and the sun and moon once more, he would be alone in darkness with the shadows of dead time.

Simon hurried down the steps.

The Tan'ja Stairs became a blur, and Simon himself was a cracked millwheel, his legs going up, down, up, down, every other step bringing a sharp pain as he forced his wounded ankle to bear the weight of his hurried descent. Shallow breaths fluted in and out of his dry mouth. If he had not been mad before, madness finally took him now. The stairs were the teeth of a mouth that wanted to swallow him, but as fast as he bounded downward, falling and not feeling the pain, clambering to his feet and plunging down to the next step, he could not escape. There were always more teeth. Always more white, even teeth. . . .

The voices that had been silent so long rose up around him like the choir of monks in the Hayholt's chapel. Simon paid them no heed. All he could do was fling himself down step after step after step. Something in the air was different, but he could not let himself pause to decide what it was: the voices were haunting him, the teeth taunting, waiting to snap closed.

Where there should have been a step, there was instead a flat white expanse of . . . something. Simon, in mid-leap downward, was brought up short and sent tumbling forward. His elbows cracked painfully against stone. He lay for a moment, whimpering, clutching his torch so hard his knuckles throbbed. Slowly he lifted his head. The air was . . . the air smelled . . . damp.

The wide landing stretched before him, then ended in

blackness. There were no more stairs, or at least none he could see.

Still making pained noises, Simon crawled forward until the blackness was just before him. As he leaned out, his arm swept a small scree of dust and gravel over the edge.

*Plink. Plink, plink.* The sound of small stones falling into water. And not falling very far.

Panting, he leaned out, holding his torch as far over the darkness as he could. He could see a reflection just a few ells below, a wavering smudge of fiery light. Hope welled up in him, and that was somehow worse than any of his pain.

*It's a trick,* he mourned. *It's another trick. It's dust . . . dust . . . dust . . .*

Still, he crawled around the edge of the landing, looking for a way down. When he discovered a small and elegantly carved staircase, he crab-climbed down the steps on his hands and knees. The stairwell ended in a circular landing and a small spit of pale stone that stretched out over the blackness. The torch light did not reveal how far it extended, but he could see the sweep of the pool's sides as they vanished away into the shadows in either direction. It was huge—almost a small lake.

Simon dropped onto his stomach and extended his hand, then stopped, sniffing. If this great pond were full of Perdruinese Fire and he brought his torch close, there would be nothing of Simon left but a scrap of cinder. But there was no oily smell. He dipped his hand in and felt the water close over it, cold and just as wet as wet should be. He sucked his fingers. There was a faint metallic tang—but it *was* water.

*Water!*

He scooped it up in a double handful and lifted it to his mouth, more dribbling on his chin and neck than went down his throat. It seemed to tingle and sparkle on his tongue and fill his veins with warmth. It was glorious—better than any liquor, more wonderful than any drink he had ever tasted. It was water. He was alive.

Simon was light-headed with joy. He drank until he

was uncomfortably full, until his stomach pressed against the wasteband of his breeches; the cool, slightly tangy water felt so splendidly wet that it was difficult to stop. He poured it over his head and face, splashing so vigorously that he almost doused the torch, which made him laugh until the echoes crisscrossed. When he had moved his light up the stairwell to safety, he went back and drank more, then took off his ragged shirt and breeches and scrubbed himself all over, letting the water run off him in wonderfully wasteful excess. At last his fatigue overcame him. He lay singing happily until he fell asleep on the wet stone.

Simon awakened slowly, as if swimming upward from a great depth. For long moments he did not know where he was or what had happened. The powerful rush of dream-pictures had come to him again, whirling through his sleeping head like leaves in a great windstorm. The sword-bearing men were part of it, but there had also been a flash of shields as an armored host rode out through a tall silver gate, a splintery array of towers in rainbow hues, a glint of yellow as a raven cocked its head to reveal a bright eye, a circle that flashed gold, a tree with bark pale as snow, a dark wheel turning. . . .

Simon rubbed his temples, trying to clear away the clinging images. His head, which had felt hollow and airy when he was bathing himself, now throbbed and pounded. He groaned and sat up. He would be plagued by dreams, it seemed, no matter what happened. But there were other things to think about, things about which he could *do* something—or at least try. Food. Escape.

He looked up to where his torch lay on one of the steps of the narrow staircase. He had been foolish, risking his light with all that splashing. And it would not burn much longer. He had found water, but his predicament was still deathly grim.

The light of the torch suddenly seemed to grow. Simon squinted, then realized it was not the torch, but that rather the whole great chamber was filling with smoky light.

And there was ... *something* ... very near. Something strong. He could feel it like hot breath on his neck.

Simon rolled over, conscious of his nakedness, his helplessness. He could see the great pool more clearly, could make out the fantastically elaborate carvings that covered the near walls and ceiling far overhead, but even with the spreading light he still could not see the pool's far side: a sort of mist seemed to hang over the water, obscuring his view.

As he gaped, a shadowy figure appeared in the the mist at the pool's center, a shape exaggerated by the gray fog and directionless light. It was tall and billow-cloaked, with horns ... antlers ... growing from its head.

The figure bowed—not in reverence, it seemed, but in despair.

*Jingizu.*

The voice rolled through Simon's mind, mournful yet angry, powerful and cold as ice that cracked and split stone. The mist swirled and eddied. Simon felt his own thoughts swept away before it.

*Jingizu. So much sorrow.*

For a moment, Simon's spirit flickered like a candle in a storm wind. He was being extinguished by the force of the thing that hovered in the mists. He tried to scream, but could not; he was being eaten by its terrible emptiness. He felt himself dwindling, fading, vanishing....

The light shifted again, then abruptly died. The pool became a wide black oval once more, and the only light was the dim yellow glow of his guttering torch.

For some moments, Simon lay gasping for air like a fish dragged into a boat. He was afraid to move, to make a sound, terrified the shadowy thing would return.

*Merciful Aedon, give me rest.* The words of the old prayer came up unbidden. *In Your Arms will I sleep, upon Your bosom ...*

He no longer had the slightest urge to cross over to the dream-side, to join the ghosts of this place. Of all the things he had seen and felt since tumbling down into the ground, this place seemed the strangest, the most terrifyingly powerful. Water or no water, he could not stay. And soon his light would be gone, and the darkness would swallow him.

Quivering, he kneeled at the bottom of the stairwell and drank his fill once more. Cursing the lack of a water skin, he dragged on his breeches and boots, then dunked his shirt into the pool. It would stay wet for a while and he could squeeze out water when he needed it. He picked up the torch and began searching for a way out. His ankle had stiffened, but for the moment the pain was unimportant. He had to leave this place.

The pool, which a moment before had been a fount of terrifying visions, was now only a silent circle of black.

# 15

# A Meandering of Ink

Miriamele was as gentle with the bandages as she could be, and Binabik said not a word, but she could tell that the pain of his blistered hands was fierce.

"There." She tied a careful knot. "Now just let them alone for a while. I'll get us something to eat."

"All that digging, and with nothing for result," the troll said mournfully. He examined his cloth-wrapped paws. "Dirt and more dirt and more dirt."

"At least those . . . things didn't come back." The sun had dropped behind the western horizon; Miriamele was finding it difficult to see into the depths of the pack. She sat down and smoothed her cloak across her lap, then dumped out the contents. "Those diggers."

"I am almost wishing that they had, Miriamele. I would have been getting some pleasure in killing more of them. Like Qantaqa, I would be growling as their blood came out."

Miriamele shook her head, disturbed by Binabik's uncharacteristic savagery, but also worried by her own hollowness. She felt no such anger—there was almost nothing inside her at all. "If he . . . survived, then he will find a way to come back to us again." The ghost of a smile crept across her face. "He's stronger than I ever thought he might be, Binabik."

"I remember when I was first meeting him in the forest," the little man said. "Like a hatchling, like the young of a bird, he looked to me, his hair pointing up and every other way. I was thinking then, 'Here is one who would be quickly dying if I had not found him.' He seemed to me as helpless as the most wobbling-legged of lambs gone stray from the herd. But he has surprised me many times since then, many times." The troll fluted a sigh. "If there was something beneath his falling beside more dirt and *boghanik,* then I am thinking he will find a way out."

"Of course he will." Miriamele stared at the array of wrapped bundles in her lap. Her eyes were misty, and she had forgotten what she was looking for. "Of course he will."

"So we will go on, and trust in the luck that has kept him well for so long a time in all the moments of terrible peril." Binabik spoke as though afraid he would be contradicted.

"Yes. Certainly." Miriamele brought her hands to her face, kneading her temples as though that might make her scattered thoughts more manageable. "And I will say a prayer for Elysia the Mother of God to look after him."

*But many prayers are said every day,* she thought. *And only a few are answered. Curse you, Simon, why did you go away?*

Simon was almost a stronger presence lost than he had been while still with them. Miriamele, despite the deep affection she felt for Binabik, found it difficult to sit with him over the thin stew she had made for their supper: that they should be alive and eating seemed an insult to their absent friend. Still, they were both grateful for the bit of meat—a squirrel that Qantaqa had brought back. Miriamele wondered whether the wolf had done her own hunting first or felt she should bring a prize to her master before pursuing her own needs, but Binabik professed not to know.

"She only brings me such things on occasion, and usually when I am sad or hurt." He showed a tiny flash of teeth. "This time I am both things, I suppose."

"Bless her for it anyway," Miriamele said, and meant it. "Our larder is nearly bare."

"I am hoping . . ." the troll began, then abruptly fell silent. Miriamele was quite sure that he was thinking about

Simon, who even if he survived would be somewhere beneath the ground without food. Neither of them spoke more until the meal was finished.

"So now what is the thing to be doing?" Binabik asked gently. "I do not wish to seem . . .".

"I am still going to find my father. Nothing has changed that."

Binabik looked at her but did not speak.

"But you do not have to come with me." Disliking the sound of her voice, she added: "It might be better if you don't. Maybe if Simon finds his way out he will come to this place. Someone should wait for him. And anyway, this is not your duty, Binabik. He's my father, but he's your enemy."

The troll shook his head. "When we come to the place at which no back-turning can happen, then I will decide. This is not seeming a safe spot to me for waiting." He looked briefly over to the distant Hayholt; in the evening light the castle was only a blackness that contained no stars. "But perhaps I could stay hidden somewhere with Qantaqa and come at certain times to look." He made an open-handed gesture. "Still, it is too soon for such thinking. I do not even know what plan you have made for your castle entrance." He turned and waved toward the invisible keep. "You may have some way for persuading your father the king, but you would not be taken to him if you present yourself at the gate, I am thinking. And if Pryrates is receiving you, he may decide it is of more convenience for you to be dead and not interfere with his plans for your father. You would become vanished."

Miriamele twitched involuntarily. "I am not stupid, Binabik, no matter what my uncle and others may think. I have some ideas of my own."

Binabik spread his palms. "I do not think you are anything like being stupid, Miriamele. I am not knowing anyone who thinks that."

"Perhaps." She got to her feet and walked across the damp grass toward her pack. Rain was coming down in a light mist. After rummaging in the bag, she found the bundle she had sought and carried it back to the small fire. "I spent a long time on Sesuad'ra making these."

Binabik unrolled the bundle, then slowly smiled. "Ah."

"And I copied them onto hides as well," she said with more than a little pride, "because I knew they would last that way. I saw those scrolls you and Sis ... Sis ..."

"Sisqinanamook," Binabik said, frowning over the skins. "Or 'Sisqi' is easier for lowlander tongues." His face went blank for a moment, then his features resumed life and he looked up at Miriamele. "So you copied the maps that Count Eolair was bringing."

"I did. He said that they were of the old dwarrow tunnels. Simon came out of the castle through them, so I thought that might be a way to get back in without being caught."

"It is not all being tunnels." Binabik stared at the meandering lines drawn on the skins. "The old Sithi castle is beneath the Hayholt, and it was of great largeness." He squinted. "These are not easy for reading, these maps."

"I wasn't sure what any of it meant, so I copied it all, even the little drawings and marks on the side," Miriamele said humbly. "I only know that these are the right maps because I asked Father Strangyeard." She felt a sudden bite of fear. "They *are* the right maps, aren't they?"

Binabik nodded slowly, black hair bouncing against his forehead. "They are looking like maps of this place, indeed—see, there is what you call the Kynslagh." He pointed to a large curving crescent at the edge of the topmost map. "And this must be Swertclif which lies beneath us even now."

Miriamele leaned forward to look, following Binabik's small finger with eager attention. A moment later, she felt a wash of intense sadness. "If that's where we are, the spot where Simon fell through has no tunnels."

"Perhaps." Binabik sounded genuinely unsure. "But maps and charts are being made at particular times, Miriamele. Just as likely it is that other tunnels have been made since the drawing of this thing."

"Elysia, Mother of Mercy, I hope that's true."

"So where was Simon emerging from his tunnels?" Binabik asked. "I seem to have a memory that it was . . ."

"In the lich-yard, just on the other side of the wall from Erchester," Miriamele finished for him. "I saw him there, but he ran away when I called to him. He thought I was a ghost."

"There are many tunnelings that seem to emerge around that place. But these were made long before Erchester and the rest were being built. I am doubting these landmarks still remain." He looked up as Qantaqa returned from her hunting, her shaggy pelt pearled with rain.

"I think I know more or less where he must have come up," Miriamele said. "We can look, anyway."

"That we will do." Binabik stretched. "Now, one more night we will be sleeping in this place. Then down to the horses."

"I hope they've had enough to eat. We didn't expect to leave them this long."

"I can be promising you that if they were finishing the grass, the next thing they chewed through would be the leather traces that held them. The horses will not suffer for want of finding food, but we may not be finding the horses."

Miriamele shrugged. "As you are always saying, there's nothing we can do about it until we get there."

"I say it because it has a great truthfulness," Binabik replied gravely.

※

Rachel the Dragon knew what she would find, but her resignation did not make it less of a blow. For the eighth day in a row, the food and water she had put out were untouched.

Offering a sad prayer for patience to Saint Rhiappa, Rachel gathered up those things that would not keep and put them in her sack. She would eat the small apple and the bit of hardening bread tonight. She replaced the neglected offerings with fresh ones, then lifted the lid on the bowl of water to make sure it was still clean and drinkable.

She frowned. Where was that poor man Guthwulf? She hated to think of him wandering blind in the darkness, unable to find his way back to the regular meals that she had been providing him. She was half-tempted to go and look for him—had in fact roamed a little wider than normal in the last few days—but knew that it would be inviting trouble. The farther down into these tunnels she went, the greater the chance that she would fall and hit her head, or tumble into a hole. Then she would be helpless. She might worry about blind Guthwulf, but no one at all was worrying about old Rachel.

These thoughts made her frown deepen. Just as such things might happen to her, so might they have happened to Guthwulf. He might be only a few furlongs away, lying injured. The thought of someone needing her care when she could not give it was like an itch inside of her, a hot frustration. Once she had been the mistress of all the castle servants, a queen of sorts; now she could not even do what was necessary for one poor sightless madman.

Rachel shouldered her bag and stumped back up the stairs, heading toward her hidden sanctuary.

When she had pulled aside the tapestry and pushed the door inward on its well-oiled hinges, she lit one of her lanterns and looked around. In a way, it was almost restful living in such a solitary fashion: the place was so small it was easy to keep clean, and since only she came here, she knew that everything was done in just the right way.

Rachel set the lamp on the stool she used as a table and pulled her chair next to it, wincing. The damp was in her bones tonight, and her extremities ached. She did not feel much like sewing, but there was little else to do, and it was still at least an hour before the time she would go to bed. Rachel was determined not to lose her routine. She had always been one to wake up just moments before the horn blare of the night sentries giving over duty to the morning watch, but these days only her morning trip upstairs to get water from the room with an outside window helped her retain a connection with the world beyond. She did not want anything to strain the tenuous contact with her old life, so she would sew for at least an hour before she allowed herself to lie down, no matter how her fingers cramped.

She took out her knife and cut the apple into small sections. She ate it carefully, but when she was finished her teeth and gums hurt, so she dipped the heel of bread into her water cup to soften before she ate it. Rachel grimaced. Everything hurt tonight. There was a storm coming, that seemed sure—her bones told her. It didn't seem fair. There had only been a few days in the past week when she had actually been able to see sunlight out of the window upstairs, and now even that was to be snatched away.

Rachel found her needlework hard going. Her mind kept flittering away, something that normally would not have affected her stitchery at all, but which tonight was causing her to stop for long moments between every few movements of the needle.

*What would things have been like if Pryrates hadn't come?* she wondered.

Elias might not have been a wonderful king like his sainted father, but he was strong and shrewd and capable. Perhaps he would have outgrown his churlishness and his bad companions; the castle would have remained in her control, the long tables snowy with their spotless cloths, the flagstones swept and mopped to a high gleam. The chambermaids would be working industriously—under Rachel's stern gaze, *everyone* worked industriously. Well, almost everyone . . .

Yes, Simon. If the red priest hadn't come to blight their lives, Simon would still be here. Perhaps he would have found some work to suit him by now. He would be bigger—oh, they grew so quickly at that age—maybe even with a man's beard, although it was hard to imagine anything manly about young Simon. He would come by sometimes to visit her at the end of the day, maybe even share a cup of cider and a little talk. She would keep a careful eye that he wasn't getting too big for his breeches, that he wasn't making a fool of himself over the wrong sort of girls—it wouldn't do to let that boy get too far out of hand. . . .

Something wet fell onto her hand. Rachel started.

*Crying? Crying, you old fool? After that mooncalf boy?* She shook herself angrily. *Well, he's in better hands than yours now, and tears won't bring him back.*

Still, it would have been nice to see him grown, a man, but still grinning that same impudent grin. . . .

Rachel put down her needlework in disgust. If she was not going to get any sewing done, it was a waste of time to pretend. She would find something else to do, instead of just sitting in her chair moping and dreaming like some ancient crone beside the fireplace. She wasn't dead yet. There was still work for her to do.

Someone *did* need her. Pacing slowly back and forth in the tiny chamber, ignoring the dull throb of her joints, Rachel decided that she would indeed go and look for Earl Guthwulf. She would be careful, and she would keep as safe as she could, but it was her Aedonite duty to find out whether the poor man was hurt somewhere, or sick.

Rachel the Dragon began making plans.

🌸

A great curtain of rain swept across the lich-yard, bending the knee-high grass and splattering on the old tumbled stones.

"Did you find anything?" Miriamele called.

"Nothing that is pleasant." She could barely hear the troll for the hissing of the rain. She bent closer to the crypt door. "I am finding no tunnel," he elaborated.

"Then come out. I'm soaking wet." She pulled her cloak tight and looked up.

Beyond the lich-yard, the Hayholt loomed, its spires dark and secretive against the muddy gray sky. She saw light glimmering in the red windows of Hjeldin's Tower and crouched lower in the grass, like a rabbit covered by the shadow of a hawk. The castle seemed to be waiting, quiet and almost lifeless. There were no soldiers on the battlements, no pennants fluttering atop the roofs. Only Green Angel Tower with its sweep of pure white stone seemed somehow alive. She thought of the days she had hidden there, spying on Simon as he daydreamed through idle afternoons in the bell chamber. As constricting and smothering as the Hayholt had seemed to her then, it had been a comparatively cheerful place. The castle that stood before her now waited like some ancient hard-shelled creature, like an old spider brooding at the center of its web.

*Can I actually go there?* she wondered. *Maybe Binabik is right. Maybe I am being stubborn and headstrong to think I can do anything at all.*

But the troll might be wrong. Could she afford to gamble? And more importantly, could she walk away from her father, knowing that the two of them might never again meet on this earth?

"You were speaking the truth." Binabik slipped out through the crypt door, shielding his eyes with his hand. "The rain is falling down very strongly."

"Let's go back to where we left the horses," Miriamele said. "We can shelter there. So you found nothing?"

"Another place with no tunnels." The troll wiped mud from his hands onto his skin breeches. "But there were quite a few dead people, none of them good to be spending time with."

Miriamele made a face. "But I'm sure that Simon came up here. It has to be one of these."

Binabik shrugged and set out toward the clutch of wind-rattled elms along the lich-yard's south wall. As he walked, he pulled up his hood. "Either you are remembering it with some slight wrongness, or the tunnel is hidden in a way I cannot discover. But I have scrabbled in all the walls, and been lifting all the stones . . ."

"I'm certain it's not you," she said. A flare of lightning lit the sky; the thunder followed a few moments later. Suddenly an image of Simon struggling in the dark earth appeared before her mind's eyes. He was gone, lost forever, despite all the brave things she and the troll had said. She gasped and stumbled. Tears coursed down her rain-wet cheeks. She stopped, sobbing so hard she could not see.

Binabik's small hand closed about hers. "I am here with you." His own voice trembled.

They stood together in the rain for a long time. At last Miriamele grew calmer. "I'm sorry, Binabik. I don't know what to do. We have spent the whole day searching and it hasn't done us any good." She swallowed and wiped water from her face. She could not speak of Simon. "Perhaps we should give up. You were right: I could never walk up to that gate."

"Let us make ourselves dry, first." The little man tugged her forward, hurrying them toward shelter. "Then we will talk over what are the things we should do."

"We have looked, Miriamele," said Binabik. The horses made anxious noises as the thunder caromed across the sky once more. Qantaqa stared up at the clouds as though the great sound were something she would like to chase and catch. "But if you wish it, I will wait and look again when the rain is gone—perhaps the searching would be safer by night."

Miriamele shuddered at the thought of exploring the graves after dark. Besides, the diggers had proved that there was far more to fear in these crypts than just the restless spirits of the dead. "I don't want you to do that."

He shrugged. "Then what is your wishing?"

She looked at the map. The wandering lines of ink were nearly invisible in the dark, storm-curtained afternoon. "There are other lines that must be other tunnels going in. Here's one."

Binabik screwed up his eyes as he studied the map. "That one is seeming to me to come out in the rock wall over the Kynslagh. Very difficult it would be to find, I think, and it would be even more beneath the nose of your father and his soldiers."

Miriamele nodded sadly. "I think you're right. What about this one?"

The troll considered. "It is seeming to be in the place the town now stands."

"Erchester?" Miriamele looked back, but could not see over the tall lich-yard wall. "Somewhere in Erchester?"

"Yes, are you seeing?" He traced the line with his short finger. "If this is the little forest called Kynswood, and this is where we are now standing . . ."

"Yes. It must be almost in the middle of the town." She paused to consider. "If I could disguise ˎmy face, somehow . . ."

"And I would be disguising my height and my troll-ness?" Binabik asked wryly.

She shook her head, feeling the idea solidify. "No. You wouldn't need to. If we took one horse, and you rode with me, people would think you were a child."

"I am honored."

Miriamele laughed a little wildly. "No, it would work! No one would look at you twice if you kept your hood pulled low."

"And what would we do with Simon's horse, and with Qantaqa?"

"Perhaps we could bring them with us." She didn't want to give up. "Maybe they would think Qantaqa was a dog."

Now Binabik laughed, too, a sudden huff of mirth. "It is one thing to make people be thinking a small man like me is a child, but unless you could find a cloak for her as well, no one will ever have belief that my companion is anything but a deadly wolf from the White Waste."

Miriamele looked at Qantaqa's shaggy gray bulk and nodded sadly. "I know. It was just a thought."

The troll smiled. "But the rest of your idea is good. There are just a few things we must do, I am thinking. . . ."

They finished their work in a grove of linden trees on the edge of a fallow field just west of the main road, a few furlongs from Erchester's northernmost city gate.

"What did you put in this beeswax, Binabik?" Miriamele scowled, probing with her tongue. "It tastes terrible!"

"That is not for touching or tasting," he said. "It will

come loose. And the answer is being, just a little dark mud for color."

"Does it really look like teeth are missing?"

Binabik cocked his head, eyeing the effect. "Yes. You are appearing very scruffy and not-princess-like."

Miriamele ran her hand through her dirt-matted hair and carefully stroked her muddy face. *I must be a sight.* She could not help being pleased for some reason. *It is like a game, like a Usires Play. I can be anyone I want to.*

But it was not a game, of course. Simon's face loomed before her; she abruptly and painfully remembered what she was doing, what dangers it would bring—and what had already been lost so that she could get to this place.

*It is to end the pain, the killing,* she dutifully reminded herself. *And to bring my father back to his senses.*

She looked up. "I'm ready, I suppose."

The troll nodded. He turned and patted Qantaqa's broad head, then led the wolf a short distance away and crouched beside her, burying his face in her neck fur to whisper in her ear. It was a long message, of which Miriamele could hear only the throaty clicking of trollish consonants. Qantaqa twisted her head to the side and whined softly but did not move. When Binabik had finished, he patted her again and touched his forehead to hers.

"She will not let Simon's horse stray far away," he said. "Now it is time for us to be going forward."

Miriamele swung up into the saddle, then leaned down to extend a hand to the little man; he scrambled up and seated himself before her. She tapped her heels against the horse's side.

When she looked back, Simon's horse Homefinder was cropping grass at the base of a rain-dripping tree. Qantaqa sat erect, ears high, yellow eyes intent on her master's small back.

The Erchester Road was a sea of mud. The horse seemed to spend almost as much time unsticking itself as it did walking.

The city gate proved to be unbolted. The delicately-weighted portal swung open with only a light push from Miriamele, creaking gently. She waded back across the muddy wagon ruts and remounted, then they rode in between the tall gate towers, rain drizzling down on them from the clotted gray skies.

"There are no guards," she whispered.

"There is no one at all that I am seeing."

Just inside the gate lay Battle Square, a vast expanse of cobblestones with a green in the center, the site of countless parades and festivals. Now the square was empty but for a few stark-ribbed dogs rooting in debris at the mouth of one of the alleys. The square looked as though it had been unused for some time, forgotten by all except the scavengers. Wide puddles rippled beneath the rain. The green had become a desolate patch of pockmarked mud.

The echo of the horse's hooves caught the dogs' attention. They stared, tongues lolling, dark eyes wary; a moment later the pack turned and fled splashing down the alleyway.

"What has happened here?" Miriamele wondered.

"I think we can be guessing," said Binabik. "You saw other nearby towns and villages, and I saw such emptiness all through the snowy lands of the north. And this place, do you see, is closest of all to what has happened at the Hayholt."

"But where have all the people gone? From Stanshire, from Hasu Vale, from . . . from here? They didn't just disappear."

"No. Some may have been dying when the harvests were not coming in, but others have just gone to the south, I am thinking. This year has been a fearful enough thing for those of us who are having some knowledge of what is happening. For those who were living here, it must have seemed that they were suddenly finding themselves under a curse."

"Oh, Merciful Elysia." Her unhappiness was strangely mixed with anger and pity. "What has my father done?"

Binabik shook his head.

As they entered broad Main Row, there at last appeared some signs of human life: from the cracks of a few shuttered windows firelight flickered, and somewhere farther up the thoroughfare a door banged shut. Miriamele even thought she could hear a faint voice raised in prayer, but somehow she could not imagine a person from whom such a ragged sound would come; rather, it seemed that some wandering spirit had left behind its mournful cry.

As they turned the bend in Main Row, a figure in a ragged cloak appeared from one of the narrow cross streets in front of them and went shambling slowly away up the road. Miriamele was so surprised to see an actual person that she reined up and sat staring for long moments. As if sensing the presence of strangers, the figure turned; for an instant a look of fear showed on the wrinkled face beneath the hood—it was difficult to tell if it was a man or a woman—then the cloaked shape scuttled rapidly forward and vanished down an alleyway. When Miriamele and Binabik drew even with the place, there was no sign of anyone. All the doors that faced the narrow byway looked as though they had been boarded up for some time.

"Whoever that was, *they* were scared of *us*." Miriamele could not keep the pained surprise out of her voice.

"Can you feel blame for them about that?" The little man waved his hand at the haunted streets. "But it is no matter. I am not doubting that many ghastly things have been happening here—but it is not our task to be worrying about such happenings. We are looking for something."

"Of course," Miriamele replied quickly, but her mind did not fix easily on what the little man was saying. It was hard to tear her eyes from the mud-spattered walls, the gloomy, empty streets. It looked as though a great flood had rushed through and swept all the people away. "Of course," she said again. "But how will we find it?"

"On the map, the tunnel end looked as though it was being in the center of the town. Are we going in that direction?"

"Yes. Main Row goes through town all the way up to the Nearulagh Gate."

"Then what is that thing being?" Binabik pointed. "It

seems to block any going forward." A few furlongs
ahead, a huge dark mass straddled the road.

"That?" Miriamele was still so disoriented that it took
her a long moment to recognize it. "Oh. That's the back
of Saint Sutrin's—the cathedral."

Binabik was silent for some moments. "And it is at the
center of the town?"

"More or less." Something in the tone of the troll's
voice finally dragged her attention back from the
dreamlike emptiness of Main Row. "Binabik? What is it?
Is something wrong?"

"Let us just wait until we are seeing it from more
closely. Why is there no golden wall? I thought from the
traveler's tales told to me that such a wall was being a famous thing about this Saint Sutrin's."

"It's on the other side—the side that faces the castle."

They continued up Main Row. Miriamele wondered
whether there might be people here after all—if instead of
almost deserted, the city might actually be full-tenanted.
Perhaps if all the inhabitants were as fearful as the one
she had seen, they were even now watching quietly from
behind shuttered windows and through cracks in the
walls. Somehow that was just as bad as imagining the
people of Erchester all gone.

Or perhaps it was something stranger still. On either
side of the road, the stalls which had once housed the various small merchants were empty, but now she thought
she could feel a sort of anticipation, as though these hollow holes waited to be filled with some new kind of
life—something as unlike the farmers, peasants, and
townsfolk who had once bustled through their lives here
as mud was unlike dry, sunlit soil.

The golden facade of Saint Sutrin's had been peeled
away by scavengers; even the famous stone reliefs were
gouged almost into unrecognizability, as though the gold
that had covered them had been smashed loose with ham-
mers in the course of a single hasty hour.

"It was beautiful." Miriamele had not much room left

for sadness or surprise. "When the sun was on it, it looked like the church was covered in holy flames."

"In times of badness, gold is being worth more than beauty," Binabik mused, squinting up at the crushed faces of the saints. "Let us go and try the door."

"Do you think it's here? The tunnel?"

"You saw from the map that it was coming up in the center of this town of Erchester. I am guessing that this place goes deeper than any other in the town."

The great wooden doors did not open easily, but Miriamele and Binabik both lowered their shoulders; the hinges groaned and the doors grated open almost a cubit, allowing them to slip inside.

The forechamber had also lost much of its decoration. The pedestals on either side of the door were empty, and the huge tapestries that had once made the chamber walls into windows that looked out on the days of Usires Aedon now lay crumpled on the flagstones, crisscrossed with muddy footprints. The room stank of damp and decay, as though it had been long deserted, but light glowed from the great chapel beyond the forechamber doors.

"Someone is here," Miriamele said quietly.

"Or at least they are still coming for lighting the candles."

They had only taken a few steps when a figure appeared in the inner doorway.

*"Who are you? What do you seek in God's house?"*

Miriamele was so surprised to hear another human voice that for a moment she did not reply. Binabik took a step forward, but she put her hand on his shoulder. "We are travelers," she said. "We wanted to see Saint Sutrin's. The doors were never closed in the past."

"Are you Aedonites?"

Miriamele thought there was something familiar about the voice. "I am. My companion is from a foreign land, but he has been of service to Mother Church."

There was a moment's hesitation before the man spoke again. "Enter, then, if you swear you are not enemies."

Miriamele doubted from the tremulousness of his tone

that the man speaking could have stopped them if they *were* enemies, but she said: "We are not. Thank you."

The shadowy figure vanished from the doorway and Miriamele led Binabik through. She was still wary. In this haunted city, anyone could live in a cathedral. Why not then use it as a trap spider used its burrow, as a lure to the incautious?

It was not much warmer inside than out, and the great chapel was thick with shadows. Only a dozen candles burned in the huge room, and their light was scarcely enough to illuminate the vaulting high overhead. Something was strange about the dome as well. After a few moments' scrutiny, Miriamele realized that all of the glass was gone but for a few splinters clinging to the lead frame. A solitary star glimmered in the naked sky.

"Smashed by the storm," a voice said beside her. She flinched, startled. "All our lovely windows, the work of ages, shattered. It is a judgment on Mankind."

Standing beside her in the dim light was an old man in a dirty gray robe, his face sagging into a thousand wrinkles, his white-wisped, balding head covered with a lop-sided hat of strange shape. "You look so sad," he murmured; his accent marked him as an Erkynlander. "Did you ever see our Saint Sutrin's before . . ." he hesitated, as he tried to find a word, but could not. "Did you ever see it . . . before?"

"Yes." Miriamele knew it was better policy to profess ignorance, but the old man seemed so pathetically proud that she did not have the heart. "I saw it. It was very beautiful."

"Only the great chapel in the Sancellan Aedonitis could compare," he said wistfully. "I wonder if it still stands? We hear little from the South these days."

"I am sure it does."

"Ah, yes? Well, that is very good." Despite his words, he sounded faintly disappointed that his cathedral's rival had not suffered a similarly ignoble fate. "But, may our Ransomer forgive us, we are poor hosts," he said suddenly, catching Miriamele's arm with a gently trembling claw. "Come in and shelter from the storm. You and your son—" he gestured to Binabik, who looked up in surprise; the old man had already forgotten what Miriamele had told him, "—will be safe here. They have taken our beautiful things, but they have not taken us from the watchfulness of God's eye."

He led them up the long aisle toward the altar, a block of stone with a rag stretched over it, mumbling as he went about the wonderful things that had once stood here or there and the horrible things that had happened to them. Miriamele was not listening to him closely: she was preoccupied by the scatter of shadowy human shapes which leaned against the walls or lay in corners. One or two were draped lengthwise across the benches as though in sleep. All together, there seemed to be several dozen people in the huge chapel, all silent and apparently unmoving. Miriamele had a sudden, horrid thought. "Who are all these folk?" she asked. "Are they . . . dead?"

The old man looked up, surprised, then smiled and shook his head. "No, no, they are pilgrims like yourself, travelers who sought a safe haven. God led them here, and so they shelter in His church."

As the old man recommenced his description of the splendors of Saint Sutrin's as it once had been, Miriamele felt a tug at her sleeve.

"Ask him whether there is anything beneath this place like that thing we are searching," the troll whispered.

When the man paused for a moment, Miriamele seized her chance. "Are there tunnels beneath the cathedral?"

"Tunnels?" The question set an odd light burning in the old man's rheumy eye. "What do you mean? There are the catacombs, where all the bishops of this place lie resting until the Day of Weighing-Out, but no one goes there. It is . . . holy ground." He seemed disturbed, staring past the altar at nothing Miriamele could see. "That is not a place for any traveler. Why do you ask?"

Miriamele did not wish to upset him any further. "I was told once that there was a . . . a holy place here." She bowed her head. "Someone dear to me is in danger. I had thought that maybe there was a special shrine. . . ." What had seemed a lie had come to her quickly, but as she thought about it, she realized it was only truth: someone dear to her *was* in peril. She should light a candle for Simon before they left this place.

"Ah." The old man seemed mollified. "No, it is not that sort of place, not at all. Now come, it is almost time for the evening *mansa*."

Miriamele was surprised. So the rites were still celebrated here, even though the church seemed little more than a shell. She wondered what had happened to fat, blustering Bishop Domitis and all his priestly underlings.

The man led them to the first row of benches facing the altar, then gestured for them to sit down. The irony did not escape Miriamele: she had often sat there before at her father's side, and at her grandfather's before that. The old man walked to a place behind the stone and its ragged covering, then lifted his arms in the air. "Come, my friends," he said loudly. "You may return now."

Binabik looked at Miriamele. She shrugged, unsure of what the man wanted them to do.

But they were not the ones who had been addressed. A moment later, whirring and flapping, a host of black shapes descended from the shadowy wreckage of the dome. Miriamele gave out a little squeak of surprise as the ravens settled upon the altar. Within moments almost a score of them stood wing to wing on the altar cloth, oily feathers gleaming in the candlelight.

The old man began to speak the *Mansa Nictalis*, and as he did, the ravens preened and ruffled.

"What is this thing?" Binabik asked. "It is not a part of your worship that I have heard of."

Miriamele shook her head. The old man was clearly mad. He was addressing the Nabbanai words to the ravens, who strutted back and forth along the altar giving voice to harsh, grating cries. But there was something else about the scene that was almost as strange as the eerie ceremony, some elusive thing. . . .

Abruptly, as the old man lifted his arms and made the ritual sign of the Great Tree, she recognized him. This was Bishop Domitis himself at the altar—or his wasted remains, since he seemed shriveled to half his previous weight. Even his voice was different: deprived of the great bellows of flesh, it had become reedy and thin. But as he rolled into the sonorous cadences of the *mansa,* much of the old Domitis seemed to return; in her weary mind she could see him again as he once had been, swelled bullfrog-great with self-importance.

"Binabik," she whispered. "I know him! He is the bishop of this place. But he looks so different!"

The troll was eyeing the capering ravens with a mixture of amusement and uneasiness. "Can you then be persuading him to help us?"

Miriamele considered. "I don't think so. He seems very protective of his church, and he certainly didn't seem to want us wandering around down in the catacombs."

"Then I am thinking that is just the place we must go," Binabik said quietly. "We must be looking for the chance to come to us." He looked up at Domitis, who stood with head thrown back and eyes closed, his arms widespread as if in imitation of his avian congregation. "I have something that I must be doing now. Wait for me here. It will take me only a little time." He got up quietly from the bench, then turned and moved quickly back down the aisle toward the front of the cathedral.

"Binabik!" Miriamele called softly, but the troll only raised his hand before disappearing into the forechamber. Unsettled, she turned reluctantly to watch the rest of the odd performance.

Domitis seemed to have completely forgotten the presence of anyone but himself and the ravens. A pair of these had flown up from the altar to settle on his shoulders. They clung there as he swayed; as he windmilled his arms in the fervor of his speech, they flapped their great black wings to maintain balance on their perches.

Finally, as the bishop began the last stages of the *mansa,* the whole flock of birds rose up and began circling his head like a croaking thundercloud. Whatever humor the ritual had held was gone: Miriamele suddenly found the whole thing frightening. Was there no corner of the world left that had not succumbed to madness? Had *everything* been corrupted?

Domitis intoned the last Nabbanai phrases and fell silent. The ravens circled a few moments more, then went whirling up toward the ruptured dome like a whirlwind, vanishing into the shadows with only the echoes of their rasping cries left hanging in the air behind them. When even those had died and the cathedral had fallen quiet, Bishop Domitis, now almost gray with expended effort, bent down behind the altar.

When some time had passed and he had not stood up again, Miriamele began to wonder whether the old man had fallen into some sort of fit, or had perhaps even dropped dead. She got to her feet and moved cautiously toward the altar, keeping an eye cocked toward the ceiling as she went, half-fearing that at any moments the ravens might descend again, talons and beaks flailing. . . .

Domitis was curled on a ragged blanket behind the altar, snoring softly. In repose, the loose skin of his face seemed even more formless, sagging into long folds so that he seemed to wear a mask of melted candlewax. Miriamele shuddered and hurried back to her chair, but after a few moments even that began to feel too exposed. The room was still full of silent figures, but it was not difficult to imagine that they were only feigning sleep, waiting to be sure her companion was not returning before they rose and came toward her. . . .

Miriamele waited for what seemed a long time. The forechamber was colder even than the broken-domed chapel, but escape was within reach at a moment's notice. A little of the night wind slipped through the partially open door, which made her feel closer to freedom and hence a great deal safer, but she still jumped when the door hinges screeched.

"Ah," said Binabik, slipping inside, "it is still raining with great forcefulness." He shook water onto the stone floor.

"Bishop Domitis has gone to sleep behind the altar. Binabik, where did you go?"

"To take your horse back to where Homefinder and Qantaqa wait. Even if we are not finding what we seek here, we can easily travel through the town by walking. But if we find a tunnel-entering-place, I am fearing that we would come back at a later time to find your horse as part of some hungry person's soup."

Miriamele had not thought of that, but she did not doubt that he was right. "I'm glad you did it. Now what should we do?"

"Go hunting for our tunnel," said Binabik.

"When Bishop Domitis was talking about the catacombs, he kept looking over to the back of the cathedral, that wall behind the altar."

"Hmmm." The troll nodded. "You are wise for noticing and remembering. That is, I am thinking, the first place we should search."

"We have to be quiet—we don't want to wake him up."

"Like snow-mice we will be, our pads whispering on the white crust." Binabik squeezed her hand.

Her worries about the slumbering Domitis were unfounded. The old man was snoring thinly but emphatically, and did not even twitch as they padded by. The great wall behind the altar, which had once been covered in a tiled representation of Saint Sutrin's martyrdom, was now only crumbling mortar with a few remaining spots of ceramic color. At one end of the wall, tucked behind a rotting velvet drapery, stood a low door. Binabik gave it a tug and it opened easily, as though it had been used with some frequency. The troll peered inside, then turned. "Let us be taking some candles," he murmured. "That way we can be saving the torches in our packs for a later time."

Miriamele went back and plucked two of the candles from the sconces. She felt a little shame, since Domitis had been kind to them in his own strange way, but she reasoned that their greater goal outweighed the sin of theft, and would benefit the bishop as well—maybe one day he would even see his beloved cathedral rebuilt. She could not help wondering if the ravens would be welcome then. She hoped not.

Each holding a candle, Miriamele and Binabik went carefully down the narrow staircase. Centuries of human traffic had worn a groove like a dry river bed in the center of the stone steps. They stepped off the stairs into the low-ceilinged catacombs and stopped to look around. The walls on either side were honeycombed with niches, each containing a silent stone effigy of a figure in repose, most wearing the robes and other symbols of church office. But for these, the narrow halls seemed entirely empty.

Binabik pointed at one turning that seemed less traveled. "This way, I am thinking."

Miriamele peered down the shadowy tunnel. The pale plaster walls were unmarked; no would-be saints lay here, it seemed. She took a deep breath. "Let's go."

In the cathedral above, a pair of ravens dropped down from the ceiling and, after circling briefly, settled on the altar. They stood side by side, bright eyes glaring at the door to the catacombs. Nor were they the only observers. A figure detached itself from the shadows along the wall and crept silently across the cathedral. It moved past the altar, stepping just as carefully as had Miriamele and the troll, then paused for a while outside the vault door as though listening. When a short time had passed, the dark shape slipped through the doorway and went pattering quietly down the stairs.

After that, nothing was heard in the dark cathedral but the bishop's even snoring and the faint rustle of wings.

# 16

# Roots of the White Tree

**Simon stared** at the amazing thing for a long time. He took a step closer, then danced back nervously. How could it be? It must be a dream-picture, like so many other illusions in these endless tunnels.

He rubbed his eyes and then opened them again: the plate still stood in the niche by the stair landing, chest-high. On it, arranged as prettily as at a royal banquet, was a small green apple, an onion, and a heel of bread. An unadorned bowl with a cover stood beside it.

Simon shrank back, looking wildly from side to side. Who would do such a thing? What would make someone leave a perfectly good supper in the middle of an empty stairwell in the depths of the earth? He raised his guttering torch to inspect the magical offering once more.

It was hard to believe—no, it was impossible. He had been wandering for hours since leaving the great pool, trying to stay on an upward course but not at all sure that the curving bridges, downsloping corridors, and oddly-constructed stairways were not taking him even further into the earth, no matter how many steps he climbed. All that time the flame of his torch had been growing fainter, until it was little more than a wisp of blue and yellow which might be blown out by any errant breeze. He had all but convinced himself that he would be lost forever, that he would starve and die in darkness—and then he had found this . . . this *miracle*.

It was not just the food itself, although the sight of it filled his mouth with saliva and made his fingers twitch.

No, it meant there must be people somewhere nearby, and likely light and fresh air as well. Even the walls, which were rough-cobbled human work, spoke of the surface, of escape. He was as good as saved!

*Hold a moment.* He caught himself with hand outstretched, almost touching the skin of the apple. *What if it's a trap? What if they know someone is down here, and they're trying to lure him out?*

But who would "they" be? No one could know he was down here but his friends and the bestial diggers and the shadowy ghosts of the Sithi in their dream-castle. No, someone had brought supper down here, then for some reason had walked away, forgetting it.

If it was even real.

Simon reached, ready for the food to vanish, to turn to dust . . . but it did not. His hand closed on the apple. It was hard beneath his fingers. He snatched it up, sniffed it briefly—what did poison smell like, anyway?—and then took a bite.

*Thank you, merciful Usires. Thank you.*

It was . . . wonderful. The fruit was far from ripe, the juice tart, even sour, but it felt like he held the living green earth in his hand again, that the life of the sun and wind and rain was crisping between his teeth and tongue, running down his throat. For a moment he forgot all else, savoring the glory of it.

He lifted the cover from the bowl, sniffed to make sure it was water, then drank it down in thirsty gulps. When the bowl was empty, he grabbed the plate of food and darted back down the corridor, searching for a place to hide and eat in safety.

Simon fought with himself to make the apple last, even though each bite seemed like a year of his life given back to him. When he had finished it, and had licked every bit of juice from his fingers, he stared longingly at the bread and onion. With masterful self-control, he tucked them both into the pockets of his breeches. Even if he found his way back to the surface, even if he was near some place where people were, there was no guarantee he would be fed. If he came up within Erchester or one of the small villages along the Kynslagh, he might find a place to hide and even some allies; if he came up in the Hayholt, all hands might be turned against him. And if he was wrong about what the plate signified—well, he would be grateful to have the rest of the meal when the thrilling effect of an entire apple wore off.

He picked up the torch—it was even dimmer now, the flames a transparent azure—and stepped back out into the corridor, then paced forward until he reached the branching place. A chill passed through him. Which way had he turned? He had been in such a hurry to put distance between himself and anyone who might return for the food that he had acted without his normal care. Had he turned left, as he should have? Somehow that did not seem correct.

Still, he could do nothing but trust to the way he had done it so far. He took the rightward branching. Within moments, he became convinced that he had chosen wrongly: this way led down. He retraced his steps and took another of the corridors, but this one also sloped away downward. A few moments' examination proved that *all* the branches went down. He walked back toward where he had eaten the apple and found the stem he had dropped, but when he held the guttering torch close to the ground he saw that the only footprints on the dusty floor led back the way he had come.

*Curse this place! Curse this mad maze of a place!*

Simon trudged back to the branching. Something had happened, it was clear—the tunnels had shifted again in some strange way. Resigned, he chose the downward path that seemed least steep and started on his way again.

The corridor twisted and turned, leading him back into the depths. Soon the walls again showed signs of Sithi work, hints of twining carvings beneath the centuries of grime. The passageway widened, then widened again. He stepped out into a vast open area and knew it only from the far-ranging echoes of his bootheels: his torch was little more now than a smoldering glow.

This cavernous place seemed as high-ceilinged as that

whioh had held the great pool. As Simon moved forward
and his eyes adjusted to the greater dimensions, his heart
lifted. It was like the chamber of the pool in another way
as well: a great staircase ran upward into the darkness,
following the curve of the walls. Something else gleamed
faintly in the middle of the chamber. He moved closer,
and the dying light of his torch revealed a great circle of
stone that might have been the base of a fountain; at its
center, set in black earth but stretching up to many times
Simon's height, was a tree. Or at least it *seemed* to be a
tree—there was a suggestion of humped and knotted roots
at the bottom and amazingly tangled branches above—but
no matter how close he held the torch, he could see no detail of it, as though it were draped in clinging shadow.

As he leaned nearer, the shadow-tree rattled in an
unfelt wind, a sound like a thousand dry hands rubbing
against each other. Simon leaped back. He had been about
to touch it, certain it was carved stone. Instead he turned
and hurried past it to the base of the winding stairway.

As he circled around the perimeter of the chamber,
picking his way up the steps by fading torchlight, he was
still intensely aware of the tree standing at the room's
center. He could hear the breathing sound of its leaves as
they moved, but he could *feel* its existence even more
strongly; it was as palpable in the darkness as someone
lying beside him in a bed. It was not like anything he had
felt before—less starkly powerful than the pool, perhaps,
but somehow more subtle, an intelligence vast, old, and
unhurried. The pool's magic was like a roaring bonfire—
something that could burn or illuminate, but would do
neither unless someone was present to use its power. Simon could not imagine anyone or anything *using* the tree.
It stood and dreamed and waited for no one. It was not
good or evil, it simply was.

Long after he had left the base of the stairway behind
him, he could feel its living presence.

The light from his torch grew less and less. At last, after he had climbed some hundreds of steps, it finally died.
Having anticipated its passing for so long did not make
the moment any less dreadful: Simon slumped down and

sat in complete darkness, too tired even to weep. He ate a mouthful of bread and some onion, then squeezed some of the last of the water from his drying shirt. When he had finished, he took a deep breath and began to crawl up the stairs on his hands and knees, feeling before him in the blackness.

It was hard to tell whether the voices that followed him were phantoms of the underground realm or the chattering of his own drifting thoughts.

*Climb up. All will be ready soon.*

*On your knees again, mooncalf?*

Step after stone step passed beneath his hands. His fingers were numb, his knees and shins aching dully.

*The Conqueror is coming! Soon all will be ready.*

*But one is missing!*

*It does not matter. The trees are burning. All is dead, gone. It does not matter.*

Simon's mind wandered as he clambered up the winding track. It was not hard to imagine that he had been swallowed whole, that he was in the belly of some great beast. Perhaps it was the dragon—the dragon that was spoken of in the inscription on his ring. He stopped and felt his finger, reassured by the feel of the metal. What had Binabik said the inscription meant? *Dragon* and *Death?*

*Killed by a dragon, maybe. I've been swallowed by one, and I'm dead. I'll climb around and around inside it forever, here in the dark. I wonder if anyone else has been swallowed? It's so lonely. . . .*

*The dragon is dead,* the voices told him. *No, the dragon is death,* others assured him.

He stopped and ate a little more of his food. His mouth was dry, but he did not take more than a few drops of water before resuming his four-legged climb.

Simon stopped to catch his breath and rest his aching leg for perhaps the dozenth time since entering the stairwell. As he crouched, panting, light suddenly flickered around him. He thought wildly that his torch had blazed again, until he remembered that the dead brand was stuck beneath his belt. For a startlingly beautiful moment the whole stairwell seemed full of pale golden light, and he looked up the shaft into infinite distance, up past a shrinking spiral of stairs to a hole that led straight to heaven. Then, with a silent concussion, a ball of angry flame bloomed in the heights above him, turning the very air red, and for a moment the stairwell became hot as forge fire. Simon shouted in fear.

*No!* the voices screamed. *No! Speak not the word! You will summon Unbeing!*

There was a crack louder than any thunder, then a blue-white flash that dissolved everything in pure light. An instant later everything was black once more.

Simon lay on the stairs, panting. Was it truly dark again, or had the flare blinded him? How could he know?

*What does it matter?* asked a mocking voice.

He pressed his fingers against his closed eyelids until faint sparkles of blue and red moved in the darkness, but it proved nothing.

*I will not know unless I find something that I know I should be able to see.*

He had a hideous thought. What if, blinded, he crawled past a way out, a lighted doorway, a portal open to the sky?

*Can't think. I'll climb. Can't think.*

He struggled upward. After a while he seemed to lose himself entirely, drifting away to other places, other times. He saw Erchester and the countryside beyond as they had looked from the bellchamber atop Green Angel Tower—the rolling hills and fenced farms, the tiny houses and people and animals laid out below him like wooden toys on a green blanket. He wanted to warn them all, tell them to run away, that a terrible winter was coming.

He saw Morgenes again. The lenses that the old man wore glinted in a beam of afternoon light, making his eyes flash as though some greater-than-ordinary fire burned within him. Morgenes was trying to tell him something, but Simon, young, stupid Simon, was watching a fly buzzing near the window. If only he had listened! If only he had known!

And he saw the castle itself, a fantastic hodgepodge of towers and roofs, its banners rippling in a spring wind. The Hayholt—his home. His home as it had been, and would never be again. But, oh, what he would give to turn Time in its track and send it rolling backward! If he could have bargained his soul for it . . . what was a soul worth, anyway, against the happiness of home restored?

The sky behind the Hayholt lightened as if the sun had emerged from behind a cloud. Simon squinted. Perhaps it was not spring after all—perhaps it was high summer. . . ?

The Hayholt's towers faded, but the light remained.

*Light!*

It was a faint, directionless sheen, no brighter than moonglow through fog—but Simon could see the dim form of the step before him, his dirt-crusted, scabby hand flattened upon it. He could see!

He looked around, trying to determine the source of the light. As far as he could see ahead of him, the steps wound upward. The light, faint as swamp-fire, came from somewhere above.

He got to his feet, swayed woozily for a moment, then began to walk upright once more. At first the angle seemed strange and he had to clutch the wall for support, but soon he felt almost human. Each step, laborious as it seemed, was taking him closer to the light. Each twinge of his wounded ankle was taking him nearer to . . . what? Freedom, he hoped.

What had seemed an unlimited vista during the blinding flash of light now abruptly closed off above him. The stairs opened out onto a broad landing, but did not continue upward. Instead, the stairwell had been sealed off with a low ceiling of crude brick, as though someone had tried to cork the stair-tower like the neck of a bottle—but light leaked through at one side. Simon shuffled toward the glow, crouching so that he would not bump his head, and found a place where the bricks had fallen down, leaving a crevice that seemed just wide enough for a single person to climb. He jumped, but his hands could only touch the rough brick lining the hole; if there was an up-

per side, it was out of his reach. He jumped again, but it
was useless.

Simon stared up at the opening. A heavy, defeated weariness descended on him. He slumped down to the landing
and sat for a moment with his head in his hands. To have
climbed so far!

He finished off the heel of bread and weighed the onion
in his hand, wondering if he should just eat it; at last, he
put it away again. It wasn't time to give up yet. After a
few moments of thought, he crawled over to the scatter of
bricks that had crumbled loose from the ceiling and began
piling them one atop the other, trying to find an arrangement that was stable. When he had made the sturdiest pile
he could, he clambered atop it. Now, as he reached up, his
hands stretched far into the crevice, but he still could not
feel any upper surface. He tensed his muscles, then
leaped. For a moment, he felt a lip at the upper part of the
hole; an instant later his hands failed their grip and he slid
back down, tumbling from the pile of bricks and twisting
his sore ankle. Biting his lip to keep from shouting at the
pain, he laboriously stacked the bricks again, climbed
atop them, crouched, and jumped.

This time he was prepared. He caught the top of the
hole and hung, wincing. After taking a few strong
breaths, he pulled upward, his whole body trembling with
the strain.

*Farther, farther, just a little farther . . .*

The broken edges of brick passed before him. As he
pulled himself higher, his elbows pushed against the
brick, and for a moment it seemed that he would be
trapped, wedged and left hanging in the hole like a game
bird. He sucked in another breath, clenched his teeth
against the pain of his arms, and pulled. Quivering, he
inched higher; he braced himself for a short moment
against the back of the hole, then pulled again. His eyes
rose past the top of his hole, then his nose, then his chin.
When he could, he threw his arm out onto the surface and
clutched, pressing his back against the brick, then brought
the other arm out as well. Using his elbows as levers, he
worked his way up out of the crevice, ignoring the scrape

of stone along his back and sides, then slid forward onto
his chest and kicked like a swimmer until the whole of
his length was lying on dank stone, safe.

Simon lay for a long time, sucking air, trying not to
think about how much his arms and shoulders hurt. He
rolled over on his back and stared up at another ceiling of
stone, this one only a little higher above him than the last
had been. Tears trickled down his cheeks. Was this to be
the next variation in his torments? Would he be forced to
pull himself up by sheer strength through hole after hole,
forever? Was he damned?

Simon pulled the wet shirt from his breeches and
squeezed it to get a few drops into his mouth, then sat up
and looked at what was around him.

His eyes widened; his heart seemed to expand inside
his chest. This was something different.

He was sitting on the floor of what was obviously a
storeroom. It was human-made, and full of human implements, although none seemed to have been touched for
some time. In one corner was a wagon wheel with two of
its spokes missing. Several casks stood against another
wall, and beside them were piled cloth sacks bulging with
mysterious contents. For a moment, all Simon could think
about was the possibility that they might contain food.
Then he saw the ladder beside the far wall, and realized
where the light was coming from.

The upper part of the ladder vanished through an open
hatch door in the ceiling, a square full of light. Simon
stared, gape-mouthed. Surely someone had heard his an-
guished prayers and had set it there to wait for him.

He roused himself and moved slowly across the room,
then clutched the rungs of the ladder and looked upward.
There was light above, and it seemed like the clean light
of day. After all this time, could such a thing be?

The room above was another storeroom. It had a hatch
door and ladder as well, but in the upper part of the wall
there was a small, narrow window—through which Simon could see gray sky.

*Sky!*

He had thought that he had no more tears to cry, but as

he stared at the rectangle of clouds, he began to weep, sobs of relief like a lost child reunited with a parent. He sank to his knees and offered a prayer of thanks. The world had been given back to him. No, that was not true: *he* had found the world once more.

After resting a few moments, he mounted the ladder. On the upper side of the hatchway he found a small chamber full of masonry tools and jars of paint and whitewash. This room had an ordinary door and ordinary rough plaster walls. Simon was delighted. Everything was so blessedly ordinary! He opened the door carefully, suddenly aware that he was in a place where people lived, that much as he wished to see another face and hear a voice that did not issue from empty shadows, he had to be cautious.

Outside the door lay a huge chamber with a floor of polished stone, lit only by small high windows. The walls were covered with heavy tapestries. On his right, a wide staircase swept upward and out of sight; across the chamber a smaller set of steps rose to a landing and a closed door. Simon looked from side to side and listened, but there seemed no one about but him. He stepped out.

Despite all the cleaning implements in the various storerooms, the large chamber did not seem to have benefited from their use: pale freckles of mold grew on the tapestries and the air was thick with the damp, close smell of a place long-untended.

The astonishment of being in daylight again, the glory of escape from the depths, was so strong that Simon did not realize for some time that he stood in a place he knew well. Something in the shape and arrangement of the windows or some dimly-perceptible detail in one of the fading tapestries finally pricked his memory.

*Green Angel Tower.* The awareness came over him like a dream, the familiar turned strange, the strange become familiar. *I'm in the entry hall. Green Angel Tower!*

That surprising recognition was followed by one much less pleasant.

*I'm in the Hayholt. In the High King's castle. With Elias and his soldiers. And Pryrates.*

He stepped back into the shadows along the wall as though any moment the Erkynguard would crash through the tower's main door to take him prisoner. What should he do?

It was tempting to consider climbing up the wide staircase to the bellchamber, the place that had been his childhood refuge. He could look down and see every corner of the Hayholt; he could rest and try to decide what to do next. But his swollen ankle was throbbing horridly, and the thought of all those steps made him feel weak.

First he would eat the onion he had saved, he decided. He deserved a small celebration. He would think later.

Simon slipped back into the closet, then considered that even that place might be a little too frequented. Perhaps the tower's entry chamber only *seemed* unvisited. He clambered down the ladder into the storeroom beneath, grunting softly at the ache in his arms and ankle, then pulled the onion from his pocket and devoured it in a series of greedy bites. He squeezed the last of his water down his throat—whatever else might happen, rain was sluicing through all the castle gutters and drizzling down past the windows, so soon he would have all the water he wanted—and then lay back with his head resting against one of the sacks and began organizing his thoughts.

Within moments he fell asleep.

🌟

*"We tell lies when we are afraid," said Morgenes.*

*The old man took a stone from his pocket and tossed it into the moat. There was a flirt of sunlight on the ripples as the stone disappeared. "Afraid of what we don't know, afraid of what others will think, afraid of what will be found out about us. But every time we tell a lie, the thing that we fear grows stronger."*

*Simon looked around. The sun was vanishing behind the castle's western wall; Green Angel Tower was a black spike, boldly silhouetted. He knew this was a dream. Morgenes had said this to him long ago, but they had been in the doctor's chambers standing over a dusty book at the* time, not outside in the fading afternoon. And in any case, Morgenes was dead. This was a dream, nothing more.

"It is, in fact, a kind of magic—perhaps the strongest of all," Morgenes continued. "Study that, if you wish to understand power, young Simon. Don't fill your head with nattering about spells and incantations. Understand how lies shape us, shape kingdoms."

"But that's not magic," Simon protested, lured into the discussion despite himself. "That doesn't do anything. Real magic lets you . . . I don't know. Fly. Make bags of gold out of a pile of turnips. Like in the stories."

"But the stories themselves are often lies, Simon. The bad ones are." The doctor cleaned his spectacles on the wide sleeve of his robe. "Good stories will tell you that facing the lie is the worst terror of all. And there is no talisman or magic sword that is half so potent a weapon as truth."

Simon turned to watch the ripples slowly dissipating. It was wonderful to stand and talk with Morgenes again, even if it was only a dream. "Do you mean that if I said to a great dragon like the one that King John killed: 'You're an ugly dragon,' that would be better than cutting its head off with a sword?"

Morgenes' voice was fainter. "If you had been pretending it wasn't a dragon, then yes, that would be the best thing to do. But there is more, Simon. You have to go deeper still."

"Deeper?" Simon turned back, angry now. "I've been down in the earth, Doctor. I lived and I came up again. What do you mean?"

Morgenes was . . . changing. His skin had turned papery and his pale hair was full of leaves. Even as Simon watched, the old man's fingers began to lengthen, changing into slender twigs, branching, branching. "Yes, you have learned," the doctor said. As he spoke, his features began to disappear into the whorls on the white bark of the tree. "But you must go deeper still. There is much to understand. Watch for the angel—she will show you things, both in the ground and far above it."

"Morgenes!" Simon's anger was all gone. His friend

*was changing so swiftly that there was almost nothing manlike left of him, only a faint suggestion in the shape of the trunk, an unnatural trembling in the tree's limbs. "Don't leave me!"*

"But I have left you already," the doctor's voice murmured. "What you have of me is only what is in your head—I am part of you. The rest of me has become part of the earth again." The tree swayed slightly. "Remember, though—the sun and stars shine on the leaves, but the roots are deep in the earth, hidden ... hidden. ..."

Simon clutched at the tree's pale trunk, his fingers scrabbling uselessly against the stiff bark. The doctor's voice was silent.

Simon sat up, nightmare-sweat stinging his eyes, and was horrified to discover himself in darkness.

*It was all a dream! I'm still lost in the tunnels, I'm lost. ...*

A moment later he saw starlight through the storeroom's high window.

*Mooncalf. Fell asleep and it got dark outside.*

He sat up, rubbing his sore limbs. What was he to do now? He was hungry and thirsty, and there seemed little chance that he would find anything to eat here in Green Angel Tower. Still, he was more than a little reluctant to leave this relatively safe place.

*Have I climbed out of the dark ground only to starve to death in a closet?* he chided himself. *What kind of knight would do that?*

He got to his feet and stretched, noting the dull ache in his ankle. Perhaps just a foray out to get some water and see the lay of the land. Certainly it would be best to do such things while it was still dark.

Simon stood uncertainly in the shadows outside Green Angel Tower. The Inner Bailey's haphazard roofs made a familiar jumble against the night sky, but Simon did not feel at all comfortable. It was not just that he was an outlaw in his childhood home, although that was disconcerting enough: there was also something strange in the air that he could not name, but which he nevertheless could sense quite clearly. The maddening slipperiness of the world belowground had somehow seeped up into the everyday stones of the castle itself. When he tilted his head to one side, he could almost see the buildings ripple and change at the edge of his sight. Faint blurs of light, like phantom flames, seemed to flicker along the edges of walls, then quickly vanish.

The Hayholt, too? Had all the world broken loose from its moorings? What was happening?

With some difficulty, he nerved himself to go exploring.

Although it seemed the great castle was deserted, Simon soon discovered it was not. The Inner Bailey was dark and quiet, but voices whispered down corridors and behind closed doors, and there were lights in many of the higher windows. He also heard snatches of music, odd tunes and odder voices that made him want to arch like a cat and hiss. As he stood in the deep concealing shadows of the Hedge Garden, he decided that the Hayolt had somehow become spoiled, a fruit left to sit for too long now grown soft and rotten beneath the outer shell. He could not quite say what was wrong, but the whole of the Inner Bailey, the place that had been the center of Simon's childhood world, seemed to have sickened.

He went stealthily to the kitchen, the lesser pantry, the chapel—even, in a moment of high daring, to the antechamber of the throne room, which opened onto the gardens. All the outer doors were barred. He could find no entrance anywhere. Simon could not remember any time before when that had been so. Was the king frightened of spies, of a siege? Or were the barriers not to keep out intruders, but to make sure that those who were inside remained there? He breathed quietly and thought. There were windows that could not be closed, he knew, and other secret ways—but did he want to risk such difficult entrances? There might be fewer people about at night, but judging by the barred doors, those who were up, especially if they were sentries, would be even more alert to unexpected noises.

Simon returned to the kitchen and pulled himself up into the branches of a small, barren apple tree, then climbed from there onto the ledge of the high window. The thick glass was gone, but the window slot had been wedged full of stones; there would be no way to remove them without making a terrible clatter. He cursed silently and descended.

He was sore and still terribly hungry, despite the luxury of a whole onion. He decided that he had wasted his time on the doors of the Inner Bailey. On the far side of the moat, though, the Middle Bailey might prove less well-protected.

There were several distressingly naked patches of ground between the two baileys. Despite not having seen a single guard or, in fact, a single other person, Simon had to force himself to cross these open stretches; each time he dashed for the safety of shadows as soon as he was clear. The bridge across the moat was the most un-nerving part. He began to cross it and then changed his mind twice. It was at least thirty ells long, and if someone appeared while he was in the middle, he would be as ob-vious as a fly walking on a white wall.

At last he blew out a shaky breath, drew in a deep gasp of air, and sprinted across. His steps sounded as loud to him as thunder. He forced himself to slow down and cross at a silent walk, despite the thumping of his heart. When he reached the far side he ducked into a shed where he sat until he felt steady again.

*You're doing well,* he told himself. *No one's around. Nothing to fear.*

He knew that was a lie.

*Plenty to fear,* he amended. *But no one's caught you yet. Not in a while, anyway.*

As he got to his feet, he could not help wondering why the bridge over the moat had been down in the first place if all the doors were barred and windows blocked against some feared attack.

*And why wasn't Green Angel Tower locked up?* He could think of no answer.

Before he had taken a hundred paces across the muddy

thoroughfare in the center of Middle Bailey, he saw
something that made him shrink back into the darkness
again, his terrors suddenly returned—this time with reason.

An army was camped in the bailey.

It had taken him some long moments to realize it, since
so few fires burned, and since the tents were made of
dark cloth that was almost invisible in the night, but the
entire bailey seemed to be full of armed men. He could
see perhaps a half dozen on the nearer outskirts, sentries
by the look of them, cloaked and helmeted and carrying
long pikes. In the dim light he could not see much of their
faces. Even as he stood hidden in a crack between two of
the bailey's buildings, wondering what to do next, another
pair of cloaked and hooded figures passed him. They also
carried long spears, but he could see immediately that
they were different. Something in the way they carried
themselves, something in their graceful, deceptively swift
strides, told him beyond doubt that these were Norns.

Simon sank farther back into the concealing darkness,
trembling. Would they know he was here? Could they . . .
smell him?

Even as he wondered, the black-robed creatures paused
only a short way from his hiding place, alert as hunting
dogs. Simon held his breath and willed himself to total
stillness. After a long wait, the Norns abruptly turned in
unison, as though some wordless communication had
passed between them, and continued on their way. Simon
waited a few shaky moments, then cautiously poked his
head around the wall. He could not see them against the
darkness, but he could see the human soldiers move out
of their way, quick as men avoiding a snake. For an instant the Norns were silhouetted against one of the
watchfires, twin hooded shapes that seemed oblivious to
the humans around them. They slipped from the light of
the fire and vanished once more.

This was something unexpected. Norns! The White
Foxes, here in the Hayholt itself! Things were worse even
than he had imagined. But hadn't Geloë and the others
said that the immortals couldn't come back here? Perhaps

they had meant that Ineluki and his undead servitors couldn't return. But even if that last was true, it seemed little solace just now.

So the Middle Bailey was full of soldiers, and there were Norns moving freely around the keep, silent as hunting owls. Simon's skin prickled. He had no doubt that the Outer Bailey was also full of Black Rimmersmen, or Thrithings mercenaries, or whatever cutthroats Elias had bought with Erkynland's gold and the Storm King's magic. It was hard to believe that many of the king's own Erkynguard, even the most ruthless, would remain in this haunted place with the corpse-faced Norns: the immortals were too frighteningly different. It had been easy to see in just a brief instant that the soldiers in the Middle Bailey were frightened of them.

*Now I have a reason to escape besides just my own skin. Josua and the others need to know what is going on in here.* He felt a momentary surge of hope. *Maybe knowing the Norns are here with Elias will bring Jiriki and the rest of the Sithi. Jiriki's kin would have to help the mortals then, wouldn't they?* Simon tried to think carefully. *In fact, I should try to escape now—if I can. What good will I do Josua or anyone else if I don't get out?*

But he had barely learned anything. He was exactly what any war leader most valued—an experienced eye in the middle of the enemy camp. Simon knew the Hayholt like a farmer knew his fields, like a blacksmith knew his tools. He owed it to his good fortune in surviving this far—good fortune, yes, he reminded himself, but his wits and resourcefulness had helped him, too—to take all he could from the situation.

So. Back to the Inner Bailey. He could last a day or two without food if necessary, since water seemed to be abundantly available. Plenty of time to spy out what useful things he could, then find a way out past the soldiers to freedom. If he had to, he could even make his way back under the castle and through the dark tunnels again. That would be the surest way to escape undetected.

*No. Not the tunnels.*

It was no use pretending. Even for Josua and the others, that was something he could not do.

He was approaching the bridge to the Inner Bailey when a loud clatter made Simon pull back into the shadows once more. When he saw the group of mounted shapes riding out onto the span, he silently thanked Usires for not bringing him to the bridge a few moments earlier.

The company seemed made up of armored Erkynguardsmen, strangely dispirited-looking for all their martial finery. Simon had only a moment to wonder what their errand might be when he saw a chillingly familiar bald head in their midst.

*Pryrates!* Simon pushed back against the wall, staring. A choking hatred rose up inside of him. There the monster was, not three score paces away, his hairless features limned by faint moonlight.

*I could be on him in a moment,* he thought wildly. *If I walked up slowly, the soldiers wouldn't worry—they'd just think I was one of the mercenaries who'd drunk too much wine. I could crush his skull with a rock....*

But what if he failed? Then he would easily be captured, any use he might be to Josua finished before it had begun. And worse, he would be the red priest's prisoner. It was just as Binabik had said: how long would it be until he told Pryrates every secret about Josua, about the Sithi and the swords—until he begged to tell the alchemist anything he wanted to hear?

Simon could not help shuddering like a taunted dog at the end of a rope. The monster was so close...!

The company of horsemen stopped. The priest was berating one of the Erkynguards, his raspy voice faint but unmistakable. Simon leaned as far forward as he could without losing the shadow of the wall, cupping his hand behind his ear so that he could hear better.

". . . or I will ride *you!*" the priest spat.

The soldier said something in a muffled voice. Despite his height and the sword he wore sheathed on his hip, the man cowered like a terrified child. No one dared speak sharply to Pryrates. That had been true even before Simon had fled the castle.

"Are you mad or just stupid?" Pryrates' voice rose. "I cannot ride a lame horse for days, all the way to Wentmouth. Give me yours."

The soldier got down, then handed the reins of his mount to the alchemist. He said something else. Pryrates laughed.

"Then you will lead mine. It will not hurt you to walk, I think, since it was your idiocy that . . ." The rest of his mocking remark was too soft to hear, but Simon thought he heard another reference to Wentmouth, the rocky height in the south where the Gleniwent River met the sea. Pryrates pulled himself up into the guardsman's saddle, his scarlet robe appearing for a moment from beneath his dark cloak like a bloody wound. The priest spurred down off the bridge and onto the mud of the Middle Bailey. The rest of the company followed after him, trailed on foot by the soldier leading Pryrates' horse.

As they passed by his hiding spot, Simon found that he was clutching a stone in his hand; he could not remember picking it up. He stared at the alchemist's head, round and bare as an eggshell, and thought about what pleasure he would feel to see it cracked open. That evil creature had killed Morgenes, and God Himself alone knew how many others. His fear mysteriously fled, Simon struggled against the almost overwhelming urge to shout his fury and attack. How could the good ones like the doctor and Geloë and Deornoth die when such a beast was allowed to live? Killing Pryrates would be worth the loss of his own life. An unimaginable vileness would be gone from the world. *Doing the necessary*, Rachel would have called it. *A dirty job, but one as needs doing.* But it seemed his life was not his to give.

He watched the company troop past. They circled around the tents and vanished, moving toward the Lesser Gate that led to the outermost bailey. Simon dropped the rock he had been clutching into the mud and stood, trembling.

A thought came to him suddenly, an idea so wild and mad that he frightened himself. He looked up at the sky, trying to guess how much time remained until dawn. By the chill, empty feel of the air, he felt sure the sun was at least a few hours away.

Who was most likely to have taken Bright-Nail from the mound? Pryrates, of course. He might not even have told King Elias, if that suited his purposes. And where would it be if that was true? Hidden in the priest's stronghold—in Hjeldin's Tower.

Simon turned. The alchemist's tower, unpleasantly squat beside the pure sweep of Green Angel, loomed over the Inner Bailey wall. If there were lights inside, they were hidden: the scarlet windows were dark. It looked deserted—but so did everything else at the center of the great keep. The whole of the Hayholt's interior might have been a mausoleum, a city of the dead.

Did he dare to go inside—or at least try? He would have to have light. Perhaps there were extra torches or a hooded lantern he could use somewhere in Green Angel Tower. It would be a fearful, terrible risk. . . .

If he had not seen Pryrates leaving with his own eyes, if he had not heard the red priest talk of riding to Wentmouth, Simon would not even have thought of it: just the idea of making his way into the ill-omened tower when hairless, black-eyed Pryrates might be sitting inside, waiting like a spider at the center of his web, made his stomach heave. But the priest was gone, that was undeniable, and Simon knew he might never have such a chance again. What if he found Bright-Nail?! He could take it and be gone from the Hayholt before Pryrates even returned. *That* would be a satisfying trick to play on the red-robed murderer. And wouldn't it be fine to ride into Prince Josua's camp and show them Bright-Nail flashing in the sun? Then he would *truly* be Simon, Master of the Great Swords, wouldn't he?

As he moved quickly and quietly across the bridge, he found himself staring at the bailey wall before him. Something about it had changed. It had grown . . . lighter.

The sun was coming up, or at least as much of the sun as would appear on this gray day. Simon hurried a little. He had been wrong.

*A few more hours, eh? You've been lucky. What if you'd*

*been rattling around outside the door of Hjeldin's Tower,
when the sun came up? Mooncalf, still a mooncalf.*

Still, he was not entirely unrepentant. Knights and heroes had to .be bold, and what he was considering now was a bold plan indeed. He would simply have to wait until tomorrow night's darkness to accomplish it. It would be a marvelous,· brave thing to do.

But even as he hurried back toward his hiding hole in Green Angel Tower, he wished his friends were around to talk him out of it.

The sun had set a few hours before. A fine drizzle was descending from the night sky. Simon stood in Green Angel Tower's doorway and prepared himself to step out.

It was not easy. He was still feeling weak and hungry, although after sleeping the day away he had found the remains of someone's supper, a crust of bread and a scanty rind of cheese, on a plate in an alcove off the tower's antechamber. Both bread and cheese were dry, but still seemed only hours old, not days or weeks; even as he gobbled them down he had wondered whose meal it had been. Did Barnabas the sexton still care for the tower and its great bells? If so, he was doing a poor job.

Thinking of Barnabas had made Simon realize that not once in the time he had returned had he heard Green Angel's bells. Now, as he stood in the doorway of the tower, waiting for darkness, the thought came to him again. The great echoing cry of the bronze bells had been the heartbeat of the Hayholt as he had known it, an hourly reminder that things went on, that time passed, that life continued. But now they were silent.

Simon shrugged and stepped out. He paused to cup his hands beneath a stream of rainwater running down from the roof, then drank thirstily. He wiped his hands on his breeches and stared at the shadow of Hjeldin's Tower against the violet sky. There was nothing left to do. There was no reason to wait any longer.

Simon made his way along the outer perimeter of the bailey, using the cover of the buildings to keep himself hidden from any eyes that might be watching. He had al-

most walked into the arms of Pryrátes and the soldiers the
night before; despite the seeming emptiness of the keep,
he would take nothing for granted. Once or twice he
heard wisps of conversation drift past, but he saw no
living people who might have been responsible. A long,
sobbing laugh floated by. Simon shivered.

As he moved out around the edge of one of the out-
buildings, he thought he saw a flicker of light in the tower's upper windows, a momentary gleam of red like a
coal that still hid smoldering life. He stopped, cursing
quietly to himself. Why should he be so sure that just because Pryrates was gone, the tower would be empty? Perhaps the Norns lived there.

But perhaps not. Surely even the priest needed servants
to look after him, to sweep the floors and light the lamps,
just as Simon had once done for Doctor Morgenes. If anyone moved inside the tower, it was likely some terrified
castle-dweller forced to labor in the red priest's stronghold. Perhaps it was Rachel the Dragon. If so, Simon
would rescue her as well as Bright-Nail. Wouldn't she be
astonished—he would have to be careful not to frighten
her too badly. She must have wondered where in the
world her wayward scullion had gone.

Simon turned before he reached the tower doors and
clambered into a patch of ivy growing along the bailey
wall. Hero or not, he was no fool. He would wait to see
if there was any sign the tower was occupied.

He huddled, holding his knees. The bulk of the tower
overhead, its blunt dark stones, made him uncomfortable.
It was hard not to feel it waited for him like a giant
feigning sleep, anticipating the moment when Simon
would come within reach. . . .

Time seemed to pass very slowly. When he could stand
the waiting no longer, he dragged himself out of the ivy,
which seemed to cling more strongly than it should. No
one had come near the doorway; no one was moving anywhere about the Inner Bailey. He had seen no more lights
in the windows, nor had he heard anything but the moaning of the wind in the towertops. It was time.

But how to get in? There was scarcely any chance he

would be able to unlock the huge black doors—someone as secretive as Pryrates must have bolts on his fortress gateway that could keep out an army. No, it would undoubtedly take climbing. The gatehouse that stood around and over the front door was probably his best chance. From the top of it he could perhaps find a way up to one of the upper windows. The stones of the walls were heavy and crudely set: climbing holds should not be too difficult to find.

He ducked into the shelter of the gatehouse and paused for a moment to look at the black timbers of the front doors. They were indeed massive—Simon guessed that even men with axes would not penetrate them in anything less than half a day. Testing, he grasped one of the massive door handles and pulled. The right side door swung out silently, startling Simon so that he stumbled backward, out into the thin rain.

The doors were open—unlocked! For a moment he wanted only to run, certain it was a trap set just for him; but as he stopped, hands raised as though to ward off a blow, he realized that was unlikely. Or perhaps there were more certain protections inside. . . ?

Simon hesitated a moment longer, his heart rattling.

*Don't be a fool. Either go in or stay out. Don't stand around in the middle of everything waiting to be noticed by someone.*

He clenched his fists and stepped through, then pulled the door shut behind him.

There was no need yet for the torch in his belt, which he had refurbished with oil from one of Green Angel Tower's storage rooms: one already burned in a bracket on the wall of the high antechamber, making shadows shiver in the corners. Simon could not help wondering who had lit it, but quickly dismissed the useless thought: he could only begin looking, try to move quietly, and listen for anyone else who might be in Hjeldin's Tower with him.

He walked across the antechamber, dismayed by the loud hiss his boot soles made rubbing on the stone. Stairs led upward along one wall to the highest, darkest parts of the tower. They would have to wait.

So many doors! Simon chose one and opened it gently. The torchlight bleeding in from the antechamber revealed a room filled entirely with furnishings made from bones that had been tied and glued together, including one large chair which had, as if in mockery of the High King's throne, an awning made entirely from skulls—human skulls. Many of the bones still had bits of dark dry flesh stuck to them. From somewhere in the room came the fizzing chirp of what sounded like a cricket. Simon felt his stomach rising into his throat and hurriedly shut the door.

When he had recovered a little he took his own brand and lit it from the wall torch. If he was really going to look for the sword, he would have to be able to see even into the dark corners, no matter what he might find there.

He went back to the bone room, but further inspection turned up nothing but the dreadful furnishings, an incredible array of bones. Simon hoped some of them were animal bones, but doubted it. The insistent buzz of the cricket drove him out once more.

The next chamber was filled wall to wall with tubs covered by stretched nets. Things Simon could not quite make out slithered and splashed in dark fluid; from time to time a slippery back or an oddly-terminated appendage pushed against the netting until it bulged upward. In another room Simon found thousands of tiny silvery figures of men and women, each carved with amazing accuracy and realism: each little statue was a perfect representation of a person frozen in a position of fear or despair. When Simon lifted one of them, the shiny metal felt slippery and strangely warm against his skin. A moment later, he dropped it and backed quickly out of the room. He was sure he had felt it squirm in his grip.

Simon made his way from one room to the next, continuously disturbed by what he found, sometimes by the sheer unpleasantness of the priest's possessions, sometimes by their incomprehensibility. The last room on the ground floor contained a few bones as well, but they were far too large to belong to anything human. They were boiling in a great vat that hung above an oil flame, filling the damp room with a powerful but unrecognizable stink. Viscous black fluid ran in oozing drops from a spigot on the vat's side into a wide stone bowl. The fetid steam swirling up made Simon's head reel and the scar on his cheek sting. A quick search discovered no trace of the sword, and he retreated gratefully to the relatively clean air outside.

After hesitating a moment, he climbed the stairs to the next level. There was undoubtedly more to be discovered beneath the tower, down in its catacombs—but Simon was in no hurry to do that. He would put such a search off for last, and pray that he found the sword before then.

A room full of glass beakers and retorts much like things Morgenes had possessed, a chamber whose walls and ceiling were draped with inordinately thick spiderwebs—his search of that one was brief and perfunctory—another which seemed an indoor jungle full of trailing vines and fat, rotting blossoms, Simon passed through them all, feeling more and more like some peasant boy from a story who had entered a witch's magical castle. Some of the chambers had contents so dreadful he could do no more than peer for a moment into the shadowed interior before shoving the door closed again. There were some things he simply could not force himself to do: if the sword was in one of these rooms, it would have to remain unrescued.

One room that did not at first seem so dreadful held only a single small cot, oddly woven from a mesh of leather straps. At first he thought this might be the place Pryrates slept . . . until he saw the hole in the stone floor and the stains beneath the cot. He left quickly, shuddering. He didn't think he could spend much longer in this place and keep his sanity.

On the fifth floor of the priest's storehouse of nightmares, Simon hesitated. This was the level at which the great red windows were set: if he moved from room to room with his torch, it was quite possible someone elsewhere in the keep might notice the moving flicker of light in what should be an empty tower. After some consideration, he set his torch in one of the high brackets on the wall. He would have to search in near-darkness, Simon realized, but he had spent enough time below ground that he thought he might be better suited for that than almost anyone except a Sitha . . . or a Norn.

Only three chambers opened off the landing. The first was another featureless room with a cot, although this one had no drain in the floor. Simon had no problem believing that this was indeed Pryrates' sleeping place: something in the stark emptiness of the room seemed appropriate. Simon could picture the black-eyed priest lying on his back staring up into nothing, plotting. There was also a privy, a strangely natural possession for someone so unnatural.

The second chamber was some sort of reliquary. The entire room was lined with shelves, and every inch of shelf space was taken up by statues. These were not all of a type, like the silver figurines on the first floor, but all shapes and sizes, some that looked like saint's icons, others lopsided wooden fetishes that might have been carved by children or lunatics. It was fascinating, in a way. Had Simon not felt the terror of this strange tower all around him, the incredible risk he was taking just being here, he might have liked to take some time to look at the bizarre collection. Some were made from wax and had candle wicks protruding from the heads, others were little more than conglomerations of bones and mud and feathers, but each was recognizably a figure of some sort, although many seemed more animal than human. But nowhere was there anything like a sword. The eyes of some of the images seemed to follow Simon as he backed out again.

The last and largest room was perhaps the red priest's study. Here the great scarlet windows were most visible, since they covered a large part of the curved wall, although with night sky outside they were dark. The room itself was littered with scrolls and books and a collection of other objects as haphazardly odd and dispiriting as anything he had seen in any of the other chambers. If he could not find the sword here, his only hope was the catacombs beneath the tower. The roof above was full of star-gazing equipment and other strange machinery—he had seen that late in the afternoon from one of Green Angel Tower's narrow windows; Simon doubted there would be anything so valuable hidden out there, but he would look anyway. No sense avoiding anything that might save him a trip down below Hjeldin's monument. . . .

The study was thick with shadows and extremely cluttered, almost the entire floor covered with objects, although the walls were curiously empty of furnishings or anything else. At the room's center a high-backed chair faced away from the door toward the high windows. It was surrounded by free-standing cabinets, each one overflowing with parchments and heavy bound books. The wall beneath the windows, Simon saw by the faint torchlight, was covered in pale, painted runes.

He took a few steps toward the wall, then stumbled slightly. Something was wrong: he felt an odd tingling, a faintly nauseating unsteadiness in his bones and his guts. A moment later, a hand shot out from the darkness of the chair and fastened onto his wrist. Simon screamed and fell down, but the hand did not let go. The powerful grip was cold as frost.

"What have we here?" a voice said. "A trespasser?"

Simon could not yank himself free. His heart sped so swiftly that he thought he would die of fear. He was pulled slowly back onto his feet, then tugged around the chair until he could look into the pale face that gazed at him from its shadows. The eyes that met his were almost invisible, faint smears of reflected light that nevertheless seemed to hold him just as strongly as the bony hand on his wrist.

"What have we here?" his captor repeated, and leaned forward to stare at him.

It was King Elias.

# 17

# An Ember in the Night Sky

✤

**Despite the urgency** of his errand and the dull ache
of his tailbone, Tiamak could not help pausing in wonder
to watch the proceedings on the broad hillside.

It occurred to him that he had spent so much of his life
reading scrolls and books that he had found very little
chance to experience the sort of things about which they
were written. Except for his brief stay in Ansis Pellipé
and his monthly forays to the Kwanitupul market, the
hurly-burly of life had not intruded much on his hut in the
banyan tree. Now, in this last year, Tiamak had been
caught up in the great movements of mortals and immortals. He had fought monsters beside a princess and a
duke. He had met and spoken with one of the legendary
Sithi. He had seen the return of the greatest knight of the
Johannine Age. Now, as though the pages of one of Doctor Morgenes' dusty volumes had taken on magical life,
he stood beneath cloudy skies watching the surrender of
an army after a life or death struggle in the famous
Onestrine Pass. Surely any scholar worth his quill pen
would give everything he had to be here.

Then why, Tiamak wondered, did he feel such intense
longing to see his banyan tree again?

*I am as They Who Watch and Shape have made me*, he
decided. *I am not a hero, like Camaris or Josua or even
poor Isgrimnur. No, I belong with Father Strangyeard
and the others like us—the small, the quiet. We do not
want the eyes of people on us all the time, waiting to see
what we do next.*

Still, when he considered some of the things he had seen and even done, he was not quite sure that he would have passed them up, even if given a choice.

*As long as I can keep dodging She Who Waits to Take All Back a while longer, that is. I would not mind having a family some day. I would not mind a wife and children who would fill the house with some laughter when I am old.*

But that would mean finding a Wran-bride, of course. Even had he any taste for the tall, fish-skinned women of the drylander cities, he doubted any of them would be eager to live on crab soup in a tree house in the marsh.

Tiamak's thoughts were interrupted by Josua's voice. He started to move toward the prince to deliver his message, but found his way blocked by several large soldiers who, caught up as they were with the spectacle before them, seemed in no hurry to make room for the small man.

"I see you are here already," the prince said to someone. The Wrannaman stood on his tiptoes, straining to see.

"Where else would I go, Prince Josua?" Varellan rose to greet the victor. Benigaris' younger brother, even with cuts and bruises on his face and his arm in a sling, looked strangely unsuited to his role as war-leader. He was tall, and handsome enough in a thin, pale way, but his eyes were watery and his posture apologetic. He looked, Tiamak thought, like a sapling that had not received enough sun.

Josua faced him. The prince wore still a torn surcoat and battered boots, as though the battle had ended only moments ago instead of two full days before. He had not left camp in that time, engaged in so many duties that Tiamak doubted he had slept more than an hour here or there. "There is no need for shame, Varellan," Josua said firmly. "Your men fought well, and you did your duty."

Varellan shook his head furiously, looking for a moment like an unhappy child. "I failed. Benigaris will not care that I did my duty."

"You failed in one thing," Josua told him, "but your

failure may bring more good than you know—although not much of it will come to your brother."

Camaris stepped up silently to stand beside the prince. Varellan's eyes opened wider, as though his uncle were some larger-than-life monster—as, Tiamak thought, in a way he was. "I cannot be happy about what has happened, Prince Josua," said Varellan tightly.

"When we are finished with this, you will find out things that may change your mind."

Varellan grimaced. "Have I not heard enough of such things already? Very well, then let us be finished. You already took my war banner. I would have preferred to give this to you on the battlefield as well."

"You were wounded." Josua spoke as though to a son. "There is no shame in being carried off the field. I knew your father well: he would have been proud of you."

"I wish I could believe that." Varellan, made awkward by the arm sling, pulled a slender golden rod from his belt; a carving of a high-crested bird's head sat atop it. He winced as he knelt. "Prince Josua, here is my commission, the warmaster's baton of the Benidrivine House. For those men who are in my command, I give you our surrender. We are your prisoners."

"No." A stirring of surprise went through the watchers at Josua's words. "You do not surrender to me."

Varellan looked up, puzzled and sullen. "My lord?"

"You have not surrendered your Nabbanai soldiers to a foreign army. You have been defeated by the rightful heir of your household. Despite your brother's patricide—I know you do not believe me yet, Varellan—the Benidrivine House still will rule, even when Benigaris is in shackles." Josua stepped back. "It is to Camaris-sá-Vinitta you surrender, not to me."

Camaris seemed more surprised than Varellan. The old knight turned questioningly to Josua; then, after a moment's hesitation, he extended a long arm and gently took the baton from the young man's hand.

"Rise, nephew," he said. "You have brought only honor on our House."

Varellan's face was a confusion of emotions. "How can

that be?" he demanded. "Either you and Josua are lying and I have lost our most important pass to a usurper, or I have sent hundreds of brave soldiers to die in the cause of the man who murdered my father!"

Camaris shook his head. "If your error was innocent, then there is no blame." He spoke with a curious heaviness, and his gaze seemed fixed on something other than the suffering young man before him. "It is when evil is done by choice, however small or foolish the undertaking may seem, that God mourns." He looked to Josua, who nodded. The old knight then turned to face the watching soldiers and prisoners. "I declare that all who will fight with us to free Nabban shall themselves be free men," Camaris cried, loud enough that even the most distant parts of the gathering could hear him. He raised the baton, and for a moment the battle-light seemed to be on him again. "The Kingfisher House will restore its honor."

There was a loud shout from the men. Even Varellan's defeated army seemed surprised and heartened by what they had seen.

Tiamak took the onset of more general celebration to elbow his way through the crowd of soldiers and sidle up to Josua; the prince was having a few quiet words with Varellan, who was still angry and bewildered.

"Your Majesty?" The Wrannaman stood by the prince's elbow, uncomfortably conscious of his small stature in the midst of all these armored giants. How could little Binabik and his troll-kin—none of them much more than two-thirds Tiamak's size—stand it?

Josua turned to see who had spoken. "A moment, please, Tiamak. Varellan, this goes far deeper than even what your brother did at Bullback Hill. There are things that you must hear that will seem strange beyond belief— but I am here to tell you that in these days, the impossible has become the actual."

Tiamak did not want to stand waiting for Josua to tell the whole story of the Storm King's war. "Please, your Majesty. I have been sent to tell you that your wife, Lady Vorzheva, is giving birth."

"What?!" Josua's attention was now complete. "Is she well? Is anything amiss?"

"I cannot say. Duchess Gutrun sent me as soon as the time came. I rode all the way from the monastery. I am not used to riding." Tiamak resisted the temptation to rub his aching rump, deciding that as casual as his relations with nobility had become, there were perhaps some boundaries still. But he did ache. There was something foolishly dangerous about riding around on an animal so much bigger than he was. It was a drylander custom he did not see himself adopting.

The prince looked helplessly at Varellan, then at Camaris. The old knight's lips creased in a ghostly smile, but even this seemed to have pain in it. "Go, Josua," he said. "There is much I can tell Varellan without you." For a moment he paused and his face seemed to crumple; tears welled in his eyes. "May God give your wife a safe birthing."

"Thank you, Camaris." Josua seemed too distracted to take much note of the old man's reaction. He turned. "Tiamak. I apologize for my bad manners. Will you ride back with me?"

The Wrannaman shook his head. "No, thank you, Prince Josua. I have other things I need to do."

*And one of them is recover from the ride here,* he added silently.

The prince nodded and hurried away.

"Come," Camaris was saying as he laid his long arm across Varellan's shoulder. "We need to talk."

"I'm not sure that I wish to hear what you will tell me," the young man replied. He seemed only half-joking.

"I am not the only one who should speak, nephew," the old knight said. He wiped his eyes with his sleeve. "There is much I would hear from you of my home and of my family. Come."

He led Varellan off toward the row of tents pitched along the ridge-line. Tiamak watched them go with a faint sense of disappointment.

*There it is. I may be in the thick of things, but I am still an outsider. At least if this were written in a book, I would*

*know what they will say to each other. There is indeed
something to be said for a lonely banyan tree.*

After a few moments watching the retreating figures,
Tiamak shivered and wrapped his cloak closer about himself. The weather had turned cold again; the wind seemed
to have knives in it. He decided it was time to go in
search of a little wine to relieve the aching of his back
and fundament.

⚜

The mist that surrounded Naglimund was poisonously
chill. Eolair would have given much to be in front of the
fire in his great hall at Nad Mullach, with war a distant
memory. But war was here, waiting just a short distance
up the slope.

"Stand fast," he told the Hernystiri who huddled behind him. "We will move soon. Remember—they all
bleed. They all die."

"But we die faster," one of the men said quietly.

Eolair did not have the heart to rebuke him. "It is the
waiting," he murmured to Isorn. The duke's son turned a
pale face toward him. "These are brave men. It is the
waiting and the not-knowing that undoes them."

"It is not just that." Isorn gestured with his chin toward
the fortress, a craggy shadow in the mists. "It is this
place. It is the things we fight."

Eolair ground his teeth together. "What is keeping the
Sithi? It might be different if we could understand what
our allies are doing. I swear, it seems they are waiting for
the wind to change or some particular birds to fly overhead. It is like fighting beside an army of scryers."

Isorn, despite his own tension, turned a look of pity on
the count. Eolair felt it almost as a rebuke. "They know
best how to battle their kinfolk."

"I know, I know." Eolair slapped at his sword-hilt.
"But I would give much . . ."

A high-pitched note sang along the hillside. Two more
horns joined in.

"Finally!" the Count of Nad Mullach breathed. He

turned in the saddle. "We follow the Sithi," he called to his men. "Stay together. Protect each other's backs, and do not lose yourselves in this gods-cursed murk."

If Eolair expected to hear an answering shout from the men, he was disappointed. Still, they followed him as he spurred up the slope. He looked back and saw them wading through the snow, grim and silent as prisoners, and he wished again he had brought them to some better fate.

*What should I expect? We are fighting an unnatural enemy, our allies are no less strange, and now the battle is not even on our own soil. It is hard for the men to see this is for the good of Hernystir, let alone for the good of their villages and families. It is hard for me to see that, though I believe it.*

The mists swirled about them as they drove toward Naglimund's shadowy wall. Beyond the gap he could see only the faintest signs of moving shapes, although a trick of hearing made the shrill cries of the Norns and the bird-like war-songs of the Sithi seem to echo all around. Suddenly the great hole in the wall was before them, a mouth opening to swallow the mortals whole.

As Eolair rode through, the air was torn by a flash of light and a booming crash. For a moment all seemed to go inside out; the mist turned black, the shadowy forms before him white. His horse reared, screaming, and fought the reins. A moment later another great smear of light rubbed against his eyes, blinding him. When Eolair could see again, his terrified horse was heading back toward the breach in the wall, right into the reeling mass of the count's own troop. Eolair yanked furiously at the reins, to no effect. With a strangled curse, he pulled himself free of the stirrups and rolled out of the saddle, then crashed to the snowy ground as his mount ran wildly, scattering the reeling soldiers before him and trampling several.

As he lay struggling to catch his breath, Eolair felt rough hands close on him and drag him to his feet. Two of his Hernystirmen were staring at him, eyes wide with fear.

"That ... that light ..." one of them stammered.

"My horse ran mad," the count shouted above the din.

He smacked snow loose from his leggings and surcoat and strode forward. The men fell in behind him. Isorn's horse had not bolted; still mounted, the young Rimmersman had vanished somewhere in the mists ahead.

Naglimund's inner court looked like some kind of nightmarish foundry. Mist hung everywhere like smoke, and flames leaped periodically from the high windows and traveled along the stone walls in great blazing curtains. The Sithi were already at close quarters with the Norn defenders; their shadows, magnified by flames and fog, stretched out across the castle like warring gods. For a moment Eolair thought he knew what Maegwin saw. He wanted to fall down on his face until it all went away.

A horseman appeared out of the fog. "They are hard pressed before the inner keep," Isorn called. He had a bloody streak down his jaw. "That is where the giants are."

"Oh, gods," Eolair said miserably. He waved his men to follow, then set out at a lope after Isorn. His boots sank into the snow at each step, so that he felt as though he labored up a steep hill. Eolair knew his mail-coat was too heavy to let him run for very long. He was breathing hard already, and not one blow struck.

The battle before the inner keep was a chaos of blades and mist and near-invisible foes into which Eolair's men quickly vanished. Isorn stopped to pick up a fallen pike and ride against a bloodied giant who held half a dozen Sithi at bay with his club. Eolair sensed movement nearby and turned find a dark-eyed Norn rushing toward him waving a gray ax. The count traded strokes with his attacker for a moment, then his foot slipped and he dropped to a knee. Before his foe could take advantage, he scooped a handful of snow and flung it up in a white shower toward the Norn's face. Without waiting to see if it had distracted his opponent, Eolair lunged forward, sweeping his sword around at ankle-height. There was a resounding crunch of steel against bone and his enemy fell atop him.

The next moments passed in what seemed a profound

stillness. The sounds of battle dropped away, as though he
had passed through into some other realm—a silent world
only a cubit wide and a few inches deep where nothing
existed but his own panicked struggle, his failing wind,
and the bony fingers clawing at his throat. The white face
hovered before him, grinning mirthlessly like some
Southern devil mask. The thing's eyes were flat dark peb-
bles; its breath smelled like a cold hole in the ground.

Eolair had a dagger at his belt, but he did not want to
let go even an instant to reach for it. Still, despite his advantage in size, he could feel his hands and arms losing
their strength. The Norn was gradually crushing the muscles of Eolair's neck, closing his windpipe. He had no
choice.

He released his grip on the Norn's wrists and snatched
at his sheath. The fingers on his throat tightened and the
silence began to hiss; blackness spread across the cubit-
wide world. Eolair hammered with the knife at the thing's
side until the pressure slackened, then he clutched his
dying enemy like a lover, trying to prevent the Norn from
reaching any weapon of its own. At last the body atop
him ceased struggling. He pushed and the Norn rolled off,
flopping into the snow.

As Eolair lay gasping for breath, the dark-haired head
of Kuroyi appeared at the edge of his cloudy vision. The
Sitha seemed to be deciding whether the count would live
or not; then, without saying a word, he vanished from
Eolair's view.

Eolair forced himself to sit up. His surcoat was sodden
with the Norn's fast-cooling blood. He glanced at the
sprawled corpse, then turned to stare, arrested even in the
midst of chaos. Something about the shape of his enemy's
face and slender torso was . . . wrong.

It was a woman. He had been fighting a Norn woman.

Coughing, each breath still burning in his throat, Eolair
struggled to his feet. He should not feel ashamed—she
had almost killed him—but he did.

*What kind of world. . . ?*

As the silence in his head receded, the singing of Sithi
and Cloud Children pressed in on him anew, combining

with the more mundane screams of anger and shrieks of pain to fill the air with a complicated, frightening music.

Eolair was bleeding in a dozen places and his limbs felt heavy as stone. The sun, which had been shrouded all day, seemed to have gone down into the west, but it was hard for him to tell whether it was sunset or the leaping flames that stained the mists red. Most of the defenders of Naglimund's inner keep had fallen: only a final knot of Norns and the last and largest of the giants remained, all backed into a covered passageway before the keep's tall doors. They seemed determined to hold this ground. The muddy earth before them was piled with bodies and drenched with blood.

As the battle slackened, the count ordered his Hernystirmen back. The dozen who still stood were dull-eyed and sagging with weariness, but they demanded to see the battle through to the end; Eolair felt a fierce love for them even as he cursed their idiocy out loud. This was the Sithi's fight now, he told them: long weapons and swift reflexes were needed, and the staggering mortals had nothing left to offer but their failing bodies and brave hearts. Eolair held to his call for retreat, sending his men toward the relative safety of Naglimund's outwall. He was desperate to bring some of them out of this nightmare alive.

Eolair remained to hunt for Isorn, who had not answered the war horn's summons. He stumbled along the outskirts of the struggle, ignored by the Sithi warriors trying to force the giant out of the shelter of the arched doorway, where he was inflicting terrible injuries even in his dying moments. The Sithi seemed in a desperate hurry, but Eolair could not understand why. All but a few of the defenders were dead; those who remained were protecting the doors to the inner keep, but whoever was still inside seemed content to let them die doing so rather than try to bring them inside. Eventually, the Sithi would pick them off—Jiriki's folk had few arrows left, but several of the Norns had lost their shields, and the giant, half-concealed behind one of the arch pillars, already had a half-score of feathered shafts lodged in his shaggy hide.

Where Eolair walked, the bodies of mortals and immortals alike lay scattered as if the gods had flung them down from heaven. The count passed by many faces he recognized, some of them young Hernystirmen with whom he had sat at the campfire only the night before, some Sithi whose golden eyes stared up into nothing.

He found Isorn at last, on the far side of the keep. The young Rimmersman was lying on the ground, limbs awkwardly splayed, his helmet tumbled beside him. His horse was gone.

*Brynioch of the Skies!* Eolair had spent hours in the freezing wind, but when he saw his friend's body, he went colder still. The back of Isorn's head was soaked with blood. *Oh, gods, how will I tell his father?*

He hurried forward and grasped Isorn's shoulder to turn him over. The young Rimmersman's face was a mask of mud and fast-melting snow. As Eolair gently wiped some of it away, Isorn choked.

"You live!"

He opened his eyes. "Eolair?"

"Yes, it's me. What happened, man? Are you badly wounded?"

Isorn took in a great rasping wheeze of breath. "Ransomer preserve me, I don't know—it feels like my head is split open." He lifted a shaking hand to his head, then stared at his reddened fingers. "One of the Hunën struck me. A great hairy thing." He sagged back and closed his eyes, giving Eolair another fright before he opened them again. He looked more alert, but what he said belied it. "Where's Maegwin?"

"Maegwin?" Eolair took the young man's hand. "She is in the camp. You are inside Naglimund, and you've been hurt. I'll go find some folk to help me with you ..."

"No," Isorn said, impatient despite his weakness. "She was here. I was chasing her when ... when the giant clubbed me. He did not strike me full."

"Maegwin ... here?" For a moment it was as though

the northerner had begun speaking another tongue. "What do you mean?"

"Just as I said. I saw her walk past the outskirts of the fighting, right through the courtyard, heading around the keep. I thought I was seeing things in the mist, but I know she's been strange. I followed, and saw her just . . . there . . ." he winced at the pain as he pointed toward the far corner of the blocky keep, "and followed. Then that thing caught me from behind. Before I knew it, I was lying here. I don't know why it didn't kill me." Despite the chill, sweat beaded on his pale forehead. "Perhaps some of the Sithi came up."

Eolair stood. "I'll get help for you. Don't move any more than you have to."

Isorn tried to smile. "But I wanted to take a walk in the castle gardens tonight."

The count draped his cloak over his friend and sprinted back toward the front of the keep, skirting the siege of the keep's great doors. He found his Hernystirmen huddled beside a gap in the outwall like sheep terrified of thunder, and took four of the healthiest back to carry Isorn to the camp. As soon as he saw they had him safe, he returned to his search for Maegwin; it had taken all the restraint he possessed to see his friend out of harm's way first.

It did not take him long to find her. She was curled on the ground at the back of the keep. Although he could see no marks of violence on her anywhere, her skin felt deathly cold to his touch. If she breathed, he could find no sign of it.

When his wits returned sometime later, he was carrying Maegwin's limp body in his arms, staggering across the camp at the base of the hill below Naglimund. He could not remember how he had gotten there. Men's faces looked up as he approached, but at that moment their expressions had no more meaning for him than the bright eyes of animals.


"Kira'athu says that she is alive, but very close to death," said Jiriki. "I bring you my sorrow, Eolair of Nad Mullach."

As the count looked up from Maegwin's pale, slack face, the Sitha healer rose from the far side of the pallet and went quietly past Jiriki and out of the tent. Eolair almost called her back, but he knew that there were others who needed her help, his own men among them. It was clear that there was little more she could do here, although Eolair could not have said what exactly the silver-haired Sitha woman had done; he had been too busy willing Maegwin to live to pay attention, clutching the young woman's cold hand as though to lend her some of his own feverish warmth.

Jiriki had blood on his face. "You've been hurt," Eolair pointed out.

"A cut, no more." Jiriki made a flicking movement with his hand. "Your men fought bravely."

Eolair turned so he could speak without craning his neck, but he retained his grip on Maegwin's fingers. "And the siege is over?"

Jiriki paused for a moment before replying. Eolair, even in the depth of his mourning, felt a sudden fear.

"We do not know," the Sitha finally said.

"What does that mean?"

Jiriki and his kin had a quality of stillness in them at all times that marked them off from Eolair and his mortal fellows, but even so it was clear that the Sitha was disturbed. "They have sealed the keep with the Red Hand still inside. They have sung a great Word of Changing and there is no longer a way in."

"No way in? How can that be?" Eolair pictured huge stones pushed against the inside of the entrance. "Is there no way to force the doors?"

The Sitha moved his head in a birdlike gesture of negation. "The doors are there, but the keep is not behind them." He frowned. "No, that is misleading. You would think us mad if I told you that, since the building clearly still stands." The Sitha smiled crookedly. "I do not know if I can explain to you, Count. There are not words in any mortal tongue that are quite right." He paused. Eolair was astonished to see one of the Sithi looking so distraught, so

... human. "They cannot come out, but we cannot enter in. That is enough to know."

"But you brought down the walls. Could you not knock down the stones of the keep as well?"

"We brought down the walls, yes, but if the Hikeda'ya had been given time earlier to do what they have now accomplished, those walls would still be standing. Only some all-important task could have kept them from doing that before we laid siege. However, even if we now took down every stone of the keep and carried it a thousand leagues away, we still could not reach them—but they would still be there."

Eolair shook his head in weary confusion. "I do not understand, Jiriki. If they cannot come out and the rest of Naglimund is ours, then there is no worry, is there?" He had reached his limit with the vague explanations of the Peaceful Ones. He wanted only to be left in peace with Lluth's dying daughter.

"I wish it were so. But whatever purpose brought them here is still not understood—and it is likely that as long as they can stay in this place, close to the A-Genay'asu, they can still do what they came to do."

"So this whole struggle has been for nothing?" Eolair let go of Maegwin's hand and rose to his feet. Rage flared within him. "For nothing? Three score or more brave Hernystirmen slaughtered—not to mention your own people—and Maegwin . . ." he waved helplessly, ". . . like *this!* For *nothing?!*" He lurched forward a few steps, arm raised as though to strike at the silent immortal. Jiriki reacted so swiftly that Eolair felt his wrists caught and held in a gentle yet unbreakable grip before he saw the Sitha move. Even in his fury, he marveled at Jiriki's hidden strength.

"Your sorrow is real. So is mine, Eolair. And we should not assume that all has been for naught: we may have hindered the Hikeda'ya in ways we do not yet realize. Certainly we are alerted now, and will be on our guard for whatever the Cloud Children may do. We will leave some of our wisest and oldest singers here."

Eolair felt his anger subside into hopelessness. He

slumped, and Jiriki released his arms. "Leave them here?" he asked dully. "Where are you going? Back to your home?" A part of him hoped that it was true. Let the Sithi and their strange magics return to the secret places of the world. Once Eolair had wondered if the immortals still existed. Now he had lived and fought with them, and doing so had experienced more horror and more pain than he had ever thought possible.

"Not to our home. Here, do you see?" Jiriki lifted the tent flap. The night sky had cleared; beyond the campfires hung a canopy of stars. "There. Beyond what we call the Night Heart, which is the bright star above the corner of Naglimund's outwall."

Puzzled and irritated, Eolair squinted. Above the star, high in the sable sky, was another point of light, red as a dying ember.

"That one?" he asked.

Jiriki stared at it. "Yes. It is an omen of terrible power and significance. Among mortal peoples, it is called the Conqueror Star."

The name had a disturbingly familiar sound, but in his grief and emptiness Eolair could summon no memories. "I see it. What does it mean?"

Jiriki turned. His eyes were cold and distant. "It means the Zida'ya must return to Asu'a."

For a moment the count did not understand what he was being told. "You are going to the Hayholt?" he said finally. "To fight Elias?"

"It is time."

The count turned back to Maegwin. Her lips were bloodless. A thin line of white showed between her eyelids. "Then you will go without me and my men. I have had enough of killing. I will take Maegwin back so she may die in Henystir. I will take her home."

Jiriki lifted a long-fingered hand as though he would reach out to his mortal ally. Instead, he turned and pulled the tent flap open once more. Eolair expected some dramatic gesture, but the Sitha only said: "You must do what you think best, Eolair. You have given much already." He slid out, a dark shadow against the starlit sky, then the flap fell back into place.

Eolair slid down beside Maegwin's pallet, his mind full of despair and confusion. He could not think any more. He laid his cheek against her unmoving arm and let sleep take him.

"How are you, old friend?"

Isgrimnur groaned and opened his eyes. His head pounded and ached, but that was as nothing to the pain below his neck. "Dead. Why don't you bury me?"

"You will outlive us all."

"If it feels like this, that is no gift." Isgrimnur sat a little straighter. "What are you doing here? Strangyeard told me that Varellan was to surrender today."

"He did. I had business here at the monastery."

The duke stared at Josua suspiciously. "Why are you smiling? It doesn't look a thing like you."

The prince chuckled. "I am a father, Isgrimnur."

"Vorzheva has given birth?" The Rimmersman shot out his furry paw and clasped Josua's hand. "Wonderful, man, wonderful! Boy or girl?"

The prince sat down on the bed so that Isgrimnur would not have to stretch so far. "Both."

"Both?" Isgrimnur's look turned to suspicion again. "What nonsense is that?" Realization came, if slowly. "Twins?"

"Twins." Josua seemed on the verge of laughing aloud with pleasure. "They are fine, Isgrimnur—they are fat and healthy. Vorzheva was right, Thrithings-women are strong. She hardly made a noise, though it took forever for them both to come."

"Praise Aedon," the Rimmersman said; he made the sign of the Tree. "Both babies and their mother, all safe. Praise be." Moisture appeared in the corner of his eye. He wiped it away brusquely. "And you, Josua, look at you. You are practically dancing. Who would have thought fatherhood would suit you so?"

The prince still smiled, but something more serious was beneath. "I have something to live for, now, Isgrimnur. I did not understand it would be like this. They must come to no harm. You should see them—perfect, perfect."

"I will see them." Isgrimnur began struggling with his covers.

"You will not!" Josua was shocked. "You will not get out of that bed. Your ribs . . ."

"Are still where they're supposed to be. They've just been dented by a tipped-over horse. I've felt worse. Most of the punishment was taken by my head, and that is all bone, anyway."

Josua had grasped Isgrimnur's broad shoulders, and for a moment it seemed that he would actually try to wrestle the duke back into bed. Reluctantly, he let go. "You're being foolish," he said. "They are not going anywhere."

"Nor will I be either if I never move around." Grunting with pain, Isgrimnur put his bare feet down on the cold stone floor. "I saw what happened to my father Isbeorn. When he was thrown from his horse, he stayed in bed the whole winter. After that he could never walk again."

"Oh, goodness. What is he . . . what is he doing?" Father Strangyeard had appeared in the doorway, and was staring at the duke with profound unhappiness.

"He is getting up to see the children," said Josua in a tone of resignation.

"But . . . but . . ."

"Blast you, Strangyeard, you sound like a chicken," Isgrimnur growled. "Make yourself useful. Get me something to sit on. I am not such a fool that I am going to stand up in there while I make faces at Josua's heirs."

The priest, alarmed, hurried back out again.

"Now come and help me, Josua. It's too bad we don't have one of those Nabbanai harnesses for lifting an armored man onto a horse."

The prince braced himself against the edge of the bed. Isgrimnur grabbed Josua's belt and pulled himself upright. By the time he was standing, the duke was breathing heavily.

"Are you well?" Josua asked worriedly.

"No. I hurt damnably. But I'm on my feet, and that's something." He seemed reluctant to move further. "How far is it?"

"Just down the hall a short way." Josua slid his shoulder under the older man's arm. "We will go slowly."

They moved carefully out into the long, cool hallway. After a couple of dozen paces, Isgrimnur stopped to rest. "I will not be able to sit a horse for a few days, Josua," he said apologetically.

"A few days!" Josua laughed. "You brave old fool. I will not let you on a horse for a month at least."

"I won't be left behind, damn you!"

"No one is going to leave you behind, Isgrimnur. I am going to need you more than ever in the days ahead, whether you can fight or not. My wife is not going to ride, either. We will find a way to get you to Nabban, and to wherever we go from there."

"Traveling with the women and children." The disgust in his voice did not mask the fear.

"Only until you are healed," Josua soothed him. "But don't lie to me, Isgrimnur. Don't tell me that you are ready when you are not. I mean it when I say that I need you, and I will not have you making yourself so weak that your wounds don't heal." He shook his head. "I should be hanged for letting you get out of bed."

The duke was a little cheerier. "A new father cannot refuse a request. Didn't you know that? An old Rimmersgard custom."

"I'm sure," said Josua sourly.

"And besides, even with smashed ribs, I could beat you the best day of your life."

"Come on, then, old war-horse," the prince sighed. "You can tell me about it when we get you to a bench."

Duchess Gutrun left the protective circle around Vorzheva's bed to give Isgrimnur a furious scolding for leaving his bed. She had been running back and forth between the two rooms for days, and was plainly exhausted. The duke did not argue, but sank onto the bench

Strangyeard had dragged in with the air of an unrecalcitrant child.

Vorzheva was propped against a mound of blankets with an infant in each arm. Like Gutrun, she was pale and obviously tired, but this did not diminish the proud serenity that shone from her like a lantern's hooded glow. Both babies were swaddled so that only their black-haired heads peeped out. Aditu squatted near Vorzheva's right shoulder, staring at the nearest child with rapt interest.

When he had caught his breath, Isgrimnur leaned forward, stealing a glance at the Sitha woman. There seemed a strange hunger in her eyes, and for a moment the duke was reminded of old stories about the Sithi stealing mortal children. He pushed away the disconcerting thought.

"They look fine," he said. "Which is which?"

"The boy is in my right arm. And this is the girl."

"And what will they be called?"

Josua took a step closer, staring down at his wife and children with unalloyed pride. "We will name the boy Deornoth, in memory of my friend. If he grows up half so noble a man, I will be proud." He shifted his gaze to the other small, sleeping face. "The girl is Derra."

"It is the Thrithings word for star." Vorzheva smiled. "She will burn bright. She will not be like my mother and sisters, a prisoner of the wagons."

"Those are good names," Isgrimnur said, nodding. "When is the First Blessing to be?"

"We leave here in three days' time," Josua replied, still staring at his family. "We will have the ceremony before we ride." He turned. "If Strangyeard can do it then, that is."

"Me?" The archivist looked around as though there might be someone else of that name in the room. "But we are in Nabban, now, Josua. There is a church on every hillside. And I have never performed a First Blessing."

"You married Vorzheva and me, so of course we would have no one else," Josua said firmly. "Unless you do not want to."

"Want to? I shall be honored, of course. Of course! Thank you, Prince Josua, Lady Vorzheva." He began to edge toward the door. "I had better find a copy of the ceremony and learn it."

"We're in a monastery, man," Isgrimnur said. "You shouldn't have to look far."

But Strangyeard had already slipped out. The duke felt sure that the attention had been too much for him.

Gutrun made a brisk throat-clearing noise. "Yes. Well, if all of you are quite finished with your talking, I think it's time for Vorzheva and the little ones to get some rest." She turned on her husband. "And *you* are going back to bed, you stubborn old bear. It nearly stopped my heart when I saw you carried back here on a sling, and it was just as bad when I saw you staggering in today. Have you no sense, Isgrimnur?"

"I'm going, Gutrun," he mumbled, embarrassed. "Don't bully me."

Aditu's voice was quiet, but her melodious tones carried surprisingly well. "Vorzheva, may I hold them for a moment?"

"She needs to rest." Gutrun was sharp; Isgrimnur thought he saw something beyond her usual firmness in her eyes—a touch of fear, perhaps. Had she had the same thought he had? "The babies, too."

"Just for a moment."

"Of course," said Vorzheva, although she, too, looked a little startled. "You had only to ask."

Aditu leaned down and carefully took the children, first the girl, then the boy, and balanced them in her arms with great care. For a long moment she looked at both of them in turn, then she closed her eyes. Isgrimnur felt an inexplicable touch of panic, as though something fearful had been set into motion.

*"They will be as close as brother and sister can be,"* Aditu intoned, her voice suddenly solemn and powerful, *"although they will live many years apart. She will travel in lands that have never known a mortal woman's step, and will lose what she loves best, but find happiness with what she once despised. He will be given another name. He will never have a throne, but kingdoms will rise and fall by his hand."* The Sitha's eyes opened wide, but

seemed to gaze far beyond the confines of the room. _"Their steps will carry them into mystery."_ After a moment her eyes closed; when they opened once more, she seemed as natural as it was possible for a Sitha to seem to mortals.

"Is this some curse?" Gutrun was frightened but angry. "What right have you to put Sithi magics on these Aedonite children?"

"Peace, wife," Isgrimnur said, although he, too, was shaken by what he had seen.

Aditu handed the children back to Vorzheva, who stared at the Sitha in superstitious bafflement.

Josua also seemed unhappy, but he was clearly trying to keep his voice even. "Perhaps it was meant as a gift. Still, Aditu, our customs are not yours. . . ."

"This is _not_ something we Sithi do." Aditu seemed a little surprised herself. "Oh, sometimes there are prophesies that go with certain of our births, but it is not a regular custom. No, something . . . came to me. I heard a voice in my ear, as one sometimes does on the Road of Dreams. For some reason I thought it was . . . young Leleth."

"But she is down the hall, next to my room," said Isgrimnur. "She has been asleep for weeks—and she never talked when she was awake. What nonsense is this?"

"I do not know." Aditu's golden eyes were bright. Her own surprise gone, she seemed to be enjoying the discomfiture she had caused. "And I am sorry if I made anyone frightened."

"That is enough," Gutrun said. "This is upsetting Vorzheva."

"I am not upset," said the new mother mildly. She, too, had recovered some of her good humor. Isgrimnur wondered if things like this happened among her wagon-folk. "But I am now tired."

"Let us get you back to bed, Isgrimnur." Josua darted a last worried glance at his wife. "We will think on this later. I suppose Aditu's . . . words . . . should be written down—although if they are true, I do not know that I wish to know the future. Perhaps they are better forgotten."

"Please forgive me," Aditu said to him. "Someone wanted those words spoken. And I do not think they portend ill. Your children seem fated for great things."

"I am not sure that any such portent could be good," Josua replied. "I, for one, have had quite enough of great things." He moved to Isgrimnur's side and helped the duke to rise.

When they were in the corridor again, Isgrimnur asked: "Do you think that was a true prophesy?"

Josua shook his head. "I have been living with dreams and omens too long to say it could not be, but as with all such things, it no doubt has its tricks and twists." He sighed. "Mother of Mercy, old friend, it seems that even my children will not be free of the mysteries that plague us."

Isgrimnur could think of nothing to say to comfort the prince. Instead, he changed the subject. "So Varellan has surrendered. I wish I had been there to see the end of the battle. And is Camaris well? And Hotvig and the rest?"

"Both wounded, but not seriously. We are in surprisingly good strength, thanks to Seriddan and the other Nabbanai barons."

"So we march on to the city itself. Where do you think Benigaris will try to draw his line?"

Bent beneath Isgrimnur's broad arm, the prince shrugged. "I do not know. But he will draw it, never fear—and we may not come out of that battle so luckily. I do not like to think about fighting house to house down the peninsula."

"We will get the lay of the land, Josua, then decide." As they reached his bedside, Isgrimnur found himself looking forward to getting into bed as eagerly as a young man might anticipate a day free from chores.

*You're turning soft,* he told himself. But at this moment, he did not care. It would be good to lay his aching bones down.

"The children are splendid, Josua." He adjusted himself on the pallet. "Do not fret on Aditu's words."

"I always fret," the prince said, smiling weakly. "Just as you always bluster."

"Are we really so set in our habits?" Isgrimnur yawned to cover a grimace at the fierce aching of his ribs and back. "Then maybe it is time for the young ones to push us aside."

"We must leave them a better world than this one if we can. We have made a terrible muck of the one we were given." He took Isgrimnur's hand for a moment. "Sleep now, old friend."

Isgrimnur watched the prince walk out, happy to see that some of the bounce still remained in his step.

*I hope you get the chance to see those two children grow. And that they get to do it in that better world you spoke of.*

He leaned back and closed his eyes, waiting for the welcome embrace of sleep.

# 18

# The Shadow King

❧

**Simon's entire life** had shrunk to the length of two arms, his and the king's. The room was dark. Elias held him in a cold-fingered grip as unbreakable as any manacle.

"Speak." The voice was accompanied by a puff of vapor like dragon-spume, although Simon's own breath was invisible. "Who are you?"

Simon struggled for words, but could make no sound. This was a nightmare, a terrible dream from which he could not awaken.

"Speak, damn you. Who are you?" The faint gleam of the king's eyes narrowed, almost vanishing into the shadows that hid his face.

"N–n–nobody," Simon stammered. "I ... I'm n–nobody. . . ."

"Are you?" There was note of sour amusement. "And what brings you here?"

Simon's head was empty of thoughts or excuses. "Nothing."

"You are nobody ... and your business is nothing." Elias laughed quietly, a sound like parchment being torn. "Then you certainly belong in this place, with all the other nameless ones." He tugged Simon a step closer. "Let me look at you."

Simon was forced in turn to look directly at the king. It was hard to see him clearly in the faint light, but Simon thought he did not look quite human. There was a sheen to his pale arm, faint as the glow of swamp water, and al-

though the chamber was dank and very cold, all of Elias'
skin that Simon could see was beaded with moisture.
Still, for all his fevered look, the king's arm was knotted
with muscle and his grip was like stone.

A shadowy something lay against the king's leg, long
and black. A sheath. Simon could feel the thing that was
in it, the sensation as faint yet unmistakable as a voice
calling from far away. Its song reached deep into the secret part of his thoughts . . . but he knew he could not let
it fascinate him. His real danger was far more immediate.

"Young, I see," Elias said slowly. "And fair-skinned.
What are you, one of Pryrates' Black Rimmersmen? Or
Thrithings-folk?"

Simon shook his head but said nothing.

"It is all the same to me," Elias murmured. "Whatever
tools Pryrates chooses for his work, it is all the same to
me." He squinted at Simon's face. "Ah, I see you flinch.
Of course I know why you are here." He laughed harshly.
"That damned priest has his spies everywhere—why
would he not have one in his own tower, where he keeps
secrets that he will not show even to his master, the
king?"

Elias' clutch loosened for a moment. Simon's heart
sped again in anticipation that he might be able to make
a try for freedom, but the king was only settling himself
in a different position; before Simon could do more than
think about escape, the claw tightened again.

*But it's something to watch for,* Simon told himself,
struggling to keep hope from dying. *Oh, if he does, I pray
I can get the door downstairs open again!*

A sudden tug on his arm dragged Simon to his knees.

"Down, boy, where I can see you without stretching
my neck. Your king is tired and his bones ache." There
was a moment of silence. "Strange. You do not have the
face of a Rimmersman or Thrithings-rider. You look more
like one of my Erkynlandish peasants. That red hair! But
they say that the grasslanders were of Erkynland once,
long ago. . . ."

The sense of being in a dream returned. How could the
king see the color of his hair in this darkness? Simon

struggled to make his breathing even, to keep his fear down. He had faced a dragon—a real dragon, not a human one like this—and he had also survived in the black dreadfulness of the tunnels. He must keep his wits about him and watch for any opportunity.

"Once all of Erkynland—all of the lands of Osten Ard—were like the grasslands," Elias hissed. "Nothing but petty tribes squabbling over pastureland, horse-stealing savages." He took a deep breath and let it out slowly; the odor was strangely like metal. "It took a strong hand to change that. It takes a strong hand to build a kingdom. Do you not think that the hill-folk of Nabban cried and wailed when the Imperator's guardsmen first came? But their children were thankful, and their children's children would have had it no other way. . . ."

Simon could make no sense of the king's rambling, but felt a fluttering of hope as the deep voice trailed off and silence fell. After waiting for a score of rapid heartbeats, Simon pulled as gently as he could, but his arm was still held. The king's eyes were hooded and his chin appeared to have sunk onto his chest. But he was not sleeping.

"And look what my father built," Elias said abruptly. His eyes opened wide, as though he could see beyond the shadowed room and its disturbing furniture. "An empire such as the old Nabbanai masters only dreamed about. He carved it out with his sword, then protected it from jealous men and vengeful immortals. Aedon be praised, but he was a man—a *man!*" The king's fingers tightened on Simon's wrist until it felt as though the bones were grinding together. Simon let out a gasp of pain. "And he gave it to me to tend, just the way one of your peasant ancestors passed his son a small patch of land and a raddled cow. My father gave me the world! But that was not enough—no, it was not enough that I hold his kingdom, that I keep its borders strong, that I protect it from those who would take it away again. No, that is only part of ruling. Only part. And it is not enough."

Elias seemed completely lost now, droning away as if to an old friend. Simon wondered if he was drunk, but there was no liquor on his breath, only that strange leaden smell. Simon's sense of being trapped rose again, choking him. Would he be kept here by the mad king until Pryrates returned? Or would Elias tire of talking and administer king's justice himself to the captured spy?

"This is what your master Pryrates will never understand," Elias continued. "Loyalty. Loyalty to a person, or loyalty to a cause. Do you think he cares what happens to you? Of course you don't—even a peasant lad like you is not so thick. It would be hard to spend a moment in the alchemist's company without knowing his only loyalty is to himself. And that is where he does not understand me. He only serves me because I have power: if he could wield the power himself, he would happily slit my throat." Elias laughed. "Or he would try, in any case. I wish he *would* try. But I have a greater loyalty, to my father and to the kingdom he built, and I would suffer any pain for it." His voice broke suddenly; for a moment, Simon felt sure the king would weep. "I *have* suffered. God Himself knows that I have. Suffered like the damned souls roasting in Hell. I have not slept . . . have not slept . . ."

Again the king fell silent. Made wary by the last such pause, Simon did not move, despite the dull throbbing of his knees pressed against the hard stone floor.

When he spoke again, Elias' voice had lost some of its harshness; he sounded almost like an ordinary man. "Look you, boy, how many years do you have? Fifteen? Twenty? If Hylissa had lived, she might have borne me a son like you. She was beautiful . . . shy as a young colt, but beautiful. We never had a son. That was the problem, you know. He might have been your age now. Then none of this would have happened." He pulled Simon closer; then, horribly, he rested a cold hand atop Simon's head as though performing some ritual blessing. Sorrow's double-guarded hilt was only a few inches away from Simon's arm. There was something dreadful about the sword, and the idea that it might touch his flesh made Simon want to pull away screaming, but he was even more terrified by what might happen if he woke the king from this strange speaking dream. He held his arm rigid, and did not move even as Elias began slowly to stroke his hair, though it sent chills down his neck.

"A son. That is what I needed. One that I could have raised as my father raised me, a son that could understand what was needed. Daughters ..." He paused and took several rasping breaths. "I had a daughter. Once. But a daughter is not the same. You must hope that the man she marries will understand, will have the right blood, for he will be the one who rules. And what man who is not his own flesh and blood can a father trust to inherit the world? Still, I would have tried. I would have tried ... but she would not have it. Damned, insolent child!" His voice rose. "I gave her everything—I gave her life, curse her! But she ran away! And everything fell to ashes. Where was my son? Where was he?"

The king's hand tightened in Simon's hair until it seemed he must tear it loose from the scalp. Simon bit his lip to keep silent, frightened again by the turn Elias' madness had taken. The voice from the shadows of the chair was growing louder. "Where have you been? I waited until I could not wait any longer. Then I had to make my own arrangements. A king cannot wait, you see. Where were you? A king cannot wait. Otherwise things begin to fall apart. Things fall apart, and everything my father gave me would be lost." His voice rose to a shout. "*Lost!*" Elias leaned forward until his face was only a handbreadth from Simon's. "Lost!" he hissed, staring. His face was glossy with sweat. "Because you did not come!"

A rabbit in the fox's jaw, Simon waited, heart hammering. When the king's hand loosened in his hair he ducked his head, waiting for the blow to fall.

"But Pryrates came to me," Elias whispered. "He had failed me in his first task, but he came to me with words, words like smoke. There was a way to make things right." He snorted. "I knew that he only wanted power. Don't you see, that is what a king does, my son. He uses those who seek to use *him.* That is the way of it. That is what my father taught me, so listen well. I have used him as he has used me. But now his little plan is unraveling and he thinks to hide it from me. But I have my own ways of knowing, do you see? And I need no spies, no peasant boys skulking about. Even did I not hear the voices that howl through the sleepless nights, still the king is no fool. What is this trip to Wentmouth, that Pryrates should go there yet again even as the red star is rising? What is at Wentmouth but a hill and a harbor flame? What is to be done there that has not been done already? He says it is part of the great design, but I do not believe him. I do not believe him."

Elias was panting now, hunched over with his shoulders moving as though he tried to swallow and could not. Simon leaned away, but his arm was still firmly prisoned. He thought that if he flung himself backward as hard as he could he might break free, but the idea of what would happen if he failed—if he only brought the king's attention back to where he was and what he was doing—was enough to make him stay shivering on his knees beside the chair. Then the king's next words pushed thought of escape from his mind.

"I should have known that there was something wrong when he told me about the swords," the king grated. "I am no fool, to be frightened with such kitchen tales, but that sword of my father's—it burned me! Like it was cursed. And then I was given . . . the other one." Although it hung at his hip only a few scant inches away, the king did not look at Sorrow, but instead turned his haunted stare up toward the ceiling. "It has . . . changed me. Pryrates says it is for the best. Said that I will not gain what he promised me unless the bargain is kept. But it is inside me like my own blood now, this sorcerous thing. It sings to me all through the night hours. Even in the daytime it is like a demon crouched beside me. Cursed blade!"

Simon waited for the king to say more, but Elias had fallen into another rough-breathing silence, his head still tilted back. At last, when it seemed that the king had truly fallen asleep, or had forgotten entirely what he had been saying, Simon nerved himself to speak.

"A—and your f–f–father's sword? Where is it?"

Elias lowered his gaze. "It is in his grave." His eyes

held Simon's for a moment, then the muscles of his jaw tightened and his teeth appeared in a mirthless grin. "And what is it to you, spy? Why does Pryrates wish to know about that sword? I have heard it spoken of in the night. I have heard much." His hand reached up and the fingers wrapped around Simon's face like bands of steel. Elias coughed harshly and wheezed for breath, but his clutch did not loosen. "Your master would have been proud of you if you had escaped to tell him. The sword, is it? The sword? Is that part of his plan, to use my father's sword against me?" The king's face was streaming sweat. His eyes seemed entirely black, holes into a skull full of twittering darkness. "What does your master plan?" He heaved in another difficult breath. "T–t–tell me!"

"I don't know anything!" cried Simon. "I swear!"

Elias was shaken by a wracking cough. He slid back in the chair, letting go of his prisoner's face; Simon could feel the icy burn where the fingers had been. The hand on his wrist tightened as the king coughed again and gasped for breath.

"God curse it," Elias panted. "Go find my cupbearer."

Simon froze like a startled mouse.

"Do you hear me?" The king let go of Simon's wrist and waved at him angrily. "Get the monk. Tell him to bring my cup." He sucked in another draught of air. "Find my cupbearer."

Simon pushed himself back along the stone until he was out of the king's reach. Elias was sunken in shadow once more, but his cold presence was still strong. Simon's arm throbbed where the king had squeezed it, but the pain was as nothing next to the heartbreaking possibility of escape. He struggled to his feet, and doing so, knocked over a stack of books; when they thumped to the floor Simon cringed, but Elias did not move.

"Get him," the king growled.

Simon moved slowly toward the door, certain that at any moment he would hear the king lurch to his feet behind him. He reached the landing, out of sight of the chair; then, within a moment, he was on the stairway. He did not even grab for his torch, though it was within

arm's reach, but hurried down the stairs in darkness, his
feet as surefooted as if he walked a meadow in sunlight.
He was free! Beyond all hope, he was free! Free!

On the stairs just above the first landing a small, dark-
haired woman stood. He had a momentary glimpse of her
yellowish eyes as she stepped out of his way. Silent, she
watched him pass.

He hit the tower's outside doors at a rush and burst
through into the foggy, moonlit Inner Bailey, feeling as
though he could suddenly sprout wings and mount up into
the clouded sky. He had only taken two steps before the
cat-silent, black-cloaked figures were upon him. They
caught him as firmly as the king had, holding both his
arms pinioned. The white faces stared at him dispassionately. The Norns did not seem at all surprised to have
captured an unfamiliar mortal on the steps of Hjeldin's
Tower.

♣

As Rachel shrank back in alarm, the bundle in her hand
fell to the rough stone floor. She flinched at the noise it
made.

The crunch of footsteps grew louder and a glow like
dawn crept up the tunnel: they would be upon her in a
moment. Backed into a crevice in the stone wall, Rachel
looked around for somewhere to hide her lamp. At last, in
desperation, she put the treacherously bright thing between her feet and bent over it, draping her cloak around
her like a curtain so that its hem spread out onto the
ground. She could only hope that the torches they carried
blinded them to the light that must leak from beneath. Rachel clenched her teeth and silently prayed. The oily
smell of the lamp was already making her feel ill.

The men who were approaching moved at a leisurely
pace—far too leisurely to miss an old woman hiding behind her cloak, she was fearfully certain. Rachel thought
she would die if they stopped.

". . . they like those white-skinned things so much, they
should put *them* to work," a voice said, becoming audible

above the noise of footfalls. "All the priest has us doing is carrying away stones and dirt and running errands. That's no job for guardsmen."

"And who are you to say?" another man asked.

"Just because the king gives Red-robe a free hand doesn't mean that we . . ." the first began, but was interrupted.

"And I suppose *you* would tell him otherwise?" a third cackled. "He would eat you for supper and toss the bones away!"

"Shut your mouth," the first snapped, but there was not much confidence in his tone. He resumed more quietly. "All the same, there's something dead wrong down here, dead wrong. I saw one of those corpse-faces waiting in the shadows to talk to him. . . ."

The scrape of boots on stone diminished. Within a few moments, the corridor was silent again.

Gasping for air, Rachel flapped her cloak out of the way and staggered from the alcove. The fumes of the lamp seemed to have seeped right into her head; for a moment the walls tilted. She put a hand out to steady herself.

*Blessed Saint Rhiap,* she breathed voicelessly, *thank you for protecting your humble servant from the unrighteous. Thank you for making their eyes blind.*

More soldiers! They were all over the tunnels beneath the castle, filling the passageways like ants. This group was the third that she had seen—or, in this instance, heard—and Rachel did not doubt there were many more that she had not. What could they want down here? This part of the castle had lain unexplored for years, she knew—that was what had given her the courage to search here in the first place. But now something had caught the attention of the king's soldiers. Pryrates had put them to work digging, it seemed—but digging after what? Could it be Guthwulf?

Rachel was full of frightened anger. That poor old man! Hadn't he suffered enough, losing his sight, driven out of the castle? What could they want with him? Of course, he had been the High King's trusted counselor before he had fled: perhaps he knew some secrets that the king was desperate to have. It must be terribly important to set so many soldiers tracking around in this dreary underworld.

It *must* be Guthwulf. Who else would there be to search for down here? Certainly not Rachel herself: she knew she counted for little in the games of powerful men. But Guthwulf—well, he had fallen out with Pryrates, hadn't he? Poor Guthwulf. She had been right to look for him—he was in terrible danger! But how could she continue her search with the passageways crawling with the king's men—and worse things, if what the guardsmen seemed to be saying was true? She would be lucky if she made her own way back to sanctuary undiscovered.

*That's so,* she told herself. *They nearly had you that time, old woman. It's a presumption to expect the saint to save you again if you persist in foolishness. Remember what Father Dreosan used to say: 'God can do anything, but He does not protect the prideful from the doom they summon.'*

Rachel stood in the corridor while she waited for her breathing to slow. She could hear nothing in the corridor but her own swift-drumming heartbeat.

"Right," she said to herself. "Home. To think." She turned back up the corridor, clutching her sack.

The stairs were hard going. Rachel had to stop frequently to rest, leaning against the wall and thinking angry thoughts about her increasing infirmity. In a better world, she knew, a world not so smirched with sin, those who walked the path of righteousness would not suffer such twinges and spites. But in this world all souls were suspect, and adversity, as Rachel the Dragon had learned at her mother's knee, was the test by which God weighed them. Surely the burdens she carried now would lighten her in the Great Scales on that fated day.

*Aedon Ransomer, I hope so,* she thought sourly. *If my earthly burdens get any heavier, on the Day of Weighing-Out I will float away like a dandelion seed.* She grinned wryly at her own impiety. *Rachel, you old fool, listen to you. It's not too late to endanger your soul!*

There was something oddly reassuring in that thought. Strengthened, she renewed her assault on the stairs.

She had passed the alcove and climbed a flight past it before she remembered about the plate. Surely nothing would be different than when she had looked on her way down that morning ... but even so, it would be wrong to shirk. Rachel, Mistress of Chambermaids, did not shirk. Although her feet ached and her knees protested, although she wanted nothing but to stagger to her little room and lie down, she forced herself to turn and go back down the stairs.

The plate was empty.

Rachel stared at it for long moments. The meaning of its emptiness crept over her only gradually.

Guthwulf had come back.

She was astonished to find herself clutching the plate and weeping. *Doddering old woman,* she berated herself. *What on God's earth are you crying for? Because a man who has never spoken to you or known your name—who likely doesn't even know his own name any more—came and took some bread and an onion from a plate?*

But even as she scolded herself she felt the dandelion-seed lightness that she had only imagined earlier. He was not dead! If the soldiers were looking for him, they had not yet found him—and he had come back. It was almost as though Earl Guthwulf had known how worried she was. That was an absurd thought, she knew, but she could not help feeling that something very important had happened.

When she had recovered, she wiped her tears briskly with her sleeve, then took cheese and dried fruit from her sack and filled the plate again. She checked the covered bowl; the water was gone too. She emptied her own water skin into the bowl. The tunnels were a dry and dusty place, and the poor man would certainly be thirsty again soon.

The happy chore finished, Rachel resumed her ascent, but this time the stairs seemed gentler. She had not found him, but he was alive. He knew where to come, and would come again. Perhaps next time he would stay and let her speak to him.

But what would she say?

*Anything, anything. It will be someone to talk to. Someone to talk to.*

Singing a hymn beneath her breath, Rachel made her way back to her hidden room.

✻

Simon's strength seemed to drain out. As the Norns took him across the Inner Bailey courtyard his knees gave way. The two immortals did not falter, but lifted him by the arms until only his toes dragged along the ground.

By their silence and their frozen faces they might have been statues of white marble magicked into movement; only their black eyes, which flicked back and forth across the shadowy courtyard, seemed to belong to living creatures. When one of them spoke quietly in the hissing, clicking tongue of Stormspike, it was as surprising as if the castle walls had laughed.

Whatever the thing had said, its fellow seemed to agree. They turned slightly and bore their prisoner toward the great keep that contained the Hayholt's chief buildings.

Simon wondered dully where they were taking him. It didn't seem to matter much. He had been small use as a spy—first walking into the king's clutches, then practically throwing himself into the arms of these creatures—and now he would be punished for his carelessness.

*But what will they do?* Exhaustion battled with fear. *I won't tell them anything. I won't betray my friends. I won't!*

Even in his numb state, Simon knew that there was little chance that he would keep his silence when Pryrates returned. Binabik was right. He had been a wretched, damnable fool.

*I will find a way to kill myself if I have to.*

But could he? The Book of Aedon said it was a sin . . . and he was afraid to die, afraid to set out on that dark journey by his own choice. In any case, it seemed unlikely that he would be given any chance for such an escape. The Norns had taken his Qanuc bone knife, and they seemed capable of effortlessly countering anything he might try.

The walls of the inner keep, covered in carvings of mythical beasts and only slightly better-known saints, appeared through the gloom. The door was half-open; deep shadow lay beyond. Simon struggled briefly, but he was held far too firmly by unyielding white fingers. He stretched his neck in desperation, trying to get a last view of the sky.

Hanging in the murky northern night between Pryrates' stronghold and Green Angel Tower was a spot of shimmering red light—an angry scarlet star.

The poorly lit corridors went on and on. The Hayholt had always been called the greatest house of all, but Simon was dully surprised at how large it truly was. It almost seemed that new passageways were being created just on the far side of every door. Although the night outside had been calm, the corridors were full of chilly breezes; Simon saw only a few, flitting shapes at the far ends of passageways, but the shadows were lively with voices and strange sounds.

Still clutching him firmly, the Norns dragged Simon through a doorway that opened onto a steep, narrow stairwell. After a long climb down, during which he was wedged so close between the two silent immortals that he thought he could feel their cold skin drawing the heat from his body, they reached another empty corridor, then quickly turned down into another stairwell.

*They're taking me down to the tunnels,* Simon thought in despair. *Down into the tunnels again. Oh, God, down into the dark!*

They stopped at last before a large door of iron-bound oak. One of the Norns produced a great crude key from its robe and pushed it into the lock, then tugged the door open with a flick of its white wrist. A billow of hot, smoky air pushed out, stinging Simon's nose and eyes.

He wavered stupidly for a long moment, waiting for whatever would happen next. At last he looked up. The Norns' flat, expressionless black eyes stared back at him. Was this the prison chamber, he wondered? Or was this the place where they threw the bodies of their victims?

He found the strength to speak. "If you want me to go in there, then you might as well make me go in." He stiffened his muscles to resist.

One of the Norns gave him a push. Simon caught at the door and teetered for a moment on the threshold, then overbalanced and toppled through into emptiness.

There was no floor.

A moment later he discovered that there *was* a floor, but that it was several cubits lower than the doorway. He hit on broken stone and tumbled forward with a shout of startlement and pain. He lay for a moment, panting, and stared up at the play of firelight across the surprisingly high ceiling. The air was full of strange hissing noises. The lock clanked overhead as the key was turned.

Simon rolled over and found that he was not alone in this place. A half-dozen strangely clad men—if they were men: their faces were almost entirely covered by dirty rags—stood a short distance away, staring at him. They made no move toward him. If they were torturers, Simon thought, they must be tired of their work.

Beyond them lay a large cavern that seemed to have been fitted for animals rather than men. A few ragged blankets were piled against the walls like empty nests; a trough of water, reflecting the scarlet glow, seemed full of molten metal. Instead of a solid stone wall, which Simon would have expected to see at the back of a prison chamber, the far side of the cavern was an opening into some bigger place beyond, a great space full of flickering, fiery light. Somewhere a pained voice cried out.

He stared, amazed. Had he been carried all the way down to the flame pits of Hell? Or had the Norns built their own version to torment their Aedonite prisoners?

The figures before him, which had been standing stolidly as grazing animals, suddenly dispersed and moved quickly to the sides of the cavern. Simon saw a terrifyingly familiar silhouette appear in the open space between the two caverns. Without thinking, he scuttled to one side and pushed himself back into a shadowed recess, then pulled a stinking blanket up to his eyes.

Pryrates still had his back to the smaller cavern and to Simon, shouting to someone out of sight; the alchemist's head reflected an arc of fire. After a few last words, he turned and came forward, bootheels crunching in shattered stone. He crossed the cavern and climbed stone stairs to the narrow ledge, then pushed the flat of his hand against the door. It swung outward, then thumped shut again behind him.

Simon had thought himself beyond any further fear or surprise, but now he was slack-mouthed with astonishment. What was Pryrates doing here when he had said he was going to Wentmouth? Even the king thought he had gone to Wentmouth. Why should the alchemist deceive his master?

*And where is "here" anyway?*

Simon looked up quickly at a sound nearby. One of the rag-masked figures was approaching him, moving with the aching slowness of a very old man. The man, for his eyes above the cloth were clearly human, stopped before Simon and stared at him for a moment. He said something, but it was too muffled for Simon to understand.

"What?"

The man reached up and slowly peeled the stiff cloth away from his face. He was almost impossibly gaunt, and his seamed face was covered with gray whiskers, but there was something about him that suggested he might be younger than he looked.

"Lucky this time, eh?" said the stranger.

"Lucky?" Simon was puzzled. Had the Norns put him in with madmen?

"The priest. Lucky that'un had other business this time. Lucky there be no more . . . tasks he needs prisoners for."

"I don't know what you're talking about." Simon stood up out of his crouch, feeling the bruises from his most recent fall.

"You . . . you be no forge man," said the stranger, squinting. "Dirty you be, but there's no smoke on you."

"The Norns captured me," Simon said after a moment's hesitation. He had no reason to trust this man—but he had no reason not to. "The White Foxes," he amended when he saw no recognition on the other's gaunt face.

"Ah, those devils." The man furtively made the sign of the Tree. "We see 'em sometimes, but only at a ways off. Godless, unnatural things they be." He looked Simon up and down, then moved a little closer. "Don't tell no one else that you be not a forge man," he whispered. "Here, come here."

He led Simon a little to one side. The other masked men looked up, but seemed little interested in the newcomer. Their eyes were empty as the stares of landed fish.

The man reached down into a snarl of blankets and at last clawed up a smoke-mask and a dirty, tattered shirt. "Here, take this—was Old Bent Leg's, but won't miss it where he be gone. Look like everyone else, you will."

"Is that good?" Simon was finding it hard to keep his overstuffed head working. He was in the forge, it seemed. But why? Was this his only punishment for spying, to work in the castle's foundry? It seemed surprisingly mild.

"If you don't want to get worked to death," the man said, then began coughing, long dry rasps that sounded as though they came all the way up from his feet. It was some time before he could talk again. "If Doctor sees you be a new 'un," he wheezed, "he'll get his work out of you, never fear. And more. A right bad 'un, he be." The man said it very convincingly. "Don't want him noticing you."

Simon looked down at the soiled scraps of cloth. "Thank you. What's your name?"

"Stanhelm." The man coughed again. "And don't tell others you be new either, or they'll run to Doctor so fast your eyes'll pop out. Tell 'em you worked with ore buckets. Those 'uns sleep in 'nother hole on t'other side, but White Foxes and soldiers dump all runaways back through this door, 'matter which side 'uns ran from." He reflected sadly. "Few of us left and work to do. That's why 'uns brought you back and didn't kill you. What be your name, lad?"

"Seoman." He looked around. The other forge men had fallen back into unheeding silence. Most had curled themselves up on their thin blankets and closed their eyes. "Who is this Doctor?" For a split instant the sound of the name had filled him with wild hope, but Morgenes, even if he had lived through the dreadful blaze, would never be someone to occasion fear in men like these.

"You'll meet 'un soon enough," Stanhelm said. "Don't be in no hurry."

Simon wrapped the strip of cloth about his face. It smelled of smoke and dirt and other things, and did not seem very easy to breathe through. He told Stanhelm so.

"You keep it wet. Thank Ransomer Himself you've got it, you will. Otherwise, fire goes right down your throat and burns innards." Stanhelm prodded the shirt with a blackened finger. "Put that on, too." He looked nervously over his shoulder at his fellow forge workers.

Simon understood. As soon as he pulled on the shirt, he would no longer be different—he would not draw attention. These were bent, almost broken men, that was clear. They did not want to be noticed if they could avoid it.

When his head poked free of the neck hole and he could see again, a looming shape was lurching toward him. For an instant, Simon thought one of the snow-giants had somehow found its way south to the Hayholt.

The great head turned slowly from side to side. The mask of ruined flesh wrinkled in anger.

"Too much sleeping, little rat-men," the thing rumbled. "Work to do. The priest wants everything finished now."

Simon thanked Usires for the tattered fabric that made him another faceless captive. He knew this one-eyed monster.

*Oh, Mother of Mercy. They've given me to Inch.*

# 19

# Cunning as Time

※

**"Do you think** Simon could be down here somewhere?"

Binabik looked up from his dried mutton, which he had
been tearing into small pieces. It was the morning meal,
if morning could be said to exist in a sunless, skyless
place. "If he is," the little man said, "I am thinking there
is only a small chance we will find him. I am sorry,
Miriamele, but here there are many leagues of tunnels."

Simon wandering alone and in darkness. The thought
hurt too much—she had been so cruel to him!

Desperate to think of something else, she asked: "Did
the Sithi really build all this?" The walls stretched high
above, so that the torchlight failed before it found the upper reaches. They were roofed over by purest black; but
for the absence of stars and weather, she and the troll
might be sitting beneath the open night sky.

"With help they built it. The Sithi were having the as-
sisting of their cousins, I have read—in fact, they were
the people who were making the maps you copied. Other
immortals, masters of stone and earth. Eolair said some
still are living beneath Hernystir."

"But who could live down here?" she wondered.
"Never seeing the day . . ."

"Ah, you are not understanding." The troll smiled.
"Asu'a was full of light. The castle you were living in
had its building on the top of the Sithi's great house.
Asu'a was buried so that the Hayholt could be born."

"But it won't *stay* buried," Miriamele said grimly.

Binabik nodded. "We Qanuc have a believing that the spirit of a murdered man cannot rest, and stays on in the body of an animal. Sometimes it is following the one who killed him, sometimes it is staying in the place he was loving most. Either way, there is no rest for it until the truth has been discovered and the crime has been given its punishment."

Miriamele thought of the spirits of all the murdered Sithi and shivered. She had heard more than a few strange echoes since they had entered the tunnels beneath Saint Sutrin's. "They can't rest."

Binabik cocked an eyebrow. "There is more here than just restless spirits, Miriamele."

"Yes, but that's what the . . ." she lowered her voice ". . . that's what the Storm King is, isn't he? A murdered soul looking for vengeance."

The troll looked troubled. "I am not happy to be talking of such things here. And he brought his own death upon him, I am remembering."

"Because the Rimmersmen had surrounded this place and were going to kill him anyway."

"There is truth in what you say," Binabik admitted. "But please, Miriamele, no more. I do not know what things are in this place, or what ears might be listening, but I am thinking that the less we speak of such matters, the happier we will be. In many ways."

Miriamele inclined her head, agreeing. In fact, she wished now she had never mentioned it. After more than a day wandering in these disturbing shadows, the thought of the undead enemy was already close enough.

They had not penetrated far into the tunnels the first night. The catacomb passages beneath Saint Sutrin's had gradually become wider and wider, and soon had begun to slant steadily downward into the earth; after the first hour, Miriamele thought that they must have descended beneath even the bed of the many-fathomed Kynslagh. They had soon found a relatively comfortable spot to stop and eat a meal. After sitting down for a short while, both of them had realized just how weary they truly were, so they had spread their cloaks and slept. Upon awaking, Binabik had relit their torches from his firepot—a tiny earthenware jug in which a spark was somehow kept smoldering—and after a few bites of bread and some dried fruit washed down with warm water, they had set out again.

The day's traveling had brought them down many twisting paths. Miriamele and Binabik had done their best to stay close to the general directions on the dwarrow map, but the tunnels were snaky and confusing; it was hard to feel very confident that they were following the correct course. Wherever they were, though, it was clear that they had left the realms of humankind. They had descended into Asu'a—in a way, they had circled back into the past. Trying to fall asleep, Miriamele had found her thoughts reeling. Who could know the world had so many secrets in it?

She was no less overwhelmed this morning. A well-traveled child, even for a king's daughter, she had seen many of the greatest monuments of Osten Ard, from the Sancellan Aedonitis to the Floating Castle at Warinsten—but the minds that had conceived this strange hidden castle made even the most innovative human builders seem timid.

Time and falling debris had crushed much of Asu'a into dust, but enough of it remained to show how matchless it had been. Spectacular as the ruins of Da'ai Chikiza had seemed, Miriamele quickly decided, these far surpassed them. Stairways, seemingly unsupported, rose and twisted into darkness like cloth streamers bending in the wind. Walls curved upward, then spread out overhead into spectacular fan-shaped arrays of multicolored, attenuated rock, or bent back on themselves in rippling folds; every surface was alive with carvings of animals and plants. The makers of this place seemed able to stretch stone like hot sugar-candy and etch it like wax.

What had clearly been streambeds, although they now held only sifting dust, ran in and out from one room to the other along the broken floors, stitched by tiny, ornate bridges. Overhead, great sconces shaped like fantastically unlikely flowers grew downward from the carved vines and leaves that festooned the ceilings. Miriamele could not help wishing she could have seen them when they had bloomed full of light. Judging by the traces of color that still remained in the grooves of the stone, the palace had been a garden of colors and radiance almost beyond imagining.

But although chamber after ruined chamber dazzled her eyes, there was also something about these endless halls that set her teeth on edge. For all their beauty, they had clearly been made for inhabitants who saw things differently than a mortal could: the angles were strange, the arrangements unsettling. Some high-arched chambers seemed far too vast for their furnishings and decorations, but other rooms were almost frightening in their closeness, so cramped and tangled with ornament that it was hard to imagine more than one person occupying them at any given time. Stranger still, the remnants of the Sithi castle did not seem entirely dead. In addition to the faint sounds which might be voices and the odd shifts of the air in what should be a windless place, Miriamele saw an elusive shimmer everywhere, a hint of unseen movement at the corner of her eye, as though nothing was quite real. She imagined she could blink and find Asu'a restored—or, equally likely, find bare cavern walls and dirt.

"God is not here."

"What is that you are saying?" asked Binabik.

Their meal finished, they were walking again, carrying their packs down a long, high-walled gallery, across a narrow bridge that stretched through emptiness like the flight of an arrow. The torchlight did not reach past the darkness below them.

She looked up, embarrassed. "I'm not sure. I said, 'God is not here.' "

"You are not liking this place?" Binabik showed a small yellow smile. "I have fear of these shadows, too."

"No—I mean, yes, I'm afraid. But that's not what I

meant." She held her torch higher, staring at a string of carvings on the wall beyond the gap. "The people who lived here weren't anything like us. They didn't think about us. It's hard to believe it's the same world as the one I know. I was taught to believe that God is everywhere, watching over everything." She shook her head. "It's hard to explain. It seems like this place is out of God's sight. Like the place itself doesn't see Him, so He doesn't see it."

"Is that making you more afraid?"

"I suppose so. It just seems as though the things happening here don't have much to do with the things I was taught."

Binabik nodded solemnly. In the yellow torchlight, he looked less like a child than he sometimes did. Outlined by shadow, his round face had an air of gravity. "But some would be saying that the things happening are exactly what your church is telling of—a battle between the armies of goodness and badness."

"Yes, but it can't be that simple," she said emphatically. "Ineluki—was he good? Bad? He tried to do what was right for his people. I just don't know any more."

Binabik paused, then reached out a small hand to take hers. "Your questions are sensible ones, and I am not thinking that we should hate . . . our enemy. But do not be naming him, please!" He squeezed her fingers for emphasis. "And make yourself assured of one thing: whatever he was being once, he has now become a dangerous thing, more dangerous than anything you know or can be thinking about. Do not be forgetting that! He will kill us and all of the people we love if his wishes are done. Of that I have certainty."

*And my father?* she wondered. *Is he only an enemy now, too? What if somehow I find my way to him, but there is nothing left of what I loved? That will be like dying. I won't care what happens to me then.*

And then it came to her. It was not that God was not watching, it was that no one was going to tell her right from wrong; she had not even the solace of doing something just because someone else had ordered her not to.

Whatever decisions she made, she would have to make herself, then live by them.

She held Binabik's hand for a moment longer before they resumed walking. At least she had the company of a friend. What would it be like to be alone in such a place?

By the time they had slept three times in the ruins of Asu'a, even its crumbling magnificence could no longer hold Miriamele's attention. The dark halls seemed to breed memories—unimportant pictures of her childhood in Meremund, her days as a captive princess in the Hayholt. She felt herself suspended between the Sithi's past and her own.

They found a wide staircase leading upward, an expanse of dusty steps with balusters carved into the form of rose hedges. When Binabik's inspection of the map suggested that this was part of their path, she felt a rush of happiness. They would be going upward, after so long in the depths!

But something more than an hour plodding up the apparently endless stairs soon cooled even that excitement; Miriamele's mind went wandering again.

*Simon is gone, and I never had a chance to . . . to really talk to him. Did I love him? It would never have come to anything—how could he care for me after I told him about Aspitis? But perhaps we could have been friends. But did I love him?*

She looked down at her booted feet, climbing, climbing, the stairs passing beneath her like a slow waterfall.

*It's useless to wonder . . . but I suppose I did.* Thinking this, she felt something vast and unformed struggling inside her, a grief that threatened to turn into madness. She fought it down, afraid of its strength. *Oh, God, is this all there is to life? To have something precious and to realize it only after it's too late?*

She almost stumbled over Binabik, who had stopped abruptly on the step above her, his head nearly even with hers. The troll lifted a hand to his mouth, warning her to be silent.

They had just mounted past a landing where several

archways led outward from the staircase, and at first
Miriamele thought the quiet noise must come from one of
them, but Binabik pointed up the stairwell. His meaning
was clear: someone else was on the stairs.

Miriamele's contemplative mood evaporated. Who
could be walking these dead halls? Simon? That seemed
too much to hope. But who else would be roaming the
shadow-world? The restless dead?

Even as they backed down toward the landing, Binabik
fumbled his walking-stick into two pieces, pulling free
the section that held a knife blade. Miriamele felt for her
own knife as the sound of footfalls grew louder. Binabik
shrugged off his pack and dropped it quietly to the stone
floor near Miriamele's feet.

A shape came down the darkened stairwell, moving
slowly and confidently into the torchlight. Miriamele felt
her heart pressing against her ribs. It was a man, one she
had not seen before. In the depths of his hood, his eyes
bulged as though with surprise or fright, but his teeth
were bared in a bizarre grin.

A moment passed before Binabik gasped in recognition. "Hangfish!"

"You know him?" Her voice sounded shrill to her, the
quaver of a frightened little girl.

The troll held the knife before him as a priest might a
holy Tree. "What do you want, Rimmersman?" he demanded. "Are you lost?"

The smiling man did not reply, but stretched his arms
wide and took another step downward. There was something terribly but indefinably wrong about him.

"Get away, you!" she cried. Involuntarily, she took another step backward toward one of the arched doorways.
"Binabik, who is he?"

"I know who he was," the troll said, still brandishing
the knife. "But I am thinking he has become something
else. . . ."

Before Binabik had finished speaking, the pop-eyed
man moved, scuttling down the stairs with shocking
speed. In an eye-blink he had closed with the troll, grabbing the wrist of Binabik's knife hand and wrapping his

other arm around the little man. After a moment's struggle, the two tumbled to the floor and rolled off the landing to the steps below. Binabik's torch flew free and bounced down the stairs ahead of them. The troll gasped and grunted with pain, but the other was silent.

Miriamele had scarcely an instant to stare openmouthed before several large hands snaked out of the shadowy archway and folded around her, seizing her wrists and clutching at her waist, the fingers rough but somehow tentative where they touched her skin. Her own torch was knocked to the ground. Before she had finished drawing breath to shout her alarm, something was pulled down over her head, shutting out the light. A sweet odor filled her nose and she felt herself slipping away, halfformed questions dissolving, everything fading.

❧

"Why will you not come and sit beside me?" said Nessalanta, like a spoiled child denied a treat. "I have not spoken to you for days."

Benigaris turned from the railing of the rooftop garden. Below him, the first fires of evening had been lit. Great Nabban twinkled in the lavender twilight. "I have been occupied, Mother. Perhaps it has escaped your attention that we are at war."

"We have been at war before," she said airily. "Merciful God, such things never change, Benigaris. You wanted to rule. You must grow up and accept the burdens that come with it."

"Grow up, is it?" Benigaris turned from the railing with his fists clenched tight. "It is you who are the child, Mother. Do you not see what is happening? A week ago we lost the Onestrine Pass. Today I have been told that Aspitis Preves has taken to his heels and Eadne Province has fallen! We are losing this war, damn you! If I had gone myself instead of sending that idiot brother of mine ..."

"You are not to say a word against Varellan,"

Nessalanta snapped. "Is it his fault that your legion was full of superstitious peasants who believe in ghosts?"

Benigaris stared at her for a long moment; there was no love in his gaze. "It *is* Camaris," he said quietly.

"What?"

"It is Camaris out there, Mother. You can say anything you wish, but I have heard the reports from the men who have been on the battlefield. If it is not him, then it is one of our ancestors' old war gods returned to earth."

"Camaris is dead," she sniffed.

"Did he elude some trap you set for him?" Benigaris moved a few steps closer. "Is that how my father became duke of Nabban in the first place—because you arranged to have Camaris killed? If so, it appears you failed. Perhaps for once you chose the wrong tool."

Nessalanta's face contorted in fury. "There are no tools in this country strong enough for my will. Don't I know that!" She stared at her son. "They are all weak, all dull-edged. Blessèd Ransomer, if only I had been born a man—then none of this would have happened! We would not be bowing to any northern king on a chair of bones."

"Spare me your dreams of glory, Mother. What did you arrange for Camaris? Whatever it was, he seems to have survived it."

"I did nothing to Camaris." The dowager duchess rearranged her skirts, recovering a little of her calm. "I admit that I was not unhappy when he fell into the ocean—for a strong man, he was the weakest of all. Quite unsuitable to rule. But I had nothing to do with it."

"I almost believe you, Mother. Almost." Benigaris smiled thinly. He turned to find one of his courtiers standing in the doorway, looking out with poorly-hidden apprehension. "Yes? What do you want?"

"There . . . there are many folk asking for you, my lord. You said you wished to be told . . . ."

"Yes, yes. Who is waiting?"

"The Niskie, for one, my lord. He is still outside the audience chamber."

"Have I not enough to occupy me? Why won't he take

the hint and go? What does the damned sea-watcher want, anyway?"

The courtier shook his head. The long feather in his cap swayed before his face, fluttered by the evening breeze. "He will not speak to any but you, Duke Benigaris."

"Then he will sit there until he dries out and lies gasping on the floor. I have no time to listen to Niskie chatter." He turned to look out over the lights of the city. "And who else?"

"Another messenger from Count Streáwe, Lord."

"Ah." Benigaris pulled at his mustache. "As expected. I think we will let that wine sit in the cask a little longer. Who else?"

"The astrologer Xannasavin, Lord."

"So he has arrived at last. Very grieved, I'm sure, to keep his duke waiting." Benigaris nodded slowly. "Send him up."

"Xannasavin is here?" Nessalanta smiled. "I'm sure he has wonderful things to tell us. You'll see, Benigaris. He'll bring us good news."

"No doubt."

Xannasavin appeared within moments. As though to take attention away from his own lean height, the astrologer carefully lowered himself to his knees.

"My lord, Duke Benigaris, and my lady, Duchess Nessalanta. A thousand, thousand pardons. I came as soon as I received your summons."

"Come and sit beside me, Xannasavin," said the duchess. "We have seen too little of you lately."

Benigaris leaned against the railing. "My mother is right—you have been much absent from the palace."

The astrologer rose and went to sit near Nessalanta. "My apologies. I have found that sometimes it is best to get away from the splendor of court life. Seclusion makes it easier to hear what the stars tell me."

"Ah." The duke nodded as though some great riddle had been solved. "That is why you were seen in the marketplace dickering with a horse merchant."

Xannasavin flinched minutely. "Yes, my lord. In fact, I

thought it might help me to ride beneath the night sky. Your court is so full of pleasurable distractions, and these are important times. I felt my mind should be clear so I might better serve you."

"Come here," Benigaris said.

The astrologer rose from his seat, smoothing the folds from his dark robe, then went to stand beside the duke at the garden railing.

"What do you see in the sky?"

Xannasavin squinted. "Oh, many things, my lord. But if you wish me to read the stars aright, I should go back to my chamber and get my charts. . . ."

"But the last time you were here, the sky was so full of good fortune! You needed no charts then!"

"I had studied them for long hours before coming up, my . . ."

Benigaris put his arm around the astrologer's shoulder. "And what of the great victories for the House of the Kingfisher?"

Xannasavin squirmed. "They are coming, my lord. See, look there in the sky." He pointed toward the north. "Is that not as I foretold to you? Look, the Conqueror Star!"

Benigaris turned to follow Xannasavin's finger. "That little red spot?"

"Soon it will fill the sky with flame, Duke Benigaris."

"He did predict that it would rise, Benigaris," Nessalanta called from her chair. She seemed disgruntled at being left out. "I'm sure everything else he said will come true as well."

"I'm certain it will." Benigaris stared at the crimson pinhole in the evening sky. "The death of empires. Great deeds for the Benidrivine House."

"You remember, my lord!" Xannasavin smiled. "These things that worry you are only temporary. Beneath the great wheel of heaven, they are only a moment of wind across the grass."

"Perhaps." The duke's arm was still draped companionably across the astrologer's shoulders. "But I worry for you, Xannasavin."

"My lord is too kind, to spare a thought for me in his time of trial. What is your worry, Duke Benigaris?"

"I think you have spent too much time looking up at the sky. You need to widen your view, look down at the earth as well." The duke pointed to the lanterns burning in the streets below. "When you stare at something too long, you lose sight of other things that are just as important. For instance, Xannasavin, the stars told you that glory would come to the Benidrivine House—but you did not listen closely enough to the marketplace gossip that Lord Camaris himself, my father's brother, leads the armies against Nabban. Or perhaps you *did* listen to the gossip, and it helped you make your sudden decision to take up riding, hmm?"

"M—my lord wrongs me."

"Because, of course, Camaris is the oldest heir of the Benidrivine House. So the glory for the house that you spoke of might very well be *his* victory, might it not?"

"Oh, my lord, I do not think so. . . !"

"Stop it, Benigaris," Nessalanta said sharply. "Stop bullying poor Xannasavin. Come sit by me and we will have some wine."

"I am trying to help him, Mother." Benigaris turned back to the astrologer. The duke was smiling, but his face was flushed, his cheeks mottled. "As I said, I think you have spent too much time staring at the sky, and not enough paying attention to more lowly things."

"My lord . . ."

"I will remedy that." Benigaris abruptly stooped, dropping his arm down to Xannasavin's hip and wrapping his other arm around it. He straightened, grunting with the effort; the astrologer swayed, his feet a cubit off the ground.

"No, Duke Benigaris, no. . . !"

"Stop that!" shrieked Nessalanta.

"Go to hell." Benigaris heaved. Xannasavin toppled over the railing, his arms grabbing at nothing, and plummeted out of sight. A long moment later a wet smack echoed up from the courtyard.

"How . . . how *dare* you. . . ?!" Nessalanta stammered,

her eyes wide with shock. Benigaris rounded on her, face contorted with rage. A thin stream of blood trickled down his forehead: the astrologer had pulled loose some of his hair.

"Shut your mouth," he snarled. "I ought to throw you over, too, you old she-wolf. We are losing this war— losing! You may not care now, but you are not so safe as you think. I doubt that whey-faced Josua will let his army rape women and kill prisoners, but the people who whisper in the market about what happened to Father know you are just as guilty as I am." He wiped blood from his face. "No, I don't need to do you in myself. Likely there are more than a few peasants sharpening their knives right now, just waiting for Camaris and the rest to show up at the gates before they start the festival." Benigaris laughed angrily. "Do you think the palace guard is going to throw their lives away protecting you when it's plain that everything is lost? They're just like the peasants, Mother. They have lives to lead, and they don't care who sits on the throne here. You old fool." He stared at her, his mouth working, fists trembling.

The dowager duchess shrank back in her chair. "What are you going to do?" she moaned.

Benigaris threw out his arms. "I am going to fight, damn you. I may be a murderer, but what I have I will keep—until they take it from my dead hands." He stalked to the doorway, then turned. "And I do not want to see you again, Mother. I don't care where you go or what you do ... but I do not want to see you."

He pushed through the door and disappeared.

"Benigaris!" Nessalanta's voice rose to a scream. "Benigaris! Come back!"

The silent monk had wrapped the fingers of one hand around Binabik's throat; even as he pressed down, his other hand brought the troll's own knife-hand up, forcing the blade closer and closer to Binabik's sweating face.

"Why ... are ... you. . . ?" The fingers cinched tighter,

cutting off the little man's air and his words. The monk's pale, sweating face hung close; it gave off a feverish heat.

Binabik arched his back and heaved. For a moment he partially broke the monk's hold, and he used that sliver of freedom to kick himself off the edge of the stair, tumbling them both over so that when they rolled to a halt, Binabik was on top. The troll leaned forward, putting all his weight behind his knife, but Hengfisk held it away with one hand. Although he was thin, the monk was nearly twice the troll's size; only the odd jerkiness of his movements seemed to be keeping him from a swift victory.

Hengfisk's fingers slithered around the troll's neck once more. Frantic, Binabik tried to push the hand away with his jaw, but the monk's grip was too strong.

"Miriamele!" Binabik gasped. "Miriamele!" There was no answering cry. The troll was choking now, fighting for breath. He could not force his blade closer to Hengfisk's relentlessly smiling face or dislodge the hand around his throat. The monk's knees rose and squeezed Binabik's ribs so that the little man could not wriggle free.

Binabik·turned his head and bit Hengfisk's wrist. For a moment the fingers at his neck clamped even more tightly, then skin and muscle parted beneath the troll's teeth; hot blood welled in his mouth and spilled down his chin.

Hengfisk did not cry out—his grin did not even slacken—but he abruptly twisted, using his legs to throw Binabik to one side. The troll's knife slipped from his hand and skittered free, but he was too occupied trying not to skid off the edge of the step and down into darkness to do anything about it. He came to a halt, palms flat on the stone, feet dangling beneath the baluster and past the brink, then pulled himself forward with hands and knees, desperate to recover his knife. It was lying only inches from Hengfisk, who crouched against the wall, protuberant eyes glaring at the troll, hand drizzling red onto the stair.

But his grin had vanished.

"Vad. . . ?" Hengfisk's voice was a hollow croak. He looked from side to side and up and down, as though he suddenly found himself somewhere unexpected. The expression he turned at last on Binabik was full of confused horror.

"Why are you attacking me?" Binabik rasped. Blood was smeared on his chin and cheeks. He could barely speak. "We were not having friendship ... but ..." He broke off in a fit of coughing.

"Troll. . . ?" Hengfisk's face, which moments before had been stretched in glee, had gone slack. "What. . . ? Ah, horrible, so horrible!"

Astonished by the change, Binabik stared.

"I cannot ..." The monk seemed overwhelmed with misery and bafflement. His fingers twitched. "I cannot ... oh, merciful God, troll, it is so *cold*. . . !"

"What has happened to you?" Binabik pulled himself a little nearer, keeping a watchful eye on the dagger, but though it lay only a short distance from Hengfisk's hand, the monk seemed oblivious.

"I cannot tell. I cannot speak it." The monk began to weep. "They have filled me ... with ... pushed me aside ... how could my God be so cruel. . . ?"

"Tell me. Is there some helping thing I can do?"

The monk stared at him, and for a brief moment something like hope flickered in his bulging, red-rimmed eyes. Then his back stiffened and his head jerked. He screamed with pain.

"Hengfisk!" Binabik threw his hands up as though to ward off whatever had stabbed at the monk.

Hengfisk jerked, arms extended straight out, limbs shaking. "Do not. . . !" he shouted. "*No!*" For an instant he seemed to master himself, but his gaunt face, when he turned it back to Binabik, began to ripple and change as though serpents roiled beneath the flesh. "They are false, troll." There was a terrible, deathly weight to his words. "False beyond believing. But as cunning as Time itself." He turned awkwardly and took a few staggering steps down the stairway, passing so close that Binabik could have reached out to touch him. "Go," the monk breathed.

Unnerved even more than he had been by the attack, Binabik crawled forward and picked up his knife. A sound behind him made him whirl. Hengfisk, his lips skinned back in a grin once more, was lurching up the steps. Binabik had time only to lift his arms before the monk fell upon him. Hengfisk's stinking robe wrapped around them both like a shroud. There was a brief struggle, then stillness.

Binabik crawled out from beneath the body of the monk. After regaining his breath, he rolled Hengfisk over onto his back. The hilt of his bone knife protruded from the monk's left eye. Shuddering, the troll pulled the blade free and wiped it on the dark robe. Hengfisk's last smile was frozen on his face.

Binabik picked up his fallen torch and stumbled back up the steps to the landing. Miriamele had vanished, and the packs that had contained their food and water and other important articles were gone, too. Binabik had nothing but his torch and his walking stick.

"Princess!" he called. The echoes caromed into the emptiness beyond the stairs. "Miriamele!"

Except for the body of the monk, he was alone.

**⚜**

"He must have gone mad. Are you certain that is what he wants?"

"Yes, Prince Josua, I am certain. I spoke to him myself." Baron Seriddan lowered himself onto a stool, waving away his squire when the young man tried to take his cloak. "You know, if this is not a trick, we could hardly wish for a better offer. Many men will die before we take the city walls, otherwise. But it *is* strange."

"It is not at all what I expected of Benigaris," Josua admitted. "He demanded that it be Camaris? Is he so tired of life?"

Baron Seriddan shrugged, then reached out to take the cup his squire brought him.

Isgrimnur, who had been watching silently, grunted. He understood why the baron and Josua were puzzled. Certainly Benigaris was losing—in the last month, the coalition assembled by Josua and the Nabbanai barons had pushed the duke's forces back until all that remained in Benigaris' control was the city itself. But Nabban was the greatest city in Osten Ard, and its seaport made a true siege difficult. Some of Josua's allies had provided their own house navies, but these were not enough to blockade the city and starve it into submission. So why should the reigning Duke of Nabban offer such an odd bargain? Still, Josua was taking the news as though it were *he* who would have to fight Camaris.

Isgrimnur shifted his aching body into a more comfortable position. "It sounds mad, Josua—but what have we to lose? It is Benigaris who is trusting our good faith, not the other way around."

"But it's madness!" Josua said unhappily. "And all he wants if he wins is safe passage for himself and his family and servants? Those are surrender terms—so why should he wish to fight for them? It makes no sense. It must be a trick." The prince seemed to be hoping someone would agree with him. "This sort of thing has not been done in a hundred years!"

Isgrimnur smiled. "Except by you, just a few short months ago in the grasslands. Everyone knows *that* story, Josua. They'll be telling it around the campfires for a long time."

The prince did not return his smile. "But I used a trick to force Fikolmij into that! And he never dreamed that his champion might lose. Even if Benigaris does not believe that this is truly his uncle, he must have heard what sort of warrior he is! None of it makes sense!" He turned to the old knight, who had been sitting in the corner, still as a statue. "What do you think, Sir Camaris?"

Camaris spread his broad hands palms upward before him. "It must end. If this is how the ending will come, then I will play my part. And Baron Seriddan speaks truly: we would be fools to throw away this chance out of suspicion. We may save many lives. For that alone, I would do whatever is needed."

Josua nodded. "I suppose so. I still do not understand the why of it, but I suppose I must agree. The people of Nabban do not deserve to suffer because their lord is a patricide. And if we accomplish this, we have a greater task before us—one for which we will need our army whole and strong."

*Of course, Josua's down-mouthed,* Isgrimnur realized. *He knows that we have horrors before us that may overshadow the slaughter in the Onestrine Pass so gravely that we think back on that battle as a day of sport. Only Josua, of all of us in this room, survived the siege of Naglimund. He's fought the White Foxes. Of course he's grim.*

Out loud, he said: "Then it's settled. I just hope somebody will help me find a stool for my fat old backside so I can watch it happen."

Josua looked at him a little sourly. "It is not a tourney, Isgrimnur. But you will be there—we all will. That seems to be what Benigaris wants."

※

*Rituals,* Tiamak thought. *My people's must seem as odd to the drylanders as these to me.*

He stood on the windy hillside, watching as Nabban's great city gates swung wide. A small procession of horsemen emerged, the leader dressed in plate armor that gleamed even beneath the cloudy afternoon skies. One of the other riders carried the huge blue and gold banner of the Kingfisher House. But no horns blew.

Tiamak watched Benigaris and his party ride toward the place where the Wrannaman stood with Josua's company. As they waited, the wind grew stronger. Tiamak felt it through his robe and shivered.

*It is bitterly cold. Too cold for this time of year, even near the ocean.*

The riders stopped a few paces short of the prince and his followers. Josua's soldiers lounged in scattered ranks about the bottom of the hillside, caught up in the moment and watching attentively. Faces also peered from the windows and rooftops of outer Nabban and from the city walls. A war had been abruptly halted so that this moment could take place. Now all the participants stood waiting, like toys set up and then forgotten.

Josua stepped forward. "You have come, Benigaris."

The leading rider pushed up the visor of his helm. "I have, Josua. In my way, I am an honorable man. Just like you."

"And you intend to abide by the terms you gave Baron Seriddan? Single combat? And all you ask if you win is safe conduct for your family and retainers?"

Benigaris flexed his shoulders impatiently. "You have my word. I have yours. Let us get on with this. Where is . . . the great man?"

Josua looked at him with some distrust. "He is here."

As the prince spoke, the circle of people behind him parted and Camaris stepped forward. The old knight wore chain mail. His surcoat was without insignia, and he held the antique sea-dragon helmet under his arm. Tiamak thought that Camaris looked even more unhappy than usual.

As he stared at the old man's face, Benigaris' sour smile curled the ends of his mustaches. "Ah. I was right. I told her." He nodded toward the knight. "Greetings, Uncle."

Camaris said nothing.

Josua lifted his hand. He seemed to be finding the scene increasingly distasteful. "So, then. Let us get on with it." He turned to the Duke of Nabban. "Varellan is here, and he has not been mistreated. I promise that whatever happens, we will treat your sister and mother with kindness and honor."

Benigaris stared at him for a long moment, his eyes cold as a lizard's. "My mother is dead." He snapped his visor down, then turned his horse and rode a short way back up the hillside.

Josua wearily beckoned Camaris. "Try not to kill him."

"You know I can promise nothing," the old knight said. "But I will grant him quarter if he asks."

The wind grew sterner. Tiamak wished he had taken up drylander clothing more completely: breeches and boots would be a decided improvement over the bare legs and sandals that his robe barely protected from the cold. He shivered as he watched the two riders turn toward each other.

*He Who Bends the Trees must have woken up angry,* he thought, echoing something his father had often said. The idea sent a deeper chill through him than had the wind. *But I do not think that it is the weatherlord of the Wran who sends this cold. We have another enemy, one who has lain quiet for a long time—and there is no question that he can command wind and storms.*

Tiamak stared up at the hillside where Camaris and Benigaris faced each other across a distance that a man could walk in a few short moments. They were only separated by a short span, and were bound close by ties of blood, but it was clear that an impassable gulf stretched between them.

*And meanwhile the Storm King's wind blows,* Tiamak thought. *As these two, uncle and nephew, dance some mad drylander ritual . . . just like Josua and Elias. . . .*

The two riders abruptly spurred toward each other, but they were nothing but a blur to Tiamak. A sickening notion had crept over him, black and frightening as any storm cloud.

*We have been thinking all along that King Elias was the tool of Ineluki's vengeance. And the two brothers have gone brawling from Naglimund to Sesuad'ra, biting and scratching at each other so that Prince Josua and the rest of us have had no chance to do anything but survive. But what if Elias is as benighted about what the Storm King plans as we are? What if his purpose in some vast plan is only to keep us occupied while that dark, undead thing pursues some completely different end?*

Despite the cold air on the hill, Tiamak felt beads of sweat cooling on his forehead. If this was true, what could Ineluki be planning? Aditu swore that he could never come back from the void into which his death spell had cast him—but perhaps there was some other revenge he schemed for that was far more terrible than simply ruling humankind through Elias and the Norns. But what could it be?

Tiamak looked around for Strangyeard, anxious to share this worry with his fellow Scrollbearer, but the priest was hidden by the milling crowd. The people around the Wrannaman were shouting excitedly at something. It took the distracted Tiamak a moment to realize that one of the mounted men had unhorsed the other. A brief stab of fear was allayed when he saw that it was gleaming-armored Benigaris who had fallen.

A murmur ran through the crowd when Camaris dismounted. Two boys ran forward to lead the horses away.

Tiamak put aside his suspicions for the moment and squeezed between Hotvig and Sludig, who were standing just behind the prince. The Rimmersman looked down in annoyance, but when he saw Tiamak he grinned. "Knocked him rump over plume! The old man is giving Benigaris a stern lesson!"

Tiamak winced. He could never understand his companions' pleasure at such things. This "lesson" might end in death for one of the two men who were now circling each other, shields up and longswords at the ready. Black Thorn looked like a stripe of emptiest night.

At first it seemed the combat would not last long. Benigaris was an able fighter, shorter than Camaris but stocky and broad-shouldered; he swung the heavy blade as easily as a smaller man might have brandished Josua's Naidel, and was well-trained in the use of his shield. But to Tiamak, Camaris seemed another kind of creature entirely, graceful as a river otter, swift as a striking serpent. In his hands, Thorn was a complicated black blur, a web of glinting darkness. Although he knew nothing good of Benigaris, Tiamak could not help feeling sorry for him. Surely this whole ridiculous battle would be over in a few moments.

*The sooner Benigaris gives up,* Tiamak thought, *the sooner we can get out of this wind.*

But Benigaris, it rapidly became clear, had other plans. After looking almost helpless through the first score of strokes, Nabban's duke suddenly took the battle to Camaris, crashing blow after blow on the old knight's shield and deflecting those that his opponent returned.

Camaris was forced back, and Tiamak could feel the worry that ran through Josua's party like a whisper.

*He is an old man, after all. Older than my father's father was when he died. And perhaps he has even less heart for this battle than for others.*

Benigaris rained strokes against Camaris' shield, trying to push home his advantage as the old knight gave ground; the duke was grunting so loudly that everyone on the hillside could hear him above the clang of iron. Even Tiamak, with almost no knowledge of drylander swordplay, wondered how long he could keep up such an attack.

*But he doesn't necessarily have to last a long time,* Tiamak realized. *Just until he beats down Camaris' guard and finds an opening. He is gambling.*

For a moment Benigaris' gamble appeared to have paid. One of his hammering blows caught Camaris with his shield too low, skimmed off its upper edge and struck the old knight on the side of the helmet, staggering him. The crowd made a hungry sound. Camaris regained his footing and lifted his shield as though it had become almost impossibly heavy. Benigaris waded in.

Tiamak was not quite sure what happened next. One moment the old knight was in a crouch, shield raised in what looked like helplessness against Benigaris' battering sword; the next, he had somehow caught Benigaris' shield with his own and knocked it upward, so that for a moment it hung in the air like a blue and gold coin. When it fell to the earth, Thorn's black point was at the duke's gorget.

"Do you yield, Benigaris?" The voice of Camaris was clear, but there was a hint of a weary tremor.

In answer, Benigaris knocked Thorn aside with a mailed fist, then thrust his own blade at Camaris' unprotected belly. The old man seemed to contort as the sword touched his mail-clad midsection. For an instant Tiamak thought he might have been skewered, but instead Camaris whirled all the way around. Benigaris' sword slid past him, and as Camaris finished his circular turn Thorn came with him in a flat, deadly arc. The black

blade crunched into Benigaris' armor just below his ribs.
The duke was driven to one knee; he wobbled for an instant, then collapsed. Camaris pulled Thorn free of the rent in the breast plate and a freshet of blood followed it.

Beside Tiamak, Sludig and Hotvig were cheering hoarsely. Josua did not seem so happy.

"Merciful Aedon." He turned to look at his two captains with more than a little anger, but his eye lit on the Wrannaman. "At least we can thank God Camaris was not killed. Let us go to him, and see what we can do for Benigaris. Did you bring your herbs, Tiamak?"

The marsh man nodded. He and the prince began to push their way forward through the knot of people that was quickly forming around the two combatants.

When they reached the center of the crowd, Josua put a hand on Camaris' shoulder. "Are you well?"

The old man nodded. He appeared exhausted. His hair hung down his forehead in sweaty twists.

Josua turned to the fallen Benigaris. Someone had removed the duke's helmet. He was pale as a Norn and there was a froth of blood on his lips. "Lie still, Benigaris. Let this man look at your wound."

The duke turned his bleary eyes on Tiamak. "A marsh man!" he wheezed. "You are a strange one, Josua." The Wrannaman kneeled down beside him and began looking for the catch-buckles on the breastplate, but Benigaris struck his hands away. "Leave me alone, damn you. Let me die without having some savage paw at me."

Josua's mouth tightened, but he motioned Tiamak to step back. "As you wish. But perhaps there is something that can be done for you. . . ."

Benigaris barked a laugh. A bubble of bloody spittle caught in his mustache. "Let me die, Josua. That is what is left for me. You can have . . ." he coughed more red froth, ". . . you can have everything else."

"Why did you do it?" Josua asked. "You must have known you could not win."

Benigaris mustered a grin. "But I frightened you all, didn't I?" His face contorted, but he regained control. "In any case, I took what was left to me . . . just as my mother did."

"What do you mean?" Josua stared at the dying duke as though he had never seen anything quite like him.

"My mother realized . . . with help from me . . . that her game was over. There was nothing left but shame. So she took poison. I had my own way."

"But you could have escaped, surely. You still control the seas."

"Escape to where?" Benigaris spat another scarlet gobbet. "To the loving arms of your brother and his pet wizard? And in any case, the damnable docks belong to Streáwe now—I thought I was holding him prisoner, but he was gnawing away at my power from within. The count is playing us all off each other for his own profit." The duke's breath sawed in and out. "No, the end had come—I saw it as soon as the Onestrine Pass fell. So I chose my own death. I was duke less than a year, Josua. No one would ever have remembered me as anything but a father-murderer. Now, if anyone survives, I will be the man who fought Camaris for the throne of Nabban . . . and damned near won."

Josua was looking at Benigaris with an expression that was not quite recognizable. Tiamak could not let the question go unasked.

"What do you mean, 'if anyone survives'?"

Benigaris looked at the Wrannaman with contempt. "It talks." He slowly turned back to the prince. "Oh, yes," he said, his labored breathing not disguising his relish, "I forgot to tell you. You have won your prize—but you may not get much joy from it, Josua."

"I almost felt sorry for you, Benigaris," the prince said. "But the feeling has passed." He stood up.

"Wait!" Benigaris raised a bloody hand. "You really should know this, Josua. Stay just a moment. I won't embarrass you long."

"Speak."

"The ghants are crawling up out of the swamps. The riders have begun coming in from the Lakelands and the coast towns along Firannos Bay bearing the tale. They are swarming. Oh, there are more of them than you can imagine, Josua." He laughed, bringing up a fresh welter of blood. "And that's not all," he said gleefully. "There was another reason I had no desire to flee Nabban by boat. The kilpa, too, seem to have gone mad. The Niskies are terrified. So you see, not only did I buy myself a clean and honorable death . . . but it is a death you and yours might find yourself envying very soon."

"And your own people?" Josua asked angrily. "Do you care nothing for them? If what you say is true, they are already suffering."

"My people?" Benigaris wheezed. "No more. I am dead, and the dead have no loyalty. And in any case, they are your people now—yours and my uncle's."

Josua stared at him for a long moment, then turned and strode away. Camaris tried to follow him, but he was quickly surrounded by a curious mob of soldiers and Nabbanai citizens and could not break away.

Tiamak was left to kneel beside the fallen duke and watch him die. The sun was almost touching the horizon, and cold shadows were stretching across the hillside, when Benigaris finally stopped breathing.

# 20

# Prisoned on the Wheel

**Simon had at first** thought the great underground forge was someone's attempt to recreate Hell. After he had been captive there for nearly a fortnight, he was certain of it.

He and the other men seemed barely to have fallen into their ragged nests at the end of one backbreaking day before one of Inch's assistants—a handful of men less terrifying but no more humane than their master—was braying at them to get up and start the next. Almost dizzy with weariness before the work had even begun, Simon and his fellow prisoners would gulp down a cupful of thin porridge that tasted of rust, then stumble out to the foundry floor.

If the cavern where the workers slept was unpleasantly hot, the vast forge cavern was an inferno. The stifling heat pressed against Simon's face until his eyeballs felt dry as walnut shells and his skin seemed about to crisp and peel away. Each day brought a long, dreary round of backbreaking, finger-burning labor, made bearable only by the man who brought the water dipper. It seemed eons between drinks.

Simon's one piece of luck was that he had fallen in with Stanhelm, who alone among the wretches working in the forge seemed to have retained most of his humanity. Stanhelm showed the new prisoner the spots to go and catch a breath where the air was a little cooler, which of Inch's minions to avoid most scrupulously, and, most importantly, how to look like he belonged in the forge. The older man did not know that Simon had a particular reason to stay nameless and unnoticed, but sensibly believed that no one should invite Inch's attention, so he also taught the new prisoner what was expected of all the workers, the greatest part of which was cringing subservience; Simon learned to keep his eyes lowered and work fast and hard whenever Inch was near. He also tied a strip of rag around his finger to cover his golden ring. He was unwilling to let such a precious thing out of his grasp, but he knew it would be a terrible mistake to let others see it.

Stanhelm's work was to sort bits of waste metal for the crucibles. He had Simon join him at it, then taught his new apprentice how to tell copper from bronze and tin from lead by tapping the metal against stone or scratching its surface with a jagged iron bar.

A strange jumble of things passed through their hands on the way to the smelter, chains and pots and crushed bits of plating whose original purpose was unguessable, wagon rims and barrel bands, sacks full of bent nails, fire irons, and door hinges. Once Simon lifted a delicately wrought bottle rack and recognized it as something that had hung on the wall of Doctor Morgenes' chamber, but as he stared, caught for a moment in an eddying memory of a happier past, Stanhelm nudged him in warning that Inch was approaching. Simon hurriedly tossed it into the pile.

The scrap metal was carried to the row of crucibles that hung in the forge fire, a blaze as large as a house, fed with a seemingly unending supply of charcoal and heated by bellows that were themselves pumped by the action of the foundry's massive water wheel, which was three times as high as a man and revolved ceaselessly, day and night. Fanned by the bellows, the forge fire burned with such incredible ferocity that it seemed a miracle to Simon the very stone of the cavern did not melt. The crucibles, each containing a different metal, were moved by a collection of blackened chains and pulleys which were also connected to the wheel. Yet another set of chains, so much larger than the links that moved the crucibles that they seemed made to shackle giants, extended upward from the wheel's hub and vanished into a darkened crevice in the forge chamber's roof. Not even Stanhelm wanted to talk about where those went, but Simon gathered it had something to do with Pryrates.

In stolen moments, Stanhelm showed Simon the whole process, how the scrap was melted down to a glowing red liquid, then decanted from the crucibles and formed into sows, long cylindrical chunks of raw metal which, when cool, were carried away by sweating men to another part of the vast chamber where they would be shaped into whatever it was that Inch supplied to his king. Armor and weapons, Simon guessed, since in all the great quantities of scrap, he had seen almost no articles of war that were not damaged beyond use. It made sense that Elias wished to convert every unnecessary bit of metal into arrow heads and sword blades.

As the days passed, it became more and more clear to Simon that there was little chance he would escape from this place. Stanhelm told him that only a few prisoners had escaped during the past year and all but one had quickly been dragged back. None of the recaptured had lived long after returning.

*And the one who escaped was Jeremias,* Simon thought. *He only managed it because Inch was foolish enough to let him go upstairs on an errand. I doubt I will get such a chance.*

The feeling of being trapped was so powerful, the impulse to flee so intense, that at times Simon could hardly stand it. He thought obsessively about being carried upward by the great water wheel chains to whatever dark place they went. He dreamed of finding a tunnel leading out of the great chamber, as he had during his first escape from the Hayholt, but they were all filled in now, or led only to other parts of the forge. Supplies from the outside came with Thrithings mercenary guards armed with spears and axes, and the arrival of anything was always supervised by Inch or one of his chieftains. The only keys hung rattling on Inch's broad belt.

Time was growing short for his friends, for Josua's cause, and Simon was helpless.

*And Pryrates has not left the castle, either. So it is*

_likely only a matter of time until he comes back here._
_What if he is not in such a hurry next time? What if he_
_recognizes me?_

Whenever he seemed to be alone and unwatched, Simon
hunted for anything that might help him to escape, but he
found little that gave him any hope. He pocketed a piece
of scrap iron and took to sharpening it against the stone
when he was supposed to be sleeping. If Pryrates discovered him at last, he would do what damage he could.

Simon and Stanhelm were standing near the scrap pile,
panting for breath. The older man had cut himself on a
jagged edge and his hand was bleeding badly.

"Hold still." Simon tore a piece from his ragged
breeches for a bandage and began to wrap it around
Stanhelm's wounded hand. Exhausted, the older man
wobbled from side to side like a ship in high winds.
"Aedon!" Simon swore unhappily. "That's deep."

"Can't go no more," Stanhelm muttered. Above the face
mask, his eyes had finally taken on the lifeless glaze that
marked the rest of the forge's laborers. "Can't go no more."

"Just stand there," Simon said, pulling the knot tight.
"Rest."

Stanhelm shook his head hopelessly. "Can't."

"Then don't. Sit down. I'll go find the dipper man, get
you some water."

Something large and dark passed before the flames,
blocking the light like a mountain obscuring a sunset.

"Rest?" Inch lowered his head, peering first at
Stanhelm, then at Simon. "You are not working."

"He h–hurt his hand." Avoiding the overseer's eyes, Simon stared instead at Inch's broad shoes, noting with
numbed bemusement that one flat, blunt toe poked
through on each. "He's bleeding."

"Little men are always bleeding," Inch said matter-of-factly. "Time to rest later. Now there is work to do."

Stanhelm swayed a little, then abruptly sagged and sat
down. Inch stared at him, then stepped closer.

"Get up. Time to work."

Stanhelm only moaned softly, cradling his injured hand.

"Get up." Inch's voice was a deep rumble. "Now."

The seated man did not look at him. Inch leaned down and smacked Stanhelm on the side of the head so hard that the forge worker's head snapped to one side and his body rocked. Stanhelm began to cry.

"Get up."

When this did not produce any better results, Inch lifted his thick fist high and struck Stanhelm again, this time knocking him into a splay-limbed sprawl.

Several of the other forge workers had stopped to stare, watching Stanhelm's punishment with the crushed calm of a flock of sheep who have seen one of their number taken by a wolf, and know that for a while at least they are safe.

Stanhelm lay silent, only barely moving. Inch lifted his boot above the man's head. "Get up, you."

Simon's heart was racing. The whole thing seemed to be happening too fast. He knew he would be a fool to say anything—Stanhelm had clearly reached his breaking point and was as good as dead. Why should Simon risk everything?

*It's a mistake to care about people,* he thought angrily.

"Stop." He knew it was his own voice, but it sounded unreal. "Let him be."

Inch's wide, scarred face swung around slowly, his one good eye blinking in the scorched flesh. "You don't talk," he growled, then gave Stanhelm an offhand kick.

"I said . . . let him be."

Inch turned away from his victim and Simon took a step backward, looking for someplace to run. There was no turning back now, no escape from this confrontation. Terror and long-suppressed rage battled inside him. He yearned for his Qanuc knife, confiscated by the Norns.

"Come here."

Simon took another step backward. "Come and get me, you great sack of guts."

Inch's ruined face screwed up in a snarl and he lunged forward. Simon darted out of his reach and turned to run across the chamber. The other workers gaped as the master of the forge lumbered after him.

Simon had hoped to tire the huge man, but had reckoned without his own weariness, the weeks of injury and deprivation. Within a hundred strides he felt his strength ebbing, although Inch still plodded some distance behind him. There was nowhere to hide, and there was no escape from the forge; better to turn and fight in the open, where he could best use whatever advantage of speed still remained to him.

He bent to pick up a large chunk of stone. Inch, certain that he had Simon captured, but wary of the stone, moved steadily but slowly closer.

"Doctor Inch is master here," he rumbled. "There is work to do. You . . . you have . . ." He growled, unable to find words to describe the magnitude of Simon's crimes. He took another step forward.

Simon flung the stone at his head. Inch dodged and it thumped heavily against his shoulder instead. Simon found himself filling with a dark exhilaration, a rising fury that surged through him almost like joy. This was the creature who had brought Pryrates to Morgenes' chamber! This monstrosity had helped kill Simon's master!

"Doctor Inch!" Simon shouted, laughing wildly as he bent for another stone. "*Doctor?!* You are not fit to call yourself anything but Slug, but Filth, but Half-Wit! Doctor! Ha!" Simon flung the second stone, but Inch sidestepped and it clattered across the cavern floor. The big man leaped forward with startling speed and hit Simon a glancing blow that knocked him off his feet. Before he could regain his balance, a wide hand closed on his arm. He was jerked upright, then flung headfirst across the stone floor. Tumbling, he hit his head, then lay for a moment, dazed. Inch's meaty hands closed on him again. He was lifted up, then something struck his face so hard that he heard thunder and saw lightning. He felt his cloth mask pull away. Another blow rocked him, then he was free and toppling to the ground. Simon lay where he had fallen, struggling to understand where he was and what had happened.

"You make me angry . . ." said a deep voice. Simon waited helplessly for another blow, hoping it would be strong enough to take away the pain in his head and the sickness in his guts forever. But for long moments nothing happened.

"The little kitchen boy," Inch said at last. "I know you. You are the kitchen boy. But you have hair on your face!" There was a sound like two stones being rubbed together. It took some time for Simon to realize that Inch was laughing. "You came back!" He sounded as pleased as if Simon were an old friend. "Back to Inch—but I am Doctor Inch now. You laughed at me. But you won't laugh any more."

Thick fingers squeezed him and he was jerked up from the floor. The sudden movement filled his head with blackness.

Simon struggled to move but could not. Something held him with his arms and legs extended, stretched to their utmost.

He opened his eyes to the tattered moon face of Inch.

"Little kitchen boy. You came back." The huge man leaned closer. He used one hand to pinion Simon's right arm against whatever stood behind, then raised the other, which clutched a heavy mallet. Simon saw the spike being held against his wrist and could not hold back his shout of terror.

"Are you afraid, kitchen boy? You took my place, the place that should have been mine. Turned the old man against me. I didn't forget." Inch raised the mallet and brought it down hard against the head of the spike. Simon gasped and twitched helplessly, but there was no pain, only a tightening of the pressure on his wrist. Inch hammered the spike in deeper, then leaned back to examine his work. For the first time Simon realized that they were high above the cavern floor. Inch was standing on a ladder that leaned against the wall just below Simon's arm.

But it *wasn't* the wall, Simon saw a moment later. The rope around his wrist was now spiked to the forge's immense water wheel. His other wrist and both ankles had already been secured. He was spread-eagled a few cubits beneath the wheel's edge, ten cubits above the ground.

The wheel was not moving, and the sluice of dark water seemed farther away than it should.

"Do whatever you want." Simon clenched his teeth against the scream that wanted to erupt. "I don't care. Do anything."

Inch tugged at Simon's wrists again, testing. Simon could begin to feel the downward pull of his weight against the bonds and the slow warmth in the joints of his arms, precursor of real pain.

"Do? I do nothing." Inch placed his huge hand on Simon's chest and gave a push, forcing Simon's breath out in a surprised hiss. "I waited. You took my place. I waited and waited to be Doctor Inch. Now *you* wait."

"W—wait for what?"

Inch smiled, a slow spread of lips that revealed broken teeth. "Wait to die. No food. Maybe I will give you water—it will take longer that way. Maybe I will think of . . . something else to do. Doesn't matter. You will wait." Inch nodded his head. "Wait." He pushed the mallet's handle into his belt and climbed down the ladder.

Simon craned his neck, watching Inch's progress with stupefied fascination. The overseer reached the bottom and waved for a pair of his henchmen to take the ladder away. Simon sadly watched it go. Even if he somehow escaped his bonds, he would surely fall to his death.

But Inch was not finished. He moved forward until he was almost hidden from Simon's view by the great wheel, then pulled down on a thick wooden lever. Simon heard a grinding noise, then felt the wheel jerk, its sudden motion rattling his bones. It slipped downward, shuddering as it went, then splashed into the sluice, sending another jolt through Simon.

Slowly . . . ever so slowly . . . the wheel began to turn.

At first it was almost a relief to be rotated down toward the ground. The weight shifted from both his arms to his wrist and ankle, then gradually the strain moved to his legs as the chamber turned upside down. Then, as he rolled even further downward, blood rushed to his head until it felt as though it would burst out through his ears.

At the bottom of his revolution, water splashed just beyond him, almost wetting his finger tips.

Above the wheel, the immense chains were again reeling up into darkness.

"Couldn't stop it for long," rumbled a downside-up Inch. "Bellows don't work, buckets don't work—and the Red Rat Wizard's tower don't turn." He stood staring for a moment as Simon slowly began to rise toward the cavern ceiling. "It does lots of things, this wheel." His remaining eye glittered in the light from the forge. "Kills little kitchen boys."

He turned and lumbered off across the chamber.

It didn't hurt that much at first. Simon's wrists were so securely bound, and he was stretched so tightly against the wheel's wide rim, that there was very little movement. He was hungry, which kept him clearheaded enough to think; his mind revolved far more swiftly than the prisoning wheel, circling through the events that had brought him to this place and through dozens of unlikely possibilities for escape.

Perhaps Stanhelm would come when it was sleeping time and cut him loose, he told himself. Inch had his own chamber somewhere in another part of the forge: with luck, Simon could be freed without the hulking overseer even knowing. But where would he go? And what made him think that Stanhelm was still alive, or if he was, that he would risk death again to save a person he barely knew?

Someone else? But who? None of the other foundrymen cared if Simon lived or died—nor could he much blame them. How could you worry about another person when every moment was a struggle to breathe the air, to survive the heat, to perform backbreaking work at the whim of a brutish master?

And this time there were no friends to rescue Simon. Binabik and Miriamele, even should they somehow make their way into the castle, would surely never come here. They sought the king—and had no reason to believe Simon still lived, anyway. Those who had rescued him from danger in the past—Jiriki, Josua, Aditu—were far away, on the grasslands or marching toward Nabban. Any friends who had once lived in the castle were gone. And even if he somehow managed to free himself from this wheel, where would he go? What could he do? Inch would only catch him again, and next time the forge-master might not devise such a gradual torment.

He strained again at his bonds, but they were heavy ropes woven to resist the strains of forge work and they gave not at all. He could work at them for days and only tear the skin from his wrists. Even the spikes that held the knotted ropes against the wheel's timbers were no help: Inch had carefully driven them between the strands so that the rope would not split.

The burning in his arms and legs was worsening. Simon felt a drumbeat of real dread begin inside him. He could not move. No matter what happened, no matter how bad it got, no matter how much he screamed and struggled for release, there was nothing he could do.

It would almost be a relief, he thought, if Pryrates came and found that Inch held him prisoner. The red priest would do terrible things to him, but at least they would be different terrible things—sharp pains, long pains, little ones and great ones. This, Simon could tell, was only going to become steadily worse. Soon his hunger would become a torment as well. Most of a day had passed since he had last eaten, and he was already thinking on his last bowl of scum-flecked soup with a regret bordering on madness.

As he turned upside-down once more, his stomach lurched, momentarily freeing him from hunger. It was little enough to be grateful for, but Simon's expectations were becoming very slight.

The pain that burned his body was matched by a fury that grew within him as he suffered, a helpless rage that could find no outlet and so began to gnaw at the very foundations of his sanity instead. Like an angry man he had once seen in Erchester, who threw everything in his house out of the window, piece by piece, Simon had nothing to fling at his enemies but what was his own—his beliefs, his loves, his most cherished memories.

Morgenes and Josua and Binabik and the others had used him, he decided. They had taken a boy who could not even write his own name and had made him a tool. Under their manipulation and for their benefit he had been driven from his home, had been made an exile, had seen the death of many he held dear and the destruction of much that was innocent and beautiful. With no say in his own destiny he had been led this way and that, and told just enough half-truths to keep him soldiering on. For the sake of Josua he had faced a dragon and won—then the Great Sword had been taken from him and given to someone else. For Binabik's sake he had stayed on in Yiqanuc—who could say that Haestan would have been killed if the company had left earlier? He had come with Miriamele to protect her on her journey, and had suffered because of it, both in the tunnels and now on this wheel where he would likely die. They had all taken from him, taken everything he had. They had used him.

And Miriamele had other crimes to answer for. She had led him on, treated him like an equal even though she was a king's daughter. She had been his friend, or had said she was, but she had not waited for him to come back from the quest to the northern mountains. No, instead she had gone off on her own without even a word left for him, as though their friendship had never existed. And she had given herself to another man—delivered her maidenhood to someone she did not even like! She had kissed Simon and let him think that his hopeless love had some meaning . . . but then she had thrown her own deeds in his face in the cruelest manner possible.

Even his mother and father had abandoned him, dying before he could ever know them, leaving him with no life and no history but what the chambermaids had given him. How could they!? And how could God let such a thing be?! Even God had betrayed him, for God had not been there. He was said to watch all creatures of His world, but He obviously cared little for Simon, the least of His children. How could God love someone and leave them to suffer as Simon had suffered, for no fault other than trying to do right?

Yet with all his fury at these so called friends who had abused his trust, he had greater hatred still for his enemies: Inch, the brute animal—no, worse than any animal, for an animal did not torture; King Elias who had thrown the world into war and blighted the earth with terror and famine and death; silver-masked Utuk'ku, who had set her huntsman after Simon and his friends and had killed wise Amerasu; and the priest Pryrates, Morgenes' murderer, who had nothing in his black soul but self-serving malice.

But the greatest author of all Simon's suffering, it seemed, was he whose ravening hatred was so great that even the grave could not contain it. If anyone deserved to be repaid in torment, it was the Storm King. Ineluki had brought ruin to a world full of innocents. He had destroyed Simon's life and happiness.

Sometimes Simon felt that hate was keeping him alive. When the agony became too strong, when he felt life slipping away, or at least passing out of his control, the need to survive and revenge himself was something to which he could cling. He would stay alive as long as he could, if only to return some measure of his own suffering to all who had abused him. Every miserable lonely night would be recompensed, every wound, every terror, every tear.

Revolving through darkness, in and out of madness, Simon made a thousand oaths to repay pain for pain.

At first it seemed a firefly, flitting on the edge of his vision—something small that glowed without light, a point of not-black in a world of blackness. Simon, his thoughts floundering in a wash of ache and hunger, could make no sense of it.

"*Come,*" a voice murmured to him. Simon had been hearing voices through this entire second day—or was it the third?—upon the wheel. What was another voice? What was another speck of dancing light?

"*Come.*"

Abruptly he was pulled free, free of the wheel, free of the ropes that burned his wrists. He was tugged onward by the spark, and could not understand how escape could be accomplished so easily . . . until he looked back.

A body hung on the slowly circling rim, a naked white-skinned form sagging in the ropes. Flame-hued hair was sweat-plastered on its brow. Chin sagged on chest.

*Who is that?* Simon wondered briefly . . . but he knew the answer. He viewed his own form with dispassion. *So that's what I looked like? But there's nothing left in it—it's like an empty jar.*

The thought came to him suddenly. *I'm dead.*

But if that was so, why could he still dimly feel the ropes, still feel his arms yanked to the straining length of their sockets? Why did he seem to be both in and out of his body?

The light moved before him again, summoning, beckoning. Without will, Simon followed. Like wind in a long dark chimney, they moved together through chaotic shadows; almost-things brushed at him and passed through him. His connection to the body hanging upon the wheel grew more tenuous. He felt the candle of his being flickering.

*"I don't want to lose me! Let me go back!"*

But the spark that led him flew on.

Swirling darkness blossomed into light and color, then gradually took on the shapes of real things. Simon was at the mouth of the great sluice that turned the water wheel, watching the dark water tumble down into the depths below the castle, headed for the foundry. Next he saw the silent pool in the deserted halls of Asu'a. Water trickled down into the pool through the cracks in the ceiling. The mists that floated above the wide tarn pulsed with life, as though this water was somehow revivifying something that had long been almost lifeless. Could that be what the flickering light was trying to show him? That water from the forge had filled the Sithi pool? That it was coming to life again?

Other images flowed past. He saw the dark shape that grew at the base of the massive stairwell in Asu'a, the tree-thing he had almost touched, whose alien thoughts he had felt. The stairway itself was a spiraling pipe that led from the roots of the breathing tree up to Green Angel Tower itself.

As he thought of the tower, he abruptly found himself staring at its pinnacle, which reared like a vast white tooth. Snow was falling and the sky was thick with clouds, but somehow Simon could see through them to the night sky beyond. Hovering low in the northern darkness was a fiery ember with a tiny smear of tail—the Conqueror Star.

*"Why have you brought me here, to all these places?"* Simon asked. The spot of light hovered before him as though listening. *"What does this mean?"*

There was no answer. Instead, something cold splashed against his face.

Simon opened his eyes, suddenly very much an inhabitant of his painful flesh once more. A distorted shape hung upside down from the ceiling, piping like a bat.

No. It was one of Inch's henchmen, and Simon himself was hanging head-down at the lowest point of the wheel's revolution, listening to the axle squeak. The henchman turned another dipper full of water over Simon's face, pouring only a little of it into his mouth. He gasped and choked, trying to swallow, then licked his chin and lips. As Simon began his upward turn, the man walked away without a word. Little drops ran down from Simon's head and hair, and for a while he was too busy trying to catch and swallow them before they dripped away to wonder at his strange vision. It was only when the wheel brought him down the other side again that he could think.

*What did that mean?* It was hard to hold a coherent thought against the fire in his joints. *What was that glowing thing, what was it trying to show me? Or was it just more madness?*

Simon had experienced many strange dreams since Inch had left him—visions of despair and exaltation, scenes of impossible victory over his enemies and of his friends suffering dreadful fates, but he had also dreamed of far less meaningful things. The voices he had heard in the tunnels had returned, sometimes as a faint babble barely audible above the splashing and groaning of the wheel, other times clear as someone whispering in his ear, snatches of speech that always seemed just tantalizingly beyond his comprehension. He was beset by fantasies, dizzy as a storm-battered bird. So why should this vision be any more real?

*But it felt different. Like the difference between wind on your skin and someone touching you.*

Simon clung to the memory. After all, it was something to think about, something beside the horrible gnawing in his stomach and fire in his limbs.

*What did I see? That the pool down below the castle is alive again, filled up by the water that's splashing right under this wheel? The pool! Why didn't I think of it before? Jiriki—no, Aditu—said that there was something in Asu'a called the Pool of Three Depths, a Master Witness. That must be what I saw down there. Saw? I drank from it! But what does that matter, even if it's true?* He struggled with his thoughts. *Green Angel Tower, that tree, the pool—are they all linked somehow?*

He remembered his dreams of the White Tree, dreams that had plagued him for a long time. At first he had thought it was the Uduntree on frozen Yijarjuk, the great ice waterfall that had stunned him with its magnificence and improbability, but he had come to think it had another meaning as well.

*A white tree with no leaves. Green Angel Tower. Is something going to happen there? But what?* He laughed harshly, surprising himself by the rasping noise—he had been silent for many, many hours. *And what can I do about it anyway? Tell Inch?*

Still, something *was* happening. The Pool was alive, and Green Angel Tower was waiting for something . . . and the water wheel kept turning, turning, turning.

*I used to dream about a wheel, too—a great wheel that spun through Time, that pulled the past up into the light and pushed everything alive down into the ground . . . not a huge piece of wood paddling dirty water, like this.*

Now the wheel was carrying him down once more, tipping him so that the blood again rushed to his head and made his temples pound.

*What did the angel tell me in that other dream?* He grimaced and choked back a cry. The pain as it moved to his legs felt like someone jabbing him with long needles. *"Go deeper,"* she said. *"Go deeper."*

Time's walls began to crumble around Simon, as
though the wheel that carried him, like the wheel that had
haunted his dreams, plunged directly through the fabric of
the living moment, pushing it down into the past and
dredging up old history to spill across the present. The
castle below him, Asu'a the Great, dead for five centuries, had become as real as the Hayholt above. The deeds
of those who were gone—or those like Ineluki who had
died but still would not go—were as vital as those of living men and women. And Simon himself was spun between them, a bit of tattered skin and bone caught on the
wheel-rim of Eternity, dragged without his consent
through the haunted present and the undying past.

Something was touching his face. Simon surfaced from
delirium to feel fingers trailing across his cheek; they
caught in his hair for a moment, then slid free as the
wheel pulled him away. He opened his eyes, but either he
could not see or the torches in the chamber had all been
extinguished.

"What are you?" asked a quavering voice. It was just to
one side, but he was moving away from it. "I hear you
cry out. Your voice is not like the others. And I can feel
you. What are you?"

The inside of Simon's mouth was swollen so that he
could barely breathe. He tried to speak, but nothing came
out except a soft gargle of noise.

"What are you?"

Simon struggled to answer, wondering even as he did
so if this was another dream. But none of those, for all
their rustlingly intrusive presence, had touched him with
solid flesh.

An eternity of time seemed to pass as he made his way
to the top of the wheel where the great chains sawed noisily upward, then began his downward turn again. By the
time he reached the bottom he had worked up enough spit
for something close to speech, although the effort tore at
his aching throat.

*"Help . . . me . . ."*

But if someone was there, they did not speak or touch him again. His circle continued, uninterrupted. In darkness, alone, he wept without tears.

The wheel turned. Simon turned with it. Occasionally water splashed on his face and trickled into his mouth. Like the Pool of Three Depths, he thirstily absorbed it to keep the spark inside him alive. Shadows flitted through his mind. Voices hissed in the porch of his ear. His thoughts seemed to know no boundary, but at the same time he was trapped in the shell of his tormented, dying body. He began to yearn for release.

The wheel turned. Simon turned with it.

He stared into a grayness without form, an infinite distance that seemed somehow near enough to touch. A figure hovered there, faintly glimmering, gray-green as dying leaves—the angel from the tower-top.

*"Simon,"* the angel said. *"I have things to show you."*

Even in his thoughts, Simon could not form the words to question her.

*"Come. There is not much time."*

Together they passed through things, moving crossways to another place. Like a fog evaporated by strong sun, the grayness wavered and melted away, and Simon found himself watching something he had seen before, although he could not say where. A young man with golden hair moved carefully down a tunnel. In one hand was a torch, in the other a spear.

Simon looked for the angel, but there was only the man with the spear and his stance of fearfully poised expectation. Who was he? Why was Simon being shown this vision? Was it the past? The present? Was it someone coming to rescue him?

The stealthy figure moved forward. The tunnel widened, and the torchlight picked out the carvings of vines and flowers that twined on the walls. Whenever this might be, the past, future, or present, Simon now felt sure that he knew *where* it was happening—in Asu'a, in the depths below the Hayholt.

The man stopped abruptly, then took a step backward, raising his spear. His light fell upon a shape that bulked huge in the chamber before him, the torch-glare glittering on a thousand red scales. An immense clawed foot lay only a few paces from the archway in which the spearman stood, the talons knives of yellow bone.

*"Now look. Here is a part of your own story...."*

But even as the angel spoke, the scene faded abruptly.

Simon awoke to feel a hand on his face and water running between his lips. He choked and spluttered, but at the same time did his best to swallow every life-preserving drop.

"You are a man," a voice said. "You are real."

Another draught of water was poured over his face and into his mouth. It was hard to swallow while dangling downside-up, but Simon had learned in his hours on the wheel.

*"Who...?"* he whispered, forcing the word out through cracked lips. The hand traced across his features, delicate as an inquisitive spider.

"Who am I?" the voice asked. "I am the one who is here. In this place, I mean."

Simon's eyes widened. Somewhere in another chamber a torch still burned, and he could see the silhouette before him—the silhouette of a real person, a man, not a murmuring shadow. But even as he stared, the wheel drew him up again. He felt sure that when he came back around this living creature would be gone, leaving him alone once more.

"Who am I?" the man pondered. "I had a name, once—but that was in another place. When I was alive."

Simon could not stand such talk. All he wanted was a person, a real person to speak with. He let out a strangled sob.

"I had a name," the man said, his voice becoming quieter as Simon rotated away. "In that other place, before everything happened. They called me Guthwulf."

# PART TWO

✥

# The
# Blazing Tower

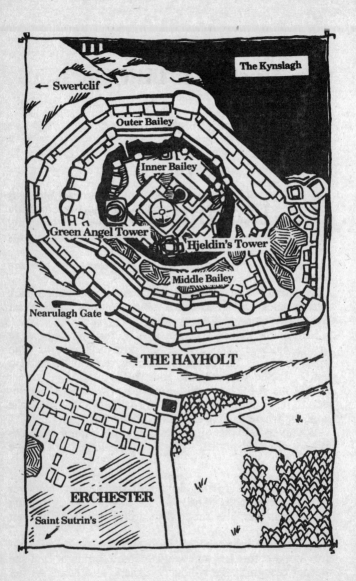

The Kynslagh

← Swertclif

Outer Bailey

Inner Bailey

Green Angel Tower

Hjeldin's Tower

Middle Bailey

Nearulagh Gate

THE HAYHOLT

ERCHESTER

Saint Sutrin's

# 21

# The Frightened Ones

✦

**Miriamele awakened** slowly into darkness. She was moving, but not of her own power, carried by somebody or something as though she were a bundle of clothing. The cloying sweetness was still in her nose. Her thoughts were muddy and slow.

*What happened? Binabik was fighting that terrible grinning man. . . .*

She dimly remembered being grasped and pulled back into darkness. She was a prisoner . . . but of whom? Her father? Or worse . . . far worse . . . Pryrates?

Miriamele kicked experimentally, but her legs were firmly held, restrained by something less painful than ropes or chains, but no more yielding; her arms were also pinioned. She was helpless as a child.

"Let me go!" she cried, knowing it was useless, but unable to restrain her frustration. Her voice was muffled: the sack, or whatever it was, still covered her face.

Whoever held her did not reply; the bumpy progress did not slow. Miriamele struggled a bit longer, then gave up.

She had been drifting in a half-sleep when whoever carried her stopped. She was set down with surprising gentleness, then the sack was carefully lifted from her head.

At first the light, though dim, hurt her eyes. Dark figures stood before her, one leaning so close that at first she did not recognize the silhouetted shape as a head. As her eyes adjusted, she gasped and scrambled backward until hard stone halted her. She was surrounded by monsters.

The nearest creature flinched, startled by her sudden movement. Like its fellows, it was more or less man-like, but it had huge dark eyes with no whites, and its gaunt, lantern-jawed head bobbed on the end of a slender neck. It reached out a long-fingered hand toward her, then drew it back as though it feared she would bite. It said a few words in a tongue that sounded something like Hernystiri. Miriamele stared back in horrified incomprehension. The creature tried again, this time in halting, oddly-accented Westerling.

"Have we brought harm to you?" The spidery creature seemed genuinely worried. "Please, are you well? Is there aught we can give to you?"

Miriamele gaped and tried to slide out of the thing's reach. It did not seem inclined to hurt her—at least not yet. "Some water," she said at last. "Who are you?"

"Yis-fidri am I," the creature replied. "These others are my fellows, and that is my mate Yis-hadra."

"But *what* are you?" Miriamele wondered if the seeming kindness of these creatures could be a trick of some sort. She tried to look unobtrusively for her knife, which was no longer sheathed at her waist; as she did so, she took in her surroundings for the first time. She was in a cavern, featureless but for the rough surface of the rock. It was dimly illuminated, all glowing pink, but she could see no source for the light. A few paces away, the packs she and Binabik had carried lay beside the cavern wall. There were things inside them she could use as a weapon if she had to. . . .

"What are we?" The one called Yis-fidri nodded solemnly. "We are the last of our people, or at least the last who have chosen this way, the Way of Stone and Earth." The other creatures made a musical sound of regret, as though this meaningless remark had great significance. "Your people have known us as dwarrows."

"Dwarrows!" Miriamele could not have been more surprised had Yis-fidri announced they were angels. Dwarrows were creatures of folktale, goblins who lived in the earth. Still, as unbelievable as it seemed, they stood here before her. And more, there was something almost familiar in Yis-fidri's manner, as though she had known him or someone like him before. "Dwarrows," she repeated. She felt a terrified laugh bubbling inside her. "Yet another story springs to life." She sat up straighter, trying to hide her fright. "If you mean me no harm, then take me back to my friend. He is in danger."

The saucer-eyed creature looked mournful. He made a melodious sound and one of the other dwarrows stepped forward with a stone bowl. "Take of this and drink. It is water, as you asked."

Miriamele sniffed at it suspiciously for a moment, then realized that if they could bring her here so easily the dwarrows had little need to poison her. She drank, savoring the feel of the chill, clean water on her dry throat. "Will you take me back to him?" she asked again when she had finished.

The dwarrows looked nervously at each other, heads wavering like poppies in a windy field. "Please, mortal woman, ask not for that," Yis-fidri said at last. "You were in a perilous place—more perilous than you can know—and you carried something there which you should not have. The balance is exceeding delicate." The words sounded stilted and almost comical, but his reluctance was very clear.

"Perilous!?" A spark of indignation kindled. "What right do you have to snatch me away from my friend? I will decide what is perilous for me!"

He shook his head. "Not for you—or not for you only. Dreadful things are in the balance, and that place . . . it is not good." He seemed very uncomfortable, and the other dwarrows swayed a little behind him, humming nervously to themselves. Despite her unhappiness, Miriamele almost laughed at the odd spectacle. "We cannot let you go there. We are deeply sorry. Some of our number will return and look for your friend."

"Why didn't you help him? Why couldn't you bring him with us if it was so important that we not be there?"

"We were sorely afraid. He did fight with an Unliving

One, or so it seemed. And the balance is very delicate there."

"What does that mean?!" Miriamele stood up, for a moment more angry than fearful. "You cannot do this!" She began to edge toward a shadowy place on the cavern wall that she thought might be a tunnel mouth. Yis-fidri reached out and caught at her wrist. His thin fingers were callused and hard as stone. There was deceptive strength, great strength, in this slender dwarrow.

"Please, mortal woman. We will tell you all that we are able. Content yourself for now to stay with us. We will seek for your friend."

She struggled, but it was hopeless. She might have been pulling against the weight of the earth.

"So," she said at last. Fright was turning to hopelessness. "I have no choice. Tell me what you know, then. But if Binabik is hurt because of what you've done, I'll ... I'll find a way to punish you, whoever you are. I will."

Yis-fidri hung his great head like a dog being scolded. "It is not our wont to force others against their will. We have ourselves suffered too much at the hands of bad masters."

"If I must be your prisoner, at least call me by my name. I'm Miriamele."

"Miriamele, then." Yis-fidri let go of her arm. "Forgive us, Miriamele, or at least judge us not until all we have to say is heard."

She lifted the bowl and took another drink. "Tell me, then."

The dwarrow looked around at his fellows, at the circle of huge dark eyes, then began to talk.

"And how is Maegwin?" Isorn asked. His bandage gave him a strange, swollen-headed appearance. Icy air crept past the tent flap to ripple the flames of the small fire.

"I had thought she might be coming back to us," Eolair

sighed. "Last night she began to move a little and take deeper breaths. She even spoke a few words, but they were whispered. I could make no sense of them."

"But that is good news! Why are you so long-faced?"

"The Sitha woman came to see her. She said it was like a fever—that sometimes the sufferer comes near to the surface, like a drowning man coming up for air one last time, but that does not mean . . ." Eolair's voice shook. He made an effort to control himself. "The healer said that she was still just as close to death, if not closer."

"And you believe the Sitha?"

"It is not an illness of the flesh, Isorn," the count said quietly. "It is a wound to her soul, which was already damaged. You saw her in the last weeks." He twined his fingers, then untwined them. "And the Sithi know more of these things than we do. Whatever happened to Maegwin left no marks, no broken bones or bleeding cuts. Give thanks that your own injury is something that can be mended."

"I do, by my faith." The young Rimmersman frowned. "Ah, Merciful Usires, Eolair, that is more grim news, then. And is there nothing anyone can do?"

The count shrugged. "The healer says it is beyond her powers. She can work only to make Maegwin comfortable."

"A cursed fate for such a good woman. Lluth's family is haunted somehow."

"No one would have said so before this year." Eolair bit his lip before continuing. His own sorrow grew until it seemed it must escape or kill him. "But, Murhagh's Shield, Isorn, no wonder that Maegwin sought the gods! How could she not think they had deserted us? Her father killed, her brother tortured and hacked to pieces, her people driven into exile?" He fought for a breath. "*My* people! And now poor Maegwin, maddened and then left dying in the snows of Naglimund. It is more than the absence of the gods—it is as though the gods were determined to punish us."

Isorn made the sign of the Tree. "We can never know

what Heaven plans, Eolair. Perhaps there are greater designs for Maegwin than we can understand."

"Perhaps." Eolair pushed down his anger. It was not Isorn's fault that Maegwin was slipping away, and everything he said was kind and sensible. But the Count of Nad Mullach did not want kindness and sense. He wanted to howl like a Frostmarch wolf. "Ah, Cuamh bite me, Isorn, you should see her! When she is not lying still as death, her face stretches in terror, and her hands clutch," he raised his own hands, fingers curled, "like this, as if she sought something to save her." Eolair slapped his palms against his knees in frustration. "She needs something, and I cannot give it to her. She is lost, and I cannot find her to bring her back!" He gasped raggedly.

Isorn stared at his friend. The light of understanding kindled in his eyes. "Oh, Eolair. Do you love her?"

"I don't know!" The count put his hands to his face for a moment before continuing. "I thought once I might be coming to it, but then she turned harsh and cold to me, pushing me away whenever she could. But when the madness came over her, she told me that she had loved me since she was a child. She was certain I would scorn her, and did not like to be pitied, so she kept me ever at bay so I would not discover the truth."

"Mother of Mercy," Isorn breathed. He reached out his freckled hand and grasped Eolair's. The count felt the broad strength of the contact and held on for a long moment.

"Life is already a confounding maze without wars between immortals and such. Ah, gods, Isorn, will we never have peace?"

"Someday," said the Rimmersman. "Someday we must."

Eolair gave his friend's hand a parting squeeze before he let it go. "Jiriki said the Sithi plan to leave within two days. Will you go with them, or back to Hernystir with me?"

"I am not sure. The way my head feels, I cannot ride at anything like speed."

"Then go with me," the count said as he rose. "We are in no hurry, now."

"Be well, Eolair."

"And you. If you like, I'll come back later with some of that Sithi wine. It would do you miles of good, and take the sting of that wound away."

"It will take more than that away," Isorn laughed. "My wits will go, too. But I do not care. I am going nowhere, and am expected to do nothing. Bring the wine when you can."

Eolair patted the younger man's shoulder, then pushed out through the door flap into the biting wind.

As he reached the place where Maegwin lay, he was struck again by the power of Sithi craft. Isorn's small tent was well-made and sturdy, but cold air crept in on all sides and melting snow seeped through at the base. Maegwin's tent was of Sithi make, since Jiriki had wished her to rest in as much comfort as she could, and though its glistening cloth was so thin as to be translucent, stepping across the threshold was like walking into a well-built house. The storm that gripped Naglimund could have been leagues away.

But why should that be so, Eolair wondered, when the Sithi themselves seemed almost unaware of cold or damp?

Kira'athu looked up as Eolair entered. Maegwin, stretched out on the pallet beneath a thin blanket, was moving restlessly, but her eyes were still closed and the deathlike pallor had not left her face.

"Any change?" Eolair asked, knowing the answer already.

The Sitha gave a small, sinuous shrug. "She is fighting, but I do not think she has the strength to break the grip of whatever has her." The Sitha seemed emotionless, her golden eyes unrevealing as a cat's, but the count knew how much time she spent at Maegwin's side. They were just different, these immortals; it was senseless trying to judge them by their faces and even voices. "Has she spoken any words to you?" Kira'athu asked suddenly.

Eolair watched as Maegwin's fingers clawed at the blanket, scrabbling for something that was not there. "She has spoken, yes, but I could not hear her well. And what I did hear was only babble. There were no words in it I recognized."

The Sitha raised a silvery eyebrow. "I thought I heard ..." She turned to look at her ward, whose mouth now moved soundlessly.

"Thought you heard what?"

"The speech of the Garden." Kira'athu spread her hands, curving the fingers to meet the thumbs. "What you would call Sithi speech."

"It is possible that she learned some in the time we have all traveled and fought together." Eolair moved closer. It tugged at his heart to see Maegwin's hands searching restlessly.

"It is possible," the healer agreed. "But it seemed spoken as the Zida'ya would speak it ... almost."

"What do you mean?" Eolair was confused and more than a little irritated.

Kira'athu rose. "Forgive me. I should speak to Jiriki and Likimeya about it rather than trouble you. And it matters little, in any case, I think. I am sorry, Count Eolair. I wish I could give you happier news."

He sat down on the ground at Maegwin's side. "It is not your fault. You have been very kind." He reached out his hand so Maegwin could grip it, but her cold fingers moved skittishly away. "Bagba bite me, what does she want?"

"Is there something she usually carries with her or wears about her neck?" Kira'athu asked. "Some amulet or other thing that gives her comfort?"

"I can think of nothing like that. Perhaps she needs water."

The Sitha shook her head. "I have given her to drink."

Eolair leaned down and began fumbling absently in the saddlebags that contained the strew of Maegwin's belongings. He took out a scarf of warm wool and pressed it into her hands, but Maegwin only held it a moment before pushing it away. Her hands began to search again as she murmured wordlessly in her throat.

Desperate to give Maegwin some kind of comfort, he began to pull other things out of the bags, placing them one at a time beneath her fingers—a bowl, a wooden bird that had apparently come from the Taig's Hall of Carvings, even the hilt of a sheathed knife. Eolair was not very happy to find this last. Afraid that with her mind clouded she might do herself an injury, he had forbidden her to bring it from Hernysadharc. Maegwin had apparently flouted his orders. But none of these things, nor the other small objects he gave to her, seemed to soothe her. She pushed them away, the movements of her hands angry and abrupt as a small child's, although her face was still empty.

His fingers closed on something heavy. He lifted it out and stared at the chunk of cloudy stone.

"What is that?" Kira'athu was surprisingly sharp.

"It was a gift from the dwarrows." He lifted it so she could see its face. "See, Yis-fidri carved Maegwin's name upon it—or so he told me."

Kira'athu took the stone from him and turned it in her slender fingers. "That is indeed her name. Those are the craft-runes of the Tinukeda'ya. Dwarrows, do you say?"

Eolair nodded. "I led Jiriki to their place in the earth, Mezutu'a." He took the stone back and held it, weighing it, watching the firelight become confused in its depths. "I did not know she had this with her."

Maegwin suddenly moaned, a deep sound that made the count flinch. He turned hurriedly to the bed. She made another sound which seemed to have words in it.

"*Lost,*" Kira'athu murmured, moving closer.

Eolair's heart clenched. "What do you mean?"

"That is what she said. She is speaking in the Garden-tongue."

The count stared at Maegwin's furrowed brow. Her mouth moved again, but no sound came but a wordless hiss; her head whipped from side to side upon the pillow. Suddenly, her hands reached out and scrabbled at Eolair's. When he released the stone to take them, she snatched it from him and pulled it against her breasts. Her feverish writhing subsided and she fell silent. Her eyes were still closed, but she seemed to have fallen back into a more peaceful sleep.

Eolair watched, dumbfounded. Kira'athu bent over her and touched her brow, then smelled her breath.

"Is she well?" the count asked finally.

"She is no closer to us. But she has found a little rest for a while. I think that stone was what she sought."

"But why?"

"I do not know. I will speak to Likimeya and her son, and anyone else who might have some knowledge. But it changes nothing, Eolair. She is the same. Still, perhaps where she walks, on the Dream Road or elsewhere, she is less afraid. That is something."

She pulled the blanket up over Maegwin's hands, which now clasped the dwarrow-stone as though it were a part of her.

"You should rest yourself, Count Eolair." The Sitha moved to the doorway. "You will be no good to her if you fall ill as well."

A breath of cold air moved through the tent as the flap opened and closed.

Isgrimnur watched Lector Velligis leave the throne room. The huge man's litter was carried by eight grimacing guards, and was led out, as it had been led in, by a procession of priests bearing sacred objects and smoking censers. Isgrimnur thought they resembled a traveling fair on its way to a new village. Spared kneeling by his injuries, he had watched the new lector's performance from a chair against the wall.

Camaris, for all his noble look, appeared uncomfortable on the high ducal throne. Josua, who had kneeled beside the chair while Lector Velligis offered his blessing, now rose.

"So." The prince dusted his knees with his hand. "Mother Church recognizes our victory."

"What choice did Mother Church have?" Isgrimnur growled. "We won. Velligis is one of those who always puts his money on the favorite—any favorite."

"He is the lector, Duke Isgrimnur," said Camaris sternly. "He is God's minister on earth."

"Camaris is right. Whatever he was before, he has been elevated to the Seat of the Highest. He deserves our respect."

Isgrimnur made a noise of disgust. "I'm old and I hurt and I know what I know. I can respect the Seat without loving the man. Did taking the Dragonbone Chair make your brother a good king?"

"No one ever claimed a kingship made its possessor infallible."

"Try telling that to most kings," snorted Isgrimnur.

"Please." Camaris raised his hand. "No more. This is a wearisome day, and there is more yet to be done."

Isgrimnur looked at the old knight. He *did* look tired, in a way that the duke had never seen. It would have seemed that freeing Nabban from his brother's killer should have brought Camaris joy, but instead it seemed to have sapped the life from him.

*It's as if he knows he's done one of the things he's meant to do—but only one. He wants to rest, but he can't yet.* The duke thought he finally understood. *I've wondered why he was so strange, so distant. He does not wish to live. He is only here because he believes God wishes him to finish the tasks before him.* Clearly any questioning of God's will, even the infallibility of the lector, was difficult for Camaris. *He thinks of himself as a dead man.* Isgrimnur suppressed a shudder. It was one thing to yearn for rest, for release, but another to feel that one was already dead. The duke wondered momentarily whether Camaris might, more than any of them, understand the Storm King.

"Very well," Josua was saying. "There is one person left we must see. I will speak to him, Camaris, if you do not mind. I have been thinking about this for some time."

The old knight waved his hand, uncaring. His eyes were like ice chips beneath his thick brows.

Josua signaled a page and the doors were thrown open.
As Count Streáwe's litter was carried in, Isgrimnur sat
back and picked up the mug of beer he had hidden behind
his chair. He took a long sip. Outside it was afternoon,
but the chamber's ceiling-high windows were barred
against the storm that lashed the seas beneath the palace,
and torches burned in the wall sconces. Isgrimnur knew
that the room was painted in delicate colors of sea and
sand and sky, but in the torchlight all was muddy and indistinct.

Streáwe was lifted from his litter and his chair was set
down at the base of the throne. The count smiled and
bowed his head. "Duke Camaris. Welcome back to your
rightful home. You have been missed, my lord." He swiv-
eled his white head. "And Prince Josua and Duke
Isgrimnur. I am honored that you have summoned me.
This is noble company."

"I am not a duke, Count Streáwe," said Camaris. "I
have taken no title, but only revenged my brother's
death."

Josua stepped forward. "Do not mistake his modesty,
Count. Camaris does rule here."

Streáwe's smile broadened, deepening the wrinkles
around his eyes. Isgrimnur thought he looked like the
most grandfatherly grandfather that God ever made. He
wondered if the count practiced before a looking glass. "I
am glad you took my advice, Prince Josua. As you see,
there were indeed many folk unhappy with Benigaris'
rule. Now there is joy in Nabban. As I came up from the
docks, people were dancing in the public square."

Josua shrugged. "That is more to do with the fact that
Baron Seriddan and the others have sent their troops into
the town with money to spend. This city did not suffer
much because of Benigaris, difficult as times are. Patricide or no, he seems to have ruled fairly well."

The count eyed him for a moment, then appeared to decide a different approach was warranted. Isgrimnur found
himself enjoying the show. "No," Streáwe said slowly,
"you are correct there. But people *know*, don't you think?
There was a sense that things were not right, and many

rumors that Benigaris had slain his father—your dear brother, Sir Camaris—to achieve the throne. There were problems that were certainly not all Benigaris' fault, but there was also much unrest."

"Unrest which you and Pryrates both helped to kindle, then fanned the flames."

Perdruin's ruler looked genuinely shocked. "You link me with Pryrates!?" For a moment his courtly mask fell away, showing the angry, iron-willed man beneath. "With that red-cloaked scum? If I could walk, Josua, we would cross swords for that."

The prince stared at him coldly for a moment, then his face softened. "I do not say you and Pryrates worked in concert, Streáwe, but that you each exploited the situation for your own ends. Very different ends, I'm sure."

"If that is what you meant, then I name myself guilty and throw myself on the mercy of the throne." The count seemed mollified. "Yes, I work in the ways I can to protect my island's interests. I have no armies to speak of, Josua, and I am always prey to the whims of my neighbors. 'When Nabban rolls over in its sleep,' it is said in Ansis Pellipé, 'Perdruin falls out of bed.' "

"Well argued, Count," Josua laughed. "And quite true, as far as it goes. But it is also said that you are perhaps the wealthiest man in Osten Ard. *All* the result of your vigilance on Perdruin's behalf?"

Streáwe drew himself up straighter. "What I have is none of your business. I understood you sought me as an ally, not to insult me."

"Spare me your false dignity, my good Count. I find it hard to believe that calling you wealthy is an insult. But you are right about one thing: we wish to speak with you about certain matters of mutual interest."

The count bobbed his head solemnly. "That is better to hear, Prince Josua. You know that I support you—remember the note I sent with my man Lenti!—and I am anxious to speak about ways that I can help you."

"That we can help each other, you mean." Josua raised his hand to still Streáwe's protest. "Please, Count, let us avoid the usual dancing. I am in a fierce hurry. There, I have given up a bargaining token already by telling you so. Now please do not waste our time with false protestations of this or that."

The old man's lips pursed and his eyes narrowed. "Very well, Josua. I find myself oddly interested. What do you want?"

"Ships. And sailors to man them. Enough to ferry our armies to Erkynland."

Surprised, Streáwe waited a moment before replying. "You intend to set sail for Erkynland now? After fighting fiercely for weeks to take Nabban, and with the worst storm in years sweeping down on us out of the north even as we speak?" He gestured toward the shuttered windows; outside, the wind wailed across the Sancelline Hill. "It was so cold last night that the water froze in the Hall of Fountains. The Clavean Bell barely rang over God's house, it was so icy. And you wish to go to sea?"

Isgrimnur felt a clutch of shock at the count's mention of the bell. Josua turned for a moment and caught the Rimmersman's eye, warning him not to speak. Obviously he, too, remembered Nisses' prophetic poem.

"Yes, Streáwe," said the prince. "There are storms and storms. We must brave some to survive others. I will take ship as soon as I can."

The count lifted his hands, showing open, empty palms. "Very well, you know your own business. But what would you have me do? Perdruin's ships are not warships, and they are all at sea. Surely Nabban's great fleet is what you need, not my trading vessels." He gestured to the throne. "Camaris is master of the Kingfisher House now."

"But you are master of the docks," Josua replied. "As Benigaris said, he thought you were his prisoner, but all the time you were gnawing him away from within. Did you use some of that gold they say fills the catacombs below your house on Sta Mirore? Or something more subtle—rumors, stories. . . ?" He shook his head. "It matters not. The thing is, Streáwe, you can help us or hinder us. I wish to discuss with you your price, whether in power or gold. There is provisioning to do as well. I want those ships loaded and on their way in seven days or less."

"Seven days?" The count showed surprise for the second time. "That will not be easy. And you have heard about the kilpa, have you not? They are running like quinis-fish—but quinis-fish do not pull sailors over the rails and eat them. Men are reluctant to go to sea in these dark days."

"So we have started the bargaining?" Josua asked. "Granted and granted. Times are difficult. What do you want, power or gold?"

Abruptly, Streáwe laughed. "Yes, we have started bargaining. But you underestimate me, Josua, or you undervalue your own coffers. You have something that might be more use to me than either gold or power—something that in fact brings both in its train."

"And what is that?"

The count leaned forward. "Knowledge." He sat up, a slow smile spreading across his face. "So now I have given *you* a bargaining token in return for your earlier gift." The count rubbed his hands in barely restrained enjoyment. "Let us speak in earnest, then."

Isgrimnur groaned softly as Josua sat down beside Perdruin's master. Despite the prince's stated hurry, it was indeed going to be a complicated dance. This was clearly something Streáwe enjoyed too much to do quickly, and something Josua took too seriously to be rushed through. Isgrimnur turned to look at Camaris, who had been silent during the whole discussion. The old knight was staring at the shuttered windows as if they were an intricately absorbing picture, his chin resting on his hand. Isgrimnur made another noise of pain and reached for his beer. He sensed a long evening ahead.

Miriamele's fear of the dwarrows was dwindling. She was beginning to remember what Simon and others had told her of Count Eolair's journey to Sesuad'ra. The count had met dwarrows—he called them *domhaini*—in

tho mines below Hernystir's mountains. He had called
them friendly and peaceful, and that seemed to be true:
except for snatching her from the stairs, they had not
harmed her. But they still would not let her go.

"Here." She gestured to the saddlebags. "If you are so
certain that something I am carrying is harmful, or dangerous, or . . . or whatever, search for yourselves."

As the dwarrows conferred in anxious, chiming voices,
Miriamele considered escape. She wondered if dwarrows
ever slept. But where had they brought her? How could
she find her way out, and where would she go then? At
least she still had the maps, although she doubted she
could read them as efficiently as Binabik had.

Where *was* Binabik? Was he alive? She felt almost ill
as she remembered the grinning thing that had attacked
the troll. Another friend was lost somewhere in the shadows. The little man had been right—this had been a foolish journey. Her own stubbornness had perhaps brought
death to her two closest friends. How could she live with
that knowledge?

By the time the dwarrows had finished their discussion,
Miriamele did not much care what they had decided.
Gloom had settled on her, sapping her strength.

"We will search among your possessions, by your
leave," Yis-fidri said. "In respect of your customs, my
wife Yis-hadra only will touch them."

Miriamele was bemused by the dwarrow's circumspec-
tion. What did they think she had brought down into the
earth, the dainty small-clothes of a castle-dwelling princess? Tiny, fragile keepsakes? Scented notes from admir-
ers?

Yis-hadra approached timidly and began to examine the
contents of the saddlebags. Her husband came and
kneeled beside Miriamele. "We are sorely grieved that
things should be thus. It is truly not our way—never have
we pressed our will by force on another. Never." He
seemed desperate to convince her.

"I still do not understand the danger you fear."

"It was the place you and your two companions
walked. It is . . . it is—there are no words that I know in

mortal tongues to explain." He flexed his long fingers. "There are ... powers, things which have been sleeping. Now they awaken. The tower stairwell in which you climbed is a place where these forces are strong. Every day they become stronger. We do not yet understand what is happening, but until we do, nothing must happen which might upset the balance. . . ."

Miriamele waved for him to stop. "Slowly, Yis-fidri. I am trying to understand. First of all, that ... thing that attacked us on the stairs was not a companion of ours. Binabik seemed to recognize him, but I have never seen him before."

Yis-fidri shook his head, agitated. "No, no, Miriamele. Be not insulted. We know that what your friend fought was no companion—it was a walking hollowness full of Unbeing. Perhaps it was a mortal man once. No, I meant that companion who followed a little behind you."

"*Behind* us? There were only two of us. Unless ..." Her heart skipped. Could it have been Simon, searching for his friends? Had he only been a short distance away when she had been taken? No, that would be too cruel!

"Then you were followed," Yis-fidri said firmly. "For good or ill, we cannot say. We just know that three mortals were upon the stairs."

Miriamele shook her head, unable to think about it. Too much confusion was piled atop too much sorrow.

Yis-hadra made a birdlike sound. Her husband turned. The she-dwarrow held up Simon's White Arrow.

"Of course," Yis-fidri breathed. The other dwarrows leaned closer, watching raptly. "We felt it, but knew it not." He turned to Miriamele. "It is not our work or we would know it as verily as you know your own hand at the end of your arm. But it was made by Vindaomeyo, one of the Zida'ya to whom we taught our skills and craft. And see," he reached to take it from his wife, "here is a piece of one of the Master Witnesses." He pointed to the cloudy blue-gray arrowhead. "No surprise that we felt it."

"And carrying it on the stairwell was a danger somehow?" Miriamele wanted to understand, but terror had battered her for a long time, and weariness was now pulling at her like an undertow. "How could that be?"

"We will explain if we can. Things are changing. Balances are delicate. The red stone in the sky speaks to the stones of the earth, and we Tinukeda'ya hear the voices of those stones."

"And these stones tell you to snatch people off the staircase?" She was exhausted. It was hard not to be rude.

"We did not wish to come here," Yis-fidri said gravely. "Things that happened in our home and elsewhere drove us ever southward, but when we reached this place through the old tunnels, we realized that the menace here is even greater. We cannot go forward, we cannot go back. But we must understand what is happening so that we can decide how best to escape it."

"You're going to run away?" Miriamele asked. "That's why you're doing all these things? To give yourself a chance to run away?"

"We are not warriors. We are not our once-masters, the Zida'ya. The way of the Ocean Children has always been to make do, to survive."

Miriamele shook her head in frustration. They had trapped her and torn her away from her friend, but only so they could escape something she did not understand. "Let me go."

"We cannot, Miriamele. We are sorry."

"Then let me go to sleep." She crawled away toward the wall of the cavern and curled herself in her cloak. The dwarrows did not hinder her, but began talking among themselves again. The sound of their voices, melodious and incomprehensible as cricket calls, followed her down into sleep.

# 22

# A Sleeping Dragon

✦

**Oh, please, God,** *don't let him be gone!*

The wheel carried Simon upward. If Guthwulf still spoke in the darkness below, Simon could not hear him above the creak of the wheel and the clanking of the heavy chains.

Guthwulf! Could it be the same man Simon had so often glimpsed, the High King's Hand with his fierce face? But he had led the siege against Naglimund, had been one of King Elias' most powerful friends. What would he be doing here? It must be someone else. Still, whoever he was, at least he had a human voice.

"Can you hear me?" Simon croaked as the wheel brought him down again. Blood, regular as the tide at evening, was rushing into his head once more.

"Yes," Guthwulf hissed. "Don't speak so loudly. I have heard others here, and I think they would hurt me. They would take away all I have left."

Simon could see him, a dim, bent figure—but large, as the King's Hand had been, broad shoulders evident despite his stoop. He held his head in an odd way, as though it hurt him.

"Can I have . . . more water?"

Guthwulf dipped his hands into the sluice beneath the wheel; as Simon swung low enough to reach, he poured the water over the prisoner's face. Simon gasped and begged for more. Guthwulf filled his palms three more times before Simon rose out of reach. "You are on . . . on

a wheel?" the man said, as though he could not quite believe it.

His thirst quenched for the first time in days, Simon
wondered at the question. Was he simple-minded? How
could anyone who wasn't blind doubt it was a wheel?

Suddenly Guthwulf's odd way of holding his head
made sense. Blind. Of course. No wonder he had felt at
Simon's face.

"Are you . . . Earl Guthwulf?" Simon asked as the
wheel headed downward again. "The Earl of Utanyeat?"
Remembering what his benefactor had said, he kept his
voice low. He had to repeat the question when he was
nearer.

"I . . . think I was." The earl's hands hung limply, dripping. "In another life. Before my eyes were gone. Before
the sword took me. . . ."

The sword? Had he been blinded in battle? In a duel?
Simon dismissed the thought: there were more important
things to think about. His belly was full of water, but
nothing else. "Can you bring me food? No, can you free
me? Please!? They are tormenting me, torturing me!" So
many words rasped his tender throat and he broke into a
fit of coughing.

"Free you. . . ?" Guthwulf sounded distinctly shaken.
"But . . . you do not wish to be here? I'm sorry, things are
. . . so different. I have trouble remembering."

*He's a madman. The only person who might help me,
and he's mad!*

Aloud, he said: "Please. I am suffering. If you don't
help me, I'll die here." A sob choked him. Talking about
it suddenly made it real. "I don't want to die!"

The wheel began to carry him up again.

"I . . . could not. The voices will not let me do anything," Guthwulf whispered. "They tell me that I must go
and hide, or someone will take everything I have from
me." His voice took on a horribly wistful tone. "But I
could hear you there, making noises, breathing. I knew
you were a real thing, and I wanted to hear your voice. I
have not spoken to anyone for so long." His words grew

faint as the wheel took Simon away. "Are you the one who left me food?"

Simon had no idea what the blind man was talking about, but heard him hesitating, troubled by Simon's pain. "I did!" He tried to be heard above the wheel without shouting. Was the man out of hearing? "I did! I brought you food!"

*Please let him be there when I get back,* Simon prayed. *Please let him be there. Please.*

As Simon neared the bottom again, Guthwulf reached out his hand once more and let it trail across Simon's features. "You fed me. I do not know. I am afraid. They will take everything from me. The voices are so loud!" He shook his shaggy head. "I cannot think now. The voices are very loud." Abruptly, he turned and lurched away across the cavern and vanished into the shadows.

"Guthwulf!" Simon cried. "Don't leave me!"

But the blind man was gone.

The touch of a human hand, the sound of a voice, had awakened Simon to his terrible pain once more. The passing hours or days or weeks—he had long since given up trying to mark time—had begun to smear into a gradually increasing nothingness; he had been floating in fog, drifting slowly away from the lights of home. Now he was back again, and suffering.

The wheel turned. Sometimes, when all the forge chamber's torches were lit, he saw masked, soot-blackened men hustling past him, but none ever spoke to him. Inch's helpers brought him water with excruciating infrequency, and did not waste words on him when they did. On a few occasions he even saw the huge overseer standing silently, watching as the wheel bore Simon around. Strangely, Inch did not seem interested in gloating: he came only to inspect Simon's misery, as a householder might pause to mark the progress of his vegetable garden while on the way to some other duty.

The pain in Simon's limbs and belly was so constant that he could not remember what it was like to feel any other way. It rolled through him as though his body were only a sack to contain it—a sack being tossed from hand to hand by careless laborers. With each rotation of the wheel, the pain rushed to Simon's head until it seemed his skull would burst, then pushed through his empty, aching guts to lodge in his feet once more, so that it seemed he stood on blazing coals.

Neither did the hunger go away. It was a gentler companion than the agony of his limbs, but still a dull and unceasing hurt. He could feel himself becoming less with every revolution—less human, less alive, less interested into holding onto whatever made him Simon. Only a dim flame of vengefulness, and an even dimmer spark of hope that someday he might come home to his friends, kept him clinging to the remains of his life.

*I am Simon,* he told himself until it was hard to remember what that meant. *I won't let them take that. I am Simon.*

The wheel turned. He turned with it.

❦

Guthwulf did not return to speak to him. Once, as he floated in a haze of misery, Simon felt the person who gave him water touch his face, but he could not move his lips to make a sound of inquiry. If it was the blind man, he did not stay.

Even as Simon felt himself shrinking away to nothingness, the forge chamber seemed to grow larger. Like the vision the glowing speck had shown him, it seemed opened to the entire world—or rather, it seemed that the world had collapsed in upon the foundry, so that often Simon felt himself to be in many different places at the same moment.

He felt himself trapped upon the empty, snow-chilled heights, burning with the dragon's blood. The scar upon his face was a searing agony. Something had touched him there, and changed him. He would never be the same.

Below the forge, but also inside Simon, Asu'a stirred. The crumbled stone shivered and bloomed anew, gleaming like the walls of Heaven. Whispering shadows became golden-eyed, laughing ghosts. Ghosts become Sithi, hot with life. Music as delicately beautiful as dew-spotted spiderwebs stretched through the resurrected halls.

A great red streak climbed into the sky above Green Angel Tower. The heavens surrounded it, but the other stars seemed only timid witnesses.

And a great storm rolled down out of the north, a whirling blackness that vomited wind and lightning and turned everything beneath it to ice, leaving only dead, silent whiteness in its wake.

Like a man floundering in a whirlpool, Simon felt himself at the center of powerful currents with no strength to alter them. He was a prisoner of the wheel. The world was turning toward some mighty, calamitous change, but Simon could not even lift his hand to his burning face.

"*Simon.*"

The fog was so thick he could not see. Gray blankness surrounded him. Who called him? Couldn't they see he needed to sleep? If he waited, the voice would go away. Everyone went away if he waited long enough.

"*Simon.*" The voice was insistent.

He did not want voices any more. He wanted nothing except to go back to sleep, a dreamless, endless sleep. . . .

"*Simon. Look at me.*"

Something was moving in the grayness. He did not care. Why couldn't the voice leave him be? "*Go away.*"

"*Look at me, Simon. See me, Simon. You must reach out.*"

He tried to shut out the troubling presence, but something inside him had been awakened by its voice. He looked into the emptiness.

"*Can you see me?*"

"*No. I want to sleep.*"

"*Not yet, Simon. There are things you must do. You will have your rest someday—but not today. Please, Simon, look!*"

The moving something took on a more definite form. A

face, sad and beautiful, yet lifeless, hovered before him.
Something like wings or flowing garments moved around
it, barely distinct from the gray.

"*Do you see me?*"

"*Yes.*"

"*Who am I?*"

"*You're the angel. From the tower.*"

"*No. But that doesn't matter.*" The angel moved closer.
Simon could see the discolorations on her weathered
bronze skin. "*I suppose it is good you can see me at all.
I have been waiting for you to come close enough. I hope
you can still get back.*"

"*I don't understand.*" The words were too difficult. He
wanted only to let go, to float back into uncaring, to
sleep. . . .

"*You must understand, Simon. You must. There are
many things I must show you, and I have only a little time
left.*"

"*Show me?*"

"*Things are different here. I cannot simply tell you.
This place is not like the world.*"

"*This place?*" He labored to make sense. "*What place
is this?*"

"*It is . . . beyond. There is no other word.*"

A faint memory came to him. "*The Dream Road?*"

"*Not exactly: that road travels along the edge of these
fields, and even to the borders of the place where I will
soon go. But enough of this. We have little time.*" The angel seemed to float away from him. "*Follow me.*"

"*I . . . I can't.*"

"*You did before. Follow me.*"

The angel receded. Simon did not want her to go. He
was so lonely. Suddenly, he was with her.

"*You see,*" she said. "*Ah, Simon, I waited so long for
this place—to be here all the time! It is wonderful! I am
free!*"

He wondered what the angel meant, but he had no
strength for more riddles. "*Where are we going?*"

"*Not where, but when. You know that.*" The angel
seemed to give off a sort of joy; if she had been a flower,

Simon thought, she would have been standing in a patch of sunlight, surrounded by bees. *"It was so terrible those other times when I had to go back. I was only happy here. I tried to tell you that once, but you could not hear me."*

*"I don't understand."*

*"Of course. You have never heard my voice until now. Never my own voice, that is. You heard hers."*

There were no words, Simon realized suddenly. He and the angel were not speaking as people spoke; rather, she seemed to give him her ideas and they found a home in his head. When she talked of "her," of the other whose voice he had heard, he did not perceive it as a word, but as a feeling of a protecting, holding, loving, but still somehow dangerous, female.

*"Who is 'her'?"*

*"She has gone on ahead,"* the angel said, as though he had asked a completely different question. *"Soon I will join her. But I had to wait for you, Simon. It doesn't bother me, though. I am happy here. I'm just glad I didn't have to go back."* Simon felt "back" as a trapped, hurting place. *"Even before, when I first came here, I never wanted to go back . . . but she always made me."*

Before he could question further—before he could even decide whether, in this strange dream, he *wanted* to question further—Simon found himself in the tunnels of Asu'a. A familiar scene spread before him—the fair-haired man, the torch, the spear, the great glittering *something* that lay just beyond the archway.

*"What is this?"*

*"Watch. It is your story—or part of it."*

The spearman took a step forward, every inch of him aquiver with fearful expectation. The great beast did not move. Its red claw lay curled on the ground just a few paces before his feet.

Simon wondered if the beast slept. His own scar, or the memory of it, stung him.

*Run away, man,* he thought. *A dragon is more than you can know. Run away!*

The spearman took another cautious step, then stopped. Simon was suddenly closer, looking into the wide chambor as though he saw through the eyes of the golden-haired man. What he saw was at first hard to take in.

The room was huge, with a ceiling that stretched up beyond the limits of the torchflame. The walls had been blasted and melted by great fires.

*It's the forge,* Simon realized. *Or that's what it is now. This must be the past.*

The dragon lay sprawled across the cavern floor, red-gold, as though the countless scales mirrored the torchlight. It was larger than a house, its tail a seemingly endless coil of looping flesh. Great wings stretched from its haunches to the elongated spurs behind its front claws. It was magnificent and terrifying in a way that even the ice-dragon Igjarjuk had not been. And it was completely and utterly dead.

The spearman stared. Simon, floating in a dream, stared.

*"Do you see?"* the angel whispered. *"The dragon was dead."*

The spearman took a step forward to prod the inert claw with his spear. Reassured, he moved into the great chamber of melted stone.

Something pale lay beneath the dragon's breast.

*"It's a skeleton,"* Simon whispered. *"A person's skeleton."*

*"Hush,"* the angel said in his ear. *"Watch. This is your story."*

*"What do you mean?"*

The spearman moved toward the pile of white bones, his fingers tracing the sign of the Tree in the air. The shadow of his hand leaped across the wall. He leaned close, still moving slowly and stealthily, as though any moment the dragon might suddenly roar back to life—but the man, like Simon, could see the ragged holes where the dragon's eyes had been, the withered, blackened tongue that lolled from the gaping mouth.

The man reached down and reverently touched the human skull that lay beside the dragon's breastbone like a pearl from a broken necklace. The rest of the bones were scattered close by. They were blackened and warped.

Looking at them, Simon suddenly remembered Igjarjuk's scalding blood, and felt a pang of sadness for the poor wretch who had slain this creature and received his own death. For slain it he had, it seemed; the only bones which still hung together were a forearm and hand, and they were wrapped around the hilt of a sword driven nearly to the hilt in the dragon's belly.

The spearman stared at this odd sight for a long time, then at last lifted his head, looking wildly around the cavern as though in fear someone might be watching. His face was somber, but his eyes gleamed feverishly. In that instant Simon almost recognized him, but the grayness of his thoughts was not entirely dispersed; when the fair-haired man turned back to the skeleton, the recognition faded.

The man dropped his spear and detached the skeletal hand from the sword's hilt with trembling care. One of the fingers broke loose. The man held it for a moment, his expression unreadable, then kissed the bone and tucked it into his shirt. When the hilt was freed, the man put his torch down on the stone, then took the sword in a firm grip. He placed his boot against the dragon's arching breastbone and pulled. Muscles rippled on his arms and cords stood out in his neck, but the sword did not come free. He rested for a moment, then spat on his palms and gripped the sword again. At last it slid out, leaving a puckered hole between the gleaming red scales.

The man lifted the sword before him, his eyes wide. At first Simon thought the blade a simple, almost crude piece of work, but its lines were clean and graceful beneath the char of dragon's blood. The man regarded it with an admiration so frank that it was almost greedy, then lowered it abruptly and looked around again, as though still afraid someone might be watching. He picked up the torch and began to move back toward the chamber's arched doorway, but stopped to stare at the dragon's leg and clawed front foot. After a long moment's consideration, he kneeled and began sawing away with the blackened sword at the leg's narrowest point, just in front of the wing-spur.

It was hard labor, but the man was young and powerfully built. As he worked, he looked up anxiously, staring into the shadows of the vast room as though a thousand scornful eyes were watching him. Sweat was trickling down his face and limbs. He seemed possessed, as though some wild spirit had taken hold of him; when he had sawed almost halfway through the thing he suddenly stood and began hacking with the sword, smashing at the arm with blow after blow until bits of tissue spun away on all sides. Simon, still a helpless but fascinated observer, saw that the man's eyes were full of tears, that his youthful face was contorted in a grimace of pain and horror.

Finally the last of the flesh parted and the claw rolled free. Shivering like a terrified child, the man shoved the sword through his belt, then hefted the huge claw up onto his shoulder as though it were a side of beef. His face still full of misery, he staggered out of the chamber and disappeared up the tunnel.

*"He felt the Sithi ghosts,"* the angel whispered to him. Simon had been so caught up in the man's private torment that he was startled by her voice. *"He felt them shame him for his lie."*

*"I don't understand."* Something was tickling his memory, but he had been in the gray for so long. . . . *"What was that? And who was the other one—the skeleton, the one who killed the dragon?"*

*"That is part of your story, Simon."* And suddenly the cavern was gone and they were in nothingness once more. *"There is much still to show you . . . and there is very little time."*

*"But I don't understand!"*

*"Then we must go deeper still."*

The gray wavered, then dissolved into another of the visions that had come to him in sleep upon the Tan'ja Stairs.

A large room opened before him. A few candles made all the light, and shadows hung in the corners. The room's sole occupant sat in a high-backed chair at the room's center, surrounded by a scatter of books and scrolls.

Simon had glimpsed this person during his stairwell dream. As in that earlier vision, the man sat in the chair with a book spread open in his lap. He was past middle age, but in his calm, thoughtful features there still remained a trace of the child he had once been, an innocent sweetness only slightly diminished by a long hard life. His hair had mostly gone to gray, although it still held darker streaks and much of his short beard remained light brown. He wore a circlet on his brow. His clothes, though simple in form, were well-made and of good cloth.

As with the man in the dragon's lair, Simon felt a twinge of recognition. Before the dream, he had never seen this person—yet, in some way, he knew him.

The man looked up from his reading as two other figures entered the room. One, an old woman with her white hair caught up in a ragged scarf, came forward and knelt at the man's feet. He put his book aside, then stood and gave the woman his hand to help her up. After saying a few words that Simon could not hear—as with the dragon-dream, all these shapes seemed voiceless and remote—the man walked across the chamber and squatted beside the old woman's companion, a little girl of seven or eight years. She had been crying: her eyes were puffy and her lip trembled with anger or fright. She avoided the man's gaze, pulling fitfully at her reddish hair. She, too, wore simple clothing, an unadorned dark dress, but despite her disarray she looked well cared for. Her feet were bare.

At last the man reached out his arms for her. She hesitated, then flung herself at him and buried her face against his chest, crying. Tears came to the man as well, and he held her for a long time, stroking her back. At last, with clear reluctance, he let her go and stood. The girl ran from the room. The man watched her go, then turned to the old woman. Without saying another word, he slipped a thin golden ring from his finger and gave it to her; she nodded and wrapped her fingers around it as he leaned down and kissed her forehead. She bowed to him; then, as if her own composure was fast slipping, she turned and hurried away.

After a long moment the man walked to a book-covered chest that lay beside the wall, opened it, and withdrew a sheathed sword. Simon recognized it immediately: he had seen that sparsely decorated hilt only moments before, standing in a dragon's breast. The man held the sword carefully, but did not look at it for more than a moment; instead, he cocked his head as though he heard something. He made the Tree sign with slow deliberation, lips moving in what might have been prayer, then returned to his seat. He set the sword across his lap, then picked up his book and opened it, spreading it atop the sword. But for the set of his jaw and the faintest tremor in his fingers as he turned the pages, he might have been thinking only of a good night's sleep—but Simon knew that he was waiting for something far different.

The scene wavered and dissipated like smoke.

*"Do you see? Do you understand now?"* the angel asked, impatient as a child.

Simon felt as though he groped at a large sack. Something was inside it, and he could feel strange corners and significant bumps, but just when he thought he knew what it contained, his imagination failed. He had been in the gray fog a long time. Thinking was difficult—and it was hard to care.

*"I don't know. Why can't you just tell me, angel?"*

*"It is not the way. These truths are too strong, the myths and lies around them too great. They are surrounded on all sides by walls I cannot explain, Simon. You must see them and you must understand for yourself. But this has been your story."*

His story? Simon thought again about what he had seen, but meaning seemed to slither away from him. If he could only remember what things had been like before, the names and stories he had known before the grayness surrounded him. . . !

*"Hold to them,"* the angel said. *"If you can get back, these truths will be of use to you. And now there is one more thing I must show you."*

*"I'm tired. I don't want to see any more."* The urge for restful oblivion had returned, pulling at him like a power-

ful current. All he had gained from this visitor was confusion. Go back? To the world of pain? Why should he bother? Sleep was easier, the drowsy emptiness of not caring. He could just let go, and all would be so easy. . . .

*"Simon!"* There was fear in the angel's voice. *"Don't! You must not give up."*

Slowly the angel's verdigrised features appeared once more. Simon wanted to ignore her, but although her face was a mask of lifeless bronze, there was something in her voice, some note of true need, that would not let him.

*"Why can't I rest?"*

*"I have only a little while left with you, Simon. You were never near enough before. Then I must give you a push to send you back or you will wander here forever."*

*"Why do you care?"*

*"Because I love you."* The angel spoke with sweet simplicity that held neither obligation or reproach. *"You saved me—or you tried. And there are others I love who need you. There is only a small chance that the storm can be turned away—but it is the only chance that remains."*

Saved her? Saved the angel who stood on the tower top? Simon felt exhausting confusion tug at him again. He could not afford to wonder.

*"Then show me, if you must."*

This time the translation from gray nothing to living vision seemed more difficult, as though this place was somehow harder to reach, or as though her powers were flagging. The first thing Simon saw was a great circular shadow, and for a long time he saw nothing else. The shadow grew ragged at one edge. Tracings of light appeared there, then became a figure.

Even in the dislocated netherworld of the vision, Simon felt a stab of fear. The figure that sat at the edge of the shadowy circle wore a crown of antlers. Before it, point down, double-guarded hilt clutched in its hands, was a long gray sword.

*The enemy!* His mind was empty of names, but the thought was clear and cold. The black-hearted one, the frozen yet burning thing that caused the world's misery. Simon felt fear and hatred burning inside him so strongly that for a moment the vision flickered and threatened to vanish.

"*See!*" The angel's voice was very faint. "*You must see!*"

Simon did not want to see. His entire life had been destroyed by this monstrosity, this demon of ultimate evil. Why should he look?

*To learn the way to destroy it,* he told himself, struggling. *To keep my anger strong. To find a reason to go back to the pain.*

"Show me. I will watch."

The image strengthened. It took Simon a moment to realize that the darkness which surrounded the enemy was the Pool of Three Depths. It gleamed beneath the cloak of shadows, the stone carvings uncorrupted, the pool itself alight and scintillant, shifting as though the very water were alive. Washed by the liquidly shifting glow, the figure sat on a pedestal on a peninsula of stone with the Pool all around.

Simon dared to look closer. Whatever else it might be, this version of the enemy was a living creature, skin and bone and blood. His long-fingered hands moved fretfully on the pommel of the gray sword. His face was covered by shadow, but his bowed neck and shoulders were those of one horribly burdened.

His attention captured, Simon saw with surprise that the antlers upon the enemy's head were not horns at all, but slender branches: his crown was carved from a single circlet of some silvery-dark wood. The branches still bore a few leaves.

The enemy lifted his head. His face was strange, as were the faces of all the immortals Simon had seen—high-cheeked and narrow-chinned, pale in the shifting light, and surrounded by straight black hair, much of which hung in twisted plaits. His eyes were wide open, and he stared across the water as though in desperate search. If something was there, Simon could not see it. But it was the expression upon the enemy's face that Simon found most disconcerting. There was anger, which did not surprise him, and an implacable determination in the set of the long jaw, but the eyes were haunted. Simon had never seen such unhappiness. Behind the stern mask lurked devastation, an inner landscape that had been scoured to bare rock, a misery that had hardened into something like the stuff of the earth itself. If this being ever wept again, it would be tears of fire and dust.

*Sorrow.* Simon remembered the name of the gray sword. *Jingizu. So much sorrow.* He felt a kind of convulsion of despair and anger. He had never seen anything as terrible, as frightening, as the enemy's suffering face.

The vision wavered.

"... *Simon* ..." The angel's voice was as quiet as a leaf tumbling across the grass. "... *I must send you back.* ..."

He was alone in misty gray nothingness. "*Why did you show me that? What is it supposed to mean?*"

"... *Go back, Simon. I am losing you, and you are far away from where you should be.* ..."

"*But I need to know! I have so many questions!*"

"... *I waited for you so long. I am called to go on, Simon.* ..."

And now he did feel her slipping away. A very different kind of fear caught at him. "*Angel! Where are you?!*"

"... *I am free now* ..." Faint as feather brushing feather. "*I have waited so long.* ..."

And suddenly, as the last touch of her voice slid away, he knew her.

"*Leleth!*" he cried. "*Leleth! Don't leave me!*"

A sense of her smiling, of Leleth free and flying at last, brushed him, then was gone. Nothing came in its place.

Simon was suspended in emptiness, without direction or understanding. He tried to move as he and Leleth had moved, but nothing happened. He was lost in the void, more lost than he had ever been. He was a rag blowing through the darkness. He was utterly alone.

"*Help me!*" he screamed.

Nothing changed.

"*Help me,*" he murmured. "*Someone.*"

Nothing changed. Nothing would ever change.

# 23

# The Rose Unmade

❖

**The ship** plunged again. As the cabin timbers creaked, Isgrimnur's empty cup bounced from his hand and clanked to the floor.

"Aedon preserve us! This is horrible!"

Josua's smile was thin. "True. Only madmen are at sea in this storm."

"Don't joke," Isgrimnur growled, alarmed. "Don't joke about boats. Or storms."

"I was not jesting." The prince gripped his chair with his hand as the cabin lurched again. "Are we not mad to let the fear of a star in the sky hurry us into this attack?"

The duke glowered. "We are here. Heaven knows, I don't want to be, but we are here."

"We are here," Josua agreed. "Let us only give thanks that for now Vorzheva and the children and your Gutrun are safe in Nabban."

"Safe until the ghants get there." Isgrimnur winced, thinking of the horrid nest. "Safe until the kilpa decide to try dry land."

"Now who is the worrier?" Josua asked gently. "Varellan, as we saw, has become an able young man, and a good portion of Nabban's army stayed there with him. Our ladies are much safer than we are."

The ship shuddered and pitched. Isgrimnur felt the need to talk, to do anything besides listen to what sounded like the timbers of the hull being wrenched apart. "I have been wondering something. If the Niskies are cousins to the immortals, as Miriamele told us, then how are we to trust them? Why should they favor our fairy-folk over the Norns?" As if summoned by his words, a Niskie's song, alien and powerful, rose once more above the shouting winds.

"But they do." Josua spoke loudly. "One of the sea-watchers gave her life so Miriamele could escape. What stronger answer do you need?"

"They haven't kept the kilpa as far away as *I'd* like." He made the sign of the Tree. "Josua, we have been attacked three times already!"

"And would have been attacked more often were it not for Nin Reisu and her brother and sister Niskies, I have no doubt," said Josua. "You have been on deck. You've seen the cursed things swimming all around. The seas are choked with them."

Isgrimnur nodded somberly. He had indeed seen the kilpa—far too many of them—swarming about the fleet, active as eels in a barrel. They had boarded the flagship several times, once in daylight. Despite the agony of his ribs, the duke had killed two of the hooting things himself, then spent hours trying to wash the oily, foul-smelling blood from his hands and face. "I know," he said at last. "It is as if they have been sent by our enemy to hold us back."

"Perhaps they have." Josua poured a bit of wine into his cup. "I find it strange that the kilpa should rise and the ghants should come pouring out of the swamps at just the same moment. Our enemy's reach is long, Isgrimnur."

"Little Tiamak believes that was happening in the ghant nest when we found him—that somehow Storm-spike was using him and the other Wrannamen to talk to those bugs." The thought of Tiamak's countrymen used by the ghants, burned up like candles and then discarded, and of the hundreds of Nabbanai mariners dragged away to a hideous death by the kilpa, made Isgrimnur curl his fist and wish for something to hit. "What kind of a demon could do such things, Josua? What kind of an enemy is this, that we cannot see and cannot strike?"

"The greatest enemy we have." The prince sipped his

wine, swaying as the ship pitched again. "An enemy we must defeat, no matter the cost."

The cabin door swung open. Camaris steadied himself, then entered, his scabbard scraping the doorframe. The old knight's cloak drizzled water on the floor.

"What did Nin Reisu say?" Josua asked as he poured wine for Camaris. "Will *Emettin's Jewel* hold together for one more night?"

The old man drained his cup and stared at the lees.

"Camaris?" Josua moved toward him. "What did Nin Reisu say?"

After a moment, the knight looked up. "I cannot sleep."

The prince shared a worried look with Isgrimnur. "I do not understand."

"I have been up on deck."

Isgrimnur thought that was obvious from the water puddling on the floor. The old knight seemed even more fearfully distracted than was usual. "What's wrong, Camaris?"

"I cannot sleep. This sword is in my dreams." He pawed fitfully at Thorn's hilt. "I hear it . . . singing to me." Camaris tugged it a short way out of the scabbard, a length of pure darkness. "I carried this sword for years." He struggled for words. "I . . . felt it sometimes, especially in battle. But never this way. I think . . . I think it is alive."

Josua looked at the blade with more than a little distrust. "Perhaps you should not carry it, Camaris. You will be forced to take it up soon enough. Put it somewhere safe."

"No." The old man shook his head. His voice was heavy. "No, I dare not. There are things to learn. We do not know how to use these Great Swords against our enemy. As you said, the time is fast coming. Perhaps I can understand the song it sings. Perhaps . . ."

The prince lifted his hand as if to dispute him, then let it fall. "You must do as you think best. You are Thorn's master."

Camaris looked up solemnly. "Am I? I thought so, once."

"Come, have some more wine," Isgrimnur urged him. He tried to rise from his stool but decided against it. The battles with the kilpa had set back his recovery. Wincing, he signaled to Josua to refill the old man's cup. "It is hard not to feel haunted when the wind howls and the sea flings us about like dice in a cup."

"Isgrimnur is right." Josua smiled. "Here, drink up." The room lurched once more, and wine splashed onto his wrist. "Come, while there is more in the cup than on the floor."

Camaris was silent for long moments. "I must speak to you, Josua," he said abruptly. "Something weighs upon my soul."

Puzzled, the prince waited.

The knight's face seemed almost gray as he turned to the duke. "Please, Isgrimnur, I must talk with Josua alone."

"I am your friend, Camaris," said the duke. "If anyone is to blame for bringing you here, it's me. If something is plaguing you, I want to help."

"This is a shame that burns. I would not tell Josua, but that he needs to hear it. Even as I lie sleepless for fear of what the sword will do, God punishes me for my secret sin. I pray that if I make this right, He will give me the strength to understand Thorn and its brother swords. But please do not force me to bare this shame to you as well." Camaris looked truly old, his features slack, his eyes wandering. "Please. I beg you."

Confused and more than a little frightened, Isgrimnur nodded. "As you wish, Camaris. Of course."

Isgrimnur was debating whether he should wait in the narrow passageway any longer when the cabin door opened and Camaris emerged. The old knight brushed past, hunched beneath the low ceiling. Before Isgrimnur could get more than half his question out, Camaris was gone down the passageway, thumping from wall to wall as *Emettin's Jewel* heaved in the storm's grip.

Isgrimnur knocked at the cabin door. When the prince did not answer, he carefully pushed it open. The prince was staring at the lamp, his blasted expression that of a man who has seen his own death.

"Josua?"

The prince's hand rose as though tugged by a string. He seemed entirely leeched of spirit. His voice was flat, terrible. "Go away, Isgrimnur. Let me be alone."

The duke hesitated, but Josua's face decided him. Whatever had happened in the cabin, there was nothing he could give the prince at this moment but solitude.

"Send for me when you want me." Isgrimnur backed out of the room. Josua did not look up or speak, but continued to watch the lamp as though it were the only thing that might lead him out of ultimate darkness.

"I am trying to understand." Miriamele's head ached. "Tell me again about the swords."

She had been with the dwarrows for several days, as far as she could tell: it was hard to know for certain here in the rocky fastness below the Hayholt. The shy earth-dwellers had continued to treat her well, but still refused to free her. Miriamele had argued, pleaded—even raged for a long hour, demanding to be released, threatening, cursing. As her anger spent itself, the dwarrows had murmured among themselves worriedly. They seemed so shocked and unsettled by her fury that she had almost felt ashamed of herself, but the embarrassment passed as quickly as the anger.

*After all,* she had decided, *I did not ask to be brought here. They say their reasons are good—then let their reasons make them feel better. I shouldn't have to.*

She was convinced of, if not reconciled to, the reasons for her captivity. The dwarrows seemed to sleep very little if at all, and only a few of them at a time ever left the wide cavern. Whether they were telling her the entire truth or not, she did not doubt that there was something out there that frightened the slender, wide-eyed creatures very badly.

"The swords," said Yis-fidri. "Very well, I will try better to explain. You saw that we knew the arrow, even though we did not make it?"

"Yes." They had certainly seemed to know *something* significant was in the saddlebags, although it was possible they could have made up the story on the spot after finding it.

"We did not make the arrow, but it was crafted by one who learned from us. The three Great Swords *are* of our making, and we are bound to them."

"You made the three swords?" This was what had confused her. It did not match what she had been told. "I knew that your people made Minneyar for King Elvrit of Rimmsersgard—but not that they forged the other two as well. Jarnauga said that the sword Sorrow was made by Ineluki himself."

"Speak not his name!" Several of the other dwarrows looked up and chimed a few unsettled words which Yis-fidri answered before turning back to Miriamele. "Speak not his name. He is closer than he has been in centuries. Do not call his attention!"

*It's like being in a whole cave full of Strangyeards,* thought Miriamele. *They seem afraid of everything.* Still, Binabik had said much the same thing. "Very well. I won't say . . . his name. But that story is not what I was told. A learned man said that . . . he . . . made it himself in the forges of Asu'a."

The dwarrow sighed. "Indeed. We were the smiths of Asu'a—or at least some of our people were . . . some who had not fled our Zida'ya masters, but who were still Navigator's Children for all that, still as like to us as two chunks of ore from the same vein. They all died when the castle fell." Yis-fidri chanted a brief lament in the dwarrow tongue; his wife Yis-hadra echoed him. "He used the Hammer that Shapes to forge it—*our* Hammer— and the Words of Making that we taught to him. It might as well have been our own High Smith's hand that crafted it. In that terrible instant, wheresoever we were, scattered across the world's face ... we felt Sorrow's making. The pain of it is with us still." He fell silent for a long time. "That the Zida'ya allowed such a thing," he said at last, "is one of the reasons we have turned away from them. We were so sorely diminished by that one act that we have ever since been crippled."

"And Thorn?"

Yis-fidri nodded his heavy head. "The mortal smiths of Nabban tried to work the star-stone. They could not. Certain of our people were sought out and brought secretly to the Imperator's palace. These kin of ours were thought by most mortals to be only strange folk who watched the oceans and kept the ships safe from harm, but a small number knew that the old lore of Making and Shaping ran deep in all the Tinukeda'ya, even those who had chosen to remain with the sea."

"Tinukeda'ya?" It took a moment to sink in. "But that's what Gan Itai ... those are Niskies!"

"We are all Ocean Children," said the dwarrow gravely. "Some decided to stay near the sea which forever separates us from the Garden of our birth. Others chose more hidden and secretive ways, like the earth's dark places and the task of shaping stone. You see, unlike our cousins the Zida'ya and Hikeda'ya, we Children of the Navigator can shape ourselves just as we shape other things."

Miriamele was dumbfounded. "You're ... you and the Niskies are the same?" Now she understood the phantom of recognition that had troubled her upon first seeing Yis-fidri. There *was* something in his bones, in his way of moving, that reminded her of Gan Itai. But they looked so different!

"We are not the same any more. The act of shaping ourselves takes generations, and it changes more than just our outward seeming. But much does not change. The Dawn Children and Cloud Children are our cousins—but the sea-watchers are our sisters and brothers."

Miriamele sat back, trying to grasp what she had been told. "So you and the Niskies are the same. And Niskies forged Thorn." She shook her head. "You are saying, then, that you can feel all the Great Swords—even more strongly than you felt the White Arrow?" A sudden thought came to her. "Then you must know where Bright-Nail is—the sword that was called Minneyar!"

Yis-fidri smiled sadly. "Yes, although your King John hung it with many prayers and relics and other mortal magicks, perhaps in the hope of concealing its true nature. But you know your own arms and hands, Princess Miriamele, do you not? Would you know them any the less if they were still joined to you, but were clothed in some other mortal's jacket and gloves?"

It was strange to think of her magnificent grandfather working so hard to hide Bright-Nail's heritage. Was he ashamed of owning such a weapon? Why? "If you know these swords so well, can you tell me where Bright-Nail is now?"

"I cannot say, 'it is such and such a place,' no. But it is somewhere near. Somewhere within a few thousand paces."

So it was either in the castle or the under-castle, Miriamele decided. That didn't help much, but at least her father had not had it thrown in the ocean or carried off to Nascadu. "Did you come here because you knew the swords were here?"

"No. We were fleeing other things, routed from our city in the north. We knew already that two of the swords were here, but that meant little to us at that time: we fled away through our tunnels and they led us here. It was only as we drew close to Asu'a that we came to understand that other forces were also at work."

"And so now you're caught between the two and don't know which way to run." She said it with more than a little disapproval, but knew even so that what the dwarrows faced was much like her own situation. She, too, was driven by things bigger than herself. She had fled her father, trying to put the entire world between the two of them. Now she had risked her life and the lives of her friends to come back and find him, but feared what might happen if she succeeded. Miriamele pushed the useless thoughts away. "Forgive me, Yis-fidri. I'm tired of sitting for so long, that's all."

It had been good to rest the first day, despite her anger over her imprisonment, but now she was aching to be on her way, to move, to *do* something, whatever that might be. Otherwise, she was trapped with her thoughts. They made painful company.

"We are truly sorry, Miriamele. You may walk as much as you wish here. We have tried to give you all that you need."

It was fortunate for them that she had the packs that held the remaining provisions, she reflected. If she had been forced to subsist on the dwarrows' food—fungi and small, unpleasant burrowing creatures—she would be a much less congenial prisoner. "You cannot give me what I need as long as I am held captive," she said. "Nothing can change that, no matter what you say."

"It is too perilous."

Miriamele bit back an angry reply. She had already tried that approach. She needed to think.

Yis-hadra scraped at a bit of the cavern wall with a curved, flat-ended tool. Miriamele could not quite tell what Yis-fidri's wife was doing, but she seemed to be enjoying it: the dwarrow was singing quietly beneath her breath. The more Miriamele listened, the more the song fascinated her. It was scarcely louder than a whisper, but it had something in it of the power and complexity of Gan Itai's kilpa-singing. Yis-hadra sang in rhythm with the movement of her long, graceful hands. Music and movement together made one singular thing. Miriamele sat beside her for some time, transfixed.

"Are you building something?" she asked during a lull in the song.

The dwarrow looked up. A smile stretched her odd face. "This *s'h'rosa* here—this piece of stone that runs through the other stone . . ." she indicated a darker streak, barely visible in the glow of the rose crystal. "It wishes to . . . come out. To be seen."

Miriamele shook her head. "It wishes to be seen?"

Yis-hadra pursed her wide mouth thoughtfully. "I do not have your tongue well. It . . . needs? Needs to come out?"

*Like gardeners,* Miriamele thought bemusedly. *Tending the stone.*

Aloud, she said: "Do you carve things? All the ruins of Asu'a I've seen are covered with beautiful carvings. Did the dwarrows do that?"

Yis-hadra made an indecipherable gesture with curled fingers. "We prepared some of the walls, then the Zida'ya created pictures there. But in other places, we gave care to the stone ourselves, helping it . . . become. When Asu'a was built, Zida'ya and Tinukeda'ya still worked side by side." Her tone was mournful. "Together we made wonderful things."

"Yes. I saw some of them." She looked around. "Where is Yis-fidri? I need to talk to him."

Yis-hadra appeared embarrassed. "Is it I have said something bad? I cannot speak your tongue as I can the tongue of the mortals of Hernystir. Yis-fidri speaks more well than I."

"No." Miriamele smiled. "Nothing bad at all. But he and I were talking about something, and I want to talk to him more."

"Ah. He will come back in a little time. He has left this place."

"Then I'll just watch you work, if you don't mind.".

Yis-hadra returned the smile. "No. I will tell you something about the stone, if you like. Stones have stories. We know the stories. Sometimes I think we know their stories better than our own."

Miriamele sat down with her back against the wall. Yis-hadra continued with her task, and as she did so, she talked. Miriamele had never thought much about rocks and stone, but as she listened to the dwarrow's low, musical voice, she saw for the first time that they were in a way living things, like plants and animals—or at least they were to Yis-hadra's kind. The stones moved, but that movement took eons. They changed, but no living thing, not even the Sithi, walked alive beneath the sky long cnough to see that change. The dwarrow-folk studied and cultivated, and even in a way loved, the bones of the earth. They admired the beauty of glittering gems and shining metals, but they also valued the layered patience of sandstone and the boldness of volcanic glass. Every one of them had its own tale, but it took a certain kind of vision and wisdom to understand the slow stories that stones told. Yis-fidri's wife, with her huge eyes and careful fingers, knew them well. Miriamele found herself oddly touched by this strange creature, and for a while, listening to Yis-hadra's slow, joyful speech, she forgot even her own unhappiness.

❦

Tiamak felt a hand close around his arm.

"Is that you?" Father Strangyeard's voice sounded querulous.

"It is me."

"We shouldn't either of us be out on deck," the archivist said. "Sludig will be angry."

"Sludig would be right," Tiamak said. "The kilpa are all around us." But still he did not move. The closed quarters of the ship's cabin had been making it hard to think, and the ideas that were moving at the edge of his mind seemed too important to lose just because of a fear of the sea-creatures—however worthy of fear they might be.

"My sight is not good," Strangyeard said, peering worriedly into the darkness. He held his hand beside his good eye to shield against the strong winds. "I should probably not be walking the deck at night. But I was ... worried for you, you were gone so long."

"I know." Tiamak patted the older man's hand where it lay on the weathered rail. "I am thinking about the things I told you earlier—the idea I had when Camaris fought Benigaris." He stopped, noticing for the first time the ship's odd movement. "Are we anchored?" he asked at last.

"We are. The Hayefur is not lit at Wentmouth, and Josua feared to come too close to the rocks in darkness.

He sent word with the signal-lamp." The archivist shivered. "It makes it worse, though, having to sit still. Those nasty gray things ..."

"Then let us go down. I think the rains are returning, in any case." Tiamak turned from the rail. "We will warm some of your wine—a drylander custom I have come to appreciate—and think more about the swords." He took the priest's elbow and led him toward the cabin door.

"Surely this is better," Strangyeard said. He braced himself against the wall as the ship dipped into a trough between the waves, then handed the sloshing cup to the Wrannaman. "I had better cover the coals. It would be terrible if the brazier tipped over. Goodness! I hope everyone else is being careful, too."

"I think Sludig is allowing few others to have braziers, or even lanterns, except on deck." Tiamak took a sip of the wine and smacked his lips. "Ah. Good. No, we are the privileged ones because we have things to read and time is short."

The archivist lowered himself to the pallet on the floor, pitching gently with the motion of the ship. "So I suppose we should be back at our work again." He drank from his own cup. "Forgive me, Tiamak, but does it not seem futile to you sometimes? Hanging all our hopes on three swords, two of which are not even ours?" He stared into his wine.

"I came late to these matters, in a way." Tiamak made himself comfortable. The rocking of the ship, however pronounced, was not that different from the way the wind rattled his house in the banyan tree. "If you had asked me a year ago what chance there was that I would be aboard a boat sailing for Erkynland to conquer the High King— that I would be a Scrollbearer, that I would have seen Camaris reborn, been captured by the ghants, saved by the Duke of Elvritshalla and the High King's daughter ..." He waved his hand. "You see what I am saying. Everything that has happened to us is madness, but when we look back, it all seems to have followed logically from one moment to the next. Perhaps someday capturing and using the swords will seem just as clear in its sense."

"That is a nice thought." Strangyeard sighed and pushed his eyepatch, which had shifted slightly, back into place. "I like things better when they have already happened. Books may differ, one from the other, but at least most every book claims to know the truth and set it out clearly."

"Someday we will perhaps be in someone else's book," Tiamak offered, smiling, "and whoever writes it will be very certain about how everything came to pass. But we do not have that luxury now." He leaned forward. "Now where is the part of the doctor's manuscript that tells of the forging of Sorrow?"

"Here, I think." Strangyeard shuffled through one of the many piles of parchment scattered about the room. "Yes, here." He lifted it to the light, squinting. "Shall I read something to you?"

Tiamak held out his hand. He had an immense fondness for the Archive Master, a closeness he had not felt to anyone since old Doctor Morgenes. "No," he said gently, "let me read. Let us not put your poor eyes to any more work tonight."

Strangyeard mumbled something and gave him the sheaf of parchment.

"It is this bit about the Words of Making that sticks in my head," Tiamak said. "Is it possible that all these swords were made with these same powerful Words?"

"But why would you think so?" Strangyeard asked. His face became intent. "Nisses' book, at least as Morgenes quotes it, does not seem to say that. All the swords came from different places, and one was forged by mortals."

"There must be *something* that links them all together," Tiamak replied, "and I can think of nothing else. Why else should possessing them all give us such power?" He shuffled through the parchments. "Great magic went into their forging. It must be this magic that will bring us power over the Storm King!"

As he spoke, the song of a Niskie rose outside, piercing the mournful sound of the winds. The melody throbbed with wild power, an alien sound even more disturbing than the distant rumble of thunder.

"If only there were someone who knew of the swords' forging," Tiamak murmured in frustration; his eyes stared at Morgenes' precise, ornate characters, but did not really see them. The Niskie song rose higher, then vibrated and fell away on a note of keening loss. "If only we could speak to the dwarrows who made Minneyar—but Eolair says they were far to the north, many leagues beyond the Hayholt. And the Nabbanai smiths who forged Thorn are centuries dead." He frowned. "So many questions we have, and still so few answers. This is tiring, Strangyeard. It seems that every step forward takes us two paces back into confusion."

The archivist was silent while Tiamak looked for the well-thumbed pages that described Ineluki creating Sorrow in the forges below Asu'a. "Here it is," he said at last. "I will read."

"Just a moment," said Strangyeard. "Perhaps the answer to one is the answer to both."

Tiamak looked up. "What do you mean?" He dragged his thoughts away from the page before him.

"Your other idea was that somehow we have been purposely kept in confusion—that the Storm King has played Elias and Josua off against each other while he pursued some goal of his own."

"Yes?"

"Perhaps it is not just some secret goal he has that he wishes to conceal. Perhaps he also tries to hide the secret of the Three Swords."

Tiamak felt a glimmer of understanding. "But if all the contention between Josua and the High King has been arranged just to keep us from understanding how to use the swords, it might mean that the answer is quite simple— something we would quickly see if we were not distracted."

"Exactly!" Strangyeard, in pursuit of an idea, had lost his usual reticence. "Exactly. Either there is something so simple that we could not fail to see it if we were not caught up in the day-to-day struggle, or there is someone or someplace vital to us that we cannot reach as long as this war between brothers continues."

*They Who Watch and Shape,* marveled Tiamak, *it is good to have someone to share my thoughts with—someone who understands, who questions, who searches for meaning!* For a moment he did not even miss his home in the swamp. Aloud, he said: "Wonderful, Strangyeard. It is something well worth considering."

The archivist colored, but spoke confidently. "I remember when we were first fleeing Naglimund, Deornoth said that the Norns seemed to wish to keep us from going certain directions—at that time it was deeper into Aldheorte. Instead of trying to kill us, or capture us, they seemed to try to ... drive us." The priest wiped absently at his chill-reddened nostrils, not yet recovered from the sojourn on deck. "I think perhaps they were keeping us from the Sithi."

Tiamak put the pages he was holding down: there would be time enough for them later. "So perhaps there is something the Sithi know—perhaps even they do not realize it! He Who Always Steps on Sand, how I wish we had questioned young Simon more closely about his time with the immortals." Tiamak stood up and moved toward the cabin door. "I will go tell Sludig that we wish to talk to Aditu." He stopped. "But I do not know how she could cross from one ship to another. The seas are so dangerous now."

Strangyeard shrugged. "It will do no harm to ask."

Tiamak paused, tilting back and forth with the ship's movement, then abruptly sat down again. "It can wait until the morning, when it would be a safe crossing. There is much we can do first." He picked up the parchments again. "It could be anything, Strangyeard—anything! We must think back on all the places we have been, the people we have met. We have been reacting to only what was in front of us. Now it is up to you and me to think on what we did *not* see while we were busy watching the spectacle of pursuit and war."

"We should talk to others, too. Sludig himself has seen much, and certainly Isgrimnur and Josua should be questioned. But we do not even know what questions to ask." The priest sighed and shook his head mournfully. "Merciful Aedon, but it is a pity that Geloë is not here with us. *She* would know where to begin."

"But she is not, as you said, and neither is Binabik. So we must do it on our own. This is our fearful duty, just as it is Camaris' task to swing a sword, and Josua's to bear the burdens of leadership." Tiamak looked at the untidy mess of writings in his lap. "But you are right: it is hard to know where to begin. If only someone could tell us more about the forging of these swords. If only that knowledge had not been lost."

As the two sat, lost for a moment in glum silence, the Niskie's voice rose again, cutting through the clamor of the storm like a sharp blade.

✦

*At first the very size of the thing prevented Miriamele from understanding what it was. Its dawn-colored brilliance and massive velvety petals, the dew drops sparkling like glass globes, even the thorns, each one a great spike of dark curving wood, all seemed things that must be absorbed and considered individually. It was only after a long while—or what seemed a long while—that she could comprehend that the vast thing spinning slowly before her eyes was . . . a rose. It revolved as though its stem were being twirled by gigantic yet invisible fingers; its scent was so powerful that she felt the whole universe choked in perfume, and yet even as it smothered her, it filled her with life.*

*The wide, unbroken plain of grass above which the rose turned began to shudder. The sod buckled upward beneath the mighty bloom; gray stones appeared, tall and angular, pushing up through the earth like moles nosing toward sunlight. As they burst free, and as she saw for the first time that the long stones were joined at the bottom, she realized that what she saw was a huge hand pushing up from below the world's surface. It lifted, grass and clotted dirt tumbling away; the stony fingers spread wide, encircling the rose. A moment later the hand closed and squeezed. The huge rose ceased turning, then slowly vanished in the crushing grip. A single wide petal scudded*

*slowly from side to side as it floated to the ground  The
rose was dead. . . .*

Miriamele struggled up, blinking, her heart rattling inside her chest. The cavern was dark but for the faint pink
glow of a few of the dwarrow's crystals, as it had been
when she had drifted off to sleep. Nevertheless, she could
tell something was different.

"Yis-fidri?" she called. A shape detached itself from
the wall nearby and moved toward her, head bobbing.

"He still has not returned," said Yis-hadra.

"What happened?" Miriamele's head was throbbing as
though she had been struck a blow. "Something just happened."

"It was very strong, this one." Yis-hadra was clearly
upset: her immense eyes were wider than usual and her
long fingers twitched spasmodically. "Some . . . change is
happening here—a change in the bones of the earth and in
the heart of Asu'a." She sought for words. "It has been
happening for some time. Now it grows stronger."

"What kind of change? What are we going to do?"

"We do not know. But we will do nothing until Yis-
fidri and the others are come back."

"The whole place is falling down around our ears . . .
and you're not going to do anything?! Not even run away?"

"It is not . . . falling down. The changing is different."
Yis-hadra laid a trembling hand on Miriamele's arm.
"Please. My people are frightened. You make it worse."

Before Miriamele could say anything else, a strange silent rumble moved through her, a sound too low to hear.
The entire chamber seemed to shift—for a moment, even
Yis-hadra's odd, homely face became something unliving,
and the roseate light from the dwarrow's batons deepened
and chilled to glaring white, then azure. Everything
seemed to be skewed. Miriamele felt herself slipping
away sideways, as though she had lost her grip on the
spinning world.

A moment later, the crystal lights warmed again and
the cavern was once more as it had been.

Miriamele took several shaky breaths before she could speak. "Something ... *very* bad ... is happening."

Yis-hadra rose from her crouch, swaying unsteadily. "I must see to the others. Yis-fidri and I try to keep them from becoming too fearful. Without the Shard, without the Pattern Hall, there is little left to hold us together."

Shivering, Miriamele watched the dwarrow go. The mass of stone all around her felt like the confining walls of a tomb. Whatever Josua and old Jarnauga and the others had feared was now happening. Some wild power was coursing through the stones beneath the Hayholt just as blood ran through her own body. Surely there was only a little time left.

*Is this where it will end for me?* she wondered. *Down here in the dark, and never knowing why?*

Miriamele did not remember falling asleep again, but she awakened—more gently this time—sitting upright along the cavern wall, pillowed against the hood of her cloak. Her neck was sore, and she rubbed it for a moment until she saw someone squatting by her pack, a dim outline in the faint rose light of the dwarrow-crystals.

"You there! What are you doing?"

The figure turned, eyes wide. "You are awake," the troll said.

"Binabik?" Miriamele stared for a moment, dumbfounded, then sprang to her feet and ran to him. She caught him up in a hug that squeezed out a breathless laugh. "Mother of Mercy! Binabik! What are you doing? How did you get here?"

"The dwarrows found me wandering on the stairs," he said as she set him down. "I have been here a little time. I did not want to wake you, but I am full of hunger, so I have been searching in the packs. . . ."

"There's a little trail-bread left, I think, and maybe some dried fruit." She rummaged through her belongings. "I am so happy to see you—I didn't know what had become of you! That thing, that monk! What happened?"

"I killed him—or perhaps I was releasing him." Binabik shook his head. "I cannot say. He was himself for a moment, and warned that the Norns were ... what did he say? ... 'false beyond believing'." He took the piece of hard bread Miriamele offered. "I knew him as a man once. Simon and I met him in St. Hoderund's ruins. We were not being friends, Hengfisk and I—but to look into his eyes...! Such a terrible thing should not be done to anyone. Our enemies have much to be answering for."

"What do you think of the dwarrows? Did they tell you why they took me?" A thought occurred to her. "Are *you* a prisoner now, too?"

"I do not know if prisoner is being the correct word," Binabik said thoughtfully. "Yes, Yis-fidri was telling me much when they found me, as we were making our way back to this place. At least for a while he was."

"What do you mean?"

"There are soldiers in the tunnels," the troll replied. "And others, too—Norns, I think, although we did not see them as we did the soldiers. But the dwarrows were certainly feeling them, and I do not think they were pretending for the benefit of me. They were full of terror."

"Norns? Here? But I thought they couldn't come to the castle!"

Binabik shrugged. "Who can say? It is their deathless master who is barred from this place, but I did not think it likely the living Norns would wish to enter here. Still, if everything I have been thinking was truth was now proved false, it would no longer be a surprising thing to me."

Yis-fidri approached, then stooped and crouched beside them, the padded leather of his garments creaking. Despite his kind, sad face, Miriamele thought that his long limbs gave him something of the appearance of a spider picking its way across a web.

"Here is your companion safe, Miriamele."

"I'm glad you found him."

"And not a moment too soon did we come upon him." Yis-fidri was clearly worried. "There are mortal men and Hikeda'ya swarming through the tunnels. Only our skill in hiding the doorway to this chamber keeps us safe."

"Do you plan to stay here forever? That won't help anything." The joy of Binabik's return had worn off a little, and now she felt desperation returning. They were all trapped in an isolated cavern while the world around them seemed to be moving toward some terrible cataclysm. "Don't you feel what is happening? All the rest of your folk felt it."

"Of course we feel it." For a moment Yis-fidri almost sounded angry. "We feel more than you. We know these changes of old—we know what the Words of Making can do. And the stones speak to us as well. But we have no strength to stop what is happening, and if we call attention to ourselves, that will be the end. Our freedom is of no use to anyone."

"Words of Making. . . ?" Binabik asked, but before he could finish his question, Yis-hadra appeared and spoke softly to her husband in the dwarrow tongue. Miriamele looked past her to where the rest of the tribe huddled against the cavern's far wall. They were clearly disturbed, eyes wide in the dim light, chattering quietly among themselves with much nodding and shaking of their large heads.

Yis-fidri's thin face wore a look of alarm. "Someone is outside," he said.

"Outside?" Miriamele pulled the pack closed. "What do you mean? Who?"

"We know not. But someone is outside the hidden door to this chamber, trying to get in." He flapped his hands anxiously. "It is not mortal soldiers, for whoever it is, they have some power over things—we shielded that door to the limits of the Tinukeda'ya's art."

"The Norns?" Miriamele breathed.

"We know not!" Yis-fidri stood and put his thin arm around Yis-hadra. "But we must hope that even though they have found the door, they cannot force it. There is nothing more we can do."

"There must be another way out, isn't there?"

Yis-fidri hung his head. "We took a risk. Hiding two doors makes both of them more vulnerable, and we feared to expend too much Art when things are so unbalanced. . . ."

"Mother of Mercy!" Miriamele cried. Anger fought with

hopeless terror inside her. "So we're trapped." She turned to Binabik. "God help us, what choice do we have?"

The troll looked tired. "Are you asking if we will fight? Of course. The Qanuc are not giving their lives away. *Mindunob inik yat,* we say—'my home will be your tomb.' " His laugh was grim. "But with certainty, even the fiercest troll would rather find a way to keep his cave without himself dying."

"I found my knife," said Miriamele, drumming her fingers nervously on her leg. She struggled to keep her voice steady. Trapped! They were trapped with no way out, and the Norns were at the door! "Merciful Elysia, I wish I'd brought a bow. I only have Simon's White Arrow, but I'm sure he would approve if I feathered a Norn with it. I suppose I can use it to stab someone."

Yis-fidri looked at them in disbelief. "You could not save yourself from the Hikeda'ya with a bow and a whole quiver full of Vindaomeyo's most perfect arrows, let alone with only a knife."

"I don't think we *will* save ourselves," Miriamele snapped. "But we have come too far to let them take us as though we were frightened children." She took a breath to calm herself. "You are strong, Yis-fidri—I felt it when you carried me off. Surely you won't just let them kill you?"

"It is not our way, fighting," Yis-hadra spoke up. "We have never been the strong ones—not strong that way."

"Then stay back." Inwardly, Miriamele thought she sounded like the worst kind of boastful tavern brawler, but it was already hard enough to think about what might be coming. Just looking at the trembling, terrified dwarrows sapped her resolve, and the fear that lay beneath felt like a hole into which she might tumble and fall forever. "Take us to the door. Binabik, let's at least pick up some stones. The good Lord knows this place is full of them."

The huddled dwarrows watched them with distrust, as though the very act of preparing a resistance made them almost as dangerous as the enemy outside. Miriamele and Binabik quickly gathered a pile of stones, then Binabik broke down his walking-stick and placed the knife section in his belt, then readied the blowpipe.

"Better to use this first." He pushed a dart into the tube. "Perhaps a death they cannot see will make them a little more slow for coming in."

The doorway appeared to be only another section of the striated cavern wall, but as Miriamele and the troll stood before it, a faint silvery line began to creep up the stone.

"Ruyan guide us!" Yis-fidri said miserably. "They have breached the wards!" There was a chorus of fearful noises from his fellow.

The silver gleam crept up the rock face, then coursed across the length of a man's reach and started down again. When a whole section was bounded by a thread of light, the stone inside the glow slowly began to swivel inward, scraping as it moved against the cavern floor. Miriamele watched its ponderous movement with terrified fascination, trembling in every limb.

"Do not step to the front of me," whispered Binabik. "I will tell you when it is safe for moving."

The door ground to a halt. As a figure appeared in the narrow opening, Binabik raised his blowpipe to his mouth. The dark shape tottered and fell forward. The dwarrows moaned in fear.

"You hit him!" Miriamele exulted. She hefted a rock, ready to try for the next one through while Binabik loaded another dart . . . but no one else moved into the doorway.

"They're waiting," Miriamele whispered to the troll. "They saw what happened to the first one."

"But I was doing nothing!" said Binabik. "My dart is still unflown."

The figure raised its head. *"Close . . . the . . . door."* Each word was an agonized effort. *"They are . . . behind me. . . ."*

Miriamele gaped in astonishment. "It's Cadrach!"

Binabik stared first at her, then at the monk, who had collapsed again. He put down his walking-stick and ran forward.

"Cadrach?" Miriamele slowly shook her head. "Here?"

The dwarrows rushed past her, hurrying to shut the door.

# 24

# The Graylands

✦

**The colorless fog** went on forever, without floor or ceiling or any visible limit at all. Simon floated in the middle of nothingness. There was no movement, no sound.

"Help me!" he shouted, or tried to, but his voice never seemed to leave his own head. Leleth was gone, her last touch upon his thoughts now grown cool and distant. "Help! Someone!"

If any shared the empty gray spaces with him, they did not answer.

*And what if there is someone or something here?* Simon thought suddenly, remembering all he had been told about the Road of Dreams. *It might be something I don't want to meet.* This might not be the Dream Road, but Leleth had said it was close. Binabik's master Ookequk had met some dreadful thing while *he* walked the road—and it had killed him.

*But would that be worse than just floating here forever, like a ghost? Soon there will be nothing left of me worth saving.*

Hours went by with nothing changing. Or it might have been days. Or weeks. There was no time here. The nothingness was perfect.

After a long empty space, his weak and scattered thoughts again coalesced.

*Leleth was supposed to push me back, back to my body, to my life. Maybe I can do it myself.*

He tried to remember what it felt like to be inside his

living body, but for a long while could form only disjointed and disturbing images of the most recent days—burrowing diggers grinning into the torchlight, the Norns gathered whispering on the hilltop above Hasu Vale. Gradually he summoned a vision of the great wheel, and a naked body prisoned upon it.

*Me!* he exulted. *Me, Simon! I'm still alive!*

The figure hanging on the wheel's rim was shadowy and without much form, like a crudely carved image of Usires on His Tree, but Simon could feel the intangible connection between it and him. He tried to give the shape a face, but could not remember his own features.

*I've lost myself.* The realization crawled over him like a blanket of killing frost. *I don't remember what I look like—I don't have a face!*

The figure on the wheel, even the wheel itself, wavered and became indistinct.

*No!* He clung to the wheel, willing its circular shadow to stay before his mind's eye. *No! I'm real. I'm alive. My name is Simon!*

He struggled to remember how he had looked in Jiriki's mirror—but first had to draw up the memory of the mirror itself, its cool feel beneath his fingers, the delicate smoothness of its carvings. It had warmed at his touch until it felt like a living thing.

Suddenly he could recall his own face prisoned in the Sithi glass. His red hair was thick and unkempt, slashed by a white streak; down his cheek from eye to jaw ran the mark of the dragon's blood. The eyes did not reveal all that went on behind them. It was not a boy who looked back from Jiriki's mirror, but a rawboned young man. It was his own face, Simon realized, his own face returned to him.

He narrowed his will, straining to force his own features onto the shadowy form hanging on the wheel. As the mask of his face grew upon the dim figure, everything else became clearer, too. The forge chamber grew out of the indistinct gray nothing, faint and ghostly, but unquestionably a real place from which Simon was separated only by some short, indefinable distance. Hope flooded back into his heart.

But no matter how he tried, he could not push any farther. He wanted desperately to return—even to the wheel—yet it remained tantalizingly out of reach: the more he struggled, the greater the distance seemed between the Simon that floated in the dreamworld and his empty, slumbering body.

*I can't reach it!* Defeat pulled at him. *I can't.*

With that realization, his vision of the wheel dimmed, then vanished. The phantom forge evaporated as well, leaving him adrift once more in the colorless void.

He summoned up the strength to try again, but this time could bring into existence only the faintest glimmering of the world he had left behind. It faded swiftly. Furious, despairing, he tried again and again, but was unable to break through. At last, his will flagged. He was defeated. He belonged to the void.

*I'm lost. . . .*

For a while Simon knew nothing but hollowness and hopeless pain.

He did not know if he had slept or passed over into some other realm, but when he could feel himself think again, something else had finally come to share the emptiness. A single mote of light glowed faintly before him, like a candle flame seen through a thick fog.

"Leleth!? Leleth, is that you?"

The spark did not move. Simon willed himself toward the gleam of light.

At first he could not say if it grew nearer, or whether, like a star on the horizon, it remained remote and beyond reach no matter how he traveled. But even though Simon could not be sure that the spark was any closer, things began to change around him. Where once there had been only airy nothingness, he now began to see faint lines and shapes which gradually became sharper and more distinct until at last he could make out the forms of trees and stones—but all were transparent as water. He was passing along a hillside, but the very earth below him and the vegetation that shrouded it seemed only scarcely more real than the void that stretched overhead in place of the sky. He seemed to be moving through a landscape of clear glass, but when he lost his way for a moment and stepped into a rock in his path, he passed through it.

*Am I the ghost? Or is it this place?*

The light *was* nearer. Simon could see its warm glow reflected faintly in the fog of tree-shapes that ringed it round. He moved closer.

The radiance hovered on the edge of a ghostly valley, perched at the end of a jut of translucent stone. It was cradled in the arms of a dim, smoky figure. As he drew closer, the phantom turned. Ghost or angel or demon, it had the face of a woman. The eyes widened, although they did not quite seem to see him.

"Who is there?" The shadowy woman's face did not move, but there was no question in his mind that it was she who spoke. Her voice was reassuringly human.

"I am. I'm lost." Simon thought of how he would feel, approached in this deathly emptiness by a stranger. "I mean no harm."

A ripple passed through the woman's form, and for a moment the gleam of light she cradled against her breast glowed more brightly. Simon felt it as a spreading warmth inside him and was strangely comforted. "I know you," she said slowly. "You came to me once before."

He could make no sense of that. "I am Simon. Who are you? What is this place?"

"My name is Maegwin." She sounded uneasy. "And this is the land of the gods. But surely you know both those things. You were the gods' messenger."

Simon had no idea what she meant, but he was desperately hungry for the company of another creature, even this ghost-woman. "I am lost," he repeated. "May I stay here and talk to you?" It seemed somehow important that he have her permission.

"Of course," she said, but the uncertainty had not left her voice. "Please, be welcome."

For a moment he could see her more clearly; her sorrowful face was framed by thick hair and the hood of a long cloak. "You are very beautiful," he said.

Maegwin laughed, something Simon felt more than heard. "In case I had forgotten, you have reminded me that I am far from the life I knew." There was a pause. The glowing light pulsed. "You say you are lost?"

"I am. It's hard to explain, but I am not here—at least, the rest of me is not." He considered telling her more, but was hesitant to open himself completely even to this melancholy, harmless-seeming spirit. "Why are *you* here?"

"I wait." Maegwin's voice was regretful. "I do not know who or what I am waiting for. But I know that is what I do."

For a time the two of them did not speak. The valley shimmered below, pellucid as mist.

"It all seems so far away," Simon said at last. "All the things that seemed so important."

"If you listen," Maegwin replied, "you can hear the music."

Simon listened, but heard absolutely nothing. That in itself was astonishing, and for a moment he was overwhelmed. There was nothing at all—no wind, no birdsong, no soft babble of voices, not even the muffled bumping of his own heart. He had never imagined a quiet so absolute, a peace so deep. After all the madness and uproar of his life, he seemed to have come to the still center of things.

"I fear this place a little," he said. "I'm afraid that if I stay here too long, I won't even want to go back to my life."

He could feel Maegwin's surprise. "Your life? Are you not already long dead? When you came to me before, I thought you must be an ancient hero." She made an unhappy sound. "What have I done? Could it be that you did not know you were dead?"

"Dead?" Shock and fury and more than a little terror surged through him. "I'm not dead! I'm still alive, I just can't get back. I'm alive!"

"Then what are you doing here with me?" There was something very strange in her voice.

"I don't know. But I'm alive!" And although he said it in part to combat his own sudden apprehension, he felt it, too—ties that had grown weak but were nevertheless quite real still bound him to the waking world and his lost body.

"But surely only the dead come here? Only the dead, like me?"

"No. The dead go on." Simon thought of Leleth flying free and knew he spoke truly. "This is a waiting place—a between-place. The dead go on."

"But how can that be, when I . . ." Maegwin suddenly fell silent.

Simon's frightened anger did not dissipate, but he felt the flame of his life still inside him, a flame that had dimmed but had not yet blown out, and he was comforted. He knew he was alive. That was all he had to cling to, but it was everything.

He felt something strange beside him. Maegwin was crying, not in sounds, but in great shuddering movements that caused her entire being to waver and almost dissipate, like breeze-stirred smoke.

"What's wrong?" As odd and unsettling as all this was, he did not want to lose her, but she had become alarmingly insubstantial. Even the light she bore seemed to have grown fainter. "Maegwin? Why are you crying?"

"I have been such a fool," she keened. "Such a fool!"

"What do you mean?" He tried to reach out to her, to take her hand, but the two of them could not touch. Simon looked down and saw nothing where his body should be. It was odd, but in this dreamlike place it did not seem as terrifying as it might have elsewhere. He wondered how he looked to Maegwin. "Why have you been a fool?"

"Because I thought I knew all. Because I thought even the gods waited to see what I would do."

"I don't understand."

For a long time she did not reply. He felt her sorrow flow through him in great gusts, angry and mournful in turn. "I will explain—but first tell me who you are, how you came to be in this place. Oh, the gods, the gods!" Her sorrow threatened to sweep her away again. "I have made too many assumptions. Far, far too many."

Simon did as she asked, starting slowly and hesitantly at first, then gaining confidence as bit by bit his past returned to him. He was surprised to find that he could remember names which only a little while before had been misty holes in his memory.

Maegwin did not interrupt, but as his recitation went on she became slightly more substantial. He could see her clearly again, her bright, wounded eyes, her lips pressed together tightly as though to keep them from trembling. He wondered who had loved her, for certainly she was a woman someone could love. Who mourned for her?

When he spoke of Sesuad'ra, and of Count Eolair's mission from Hernysadharc, she broke her silence for the first time, asking him to tell more of the count and what he had said.

As Simon described Aditu, and what the Sitha-woman had said about the Dawn Children riding to Hernystir, Maegwin again began to weep.

"Mircha clothed in rain! It is as I feared. I have almost destroyed my people with my madness. I did not die!"

"I don't understand." Simon leaned a little closer, basking in the warmth of her glow. It made the strange ghostly landscape a little less empty. "You didn't die?"

The shadow-woman began to speak of her own life. Simon realized with dawning amazement that he did indeed know of her, although they had never met: she was Lluth's daughter, sister of Gwythinn the Hernystirman Simon had seen at Josua's councils in Naglimund.

The story she told, and then the further tale of dreams and misunderstandings and accidents that she and Simon pieced together from fragments and guesses, was terrible indeed. Simon, who had spent much of his time on the wheel in a fury of self-pity, found himself sickened by Magwin's losses—her father, her brother, her very home and country taken from her in a way that even he, for all his sorrows, had not experienced. And the cruel tricks that fate, with Simon's unwitting help, had played on her!

No wonder she had lost her wits and imagined herself dead. He ached for her.

When Maegwin had finished, the phantom valley again fell into total silence.

"But why are you here?" Simon finally asked.

"I do not know. I was not led here, like you. But after I touched the mind of the thing in what I thought was Scadach—in Naglimund, if that is where it was—I was nowhere at all for a time. Then I awoke to this place, this land, and knew I was waiting." She paused. "Perhaps it was you I was meant to wait for."

"But why?"

"I do not know. But it seems we fight the same fight—or rather we did fight it, since I see no way that either of us will leave this place."

Simon waited and thought. "That thing . . . that thing at Naglimund. What was it like? What did . . . what did you *feel* when you touched its thoughts?"

Maegwin struggled to find a way to explain. "It . . . it burned. Being so near to it was like putting my face in the door of a kiln—I feared it would scorch away my very being. I did not sense words, as I do from you, but . . . ideas. Hatred, as I told you—a hatred of the living. And a longing for death, for release, which was almost as strong as the longing for revenge." She made a sad noise. For a moment her light dimmed. "That was when I was first troubled about my own thoughts, for *I* felt that longing for death, too—and if I was already dead, how could I desire to be released from life?" She laughed, a bittersweet sensation that pricked at Simon's being. "Mircha shelter me! Listen to us! Even after all that has passed, this is a madness beyond all understanding, dear stranger. That you and I should be in this place, this *moiheneg*," she used a Hernystiri word or thought that Simon did not understand, "talking of our lives, although we do not even know whether we still live."

"We have stepped out of the world," Simon told her, and suddenly everything seemed different. He felt a sort of calm descend upon him. "Perhaps we've been given a gift. For a time, we've been allowed to step outside the

world. A time to rest." Indeed, he felt more like himself
than he had since he had fallen through the earth of
John's barrow. Meeting Maegwin had done much to make
him feel like a living thing again.

"A time to rest? Perhaps for you, Simon—and if that is
so, I am happy for you. But I can only look on the foolishness I made of my life and mourn."

"Was there anything else you learned from . . . from the
burning thing?" He was anxious to distract her. Her sorrow over her mistakes seemed only barely contained, and
he feared that if it overwhelmed her he would find himself alone again.

Maegwin shimmered slightly. An unfelt wind seemed
to toss her cloudy hair. "There were thoughts for which I
have no words. Pictures I cannot quite explain. Very
strong, very bright, as though they were close to the center of the flames that give that spirit life."

"What were they?" If the burning presence Maegwin
described was what he thought it was, any clue to its
plans—and by extension to the designs of its undead
master—might help avert an endless age of blackness.

*If I can even get back,* he reminded himself. *If I can escape this place.* He pushed the disturbing thought away.
Binabik had taught him to do only what he could at any
given time. *'You cannot catch three fish with two hands,'*
the little man often said.

Maegwin hesitated, then the glow began to spread. "I
will try to show you."

In the valley of glass and shadows before them, something moved. It was another light, but where the one that
Maegwin held against her breast was soft and warm, this
one blazed with a fierce intensity; as Simon watched, four
more points of radiance sprang up around it. A moment
later the central light grew into a licking flame, stretching
upward—but even as the flame grew, it changed color,
becoming paler and paler until it was white as frost; the
licking tendrils of fire stiffened into immobility even as
they reached up and outward. Simon gaped at what they
had become. At the center of the four-cornered ring of
flames now loomed a tall white tree, beautiful and un-

earthly. It was the thing that had haunted him so long. The white tree. The blazing tower.

"It's Green Angel Tower," he murmured.

"This is where all the thoughts of the spirit in Naglimund are bent." Maegwin's voice was suddenly weary, as though showing Simon the tree had taken nearly all her strength. "That idea burns inside it, just as those flames burn around the tree." The vision wavered and fell away, leaving only the shadowy, insubstantial landscape.

*Green Angel Tower,* Simon thought. *Something is going to happen there.*

"One other thing." Maegwin had grown markedly fainter. "Somehow it thought of Naglimund as ... the Fourth House. Does that mean something?"

Simon had a dim recollection of hearing something similar from the Fire Dancers on the hilltop over Hasu Vale, but at this moment it meant little to him. He was consumed by the thought of Green Angel Tower. The tower, and its mirror-phantom the White Tree, had haunted his dreams for almost a year. It was the last Sithi building in the Hayholt, the place where Ineluki had spoken the dreadful words that had slain a thousand mortal soldiers and had barred him forever from the living world of Osten Ard. If the Storm King desired some ultimate revenge, perhaps by giving some dread power to his mortal ally Elias, what more likely place for it to happen than the tower?

Simon felt a frustrated rage sweep over him. To know this, to see at last the outlines of the Enemy's ultimate plan, but to be helpless to do anything—it was maddening! More than ever he needed to be able to act, yet instead he was condemned to wander as an unhomed spirit while his body hung useless and unihabited.

"Maegwin, I have to find a way out of this ... this place. I must go back, somehow. Everything we have both fought for is there. Green Angel Tower in the Hayholt— that is the White Tree. I must go back!"

The shadowy figure beside him took a long time to respond. "You wish to go back to that pain? To all your suffering?"

Simon thought of all that had happened and still might happen, of his tormented body on the wheel and the agony he had fled in coming here, but it did not change his resolve. "Aedon save me, I have to. Don't you want to go back, too?"

"No." Maegwin's dim form shuddered. "No. I have no strength left, Simon. If something was not keeping me here, I would already have let go of everything that held me." She took what seemed to be a deep breath; when she spoke again, her voice trembled on the edge of weeping. "There are some I have loved, and I know now that many of them are still among the living. One in particular." She steadied herself. "I loved him—loved him until I was sick with it. And perhaps he even cared for me a little and I was too stupidly prideful to see it ... but that is not important now." Her voice grew ragged. "No, that is not true. There is nothing in the living world more important to me than that love—but it is not to be. I would not go back and start again, even if I could."

Her pain was so great that Simon was left without words. There were some things that could not be made better, he realized. Some sorrows were irreparable.

"But I believe that *you* must go back," she said. "It is different for you, Simon. And I am glad to know that, to find that there are still those who wish to live in the world. I would not wish the way I feel on anyone. Return, Simon. Save those you love if you can—and those I love, too."

"But I can't." And now his thwarted anger at last gave way to desolation. There was no way to return. He and Maegwin would be here discussing the minutiae of their lives for eternity. "I don't know why I even said it, because I can't. I've tried. I don't have the strength to find my body again."

"Try. Try once more."

"Don't you think I did? Don't you believe I tried as hard as I could? It's out of my reach!"

"If you are right, we have forever. It will do no harm to try once more."

Simon, who knew that he had already exerted his powers to the utmost and failed, choked down bitter words. She was right. If he were to be any help to his friends, if he were to have even a remote chance to gain revenge for all he and Maegwin and thousands of others had suffered, he must try again—however unlikely success might be.

He tried to empty his mind of all his fears and distractions. When he had achieved a small measure of calm, he called up the image of the waterwheel, willing it into existence so that it turned in a great smoky circle over the ghostly valley. Then he summoned the image of his own face, his particular and only face, paying special attention this time to what was *behind* the features as well, the dreams and thoughts and memories that made him Simon. He tried to make the shadowy figure bound to the wheel come alive with Simon-ness, but already felt himself at the limits of his strength.

"Can you help me, Maegwin?" As the wheel grew more substantial she had grown dimmer; she was now little more than a glow of hazy light. "I can't do it."

"Try."

He struggled to keep the wheel before him, tried to summon the pain and terror and unending loneliness that went with it. For a moment he almost felt the rough wood scraping his back, heard the splashing of the wheels and the grating clash of the great chains, but then it began to slip away once more. Fading, the wheel trembled like a reflection in a rippling pond. It had been so close, but now it was receding from his reach. . . .

"Here, Simon."

And suddenly Maegwin's presence was all around him—even, somehow, inside of him. The glow that she had cradled as long as they spoke she now passed to him; it felt warm as the sun. "I think this is why I was brought here to wait. It is time for me to go on—but it is time for you to return."

Her strength filled him. The wheel, the forge chamber,

the gnawing pain of his living body, all the things that at this moment meant life to him were suddenly very close.

But Maegwin herself was far away. Her next words seemed to come from a great distance, faint and dwindling rapidly.

*"I am going on, Simon. Take what I give you and use it: I do not need my life any more. Do what you must. I pray it will be enough. If you meet Eolair . . . no, I will tell him myself. Someday. In another place . . ."*

Her brave words did not mask her fear. Simon felt every bit of her terror as she let go and allowed herself to slip away into the dark unknown.

*"Maegwin! Don't!"*

But she was gone. The glow she had held was part of Simon, now. She had given him the only thing she had left—the bravest, most terrible gift of all.

Simon fought as he had never fought before, determined not to waste Maegwin's sacrifice. Although the living world was so close he could feel it, still some inexplicable barrier separated him from the body he had left behind—but he could not let himself fail. Using the strength Maegwin had given him, he forced himself closer, embracing the agony, the fear, even the helplessness that would be his if he returned. There was nothing he could do unless he accepted what was real. He pushed and felt the barrier ripping. He pushed again.

Murky gray turned to black, then red. As he passed back from the nether realms into the waking world, Simon screamed. He hurt. Everything hurt. He was reborn into a world of pain.

The scream continued, rasping from his dried throat and cracked lips. His hand was on fire, full of scorching agony.

*"Quiet!"* The frightened voice was very close. "I am trying . . ."

He was back on the wheel. His head was pounding, and splintered wood rubbed against his skin. But what was wrong with his hand? It felt as though someone were trying to tear it from his wrist with hot pincers. . . .

It moved! He could move his arm!

Again there came a tremulous whisper. "The voices say I must hurry. They will be coming soon."

Simon's left arm was free. As he tried to flex it, a flaming bolt of pain leaped into his shoulder—but the arm moved. He opened his eyes and goggled dizzily.

A figure hung upside down before him; beyond, the forge cavern itself was inverted as well. The dark shape was sawing at his right arm with something that caught the gleam of one of the torches at the far side of the cavern. Who was it? What was it doing? Simon could not make his crippled thoughts follow each other.

A throbbing, burning pain now crept into his right hand. What was happening?

"You brought me food. I . . . I could not leave you. But the voices say I must hurry!"

It was hard to think with both of his arms on fire, but slowly Simon began to understand. He was hanging head-downward on the wheel. Someone was cutting him free. Someone . . .

". . . Guthwulf . . . ?"

"Soon the others will notice. They will come. Do not move—I cannot see and I fear I will cut you." The blind earl was working furiously.

Simon ground his teeth as the blood rushed back into his arms, trying to choke back another scream. He had not believed such misery was possible.

*Free. It will be worth it. I'll be free. . . .* He shut his eyes again, his jaws clamped together. His other arm was loose, and now both dangled beside his head. The change of position was excruciating.

He dimly heard Guthwulf wade a few steps, then felt the rhythmic sawing begin on his ankle.

*Only a few moments,* Simon promised himself, trying desperately to stay silent. He remembered what the chambermaids had told him when, as a child, he had wept over a small hurt. *"It won't mean anything tomorrow. You'll be happy then."*

One ankle came free, and the misery of its release was equaled by the strain now put on the other. Simon turned his head and sank his teeth into his own shoulder. Anything to keep from making noise that might bring Inch or his minions.

"Almost . . ." said Guthwulf hoarsely. There was an instant of slow movement, a sense of slippage, then Simon abruptly fell. Stunned, he found himself drowning in cold water. He thrashed helplessly, but could not feel his limbs. He did not know which direction was up.

Something grasped his hair and yanked. A moment later, another hand curled chokingly around his neck beneath his chin. Simon's mouth came up out of the water, and he gasped in a long breath. For a moment his face was pressed against Guthwulf's lean stomach while his rescuer struggled to get a better grip. Then Simon was dragged forward and dumped onto the rim of the sluice. His hands still did not work properly; he clung in place with his elbows, almost oblivious to the shrieking pain of his joints. He did not want to go back into that water again.

"We must . . ." he heard Guthwulf begin, then the blind man gasped and something smashed against Simon, who slid backward and only barely retained his hold on the edge of the sluice.

"What happens here?!" Inch's voice was a dreadful rumbling growl. "You do not touch my kitchen boy!"

Simon felt hope fade, replaced with sick terror. How could this happen? It was wrong! That he should have come back from death, from nothingness, only to have Inch show up a few moments too soon—how could Fate play such a monstrous trick?

Guthwulf gave a choking cry, then Simon could hear nothing but frenzied splashing. He slowly let himself back down until his feet touched the slippery bottom of the sluice. Putting weight on his wounded legs sent a blinding cloud of black fire through his head and back, but he stood. After his torments he knew he should not even be able to move, but he still retained some of the strength given to him by Maegwin's sacrifice; he felt it smoldering in him like a low-banked fire. He forced himself to remain upright in the slow-moving water until he could see again.

Inch had waded into the sluice, and now stood waist-deep in the center like some beast of the swamps. In the dim torchlight, Simon saw Guthwulf burst up from beneath the water, struggling wildly to escape the overseer's clutches. Inch grabbed the blind man's head and pushed him back under.

"No!" Simon's crippled voice was barely louder than a whisper. If it carried across the short distance, Inch gave him no heed. Still, the silence nagged at Simon in some obscure way. Was he deaf? No, he had heard both Guthwulf and Inch. So why did the chamber seem so quiet?

Guthwulf's arms jerked above the surface, but the rest of him remained submerged in the dark waters.

Simon stumbled toward them, thrashing against the slow current. The great wheel hung unmoving above the waterway. As he saw it, Simon realized why the cavern was strangely quiet: Guthwulf had somehow managed to lift the wheel so he could cut Simon free.

As he neared Inch, the cavern began to grow lighter, as though dawn had somehow found its way down through the rock. Shadowy figures were approaching, a few of them bearing torches. Simon thought they must be soldiers or Inch's henchmen, but when they came a little closer he saw their wide, frightened eyes. The forge workers had been roused, and now came hesitantly forward to see what was causing the uproar.

"Help!" Simon rasped. "Help us! He cannot stop you all!"

The tattered men stopped, as though Simon's words alone might make them traitors, liable to Inch's punishment. They stared, too cowed even to whisper among themselves.

Inch was paying neither Simon nor his slave labor any attention. He had allowed Guthwulf to surface briefly, gasping and spitting, and now was shoving him back into the water again. Simon lifted his hands, still numb with their long binding, and struck at Inch as hard as he could.

He might as well have kicked a mountain. Inch turned to look at him. The overseer's scarred face was curiously expressionless, as though the act of violence in which he was engaged took all his attention.

"Kitchen boy," Inch boomed. "You do not run away. You are next." He reached out a huge hand and jerked Simon forward. He released his grip on drowning Guthwulf long enough to pick Simon up with both hands and throw him out of the sluiceway onto the hard stone. All Simon's breath blew out, and another rush of pain coursed through him, fiercer even than the simmering agony of his limbs. For a moment he could not make his battered body respond.

Simon sensed somebody stooping over him. Certain it was Inch come to finish the job, he curled into a ball.

"Here, lad," someone whispered, and tried to help him into a sitting position. Stanhelm, the forge worker who had befriended him, was crouching at his side. The older man seemed barely able to move: one arm curled uselessly in front of his chest, and his neck was bent at an odd angle.

"Help us." Simon struggled to rise. His chest felt dagger-stabbed with each breath.

"Nothing left of me." Even Stanhelm's speech was slurred. "But look to yon wheel, lad."

While Simon fought to make sense of this, one of Inch's helpers strode over.

"Don't touch him," he snarled. "He's Doctor's."

"Shut your mouth," said Stanhelm. The henchman lifted his hand as if to strike, but suddenly several other forge men moved in on either side of him. Some of them held bits of iron scrap, heavy and sharp-edged.

"You heard," one of them growled quietly at Inch's man. "Shut your mouth."

The man looked around, judging his chances. "You'll pay pretty when Doctor hears. He'll be done with that'un in a moment."

"Then go watch," spat another of the forge workers. The men seemed frightened, but somehow they had drawn a line: if they were not yet willing to fight back against the hulking overseer, neither would they stand by and see Inch's crony harm Simon or Stanhelm. The henchman cursed and backed off, then hurried to the safety of his master's vicinity.

"Now, lad," Stanhelm whispered. "Look to yon wheel."

Dizzied by all that was happening, Simon stared at the forge man as he tried to make sense out of his words. Then he turned slowly and saw.

The great wooden paddlewheel had been lifted up so that it hung almost twice a man's height above the watercourse. Inch, who had pursued floundering Guthwulf a short way down the sluice, now stood beneath the wheel.

Stanhelm extended a bent and shaking arm. "There. Them are the works."

Simon struggled to his feet and took a few shaky steps toward the vast framework. The lever which he had seen Inch use was cocked, secured by a rope. Simon slowly tugged the rope free, straining his burning muscles and cramped hands, then grasped the lever itself in slippery, numbed fingers. Inch had pushed Guthwulf under again; he watched his victim's suffering with calm interest. The blind man was floundering away from his tormentor, toward Simon, and now appeared to be beyond the wheel's rim.

Simon said the few words of the Elysia prayer that he could remember, then heaved on the wooden lever. It moved only slightly, but the frame that held the wheel groaned. Inch looked up and around, then gradually turned his monocular gaze toward Simon.

"Kitchen boy! You . . ."

Simon heaved again, this time lifting his feet from the ground so that all his weight hung on the lever. He screamed with the pain of holding on. The frame groaned again, then, with a grating squeal, the lever banged down and the wheel shuddered and dropped into the sluice with a thunderous splash. Inch tried to dive forward out of the way, but disappeared beneath the huge paddles.

For a moment nothing moved in the whole cavern but the wheel, which began, slowly, to revolve. Then, as if the frothing channel gave birth to a monster, Inch burst to the surface howling in anger, water running from his wide-stretched mouth.

*"Doctor!"* he spluttered, waving his fist. *"Can't kill me! Not Doctor Inch!"* Simon slumped to the ground. He had done all he could.

Inch took a sloshing step forward, then began to fly. Simon stared, overwhelmed. The world had run entirely mad.

Inch's body lifted out of the water. Only when all of him was in view could Simon see that the foundry-master's broad belt had somehow caught on the fittings of one of the vast paddle blades.

The waterwheel bore Inch upward. The giant was in a frenzy now, bellowing as he was manhandled by something even larger than he was. He twisted at the end of the blade, struggling to free himself, reaching back to smash at the wooden paddle with his fist. As the wheel swung him up toward the top of its rotation, he reached out for the great chains which twined around its axle and climbed up out of sight into the shadows of the cavern ceiling. Inch's huge hands grasped the slippery links. He clung tightly. As they pulled upward past the wheel, he was stretched to his utmost for an instant. Then the buckle of his belt snapped loose and he fell free of the paddle. He clung to the massive chain with both his arms and legs.

Inch was still not coherent, but his echoing roar changed to a note of triumph as the chains carried him slowly upward. He swung away from the wheel so he could drop into the water below, but when he let go, he fell only a little way and then tipped over. He slammed against the chain and dangled, head downward. His foot had slid through the center of one of the wide, oily links and was wedged there.

The overseer thrashed, trying to pull himself up to free his foot. Howling and sputtering, he tore his own leg bloody, but he could not drag his weight high enough. The chain carried him up toward the unseen heights.

His cries grew fainter as he vanished into the shadows overhead, then a horrendous agonized cry echoed down, a rasping gargle with nothing human in it. The wheel lurched in its rotation for a moment and stopped, bouncing a little from side to side as the current pushed at the immobilized paddle blades. Then the wheel began to turn again, forcing the obstruction through the monumental grinding gears that turned Pryrates' tower-top. A drizzle of dark fluids rained down. Bits of something more solid spattered across the waterway.

Moments later, what remained of Inch slowly descended into the light, wrapped around the huge chain like meat on a cooking skewer.

Simon stared idiotically for a moment, then bent, retching, but there was nothing in his stomach to bring up.

Someone was patting his head. "Run, lad, if you got place to go. Red priest'll come quick. His tower stopped turning for a good long time when wheel was up."

Simon squinted against the black flecks that danced before his eyes, fighting to make sense of things. "Stanhelm," he gasped. "Come with us."

"Can't. Nothing left of me." Stanhelm gestured with his chin at his twisted, badly-healed legs. "Me and others'll keep the rest shut up. Say Inch had a bit of accident. King's soldiers won't do us badly—they need us. You run. Didn't belong here."

"Nobody belongs here," Simon gasped. "I'll come back for you."

"Won't be here." Stanhelm turned away. "Go on now."

Simon clambered to his feet and stumbled toward the watercourse, pain arrowing through him with every step. A pair of forge workers had lifted Guthwulf out of the water; the blind man lay on the cavern floor, struggling for air. The men who had saved him stared, but did nothing further to help. They seemed curiously numbed and slow, like fish in a winter pond.

Simon bent and tugged at Guthwulf. The last of the strength Maegwin's sacrifice had lent him was eddying away.

"Guthwulf! Can you get up?"

The earl flailed his hands. "Where is it? God help me, where is it?"

"Where is what? Inch is dead. Get up! Hurry! Where do we go?"

The blind man choked and spat water. "Can't go! Not without ..." He rolled over and forced himself up onto hands and knees, then began scrabbling along the ground beside the watercourse, pawing as though to dig himself a hole.

"What are you doing?"

"Can't leave it. I'll die. Can't leave it." Suddenly, Guthwulf gave an animal cry of joy. "Here!"

"Aedon's mercy, Guthwulf, Pryrates will be here any moment!"

Guthwulf took a few staggering steps. He lifted something that reflected a yellow strip of torchlight. "I should never have brought it," he babbled. "But I needed something to cut the rope." He gasped in more air. "They all want to take it."

Simon stared at the long blade. Even in the shadowy forge chamber, he knew it. Against all sense, against all likelihood ... here was the sword they had sought.

"Bright-Nail," he murmured.

The blind man suddenly lifted his free hand. "Where are you?"

Simon took a few painful steps closer. "I'm here. We have to go. How did you get here? How did you come to this place?"

"Help me." Guthwulf put out his arm.

Simon took it. "Where can we go?"

"Toward the water. Where the water goes down." He began to limp along the edge of the channel. The forge workers drifted back to let them pass, watching with nervous interest.

"You're free!" Simon croaked at them. "Free!" They stared at him as though he spoke a foreign tongue.

*But how are they free, unless they follow us? The forges are still locked, the doors still barred. We should help them. We should lead them out.*

Simon had no strength left. Beside him, Guthwulf was mumbling, shuffling his feet like a lame old man. How could they save anyone? The forge workers would have to make their own way.

The water ran foaming down through a fissure in the cavern wall. As Guthwulf felt his way along the stone, Simon was momentarily certain that the blind earl had lost what few wits he had left—that they had escaped drowning once, but would now be washed down into blackness. But there was a narrow track along the edge of the watercourse, one that Simon could never have found in the shadows. Guthwulf, to whom light was useless, made his way downward, tracking the wall with his fingers as Simon struggled to help him and still remain balanced. They passed out of the last gleams of torchlight and into blackness. The water churned noisily beside them.

The darkness was so complete that Simon had to struggle to remember who he was and what he was doing. Fragments of the things Leleth had showed him floated up from his memory, colors and pictures as swirlingly confused as an oil film on a puddle. A dragon, a king with a book, a frightened man looking for faces in the shadows—what did all these things mean? Simon did not want to think any more. He wanted to sleep. To sleep . . .

The roar of the water was very loud. Simon emerged suddenly from a haze of pain and confusion to find himself leaning sideways at a precarious angle. He grabbed at the cracked wall of the fissure, pulling himself upright. "Guthwulf!"

"They speak so many tongues," the blind man murmured. "Sometimes I think I understand them, but then I am lost again." He sounded very weak. Simon could feel him trembling.

"I can't . . . go much longer." Simon clung to the rough stone. "I have to stop."

"Almost." Guthwulf took another stumbling step along the slender track. Simon forced himself away from the wall, struggling to retain his clutch on the blind man.

They trudged on. Simon felt several openings in the stone wall pass beneath his fingers, but Guthwulf did not turn. When the tunnel began to resonate with loud voices, Simon wondered if he were sliding into Guthwulf's madness, but after a short while he saw a gleam of amber torchglow on the cavern wall and realized that someone was coming down the sluiceway behind them.

"They're after us! I think it's Pryrates." He slipped and

released his hold on the blind man to steady himself. When he reached out again, Guthwulf was gone.

A moment of complete panic ended when Simon found the opening to a spur tunnel. Guthwulf was just inside. "Almost," the earl panted. "Almost. The voices—Aedon, they're screaming!—but I have the sword. Why are they screaming?"

He headed down the tunnel, lurching against the walls. Simon kept his hand against the earl's back as Guthwulf turned several more times. Soon Simon could no longer remember all the turnings. That was hopeful—whoever followed them should find it no easier.

The trudge through blackness seemed to go on and on. Simon felt bits of himself drifting away, until he thought himself a spirit again, an unhomed ghost like the one that had roamed the gray spaces alone.

*Alone except for Leleth. And Maegwin.*

Thinking of those who had helped him there, he reached down for a last increment of resolve and struggled on.

Walking in a daze, he did not notice that they had stopped until he felt Guthwulf abruptly drop forward; when Simon's hand found him again, the blind man was crawling. When Guthwulf stopped, Simon reached down and felt crumpled cloth strewn across the stone. A nest. Letting his hand travel farther across the floor, Simon touched the earl's quivering leg, then the cold metal of the sword.

"Mine," Guthwulf said reflexively. His voice was muddy with fatigue. "This, too. Safe."

At that moment, Simon no longer cared about the sword, about Pryrates or any soldiers who might be following, or even whether the Storm King and Elias might bring the whole world tumbling down around his ears. Every breath burned, and his arms and legs were a-twitch with agonizing cramps. His head hammered like the bells in Green Angel Tower.

Simon found a place of his own amid the scattered rags, then surrendered to the dark pull.

# 25

# Living in Exile

❦

**Jiriki took** his hands off the dwarrow-stone.

Eolair did not need to be told. "She is gone." The count stared at Maegwin's pale face, relaxed now as though in sleep. "Gone." He had been preparing himself for this moment, but still felt as though a huge emptiness had opened inside him, a void that would never be filled. He reached out and grasped her hands, which were still warm.

"I am sorry," said Jiriki.

"Are you?" Eolair did not look at him. "What can the short life of a mortal mean to your kind?"

The Sitha did not speak for a moment. "The Zida'ya die, just as mortals do. And when those we held in our hearts have passed from us, we, too, are unhappy."

"Then if you understand," Eolair said, struggling for control, "please leave me alone."

"As you wish." Jiriki stood, a catlike unfolding from his seat on the pallet. He seemed about to say something more, but instead went silently out of the tent.

Eolair stared at Maegwin for a long time. Her hair, damp with sweat, lay in tight curls across her forehead. Her mouth seemed to hint at a smile. It was almost impossible to believe that life had left her.

"Oh, the gods have been cruel masters," he groaned. "Maegwin, what did we do to be so ill-treated?" Tears started in his eyes. He buried his face in her hair, then kissed her cooling cheek. "It has all been a cruel, cruel trick. It has all been for nothing, if you are dead." His

body was shaken by sobs. For a while he could only rock
back and forth, clutching her hand. The dwarrow-stone
was still in her other palm, held against her breast as
though to keep it from theft.

"I never knew. I never knew. You foolish woman, why
did you tell me nothing? Why did you pretend? Now all
is gone. All is lost. . . ."

Jiriki, white hair streaming in the wind, was waiting for
him when he emerged. Eolair thought he looked like a
storm-spirit—like a harbinger of death.

"What do you want?"

"As I said, Count Eolair, I am very sorry. But there are
things I think you should know—things that I discovered
in the last moments of the Lady Maegwin's life."

*Oh, Brynioch preserve me,* he thought wearily. The
world was too much for Eolair, and he did not think he
could bear any more Sithi riddles.

"I am tired. And we must leave tómorrow for
Hernystir."

"That is why I wish to tell you now," Jiriki said patiently.

Eolair stared at him for a moment, then shrugged.
"Very well. Speak."

"Are you cold?" Jiriki asked this with the careful solic-
itousness of one who had learned that although he never
suffered from the ēlements, others did. "We can walk to
one of the fires."

"I will survive."

Jiriki nodded slowly. "That piece of stone was given to
Maegwin by the Tinukeda'ya, was it not? By those you
call *domhaini?*"

"It was a gift from the dwarrows, yes."

"It was much like the great stone you and I visited in
Mezutu'a beneath the mountain—the Shard, the Master
Witness. When I touched this small stone, I felt much of
Maegwin's thought."

Eolair was disturbed by the idea of the immortal being
with Maegwin in her last moments, being with her in a

way he could not. "And can you not leave those thoughts in peace—let them go with her to her barrow?"

The Sitha hesitated. "It is difficult for me. I do not wish to force things upon you. But there are things I think you should know." Jiriki laid his long fingers against Eolair's arm. "I am not your enemy, Eolair. We are all hostages to the whims of a mad power." He let his hand fall. "I cannot claim to know for certain all that she felt or thought. The ways of the Dream Road—the path that Witnesses such as the dwarrow-stone open—are very confusing these days, very dangerous. You remember what happened when I touched the Shard. I was reluctant even to risk the Other Pathways, but felt that if there was a chance I could help, I should."

From a mortal Eolair would have found this self-serving, but there was something about the Sitha that suggested an almost frightening sincerity. Eolair felt a little of his anger slip away.

"In that muddle of thoughts and feelings," Jiriki continued, "I did understand two things, or at least I am fairly sure that I did. I believe that at the end her madness lifted. I did not know the Maegwin that you knew, so I cannot be certain, but her thoughts seemed clear and unmuddied. She thought of you. I felt that very strongly."

Eolair took a step backward. "She did? You do not say that to soothe me, as a parent might to a child?"

The Sitha's smooth face momentarily showed surprise. "Do you mean tell you something that is not true, deliberately? No, Eolair. That is not our way."

"She thought of me? Poor woman! And I could do nothing for her." The count felt tears returning, but made no attempt to hide them. "This is no favor, Jiriki."

"It was not meant to be. These are things you deserve to know. Now I must ask you a question. There is a young mortal named Seoman who is linked to Josua. Do you know him? More importantly, did Maegwin know him?"

"Seoman?" Eolair was bewildered by the sudden shift of the conversation. He thought for a moment. "There was a young knight named Simon, tall, red-haired—is that who you mean? I think I heard some call him Sir Seoman."

"That is him."

"I doubt very much that Maegwin knew him. She never traveled to Erkynland, and I believe that was where the young man lived before running away to serve Josua. Why?" Eolair shook his head. "I do not understand this."

"Nor do I. And I fear what it might mean. But in those last moments, it seemed Maegwin thought also of young Seoman, almost as though she had seen him or spoken with him." Jiriki frowned. "It is our ill luck that the Dream Road is so murky now, so unrewarding. It was all I could do to glean that much. But something is happening in Asu'a—the Hayholt—and Seoman will be there. I fear for him, Count Eolair. He is ... important to me."

"But that is where you are going anyway. That is fortunate, I suppose." Eolair did not want to think any more. "I wish you luck finding him."

"And you? Even if Seoman had some significance for Maegwin? Even if she had some message from him, or for him?"

"I am done with that—and so is she. I will take her back to Erkynland to be buried on the mountain beside her father and brother. There is much to do to rebuild our country, and I have been absent too long."

"What help can I give you?" Jiriki asked.

"I want no more help." Eolair spoke more sharply than he had intended. "We mortals are very good at burying our dead."

He turned and walked away, pulling his cloak tight against the flurrying snows.

Isgrimnur limped out onto the deck, cursing his aching body and his halting progress. He did not notice the shadowy figure until he had nearly stumbled into it.

"Greetings, Duke Isgrimnur." Aditu turned and regarded him for a moment. "Is it not chill weather for one of your folk to be out in the wind?"

Isgrimnur hid his startlement by an elaborate readjustment of his gloves. "Perhaps for the southern folk like Tiamak. But my people are Rimmersmen, my lady. We are hardened to the cold."

"Am I your lady?" she said with amusement. "I certainly hold no mortal title. And I cannot believe that Duchess Gutrun would approve of any other meaning."

He grimaced, and was suddenly grateful for the chill wind on his cheeks. "It is just politeness, my la ..." He tried again. "I find it difficult to call by their first name someone who ... who ..."

"Who is older than you are?" She laughed, a not unpleasant sound. "Another problem for which I am to blame! I truly did not come to you mortals to discomfort you."

"Are you really? Older than me?" Isgrimnur was not sure if it was a polite question—but after all, she had brought it up.

"Oh, I should think so ... although my brother Jiriki and I are both accounted quite young by our folk. We are both children of the Exile, born since Asu'a fell. To some, like my uncle Khendraja'aro, we are barely even real people, and certainly not to be trusted with any responsibility." She laughed again. "Oh, poor Uncle. He has seen so many outrageous things happen in these last days—a mortal brought to Jao é-Tinukai'i, the breaking of the Pact, Zida'ya and humans fighting side by side again. I fear that he will finish his present duty to my mother and Year-Dancing House and then simply let himself die. Sometimes it is the strongest who are the most brittle. Do you not think so?"

Isgrimnur nodded. For once, he understood what the Sitha-woman meant. "I have seen that, yes. Sometimes those who act the strongest are really the most frightened."

Aditu smiled. "You are a very wise mortal, Duke Isgrimnur."

The duke coughed, embarrassed. "I am a very old, very sore mortal." He stared out across the choppy bay. "And tomorrow we make landfall. I am glad we have been able to shelter here in the Kynslagh—I don't think most of us could have taken much more of the storms and the kilpa on the open sea, and God knows I hate boats—but I still don't understand why Elias has not lifted a hand in his own defense."

"He has not yet," Aditu agreed. "Perhaps he feels that his Hayholt walls are defense enough."

"Could be." Isgrimnur voiced the fear that others in the prince's fleet shared. "Or perhaps he is expecting allies—the kind of allies he had at Naglimund."

"That could also be true. Your people and my people have both wondered much about what is intended." She shrugged, a sinuous gesture that might have been part of a ritual dance. "Soon it will not matter. Soon we will learn first hand, as I think you say."

They both fell silent. The wind was not strong, but its breath was bitterly cold. Despite his rugged heritage, Isgrimnur found himself pulling his scarf higher on his neck.

"What happens to your fairy-folk when they get old?" Isgrimnur asked suddenly. "Do they just get wiser? Or do they turn silly and mawkish, as some of ours do?"

" 'Old' means something different to us, as you know," Aditu replied. "But the answer is: there are as many different answers as there are Zida'ya, as is no doubt true with mortals. Some grow increasingly remote; they do not speak to anyone, but live entirely in their own thoughts. Others develop fondnesses for things others find unimportant. And some begin to brood on the past, on wrongs and hurts and missed chances.

"The oldest one of all, the one you call the Norn Queen, has grown old in that way. She was known once for her wisdom and beauty, for grace beyond measurement. But something in her was balked and grew bent, and so she curled inward into malice. As the years almost beyond counting rolled past, all that was once admirable became twisted." Aditu had suddenly become serious in a way that Isgrimnur had not seen before. "That is perhaps the greatest sorrow of our folk, that the ruin of the world should be brought about by two who were among the greatest of the Gardenborn."

"Two?" Isgrimnur was trying to reconcile the stories he had heard of the silver-masked queen of ice and darkness with Aditu's description.

"Ineluki . . . the Storm King." She turned back to look across the Kynslagh, as though she could see the old Asu'a looming beyond the darkness. "He was the brightest-burning flame ever kindled in this land. Had the mortals not come—had your own ancestors not come, Duke Isgrimnur—and attacked our great house with iron and fire, he might have led us out of the shadows of exile and back into the light of the living world again. That was his dream. But any great dream can flower into madness." She was silent for a while. "Perhaps we must all learn to live with exile, Isgrimnur. Perhaps we must all learn to live with smaller dreams."

Isgrimnur said nothing. They stood for a while in the wind, silent but not uncomfortably so, before the duke turned and sought the warmth of the cabins.

⚜

Duchess Gutrun looked up in alarm when she felt the cold air. "Vorzheva! Are you mad? Bring those children away from the windows."

The Thrithings-woman, one child cradled in each arm, did not move. Beyond the open window stretched Nabban, vast but strangely intimate; the city's famous hills made the houses and streets and buildings seem built almost on top of each other. "There is no harm in air. On the grasslands, we live all our lives out in the open."

"Nonsense," Gutrun said crossly. "I've been there, Vorzheva, don't forget. Those wagons are almost like houses."

"But we only sleep in them. Everything else—eating, singing, loving—we do beneath the sky."

"And your men cut their cheeks with knives, too. Does that mean you're going to do that to poor little Deornoth?" She bristled at the mere thought.

The Thrithings-woman turned and gave her companion an amused look. "You do not think the little one should wear scars?" She gazed at the male infant's sleeping face, then laid a finger along his cheek, pretending to consider it. "Oh, but they are so handsome to see. . . ." She darted a sideward glance, then burst out laughing at the Rimmerswoman's horror. "Gutrun! You think I mean it for true!"

"Don't even say such things. And bring those poor babies away from the window."

"I am showing them the ocean where their father is. But you, Gutrun, you are very angry and unhappy today. Are you not well?"

"What is there to be happy about?" The duchess sank down again onto her chair and picked up her sewing, but only turned the cloth in her hands. "We are at war. People are dying. It is not even a week since we buried little Leleth!"

"Oh, I am sorry," Vorzheva said. "I did not mean to be cruel. You were very close to her."

"She was just a child. She suffered terrible things, may God grant her peace."

"She did not seem to have any pain at the end. That is something. Did you think she would come awake, after all that time?"

"No." The duchess frowned. "But that does not make the sadness less. I hope I am not the one who must tell young Jeremias when he comes back." Her voice dropped. "If he comes back."

Vorzheva looked at the older woman intently. "Poor Gutrun. It is not just Leleth, is it? You are frightened for Isgrimnur also."

"My old fellow will come back well," Gutrun muttered. "He always does." She peered up at Vorzheva, who still stood before the open window, a sweep of ash-gray sky behind her. "But what of you, who feared so much for Josua? Where is *your* worry?" She shook her head. "Saint Skendi protect us, I should not speak of such things. Who knows what ill luck it could bring?"

Vorzheva smiled. "Josua will come back to me. I had a dream."

"What do you mean? Has all that nonsense of Aditu's turned your head?"

"No." The Thrithings-woman looked down at her girl-child; Vorzheva's thick hair fell like a curtain, so that for a moment the faces of both mother and daughter were hidden. "But it was a true dream. I know. Josua came to me and said, 'I have what I always have wanted.' And he was at peace. So I know that he will win, and he will come back to me."

Gutrun opened her mouth to say something, then shut it again. Her face was fearful. Quickly, while Vorzheva still gazed at little Derra, the duchess made the sign of the Tree.

Vorzheva shivered and looked up. "Perhaps you are right, Gutrun. It *is* getting cold. I will shut the windows."

The duchess levered herself up from her chair. "Nonsense. I'll do it. You take those little ones right back and get under the blankets." She paused in front of the window. "Merciful Elysia," she said. "Look."

Vorzheva turned. "What?"

"It's snowing."

"You would think we were stopping for a visit to a local shrine," Sangfugol observed. "That these were boat-loads of pilgrims."

Tiamak was huddled with the harper and Strangyeard on a windy, snow-clad slope east of Swertclif. Below them, landing boats bounced Josua's army across the choppy Kynslagh toward the shore; the prince and the martial arm of his household were at the landing site, overseeing the complex enterprise.

"Where is Elias?" Sangfugol demanded. "Aedon's Bones, his brother is landing an army on his doorstep. Where is the king?"

Strangyeard winced ever so slightly at the oath. "You sound as though you want him to come! We know where

the High King is, Sangfugol," He gestured toward the
Hayholt, a cluster of spiky shadows almost hidden by
whirling snow. "Waiting. But we do not know why."

Tiamak sank deeper into his cloak. His bones felt frozen. He could understand that the prince might not want
them underfoot, but surely they could have found a place
to stay out of the way that was less exposed to the wind
and snow?

*At least I have drylander breeches now. But I still do
not want to end my days here, in this cold place. Please
let me see my Wran again. Let me go to the Wind Festival
one more time. Let me drink too much fern beer and play
snatch-the-feather. I don't want to die here and be un-
burned and unremembered.*

He shivered and tried to slough off such glum thoughts.
"Has the prince sent scouts toward the castle?"

Sangfugol shook his head, pleased to be knowledge-
able. "Not in close. I heard him tell Isgrimnur that stealth
was useless, since the king must have seen us coming
days ago, and heard of it long before that. Now that he
has made sure Elias has no soldiers hidden in Erchester—
soldiers! No one is there but dogs and rats!—Josua will
send outriders ahead when the company moves up to set
the siege."

As the harper went on to explain how, in his estima-
tion, the prince should go about deploying his forces,
Tiamak saw someone slogging up the hill through the
snow.

"Look!" Father Strangyeard pointed. "Who is that?"

"It's young Jeremias." Sangfugol was a little nettled to
be interrupted. "Been driven out like the rest of us, I suppose."

"Tiamak!" Jeremias called. "Come with me! Hurry!"

"Goodness!" Strangyeard fluttered his hands. "Perhaps
they've found something important!"

Tiamak was already standing. "What is it?"

"Josua says come quickly. The Sitha-woman is sick."

"Shall we come, Tiamak?" Strangyeard asked. "No, I
am sure you would rather not be crowded. And what help
or comfort could *I* give to one of the Sithi?"

The Wrannaman started down the hill, leaning into the wind. As the snow crunched beneath his feet, he was again grateful for Sangfugol's loan of boots and breeches, although both were too large.

*I am in a strange place,* he marveled. *A strange time. A marsh man wading through the snows of Erkynland to help one of the Sithi. It must be They Who Watch and Shape who have drunk too much fern beer.*

Aditu had been taken to a makeshift shelter, a cloth cargo cover that had been stretched across the bottom branches of a tree on a rise above the shoreline. Josua and Sludig and a few of the soldiers stood by awkwardly, hunched beneath the low roof. "Sludig found her," the prince said. "I feared she had surprised some of my brother's spies, but there are no marks of violence upon her and Sludig said he saw no signs of struggle. No one heard anything, either, although she was only a hundred paces up from the shore." He frowned worriedly. "It is like Leleth after Geloë died. She is sleeping, but will not wake."

Tiamak stared at the Sitha's face. With her eyes closed she appeared nearly human. "I did little for Leleth," he said, "and I have no idea what effect my herbs would have on one of the immortals. I do not know what I can do for Aditu."

Josua made a gesture of helplessness. "At least see that she is comfortable."

"Did you see anything that might have caused it?" Tiamak asked Sludig.

The Rimmersman shook his head vigorously. "Nothing. I found her as you see her, lying on the ground with no one else nearby."

"I must get back to watch over the unloading. Unless there is something . . ." Josua seemed distracted, as though even this upsetting event was not quite enough to hold his full attention. The prince had always been a bit remote, but in the day since they had made landfall, the Wrannaman had found him to be unusually preoccupied. Still, Tiamak decided, with what lay ahead of them all, the prince had a right to be a little distracted.

"I will stay with her, Prince Josua." He bent and touched the Sitha's cheek. Her skin was cool, but he had no idea whether that was unusual.

"Good. My thanks, Tiamak." Josua hesitated for a moment, then ducked out from beneath the lean-to. Sludig and the other soldiers followed.

Tiamak squatted beside Aditu. She was dressed in mortal clothes, pale breeches and a jacket made of hide, neither of them heavy enough for the weather—but Sithi cared little about weather, Tiamak reminded himself. She was breathing shallowly, and one hand was curled into a fist. Something about the way her long fingers were bent caught Tiamak's interest; he opened her hand. Her grip was surprisingly strong.

Nestled in Aditu's palm was a small round mirror, scarcely larger than an aspen leaf. Its frame was a narrow ring of what appeared to be shiny bone, minutely carved. Tiamak lifted it up and balanced it gently in his own hand. It was heavy for its size and oddly warm.

A tingling, prickling sensation crept through his fingers. He tilted the mirror so that he could see his face reflected; as he moved the angle, he could find no trace of his own features, but only roiling darkness. He brought it closer to his face and felt the tingling grow more pronounced.

Something struck his wrist. The mirror tumbled from his hand onto the damp ground.

"Leave it." Aditu withdrew her hand and let herself fall back, covering her eyes with her long fingers. Her voice was thin and strained. "Do not touch it, Tiamak."

"You are awake!" He looked at the mirror where it lay in the grass, but felt no particular urge to flout Aditu's warning.

"Yes, I am now. Were you sent to take care of me? To heal me?"

"To watch over you, anyway." He moved a little closer to her. "Are you well? Is there anything I can get you?"

"Water. Some snowmelt would be a good thing."

Tiamak scrambled out from under the heavy cloth and

scooped up a double handful of snow, then brought it back. "I have no cup or bowl."

"It does not matter." She sat up, not without effort, and received it in her cupped palms. She pushed some of it into her mouth and rubbed the rest on her face. "Where is the mirror?"

Tiamak pointed. Aditu bent and plucked it from the grass; a moment later, her hand was empty again. Tiamak had not seen where she put it. "What happened to you?" he asked. "Do you know?"

"Yes and no." She pressed her hands against her face. "You have learned something of the Witnesses?"

"A little."

"The Dream Road, the place we Zida'ya go when we use such Witnesses as the mirror you held for a moment, has been almost completely barred to us since Amerasu Ship-Born was slain in the Yásira. Because of this, I have not been able to confer with Jiriki or Likimeya my mother or any of my people since I left them. But I have been thinking about the things you and Strangyeard asked me—even though, as I told you, I have no answers myself. I agree that your questions may be very important. I hoped that since we are now closer to my kin, perhaps I could somehow let them know I needed to speak with them."

"And you failed?"

"Worse than that, I may have done something foolish. I underestimated how things have changed on the Dream Road."

Tiamak the Scrollbearer, glutton for knowledge, was starting to settle in for the tale before he remembered his nominal duty. "Is there anything else I can bring to you, Lady Aditu?"

She smiled at something, but did not explain. "No. I am well."

"Then please tell me what you meant about the Dream Road."

"I will tell you what I can—but there is a reason I said 'yes and no' when you asked whether I knew what had happened. I am not quite sure what *did* happen. The Road of Dreams was far more chaotic than I have ever found it, but that I expected. What I did not expect was some terrible *thing* to be waiting for me there."

Tiamak was uneasy. "What do you mean, a 'thing'? A demon? One of our . . . enemies?"

"It was not like that." Aditu's amber eyes narrowed in concentration. "It was . . . a structure, I suppose. Something very powerful and very strange that had been . . . built there. There is no other word. It was something as huge and menacing in its own way as the castle that Josua plans to attack here in the waking world."

"A castle?" Tiamak was mystified.

"Nothing so simple, nothing so much like anything you know. It was a construction of the Art, I believe—an intelligent construction, not like the shadow-things that spontaneously spring into being along the Other Ways. It was a maelstrom of smoke and sparks and black energies—a thing of great power, something that must have been long in the building. I have never seen or heard of anything like it. It caught me up as a whirlwind draws in a leaf, and I only barely won free again." She pressed her temples again. "I was lucky, I think."

"Is it a danger to us? And if it is, is there anything you can think of that might help solve this riddle?" The Wrannaman was reminded of his earlier thought about unfamiliar ground: this was territory about which he knew nothing.

"I find it hard to believe that such an unusual thing would *not* have something to do with Ineluki and the other events of these days." She paused, considering. "One thought I had might mean something, although it means nothing to me. When I first perceived it, I heard or felt the word '*Sumy'asu.*' In the speech of the Gardenborn, that means 'The Fifth House.'"

"The Fifth House?" repeated Tiamak, mystified.

"Yes." Aditu lay back. "It means nothing to me, either. But that was the name I heard when I first encountered this powerful thing."

"I will ask Strangyeard," said Tiamak. "And I suppose

we should tell Josua, too. In any case, he will be relieved to hear you are well."

"I am tired. I think I will lie here quietly a while and think." Aditu made a gesture unfamiliar to the Wrannaman. "My thanks to you, Tiamak."

"I did nothing."

"You did what you could." She closed her eyes and leaned back. "The Ancestors may understand all this—but I do not. I am frightened. I would give much to speak to my kin."

Tiamak rose and made his way back out onto the Kynslagh's snowy shores.

◆

The cart rolled to a stop and the wooden wheels fell silent. The Count of Nad Mullach was certain that he would be very tired of the painful sound of their creaking by the time his journey was finished.

"Here we say farewell," he called to Isorn. He left his horse in the care of one of the soldiers and walked through the snow to the young Rimmersman, who dismounted and embraced him.

"Farewell, indeed." Isorn looked to the cart and Maegwin's shrouded body. "I cannot tell you my sorrow. She deserved better. So do you, Eolair."

The count gave him a last handclasp. "In my experience," he said with more than a touch of bitterness, "the gods do not seem to care much what their servants deserve—or at least the rewards they give are too subtle for my understanding." He closed his eyes for a moment. "But enough. She is dead, and all the lamenting in the world, all the railing against Heaven, cannot bring her back. I will bury her with her loved ones and then I will help Inahwen and the rest of my folk do what they can to rebuild."

"And after that?"

Eolair shook his head. "I think that depends on whether the Sithi are able to stop Elias and his ally. I hope you do not think I wish you ill luck if I say that we may keep the caves of the Grianspog prepared in case we need them again."

Isorn smiled thinly. "You would be a fool not to."

"And you will go with them? Your own people will be looking for help, now that Skali is gone."

"I know. But I must find my family, and Josua. My wounds have healed well enough that I can ride, so I will go with the Sithi. The only mortal, I will be. It will get lonely on the way to Erchester."

Eolair smiled. "The way that Jiriki's folk ride, I do not think it will be a long journey." He looked to his ragged troop of men. He knew that they preferred crossing the blizzard-ridden Frostmarch to any more travels with the immortals. "But if things go in such a way that the men of Hernystir are needed, send word to Hernysadharc. I will find a way to come."

"I know."

"Fare you well, Isorn."

Eolair turned and walked back toward his horse. As he mounted, Likimeya and Jiriki, who had been hanging back, rode toward them.

"Men of Hernystir." Likimeya's eyes were bright beneath her black helm. "Know that we honor you. Not since the days of Prince Sinnach have your folk and ours fought side by side. Your fallen lie with our own dead, both here and in your home country. We thank you."

Eolair wanted to ask the stern-faced Sitha what value there had been in the deaths of four score Hernystiri, but this was not the time to recommence such an argument. His men stood, nervous but silent, wanting only to be on their way.

"You freed Hernystir from a great scourge," he replied dutifully. There were observances that had to be made. "We thank you and honor you, as well."

"May you find some peace at the end of your journey, Count Eolair," said Jiriki. His dark blade Indreju hung at his hip. He, too, was armored and looked every bit as much a strange warrior god as his mother. "And when you find it, may it last."

"May Heaven preserve you." Eolair swung up into his

saddle, then waved his arm, signaling the carter. The wheels slowly began to turn. Maegwin's shroud rippled in the stiff, sharp wind.

*And as for me,* he thought, *may the gods from this moment leave me alone. They have broken my people and my life. Let them now turn their attention elsewhere so we can begin to build anew.*

When he looked back, the Rimmersman and the Sithi still stood motionless, outlined by the rising sun. He raised his arm; Isorn returned the gesture of leavetaking.

Eolair looked west across the snows. "Come, my countrymen," he called to his tattered band. "We are going home."

# 26

# Song of the Red Star

*✷*

**"Here, drink."** The troll held out a water skin. "I am
Binabik of Mintahoq. Ookequk was my master. And you
are Padreic. He was speaking of you many times."

"Padreic is dead," the monk gasped. He took a sip of
water, letting some run down his chin. He was clearly exhausted. "I am a different man now." He put up a trembling hand to push the bowl away. "By all the gods, old
and new, that was a powerful ward on the door. I have not
tried to defeat such a thing in two decades. I think it almost killed me." He shook his head. "Better if it had, perhaps."

"Listen to you!" Miriamele cried. "You appear from
nowhere, but you are still spouting the same nonsense.
What are you doing here?"

Cadrach would not meet her eye. "I followed you."

"Followed me? From where?"

"All the way to Sesuad'ra—then followed after you
when you fled." He looked at the dwarrows, who had
closed the stone door and now stood in huddled colloquy
at the far end of the cavern, peering at the newcomer as
though he might be a Norn in disguise. "And there they
are—the *domhaini*." He grimaced. "I thought I felt their
clever hand in that door-ward, but I couldn't be sure. I
had never encountered one of theirs so new-minted."

Miriamele would not be distracted. "What are you
doing here, Cadrach? And who is following you?"

The monk turned his gaze down to his own hands,
which were clenched in the folds of his tattered robe. "I

fear I have brought the Norns down on you and your allies. The white monsters have been following me almost since I descended through the catacombs. I have been hard-pressed to stay ahead of them."

"So you led them to us?" Miriamele still did not know what she felt about seeing Cadrach again. Since he had deserted her and the rest of the company in the Lake Thrithing, she had done her best to put him out of her mind. She still felt shame about the argument over Tiamak's parchment.

"They will never take me again," the monk said fervently. "If I had not been able to force the door, I would have thrown myself down the Tan'ja Stairs before falling into their hands."

"But now the Norns are outside, you say, and the cavern has only one door for leaving," Binabik pointed out. "This is not much good you have done for yourself, Cadrach or Padreic or whichever name you now wear." Binabik had heard many stories about the monk from her and from Simon. Miriamele could see his respect for what the Hernystirman had once been warring with distrust of anyone who could betray one of the troll's friends. He shrugged. "Chukku's Stones! Enough of talking. Let us be seeing to important things now." He rose and padded across the cavern toward the dwarrows.

"Why did you run away, Cadrach? I told you I was sorry about Tiamak's parchment ... about all that."

The monk finally turned his eyes to hers. His gaze was curiously flat. "Ah, but you were right, Miriamele. I am a thief and a liar and a drunkard, and that is the truth of many years. That I did a few honest deeds does not change that."

"Why do you always say such things?" she demanded. "Why are you so determined to see the worst in yourself?"

The look on his face became something almost accusatory. "And why are you determined to see the best in me, Miriamele? You imagine that you know all about the world, but you are only a young girl, after all is said and done. There are limits to your imagination, to your understanding of how black a place the world truly is."

Stung, Miriamele turned away and busied herself looking in the saddlebag. He had only been back a few moments, and already she wanted to strangle him—yet she was searching diligently for something to feed him.

*I suppose I might as well keep him healthy until I decide to kill him.*

Cadrach was leaning against the cavern wall, head thrown back and eyes closed, overcome with exhaustion. She took the opportunity to look him over. He had grown even thinner since he had abandoned her on the grasslands; his face sagged, the skin deprived of its padding of flesh. Even in the pink light of the dwarrows' stones, the monk looked gray.

Binabik returned. "Our safeness may not last long. Yisfidri is telling me the door-wards will never be as strong now that they have once been forced. Not all the Norns are being masters like your monkish friend, but some of them might be. And even if none of them can open it, it is likely that Pryrates will not be prevented."

"Masters? What do you mean?"

"Lore-masters. Learned in the Art—what folk who are not Scrollbearers sometimes are calling magic."

"Cadrach said he couldn't do magic any more."

Binabik shook his head in bemusement. "Miriamele, once Padreic of Crannhyr was perhaps the most adept user of the Art in all of Osten Ard—although that was in part being so because other Scrollbearers, even the greatest, Morgenes, chose not to risk its deepest currents. It is seeming that Cadrach has not lost his skills, either—how else did he force the dwarrows' door?"

"It all happened so fast. I suppose I hadn't thought about it." She felt a brief upsurge of hope. Perhaps fate had brought the monk here for a reason.

"I did what I had to," Cadrach said abruptly. Miriamele, who had thought he was asleep, jumped. "The White Foxes would have caught me in a few more moments. But I am not what I was, troll. Working the Art takes discipline and hard work . . . and peace. I have been a stranger to those things for many years." He let his head fall back against the cavern wall. "Now the well is dry. I have no more to give. Nothing."

Miriamele was determined to have answers. "You still have not explained why you followed me, Cadrach."

The monk opened his eyes. "Because there is nothing else. The world holds nothing else for me." He hesitated, then looked at Binabik angrily, as though the little man was eavesdropping on something he had no right to hear. The words came slowly. "Because . . . because you were kind to me, Miriamele. I had forgotten what it feels like. I could not go with you to face the questions, the looks, the disgust of all those others—Duke Isgrimnur and the rest—but neither could I let go of that small touch of life . . . life as it once was. *I could not let go.*" He reached up with both hands and rubbed at the skin of his face, then laughed wretchedly. "I suppose I am not so much a dead man as I thought."

"Was it you who followed Simon and me in the forest?"

"Yes, and through Stanshire and Falshire as well. It was only when this one joined you," he indicated Binabik, "that I had to fall farther behind. That wolf has a keen nose."

"You were not much help when the Fire Dancers caught us."

Cadrach only shuddered.

"So you followed us all the way here?"

"I lost your track after Hasu Vale. It was pure luck I found you again. If you had not come to Saint Sutrin's, where I had found a sheltering roof courtesy of that madman Domitis, I think we would never have met again." He laughed again, harshly. "Think on that, my lady. *Your* luck went bad when you entered God's house."

"Enough of this." Miriamele was losing patience with Cadrach's self-loathing. "You are here. What do we do now?"

Before the monk could offer any suggestion, Yis-fidri came shambling up. The dwarrow looked mournfully at Cadrach, then turned to Miriamele and Binabik. "This

man is right in one thing. Someone else is now outside
this cavern. The Hikeda'ya have come."

There was a silence as the words sank in.

"Are you certain?" Miriamele held little hope they
were wrong, but the thought of being hemmed in the cavern with the corpse-faced Norns outside was dreadful.
The White Foxes had been fearsome enough as characters
in her uncle's tales of the fall of Naglimund, but on the
hillside above Hasu Vale she had seen them for herself.
She never wished to see them again—but she doubted she
would be so lucky. Her panic, which had abated with the
surprise of Cadrach's entrance, now returned. She was
suddenly short of breath. "You're certain it's the Norns,
not just some of my father's soldiers?"

"This man we did not expect," said Yis-fidri, "but we
know what things move through our tunnels. The door
does for now hold them out, but soon that may change."

"If these are your tunnels, you must know a way we
can escape!"

The dwarrow said nothing.

"Perhaps we will after all be using those stones we
gathered," Binabik said. "We should give thought to trying an escape before more of our enemies arrive." He
turned to Yis-fidri. "Can you tell how many are being
outside?"

The dwarrow fluted what sounded like a question to his
wife. After listening to her reply, he turned. "The number
of one hand's fingers, perhaps. But that will not be true
for long."

"That few?" Miriamele sat up. "We should fight! If
your folk will help us, surely we can defeat so few of
them and escape!"

Yis-fidri shrank back, plainly uneasy. "I have told you.
We are not strong. We do not fight."

"Listen to what the Tinukeda'ya say." Cadrach's voice
was cold. "Not that it will make much difference soon,
but I for one prefer to await the end here rather than be
spitted on one of the White Foxes' spears."

"But the end is certain if we wait. At least if we try to
escape, there is a chance."

"There is no chance either way," the monk replied. "At least here, we can make our peace and die by our own choice when it suits us."

"I cannot believe what a coward you are!" cried Miriamele. "You heard Yis-fidri! A half-dozen Norns at the most! That is not the end of the world. We have a chance!"

Cadrach turned to her. Sorrow and disgust and barely-concealed fury warred in his expression. "It is not the Norns that I fear," he said finally. "But it *is* the end of the world."

Miriamele caught something unusual in his tone, something beyond even his ordinary pessimism. "What are you talking about, Cadrach?"

"The end of the world," he repeated. He took a deep breath. "Lady, if you and I and this troll could somehow slaughter every Norn in the Hayholt—every Norn in Stormspike, too—still it would make no difference. It is too late to do anything. It was *always* too late. The world, the green fields of Osten Ard, the people of its lands . . . they are doomed. And I have known it since before I met you." He looked up imploringly. "Of course I am bitter, Miriamele. Of course I am almost mad. Because I know beyond doubt that there is no hope."

※

Simon woke from cloudy, chaotic dreams into utter darkness. Someone was moaning nearby. Every part of his body throbbed, and he could barely move his wrists and ankles. For long moments he was certain he had been captured and was bound in some black cell, but at last he remembered where he was.

"Guthwulf?" he croaked. The moans continued, unchanging.

Simon rolled over onto his stomach and crawled toward the sounds. When his swollen fingers encountered something, he stopped and explored clumsily until he found the earl's shaggy-bearded face. The blind man was blazing with fever.

"Earl Guthwulf. It's Simon. You saved me from the wheel."

"Their home is burning!" Guthwulf sounded terrified. "They cannot run—there are strangers with black iron at the gates!"

"Do you have water here? Is there food?"

He felt the blind man struggle to sit up. "Who's there? You can't take it! It sings for me. For me!" Guthwulf grabbed at something, and Simon felt a cold metal edge drag painfully along his forearm. He swore and lifted the arm to his mouth, tasting blood.

*Bright-Nail.* It seemed impossibly strange. *This fever-ridden blind man has Bright-Nail.*

For a moment he considered simply pulling it from Guthwulf's weakened grasp. After all, how could this madman's need outweigh that of entire nations? But even more troubling than the idea of stealing the sword from a sick man who had saved his life was the fact that Simon was lost without light somewhere in the tunnels beneath the Hayholt. Unless for some incomprehensible reason the blind earl kept a torch or lantern, without Guthwulf's knowledge of this maze he might wander forever in the shadows. What good would Bright-Nail be then?

"Guthwulf, do you have a torch? Flint and steel?"

The earl was murmuring again. Nothing Simon could understand seemed useful. He turned away and began to search the cavern by touch, wincing and groaning at the pain each movement caused.

Guthwulf's nesting place was small, scarcely a dozen paces wide—if Simon had been on his feet and pacing—in either direction. He felt what seemed to be moss growing in the cracks of the stone beneath him. He broke some off and smelled it: it did not seem to be the same plant that had sustained him in Asu'a's ruined halls. He put a little on his tongue, then spat it out again. It tasted even more foul than the other. Still, his stomach hurt so much that he knew he would be trying it again soon.

Except for the various rags strewn about the uneven stone floor, Guthwulf seemed to have few possessions.

Simon found a knife with half its blade snapped off. When he reached to tuck it into his belt, he suddenly realized he did not have one, nor any other clothes.

*Naked and lost in dark. Nothing left of Simon but Simon.*

He had been splashed by the dragon's blood, but afterward, he had still been Simon. He had seen Jao é-Tinukai'i, had fought in a great battle, had been kissed by a princess—but he was still the same kitchen boy, more or less. Now everything had been taken from him, but he still had what he had begun with.

Simon laughed, a dry, hoarse sound. There was a sort of freedom in having so little. If he lived to the next hour, it would be a triumph. He had escaped the wheel. What more could anyone do to him?

He put the broken knife against the wall so he could find it again, then continued his search. He encountered several objects he could see no purpose for, oddly shaped stones that felt too intricate to be natural, bits of broken pottery and splintered wood, even the skeletons of some small animals, but it was only as he reached the far side of the cavern that he found something truly useful.

His numb, stiffened fingers touched something wet. He snatched his hand away, then slowly reached out again. It was a stone bowl half full of water. On the ground beside it, as wonderful as any miracle from the Book of Aedon, was what felt like a lump of stale bread.

Simon had the bread to his mouth before he remembered Guthwulf. He hesitated, his stomach raging, then tore a piece loose and dipped it in the water and put it in his mouth. He ate two more small pieces the same way, then held the bowl carefully in his aching, trembling hand and crawled to where Guthwulf lay. Simon dipped his fingers in the water and let some dribble into the earl's mouth; he heard the blind man swallow thirstily. Next he took a morsel of bread and moistened it, then fed it to his ward. Guthwulf did not close his mouth, and seemed unable to chew or swallow it. After a moment, Simon retrieved it and ate it himself. He felt exhaustion creeping over him.

"Later," he told Guthwulf "Later you will eat, You will be well again, and so will I. Then we will leave here."

*Then I will take Bright-Nail to the tower. That is what I took back my life to do.*

"The witchwood is in flames, the garden is burning. . . ." The earl squirmed and twisted. Simon moved the bowl away, terrified it might be spilled. Guthwulf groaned. *"Ruakha, ruakha Asu'a!"*

Even from a short distance away, Simon could feel his raging heat.

The man lay on the ground, his face pressed against the stone. His clothes and skin were so dirty it was hard to see him. "That's everything, master. I swear it!"

"Get up." Pryrates kicked him in the ribs, but not hard enough to break anything. "I can scarcely understand you."

He rose to his haunches, whiskered mouth quivering in fear. "That's all, master. They run away. Down watercourse."

"I know that, fool."

The alchemist had given his soldiers no directions since they had returned from their fruitless search, and now they stood uneasily. Inch's remains had been removed from the chains that turned Pryrates' tower top; they lay in an untidy heap beside the sluice. It was obvious that most of the guardsmen wished they had been allowed to cover such of the overseer as had been recovered, but since they had received no order from Pryrates, they were studiously looking anywhere else.

"And you do not know who these people were?"

"'Twas the blind man, master. Some have seen him, but none ever catched him. He takes things sometime."

A blind man living in the caverns. Pryrates smiled. He had a reasonably good idea who that might be. "And the other? One of the foundrymen being punished, I take it?"

"That it was, master. But Inch called him something else."

"Something else? What?"

The man paused, his face a mask of terror. "Can't remember," he whispered.

Pryrates leaned down until his hairless face was only a handbreadth from the man's nose. "I can *make* you remember."

The forge man froze like a serpent-tranced frog. A small whimper escaped his throat. "I be trying, master," he squeaked, then: " 'Kitchen Boy'! Doctor Inch called him 'Kitchen Boy'!"

Pryrates straightened up. The man slumped, his chest heaving.

"A kitchen boy," the priest mused. "Could it be?" Suddenly he laughed, a rasping scrape of sound. "Perfect. Of course it would be." He turned to the soldiers. "There is nothing else for us to do here. And the king has need of us."

Inch's henchman stared at the alchemist's back. His lips moved as he worked up the nerve to speak. "Master?"

Pryrates turned slowly. "What?"

"Now . . . now that Doctor Inch be dead . . . well, who do you wish to . . . to take charge here? Here in king's forge?"

The priest looked sourly at the grizzled, ash-blackened man. "Sort that out yourselves." He gestured at the waiting soldiers, marking out half of the score of men. "You lot will stay here. Do not bother protecting Inch's cronies—I should not have left him in charge of this place so long. I want you only to make sure that wheel stays in the water. Too many important things are driven by it to risk a second occurrence of a folly like this. Remember: if that wheel stops turning again, I will make you very, very sorry."

The designated guards took up positions along the edge of the watercourse; the rest of the soldiers filed out of the forge. Pryrates' stopped in the doorway to look back. Under the impassive gaze of the guardsmen, Inch's chief honohman was quickly being surrounded by a tightening ring of grim forge workers. Pryrates laughed quietly and let the door crunch shut.

✦

Josua sat up, startled. The wind was howling fiercely, and the shape in the tent's door loomed giant-size.

"Who is there?"

Isgrimnur, who had been nodding during the long silence, snorted in surprise and fumbled for Kvalnir's hilt.

"I cannot stand it any longer." Sir Camaris swayed in the doorway like a tree in a strong wind. "God save me, God save me . . . I hear it even in my waking hours now. In the darkness it is all there is."

"What are you talking about?" Josua rose and went to the tent flap. "You are not well, Camaris. Come, sit down here beside the fire. This is no weather to be out wandering."

Camaris shook off his hand. "I must go. It is time. I can hear the song so clearly. It is time."

"Time for what? Go where? Isgrimnur, come help me."

The duke struggled to his feet, wheezing at the pain of stiff muscles and still-tender ribs. He took Camaris by the arm and found the muscles tight as wet knots.

*He is terrified! By the Ransomer, what has done this to him?*

"Come, sit." Josua urged him toward a stool. "Tell us what ails you."

The old knight abruptly pulled away and took a few staggering steps backward out into the snow. Thorn's long scabbard bumped against his leg. "They are calling, each to each. They *need*. The blade will go where it will go. It is time."

Josua followed him out onto the hillside. Isgrimnur, puzzled and worried, limped after, pulling his cloak tight against the wind. The Kynslagh lay below, a dark expanse beyond the blanketing white. "I cannot understand you, Camaris," the prince called over the wind. "What is it the time for?"

"Look!" The old man threw up an arm, pointing into the murk of storm clouds. "Do you not see?"

Isgrimnur, like Josua, looked upward to the sky. A dull spot of ember-red burned there. "The Conqueror Star?" he asked.

"They feel it. It is time." Camaris took another retreating step, wobbling as though he might at any moment tumble backward down the hill. "God grant me strength, I can resist it no longer."

Josua caught the duke's eye, silently asking his help. Isgrimnur walked forward and he and the prince again grasped Camaris' arms. "Come in from the cold," Josua begged.

Sir Camaris yanked himself free—his strength never ceased to astonish Isgrimnur—and for a moment his hand strayed to Thorn's silver-wrapped hilt.

"Camaris!" Isgrimnur was shocked. "You would draw blade against us!? Your friends!?"

The old man stared at him for a moment, his eyes curiously unfocused. Then, slowly, the duke saw his tension ease. "God help me, it is the sword. It sings to me. It knows where it wants to go. Inside." He gestured limply toward the dark bulk of the Hayholt.

"And we will take you there—and the sword, too." Josua was calm. "But there is the simple matter of breaching the walls that we must deal with first."

"There are other ways," said Camaris, but his wild energy had faded. He allowed himself to be led into Josua's tent.

Camaris downed the cup that Josua had filled for him in a single gulp, then drained a second serving. This worried Isgrimnur almost as much as the strange things the old knight had said: Camaris was reknowned as a moderate man. Still, by his haunted look, the old knight now seemed to welcome anything that might bring him relief from the agony Thorn caused him.

Camaris would say nothing more, although Josua pressed him for information in what Isgrimnur thought was an exceedingly solicitious yet awkward manner. Ever since the night on the ship, Isgrimnur had seen Josua's attitude to the old knight change, as though even the old man's presence made him dreadfully uncomfortable. Isgrimnur wondered, not for the first time, what terrible thing Camaris had told him.

After a while, the prince gave up and returned to the discussion interrupted by the knight's appearance.

"We know now that there are indeed forces still within the castle walls, Isgrimnur—considerable forces of men, mercenaries as well as the Erkynguard." Josua frowned. "My brother shows more patience than I would have suspected. Not even a sally while we were landing."

"Patience . . . or perhaps Elias has some worse fate planned for us." The duke tugged at his beard. "For that matter, Josua, we do not even know that your brother is still alive. Erchester is all but deserted, and the few people we have managed to find there wouldn't know if Fingil himself had come back from the grave and was sitting on the Dragonbone Chair."

"Perhaps." The prince sounded doubtful. "But I cannot rid myself of the feeling that I would know if Elias were dead. In any case, even if Pryrates rules him, or has even taken the throne himself, we are still faced with the Storm King and the Scroll League's angry star."

Isgrimnur nodded. "Someone is in there, right enough. Someone knows our plans. And they took your father's sword."

Josua's mood darkened. "That was a blow. Still, when I saw that Swertclif was unguarded, I had little hope left we would find it there."

"We always knew we would have to go inside the Hayholt to get that fairy-sword, Sorrow." Isgrimnur pulled at his beard again and made a noise of disgust. War was difficult enough without these magical complexities. "I suppose we can go in for two as easily as one."

"If it is even inside the walls," Josua pointed out. "That hole in the side of my father's cairn looked a hurried thing to me—not what I would have expected from Pryrates or my brother, who need hide their works from no one."

"But who else would do it?"

"We still do not know what happened to my niece and Simon and the troll."

Isgrimnur grunted. "I doubt that Miriamele or young Simon would have taken the blade and just disappeared. Where are they? They both know what Bright-Nail is worth to us."

Camaris' sudden outcry made the duke flinch.

"*All* the swords! God's Nails, I can feel them, all three! They sing to each other—and to me." He sighed. "Oh, Josua, how I wish I could silence them!"

The prince turned. "Can you truly feel Bright-Nail?"

The old knight nodded. "It is a voice. I cannot explain, but I hear it—and so does Thorn."

"But do you know where it is?"

Camaris shook his head. "No. It—the part that calls to me—is not in a place. But they wish to come together inside the walls. There is need. The time is growing short."

Josua grimaced. "It sounds as though Binabik and the others were right. Hours are marching by: if the swords are any use to us, we must find them and discover that use soon."

*Madness,* thought Isgrimnur. *Our lives, our land, ruled by madness out of old tales. What would Prester John have thought, who worked so hard to drive the fairy-folk out of his kingdom and to push the shadows away?*

"We cannot fly over those walls, Josua," he pointed out. "We've won a victory in Nabban and sailed north in such a short time that folk will talk of it for years. But we cannot fly an army into the Hayholt like a flock of starlings."

"There are other ways ..." Camaris whispered. Josua looked at him sharply, but before he could discover whether this was more singing-sword maundering or something useful, another shape appeared in the tent doorway, accompanied by a blast of chill air and a few snowflakes.

"Your pardon, Prince Josua." It was Sludig, in mail and helm. He nodded to Isgrimnur. "My lord."

"What is it?"

"We were riding the far side of Swertclif, as you asked. Searching."

"And you found something?" Josua stood, his face carefully expressionless.

"Not found something. Heard something." Sludig was obviously exhausted, as though he had ridden far and fast. "Horns in the far distance. From the north."

"From the north? How far away?"

"It is hard to say, Prince Josua." Sludig spread his hands, as though he could find the words by touch. "They were not like any horns I have heard. But they were very faint."

"Thank you, Sludig. Are there sentries on Swertclif?"

"On the near side, Highness, out of sight of the castle."

"I do not care if anyone sees them," the prince said. "I am more concerned about who might be coming down on us from the north. If you and your men are tired, ask Hotvig to take some of his grasslanders and ride down the far side toward the skirts of Aldheorte. Tell them to return immediately if they see something coming."

"I will, Prince Josua." Sludig went out.

Josua turned to Isgrimnur. "What do you think? Is the Storm King going to play the same hand he produced at Naglimund?"

"Perhaps. But you had castle walls, there. Here we have nothing before us but open land, and nothing behind us but the Kynslagh."

"Yes, but we have several thousand men here, too. And no innocents to worry over. If my brother's chief ally thinks he will find us as easy a nut to crack as before, he will be disappointed."

Isgrimnur stared at the fierce-eyed prince, then at Camaris, who held his head in his hands and stared at the tabletop.

*Is Josua right? Or are we the last raveled end of John's empire, waiting for a final pull before it falls into threads?*

"I suppose we'd better go and talk to a few of the captains." The duke got up and held his hands close to the brazier, trying to dispel some of the chill. "Better we tell them something's coming than they hear it by rumor." He made a noise of disgust. "Looks like we don't get much sleep."

⁂

Miriamele stared at Cadrach. She, who had heard him lie so many times, could not free herself of the horrifying certainty that this time he was telling the truth.

*Or the truth as he sees it, anyway,* she tried to comfort herself.

She looked at Binabik, who had narrowed his eyes in concentration, then returned to Cadrach's bleak face. "Doomed? Do you mean some danger beside that we already face?"

He met her stare. "Doomed beyond hope. And I have played no little part in it."

"What is it you are saying?" demanded Binabik.

The dwarrow Yis-fidri seemed to want little to do with this volatile and frightening conversation; he hesitated, fingers flexing.

"What I am saying, troll, is that all the scurrying about in caverns that we do here matters little. Whether we escape the White Foxes outside, whether your Prince Josua knocks down the walls, whether God Himself sends lightning down from Heaven to blast Elias to ash . . . none of it matters."

Miriamele felt her guts twist at the certainty in his voice. "Tell us what you mean."

The monk's hard face crumpled. "Aedon's mercy! Everything you have thought about me is true, Miriamele. Everything." A tear ran down his cheek. "God help me—although He has no reason to—I have done such foul things. . . ."

"Curse you, Cadrach, will you explain!"

As if this outburst had somehow pushed Yis-fidri past what he could bear, the dwarrow got up and moved away rapidly, going to join his whispering fellows on the other side of the cavern.

Cadrach wiped at his eyes and nose with his dirty

sleeve. "I told you of my capture by Pryrates," he said to
Miriamele.

"You did." And she in turn had told Binabik and others
on Sesuad'ra, so she felt no need to retell the tale now.

"I told you that after I had betrayed the booksellers,
Pryrates threw me out, thinking I was dead."

She nodded.

"That was not true—or at least it did not happen then."
He took a breath. "He set me to spy on Morgenes and
others I had known from my days as a Scrollbearer."

"And you did it?"

"If you think I hesitated, my lady, you do not know
how fiercely a drunkard and coward can cling to his
life—or how terrified of Pryrates' anger I was. You see,
I *knew* him. I knew that the injuries he had done to my
flesh in his tower were nothing set against what he could
do if he truly wished to make me suffer."

"So you spied for him?! Spied on Morgenes?"

Cadrach shook his head. "I tried—by the Tree, how I
tried! But Morgenes was no fool. He knew that I had
fallen into dreadful straits, and that the red priest knew
both of us from elder days. He gave me food and a night's
lodging, but he was suspicious. He made sure there was
nothing for me to find in either his chambers or his dis-
course that would be useful to someone like Pryrates."
Cadrach shook his head. "If anything, my efforts only
taught Morgenes that he had less time than he had
hoped."

"So you failed?" Miriamele could not see where this
was leading, but a deep dread was spreading through her.

"Yes. And I was terrified. When I went back to
Hjeldin's Tower, Pryrates was angry. But he did not kill
me, or do something worse, as I feared. Instead he asked
me more questions about *Du Svardenvyrd*. I think by then
he had already been touched by the Storm King and was
beginning to bargain with him." Cadrach's look turned
contemptuous. "As if any mortal could successfully bargain with one such as that! I doubt Pryrates has even yet
realized what has come through the door he opened."

"We will talk of what thing Pryrates has done later,"

said Binabik. "You are telling us now of things *you* have been doing."

The monk stared at him. "They are less separate than you think," he said at last. "Pryrates asked me many questions, but for one who had read *Du Svardenvyrd*—indeed, for one who knew Nisses' book so well that the memory of its words still haunts my thoughts daily—it was easy enough to see the direction behind his questions. Somehow he had been reached by the Storm King, and now Pryrates was eager to know about the three Great Swords."

"So Pryrates *does* know about the swords." Miriamele took a shaky breath. "I suppose he was the one who took Bright-Nail·from the mound, then."

Cadrach held up his hand. "Pryrates dealt with me harshly for failing with Morgenes. Then he had me send a message to old Jarnauga in the north, asking for information about the Storm King. I suspect that the alchemist was looking for ways to defend himself against his new and very dangerous friend. He made me write it as he watched, then sent it himself with a sparrow he had filched from Morgenes. He let me go free again. He was sure I would not run away when he could so easily locate me."

"But you did run away," Miriamele said. "You told me so."

Cadrach nodded. "Eventually. But not then. My fear was too great. But at the same time I knew that Jarnauga would not respond. The Rimmersman and Morgenes were closer than Pryrates realized, and I had no doubt the doctor would have already written to tell Jarnauga about my unexpected visit. In any case, Jarnauga had been living in Stormspike's shadow for years and would not have opened his mind to anyone he did not know for certain to be untouched by Ineluki's long hand. So I knew that the imposture Pryrates had forced me to commit was useless, and that when the red priest discovered it, he would have no use left for me. My only worth was as one who had read Nisses' book and as a former Scrollbearer. But I had answered all of his questions about the book, and now he would discover that the other Scrollbearers had stopped trusting me years before. . . ." He broke off, struggling again with powerful emotions.

"Go on." Miriamele spoke a little more gently than before. Whatever he had done, he seemed to be genuinely suffering.

"I was in terror—stark terror. I knew that I had only a short time before Jarnauga's inevitably unhelpful reply. I wanted desperately to flee, but Pryrates would know the moment I left Erchester, and by his use of the Art would also know where I had gone. He had marked me in that high chamber of his tower. He would find me *anywhere*." Cadrach paused, struggling for self-control. "So I thought, and thought, and thought—but not, to my shame, of a way to escape Pryrates or thwart his plans. No, in my besottedness and my fear, I thought only of ways that I could please this horrid master, that I could convince him to grant me my pathetic life." He quivered, unable for a moment to continue.

"I had thought much about his questions," the monk finally resumed. "Especially about the three Great Swords. It was clear that they had some marvelous power, and equally clear that they meant something to the Storm King. What was not clear to anyone but me, I thought, was that the sword Minneyar, one of the three, was in fact Bright-Nail, the sword that had been buried with King John."

Miriamele gaped. "You knew?"

"Anyone who read the books of history that I had would have suspected it," Cadrach replied. "I am convinced Morgenes knew, but hid it in his own book about your grandfather so that only those who knew what to look for would find it, thus keeping it from common knowledge." He had regained a little composure. "In any case, I read the same sources Doctor Morgenes did, and had long held that opinion, although I had never shared it with anyone. And the more I thought about the market-place gossip that claimed Elias would not handle his father's sword, that he had, against custom, buried it with his father, the more I felt sure that my guess was not just likely, but true.

"So I decided that if what *Du Svardenvyrd* seemed to suggest was *also* true—that the only weapons the Storm King feared were the Three Great Swords—what more pleasing gift could I bring to Pryrates than one of the swords? All three were thought to be lost. Surely if I produced one, I reasoned, Pryrates would find me useful."

Miriamele gaped at the monk in disgust and astonishment. "You . . . you traitor! Was it you who took the sword from my grandfather's barrow? And gave it to Pryrates!? God curse you if it was, Cadrach!"

"You may call curses on me all you like—and you will, with ample reason. But wait until you hear the whole tale."

*I was right to try and drown him in Emettin Bay. I wish he had never been fished out.* She waved angrily for him to continue.

"I went to Swertclif, of course," he said. "But the burial ground was closely guarded by the king's soldiers. It seemed that Elias meant to keep his father's grave safe. I waited two nights for a moment when I might get at the barrow, but no such moment came. And then Pryrates sent for me." He winced, remembering. "He had learned well from his studies. His voice was in my head—you cannot imagine how that feels! He forced me to come to him, come slinking like a disobedient child. . . ."

"Cadrach, there are Norns who are waiting outside this cavern," Binabik interrupted. "So far your story is telling us little that will help us."

The monk stared at him coldly. "Nothing will help us. That is what I am trying to explain—but I will not force you to listen."

"You will tell us everything," Miriamele declared, her rage fighting free. "We are fighting for our lives. Speak!"

"Pryrates called me to him again. As I knew he would, he told me that Jarnauga had sent only information of no worth, that it was clear the old Rimmersman did not trust me. 'You are useless to me, Padreic ec-Crannhyr,' the alchemist said.

" 'What if I can tell you something that is *very* useful?' I asked. No, that is not the right word. I begged. 'If you will leave me my life, I will serve you faithfully. There are still things I know that might help you!' He laughed when I said that—laughed!—and told me that if I could give him even a single piece of information that was truly valuable, he would indeed spare me. So I told him that I knew the Great Swords were important to him, that all were lost, but that I knew where one of them was.

" 'Do you think to tell me Sorrow is with the Norns of Stormspike?' he said scornfully. 'I know that already,' I shook my head—in fact, I had not known that myself, but I could guess how he had discovered it. 'That Thorn did not sink into the ocean with Camaris?' he continued.

"I hurriedly told him what I had discovered—that Minneyar and Bright-Nail were one and the same, that one of the Great Swords was even now buried less than a league from where we sat. In my eagerness to gain his favor, I even told him that I had tried to get it myself to bring it to him."

Miriamele scowled. "To think that I saw you as a friend, Cadrach—if you had even an idea of what this could mean to us all. . . !"

The monk ignored her, grimly following her order to finish the tale. "And when I was done . . . he laughed again. 'Oh, this is very sad, Padreic,' he hooted. 'Is this your great work of spycraft? Is this what you think will save you? I have known what Bright-Nail truly is since before you first entered this tower. And if you *had* moved it from its resting place, I would have plucked out your eyes and tongue with my own fingers. It will lie there on old John's rotting breast until the proper time. When the hour is right, the sword will come. All the swords will come.' "

Miriamele's thoughts suddenly went staggering. "The sword will come? He . . . he has known all along? Pryrates . . . wanted it left there?" She turned helplessly to Binabik, but the little man seemed just as amazed as she. "I don't understand. Elysia, Mother of Mercy, what are you telling us, Cadrach?"

"Pryrates knows all." A certain black satisfaction crept into the monk's voice. "He knew what Bright-Nail was, where it lay—and he saw no need to disturb it. I feel sure that everything your uncle and these . . ." he gestured toward Binabik, "latter-day Scrollbearers plan is already known to him. He is content to see it happen."

"But how can that be? How can Pryrates not fear the one power that can undo his master?" Miriamele was still astonished. "Binabik, what does this mean?"

The troll had lost his composure. He held up his trembling fingers, begging a moment to think. "It is much for considering. Perhaps Pryrates has a plan of some treachery against the Storm King. Perhaps he thinks to keep Ineluki's power restrained with the threatening of the swords' power." He turned to Cadrach. "He was saying 'the swords will come'? Those words?"

The monk nodded. "He knows. He *wants* Bright-Nail and the others brought here."

"But no sense in this am I seeing," said Binabik anxiously. "Why not then bring Prester John's blade in and hide it away until the time he waits is arrived?"

Cadrach shrugged. "Who can know? Pryrates has walked strange paths and learned hidden things."

As her shock lessened a little, Miriamele felt her rage at the monk return, battening on her fear. "How can you sit there so smugly? If you did *not* betray me and all I care about, it was not for lack of trying. I suppose he set you free then to spy some more? Is that why you arranged to accompany me from Naglimund? I thought you were just using me to further your own greed . . ." as she thought about it, despair seized her, "but . . . but you were working for Pryrates!" She turned away, unable to look at Cadrach any longer.

"No, my lady!" Amazingly, he sounded hurt and upset. "No, he did not release me—and I did not serve him again."

"If you expect me to believe that," she said with cold hatred, "you are truly mad."

"Is there more to your tale?" The tentative respect Binabik had earlier shown the monk had curdled into sour practicality. "Because we are still trapped here, still in danger that is most dreadful—although there is little else we can do, I am thinking, until the Norns prove they can force the dwarrows' door."

"There is a little more. No, Miriamele, Pryrates did not release me. As I told you, he had proved that I was worthless to him. I told you this much of the truth when we were in the landing boat—I was not even worth more tortures. Someone clubbed me, then I was tossed away like offal dumped behind a rich man's house. Except I was not left for dead out in the Kynswood as I told you before. Rather, I was dumped into a pit in the catacombs that run beneath Hjeldin's Tower . . . and that is where I awoke. In darkness."

He paused, as though this memory was even more painful than the ghastly things he had already told. Miriamele said nothing. She was furious and yet empty. If Cadrach's tale was true, then perhaps there really was no hope. If Pryrates was as powerful as this—if he had a strategem to constrain even the Storm King to his will— then should Miriamele somehow find her father and convince him to end the war, the red priest would still find some method to have things his own way.

No hope. It was strange to think about. As unlikely as their chances had seemed, Josua and his allies had always had the slim hope of the swords to cling to. If that was gone . . . Miriamele felt dizzy. It seemed she had walked through a familiar door only to find a chasm yawning just beyond the threshold.

"I was alive, but wounded and dazed. I was in a terrible place—no living man should have to visit the black, black places beneath Pryrates' tower. And to go upward would mean escaping *through* the tower, past Pryrates himself. I could not imagine succeeding at that. The only tiny scrap of luck I had was that he likely thought me dead. So I went . . . another way. Down."

Cadrach had to pause for a long moment and wipe the sweat from his pale face. It was not particularly warm in the cavern.

"When we were in the Wran," he suddenly said to

Miriamele, "I could not force myself to go down into the ghants' nest. That was because it was too much like ... like going into the tunnels below Hjeldin's Tower."

"You were here before?" She stared at him, her attention unwillingly held. "Here beneath the castle?"

"Yes, but not in the places you have been, the places I have followed you." He wiped at his forehead again. "Ransomer preserve me, I wish my escape had been through the parts of this vast maze you saw! The way I came was far worse." He tried to find words but gave up. "Far, far worse."

"Worse? Why?"

"No." Cadrach shook his head. "I will not tell you. There are many ways in and out of here, and not all of them are ... normal. I will speak no further on it, and if you could glimpse even a piece of what I saw, you would thank me for not telling you." He shivered. "But it felt like years that I was below the ground, and I saw and heard and felt things ... things that ..." He stopped, shaking his head again.

"Don't tell us, then. I don't believe you, in any case. How could you escape unnoticed? You said that Pryrates could find you, could summon you."

"I had—I still have—some little smatterings of the Art left to me. I was able to draw a ... a sort of fog over me. I have kept it since. That is why you were not summoned to Sesuad'ra as Tiamak and the others were. They could not find us."

"But why didn't that shield you from Pryrates before, when he summoned you—when you couldn't run away and had to spy and sneak for him like the worst sort of traitor in the world?" She was disgusted with herself for being drawn back into a discussion. She was even angrier that she had ever wasted her trust and concern on someone who could do what the monk had done. She had defended him to the world, but it was she who had been the fool. He was a traitor through and through.

"Because he thinks I am dead!" Cadrach almost shouted. "If he knew I lived, he would find me soon enough. He would blow my poor shielding fog away like a strong wind and I would be naked and helpless. By all the gods old and new, Miriamele, why do you think I was so determined to get off Aspitis' ship? As I slowly came to realize that he was one of Pryrates' servitors I could think of nothing but that he might tell his master I still lived. Aedon save us, why do you think when we met him again on the Lakelands I begged you to kill him?" He mopped more sweat from his face. "I can only guess that Pryrates did not recognize the name 'Cadrach,' although I had used it before. But I have used many names—even that red-robed demon could not know them all."

"So you were making your way to freedom through the tunnels," Binabik prompted. "*Kikkasut!* This place is indeed like our Mintahoq cave-city—most that is important happens beneath the rock."

"Freedom?" Cadrach almost sneered. "How could anyone be free who lived with the knowledge I did? Yes, I finally made my way up from the very deepest depths; I think I was quite mad by then. I headed north, away from Pryrates and the Hayholt, although at the time I had no idea of where I would go. I wound up finally in Naglimund, thinking that I would be safest in a place sworn to oppose Elias and his chief counselor. But it was soon apparent that Naglimund, too, would be' attacked and thrown down, so I took up the Lady Vorzheva's offer to accompany Miriamele south."

"You said you were not free because of the knowledge you had," said Miriamele slowly. "But you did not share that knowledge with anyone. That is perhaps the most wretched deed of all you have done, Cadrach. Fear of Pryrates might make you do terrible things, but to be free of him and still say nothing—while the rest of us have pondered and struggled and suffered and died . . ." She shook her head, trying to make her words reflect the chilly contempt she felt. "That I cannot forgive."

He looked at her without flinching. "Now you truly know me, Princess Miriamele."

A long silence fell, broken only by the faint singsong of the dwarrows muttering among themselves. Binabik was the one who ended it. "We have talked enough of these things. And I need time for pondering on what Cadrach has said. But something there is that is clear: Josua and the others search for Bright-Nail, and they have Thorn already. They plan to bring them here if they can, but they are knowing nothing of what this one says of Pryrates. If we were having no other reason for surviving and escaping, we now have one that is large." He made a close-fisted gesture. "But what is outside our door is the first thing that will prevent us. How will we be making an escape?"

"Or have we already lost the chance listening to Brother Cadrach's tale of treachery?" Miriamele took a breath. "There were a handful of Norns before—how long before there is an army?"

Binabik looked at Cadrach, but the monk had lowered his face into his hands.

"We must make an attempt at escaping. If only one of us can survive to bear the tale, then still it will be a victory."

"And even if all is lost," Miriamele said, "there will be some Norns who will not be around to see it. I would settle for even a victory like that." She meant it, she realized—and with that realization, a part of her seemed to turn cold and lifeless.

# 27

# Hammer of Pain

🔥

"**Prince Jiriki.** At last we meet." Josua bowed, then extended his left hand; the manacle he wore as a remembrance of imprisonment was a shadow on his wrist. The Sitha made a strangely-jointed bow of his own, then reached out his hand to clasp Josua's. Isgrimnur could not help marveling at such a strange scene.

"Prince Josua." The new-risen sun turned both Jiriki's white hair and the snow faintly golden. "Young Seoman told me much about you. Is he here?"

Josua frowned. "He is not, to my regret. There is much to say—much to tell you, and much we hope you can tell us." He looked up at the looming walls of the Hayholt, falsely welcoming in the dawn light. "I am not sure which of us should say to the other: 'Welcome home.' "

The Sitha smiled coldly. "This is not our home any more, Prince Josua."

"And I am not sure it is mine, either. But come, it is foolish to stand in the snow. Will you come and break your fast with us?"

Jiriki shook his head. "Thanks to you for your courtesy, but I think not yet." He looked back at the milling Sithi, who had fanned out across the hillside and were rapidly setting up camp, the first colorful tents blooming like snowflowers. "My mother Likimeya, I think, speaks with my sister; I, too, would like to spend a short time with Aditu. If you would be kind enough to come to my mother's tent by the time the sun is above the treeline, bringing those of your household you deem necessary, we will begin to talk. There is, as you said, much to tell."

The Sitha gave a sort of graceful salute, bowed again, then turned and moved away across the snow.

"That's cheek," Isgrimnur muttered. "Making you come to them."

"It *was* their castle first." Josua laughed quietly. "Even if they do not wish to reclaim it."

Isgrimnur grunted. "As long as they help us put the bastards out, I suppose we can go to their house for a visit." He squinted. "Now who's that?"

A solitary rider had crested the hilltop behind the Sithi encampment. He was taller and more solidly-built than the immortals, but he slumped wearily in the saddle.

"God be praised!" Isgrimnur breathed, then shouted for joy. "Isorn! *Hah*, Isorn!" He waved his arms. The rider looked up, then spurred his horse down the hill.

"Ah, Father," he said after he had dismounted and received a backbreaking embrace from the duke, "I cannot tell you how good it is to see you. This brave Hernystiri mount," he patted his gray horse, "kept up with the Sithi almost all the way from Naglimund. They ride so fast! But we fell behind at the end."

"No matter, no matter," Isgrimnur chortled. "I only wish your mother was not behind in Nabban. Bless you, son, it makes my heart glad to see you."

"Indeed," said Josua. "You are a happy sight. What of Eolair? What of Hernystir? Jiriki said but little."

Isorn made a weary bow. "Everything I can tell you I will, Josua. Is there something to eat here? And somewhat to drink, too?"

"Come." Isgrimnur put his arm about his tall son. "Let your old father lean on you for just a few minutes—I was smashed beneath my horse in Nabban, did you know? But I am not finished yet! We will all break fast together. Aedon has blessed us this morning."

The afternoon had turned dark and the wind had risen, clawing at the walls of the tent. Silent Sithi had put out shining globes of light which were now warming into full brightness like small suns.

Duke Isgrimnur was beginning to feel restless. His back was giving him no peace, and he had been sitting propped on cushions—and how *did* a war party of Sithi manage to carry cushions, he could not help wondering—so long that he did not think he could rise to his feet without help. Even the presence of Isorn sitting nearby was not enough to keep his thoughts from turning sour.

The Sithi had destroyed Skali and his men—that was the first news Isorn had given him. The immortals had brought the Thane of Kaldskryke's head back to Hernysadharc in a sack. Isgrimnur knew he should rejoice that the man who had stolen his dukedom and brought so much unhappiness to Rimmersgard and Hernystir was dead, but he felt mostly his own age and infirmity, as well as a certain angry shame. The revenge he had sworn so loudly at Naglimund had been taken by someone else. If he regained Elvritshalla, it would be because the Sithi had earned it for him. That did not sit well. The unhappy duke was having trouble paying attention to the things that seemed to fascinate Josua and the immortals.

"All this talk of Houses and Stars is very well," he said crossly, "but what exactly are we going to *do?*" He folded his arms across his broad chest. *Someone* had to hasten things along. These Sithi were like an army of golden-eyed Josuas, seemingly content to talk and ponder until The Day of Weighing-Out—but the reality of the Hayholt would not go away. "We have siege engines, if you know what those are. We can knock the gates down eventually, or maybe even burrow under the walls. But the Hayholt was built stronger than anything in Osten Ard, and it won't happen fast. In the meantime, your Conqueror Star is right overhead."

Likimeya, who Isgrimnur supposed was the queen of the Sithi, though no one seemed to call her by that title, turned her faintly serpentine gaze on him. It was all the Rimmersman could do to meet her stare.

*This one chills my blood. And I thought Aditu was strange.*

"You are correct, mortal. If our understanding, and the lore of your Scrollbearers is true, we have very little time." She turned to Josua. "We brought down Naglimund's walls in days—but that did not stop the Hikeda'ya from doing what they wished, or at least we do not think it did. We cannot afford to make that mistake here."

Prince Josua lowered his head, thinking. "But what else can we do? As Isgrimnur pointed out to me last night, we cannot fly over the walls."

"There are other ways into the castle you call the Hayholt," said Likimeya. The tall, black-haired Sitha beside her nodded. "We could not send an army in through those passages, nor would we wish to, but we can, and should, send a sufficient force. Ineluki has a hand in all this; he or your mortal enemies have doubtless made sure that these ways are guarded. But if we keep our foes' attention on what happens out here before the walls, we might succeed in getting a small troop inside."

"What 'other ways' do you mean?" Josua asked, frowning.

"Tunnels," said Camaris suddenly. "Ways in and out. John knew them. There is one on the cliffside below the Sea Gate." The old man had a slightly wild look, as though any moment he might begin raving again.

Likimeya nodded. The strings of polished stones braided into her hair clinked. "Just so—although I think we can choose a better entrance than the caves along the cliff. Do not forget, Prince Josua: Asu'a was ours once, and many of us were alive when it was still the great house of the Zida'ya. We know its hidden paths."

"The sword." Camaris rubbed his hand back and forth across Thorn's pommel. "It wants to go inside. It has been . . ." He broke off and fell silent. He had been strangely subdued through the entire day, but Isgrimnur could not help noticing that he seemed less daunted by the Sithi than any of the other mortals assembled in Likimeya's tent. Even Tiamak and Strangyeard, students of old lore, sat wide-eyed and silent except when forced into stammering speech.

Outside, the wind grew louder.

"That is another, and perhaps the most important, mystery," said Jiriki. "Your brother has one Great Sword, Prince Josua. This mortal knight, Sir Camaris, has another. Where is the third?"

Josua shook his head. "As I told you, it is gone from my father's barrow."

"And how will they serve us if we bring them all together?" Jiriki finished. "Still, it seems that Camaris must be one of those we send beneath the walls. We cannot afford the chance that we would gain the other two swords and have this black blade left outside." He steepled his long fingers. "I regret more than ever the fact that Eolair and I could not find the Tinukeda'ya of Mezutu'a—those you call dwarrows. They know more of sword-lore and forging than anyone, and they certainly made Minneyar. There is doubtless much they could have told us."

"Send in Camaris? Through some underground caverns?" Josua seemed more than dubious—there was an edge almost of despair to his words. "We face perhaps the greatest battle that Osten Ard has seen—certainly, it seems, one of the most important—and you say that we should send away our greatest warrior?" As Josua looked over to the old knight, Isgrimnur saw again the discomfort he had sensed earlier. What had Camaris told him?

"But surely you can see the sense of what my brother says, Prince Josua." Aditu had been almost deferentially silent through the afternoon. "If all the signs, if all the dreams and rumors and whispered lore are true, then it is the Great Swords that will thwart Ineluki's plan, not men—or even immortals—battling before the gates of the castle. That has been the wisdom by which you have planned everything."

"So because Thorn belongs to Camaris, he and he alone can take it inside? And not through the gate or over the walls with the army behind him, but like a sneak thief?"

"Thorn does not belong to me." Camaris seemed to be

struggling just to speak slowly and rationally. "Methinks it is the other way around. Merciful Aedon, let me go, Josua. I doubt I can wait much longer before this thing drives me mad."

Josua looked at the old knight for a long time; something unspoken passed between them. "Perhaps there is sense in what you all say," the prince admitted at last. "But it will be a hard thing to lose Camaris...." He paused. "To lose him for the coming battle. It will be hard on the men. They feel invincible when they follow him."

"Perhaps they should not know that he is gone," Aditu said.

Josua turned, startled. "What? How would we hide such a thing?"

"I think my sister has spoken wisely," said Jiriki. "If we hope to have a chance to send Sir Camaris into your brother's castle—and he will not be alone, Josua; there will be Zida'ya with him who know those places—but we do not wish to blow a trumpet and announce that we have done that, we must make it seem that Camaris is still here, even once the full siege has begun."

"The siege? But if our only hope is the swords and our true stroke is this company that we send in through your secret ways, what point is there in throwing away the lives of others?" the prince demanded angrily. "Are you saying we should sacrifice men in a bloody siege that we already know is starting too late to achieve success?"

Likimeya leaned forward. "We must sacrifice men and Zida'ya both." Isgrimnur caught a flicker in her amber stare that seemed almost like regret, or pain, but he dismissed it. He could not believe one so stern, so alien, felt anything but cool necessity. "Otherwise, we announce to our enemies that we have other hopes. We shout to them that we are waiting for some other stratagem to take effect."

"Why?" Isgrimnur could see that Josua was truly agonized. "Any sensible war-leader knows it is better practice to starve out a foe than to waste men's lives on thick stone walls."

"You are camped beside the Zida'ya. Those who are

even now watching from behind those stone walls have made compact with Ineluki. Some may even be our kin, the Hikeda'ya. They will know that the Dawn Children see the red star in the sky overhead. The Conqueror Star, as you call it, tells us that we have only a few days at most, that whatever your mortal sorcerer plans to do on Ineluki's behalf must happen soon. If we appear to ignore that fact, we will fool no one. We must launch the siege immediately, and your people and ours must fight as though we have no other hope. And who knows? Perhaps we do not. Not all tales end happily, Prince Josua. We Gardenborn know that all too well."

Josua turned to Isgrimnur as if for support. "So we send our finest warrior, who is also our greatest inspiration, down into the earth. And we throw away the lives of our fighting men on a siege that we know cannot succeed. Duke Isgrimnur, have I gone mad? Is this all that is left to us?"

The Rimmersman shrugged helplessly. It was dreadful to watch Josua's honest torment. "What the Sithi-folk say makes sense. I'm sorry, Josua. It galls me, too."

The prince lifted his hand in a gesture of resignation. "Then I will do as you all say. Since my brother took the throne, I have been faced with horror after horror. It seems, as one of my teachers once told me, that God shapes us with a hammer of pain on an anvil of duty. I cannot imagine what shape we will be when He is finished." He sat back, waving to the others to continue. "Make certain only that Camaris is well-defended. He carries the one thing we have that we did not already possess when my brother and the Storm King broke Naglimund—and we have lost much else since then."

Isgrimnur looked at the old knight. Camaris was lost in thought, his eyes fixed on nothing visible, his lips moving.

※

The king was lurking in the passageway above the entrance to the forge. The soldiers, already nervous, startled when they saw the cloaked shape lurch forward out of the shadows. One of them even went so far as to draw his sword before Pryrates barked at him to put up; Elias, though, seemed oblivious to what would normally be a fatal error for a young guardsman.

"Pryrates," the king rasped. "I have been searching and searching. Where is my cupbearer? My throat is so dry. . . ."

"I will help you, Majesty." The priest turned his coal-black stare on the gawking soldiers, who quickly shifted their eyes sideways or down to their own chests. "The captain will take these men back to the walls. We are finished here." He waved them away with a flapping red sleeve.

When the noise of their footfalls grew faint in the corridor, Pryrates gently took the king's arm so that Elias could lean on him. The king's staring face was parchment-white, and he licked at his lips constantly.

"Did you say you had seen my cupbearer?"

"I will take care of you, Majesty. I think we will not see Hengfisk again."

"Has he . . . has he run away to . . . them?" Elias cocked his head as though treachery might have a sound. "They are all around the walls. You must know. I can feel them. My brother, and those bright-eyed creatures . . ." He pawed at his mouth. "You said they would be destroyed, Pryrates. You said all that resisted me would be destroyed."

"And so they will be, my king." The priest induced Elias to walk down the hallway, heading him through the maze of corridors toward the residences. They passed an open window where snow blew in and melted into puddles on the floor: outside, Green Angel Tower loomed against the swirling storm clouds. "You yourself will destroy them and usher in the Golden Age."

"And then the pain will go away," Elias wheezed. "I would not hate Josua so if he had not brought me such pain. If he had not stolen my daughter, too. He *is* my brother, after all . . ." the king clenched his teeth as though something had stabbed him, ". . . because family is blood. . . ."

"And blood is powerful magic," Pryrates said, half to himself. "I know, my king. But they turned against you. That is why I found you new friends—powerful friends."

"But you cannot replace a family," said Elias, a little sadly. He winced. "Ah, God, Pryrates, I am burning up. Where is that cupbearer?"

"A little farther, Majesty. Just a little farther."

"I can feel it, you know," Elias panted. He lay back on his mattress, which had rotted through in so many places that the horsehair stuck up all around him. A stained goblet, now empty, was clutched in his hand.

Pryrates paused in the doorway. "Feel what, Majesty?"

"The star, the red star." Elias pointed at the cobwebbed ceiling. "It is hanging overhead, staring at me like an eye. I hear the singing all the time."

"Singing?"

"The song it sings—or that the sword sings to the star. I cannot tell which." His hand fell and crawled like a white spider onto the long sheath. "It sings in my head. 'It is time, it is time,' the voices say, over and over." He laughed, a cracked, jagged sound. "Sometimes I awaken to find myself walking through the castle and I cannot remember how I came there. But I hear the song, and I feel the star burning into me whether it is day or night. It has a fiery tail, like a dragon. . . ." He paused. "I will go out to them."

"What!?" Pryrates returned to the king's bedside.

"I will go out to them—Josua and the others. Perhaps that is the time the sword means. Time to show them that I am different than they know. That their resistance is foolish." He brought his hands to his face. "They are . . . they are my blood, Pryrates."

"Your Highness, I . . ." The priest seemed momentarily unsure. "They are your enemies, Elias. They wish you only harm."

The king's laugh was almost a sob. "And you mean me only well, is that right? That is why every night since you took me to that hill I have suffered dreams that God would not visit upon sinners in Hell? That is why my body aches and burns until I can barely keep from screaming out loud?"

Pryrates frowned. "You have suffered, my king, but you know the reason. The hour is coming fast. Do not let your torments be for nothing."

Elias waved his hand. "Go away. I do not wish to talk any more. I will do what I think best. I am the master of this castle—of this land." He gestured violently. "Go away, damn you. I am in pain."

The alchemist bowed. "I pray you can rest, Majesty. I will go."

Pryrates left the king staring up into the shadows of the ceiling.

After standing silently in the corridor for long moments, the priest returned to the closed door and passed his hand over hinges and frame and door latch several times, mouth working soundlessly. When he had finished he nodded, then went briskly up the corridor, bootheels clicking.

Tiamak and Strangyeard walked close together as they made their way down the hillside. Snow was no longer falling, but it was piled high on the ground; they made slow progress despite the comparatively short distance between the Sithi camp and the fires of the prince's army.

"I am going to turn to ice in a moment," Tiamak said through clicking teeth. "How do your people live like this?"

Strangyeard was shivering, too. "This is a terrible cold by any measurement. And we have thick walls to hide behind, and fires—the lucky ones do, that is." He stumbled and went down on his knees in a thick drift. Tiamak helped him back up. The bottom half of the priest's robe was covered in clinging snow. "I am tempted to curse," Strangyeard said, and laughed unmerrily; his breath hovered as a cloud.

"Come, lean on me," urged Tiamak. The priest's disarranged hair and sad face tugged at his heart. "One day you must come see the Wran. It is not all pleasant, but it is never cold."

"Just n–now that sounds very n–n–nice."

The storm clouds had been borne away by the wind, and a salting of dim stars glimmered. Tiamak stared upward. "It looks so close."

Strangyeard followed his gaze, stumbled for a moment, then righted himself. The Conqueror Star seemed to hang almost directly over the Hayholt, a burning hole in the darkness with a tail like a smear of blood. "It is close," the priest said. "I can feel it. Plesinnen wrote that such stars spout bad air over the world. Until n–now, I was never sure whether I believed him—but if there was ever a star that dripped p–pestilence, that is it." He hugged himself. "I sometimes wonder if these are the final days, Tiamak."

The marsh man did not want to think about that. "All the stars here are a little strange. I keep thinking that I recognize the Otter or the Sand Beetle, but they seem stretched and changed."

Strangyeard squinted his single eye. "The stars look odd to me, too." He shivered and lowered his gaze to the knee-high snow. "I am frightened, Tiamak."

They staggered on toward the camp, side by side.

"The worst of it," said Tiamak, holding his hands close to the fire, "is that we have no better answer to our questions than we did when Morgenes sent the first sparrow to Jarnauga. The Storm King's plan is a complete puzzle, and so is the one scheme we have to stop him." The small tent was filling with smoke despite the opening near the top, but at this moment Tiamak did not care; as a matter of fact, it felt somewhat homelike.

"That is not completely true." Strangyeard coughed and waved away some of the smoke. "We know a few things—that Minneyar is Bright-Nail, for one."

"But that Hernystirman had to come tell us that," Tiamak said crossly. "You need not feel bad, Strangyeard.

From what I heard, you did much to help them locate Thorn. But I have done little to warrant being a member of the League of the Scroll."

"You are too hard on yourself," the archivist said. "You brought the page of Nisses' book that helped bring back Camaris."

"Have you looked into his eyes, Strangyeard? Was that anything other than a curse to him? And now it seems he is losing those wits all over again. We should have left him alone."

The priest stood. "Forgive me, but this smoke ..." He pulled the tent flap open and fanned vigorously. A blast of cold air pushed much of the smoke back inside and set them both to shivering anew. "I'm sorry," he said miserably.

Tiamak gestured for him to sit down. "It is a little better. My eyes are not stinging so." He sighed. "And this talk of a Fifth House—did you see how worried the Sithi looked? They may have said they did not know what it meant, but I believe they knew something. They did not like it." The Wrannaman shrugged his thin shoulders; he had already learned from Aditu that what the Sithi did not want to discuss remained a secret. They were polite, but could be stubbornly vague when they wished. "It matters little, I suppose. The siege begins tomorrow morning, and Camaris and the others will try to make their way inside, and whatever They Who Watch and Shape decide will happen ... it will happen."

Strangyeard stared at him, his unpatched eye redrimmed and watery. "You do not seem to get much solace from your Wran gods, Tiamak."

"They are mine," the marsh man said. "I doubt yours would bring me any greater peace." He looked up, and was startled by the archivist's pained expression. "Oh! I am sorry, Strangyeard. I did not mean to be insulting. I am just angry ... and frightened, like you."

*Please, let me not lose my friends. Then I would have nothing at all!*

"Of course," the archivist said, then sighed. "And I am no different than you. I cannot escape the feeling that

something important is just before me—some simple
thing, as you mentioned. I can feel its presence, but I cannot grasp it." He stared at his knit hands. "It is infuriating. There is some obvious mistake we have made, or will
make, I am certain. It is as though I looked back and forth
through a well-known book, looking for a page I have often read, but now I cannot find it." He sighed again. "It
is no wonder we are neither of us very happy, my friend."

Tiamak warmed briefly at the word 'friend,' but then
felt his sorrow return. "Something else is worrying me,
too," he told the archivist.

"What is that?" Strangyeard leaned over and tugged the
door flap open for a moment, then let it fall shut.

"I have realized that I must go down into the deeps
with Camaris and the others."

"What? Blessed Elysia, Tiamak, what do you mean?
You are no warrior."

"Exactly. And neither Camaris nor any of the Sithi
have read Morgenes' book, or studied the archives at
Naglimund, as you did, nor shared the wisdom of
Jarnauga and Dinivan and Valada Geloë. But someone
who has must go—otherwise, what if the people of this
raiding party secure the swords and cannot guess how to
use them? We will not get a second chance."

"Oh! Well, then ... mercy! I suppose I should go,
since I have had the most time to study these things of
anyone remaining."

"Yes, Strangyeard, my good drylander friend, of all of
us, you know the most about the swords. But you have
only one eye, and the sight in that one is not good. And
you are many years older than I am, and not so used to
climbing and getting in and out of tight places. If Binabik
of Yiqanuc were here, I would let him go and wish him
well, since he is more learned in these things than I, and
at least as capable in other ways—not to mention the least
likely to get stuck in a narrow tunnel of any of us."
Tiamak wagged his head sadly. "But Binabik is gone, and
the wisewoman Geloë is gone, and all the old
Scrollbearers are dead. So it falls to me, I think. You have
taught me much in a short time, Strangyeard." He let out

another heartfelt sigh. "I have evil dreams still about being in the ghant nest, of the pictures I saw in my head, of hearing my own voice clacking away in the dark. But I fear this may be worse."

After a long silence, the priest went and pawed through his belongings, coming back at last with a skin bag. "Here. This is a strong drink made from berries. Jarnauga brought it with him to Naglimund: he said it was a shield against the cold." He laughed nervously. "Cold we certainly have, don't we? Try a little." He passed Tiamak the sack.

The liquor was sweet and fiery. Tiamak swallowed, then took another swig. He passed the bag back to Strangyeard. "It is good, but strange-tasting. I am used to sour fern beer. Try some."

"Oh, I think it too potent for me," the priest stammered. "I wanted you . . ."

"A little will help to keep out the chill—perhaps it will even help set free that elusive thought you spoke of."

Strangyeard hesitated, then lifted the sack to his lips. He took a tiny sip and worked it around his mouth, then took a little more. Tiamak was pleased to see he did not choke. "It's . . . hot," the priest said, wonderingly.

"It feels that way, does it not?" The Wrannaman sank back against one of the priest's saddlebags. "Have another, then pass it to me again. I will need more than a few swallows before I work up the nerve to tell Josua what I have decided."

The sack was mostly empty. Tiamak had heard the sentries change outside, and knew it must be near midnight. "I should go," he said. He listened to the words as he formed them, and was proud of how well-articulated they were. "I should go because I need to tell Prince Josua what I will do."

"What you will do, yes." Strangyeard was holding the wineskin by its cord strap and watching it swing back and forth. "That is good."

"So in a moment I will get up," Tiamak pointed out.

"I wish Geloë were here."

"Geloë? Here?" Tiamak frowned. "Drinking this Rimmersgard liquor?"

"No. Well, I suppose." Strangyeard reached up his free hand and set the skin swinging again. "Here to talk to us. She was a wise one. Frightening, a little—didn't she frighten you? Those eyes . . ." His forehead creased as he remembered Geloë's alarming stare. "But solid. Reassuring."

"Of course. We miss her." He got unsteadily to his feet. "Terrible thing."

"Why did those . . . things do it?" the priest wondered.

"Kill Geloë?"

"No, Camaris." Strangyeard carefully placed the skin on top of a blanket. "Why did they kill Camaris? No." He smiled, abashed. "I mean . . . why did they *try* to kill Camaris? Just him. Doesn't make sense."

"They wanted to take the sword. Thorn."

"Ah," Strangyeard replied. "Ah. P'raps so."

Tiamak struggled out through the tent flap. The chilly air was like a blow. He looked over at the priest, who had followed him out. "Where are you going?"

"With you," Strangyeard said matter-of-factly. "Tell Josua I'm going, too. Down in the tunnels."

"No, you're not." Tiamak was firm. "That would be a bad idea. I told you before."

"I'll come with you anyway. To talk with him." The priest's teeth were already chattering. "Can't let you walk in the cold by yourself." He staggered a few steps, then stopped, peering upward, and frowned broadly. "Look at that red star. Mad thing. Causing all this trouble. The stars should leave us alone." He raised his fist. "We're not afraid!" he called to the distant spot of light. "Not afraid!"

"You drank too much," Tiamak said as he took the archivist's elbow.

Strangyeard bobbed his head. "I might have done."

✦

Josua watched the archivist and the Wrannaman lurch out of his tent and into the night, then turned to Isgrimnur. "I would never have believed it."

"A drunken priest?" The duke yawned despite the tension that roiled his stomach. "That's nothing strange." There was a dull pressure behind his eyes. It was past the middle of the night, and the next day promised to be something dreadful. He needed sleep.

"Perhaps, but a drunken Strangyeard?" Josua shook his head slowly. "I think that Tiamak is right about going, though—and he is, from what you've told me, a useful fellow."

"Wiry as a hound," Isgrimnur said.. "Brave, too, and so well-spoken I'm still not used to it. I'll confess, I didn't think marsh men were that learned. Camaris could do far worse than to take Tiamak, even with his limp. That was a cockindrill bit him there, did you know?"

Josua's mind was on other things. "So that is two of our mortal contingent." He rubbed his temple. "I cannot think any more—it feels like three days have passed since this morning's sun rose. We will begin the siege tomorrow, and tomorrow evening will be time enough to make the final decision on who shall go." He rose and looked almost with tenderness at Camaris, who was stretched full-length on a pallet at the far side of the tent, moving fitfully in his sleep. The squire Jeremias, who seemed to attach himself to troubled folk, was curled up on a pile of blankets near the old knight's feet.

"Can you find your way back?" Josua asked the duke. "Take the lantern."

"I'll find my way right enough. Isorn will be up telling tales with Sludig and the rest, I have no doubt." He yawned again. "Wasn't there a time when we could stay up all night drinking, then fight in the morning, then start drinking all over again?"

"Maybe for you, Uncle Isgrimnur," Josua said with a tiny smile. "Never for me. God grant you good rest tonight."

Isgrimnur grunted, then picked up the lamp and made

his way out of the tent, leaving Josua standing in its center, staring at the sleeping Camaris.

Outside the storm clouds had dispersed. The stars spread a faint light over the Hayholt's silent walls. The Conqueror Star seemed to hang just above Green Angel Tower like a flame above a candle.

*Go away, you cursed, ill-omened thing,* he demanded, but he knew that it would not comply.

Shivering in the chill, he stumped slowly through the snow toward his tent.

"Jeremias! Boy! *Wake up!*"

The young squire sat up, fighting his way out of sleep. "What?"

Josua stood over him, half-dressed. "He's gone. He's been gone far too long." The prince snatched up his sword belt and leaned to pluck his cloak from the floor. "Put on your boots and come help me."

"What? Who's gone, Prince Josua?"

"Camaris, curse it, Camaris! Come and help me. No, rouse Isgrimnur and find some men to help. Have them bring torches."

The prince took a brand from the fire, then turned and pushed out through the door flap. He looked down at the snow, trying to make some sense out of the muddle of footprints. At last he chose a set of tracks that led downhill toward the Kynslagh. Within moments he was beyond the light of the few campfires still burning. The moon had vanished from the sky, but the Conqueror Star still burned like a signal beacon.

The trail twisted erratically, but within half a furlong it was clear that the footprints had turned toward the cliffs east of the Hayholt's seawall. Josua looked up to see a pale figure moving along the edge of the shoreline, silhouetted against the wall of empty blackness that was the Kynslagh.

*"Camaris!"* Josua called. The figure did not stop, but moved along unsteadily toward the edge, lurching like a

puppet with knotted strings. The prince began to run, floundering in the deep snow, then slowed as he reached the cliffs. "Camaris," he said, his voice deceptively calm. "Where are you going?"

The old man turned to look at him. He wore no cloak, and his loose shirt flapped in the wind. Even seen by starlight there was something odd in his posture.

"It is Josua." The prince lifted his arms as though to embrace the old man. "Come back with me. We will sit by the fire and talk."

Camaris stared as though the words were animal noises, then began to make his way down the rocks. Josua hastened forward.

"Stop! Camaris, where are you going?" He scrambled over the edge, struggling to keep his balance on the muddy slope. "Come back with me."

The old knight whirled and pulled Thorn from its scabbard. Although he seemed fearfully confused, he handled the sword with unthinking mastery. His horn Cellian dangled on its baldric, drawing Josua's eye as it swung back and forth. "It is time," Camaris whispered. He was barely audible above the waves that slapped on the shore below.

"You cannot do this." Josua reached out his hand. "We are not ready. You must wait until the others can go with you." He advanced a few slithering steps down the slope. "Come back."

Camaris abruptly swung the sword in a wide, flat arc; it was nearly invisible in the darkness, but it hissed as it passed the prince's chest.

"Aedon's Blood, Camaris, do you not recognize me?" Josua took a step back. The old man raised the sword for another stroke.

"It is *time!*" he said, and swung, this time with deadly aim.

Josua threw himself backward. His feet skidded from beneath him and he whirled his arms for a moment, struggling for balance, then fell and tumbled down the slope, through long grasses and over mud and stones, landing at last in a drift of dirty snow where he lay for long moments, wheezing in pain.

"Prince Josua?!" A head appeared at the top of the rise. "Are you down there?"

Josua dragged himself onto his feet. Camaris had made his way down to the bottom of the hill and onto the beach. Now he was a ghostly shape moving along the cliff face. "I'm here," he called to Jeremias. "Damn it, where is the duke!?"

"He's coming, but I don't see him yet," the youth said excitedly. "I ran back after I told him. Shall I come down and help you? Are you hurt?"

Josua turned and saw Camaris hesitating before one of the black openings in the cliff wall. A moment later he vanished into the hole. "No!" Josua shouted, then called up to Jeremias: "Get Isgrimnur, make him hurry! Tell him Camaris has gone into one of the caves down here—I will mark which one! We will lose him if we wait any longer. I am going to bring him out."

"You ... you ..." The squire was confused. "You're going to follow him?"

"Damn me, I can't let him go down there himself—he is mad. Aedon knows what—he might fall, be lost ... I will bring him back somehow, even if I have to outfight him myself and carry him back on my shoulder. But for God's sake, tell Isgrimnur to hurry with the torches and men. Go on, boy, run!"

Jeremias hesitated a moment longer, then vanished from the prince's sight. Josua crawled the short distance to where his torch lay sputtering on a muddy outcropping, then clambered down the slope to the beach. He quickly made his way to the place where Camaris had disappeared and found a cave mouth little different than any of the others along the cliff. Josua grabbed several stones and piled them next to the opening, then stepped in, holding the torch before him.

Isgrimnur stared at the soldiers. "What do you mean, gone?"

The man looked back at him, half-apologetic and half-defensive. "Just that, Duke Isgrimnur. The hole splits off, goes different ways. We thought we saw some marks, like from a torch-end, up on the walls, but we didn't find anybody that way. We searched the other passages, too. It's like wormholes in there, tunnels everywhere."

"And you shouted?"

"Called the prince's name loud as we could. Nobody called back."

Isgrimnur stared at the gap in the cliff wall, then looked at Sludig. "Ransomer preserve us," he groaned. "Both gone. We'll have to get the Sithi after them now." He turned to the soldier. "I'll be back before sunrise. Until then, keep looking and calling."

The man nodded. "Yes, sire."

Isgrimnur pulled at his beard for a moment, then began making his way back along the beach. "Oh, Josua," he said quietly. "You fool. And me, too. We've all been fools."

# 28

# Abandoned Ways

❧

**Binabik touched** her arm. "Miriamele, what are you thinking?"

"I'm trying to think of what we can do." Her head was pounding. The shadowed cavern seemed to be closing in. "We have to get out, somehow. We have to. I don't want to be trapped in here." She caught her breath and looked at Cadrach huddled against the wall on the far side of the cavern. "How could he do such things, Binabik? How could he betray us all that way?"

"He was not knowing you then," the troll pointed out. "So he could not be thinking that it was you he was betraying."

"But he didn't tell us afterward! He didn't tell us anything! All that time we were together."

Binabik lowered his head. "It is done. Now we must be thinking on other things." He gestured to the dwarrows, who were seated in a circle, singing quietly. "They are thinking the Norns come soon, they have said to me. Already the ward is crumbling. The door will not hold for a much lengthier time."

"And they're just going to sit and wait," said Miriamele bitterly. "I can't understand them any more than I can understand Cadrach." She stood and walked past the troll. "Yis-fidri! Why are you mooning around like this when the Norns are outside? Don't you understand what will happen to us?" She heard her voice rising shrilly, but she did not care.

The dwarrows stared up apprehensively, mouths agape.

Miriamele thought they looked like a nestful of baby birds. "We are waiting . . ." he began.

"Waiting! That's just it, you're waiting." She quivered with anger. They were all waiting for those fishbelly-white things to come in and take them—take her and the troll, too. "Then let's open the door now. Why put it off any longer? Binabik and I will fight to win free and probably be killed—killed because you brought us here to this trap against our will—and you will sit and be slaughtered. So there is no sense waiting any longer."

Yis-fidri goggled. "But . . . perhaps they will go. . . ."

"You don't believe that! Come, open the door!" Her fear beat higher, rising like storm-tossed waves. She leaned down and grabbed the dwarrow's long wrist in her hand and tugged. He was as unmovable as stone. "Get up, damn you!" she shouted, and yanked as hard as she could. Alarmed, the dwarrows burbled at each other. Yis-fidri's eyes widened in consternation; with a flick of his powerful arm he dislodged Miriamele's grip. She fell back on the cavern floor, breathless.

"Miriamele!" Binabik hurried to her side. "Are you hurt?"

She shook off the troll's helping hand and sat up. "There!" she said triumphantly. "Yis-fidri, you didn't tell the truth."

The dwarrow stared at her as though she had begun to foam at the mouth. He curled his flat fingers protectively against his chest.

"You didn't," she said, and stood. "You will push *me* away to keep me from forcing you against your will, so why not the Norns? Do you want to die, then? Because the Norns will certainly kill you, kill me, kill us all. Or perhaps they will make you slaves again—is that what you are hoping for? Why do you resist me and not resist them?"

Yis-fidri turned briefly to his wife; she stared back at him, silent and solemn-eyed. "But there is naught we can do." The dwarrow seemed to be pleading for Miriamele's understanding.

"There is *always* something you can do," she snapped.

"It may not change anything, but you will have tried. You are strong, Yis-fidri—you dwarrow-folk are very strong, and you can do many things: I watched your wife shaping stone. Maybe you have always run away before, but now there is nowhere left to hide. Stand with us, damn you!"

Yis-hadra said something in the dwarrow tongue, which brought a murmuring but swift reply from others in the group. Yis-fidri entered in, then for a long time the dwarrows argued among themselves, voices rushing and burbling like water chiming on stone.

At last Yis-hadra rose. "I will stand with you," she said. "You speak rightly. There is nowhere left to run, and we are almost the last of our kind. If we die, no one then will be left to tend and harvest the stone, no one to find the beautiful things in the earth. That would be a shame." She turned to her husband and again spoke rapidly to him. After a moment, Yis-fidri lidded his huge eyes.

"I will do as my wife does," he said with obvious reluctance. "But we do not speak for our fellow Tinukeda'ya."

"Then speak *to* them," Miriamele urged. "There is so little time!"

Yis-fidri hesitated, then nodded. The other dwarrows looked on, their strange faces fearful.

Miriamele crouched in blackness, her heart thudding. She could see nothing at all, but apparently enough light was still bleeding from the crystal batons to allow the dwarrows to see: Miriamele could hear them padding back and forth across the cavern as unhesitatingly as she herself would walk through a lamplit room.

She reached out to touch the small but reassuring shape of Binabik crouched beside her. "I'm frightened," she whispered.

"As who is not?" She felt him pat her hand.

Miriamele had opened her mouth to say something else when a slight sensation of movement passed through the stone behind her. At first she thought it was the strange shifting she had felt earlier, the thing that had so frightened Yis-hadra and the other dwarrows, but then a faint blue glow sprang up in the empty black where the door stood. It was not like any light she had seen, for it illuminated nothing else; it was only a pulsing sky-blue streak hanging in the darkness.

"They're coming," she gurgled. Her heart raced even more swiftly. All her brave words now seemed foolish. On the far side of Binabik, she heard Cadrach's harsh breathing grow louder. She half-expected him to cry out, to try to shout a warning to the Norns. She did not believe his claim that he had no Art that would help them against the Norns, nor even the strength left now to use those few skills he retained.

The blue line lengthened. A warm wind pushed through the chamber, tangible as a slap to her heightened senses. For the dozenth time since the dwarrows had darkened the cavern she tugged at the straps of her pack and wiped sweat from the handle of her dagger. She also clutched Simon's White Arrow; if the Norns grabbed her, she would stab at them with both hands. A shudder ran through her. The Norns. The White Foxes. They were only moments away....

Yis-fidri said something quiet but emphatic in the dwarrow tongue. Yis-hadra replied in the same tone from somewhere across the cavern. The sound of moving dwarrows ceased. The chamber was silent as a grave.

The blue gleam grew in a rough oval until one end of the line met the other. For a moment the heat became greater, then the glow faded. Something scraped and then fell heavily. A rush of cold air swept into the chamber, but if the door had opened, no light came through.

*Curse them!* Despair swept over her. *They are too clever to come in with torches.* She clutched her knife tighter: she was shaking so violently she feared she might drop it.

Suddenly there was a booming rumble like thunder and a high-pitched shout that came from no human throat. Miriamele's heart leaped. The great stones the dwarrows had loosened above the cavern door were tumbling down—she could hear the Norns' high-pitched, angry wailing. Another crash was followed by a scraping, grinding noise, then many voices were shouting, none of them in human languages. After a moment Miriamele felt her eyes begin to sting. She took a breath and felt it burn all the way down.

"Up!" Binabik cried. "It is poison-smoke!"

Miriamele struggled to her feet, lost in the dark and feeling as though her insides were on fire. A powerful hand gripped her and led her stumbling through the blackness. The cavern was raucous with strange cries and shrieks and the sound of smashing stone.

The next moments were blind madness. She felt herself pulled through into chilly air; within moments she could breathe again, although she still could not see. The hand that held her let go, and a moment later she caught her foot on something and crashed to the ground.

"*Binabik!*" she shouted. She tried to rise, but something had entangled her. "Where are you!?"

Miriamele was seized again, but this time was lifted bodily and carried swiftly through the noisy darkness. Something struck her a glancing blow. For a moment whoever was carrying her stopped and put her down; there was a succession of strange noises, some of them grunts or gasps of pain, then a moment later she was snatched up again.

At last she touched down again on the hard stone. The darkness was absolute. "Binabik?" she called.

There was a spark nearby, then a flash. For a moment she saw the troll standing beside a cavern wall in the midst of darkness with his hand full of flame. Then he flung whatever he held outward, and it scattered in a shower of sputtering sparks. Tiny flames burned everywhere. Frozen as if painted on a tapestry were Binabik, several dwarrows, and almost a dozen other shadowy figures, all scattered about a long, high-ceilinged cavern. The stone door that had protected them lay in pieces behind her at the far end of this outer cavern.

She had scarcely an instant to marvel at the effect of the troll's fire-starting powder before a pale-faced shape raced toward her, long knife held high. Miriamele lifted her own blade, but her ankles seemed bound somehow and she could not get her feet beneath her. The knife lashed toward Miriamele's face, but the blade stopped abruptly a hand's length from her eyes.

The dwarrow that had caught the creature's arm jerked upward. There was a sound of something snapping; a moment later the Norn was pitched headfirst across the chamber.

"Go that way," Yis-fidri gasped, pointing toward a dark hole at the near end of the cavern. In the faint, flickering light he looked even more grotesque than the enemy he had dispatched: one of his arms hung limply, and the broken shaft of an arrow wagged in his shoulder. The dwarrow flinched as another arrow shattered against the cavern wall beside him.

Miriamele reached down and disentangled her feet from what had held them—a Norn bow. Its owner lay a few paces away, just inside the entrance to the dwarrow's hiding place; a thick shard of rock jutted from his crushed chest.

"Move quickly, quickly," said Yis-fidri. "We have surprised them, but there may be more coming." His brisk tones could not hide his terror; his saucer eyes seemed to bulge. One of the other dwarrows threw a stone at the Norn archer. The motion was awkward, but the missile flew so swiftly that the white-faced immortal staggered backward before the dwarrow's arm had finished moving, then crumpled to the cavern floor.

"Run!" Binabik called. "Before more archers are coming!"

Miriamele rushed after him into the tunnel mouth, still clutching the bow. She stooped on the run to pick up a few scattered Norn arrows. She put Simon's arrow through her belt for safekeeping, and nocked one of the black arrows; as she did so, she looked back. Yis-fidri and the other dwarrows were backing after her, keeping their frightened eyes fixed on the Norns. These inched along behind them, staying out of the dwarrows' long reach, but obviously not intending to let them escape so easily. Despite the carnage, the half-dozen bodies lying scattered in the outer chamber and the breached doorway, the Norns seemed as calm and unhurried as hunting insects.

Miriamele turned and hastened her pace. Binabik had lit a torch, and she followed its light down the uneven tunnel.

"They're still following!" she panted.

"Run, then, until we find a better place for fighting," the troll called back. "Where is the monk Cadrach?"

"Don't know," Miriamele said.

*And maybe it would be better for everyone if he died back there.* The thought felt cruel but just. *Better for everyone.*

She raced along after the bobbing torch.

"Josua is gone?" Isorn was stunned. "But how could he risk himself, even for Camaris?"

Isgrimnur did not know how to answer his son's question. He tugged fiercely at his beard, trying to think clearly. "Still, there it is," he said. He stared around the tent at the rest of the unhappy faces. "I have had soldiers hunting all through the caves for hours with no luck. The Sithi are preparing to go after the two of them, and Tiamak will accompany them. There is nothing more we can do about it." He blew out, fluttering his mustache. "Yes, damn me, Josua has hamstrung us, but now more than ever we must make sure we distract Elias. We can't waste tears."

Sludig peered out through the door flap. "It is nearly dawn, Duke Isgrimnur. And snowing again. The men know something strange has happened—they are growing restless. We should decide what to do, my lord."

The duke nodded. Inwardly he cursed the fate that had dropped Josua's command into his lap. "We will do what we planned. All that has changed from yesterday's council is that Josua is gone. So we will need not one mimic, but two."

"I am ready," Isorn said. "I have Camaris' surcoat, and see," he pulled his sword from its scabbard: blade and hilt

were shiny black, "a little paint and it becomes Thorn."
He caught Isgrimnur's discomfited look. "Father, you
agreed to this and nothing has changed. Of all who can be
trusted with the secret, only I am nearly tall enough to
pass as Camaris."

The duke frowned. "It is so. But because you pretend
to be Camaris, don't believe you *are* Camaris: you need
to stay alive and on your horse so you can be seen. Take
no foolish chances."

Isorn flashed him an unhappy glance, angry after all his
experiences to be treated like a child. Isgrimnur almost
regretted his fatherly worry—almost, but not quite. "So
then. Who shall mime Josua?"

"Are there any that can fight with their left hands?"
Sludig asked.

"S'right," said Freosel. "None'll believe Josua with a
right hand."

Isgrimnur felt his frustration growing. This was
madness—like choosing courtiers to act in the Tunath's
Day pageant. "He need ·only be seen, not fight,"
Isgrimnur growled.

"But he must be somewhere in the fighting," Sludig insisted, "or no one will see him."

"I will do it," said Hotvig. The scarred Thrithings-man
lifted his arm and his bracelets jangled. "I can fight with
either hand."

"But ... but he does not look like Josua," said
Strangyeard apologetically, "... does he?" He had sobered since the duke had seen him earlier, but still seemed
distracted. "Hotvig, you are ... you are very broad in the
chest. And your hair is too light."

"He will be wearing a helm," Sludig pointed out.

"The harper Sangfugol looks much like the prince,"
Strangyeard offered. "At least he is slender and dark-
haired."

"Ha." Isgrimnur barked a laugh. "I would not send a
singer into the middle of such a bloodletting. Even if he
need not fight, he must sit his horse in the clamor of
fierce fighting." He shook his head. "But I cannot spare
you, either, Hotvig. We need your Thrithings-men—you

are our fastest horsemen, and we must be ready in case the king's knights make a sally from the gate. Who else?" He turned to Seriddan. The Nabbanai captains had been silent, stunned by Josua's disappearance. "Have you any ideas, Baron?"

Before Seriddan could reply, his brother Brindalles stood. "I am close to the prince's size. And I can ride."

"No, that is foolish," Seriddan began, but Brindalles halted him with a raised hand.

"I am not a fighter like you, my brother, but this is something I can do. Prince Josua and these folk have risked much for us. They faced imprisonment or even death at our hands to bring us the truth, and then helped us to drive Benigaris from the throne." He looked around the tent somberly. "But what good is that to us if we do not survive to enjoy it, if our children are unhomed by Elias and his allies? I am still somewhat baffled by all this talk of swords and strange magics, but if this stratagem is truly necessary, then it is the least I can do."

Isgrimnur saw his calm resolve and nodded. "It is done, then. Thank you, Brindalles, and may Aedon give you good luck. Isorn, get him into things of Josua's as will fit, then you can take whatever else of Camaris' that you need. From what Jeremias said, I doubt he took his helm with him. Freosel?"

"Yes, Duke Isgrimnur?"

"Tell the engineers to make ready. Everyone else, go to your men and make ready. God's grace on us all."

"Yes," Strangyeard said suddenly. "Yes, of course— God's grace on us all."

☸

*He Who Always Steps on Sand,* Tiamak prayed silently, *I am going into a dark place. I am far from our swamps, farther than I have ever been. Please do not lose sight of this marsh man!*

The sun was invisible beyond the storm, but the deep blue of night was beginning to pale. Tiamak looked up from the Kynslagh beach at the faint shadows that must be the turrets of the Hayholt. They seemed impossibly far away, distant and forbidding as mountains.

*Bring me out alive and I will . . . and . . .* He could not think of any promise that might tempt the protector-god. *I will honor you. I will do what is right. Bring me out alive again, please!*

The snow swirled and the wind moaned, whipping the black Kynslagh to a froth of waves.

"We go, Tiamak," Aditu said from behind him. She was near enough that he jumped in surprise at the sound of her voice.

Her brother disappeared into the black mouth of the cave. Tiamak followed; the noise of the wind began to diminish behind him.

Tiamak had been surprised to find the Sithi such a small group, and even more surprised to find Likimeya a part of it.

"But isn't your mother too important to leave your people and come down here?" he whispered to Aditu. As he scrambled down a boulder, clinging to the shining globe that Jiriki had given him, he saw Likimeya turn to look back at him with what he felt sure was disgust. He was embarrassed and angry with himself for underestimating the Sithi's keen ears.

Aditu slithered down beside him, nimble as a deer. "If someone must speak for Year-Dancing House, Uncle Khendraja'aro will be there. But the others will make their decisions as things happen, and all will do what needs to be done." She stopped to pick something off the floor and stared at it intently; it was too small for Tiamak to see. "In any case, there are things at least as important to be done down here, and so those most able to do them have come."

He and Aditu were at the back of the small company, trailing Jiriki and Likimeya, as well as Kira'athu, a small, quiet Sitha-woman, another woman named Chiya, who seemed to Tiamak inexplicably more foreign than even the rest of the alien group, and a tall, black-haired Sitha-man named Kuroyi. All moved with the odd grace

Tiamak had long noted in Aditu, and except for Aditu and her brother, none seemed to take any more notice of the Wrannaman than of a dog following in the road.

"I found sand," Aditu called to the rest of the party. She had been careful to speak Westerling all morning, even with her kin, for which Tiamak was duly grateful.

"Sand?" Tiamak squinted at the invisible something she held prisoned between finger and thumb. "Yes?"

"We are now far in from the water's edge," she said. "But this is rounded, formed by the motion of stone in water. I would say we are still on Josua's track."

Tiamak had thought the Sithi were following the prince by some kind of immortals' magic. He did not know quite what to make of this revelation. "Can't you . . . don't you just . . . *know* where the prince and Camaris are?"

Her amused smile was very human. "No. There are things we can sometimes do to make finding someone or something easier—but not here."

"Not here? Why?"

The smile went away. "Because things are changing here. Can you not feel it? It is as powerful to me as the wind was loud outside."

Tiamak shook his head. "If anything dangerous comes toward us, I hope you will tell me. This is not my marsh, and I do not know where the dangerous sands lie."

"Where we go was our place once," Aditu said seriously. "But no more."

"Do you know your way?" Tiamak looked around at the sloping tunnel, the countless crevices and nearly identical cross-passages, black beyond the range of the lighted globes. The thought of being lost here was terrifying.

"My mother does, or at least she soon will. Chiya also lived here."

"Your mother lived in this place?"

"In Asu'a. She lived there for a thousand years."

Tiamak shivered.

The company followed no logical path that Tiamak could see, but he had long resigned himself to trusting the Sithi, although there was much about them that frightened him. Meeting Aditu on Sesuad'ra had been strange enough, but she had been singular, a freak, as Tiamak himself must have seemed to the drylanders. Seeing them together, either in their great numbers on the hillside east of the Hayholt, or here in a group that, despite making many decisions without discussion, seemed always in accord, he felt for the first time the true force of their strangeness. They had ruled all of Osten Ard once. History said they had been kind masters, but Tiamak could not help wondering if they had been truly kind, or had just given no attention at all, tyrannical or otherwise, to their mortal inferiors. If that was true, they had been cruelly repaid for their heedlessness.

Kuroyi halted and the others stopped with him. He said something in the liquid Sithi speech.

"Someone is there," Aditu quietly told Tiamak.

"Josua? Camaris?" He did not want to think it could be something worse.

"We will find out."

Kuroyi turned into a passageway and took a few steps downward. A moment later he danced back out, hissing. Aditu pushed past Tiamak and ran to Kuroyi's side. "Do not run!" she called into the dark space. "I am Aditu!"

After a few moments a figure appeared, sword leveled.

"Prince Josua!" Relief flowed through Tiamak. "You are safe."

The prince stared at them for a long moment, blinking in the light of the crystal globes. "Aedon's Mercy, it is truly you." He sank down heavily onto the floor of the tunnel. "My . . . my torch burned out. I have been in darkness some time. I thought I heard footsteps, but you walk so quietly I could not be sure. . . ."

"Have you found Camaris?" Tiamak asked.

The prince shook his head miserably. His eyes were haunted. "No. I lost sight of him soon after I followed him in. He would not stop, no matter how I called. He has gone! Gone!" He struggled to control himself. "I have left my men without a leader—deserted my people! Can you take me back?" He looked imploringly around the circle of Sithi.

"The mortal Duke Isgrimnur is performing ably in your

place," said Likimeya. "We cannot afford the time to return you, nor any of our number, and you could not find your way back alone."

Josua lowered his head, bowed by shame. "I have done a foolish thing, and failed those who trusted me. It was all to find Camaris . . . but he has gone. And he has taken Thorn with him."

"Do not worry yourself over what is done, Prince Josua." Aditu spoke with surprising gentleness. "As for Camaris, do not fear. We will find him."

"How?"

Likimeya stared at Josua for a moment, then turned her glance up the passageway. "If the sword is being drawn toward Sorrow and the other blade, as seems true from what you have told us, then we know where he is bound." She looked at Chiya, who nodded. "We will go there by the straightest route, or close to it. Either we will find him, or we will reach the upper levels before him and can wait."

"But he could wander down here forever!" Josua said unhappily, and Tiamak remembered his own earlier thought.

"I do not think so," said Likimeya. "If some convergence of power is drawing the swords together—which may be our greatest hope, for it will bring Bright-Nail, too—then he will find his way, even with his wits as troubled as you say they were. He will be like a blind man searching for the fire in a cold room. He will find his way."

Jiriki extended his hand to the prince. "Come, Prince Josua. I have some food and water. Take some nourishment, then we will find him."

As the prince looked at him some of the hard edge of worry softened. "Thank you. I am grateful you found me." He took Jiriki's hand and stood, then laughed, mocking himself. "I thought . . . I thought I heard voices."

"I have no doubt you did," said Jiriki. "And you will hear more."

Tiamak could not help noticing that even the impassive

Sithi did not look entirely comfortable with Jiriki's remark.

Slowly, almost imperceptibly, Tiamak's surroundings began to change. As he and Josua followed the immortals through the twisting passages, he first noticed that the floors seemed more level, the tunnels a little more regular. Soon he began to see the undeniable marks of intelligent shapers, hard angles, arches of stone that braced the wider crossings, even a few patches in the rock walls that seemed to have been carved, although the decorations were little more than repetitive patterns like waves or twining grass stems.

"These outermost reaches were never finished," Aditu told him. "Either they were built too late in Asu'a's life, or were abandoned in favor of more useful paths."

"Abandoned?" Tiamak could not imagine such a thing. "Who would do all the work of gouging through this stone and then abandon it?"

"Some of these passages were built by my people, with the help of the Tinukeda'ya—the dwarrows as mortals call them," she explained. "And that stone-loving folk carved some just for themselves, unconcerned with finishing or keeping, as a child might make a basket of grass stems and then toss it away when it is time to run home."

The marsh man shook his head.

Mindful of their mortal companions, the Sithi stopped at last for a rest in a wide grotto whose roof was covered with a tracery of slender stalactites. In the mellow light of the globes, Tiamak thought it looked entirely magical; for a moment, he was glad he had come. The world below, it seemed, was full of wonders as well as terrors.

As he sat eating a piece of bread and a savory but unfamiliar fruit the Sithi had brought, Tiamak wondered how far they had come. It seemed they had walked most of a day, but the full distance on the surface between where they had begun and the walls of the Hayholt would not have taken a fourth of that time. Even with the circuitous track of the tunnels, it seemed they should have reached something, but they were still wandering through largely featureless caverns.

*It is like the spirit-hut of Buayeg in the old story,* he decided, only half in jest. *Small outside, big inside.*

He turned to ask Josua if he had noticed the same oddity; the prince was staring at his own piece of bread as though he was too tired or distraught to eat. Abruptly the cavern shuddered—or seemed to: Tiamak felt a sensation of movement, of sudden slippage, but neither Josua nor the Sithi seemed to move in response to it. Rather, it was as though everything in the grotto had slid to one side, but the people inside had slid effortlessly with it. It was a frightening wrench, and for a long moment after it had passed Tiamak felt as though he occupied two places at the same time. A thrill of terror ran up his spine.

"What is happening!?" he gasped.

The obvious uneasiness of the Sithi did nothing to make him feel better. "It is that which I spoke of before," said Aditu. "As we draw closer to Asu'a's heart, it is getting stronger."

Likimeya stood and slowly looked around, but Tiamak felt sure that she was using more than her eyes. "Up," she said. "Time is short, I think."

Tiamak scrambled to his feet. The look on Likimeya's stern face frightened him badly. He suddenly wished he had kept his mouth closed, that he had stayed above ground with the rest of his mortal companions. But it was far too late to turn back.

⚜

"Where are we going?" Miriamele gasped.

Yis-hadra, who had replaced her wounded husband as leader, turned to stare. "Going?" said the dwarrow. "We are fleeing. We run to escape."

Miriamele stopped, bending over to catch her breath. The Norns had attacked them twice more as they fled through the tunnels, but without archers they had been unable to overcome the terrified dwarrows. Still, two more of the stone-tenders had fallen in the fighting, and the white-skinned immortals had by no means given up. Since the last struggle, Miriamele had already spotted the pursuers once when she had entered a passageway long and straight enough to permit a backward look; in that glimpse they had truly seemed creatures of the lightless depths—pale, silent, and remorseless. The Norns seemed in no hurry, as if they were merely trailing Miriamele and her companions until more of their kind came bearing bows and long spears. It had been as much as she could do not to sink to the ground in surrender.

She knew that they had been lucky to escape the dwarrows' cavern at all. If the White Foxes had anticipated any resistance, they had doubtless expected it to be close combat in a narrow corner. Instead, the dwarrows' desperate attack in the dark and the avalanches of falling stone they had engineered had caught the immortals by surprise, permitting Miriamele and her companions to flee. But she had no illusions they could trick the cunning Norns twice.

"We could be forced to run this way forever," she told Yis-hadra. "Perhaps you can outlast them, but we can't. In any case, our people are in danger up above."

Binabik nodded. "She speaks truth to you. Escaping is not enough for us. We have need of finding our way out from this place."

The dwarrow did not reply, but looked to her husband who was limping up the passageway toward them, trailed by the last of the dwarrows and Cadrach. The monk's face was ashen, as though he had been wounded, but Miriamele saw no injuries. She turned away, unwilling to waste sympathy on him.

"They are a distance behind us, now," said Yis-fidri wearily. "They seem full content to let us run ahead." He leaned back against the wall, letting his head rest against the stone. Yis-hadra went to him and probed gently with her wide fingers at the arrow wound in his shoulder. "Sho-vennae is dead, and three others," he groaned, then fluted a few words to his wife, who gave a cry of grief. "Smashed like delicate crystals. Gone."

"If we had not run, they would all be dead anyway—

and you and the rest of us would be, too." Miriamele paused to fight back her anger and her horror of the pursuing Norns. "Forgive me, Yis-fidri. I am sorry about your people. I am truly sorry."

Sweat beaded on the dwarrow's brow, glimmering in the light of the batons. "Few mourn for the Tinukeda'ya," he replied softly. "They make us their servants, they steal from us the Words of Making, they even beg our help when they are in need—but they seldom mourn us."

Miriamele was ashamed. Surely he meant that she was as guilty of using the dwarrows—and Niskies, too, she thought, remembering Gan Itai's sacrifice—as even their one-time masters, the Sithi.

"Take us to where we can reach the world above," she said. "That is all I ask. Then go with our blessing, Yis-fidri."

Before the dwarrow could reply, Binabik suddenly spoke up. "The Words of Making. Were *all* the Great Swords being forged with these Making-Words?"

Yis-fidri looked at him with more than a little suspicion, then winced at something his wife was doing to his shoulder. "Yes. It was needful to bind their substance—to bring their being within the Laws."

"What laws are these?"

"Those Laws that cannot be changed. The Laws that make stone be stone, make water be water. They can be ..." he searched for a word, "stretched or altered for a short time, but that brings consequences. *Never* can they be undone."

One of the dwarrows at the rear of the tunnel spoke anxiously.

"Imai-an says he can feel them coming," Yis-hadra cried. "We must run."

Yis-fidri pushed himself away from the tunnel wall and the group began its uneven progress once more. Miriamele's weary heart was racing. Would there never be an end to this? "Help us reach the surface, Yis-fidri," she begged. "Please."

"*Yes!* It is more than ever important!"

Miriamele turned at the distraught tone of Binabik's

voice. The little man looked terrified. "What is it?" she asked him.

Sweat was running on his dark forehead. "I must think on this, Miriamele, but I have never had such fear as I do now. For the first time I believe I see behind the shadow that has been all our consideration, and I am thinking— Kikkasut! To be saying such words!—that the monk may have spoken rightly. There may be nothing left for our doing at all."

With those words hanging in the air, he turned from her and hastened after the dwarrows. As though his sudden despair had passed to her like a fever, she felt hopelessness enwrap her.

# 29

# The Hand of the North

❦

**The winds shrieked** around Stormspike's summit, but beneath the mountain all was silent. The Lightless Ones had fallen into a deep slumber. The corridors of Under-Nakkiga were nearly empty.

Utuk'ku's gloved fingers, slender and brittle as cricket legs, flexed upon the arm of her throne. She settled her ancient bones against the rock and let her thoughts move through the Breathing Harp, following its twistings and turnings until Stormspike fell away and she became pure mind moving through the black between-spaces.

The angry Dark One was gone from the Harp. He had moved himself to the place—if it could be called a place—where he could act in concert with her to enact the final step of their centuried scheme, but she could still feel the weight of his hatred and envy, personified in the net of storms that spread across the land above.

In Nabban, where the upstart Imperators had once ruled, snow piled high in the streets; in the great harbor high waves flung the anchored ships against each other, or drove them into the shore where their splintered timbers lay like the bones of giants. The kilpa, frenzied, struck at everything that moved across the water, and even began to make sluggish forays into the coastal towns. And deep within the heart of the Sancellan Aedonitis, the Clavean Bell hung silent, immobilized by ice just as the mortals' Mother Church was frozen by fear.

The Wran, although its interior was sheltered from the worst of the storm, nevertheless turned chillingly cold.

The ghants, undeterred as a group, though countless individuals died in the harsh weather, continued to boil out of the swamps and harry the coastal villages. Those few mortals of Kwanitupul who braved the icy winds to walk outside went only in groups, armed with iron weapons and wind-whipped torches against the ghants who now seemed to be crawling in every shadowy place. Children were kept inside, and doors and windows were shuttered even during those few hours when the storm abated.

Even Aldheorte Forest slept beneath a blanket of white, but if its ageless trees suffered beneath the freezing hand of the North, they did so in silence. In the heart of the woods Jao é-Tinukai'i lay empty, misty with cold.

All the mortal lands lay trembling beneath Stormspike's hand. The storms kept Rimmersgard and the Frostmarch an icy wasteland, and Hernystir suffered only a little less. Before the Hernystiri could truly reclaim the homes from which they had been driven by Skali of Kaldskryke, they had been forced back into the caves of the Grianspog. The spirit of the people the Sithi had loved, a spirit which had flamed high for a short time, sank back to a guttering flicker.

The storm hung low over Erkynland. Black winds bent and broke the trees and piled snow high on the houses; thunder growled like an angry beast up and down the length of the land. The storm's malevolent heart, as it seemed, full of whirling sleet and jagged lightning, pulsed above Erchester and the Hayholt.

Utuk'ku noted all this with calm satisfaction, but did not pause to savor the terror and hopelessness of the hated mortals. She had something to do, a task she had awaited since her son Drukhi's pale, cold body had been set before her. Utuk'ku was old and subtle. The irony that it was her own great-great-grandchild who had led her to her revenge at last, that he was also a scion of the very family that had destroyed her happiness, was not lost on her. She almost smiled.

Her thoughts raced on, out along the whispery threads of being until they passed into the farther regions, the places only she of all the living could go. When she felt the presence of the thing she sought, she reached out for it, praying to forces that had been old in Venyha Do'sae that it would give her what she needed to accomplish her final, long-awaited goal.

A flare of joy passed through her. The power was there, more than enough for her purposes; now all that remained was to master it and make it hers. The hour was approaching, and Utuk'ku had no need to be patient any longer.

"My eyes are not good at the best of times," Strangyeard complained. "And with this sunless day and the blowing snow, I cannot see anything! Sangfugol, tell me what is happening, please!"

"There's nothing to see, yet." They were perched on the side of one of Swertclif's foothills, looking down on Erchester and the Hayholt. The tree beneath which the pair huddled and the low wall of stones they had made provided scant protection against the wind. Despite his hooded cloak and the two blankets he had wrapped around himself, the harper was shivering. "Our army is before the walls and the heralds have blown the trumpets. Isgrimnur or someone must be reading the Writ of Demand. I still don't see any of the king's soldiers . . . no, there are some shapes moving on the battlements. I had begun to wonder if anyone was inside at all. . . ."

"Who? Who is on the battlements?"

"Aedon's mercy, Strangeyeard, I can't tell. They are shapes, that's all."

"We should be closer," the priest said fretfully. "This hillside is too distant in weather like this."

The harper darted a glance at him. "You must be mad. I am a musician, you are a librarian. We are too close as it is—we should have stayed in Nabban. But here we are, and here we will stay. Closer, indeed!" He blew into his cupped palms.

A faint clamor of horns drifted over the wind. "What is it?" Strangyeard asked. "What is happening?"

"They have finished the Writ and I suppose they've gotten no answer. That is just like Josua, to give Elias a chance to surrender honorably when we know already he will do nothing of the sort."

"The prince is ... determined to do the right thing," Strangyeard replied. "Goodness, I hope he is well. It makes me sick to think of him and Camaris wandering lost in those caverns."

"There is that Nabbanman," Sangfugol said excitedly. "He does look rather like Josua—from here, anyway." He turned suddenly toward the priest. "Did you really suggest *I* should mimic the prince?"

"You look much like him."

Sangfugol stared at him with disgust and bitter amusement. "Mother of God, Strangyeard, do me no favors." He huddled deeper into his blankets. "Imagine me riding around waving a sword. Ransomer save us all."

"But we all must do what we can."

"Yes—and what I can do is play my harp, or my lute, and sing. And if we win, I will most assuredly do that. And if we don't—well, I may do that anyway if I live, but it won't be here. But what I *cannot* do is ride and fight and convince people that I am Josua."

They were silent for a time, listening to the wind.

"If we lose, I fear there will be nowhere else to run to, Sangfugol."

"Perhaps." The harper sat unspeaking a while longer, then said: "Finally!"

"What? Is something happening?"

"They are bringing forward the battering ram—save me, but it is a frightening thing. It has a great iron head on it that looks like a real ram, with curling horns and all. But it's so big! Even with all those men, it is a miracle they can push it along." He took a sharp breath. "The king's men are firing arrows from the walls! There, someone is down. More than one. But the ram is still going forward."

"May God keep them safe," Strangyeard said quietly. "It is so cold up here, Sangfugol."

"How can anyone shoot an arrow in this wind, let alone

hit anything? Ah! Someone has fallen from the wall. That's one of theirs gone, in any case." The harper's voice rose in excitment. "It is hard to see what is happening, but our men are close to the walls now. There, someone has put up a ladder. There are soldiers swarming up it." A moment later he made a noise of surprise and horror.

"What do you see?" Strangyeard squinted his eye, trying to see through the swirling snows.

"Something was dropped on them." The harper was shaken. "A big stone, I think. I am sure they are all dead."

"May the Ransomer protect us," Strangyeard said miserably. "It has begun in earnest. Now we can only wait for the ending, whatever that may be."

⚜

Isgrimnur held his hands close to his face, trying to shield himself from the wind-flung snow. He was having great difficulty keeping track of what was happening, although the Hayholt's walls were less than five hundred cubits up the hillside from where he watched. Hundreds of armored men floundered in the drifts before the wall, busy as insects. Hundreds more, even dimmer shapes from Isgrimnur's vantage point, scurried about atop the Hayholt's walls. The duke cursed quietly. Everything seemed so damnably distant!

Freosel climbed onto the wooden platform the engineers had built between the bottom of the hill and the empty, storm-raddled husk of Erchester. The Falshireman was visibly struggling against the wind. "Ram's almost to the gates. The wind, it'll be our friend today—hard on their bowmen, it be."

"But we're not able to shoot any better," the duke snarled. "They've got free run of the walls and they're pushing our scaling ladders off easy as you please." He smacked his fist into his gloved hand. "The sun's been up for hours and all we've done is wear a few trenches in the snow."

The Falshireman looked at him quizzically. "Pardon, Sir Duke, but seems you think we should knock these walls down 'fore sunset."

"No, no. God knows the Hayholt is built strong. But I don't know how much time we have." He looked up into the murky sky. "That cursed star they all talk about is right overhead. I can almost feel it glaring. The prince and Camaris are gone. Miriamele's gone." He turned his gaze to the Hayholt, peering through the snow flurries. "And our men are going to freeze solid if we keep them out there too long. I wish we *could* knock the walls down by sunset—but I don't hold much hope."

Isorn pointed upward. The soldiers gathered around him looked up.

"There. On the walls."

Beside the helmeted heads peering through the crenellations were more than a few whose heads were bare; their faces were ghostly, and their white hair blew in the strong wind.

"White Foxes?" asked Sludig. He made the sign of the Tree.

"Indeed. And inside the Hayholt. Cursed things!" Isorn lifted his black-painted sword and waved it back and forth in challenge, but the distant figures on the walls did not seem to notice. "And curse Elias for whatever foul bargain he made."

Sludig was staring. "I have not seen them before," he cried above the tumult. "Merciful Aedon, they look like demons!"

"They *are* demons. And now the Hayholt is their nest."

"But they are doing nothing that I can see."

"Just as well," Isorn replied. "Perhaps they are too few. But they are fearsome archers. I wonder why none of them seem to have bows."

Sludig shook his head, mystified. He was unable to look away from the pale faces. "Preserve us," he said hoarsely.

❧

Baron Seriddan climbed heavily up the steps onto the platform, weighted by his armor. "What news?" Isgrimnur asked.

Seriddan took off his gloves and held his hands close to the brazier of coals. "Things go well, I suppose. Elias' men are firing on the ram and it is slow going to keep it moving uphill, but it will be against the gate soon. Some of the siege towers are also being moved into place, and they seem to be concentrating their arrows on them. We are lucky there is such wind today, and that it is so hard for the king's archers to see."

"That's what everyone keeps saying," the duke grumbled. "But I am going quietly mad here anyway. Curse Josua for leaving me this way." He scowled, then made the sign of the Tree. "Forgive me. I did not mean that."

Seriddan nodded. "I know. It is terrible not to know where he is."

"That's not all that's bothering me. There are still too many unanswered questions."

"What do you mean?"

"If all they need to do is stall us—if this flaming star truly signifies something will happen that helps Elias— then why didn't they even try to parley? And you'd think that the king would want to see his brother at the very least, if only to shout at him and call him a traitor."

"Perhaps Elias knows that Josua is not here."

Isgrimnur flinched. "How could he know that? Josua only disappeared last night!"

"You know more of these matters than I do, Duke Isgrimnur. You have been fighting the king and his magical allies a long time."

Isgrimnur walked to the front of the platform, staring at the Hayholt's shadowy walls. "Maybe they *do* know. Maybe they lured Camaris in somehow—but, damn me, that wouldn't mean Josua would come, too. They couldn't have planned on that."

"I cannot even guess," said the baron. "I only came to tell you that I'd like to take some of my men around to the western wall. I think it is time we gave them another spot to worry about."

"Go ahead. But that is another thing that troubles me: Elias doesn't seem very worried at all. With the battering ram so close, I would have expected at least one sortie to prevent us from dragging it into place."

"I cannot answer you." Seriddan clapped him on the arm. "But if this is all that the High King has left to offer, we will have the gate down in a matter of days at the most."

"We may not have days," Isgrimnur replied, frowning.

"But we do what we can." Seriddan clambered down and moved toward his horse. "Take heart, Duke Isgrimnur," he called. "Things are going well."

Isgrimnur looked around. "Jeremias!"

The boy pushed through a small knot of armored men at the back of the platform. "Yes, sire."

"See if you can find me some wine, boy. My guts are colder than my toes."

The squire hurried off toward the tents. Isgrimnur turned back to the windy, snow-smothered battlefield, glowering.

"God preserve us!" Sludig gaped in astonishment. "What are they doing?"

"Singing," said Isorn. "I saw it before the walls of Naglimund. It went on a long time." He stared at the two dozen Sithi, who had ridden forward and now stood calmly within bowshot of the walls, knee-deep in the drifting snows.

"What do you mean, *singing?*"

"It is how they fight—at least it is how they fight with their cousins, the Norns. If I understood better, I would explain it to you."

"And these are the allies we've been waiting for?" Sludig's voice rose in anger. "We battle for our lives— and they *sing?* Look! Our men are dying out there!"

"The Sithi can fight in other ways too, Sludig. You will

see that, I think. And it worked for them at Naglimund, although I don't know how. They brought the walls down."

His companion snorted derisively. "I will put my faith in the ram and the siege-towers—and in men with strong arms." He looked up at the sky. "It's getting darker. But it cannot be much past midday."

"The storm is growing thicker, perhaps." Isorn restrained his horse, which was stepping nervously. "I do not like the looks of it, though. Do you see that cloud over the towers?"

Sludig stared, following Isorn's pointing finger. He blinked. "Lightning! Is this the Sithi's doing?" Indeed, almost the only thing that could be heard over the moaning wind was the strange, rhythmic rise and fall of the immortals' voices.

"I do not know, but it might be. I watched them at it before Naglimund for days, and still I could not tell you what they do. But Jiriki told me that his people work to counter certain magicks of the Norns." Isorn winced as thunder crashed, echoing across the hillside and down through the deserted streets of Erchester behind the prince's army. The lightning flashed again, seeming for a moment to freeze everything on and before the walls of the Hayholt—men, engines of war, flurrying snowflakes, even arrows in their flight—before the storm darkness returned. Another roar of thunder sounded. The wind howled even louder. "Perhaps that is why the Norns are not among the archers," Isorn continued loudly. "Because they are preparing some trick, some spell—something we will not like much. Oh, I saw horrors at Naglimund, Sludig. I pray Jiriki's people are strong enough to hold them back."

"This is madness!" Sludig shouted. "I can see almost nothing!"

Another crash came, this one a little softer. It was not thunder. "Praise Usires! They have brought the ram against the gates," Isorn called, excited. "See, Sludig, they have struck the first blow!" The black sword raised before him, he spurred his horse forward a few steps.

With the sea-dragon helm on his head and his cloak whipping in the high wind, even Sludig could almost believe this was Camaris and not his liege-lord's son. "We must find Hotvig's riders and be ready to go in if they can breach the gate."

Sludig looked in vain for a messenger among the milling foot soldiers. "We should tell your father," he shouted.

"Go, then. I will wait. But hurry, man. Who would have thought we would be so close so soon?"

Sludig tried to say something, but it was lost in the noise of the storm. He turned his horse away and rode back down the hill toward Duke Isgrimnur's watching place.

☗

"The ram is against the gate," Sangfugol said exultantly. "Look at it! It is big as three houses!"

"The gate is bigger." Strangyeard was shivering. "Still, I am astonished that there should be so little resistance."

"You saw Erchester. Everyone has fled. Elias and his pet wizard have made this place a wasteland."

"But there seem to be men enough inside the walls to defend the castle. Why did they dig no trenches to slow the siege engines? Why did they lay up so few stones to push down on the scaling ladders?"

"The stones they had did their work," Sangfugol replied, angry that Strangyeard did not share his excitement. "The men who wound up beneath them are as dead as you could wish."

"Elysia, Mother of our Ransomer!" The priest was shocked. "Sangfugol, do not speak so of our fallen soldiers! I only meant it is strange the defenders seem so ill-prepared for a siege Elias must have known was coming for weeks, even months."

"The king has gone mad," the harper replied. "You've heard what those who fled Erkynland say. And there are few left to fight with him. This will be no different than prodding a bear out of its cave. The bear is fierce, but it is an animal for all that, and must lose out to the cleverness of men."

"Cleverness?" The archivist did his best to shake the snow off his blanket. The wind slashed bitterly even through the low barrier of stones they had erected. "What have we done that is so clever? We have been led by the nose like oxen all along."

Sangfugol waved his hand airily, although he too was trembling with cold. "Having Isorn and that Nabban fellow pose as Camaris and Josua—that was a clever idea, you must admit . . . except for your little suggestion that *I* be the one to play the prince. And going beneath the Hayholt's walls by caverns and tunnels—that is something clever indeed! The king would not think of that in a thousand years."

Strangyeard, who was rubbing his hands together furiously in an effort to keep them warm, suddenly stopped. "The king might not—but his allies must know of those tunnels." His voice shook. "Surely the Norns must know."

"That is why *our* fairy-folk have gone down after the prince and Camaris. I've seen them, Aditu's brother and mother and the rest. They can take care of themselves, I have no doubt . . . even if the Norns know about the tunnels and are waiting for them, as you seem to think."

"That is *not* what I am thinking." Strangyeard stood. Snow fell from him and was promptly snatched away by the wind. "Not what I am thinking at all. The Norns know all about the tunnels." He stepped over the low wall of stones, knocking several loose.

"Hi! What are you doing?"

"I have to find Duke Isgrimnur. We are in more danger than we suspected." He turned and waded downhill through the drifts, leaning into the wind, frail but determined.

"Strangyeard!" cried Sangfugol. "Blast it, I am not staying here by myself. I'll come with you, whatever madness you're onto." He followed the archivist over the barrier. "You are heading right toward the fighting!" he shouted. "You'll be shot with an arrow!"

"I have to find Isgrimnur," Strangyeard called back. Cursing richly, the harper hurried after him.

✦

"Isorn's right, sire," said Sludig. "If we pass through the gate, we must make a great charge. The men have already seen the Norns and they are frightened. If we hesitate, the advantage will be the king's again. Who knows what will happen if he makes a sortie, and us fighting uphill?"

Isgrimnur stared at the Hayholt's high walls. It was only when seen against a storm like this that the works of man, even such a mighty construction as the Hayholt, seemed truly small. Perhaps they actually *could* knock down the gate. Perhaps Sludig and the others were right—Elias' kingdom was a rotting fruit waiting to fall from the vine.

There was another strange, sputtering flash of lightning over the tower tops. Thunder rolled, but following close behind it came a loud crash as the great ram was swung forward into the gate.

"Go, then," Isgrimnur told Sludig. His carl had not dismounted, but had brought his steam-puffing horse to the edge of the wooden structure where the duke stood. "Hotvig and his riders are still waiting at the edge of the Kynswood. No, better yet, you stay here." Isgrimnur summoned one of the newly returned outriders and gave him a message for the Thrithings-men, then sent him on his way. "You go back to Isorn, Sludig. Tell him to hold fast and let the first of the men-at-arms go through on foot. There will be no storied charges here, at least not until I see what Elias has waiting."

As the duke spoke, the ram smashed against the Nearulagh Gate. The timbers seemed to sag inward a little way, as though the huge bolts had been loosened.

"Yes, sire." Sludig turned his charger toward the walls.

The ram's engineers swung it forward once more. The iron-plated head crunched against the barrier. A length of wood splintered away down the length of the gate, and even through the storm noises Isgrimnur could hear the excited shouts of men all across the field. The ram was pulled back and then set in motion again. The Nearulagh Gate shattered and fell inward in an explosion of broken timbers and tumbling statuary. Snow swirled in the empty space. Isgrimnur goggled, almost unable to believe the gate was down. When the snow cleared, a few score of the castle's pikemen moved into the opening, braced against attack. No great hidden army charged outward.

A long moment passed as the two forces eyed each other through the snow-flurries. It seemed no one could move, that both sides were astonished by what had happened. Then a small, golden-helmeted figure lifted a sword and spurred forward. A score of mounted knights and several hundred foot soldiers surged toward the breach in the Hayholt's walls.

"Damn me, Isorn!" Duke Isgrimnur shouted. He leaned so far forward that he nearly lost his balance and toppled from the observation platform. "Come back! Where is Sludig!? Sludig! Stop him!" Someone was tugging at his sleeve, pulling him back from the edge of the platform, but Isgrimnur paid the intruder no mind. "Can't he see that it's too easy? *Isorn!*" He knew his voice could not possibly carry above the tumult. "Seriddan! Where are you!? Ride after him—by Dror's red mallet, where are my messengers!?"

"Duke Isgrimnur!" It was Strangyeard the archivist, still pulling at his sleeve.

"Get away, damn you!" Isgrimnur roared. "I do not need a priest, I need mounted knights. Jeremias, run to Seriddan," he called. "Isorn has forced our hand. Tell the baron to ride in."

Strangyeard was undaunted. "Please, Duke Isgrimnur, you must listen to me!"

"I have no time for you now, man! My son has just charged in like a fool. He must think he *is* Camaris—after all I told him!" He stalked across the platform, satisfying himself that everyone was in as much of a furious state of excitement as he was. The priest pursued him like a dog nipping at the heels of a bull. Finally Strangyeard grasped

Isgrimnur's surcoat and yanked hard, pulling the duke off-balance and almost toppling him over.

"By all that's holy, Isgrimnur!" he shouted. "You must listen to me!"

The duke stared at the priest's reddened face. Strangyeard's eyepatch had slid almost onto his nose. "What are you on about?" Isgrimnur demanded. "We have knocked down the gates! We are at war, man!"

"The Norns must know about the tunnels," Strangyeard said urgently. Isgrimnur saw Sangfugol the harper skulking beside the platform, and wondered what both a priest *and* a harper were doing in the middle of things that did not concern them.

"What do you mean?"

"They must know. And if we can think to send somebody under the castle walls ..."

The clamor of men as they charged up the hillside toward the shattered gate, even the grumbling of thunder and the moan of the wind, were suddenly overtopped by a hideous grinding noise, a rasp like fingernails on slate. Horses reared, and several of the soldiers on the platform lifted their hands to their ears.

"Oh, merciful Aedon," said Isgrimnur, staring up at the Hayholt. "No!"

The last of Isorn's company had fought their way through the opening in the wall. At their backs, thrusting up from the snowy ground and the wreckage left by the battering ram, a second gate was rising. It climbed upward swiftly, rasping like an ogre's teeth grinding on bone. Within a few moments the wall was sealed again. The new gate, beneath a layer of snow and mud, was covered with dull iron plates.

"Oh, God help me, I was right," Isgrimnur groaned. "They have trapped Isorn and the others, Sweet Usires." He stared in sick horror as the engineers rolled the ram forward and began hammering at the second gate. The metal-clad wood did not seem to give even an inch.

"They think they have trapped Camaris," Strangyeard said. "That is what they planned to do all along."

Isgrimnur turned and grabbed at the priest's robe,

thrusting his face close to the smaller man's. "You knew? You *knew?!*"

"Goodness, Isgrimnur, no, I didn't. But I see it now."

The duke let him go and began shouting frantic orders, sending his remaining archers forward to help protect the engineers, who were receiving redoubled interest from the soldiers on the Hayholt's walls. "And find me that damn Sithi general!" he bawled. "The one in green! The fairy-folk must help us knock this new wall down!"

"But you still must listen to me, Isgrimnur," said the priest. "If the Sithi know of those tunnels, the Norns must, too. The Storm King, when he lived, was master of Asu'a!"

"What does that mean? Speak plainly, damn you!" Isgrimnur was furiously agitated. "My son is trapped in there with only a few men. We must break down this new gate and go in after him."

"I think you must look ..." Strangyeard began, when another round of excited shouts interrupted him. This time, though, they came from behind Isgrimnur.

"Coming up through Erchester!" one of the mounted men screamed. "Look! It is the White Foxes!"

"I think you must look behind you, I was going to say." Strangyeard shook his head. "If we could go beneath the walls, so could they."

Even in near-darkness it was possible to see that the host moving up Main Row was not human. White faces gleamed in the shadows. White hands held long sharp spears. Now that they had been sighted and the need for stealth was gone, they began to sing, a triumphant chant that fell painfully on Isgrimnur's ears.

The duke allowed himself one moment of utter despair. "Ransomer preserve us, we have been snared like rabbits." He patted the priest's shoulder in silent thanks, then strode to the middle of the platform. "To me, Josua's men! To me!" He waved to Jeremias, calling for his horse.

The Norns came up Main Row, singing.

# 30

# Beside the Pool

✦

"Up to the tree . . ." Guthwulf mumbled. His face beneath Simon's hand was oven-hot and slippery with sweat. "To the flaming tree. Wants to go . . ."

The earl was getting worse, and Simon did not know what to do. He was still badly hobbled by his own wounds, knew almost nothing of the healing arts, and in any case was in a lightless place with nothing that might be of use in easing Guthwulf's fever. Because of a dim recollection that fevers had to burn themselves out, he had covered the suffering earl with some of the rags strewn about the floor, but he felt like a traitor putting warm things on someone who seemed to be burning up.

Helpless, he sat down beside Guthwulf once more, listening to him rave and praying that the earl would survive. The blackness pressed in on him like the crushing depths of the ocean, making it hard to breathe, to think. He tried to distract himself by remembering the things he had seen, the places he had been. More than anything he wanted to *do* something, but at this moment there seemed to be nothing to do but wait. He did not want to be left alone and lost in the empty places again.

Something touched his leg and Simon reached out, thinking that Guthwulf in his misery was looking for a hand to hold. Instead, Simon's fingers trailed across something warm and covered with fur. He let out a shout of surprise and scrabbled back, expecting momentarily to feel rats or something worse swarming over him. When there was no further contact he crouched, huddled into himself, for a long time. Then his feelings of responsibility for Guthwulf won out and he edged back toward the earl. A squeamish exploration found the furry thing again. It shrank back as he had, but did not go far. It was a cat.

Simon laughed breathlessly, then reached out and stroked the creature. It arched beneath his hand, but would not come to him. Instead it settled against the blind man and Guthwulf's movements became less agitated, his breathing quieter. The cat's presence seemed to soothe him. Simon, too, felt a little less alone, and resolved to be careful not to frighten the animal away. He fetched some of the remaining heel of bread and offered a pinch to the cat, who sniffed it but did not take any. Simon ate a few small pieces himself, then tried to find a comfortable position to sleep in.

Simon awakened, abruptly conscious that something had happened. In the darkness it was impossible to discern any changes, but he had the inescapable feeling that things had shifted somehow, that he was suddenly in an unfamiliar place with no knowledge of how he had come there. But the rags around him were the same, and Guthwulf's labored breathing, though quieter, still rasped away nearby. Simon crawled over to the earl, gently pushed aside the warm and purring cat, and was heartened to feel much of the cramping tension gone from the blind man's limbs. Perhaps he was recovering from the fever. Perhaps the cat had been his companion and its presence had restored a little of his sanity. In any case, Guthwulf had stopped raving. Simon let the cat clamber back into the crook of the earl's arm. It felt strange not to hear Guthwulf's voice.

During the earliest hours of his fever, the earl had been almost lucid for short stretches, although he was so plagued by his voices and former solitude that it was difficult to separate truth from terrifying dream. He talked about crawling through darkness, desperate to find Bright-Nail—although, strangely, he did not seem to think of it as a sword at all, but as something alive that summoned him. Simon remembered

Thorn's disturbing vitality and thought he understood a little of what the earl meant.

It was hard to make sense out of the impressions of a half-mad blind man, but as Guthwulf spoke, Simon pictured the earl walking through the tunnels, lured by something that called to him in a voice he could not ignore. Guthwulf had gone far beyond his usual range, it seemed, and had heard and felt many terrible things. At last he had crawled, and when even those narrow ways were blocked, he had dug, fighting his way through the last cubits of earth that had separated him from the object of his obsession.

*He dug into John's barrow,* Simon realized, shuddering. *Like a blind mole after a carrot, scraping, scraping . . .*

Guthwulf had taken his prize and had somehow found his way back to his nest, but apparently even the joy of possessing the thing he had sought had not been enough to keep him in hiding. For some reason he had ventured out, perhaps to steal food from the forge—where else had the bread and water come from?—but perhaps for some deeper, more complicated reason.

*Why did he come to me?* Simon wondered. *Why would he risk being caught by Inch?* He thought again of Thorn, of how it had seemed almost to choose where it wished to go. *Maybe Bright-Nail wanted to find . . . me.*

The thought was a frighteningly seductive one. If Bright-Nail was being drawn to the great conflict that was coming, then maybe it somehow knew that Guthwulf would never willingly go up into the light again. As Thorn had chosen Simon and his fellows to bring it down from Urmsheim and back to Camaris, maybe Bright-Nail had chosen Simon to carry it up to Green Angel Tower to fight the Storm King.

Another dim recollection surfaced. *In my dream, Leleth said that the sword was part of my story. Is that what she meant?* The details were strangely misty, but he remembered the sad-faced man who had held the blade across his lap as he waited for something. *The dragon?*

Simon let his fingers trail away from the cat's back and down Guthwulf's arm until they reached Bright-Nail. The earl moaned, but did not resist as Simon gently pried his fingers away. His finger reverently traced the rough shape of the Nail, bound just below the guard. A nail from the Execution Tree of holy Usires! And some sacred relic of Saint Eahlstan was sealed inside the hollow hilt, he re-•membered. Prester John's sword. It was astonishing that a onetime scullion should ever touch such a thing!

Simon curled his hand around the hilt. It seemed to . . . fit. It lay in his hand as comfortably as though it had been made for him. All other thoughts about the blade, about Guthwulf, slid away. He sat in the dark and felt the sword to be an extension of his own arm, of himself. He stood, ignoring his aching muscles, and slashed at the lightless void before him. A moment later, horrified at the thought that he might accidentally strike Bright-Nail against the rock wall of the cavern and blunt its edge, he sat down again, then crawled away to his corner of the cavern and stretched out on the stone, clutching the sword to him as though it were a child. The metal was cold where it touched his skin, and the blade was sharp, but he did not want to let it go. Across the chamber, Guthwulf murmured uncomfortably.

Some time had passed, although Simon did not know whether he had slept or not, when he suddenly became aware that something was missing: he could no longer hear the earl breathing. For a moment, as he scrambled across the uneven floor, he clung to the wild hope that Guthwulf had grown well enough to leave the cavern, but the presence of Bright-Nail still gripped in his own fingers made that seem very unlikely: the blind man would not for a moment allow someone else to have his blade.

When Simon reached Guthwulf, the earl's skin was cool as river clay.

He did not weep, but his feeling of loss was great. His sorrow was not for Guthwulf the man, who except for these last dreamlike hours or days he had only known as a fearsome figure, but for himself, left alone once more.

Almost alone. Something bumped against his shin. The cat seemed to be trying to get his attention. It missed its companion, Simon felt sure. Perhaps it thought that somehow he could wake Guthwulf where it had failed.

"Sorry," he whispered, running his fingers down its back and gently tugging its tail. "He's gone somewhere else. I'm lonely, too."

Feeling empty, he sat for a moment and took stock of things. Now he had no choice but to brave the mazy, lightless tunnels, even though he doubted he would find his way out again without a guide. Two times he had stumbled through this haunted labyrinth, each time followed so closely by death that he heard its patient footsteps behind him; it was too much to hope that he would be lucky again. Still, there was little else he could do. Green Angel Tower stood somewhere above, and Bright-Nail must be carried there. If Josua and the others had not brought Thorn, he would do what he could, although it would doubtless end in failure. He owed that much to all those who had sold their dear lives for his freedom.

It was difficult to put Bright-Nail down—he already felt a little of Guthwulf's possessiveness, although there was nothing in the small cavern that might endanger the sword—but he could accomplish little with it clutched in his hand. He leaned it against one of the walls, then proceeded to the unpleasant task of undressing the dead earl. When he had removed Guthwulf's tattered clothing he took some of the rags scattered about the cavern and, in poor imitation of the priestly labors in the House of Preparing, wrapped the body. A part of him felt ridiculous for going to such lengths for a man who had, by all repute, been little-loved in his life, and who would lie here alone and undiscovered regardless, but Simon felt a stubborn urge to pay the blind man back. Morgenes and Maegwin had given their lives for him, and they had been given no memorial, no rites, except those in Simon's own heart. Guthwulf should not go to the Fields Beyond unheralded.

When he had finished, he stood.

*"Our Lord protect you,"*

he began, struggling to remember the words to the Prayer for the Dead,

*"And Usires His only Son lift you up.*
*May you be carried to the green valleys*
*Of His domains,*
*Where the souls of the good and righteous sing from*
*the hilltops,*
*And angels are in the trees,*
*Speaking joy with God's own voice. . . .*

"Thank you, Guthwulf," he said when the prayer was done. "I'm sorry to take the sword away from you, but I'll try to do what should be done."

He made the sign of the Tree—hoping that, despite the darkness, God would see and so take note of Guthwulf when at last the earl came before Him—then he pulled on Guthwulf's clothing and boots. A year before, he might have thought twice before donning a dead man's garb, but Simon had walked so close to death himself that he was now all practicality. It was warm and safe in the cavern, but who knew what cold winds, what sharp stones, awaited him?

As he drank off the last drops in the water bowl, the cat nudged his leg once more. "You can come with me or stay here," he told it. "Your choice." He took up Bright-Nail, then wrapped a rag around the blade just below the hilt and tied the earl's buckleless belt around the sword and his waist so his hands would be free. It was more than a slight relief to feel it against him once more.

As he felt his way toward the mouth of the cavern the cat was at his feet, twining in and out between his ankles. "You'll trip me," he said. "Stop that."

He edged a little distance along the passageway, but the creature was between his legs again and made him stumble. He reached down for it, then laughed hollowly at the stupidity of trying to catch a cat in blind darkness. The

cat moved under his hand and then slipped away in the
opposite direction. Simon paused.

"That way, not this way?" he said aloud. After a moment, he shrugged, then laughed again. Despite all the
horror behind him and before him, he felt curiously free.
"Very well, then, I'll follow you for a while. Which
means I'll probably wind up sitting next to the largest rat
hole in Osten Ard."

The cat bumped him, then slipped away up the corridor. Feeling along the walls, entirely surrounded by darkness, Simon trailed after it.

Yis-hadra stopped at the base of the stairs and chimed
anxiously to her husband. Yis-fidri replied. They bent to
examine the cracked stone baluster.

"This place," Yis-fidri said. "If you follow these steps
upward, you will come at last to the mortal castle built
atop this one."

"Where?" asked Miriamele. She dropped her bow and
pack to the tunnel floor and slumped against the stone.
"Where in the castle?"

"We know not," Yis-hadra said. "All has been built
since our day. No Tinukeda'ya touched those stones."

"And you? Where will you go?" She looked up the
stairwell. It spiraled up far beyond the weak light of the
dwarrow's batons, twisting into darkness.

"We will find another place." Yis-fidri looked at his
wife. "There are few of us left, but there are still places
that will welcome our hands and eyes."

"It is time for *our* going," Binabik said urgently. "Who
is knowing how far away the Norns are?"

Miriamele asked the dwarrows: "Why don't you come
with us? You are strong, and we can use your strength.
You should know by now that our fight is yours, too."

Yis-fidri shuddered and raised his long hands as though
to fend her off. "Do you not understand? We do not belong in the light, in the world of Sudhoda'ya. We have already been changed by you, done things that Tinukeda'ya

do not do. We have . . . we have killed some of those who
were once our masters." He murmured something in the
dwarrow-tongue and Yis-hadra and his other remaining
folk chorused unhappily. "It will take us long to learn to
live with that. We do not belong in the world above. Let
us go to find the darkness and deep places we crave."

Binabik, who had spoken much to Yis-fidri during the
last part of their flight, stepped forward and extended his
small hand. "May you find safety."

The dwarrow looked at him for a moment as if he did
not understand, then slowly put out his own spidery fingers and wrapped them around the troll's. "And you. I
will not tell you my thoughts, for they are fearful and unhappy."

Miriamele bit back words of argument. The dwarrows
wished to go. They had fulfilled the promise that she had
forced out of them. They were already frightened and
miserable; aboveground they might be less than useless,
more a responsibility than an asset. "Farewell, Yis-fidri,"
she said, then turned to his wife. "Yis-hadra, thank you
for showing me how you tend the stone."

The dwarrow bobbed her head. "May you also fare
well."

Even as she spoke, the lights of the batons flickered
and the underground chamber seemed to shift, another
convulsion without movement; a moment later, when
things were again as they had been, the remaining
dwarrows began to whisper.

"We must go now," Yis-hadra said, her dark eyes wide
with fear. She and her husband turned and led their troop
of shuffling, spindle-legged kin away into the shadows.
Within moments the corridor was as empty as if they had
never existed. Miriamele blinked.

"We must go also." Binabik started up the stairs, then
turned. "Where is the monk?"

Miriamele looked back. Cadrach, who had been at the
rear of the assembled dwarrows, was sitting on the
ground, his eyes half-closed. The flicker of Binabik's
torch made him seem to sway.

"He's useless." She bent to pick up her belongings.

"We should leave him here. Let him follow if he wants to."

Binabik frowned at her. "Help him, Miriamele. Otherwise, he is left for the Norns' finding."

She was not sure the monk didn't deserve just that, but she shrugged and went to him anyway. A tug on his arm brought him slowly to his feet.

"We're going."

Cadrach looked at her for a moment. "Ah," he said, then followed her up the ancient stairway.

✳

As the company of Sithi led them farther into the deeps below the Hayholt, Tiamak and Josua found themselves staring around in astonishment, like Lakeland farmers on their first visit to Nabban.

"What a treasure trove this is!" Josua breathed. "And to think it was below me all those years I lived here. I would gladly spend a lifetime down here, exploring, studying. . . ."

Tiamak, too, was overwhelmed. The rough corridors of the outer tunnels had given way to a decayed splendor he could never have imagined, and even now could scarcely believe. Vast chambers which seemed to have been painstakingly carved out of living rock, every surface a minutely detailed tapestry; seemingly endless stairways, thin and beautiful as spiderwebs, that curled up into shadow or stretched across black emptiness; entire rooms carved in the likeness of forest clearings or mountainsides with waterfalls, though everything in the chamber was solid stone—even as crumbling ruins, Asu'a the Great was astonishing.

*They Who Watch and Shape,* Tiamak thought, *seeing this place has made every bit of my suffering worthwhile. My lame leg, my hours in the ghant nest—I would not trade them if I must also lose the memories of this hour.*

As they wound through the dusty byways, Tiamak tore his eyes away from the wonders that surrounded him long enough to observe the strange behavior of his Sithi companions. When Likimeya and the others stopped to let the mortals rest, in a high-roofed chamber whose arching windows were clogged with dirt and rubble, Tiamak sat beside Aditu.

"Forgive me if my question is rude," he asked softly, "but do your people mourn their old home? You seem ... distracted."

Aditu inclined her head, bending her graceful neck. "In part, yes. It is sad to see the beautiful things our people built in such a state—and for those who lived here ..." she made an intricate gesture, "it is even more painful. Do you remember the chamber carved with great flowered steps—the Hall of Five Staircases, as we call it?"

"We stopped there a long time," Tiamak said, remembering.

"That was the place where my mother's mother, Briseyu Dawnfeather, died."

The marsh man thought of how Likimeya had stood expressionlessly in the center of that wide room. Who could know these immortals?

Aditu shook her head. "But such are not the greatest reasons we are, as you put it, distracted. There are ... presences here. Things that should not be."

Tiamak had himself felt more than a touch of what he thought Aditu meant—a riffle of wind on the back of his neck that seemed insistent as probing fingers, echoes that almost sounded like faint voices. "What does it mean?"

"Something is awake here in Asu'a that should not be awake. It is hard to explain. Whatever it may be, it has given a semblance of life to what should not have one."

Tiamak frowned, unsure. "Do you mean ... ghosts?"

Aditu's smile was fleeting. "If I understood First Grandmother when she taught me what the mortal word means, no. Not as such. But it is hard to show the difference. Your tongue is not suited for it, and you do not see or feel what we do."

"How can you tell?" He looked across to Josua, but the prince was staring fixedly at the ornately carved walls.

"Because if you did," Aditu replied, "I suspect you would not be sitting there so calmly." She rose and crossed the rubble-strewn floor to where her mother and Jiriki stood in quiet conversation.

In the middle of emptiness, Tiamak suddenly felt surrounded by danger. He slid closer to Josua.

"Do you feel it, Prince Josua?" Tiamak asked. "The Sithi do. They are frightened."

The prince looked grim. "We are all of us frightened. I would have liked a full night to prepare for this, but Camaris took that away from me. I try not to remember where it is we are going."

"And all with no idea of what to do when we get there," Tiamak mourned. "Was there ever a battle fought so confusedly?" He hesitated. "I have no right to question you, Prince Josua, but why *did* you follow Camaris? Surely others less crucial to our success than you could have tried to track him."

The prince stared ahead. "I was the only one there. I sought to bring him back before he was lost to us." He sighed. "I feared others would not come in time. But even more . . ."

The strange perturbation of air and stone came again, sudden and disorienting, cutting Josua off in mid-speech. The Sithi's lights jittered, although the immortals themselves seemed not to move. For a moment, Tiamak thought he sensed the presence of a host of others, a shadowy horde disposed all through the ruined halls. Then the feeling was gone and everything was as it had been but for an odd, lingering smell of smoke.

"Aedon's mercy!" Josua looked down at his feet as though surprised to discover them still on the ground. "What is this place?"

The Sithi had paused. Jiriki turned to the mortals.

"We must go faster," he said. "Can you keep up?"

"I have a lame leg," Tiamak replied. "But I will do my best."

Josua laid his hand on the Wrannaman's shoulder. "I will not leave you behind. I can carry you if need be."

Tiamak smiled, touched. "I do not think it will come to that, Prince Josua."

"Come, then. The Sithi need haste. We will try to give it to them."

They moved at a fast trot through the winding passageways. Watching the backs of the Sithi, Tiamak had little doubt that if they chose they could leave their mortal companions far behind. But they did not, and that said much: the Sithi thought that Tiamak and Josua could do something important. He ignored the pain in his leg and hurried on.

They seemed to run for hours, although Tiamak had no way of knowing if that was true: just as the substance of Asu'a itself seemed strangely unstable, so too did time move in a manner that Tiamak no longer trusted himself to interpret. The lag between steps sometimes seemed to stretch for long moments, then an instant later he would be in another part of the ruined sub-castle, still running, with no memory of the intervening journey.

*He Who Always Steps on Sand, keep me sane until I have done whatever I can do,* he prayed. Beside him, the prince too seemed in silent communication with something or someone.

For a while the Sithi were so far ahead that their lights were little more than a glow in the tunnel before them. Tiamak's own globe, jiggling in his clutch, provided inconstant light; he and Josua found themselves stumbling through wreckage they could barely see, suffering more than a few cuts and bruises, until they caught up to the immortals once more.

The Sithi had halted beneath a high archway where they stood silhouetted by a diffuse glow from the chamber beyond. As Tiamak hobbled to a stop beside them, gasping for breath, he wondered if they had finally reached the light of the upper world. As he sucked air into his lungs, he stared at the dragonlike serpent carved on the arch. Its tail stretched down one side and was carved across the dusty floor of the archway as well, then rose up the other side and back to the lintel, where the tip was clasped in its owner's mouth. There were still flecks of paint on its thousands of minute scales.

The smoky light behind the Sithi made them seem distorted, freakishly lean and without firm edges. The nearest, Jiriki, turned and looked back at the panting mortals. There was compassion on his face, but it battled with more pressing emotions. "Beyond is the Pool of Three Depths," he said. "If I tell you it is a Master Witness, you may have some idea of what kind of forces are at work here. This is one of the mightiest of the places of power; the great worms of Osten Ard once came to drink its waters and share their wordless wisdom, long before my people set foot in this land."

"Why have we stopped here?" Josua asked. "Is Camaris. . . ?"

"He may be, or he may have already been here and passed on. It is a place of potency as I said, and it is one of the sources of the change we have felt all around us. He may very well have been drawn here." Jiriki lifted his hand in warning; for the first time, Tiamak could see the weariness on the immortal's face. "Please do nothing without asking. Touch nothing except the floor where we walk. If something speaks to you, do not reply."

Tiamak was chilled. He nodded his understanding. There were a thousand questions he longed to ask, but the tension he saw in the Sithi was a strong argument for silence.

"Lead on," said Josua.

Appearing a little hesitant themselves, the Sithi stepped through the archway into a wide chamber full of indirect light. Where Tiamak could see the walls through the strange mistiness of the air, they seemed almost new-built, undamaged and ribbed with great sculpted pillars that stretched up toward the hidden ceiling. The pool, a circular expanse of scintillant water, lay in the center of the chamber. A circular staircase whose landing touched on the pool's far side spiraled up, massive yet graceful, and vanished in the mists above.

Something in the room was . . . alive. Tiamak could think of no other way to describe the sensation. Whether it was the pool itself, with its shifting blue and green glows flickering up from the depths, he could not say, but there was far more to this place than water and stone. The air was thunderstorm-taut, and he found he was holding his breath as they moved forward. The Sithi, moving as cautiously as hunters stalking a wounded boar, fanned out along the edge of the pool, growing unaccountably more distant from him with each single step. The smoky light glimmered.

"Camaris!" shouted Josua. Tiamak looked up, startled. The prince was staring at a shape beyond the farthest of the Sithi, a tall figure with a long shadow in one hand. The prince hastened around the tarn's rim; the Sithi, their attention pulled away from the pool, moved with him toward the solitary figure. Tiamak hurried after, the pain of his leg momentarily forgotten.

For an instant Tiamak thought the prince was mistaken, that whatever this shape was, it was not Camaris: for a blink of time he saw someone completely different, jet-haired and dressed in strange robes, with a branching crown upon his head. Then the chamber seemed to shudder and tip, and the Wrannaman stumbled; when he had regained his balance, he saw that it was indeed the old knight. Camaris looked up at the approaching figures and stepped back, his eyes wild with alarm, then leveled the black sword before him. Josua and the Sithi stopped beyond its reach.

"Camaris," said the prince. "It is Josua. Look, it is only me. I have been searching for you."

The old man stared at him, but the sword did not waver from its defensive position. "It is a sinful world," he replied hoarsely.

"I will go with you," said Josua. "Wherever you wish to go. Do not be afraid. I will not stop you."

Likimeya's voice was surprisingly gentle. "We can help you, *Hikka Ti-tuno*. We will not stay you, but we can make your pain less." She took a step forward, her hands held with palms upward. "Do you remember Amerasu Ship-Born?"

The old man's lips drew back in a grimace of pain or fear and he drew Thorn back as if to strike. Dark Kuroyi's sword hissed from its sheath as he stepped in front of Likimeya.

"There is no need," she said coldly. "Put up."

The tall Sitha hesitated for a moment, then slipped his witchwood sword back into place. Camaris lowered his black blade once more.

"Pity." Kuroyi sounded genuinely regretful. "I have always wondered what it would be to cross swords with the greatest of mortal warriors. . . ."

Before anyone else spoke again the light flared wildly, then the room was plunged into blackness. A moment later light returned, but this time the misty air was blue as the center of a flame. Tiamak felt a freezing wind that seemed to blow through him, and the tension of the air increased until his ears hammered.

*"How you do love mortals."* The dreadful voice sounded in his thoughts and all through his body; the words felt like insects skittering on the Wrannaman's skin. *"You cannot leave them alone."*

Tiamak and the others turned. In the roiling mists behind them a shape was forming, pale robed and silver masked, enthroned in midair above the pool. The sickly blue light did not reach much beyond the water, and the chamber was now walled with shadow. The Wrannaman felt terror seize him by the spine. He could not move, could only pray that he would be unnoticed. Stormspike's queen—for who else could it be?—was as dreadful as any nightmare vision of She Who Waits to Take All Back.

Likimeya nodded her head. She held herself stiffly, as though even speaking took much effort. "So, Eldest. You have found a way to reach the Pool of Three Depths. That does not mean that you can use it."

The masked figure did not move, but Tiamak felt something almost like triumph emanate from it. *"I silenced Amerasu—I broke her before my huntsman dispatched her. Do you think you are her equal, child?"*

"By myself, no. But I have others here with me."

*"Other children."* A pale gloved hand lifted, wavering as the mist swirled.

Tiamak was dimly aware of movement on the edge of the circle of figures around him, but could not tear his eyes away from the shimmering silver mask.

"Camaris!" Josua cried. "He is leaving."

"Go," said Jiriki. "And you, too, Tiamak. Follow him."

"But what of you?" The prince's voice cracked. "And how will we find our way?"

"He is going where he is drawn." Jiriki moved closer to his mother, who already seemed locked in some silent struggle with the Norn Queen. The muscles of Likimeya's face were rippling. "And that is where you must go, too. This is our struggle here." Jiriki turned to face the pool.

"Go!" said Aditu urgently. She tugged at Tiamak's sleeve, pulling him off-balance and sending him stumbling toward Josua. "We will call on the power of the Oldest Tree and hold her at bay as long as we can, but we cannot defeat their plan here. Utuk'ku is already drawing on the Master Witness. I can feel it."

"But what is she doing? What is happening?" Tiamak heard his voice rising in terror.

"We cannot see that," Aditu moaned. Her teeth were clenched. "We have all we can do to hold her back. You and the others must accomplish whatever remains. This is *our* battle. Now go!" She turned away from him.

The pulsing radiance of the pool grew stronger, and lavender flames kindled along the walls, leaping as though in a fierce wind. The entire chamber felt tight as a drumhead. Tiamak thought he could feel himself shrinking, twisting, being slowly crushed by the forces now unleashed. Something powerful, yet without form or substance, was beating out at him from the misty shape that hovered over the water.

Fumbling as though they were battered by gale winds, the Sithi formed into a line before the pool and linked their hands, then began to sing.

As the immortals' strange music rose, the lights of the pool flickered wildly. Tiamak stared helplessly at the glowing mists, unable to remember how to move. The walls around the pool seemed to bend inward and then push out again, bend in and push out, as though the chamber breathed. On the rim of the pool Aditu staggered and slumped forward, but her brother, who stood beside her, pulled her upright; the song of the Sithi faltered for a moment, then resumed.

In response to their wailing music, something else began to form in the mists of the pool, something that rapidly became entangled with the pale shadow of the Norn Queen. Tiamak saw it as a dim, dark shape with a wide trunk, swaying branches, and phantom leaves that fluttered as though a wind caressed them. Aditu had said "the Oldest Tree"; Tiamak could sense this huge thing's antiquity, its deep roots and spreading, nurturing strength. For a moment he felt something like hope.

As if in response, the blue lights in the water began to burn even more fiercely, until the glare filled the chamber with blinding radiance. The tree shape grew less substantial. The Wrannaman felt himself sinking down to the ground as Utuk'ku's choking, freezing might surged out from the Pool of Three Depths.

*"Tiamak!"*

The voice was distant and far behind him; it meant little. Nothing could push through the fog that was filling his ears, his heart, his thoughts. . . .

High above the center of the pool, the Norn Queen seemed a creature made entirely of ice, but something black pulsed at the heart of her, and jagged flares of purple and blue played about her head and glinted from her shining mask. She spread her arms, then clenched her gloved fists. Kuroyi abruptly shrieked and fell away from the rest of the Sithi to writhe on the ground. The dark-haired Sitha began to deform into impossibly swift-changing shapes, as though invisible hands kneaded him like dough. The other Sithi slumped and fell back; the ghost-tree vanished completely. After a few moments Aditu and her kin recovered themselves and began fighting to close the gap where Kuroyi had been. They struggled as though immersed in deep water, striving to join hands once more. The fallen Sitha had stopped struggling and lay still. There was no longer anything manlike in his form.

Something jerked at Tiamak's arm, then jerked again. He turned slowly. Josua was screaming at him, but he could not hear the words. The prince pulled him up onto his feet and dragged him, stumbling, away from the pool. Tiamak's heart was rattling as though it might burst. His

legs did not want to support him, but Josua kept tugging
until Tiamak could move on his own, then the prince
turned and lurched away in pursuit of Camaris. The old
knight was several score paces ahead, walking stiff-
legged toward the dark passages at the far side of the
wide chamber. Tiamak limped slowly after them both.

The song of the Dawn Children rose again behind him,
more raggedly this time. Tiamak did not dare look back.
Blue light throbbed all across the cavern ceiling, and the
shadows bloomed and vanished and then bloomed again.

♣

Despite the strange shifting that seemed to be going on
around him, despite the bodiless voices that sometimes
shrieked or gibbered in the blackness, Simon did not surrender to fear. He had survived the wheel and then had
passed over into the void and returned. He had won back
his life, but he did not hold it as tightly as he once had,
and so, in a way, his grip on it was more sure. What were
little things like hunger or momentary blindness? He had
been hungry before. He had wandered without light.

The cat padded silently ahead, turning at intervals to
rub against him before moving on, leading him slowly
through the twisting tunnels. He had long since given his
safety over into the animal's care. There was nothing else
to do, and no use worrying about it.

Something was happening around him, although he
could not tell exactly what that something was. The
ghostly presences and strange distortions were even stronger than before, and seemed to come now as regularly as
waves dashing themselves upon a beach, sweeping all before them, then ebbing away again. He hardened himself
to the sensations as he had hardened himself to his own
aches.

Simon felt his way along the black corridors, Bright-
Nail scraping the walls like a beetle's feeler, his fingers
trailing through dust and dank moss and cobwebs and
other things less pleasant. He could do nothing but what
he was doing. He had faced the ice-dragon and shouted

his name at it, had wandered the emptiness beyond dreams and clung to himself. He could not turn back from the task that was before him, and he would not.

Bright-Nail seemed to change along with his lightless surroundings. One moment it was a simple blade slapping against his hip, then a moment later it seemed to throb in time with the convulsions of the castle depths, becoming for a moment a living thing; at those times, it was hard to tell whether one of them was master, or whether Simon and the sword were, as he and the cat were, two creatures traveling the darkness together in strange partnership.

At such times, he could begin to hear its call in his thoughts; it was a faint presence, only a hint of the song that Guthwulf had seemed to hear, but it was growing steadily stronger. For brief moments he could almost understand it, as though it spoke to him in a language he had forgotten long ago, but which was slowly surfacing from the place in his memory where it had been buried. But Simon did not think he wanted to understand what the blade sang. Perhaps if he wandered long enough, he thought, he would indeed become like Guthwulf, and hear almost nothing but the sword's compelling music.

He hoped he would not be in darkness that long.

There came a time when the cat stopped and did not go on. It wreathed itself around his shins as though it wished to be stroked; when he bent to touch it, it pushed at his fingers with its muzzle, but did not continue on its way. He waited, finally wondering if he had not put far too much trust in a mere beast.

"Where next?" he said. His voice scarcely echoed: they were still in one of the narrower passages. "Go on, now. I'm waiting."

The cat rubbed against him, purring. After a few moments, Simon put his hands out and began searching carefully along the walls, looking for something—perhaps a doorway of some kind that did not reach the floor—which might have stopped their progress. Instead, on a shelf of rock set into the wall, nearly head high, he found a plate and a covered bowl.

*I've been here before!* he realized. *Unless some madman is leaving food all across the tunnels. But if so, bless him, bless him anyway.*

Simon said a prayer of thanks as he took the bread and dried meat and small wedge of cheese from the plate, then sat down and ate enough of each to feel happier and more prosperous than he had in a long while. He drank half the bowl of water, then after a moment's consideration, finished it off. He regretted the lack of a water skin, but if he had to carry the water without one, it might as well be inside him.

The cat was at him again, butting and purring. Simon broke off a sizable piece of the jerked meat to share with his guide—the cat took it so quickly its sharp teeth scraped his fingers—then put the remainder in the pocket of his shirt. He stood.

*P'raps he won't want to lead me anymore,* he thought. *This may have been all the little creature wanted.*

But the cat, as though some ritual had been successfully observed, slithered in and out between his ankles for a few moments, then started off again. Simon bent and felt first its head, then its back, then its tail pass beneath his fingers. He smiled an invisible smile and followed it.

It was so faint at first as to be almost unnoticeable, but gradually Simon realized that the walls around him were slowly becoming visible. The light was so dim that for hundreds of paces he thought it was only his eyes playing tricks on him, but eventually he realized that he was seeing the rough surfaces across which he dragged his hands. The cat, too, had become a real thing instead of just an idea, a hint of movement on the tunnel floor before him.

He followed the shadow-cat up through the coiling tunnels. These were rougher hewn than those which traversed the ruins of Asu'a, and he felt a growing certainty that he was back in the mortal castle once more. As he turned another bend, the dim netherlight became a torch in a wall bracket at the far end of a long passageway.

*Light! Back again!* He fell to his knees, unmindful for a moment of his aching limbs, and pressed his forehead against the stone floor. He stayed there, trembling. Light! He was in the world again.

*Thank you, Maegwin. Bless you. Thank you, Guthwulf.*

The cat was a gray shape against the gray stone. Something else tugged at his memory.

*I've seen that cat before—or have I? The Hayholt was full of cats.*

The air abruptly contracted and the walls shivered and then bowed inward as though to trap him. An image passed before his mind's eye, a great tree shivering in storm winds, its branches torn loose and spinning away. For a moment Simon felt as though he had been turned inside-out. Even when the vision had gone and all was as it had been, he remained on his knees for long moments, panting.

His four-footed guide stopped and looked around to see if he was still following, then continued on, as though the strange slippage was beneath a cat's notice. Simon clambered to his feet.

The creature paused in an archway. Simon saw a narrow staircase climbing up into darkness. The cat bumped his shin but did not move on.

"Should I go up here?" he whispered. He poked his head into the entranceway. High above, hidden by the twisting stairwell, another source of light glowed faintly.

He stared at the cat for a moment. The cat stared back, yellow eyes wide.

"Very well, then." He touched Bright-Nail, making sure the hilt was not tangled in the rags of his belt, then began to climb. After a few steps he turned and looked back. The cat still sat in the middle of the tunnel floor, watching. "Aren't you coming?"

The gray cat stood and slowly sauntered away down the corridor. Even if it had possessed the gift of speech, it could not more clearly have told him that from this point he was on his own.

Simon smiled grimly.

*I suppose there's no cat in the world stupid enough to go where I'm going.*

He turned and made his way up the shadowed stairs.

* * *

The stairwell opened at last into a broad windowless room imperfectly lit by an open hatch door in the ceiling. As he stepped out from behind the wooden screen that hid the stairway, he realized that he was in one of the storage rooms below the refectory. He had been in this place before as well, on the momentous, horrible day when he had discovered Prince Josua in Pryrates' prison cell ... but that time the storeroom had been packed to the ceilings with all manner of food and other goods. Now the barrels that remained lay empty, many in splinters. Dusty mantles of spiderweb covered the remains, and the few spatters of flour left on the floor were crisscrossed with the tracks of mice. It looked as though no one had entered the room for some time.

Up above him, he knew, stood the refectory, and the hundreds of other close-huddled buildings of the Inner Bailey. Looming over them all was the ivory spike of Green Angel Tower.

As he thought of it, he felt Bright-Nail's song grow a little more insistent.

*... go there....* It was a whisper at the farthest edge of his thoughts.

Simon found and replaced the hatchway ladder, which had toppled to the floor, then began to climb. It creaked ominously, but held. Beneath its complaining he could hear a faint murmur, as though the hissing voices of the tunnels were following him up from the dark.

The only illumination in the refectory hall was the weak and unevenly pulsing gray light that leaked in through the high windows. The remaining tables and benches were scattered, some smashed to flinders, but most were gone entirely, perhaps taken to be burned as firewood. A bleak layer of dust lay everywhere, even on those things which had suffered a violent end, as though the destruction had happened a century before. A pair of rats scurried across one of the broken tables, paying Simon no heed.

The murmuring noise he had heard was louder here. The greatest part of it was the wind moaning outside the windows, but there were still hints of voices crying out in pain or anger or fear. Simon looked up and saw tiny flecks of snow whirling in past the broken shutters. He thought he could feel Bright-Nail stir, like a hunting beast catching the scent of blood.

He looked once more around the refectory—taking note, however distractedly, of the damage visited upon his home—then moved as quietly as he could toward the eastern portico. As he approached the door, he saw that it sagged on broken hinges and he despaired of opening it without noise, but as he came closer and heard the tumult outside he realized no one would hear him even if he were to kick it loose. The menacing song of the wind had grown, but the shouting voices and other noises had become louder still, until it sounded as if a great battle were being fought just outside the refectory door.

He crouched and placed his eye against the wedge of light where the door had edged free from its frame. It was hard at first to make sense of what he saw.

There *was* a battle just outside, or at least great knots of armored men were surging back and forth across the bailey. The chaos was abetted by the snows which covered the muddy ground and blew through the air like smoke, making everything murky; what sky he could see was full of streaming black clouds.

Lightning flashed, turning all to brilliant noon one instant, then, on its disappearance, making it seem for a moment as though all light had fled. It looked like a battle at the gates of Hell, a madness of shrieking faces and terrified horses, and it raged like an angry sea all across the snow-smothered bailey. Trying to make his way through such madness would be choosing to die.

On the far side, hopelessly out of Simon's reach, Green Angel Tower stood with its ivory spire wreathed in thunderheads. Lightning burst across the sky once more, a jagged, flaring chain that seemed to encircle the tower. Thunder shook his bones. Staring upward in that instant of savage illumination, Simon saw a pale face gazing from the great bellchamber windows.

# 31

# The False Messenger

❧

**Miriamele was** staggeringly exhausted. She could not imagine how Binabik, with his shorter legs, could still be moving. She was certain they had been climbing for more than an hour. How could there be so many steps? Surely by this time they could have reached the Hayholt if they had started from the center of the earth.

Panting, she stopped to wipe sweat from her face and look back. Cadrach was two flights down, barely visible in the torchlight. The monk would not give up; Miriamele had to credit him for that.

"Binabik, wait," she called. "If I . . . if I go another step . . . my legs will fall off."

The troll paused, then turned and came back down. He handed her his water skin, and as she drank, he said: "We have almost reached to the castle. I can feel the changing of air."

Miriamele slumped down onto the wide smooth step, discarding the bow and pack she had been tempted to toss away so many times in the past hour. "What air? I haven't had any in my lungs since I don't remember when."

Binabik looked at her solicitously. "Mountain-clambering is what we Qanuc learn before we can talk. You have been doing well to stay with me."

Miramele did not bother with a reply. A few moments later Cadrach staggered up and toppled against the wall, then slid down onto the step an arm's length from her. His pale face was moist, his eyes remote. She watched him

fight for breath, and after a moment's hesitation offered
him the water skin. He took it without looking up.

"Rest, both of you," said Binabik. "Then after will be
time for the last climbing. We are near, very near."

"Near to what?" Miriamele took the water skin from
Cadrach's unresponsive fingers and had another drink,
then passed it back to the troll. "Binabik, I have been trying to find the breath to ask you—what is happening?
Something the dwarrows said, something you thought
of . . ." She held his eye, although she could see he
wished to look away. "What is it?"

The troll fell silent, but he cocked his head as though
listening. There was nothing to be heard in the stairwell
except the rough noise of their breathing. He sat down beside her.

"It was indeed something the dwarrows were saying—
although that alone would not have been making my
thoughts leap so." Binabik stared at his feet. "There are
other thoughts I have, too. Something I have been long
pondering—the 'false messenger' of Simon's dream."

"In Geloë's house," Miriamele whispered, remembering.

"And he was not the only one. A message we were receiving in the White Waste, sparrow-carried—which now
it is my thinking was sent by Dinivan of Nabban, since
Isgrimnur later heard him speak it as well—also held a
warning against false messengers."

Miramele felt a pang at the memory of Dinivan. He had
been so kind, so clever—yet he had been broken like a
kindling-stick by Pryrates. Isgrimnur's tale of the horrors
he had seen in the Sancellan Aedonitis still colored her
nightmares.

A sudden thought came to her: she had fought Cadrach
when he tried to take her out of the Sancellan, resisted
him and called him a liar until he was forced to strike her
senseless and carry her out—but he had, in fact, told her
the truth. Why hadn't he simply run and saved himself,
leaving her to make her own way?

She turned to look at him. The monk had still not

caught his breath; he lay curled against the wall, his face blank as a wax doll's.

"So long have I wondered who could be such a messenger," Binabik continued. "Many are the messengers who have come to Josua, and also to Simon and Dinivan, the two who somehow had these warnings. Which messenger was meant?"

"And now you think you know?"

Binabik started to answer, then took a breath. "Let me tell you what I am thinking. Perhaps you will be finding some flaw—you too, Cadrach. I have hope only that I am wrong." He knitted the fingers of his small hands together and frowned. "The dwarrow-folk say the Great Swords were all having their forging with the help of Words of Making—words that the dwarrows say are used for pushing back the rules of the world."

"I didn't understand that."

"I will try for explaining," Binabik said unhappily. "But truly we are having little time to talk."

"When I've caught my breath, you can talk while we're climbing."

The troll nodded. "Then here is my explaining about the world's rules. One is that things want to fall downward." He put the stopper on the water skin and then dropped it, illustrating his point. "If some *other* kind of falling is wanted—to make this fall *upward*, that might be—that is one thing that the Art is being used for. To make something that is going against the world's rules."

Miriamele nodded. Beside her, Cadrach had raised his head as though listening, but he still stared out at the opposite wall.

"But if some rule must be broken for a long time, then the Art used must have great powerfulness, just as lifting a heavy thing once and then dropping it is easier than the holding of it in the air for hours. For such tasks, the dwarrows and others who were practicing the Art used . . ."

". . . The Words of Making," Miriamele finished for him. "And they used them when the Great Swords were forged."

Binabik bobbed his head. "They did that because all the Great Swords were forged of things that had no place in Osten Ard, things which were resisting the Arts used for creating a magical weapon. This needed overcoming, but not just for a moment. *Forever* was the time that these resisting forces must be subdued, so the most powerful Words of Making were being used." He spoke slowly now. "So those blades, it is my thinking, are like the pulled-back arm of the giant sling-stones your people use to attack walled cities—balanced so that one touch sends a vast rock flying like a tiny, tiny bird. Such great power is being restrained in each one of those swords—who knows what the power of three brought together may be doing?"

"But that's good," said Miriamele, confused. "Isn't that what we need—the strength to overcome the Storm King?" She looked at Binabik's sorrowful face and her heart grew heavy. "Is there some reason we can't use it?"

Cadrach shifted against the wall, turning his gaze at last on the troll. A gleam of interest had kindled in his eyes. "But who *will* use it?" the monk asked. "That is the question, is it not?"

Binabik nodded unhappily. "That is indeed what I am fearing." He turned to the princess. "Miriamele, why is Thorn being brought here? Why are Josua and others searching for Bright-Nail?"

"To use against the Storm King," Miriamele replied. She still did not see where the troll's questions were leading, but Cadrach evidently did. A grim half-smile, as of reluctant admiration, curled the monk's lips. She wondered who the admiration was for.

"But why?" asked the troll. "What was telling us to use them against our enemy? This is not something for tricking you, Miriamele—it is what I myself have been worrying until my head feels full of sharp stones."

"Because . . ." For a moment, she could not remember. "Because of the rhyme. The rhyme that told how to drive the Storm King away."

*"When frost doth grow on Claves' bell . . ."*

Binabik recited, his voice ringing strangely in the stairwell. His face twisted in what looked like pain

> *"And Shadows walk upon the road*
> *When water blackens in the Well*
> *Three Swords must come again*
>
> *"When Bukken from the Earth do creep*
> *And Hunën from the heights descend*
> *When Nightmare throttles peaceful Sleep*
> *Three Swords must come again*
>
> *"To turn the stride of treading Fate*
> *To clear the fogging Mists of Time*
> *If Early shall resist Too Late*
> *Three Swords must come again . . ."*

"I've heard it a hundred times!" she snapped. Anger only thinly covered her fear at the little man's strange expression. "What are you saying?"

Binabik lifted his hands. "Listen, listen to what it is telling, Miriamele. All the first parts are true things—diggers, giants, the great bell in Nabban—but at the end it only speaks of turning Fate, of clearing Time . . . and of Early fighting against Late."

"So?"

"What, then, is to say that it speaks to us!?" hissed Binabik.

She was so astonished by the troll's agitation that it took several moments before his words sank in. "Do you mean to say. . . ?"

"That it could just as easily be speaking of what will be helping *the Storm King himself!* For what are we mortals being to him if not the Lateness to his Earliness? Who is turning this Fate? And whose fate is it being?"

"But . . . but . . ."

Binabik spoke on in a fury, as though the words had been unbottled after a long fermentation and now foamed free. "Where did the idea to look for this rhyming come to us? From the dreams of Simon and Jarnauga and others! The Dream Road has been long compromised—Jiriki and the other Sithi have told that to us—but we were frightened enough to believe those dreams, desperate to have some way for fighting the returning Storm King!" He paused a moment, panting. "I am sorry, but I have so much angriness at my own stupidity. . . ! We took a twig of great slenderness and hung a bridge upon it without thinking more. Now we are over the middle of the chasm." He slapped his palms against his thighs. "Scrollbearers, we are now called. *Kikkasut!*"

"So . . ." She struggled to understand the ins and outs of what the troll had said; a throb of despair had begun beating inside her. "So the dreams about Nisses' book— *those* were the false messengers? The ones that led us to this rhyme?"

"That is what I am now thinking."

"But that doesn't make sense! Why would the Storm King play such a strange trick? If we cannot defeat him, why lead us to believe we could?"

Binabik took a breath. "Perhaps he has need of the swords, but cannot bring them himself. Pryrates was telling Cadrach that he knew where Bright-Nail was and did not wish it touched. Perhaps the red priest was having no plans of his own, and was doing only the Storm King's bidding. I am thinking the dark one in the north needs the great power that is in those blades." His voice broke. "It . . . it is my great fear that all this has been a complicated game, like the Sithi's *shent*, created for making us bring the remaining swords."

Miriamele sat back against the wall, stunned. "Then Josua, Simon . . . all of us . . ."

"Have been doing the enemy's bidding all along," said Cadrach abruptly. Miriamele expected to hear satisfaction in his words, but there was none, only hollowness. "We have been his servants. The enemy has already won."

"Shut your mouth," she spat. "Damn you! If you had told us what you knew, we would likely have discovered this already." She turned to Binabik, struggling to keep her wits. "If you're right, is there anything we can do?"

The troll shrugged. "Try to be escaping, then find our way back to Josua and the others for warning them."

Miriamele stood. A few moments earlier she had been rested and ready to climb again. Now she felt as though an ox-yoke had been laid across her shoulders, a ponderous, painful weight that could not be shrugged off. There seemed little doubt that all was indeed lost. "And even if we find them, now we will have no weapons to use against the Storm King."

Binabik did not reply. The diminutive troll seemed to have shrunk even smaller. He rose and began clambering up the stairs again. Miriamele turned her back on Cadrach and followed him.

＊

Order had been overthrown; screaming, grinding chaos raged before the Hayholt's walls. Pale Norns and shaggy, barking giants were everywhere, fighting with no discernible regard for their own lives, as though their only purpose was to strike horror into the hearts of their enemies. One of the giants had lost most of an arm to a warrior's ax-blow, but as it pushed through panicked human soldiers the huge beast swung the fountaining stub as vigorously as it did the club in its remaining hand, both combining to fill the surrounding air with a mist of red. Other giants were yet unwounded, and they quickly piled terrible carnage around themselves. The Norns, almost as fierce but far more canny, gathered themselves into small rings and stood shoulder to shoulder, their needle-sharp pikes facing outward. The swiftness and battle mastery of the white-skinned immortals was such that they seemed to fell two or three humans for each one of their own number that fell . . . and as they fought, they sang. Their eerie, strident voices echoed even above the clamor of combat.

And over all hung the Conqueror Star, glowing a sickly red.

Duke Isgrimnur raised Kvalnir in the air and shouted for Sludig, for Hotvig, but his voice was swallowed by the din. He turned his horse in circles, trying to find some area where the forces were concentrated, but already his army was scattered in a thousand separate pieces. Although he had been fighting vigorously for some time, Isgrimnur still could not quite believe what was happening. They were under attack by creatures out of old stories. The battlefield, grim but familiar less than an hour before, had now become a nightmare of otherworldly punishment.

Josua's standard had been thrown down; Isgrimnur searched in vain for something he could use to give his forces a rallying point. A giant fell to the snow, thrashing as it died with a dozen arrows crackling beneath it, and the duke's horse bolted away despite his attempts to control it, pulling up at last in an eddy of calm on the part of the northeastern hillside nearest the Kynswood.

When he had steadied his mount, Isgrimnur sheathed Kvalnir and removed his helmet, then tugged his surcoat up, grunting at the pain in his back and ribs. For a moment his bulky mail prevented him from pulling the garment over his head; Isgrimnur struggled, cursing and sweating, horrified at the thought of being taken by surprise and struck down in such a ridiculous position. The surcoat ripped at the armholes and he yanked it free at last, then looked around for something to which he could tie it. One of the Norns' pikes lay on the snow. Isgrimnur unsheathed his sword, then leaned over, grunting, and hooked it up so he could grab the long shaft. As he tied the shirt sleeves to the smooth grayish wood, he stared at the bladed tip that seemed to blossom like a knife-petaled flower. When he had finished, he lifted the makeshift banner above his head and rode back into the thick of the battle, roaring a Rimmersgard war song that even he could not hear.

He had already dodged one swinging blow from an ax-wielding Norn before he realized his helm was still swinging on his saddle horn. Kvalnir bounced ineffectively from the creature's strange painted armor. Isgrimnur managed to catch the returning blow on his arm, suffering only torn mail and a shallow gouge in his flesh, but the

Norn was very nimble on the slippery snow, and was circling rapidly for another attack. The wind abruptly blew the banner across the duke's face.

*Killed by my own shirt,* was his brief thought, then the cloth flapped away again. A dark something heaved into his field of sight and the Norn staggered sideways, blood erupting from a split helmet. The new arrival wheeled about in a splash of snow and returned to ride down Isgrimnur's reeling enemy.

"You are alive," Sludig gasped, swiping his dripping ax against his cloak.

Isgrimnur took a breath, then shouted over the growing rumble of thunder. "This is a damnable mess—where's Freosel?"

Sludig indicated a knot of struggling shapes a hundred cubits away. "Come. And put your damned helmet on."

"They're coming down the walls!" someone shouted.

Isgrimnur looked over to see rope ladders unrolling at the far end of the Hayholt's sloping outwall. The darkening sky and the dizzying flashes of intermittent lightning made it hard to see anything clearly, but to Isgrimnur the men making their way down the ladders looked like mortals.

"God damn their mercenary souls!" the duke growled. "And now we're pinched from both sides. We're being forced back against the walls and we won't have the advantage of numbers much longer." He turned and looked past his small, besieged company. Across the battlefield he could see determined clumps of men, Seriddan's Nabbanai legions and Hotvig's horsemen, trying to fight their way toward his surcoat-banner, which now waved on the strut of a scaling ladder socketed in the muddy ground. The question was whether Hotvig and the rest could cut their way through before Isgrimnur's small party was crushed between the Norns and the mercenaries.

*Perhaps we should fall back toward the base of the castle walls,* he thought,—*even try to fetch up in front of that new gate.* There was little else he and Sludig and the rest could do: they were going to be forced back in any case, so they might as well pick their spot. The duke had noticed that none of Elias' soldiers were atop the gate: he guessed it might not be wide enough. If that was true, he and his small company could use it as a rearguard without having to worry about missiles from above. With their backs protected, they could hold off even the fearsome Norns until the rest of the soldiers fought through . . . or so he hoped.

*And maybe if we make ourselves a little room we can force that cursed gate, or use those ladders, and go in after Isorn. No reason Elias shouldn't have some* mortal *foxes in his henyard for a change.*

He turned back to the horde of pale, black-eyed creatures and their witchwood blades. Lightning split the sky again, eclipsing for a moment the scarlet smolder of the Conqueror Star. Dimly, Isgrimnur heard a bell tolling, and felt it in his gut and bones as well. For a moment he saw what looked like flames crawling at the edge of his vision, but then the storm-darkness fell again.

*God help us,* he thought distractedly. *That's the noon bell in the tower. And here it is black as night. Aedon, it's so dark. . . .*

✦

"Oh! Mother of Mercy!" Miriamele looked down from the balcony, horrified. Below her perch on the king's residence, the Inner Bailey was a sea of men and horses that moved in strange rippling patterns of conflict. Snow whipped and circled· in the wind, making everything indistinct. The sky was knotted with stormclouds, but the red star burned visibly behind them, its long tail casting a faint bloody glow over all. "Uncle Josua has begun the siege!" she cried. Their hurry to find him and warn him seemed to have been for nothing.

The climb up the stairs had led them at last to a door hidden in the lower recesses of the storerooms beneath the king's residence. Miriamele, who prided herself on her knowledge of the Hayholt's ins and outs, many of them discovered while in her Malachias disguise, had been shocked to discover that a passageway to old Asu'a had been beneath her nose all the time she had lived here—but there were more surprises waiting.

The second came when they emerged cautiously into the ground-level portions of the residence. Despite the howling of wind and the roar of wild voices outside, the many chambers of the residence were deserted and showed little evidence of any recent habitation. As they passed through the cold rooms and grimy hallways, Miriamele's fear of discovery had lessened, but her sense of things being wrong had grown steadily. Braced for any number of unhappy discoveries, she had entered her father's sleeping chamber only to find it not just empty, but in such a fetid and bestial state that she could not imagine who might have been living there.

Now they had emerged onto a small sheltered balcony off one of the third floor rooms, where they crouched behind its stone railing, peering through the ornamental slits at the madness below. The air smelled strongly of lightning-tang and blood.

"I fear that is true." Binabik spoke in a loud voice: between the uproar of combat and the howling winds, there was no fear of drawing attention. "People are fighting down below, and there are men and animals lying dead. But still something there is that is strange. I wish we could be seeing beyond the castle walls."

"What do we do?" Miriamele looked about frantically. "Josua and Camaris and the rest must still be outside. We have to get out to them somehow!"

The daylight, darkened by stormclouds until the whole of the castle seemed sunk in deep water, shifted and flickered strangely, then for a moment the world suddenly shouted and went white. A coil of lightning had snapped down like a fiery whip; thunder rattled the air and even seemed to shake the balcony beneath them. The lightning curled around Green Angel Tower, hung for a moment as the thunder echoes faded, then sputtered out of existence.

"How?" Binabik shouted. "I do not know this castle. What places might there be for escaping?"

Miriamele was having trouble thinking. The noises of

wind and combat made her want to scream and cover her ears; the whirling clouds overhead dizzied her. She abruptly remembered Cadrach, who had been trailing along behind them, silent and unresponsive as a sleepwalker. Miriamele turned, certain that he had taken advantage of their confusion to sneak away, but the monk was crouched in the doorway, gazing up at the tempestuous, red-shot sky with a look of resignation.

"Perhaps we could get out through the seagate," she said to the troll. "If Josua's army is at the walls above Erchester, perhaps there will be only a few . . ."

Binabik's eyes widened. "Look there!" He thrust his hand through the slitted railing to point. "Is that not. . . ? Oh, Daughter of the Mountains!"

Miriamele squinted, trying to make sense out of the madness below her, and saw that there was more to the antheap-swirl of activity than just defenders running to and from the moat-bridge that led to the Middle Bailey. In fact, there seemed to be a fight of some kind taking place on the bridge itself. A large knot of armed men in the Middle Bailey was forcing a smaller troop of riders and footmen back across the moat. As she stared, one of the horses reared and tumbled from the span, taking its rider with it into the dark water. Were Josua's forces inside the wall already, and pushing toward the Inner Bailey? Could those few on the bridge be the last of her father's defenders? But then what of all the armored men just below her who were doing nothing to support the retreating horsemen? Who were they?

And then, as the small troop on the bridge was forced back even farther, she saw what Binabik had seen. One of the riders, standing almost impossibly tall in his saddle, swung his blade high overhead. Even in the false twilight she could see that the sword was black as coal.

"Oh, God, save us." Something cold clutched at her innards. "It's Camaris!"

Binabik was leaning forward, his face pressed against the stone rails. "I am thinking I see Prince Josua, too—there, in the gray cloak, riding near to Camaris." He turned to her, his face fearful. Another jagged lightning

flash silvered the sky. "And there are so few with them—
they could not have been fighting their way inside the
walls, I am guessing. Somehow they have been tricked
into bringing the sword into the castle."

Miriamele hammered her palms against the balcony
floor. "What can we do?!"

The troll peered out through the rails again. "I am not
knowing," he half-shouted. "I have no thoughts at all!
*Kikkasut!* We will be cut in pieces if we go down to
them—and they have already been bringing the sword!
*Kikkasut!*"

"There are flames in the tower window," Cadrach said
in a loud, flat tone.

Miriamele glanced briefly at both Green Angel Tower
and Hjeldin's Tower, but except for the clot of writhing
clouds above the tall spire of the first, she could see nothing unusual.

"See!" Binabik called. "Something is happening!" He
sounded angry and puzzled. "What are they doing?"

Josua and Camaris and their small company of allies
had been driven across the bridge and onto the soil of the
Inner Bailey. But the rest of the mercenary troops milling
haphazardly inside the bailey did not step up to cut them
off; rather, a ragged gap formed in their ranks, a split
which gradually opened into a path that led from the base
of the moat-bridge to the front steps of Green Angel
Tower. As the rest of the king's soldiers pushed their way
across the bridge, Josua and his followers were forced toward the tower. Astoundingly, the mercenaries on either
side did not menace them at all until Camaris, on his pale
horse, tried to turn the troop sideways to cut his way
through the wall of enemies. The king's forces resisted
fiercely and the small company was thrown back, then
driven again across the open space toward Green Angel's
waiting steps.

"The tower!" said Miriamele. "They're forcing them to
the tower! What. . . ?"

"The Sithi-place!" Binabik sprang up suddenly, all
thought of hiding now gone. "The place where the Storm

King was making his last battle. Your father and Pryrates are wanting the swords there!"

Miriamele stood. Her knees were weak. What monstrous thing was happening before them, as relentless and inescapable as the clutch of a nightmare? "We have to go to them! Somehow! Maybe ... maybe there's still something we can do!"

Binabik grabbed his pack from the floor inside the balcony window. "Where and how are we going to them?" he asked her.

Miriamele stared at him, then at silent Cadrach. For a moment, her mind was empty of everything except the howling of the wind outside. At last, a memory fluttered up from the depths.

"Follow me." She shouldered her pack and Norn bow and ran across the damp stone toward the doorway and the residence stairs. Binabik hurried after her. She did not look back to see what Cadrach did.

꙳

Tiamak and Josua scrambled up the stairwell, silent except for their labored breath, struggling to stay close behind Camaris. A flight above them the knight climbed steadily, unheeding as a sleepwalker, his powerful legs carrying him upward two steps at a time.

"How could any stairs stretch so high?" Tiamak gasped. His lame leg was throbbing.

"There are mysteries in this place I never dreamed." Josua held his torch high, and the shadows leaped from crevice to crevice along the richly-textured walls. "Who knew a whole world still remained down here?"

Tiamak shuddered. The silver-masked Norn Queen hovering over the Sithi's sacred pool was a mystery that the Wrannaman wished he had never discovered. Her words, her chill invincibility, and especially the dreadful power that had filled the cavern of the Pool of Three Depths, had haunted him all the way up the great staircase. "Our ignorance is thrown back at us," he panted. "We are fighting things we only guessed at, or glimpsed

in nightmaroo. Now the Sithi are locked in struggle with
that . . . she-thing, fighting, dying . . . and we do not even
know why."

Josua turned his gaze from the old man's back to peer
briefly at Tiamak. "I thought that was the task of the
Scroll League. To know such things."

"Those who went before us knew more than we do,"
Tiamak replied. "And there is much that even Morgenes
and the others never learned, much hidden even to
Eahlstan Fiskerne, who they say was a true if secret
friend to the Sithi. The immortals have always been tight-
fisted with their lore."

"And who can blame them, after the harm mortals have
done with nothing more than stone and iron and fire."
Josua glanced at the marsh man again. "Ah, merciful
God, we are wasting breath on talk. I see pain on your
face, Tiamak. Let me carry you a while."

Tiamak, climbing doggedly, shook his head. "Camaris
has not slowed. We would fall farther behind, and if we
leave the stairs we might lose him again, with no Sithi
this time to help us find our way. He would be alone, and
we might wander here forever." He mounted several more
steps before he had the breath to speak again. "If need be,
let me trail behind. It is more important you stay with
Camaris than with me."

Josua did not say anything, but at last nodded unhappily.

The terrible sensation of shifting eddied away, and with
it the dancing lights that, for a moment, had made Tiamak
think the great staircase was burning. He shook his head,
trying to clear his rattled thoughts. What could be happening? The air seemed strangely hot, and he felt the
hairs on his arm and neck prickling.

"Something dreadful is happening," Tiamak cried. He
staggered in Josua's shadow, wondering if the increasing
force of the strange slippages meant that the Norn Queen
was defeating the Sithi. The thought fastened on him as
though it had claws. Perhaps she had escaped the pool.
Would she follow him and the prince up the darkened

stairs, silver mask expressionless, white robes fluttering. . . ?

"He's gone!" Josua's voice was full of horror. "But how can that be?"

"What? Gone where?" Tiamak looked up.

The torchlight revealed a place where the stairwell abruptly stopped, capped by a low ceiling of stone. Camaris was nowhere in sight.

"There is no place he could have hidden!" the prince said.

"No, look!" Tiamak pointed toward a fissure in the ceiling wide enough to allow a man to crawl through.

Josua quickly lifted Tiamak up into the hole, then held him steady while the Wrannaman probed for something to grasp. Tiamak found he could almost push his head above the surface on the far side. He pulled himself up and through, fighting against his treacherous, weary muscles, and when he lay quivering on the stone floor he called down through the fissure: "Come! It's a storeroom!"

Josua tossed up the torch. With a helping hand from Tiamak, he struggled upward through the crack. Together they raced across the room, dodging the bits of wreckage strewn about, and climbed a rickety ladder through a hatchway. Beyond this was another storeroom, this one with a small window high in the wall. Threatening black clouds roiled in the box of sky visible there, and cold wind bled through. Another hatchway led to yet one more level.

As Tiamak put his aching leg to the bottommost rung, a crash resounded back through the hatch door, a sudden and violent sound. Josua, who climbed above him, sped up the ladder and disappeared.

When Tiamak made his way to the top, he found himself in a small, shadowy room, staring at the flinders of a door strewn outward into the chamber beyond. He could see torchlight in the chamber, and figures moving. Josua's voice rang out.

*"You! May God send your black soul to hell!"*

Tiamak hurried to the doorway, then stopped, blinking as he tried to make sense of the wide circular room that

opened before him. On his left, the windows above the
tall main doors streamed with scarlet-tinted light that vied
with the dull glow of torches in the wall sconces. Just a
few cubits before the Wrannaman, Camaris stood in the
ruins of the smaller door which had blocked his own way
out into the chamber; the old knight now stood motionless, as though stunned. Josua was only an arm's length
away from Camaris, Naidel unsheathed and dangling in
his hand. Two dozen paces beyond them, on the far side
of the stone floor, a small door in the wall mirrored the
one Camaris had just burst into flinders. On Tiamak's
right, beyond a high arch, a great sweep of stairs coiled
upward out of sight.

But it was the figures on the bottom steps of this staircase that caught and held Tiamak's eye, as they had
Josua's—especially the bald man in the flapping red robe,
who stood tall in the midst of a strew of human bodies,
like a fisherman in a shallow stream. One armored man
he still held by the shoulders, though the way the soldier's gold-helmeted head wagged suggested he had long
since stopped fighting.

"Damn you, Pryrates, let him go!" cried Josua.

The priest laughed. With a shrug, he effortlessly threw
aside . . . Camaris, who clattered on the stone flags and
lay still, black blade clutched in his fist.

Tiamak stared in numb astonishment. The Camaris he
and Josua had followed still stood nearby, wavering
slightly like a tree in a stiff breeze. How could there be
two? Who sprawled there?

"Isorn!" Josua shouted, his voice ragged with grief.
Tiamak suddenly remembered, and the terror that
clutched him clamped tighter. The deception they had
conceived with the Sithi had come to this—this clutter of
motionless men? Nearly a dozen soldiers, including powerful young Isorn, and the priest had defeated them with
his bare hands? What could possibly stop Pryrates and his
immortal ally now? Josua and his companions had but
one of the Great Swords, and its wielder, Camaris,
seemed lost in a dreaming daze. . . .

"I'll have your heart for this," Prince Josua snarled,

leaping toward the stairway. Pryrates lifted his hands and a nimbus of oily yellow light flickered around the alchemist's fingers. As Naidel came flashing toward him in a wide, deadly arc, Pryrates' hand snaked out and caught the blade. The point of contact hissed like a hot stone dropped into water, then the priest grabbed Josua's sword arm and pulled him forward. The prince struggled, flailing at Pryrates with his other, handless arm, but the priest caught that too and drew Josua toward him until their faces were so close it seemed that the alchemist might kiss the prince.

"It is almost too easy," Pryrates said, laughing.

Tiamak, weak with fear, slid back into the shadows of the doorway. *I must do something—but who am I?* The Wrannaman could barely stand upright. *A little man, a nobody! I am no fighter! He would catch me and kill me like a tiny fish.*

"There is no hell deep enough for you," Josua grated. Sweat streamed down his face, and his sword arm trembled, but he seemed as helpless as a child in the priest's prisoning grip.

"And I will visit them all." Pryrates extended his arms again. The yellow light wavered around him. "You are one of the few who have balked me, Lackhand. Now you will see that your interference comes to—*nothing.*" He flung Josua against the nearby arch. The prince struck hard and slid down to lie motionless beside a man dressed in his own gray surcoat and armor—the Nabbanai baron's brother, Brindalles. The man's right arm, like Josua's, ended in a black leather cap, but Brindalles' arm was bent at an angle that made Tiamak's stomach lurch. There was no sign of life on the impostor's pale, blood-flecked face.

Tiamak shrank farther back into the shadows, but Pryrates did not even look at him. Instead, the priest moved up the stairwell, then stopped and turned to Camaris.

"Come, old one," he said, and smiled. Tiamak thought his grin as empty and mirthless as a crocodile's. "I can feel the ward solidifying, which means the time has come. You need carry your burden only a little farther."

Camaris took a step toward him, then stopped, shaking his head slowly. "No," he said hoarsely. "No. I will not let it . . ." Something of his real self had returned; Tiamak felt a faint swelling of hope.

Pryrates only crossed his arms on his scarlet breast. "It will be interesting to watch you resist. You will fail, of course. The pull of the sword is too strong for any mortal, even a tattered legend like yourself."

"Damn you," Camaris gasped. His body twitched and he shifted his balance back and forth, as though he fought some invisible thing that sought to tug him toward the stairs. The old knight sucked in a breath with a painful gasp. "What manner of creature are you?"

"Creature?" Pryrates' hairless face was amused. "I am what a man who accepts no limits can become. . . ."

While his last words still hung in the air, there was a sudden booming concussion. Where the door on the opposite side of the chamber had been, a murky cloud billowed. Several shadowy figures stumbled through, indistinguishable in the smoke.

"How exciting." Pryrates' tone was sardonic, but Tiamak saw a certain animation creep into the alchemist's face that had not been there before. The priest took a step downward and peered into the haze. A moment later he reeled back, gurgling, with a black arrow all the way through his neck, its head standing out a handspan beyond the skin. Pryrates stumbled in place for a moment, then fell and rolled down the stairs to lie beside his victims. Blood pooled beneath his head, as though his bright robes melted and ran.

Miriamele stared up and down the narrow hallways, struggling to regain her bearings. The Chancelry had been a daunting maze when she had lived in the castle, but it was even more confusing now. Familiar doors and hallways were not quite where they should be, and all the passages seemed the wrong lengths, as though the Chancelry's dimensions had somehow become shiftingly fluid.

Miriamele struggled to keep her head. She was certain she could eventually find a way through, but she feared the loss of precious time.

As she waited for her companions, the freezing wind which whistled through the unshuttered windows rolled a few crumpled parchments past her feet.

Binabik trotted around the corner. "I did not mean that you should be waiting for me," he said. "I was stopping only because I saw these. They have come through the window, I am thinking." He handed her three arrows of plainer workmanship than the Norn shafts she had scavenged earlier. "There were others, too, but they had been broken by striking on the stone walls."

Miriamele had no quiver to put them in. She slipped them into the open corner of her pack beside Simon's prize and the shafts she had saved from the tunnels. Even with Binabik's additions she still had far fewer arrows than she would have liked, but it was a relief to know that if it came to it, she need not sell her life cheaply.

*Look at me,* she marveled. *The world is ending, the Day of Weighing-Out has come at last . . . and I'm playing at soldier.*

Still, it was better than letting the terror push through. She felt it coiling inside her, and knew that if she let go of composure for even a moment she would be overwhelmed.

"I wasn't waiting." She pushed away from the wall. "Just making sure I know the way. This place was always difficult, but now it's almost impossible. And it's not just this. . . ." She gestured at the smashed furniture and the ghostly rags of parchment, the doors splintered off their hinges that lay across the passage. "There are other changes too, things I don't understand. But I think I'm right, now. We must go quietly from here, wind or no wind—we're almost to the chapel, and that's right beside the tower."

"Cadrach is coming." The troll said it as though he thought she might care.

Miriamele curled her lip. "I'm not waiting. If he can keep up, then let him." She hesitated for a moment, then pulled one of the arrows from her pack and nocked it, letting it sit loosely on the bowstring. Armed, she set off down the narrow hallway. Binabik looked back, then scurried after her.

"He has been having as much hurt as us, Miriamele," said the troll. "Maybe more. Who can say what things he or she would be doing under Pryrates' torturing?"

"The monk has lied to me more times than I can count." The thought of his betrayals burned so fiercely inside her that for a moment she was not even afraid. "One word of truth about the swords, about Pryrates, might have saved us all."

Binabik's face was unhappy. "We are not losing everything yet."

"Not yet."

Cadrach caught up to them in the chaplain's walking hall. The monk said nothing—perhaps in part because he was fighting for breath—but fell in behind the troll. Miriamele allowed herself one icy stare.

As they reached the door, everything seemed to shift again. For a moment Miriamele thought she saw pale flames running up the walls; she struggled not to cry out as, for a dreadful instant, she felt herself torn apart. When the sensation passed, she did not feel as though she had been completely restored.

Long moments passed before she felt able to speak.

"The ... chapel is on ... the other side." Despite the incessant keening of the wind beyond the walls, Miramele whispered. The terror inside her was struggling to break free and it took all her strength to keep it in place. Binabik was wide-eyed and unusually pale; Cadrach looked ill, his forehead moist, his gaze fever-bright. "On the far side there is a short hallway that leads directly into the tower. Look to your feet. With all these broken things about, you might trip and hurt yourself—" she pointedly addressed her concern only to Binabik, "—or make enough noise that whoever is inside will hear us coming."

The troll smiled wanly. "Like hare's feet are the steps of the Qanuc," he whispered. "Light on snows or rock."

"Good." Miriamele turned to stare at the monk, trying

to divine what further treachery might lurk behind his watery gray eyes, then decided it did not matter. There was little Cadrach could do to worsen their situation: the time for stealth would be over in moments, and what had been their greatest hope seemed now to have been turned against them.

"Follow me, then," she told Binabik.

As she opened the door into the transept of the chapel, the cold reached out and grasped at her; a cloud of her steaming breath hung in the air. She paused for a moment and listened before leading her companions out onto the wide chapel floor. Snow had drifted into the corners and against the walls, and pools of water lay everywhere on the stone. Most of the benches were gone; the few tapestries that remained flapped in ragged, moldy strips. It was hard to believe it had once been a place of comfort and refuge.

The storm and the clamor of the struggle outside were also louder here. When she looked up, she learned the reason.

The great dome overhead had been ruptured, the glass saints and angels all tumbled and shattered into colored dust. Miriamele trembled, awed even after all she had experienced to see a familiar thing so changed. Snowflakes swirled lazily downward, and the storm-darkened sky, touched with the bloodlight of the flaming star, twisted in the broken frame like an angry face.

As they made their way across the front of the apse, past the altar, Miriamele saw that other forces beside impersonal nature had worked desecration here: crude hands had smashed the faces of the holy martyrs' statues, and had smeared others with blood and worse things.

Despite the dangerous footing, they made their way silently across to the far transept. She led them down a slender passageway to a door set deeply into the rock. She stooped and listened at the keyhole, but could hear nothing through the echoing din that leaked from above. A strange, painful, prickling sensation came over her, as though lightning were in the air—but lightning *was* in the air, she reminded herself.

"Miriamele. . . ." Cadrach sounded frightened.

She ignored him, trying the latch. "Locked," she said quietly, then shrugged against the crawling itch, which was worsening. "And too heavy for us to knock down."

"Miriamele!" Cadrach pulled at her sleeve. "Some kind of barrier is being formed. We will be trapped."

"What do you mean?"

"Can you not sense it pushing in on us? Feel your skin creep? A barrier is being formed and drawn inward to surround the tower. Pryrates' work—I feel his heedless power."

She stared at the monk, but there was no sign of anything but unfeigned concern on his face. "Binabik?" she asked.

"I am thinking he speaks rightly." He, too, was beginning to twitch. "We will be squeezed in a most comfortless way."

"Cadrach, you opened the dwarrows' door. Open this one."

"This is a simple lock, Lady, not a door-warding spell."

"But you have been a thief, too!"

He shivered. Wisps of hair were beginning to stand upright on his head, and Miriamele could feel a stirring on her own arms and scalp. "I have no lockpicks, no tools—it is useless. Perhaps it is just as well. I wager it will be a quick death."

Binabik hissed in exasperation. "I am not wanting any death, of quickness *or* slowness, if it can be escaped." He stared at the door for a moment, then threw down his pack and began to rummage in it.

Miriamele watched helplessly. The oppressive feeling was growing by the moment. Praying they could find some other way into the tower, she hurried back up the passageway, but within a dozen strides the air seemed to become grossly thicker, harder to breathe. A strange humming was in her ears and her skin burned. Unwilling to give up so easily, she took a few more steps; each was more difficult than the last, as though she waded in deepening mud.

"Come back!" Cadrach cried. "That will do you no good!"

She turned with difficulty and made her way back to the door. "You were right, there is no going back. But this thing, this barrier, moves so slowly!"

The monk was scratching frenziedly at his arms. "Such things take a certain time to appear, and the priest has expended much power summoning it. He obviously intends nothing should go in or come out."

Binabik had found a small leather sack and was rooting in it. "How do you know it's Pryrates?" Miriamele asked. "Perhaps it's . . . the other."

Cadrach shook his head mournfully, but there was a hard core of rage beneath. "I know the red priest's work. Gods! I shall never forget the feeling of his filthy presence in my head, in my thoughts. . . ."

"Miriamele, Cadrach," the troll said. "Lift me up."

They bent and raised him from the floor, then moved at his direction to the side of the door. The air seemed to be tightening around them: the effort to lift tiny Binabik seemed tremendous. The troll climbed until he stood with his feet on their quivering shoulders.

"It's . . . hard to . . . breathe," Miriamele panted. Something was buzzing in her ears. Cadrach's mouth hung open and his chest heaved.

"No speaking." Binabik reached up and poured a handful of something into the door's upper hinge.

Miriamele's ears were hammering now; she felt squeezed, as though held in a huge, crushing fist. A constellation of sparks spun in the shadows before her.

"Turn away your faces," Binabik gasped, then took something from his hand and smacked it sharply against the hinge.

A sheet of light filled Miriamele's eyes. The throttling fist became a giant open hand that slapped her away from the door. Despite the force, she fell backward only a little way and retained her feet, buoyed by the unseen but encroaching barrier. Binabik toppled from her shoulders and fell onto the ground between her and Cadrach.

When she could see again, the door lay a-tilt in its frame, half-obscured by drifting smoke.

"Through!" she said, and tugged the troll's arm. He snatched up his pack, then they pushed into the dark space, stumbling on the tipped door. For a moment Miriamele stuck in the doorway, her pack wedged, her bow snagged on the broken hinge, but she fought free at last. When they had passed over into Green Angel Tower's broad antechamber, the pressure was suddenly gone.

"Lucky we are the hinges were outside," Binabik gasped, fanning the air.

Miriamele stopped and stared. Through the murk she could see a flash of bright red on the tower's staircase. A moment later the smoke had cleared enough that she could clearly see Pyrates' gleaming pink skull. Bodies lay scattered at his feet, and Camaris stood before him in the room's center. The old man was staring at the priest with such hopeless misery that Miriamele felt her heart tear in her breast.

Grinning, Pyrates turned from the old knight and took a step down, swiveling his bottomless black eyes toward the doorway where she stood. The door's destruction seemed to have startled him no more than the fall of a tumbling leaf. Without thinking, Miriamele lifted her bow, straightened the arrow, drew, and fired. She aimed for the widest part of the priest's body, but the shaft flew high. It seemed a miracle when she saw Pyrates stumble backward. When she saw that the arrow stood from his throat, she was too dumbfounded at her own shot even to feel joy. The priest fell and rolled bonelessly down the few remaining steps to the antechamber floor.

"Chukku's Stones!" the troll gasped. "You have ended him."

"Uncle Josua!" she shouted. "Where are you? Camaris! It's a trick! They *wanted* us to bring the swords!"

*I've killed him!* The thought was a quiet bloom of exultation deep inside her. *I've killed the monster!*

"The sword must not be going any farther," cried Binabik.

The old knight took a few lurching steps toward them,

but even with Pryrates facedown on the floor, dead or dying, Camaris still seemed in the grip of some terrible power. Of Josua there was no sign; but for the old man, all in the chamber lay motionless.

Before anyone could speak again a bell rang in the tower high above, monstrously loud, lower and deeper than any bell Miriamele had ever heard. The very stones of the wide room shuddered, and she felt its tolling strike into her bones. For an instant the antechamber seemed to melt away, the waterstained tapestries replaced by walls of gleaming white. Lights glittered everywhere, like fire-flies. As the cry of the bell faded, the illusion flickered and disappeared.

As Miriamele struggled to regain her wits, a figure rose slowly near the foot of the stairs, grasping at the stone arch for support. It was Josua, his cloak hanging raggedly, his thin shirt torn at the neck.

"Uncle Josua!" Miriamele hastened toward him.

He stared at her, eyes wide and, for a brief moment, uncomprehending. "You live," he said at last. "Thank God."

"It's a trick," she said even as she threw her arms around him. The small return of hope, when the greatest perils still remained, was painful as a knife-wound. "The false messenger—that was the rhyme about the swords! It was a trick. They *wanted* the swords here, wanted us to bring them!"

He gently disengaged himself. A trickle of blood showed along his high hairline. "Who wanted the swords? I do not understand."

"We were fooled, Prince Josua." Binabik came forward. "It has been the planning of Pryrates and the Storm King all along that the swords should be brought here. I am thinking the blades will be used in some great magic."

"We didn't find Bright-Nail," Miriamele said urgently. "Do you have it?"

The prince shook his head. "The barrow was empty."

"Then there's hope! It's not here!"

Josua opened his mouth to reply, but a loud moan of pain from Camaris stopped him.

"Ah, God, why do You torment me?" the old man cried. He lifted his free hand to his head as though he had been struck by a stone. "It is wrong—that answer is wrong!"

The prince's face was full of startled concern. "We must take him out of this place. Something in the sword drew him here. While he still has his wits about him, we must get him outside again."

"But Pryrates was making some barrier around the tower," said Binabik anxiously. "Our only hope is that now . . ."

"This is my punishment!" cried Camaris. "Oh, my God, there is too much blackness, too much sin. I am sorry . . . so sorry!"

Josua took a step toward him, then leaped away again as Thorn flickered through the air. The prince backed toward the stairwell, trying to keep himself between Camaris and whatever called him so powerfully.

"The thing Pryrates has begun is not yet being finished," Binabik shouted. "The sword must not be going further!"

Josua danced back from another awkward blow. He held Naidel before him, but seemed reluctant even to use it for defense, as though fearing he might hurt the old man. Miriamele, full of fluttering panic, knew that the prince would be killed if he did not resist with all his power.

"Uncle Josua! Fight back! Stop him!"

As Josua backed up the wide stairway and Camaris reached the bottom step, Binabik bolted from her side. He leaped across the motionless bodies lying before the stairs and threw himself at the back of the old knight's legs, knocking Camaris down. As Miriamele hurried forward to help the troll, another figure came up beside her. She was amazed to see that it was the Wrannaman, Tiamak.

"Take one of his arms, Lady Miriamele." The marsh man's eyes were wide with fear and his voice shook, but he was already reaching down. "I will take the other."

Although Binabik had wrapped both his arms and legs around the old knight's knees, Camaris was already beginning to rise. Miriamele grasped at the hand that sought to pull Binabik loose, but it slipped from her sweating grip. She clutched again at his upper arm and this time hung on as Camaris' long muscles bunched beneath her. A moment later all four of them tumbled to the floor again, landing among the scatter of bodies. Miriamele found herself staring down into the half-open eyes of Isorn, whose slack face was as white as one of the Norns. A scream tried to force its way out of her, but she was clinging so fiercely to Camaris' flailing arm that she could not think much about Isgrimnur's son. There was only the scent of fear-sweat and rolling bodies.

She caught a glimpse of Josua, who stood a short distance away on the stairs. Camaris again began to climb to his feet, dragging his attackers up with him.

"Josua," she panted. "He'll . . . get away from us! Kill him . . . if you have to . . . but stop him!"

The prince only stared. Miriamele could feel the old knight's tremendous strength. He would shake them off in a few moments.

"Kill him, Josua!" she screamed. Camaris was half-standing now, but Tiamak was draped around his sword arm; the knight's chest and stomach were unprotected.

"Something!" Binabik grunted in pain, struggling to hold Camaris' legs together. "Be doing something!"

But Josua only took a hesitant step forward, Naidel hanging slack in his hand.

Miriamele let go with one arm and hurriedly groped for Camaris' sword belt. When she had it, she slid off his arm and grasped the belt with both hands, then braced her legs against the bottom step and pulled backward as hard as she could. The old man swayed for a moment, but the tangling weight of Tiamak and Binabik were making his movements clumsy and he could not keep his balance. He tottered, then fell backward as heavily as an axed tree.

Miriamele's legs were caught beneath the knight. His collapse knocked the breath from her. When Camaris stirred after a long moment, she knew she did not have the strength to pull him down again.

"Ah, God," the knight murmured to the ceiling. "Free me from this song! I do not wish to go—but it is too strong for me. I have paid and paid. . . ."

Josua seemed almost as wracked with torment as Camaris. He took another step downward, then paused before backing up again. "Merciful God," said the prince. "Merciful God." He straightened, blinking. "Keep Camaris there as long as you can. I think I know who is waiting at the top of the stairs." He turned away.

"Come back, Josua!" cried Miriamele. "Don't go!"

"There is no time left," he called over his shoulder as he mounted upward. "I must get to him while I can. He is waiting for me."

She suddenly realized who he meant. "No," she whispered.

Camaris was still lying on the floor, but Binabik had not let go of the knight's legs. Tiamak had been flung to one side; he crouched at the foot of the stairs, rubbing a bruised arm and staring at Camaris with fearful anticipation.

"Tiamak, follow him," pleaded Miriamele. "Follow my uncle. Hurry! Don't let them kill each other."

The Wrannaman's eyes widened. He looked at her, then back to Camaris, his face solemn as a frightened child's. At last he clambered to his feet and hobbled up the stairs after Josua, who had already disappeared into the shadows.

Camaris drew himself into a sitting position. "Let me up. I do not wish to hurt you, whoever you are." His eyes were fixed on some distant point beyond the antechamber. "It is calling me."

Miriamele pulled herself free and, trembling, took his hand. "Sir Camaris, please. It is an evil spell that is calling you. Don't go. If you take the sword there, everything you have fought for may be destroyed."

The old knight lowered his pale eyes to meet hers. His face was bleak, drawn with terrible strain. "Tell the wind not to blow," he said hoarsely. "Tell the thunder not to roar. Tell this cursed sword not to sing and pull at me." But he seemed to sag, as though for a moment the summoning grew less powerful.

A wordless cry like a howl of animal fear rang through the antechamber. Miriamele suddenly remembered

Cadrach. She whirled to look at him where he crouched by the doorway, but the monk yowled again and pointed.

Pryrates was climbing slowly to his feet, loose-limbed as a drunkard. The arrow still protruded from either side of his neck. A faint, putrescent glow played about the torn flesh.

*But he's dead!* Horror gusted through her. *He's dead! Sweet Elysia, Mother of God, I killed him!*

The priest staggered a step, groaning, then turned his sharklike gaze toward Miriamele. His voice was even harsher than before, ripped raw. "You . . . *hurt* me. For that, I will . . . I will keep you alive a long time, womanchild."

"Daughter of the Mountains," Binabik said hopelessly. He still clung to the old knight's legs. Camaris lay staring at the ceiling, oblivious to all but the call from above.

Swaying, the priest reached up and grasped the black shaft just behind the arrowhead and snapped it off, bringing a fresh dribble of blood from the wound. He took a couple of whistling breaths, then grasped the feathers and drew the rest of the arrow back out through his throat, his face stretched in a rictus of agony. He stared at the blood-smeared thing for a moment before tossing it disdainfully onto the floor.

"A Nakkiga shaft," he rasped. "I should have known. The Norns make strong weapons—but not strong enough." The bleeding had stopped, and now a tiny wisp of smoke wafted from one of the holes in his neck.

Miriamele had nocked another arrow, and now tremblingly drew her bow and leveled the black point at his face. "May . . . may God send you to Hell, Pryrates!" She struggled to form the words without falling into panicked shrieking. "What have you done with my father?!"

"He is upstairs." The priest laughed suddenly. He stood now without wavering, and seemed almost gleefully drunk on his own display of power. "Your father is waiting. The time we have both waited for is come. I wonder who shall enjoy it more?" Pryrates lifted his fingers and curled them. The air grew momentarily hotter around Miriamele's hand, then the arrow snapped. The suddenly empty bow almost flew from her grasp.

"It is not so pleasant tugging out arrows that I will stand and let you feather me all day, girl." Pryrates turned to look back across the antechamber at Cadrach. The broken doorway behind the monk, barred by the alchemist's ward, was full of shifting, crimson-streaked shadows. The priest beckoned. "Padreic, come here."

Cadrach gave a low moan, then stood and took a lurching step.

"Don't do it!" Miriamele called to him.

"Do not be so cruel," said Pryrates. "He wishes to attend his master."

"Fight him, Cadrach!"

The priest cocked his head. "Enough. Soon I shall have to go and attend to *my* duties." He lifted his hand again. "Come here, Padreic."

The monk staggered forward, sweating and mumbling. As Miriamele watched helplessly, he sank into a heap at Pryrates' feet, face pressed against the stone. He edged forward, quivering, and laid his cheek against one of the priest's black boots.

"That is better," Pryrates crooned. "I am glad you are not so foolish as to challenge me—glad that you *remember*. I feared you had forgotten me during your travels. And where *have* you been, little Padreic? You left me and went to keep company with traitors, I see."

"It is you who are being the traitor," Binabik shouted at him. He grimaced as Camaris shifted, trying at last to break the troll's grip on his legs. "To Morgenes, to my master Ookequk, to all who were taking you in and teaching you their secrets."

The priest looked up at him, amused. "Ookequk? So you are the fat troll's errand boy? This is splendid, indeed. All of my old friends gathered here to share this day with me."

Camaris was clambering to his feet. Binabik struggled to retain his hold, but the old man reached down and effortlessly dislodged him, then straightened, black Thorn dangling in his hand. He took a few hesitant steps toward the stairs.

"Soon, now," said Pryrates. "The call is very strong."

He turned his attention to Miriamele. "I fear the rest of our conversation will have to wait. The ritual will soon reach a delicate moment. It would be good for me to be there."

Miriamele was desperate to distract him, to keep him away from her uncle and father. "Why do you do this, Pryrates? What can you gain?"

"Gain? Why, everything. Wisdom such as you cannot even imagine, child. The entire cosmos laid naked before me, unable to hide even its smallest secret." He extended his arms, and for a moment seemed almost to grow. His robe billowed, and eddies of dust whirled away across the chamber. "I will know things at which even the immortals can only guess."

Camaris suddenly cried out as though he had been stabbed, then stumbled toward the wide staircase. As he did, the great bell tolled again from somewhere above, making everything shiver and rock. The room wavered before Miriamele's eyes; flames licked up the walls, then vanished as the echoes faded away.

Miriamele's head was reeling, but Pryrates seemed unaffected. "That means the moment is very near," he said. "You hope to detain me while Josua confronts his brother." The priest shook his hairless head. "Your uncle can no more halt what is to come than he could carry this castle away on his shoulders. And neither can you. I hope I can find you when everything is finished, little Miriamele—I am not quite sure what will remain, but it would be a shame to lose you." His cold eyes flicked over her. "There is so much we will do. And we will have as long as we want—forever, if need be."

Miriamele felt her heart smothered in an icy fist.

"But you've failed!" she shouted at him. "The other sword isn't here! You've failed, Pryrates!"

He smiled mockingly. "Have I?"

She turned as something moved just at the edge of her vision. Camaris' resistance had faded at last, and he was shambling up the first flight of stairs; within moments he had vanished around the spiraling stairwell. She watched the old man go with dull resignation. They had done everything they could, but it had not been enough.

Pryrates stepped past Binabik and Miriamele to follow the old knight, then stopped at the base of the steps and slapped at his neck. He turned slowly to stare at the troll, who had just taken his blowpipe from his lips. Pryrates plucked something from behind his ear and examined it. "Poison?" he asked. "You are a fitting apprentice for Ookequk. He was always slow to learn."

He dropped the dart on the floor and ground it beneath his black boot, then mounted the stairs.

"He is fearing nothing," Binabik whispered, awed. "I do not . . ." He shook his head.

Miriamele stared at the priest's red garment until it had disappeared into the shadows. Her gaze moved down to the sad, broken bodies of Isorn and the other soldiers. The flame of her anger, which had nearly been extinguished by fear, suddenly sprang up again.

"My father is up there."

On the floor beside them, Cadrach lay weeping with his face buried in his sleeve.

Tiamak hurried up the stairs.

*All our calculations, all our clever plans, our hopes,* he mourned. *All for nothing. The swords were a trick, they said. We have been foolish, foolish. . . .*

He scrambled upward, ignoring the flare of pain each step brought as he fought to keep close to Josua, who was a slender gray shadow moving through the near-darkness above him. Tiamak's mouth was dry. *Something* waited at the top of these stairs.

*Death,* he thought. *Death, crouching like a ghant in the treetops.*

From somewhere above the bell thundered again, a shuddersome impact that shook him as an angry parent shakes a child. Flames flickered again before his eyes, and the very substance of things seemed to shred apart. It seemed an agonizingly long time before he could see the steps before him once more, and could make his clumsy, nerveless legs do what he bade them. The tower . . . was it coming to life? When everything else was about to die?

*Why did she send me? What can I do? He Who Always Steps on Sand, I am so frightened!*

Prince Josua pulled farther ahead, then disappeared from view, but the lame Wrannaman climbed on. Quick glances through the tower windows showed him brawling chaos raging across the unfamiliar terrain below. The Conqueror Star glared like an angry eye overhead. Snow cluttered the reddened skies, but he could make out the faint shapes of men swarming over the walls, small skirmishes forming along the battlements, other combats spilling across the open ground around the tower. For a moment Tiamak felt hope, guessing that Duke Isgrimnur and the rest of Josua's army must be forcing their way in—until he remembered the ward with which Binabik said the tower was sealed. Isgrimnur and the others would be unable to prevent whatever was to happen here.

So much was confusing. What exactly had Miriamele and the troll meant about the swords? They were a trick, somehow—and, more importantly, Pyrates and Elias wanted them brought here. But why? What had they planned? Clearly, Utuk'ku's presence beneath the castle had something to do with it. The Sithi had said they could slow her but not stop her. There had been some vast power in the Pool of Three Depths, and Tiamak felt sure the Norn Queen intended to harness it. The Sithi had been struggling to slow her, but they had seemed to be failing at even that task.

Tiamak heard Josua's voice close by. He paused, quivering, afraid to go the final steps. Suddenly he did not want to see whatever the prince had found at the top of the stairs. He squeezed his eyes tightly shut and prayed with all his strength that he would wake up in his banyan-tree hut once more, everything that had happened just an evil dream. But the sound of the restless winds outside never faded, and when he opened his eyes the pale, polished walls of Green Angel Tower's stairwell still surrounded him. He knew he must go on, although every hammerblow of his heart urged him to flee back down the stairs. His legs too weak to hold him upright, he sank to the stone, then climbed the last few steps on his hands and knees, until his head rose past the top step into cold wind and he found himself inside the airy bellchamber.

The huge bronze bells hung beneath the vaulted ceiling like poisonous green marsh flowers, and indeed, despite the buffeting wind, the chamber was filled with the odor of decaying flesh that such flowers produced. Around the center of the chamber a cluster of dark pillars rose to the ceiling, and on all four sides great arched windows opened out onto swirling snow and angry crimson clouds. Josua stood a few steps before Tiamak, facing the north window. The prince's attitude was stiff, as though he did not know what to do, how to stand. Facing him, seated before the window on a simple wooden stool, was his brother Elias.

The king wore a dark iron crown on his pale brow, and held in his hands a long gray something that Tiamak could not quite see. It had something of the shape of a sword, but Tiamak's eyes could not fasten on it properly, as though it did not entirely reside within the natural world. The king himself was dressed in full royal pomp, but his clothes were stained, and his cloak where the wind caught and lifted it showed more holes than cloth.

"Throw it away?" Elias said slowly. His eyes were still downcast, and he replied to whatever Josua had said with the air of one who had been daydreaming. "Throw it away? But I could never do that. Not now."

"For God's love and mercy, Elias!" Josua said desperately, "it is killing you! And it is meant to do more—whatever Pryrates has told you, he plans only evil!"

The king lifted his head, and Tiamak, though he was behind Josua and hidden by the shadows in the stairwell, could not help recoiling in horror. The red light from the windows played across the king's colorless face; muscles writhed beneath the skin like worms. But it was his eyes that made Tiamak choke back a shout of fear. A dull gleam smoldered in them, an inhuman light like the pallid glare of marsh-candles.

"Aedon save us," Josua gasped.

"But this is *not* Pryrates' plan." Elias' lips pulled back in a stiff smile, as though he could no longer make his face work properly. "I am the High King, do not forget: everything moves at my will. It is *my* plan. The priest has only done my bidding, and soon I will have no further need of him. And *you* ..." he rose, unfolding himself with odd jerking movements until he stood at full height, the uncertain gray thing still resting point-down on the floor, "... you were my brother. Once."

"Once!?" Josua shouted. "Elias, what has happened to you? You have become something foul—something demonic!" He took a step back and almost fell into the hole of the stairwell, then turned Naidel's hilt in his trembling hand and made the sign of the Tree over his own breast. Thunder growled outside and the light flickered, but the king only stared at him blankly.

"I am no demon," the king said. He seemed to be considering the matter carefully. "No. But soon I will be more—much more—than a man. I can feel it already, feel myself opening to the winds that cry between stars, feel myself as a night sky where comets flare...."

"May Usires the Ransomer forgive me," Josua breathed. "You are correct, Elias. You are no longer my brother."

The king's calm expression twisted into rage. "And whose is the fault?! You have envied me since you were a child and have done your best to destroy me. You took my wife from me, my beloved Hylissa, stole her and gave her to Death! I have not had a moment's peace since!" The king lifted a twitching hand. "But that was not enough—no, cutting out my heart was not enough for you, but you would have my rightful kingship, too! So you covet my crown, do you?" he bellowed. "Here, take it!" He wrenched at the dark circlet as Josua stared. "Cursed iron—it has burned me until I thought I would go mad!" Elias grunted as he ripped it free and cast it to the floor. A seared shadow-crown of torn, blackened flesh remained on his brow.

Josua took a step back, eyes wide with horror and pity. Tears ran down his cheeks. "I pray ... Aedon's mercy! I pray for your soul, Elias." The prince lifted his leather-capped arm as though to push away what he saw. "Ah, God, you poor man!" He stiffened, then raised Naidel and extended it until the point trembled before the king's breast. "But you *must* surrender that cursed sword. There are only moments before Pryrates comes. I cannot wait."

The king dropped his chin, peering out at Josua from beneath his eyebrows, head lolling as if his neck was broken. A thick droplet of blood oozed from the place where the crown had been. "Ah. Ah. Is it that time, then? I grow confused, since everything has already happened—or so it seems . . ." He swept up the gray thing, and for a moment it hardened into existence, a long mottle-bladed sword with a double guard, streaked with fiery gleams. Tiamak quailed, but stayed where he was, unable to look away. The blade seemed a piece of the storm-tortured sky. "Very well. . . ."

Josua leaped forward with a wordless cry, Naidel darting like lightning. The king flicked Sorrow and knocked the blow aside, but did not return the thrust. Josua danced back, shaking as though fevered; Tiamak wondered if merely having the gray sword touch his own made him quiver so. The prince waded in again, and for long moments he strove to break through his brother's guard. Elias seemed to fight in a sort of dream, moving in sudden spasms, but only enough to block Josua's attacks, waiting until the last moment each time as though he knew where the prince would strike.

Josua at last drew back, gasping for breath. The sweat on his brow gleamed as lightning flickered in the distance.

"You see," Elias said, "it is too late for such crude methods." He paused for a moment; a rumble of thunder gently shook the bells. "Too late." The smoky light in his eyes flared as he lifted Sorrow. "But it is not too late for me to enjoy a little repayment for all the evil you have done me—my wife dead, my throne made unsafe, my daughter's heart poisoned against me. Later I will have other concerns. But for this time I can think on *you,* once-brother." He stepped forward, the sword a shadowy blur.

Josua fought a desperate battle of resistance, but the

king had a more than human strength. He quickly backed Josua against the southern window, then, despite the strange stiffness of his movements, kept the prince pinned there with heavy blows that Josua only barely managed to keep from his vital spots. Slender Naidel was not enough to hold the king away, and within instants Josua tottered against the window-ledge, unable to protect himself any longer. Elias abruptly reached out and grasped Naidel by the blade, then yanked it from Josua's grip. Tiamak, desperate beyond sense, clambered up out of the stairwell and flung himself at the king's back as Sorrow rose overhead. The Wrannaman dragged at Elias' sword arm.

It was not enough to save the prince. Josua flung up his arms to protect himself, but the gray blade hammered down at his neck. Tiamak did not see the sword bite, but he heard the awful smash of impact and felt it shiver up the king's arm. Josua's head jerked and he flew to one side, blood streaming from his neck. He collapsed like an empty sack, then lay still.

Thrown off his balance, the king staggered sideways, then reached up and grasped the back of Tiamak's neck with his free hand. For a moment the Wrannaman's hands closed on Sorrow; the sword was so cold that it burned him. A horrible lance of chill pierced Tiamak's chest and his arms lost their feeling. He had time only to let out a scream of anguish for his pain, for Josua, for all that had gone so terribly wrong, then the king tugged him free and threw him aside. Tiamak felt himself skid across the bellchamber's stone floor, helpless, then something smashed against his head and neck.

He lay on his side, crumpled against the wall.

Tiamak was unable to speak or move. His already fading vision blurred as his eyes filled with tears. A great noise suddenly boomed through the chamber, shaking even the floor beneath him. Red light bloomed even more brightly beyond the windows, as though flames surrounded the tower—for a moment they leaped high enough that he could see them, and see the king's firedrawn silhouette in the window. Then they were gone.

The bell had rung a third time.

# 32

# The Tower

✦

**Simon paused** at the throne room door. Despite the
strange calm he had felt on his trip through the Hayholt's
underbelly, despite Bright-Nail hanging on his hip, his
heart was thudding in his chest. Would the king be waiting silently in the dark, as in Hjeldin's Tower?

He pushed through the doorway, one hand falling to his
sword hilt.

The throne room was empty, at least of people. Six silent figures flanked the Dragonbone Chair, but Simon
knew them of old. He stepped inside.

The heraldic banners that had hung along the ceiling
had fallen, worried free by the teeth of the wind that
streamed in through the high windows. Flattened beasts
and birds lay in tangled piles, a few of them even draped
limply across the bones of the great chair. Simon stepped
over a waterstained pennant; the falcon stitched upon it
stared, eye wide as though shocked by its tumble from the
heavens. Nearby, partially covered by other damp banners, lay a black cloth with a stylized golden fish. As Simon looked at it, a memory came drifting up.

The tumult was growing outside. He knew he had little
time to spare, but the wisp of memory teased him. He
moved toward the black malachite statues. The pulsing
storm light made their features seem to writhe, and for a
moment Simon worried that the same magics that made
the entire castle shift and change might be bringing the
stone kings to life, but to his relief they remained frozen,
dead.

Simon stared at the figure standing just to the right of the great chair's yellowed arm. Eahlstan Fiskerne's face was lifted as though he looked to a glory beyond the windows, beyond the castle and its towers. Simon had gazed many times at the martyr-king's face, but this time was different.

*He's the one I saw,* he realized suddenly. *In the dream Leleth showed me. He was reading his book and waiting for the dragon. She said: "This is a part of your story, Simon."* His eyes dropped to the thin circlet of gold around his own finger. The fish symbol scribed on the band looked back at him. What was it Binabik had told him the Sithi writing on the ring meant? Dragons and death?

*"The dragon was dead."* That was what Leleth had whispered in that not-place, the window onto the past.

*And King Eahlstan is a part of my story?* Simon wondered. *Is that what Morgenes entrusted to me when he sent this ring to me? The greatest secret of the League of the Scroll—that its founder killed the dragon, not John?*

Simon was Eahlstan's messenger, across five centuries. It was a weight of honor and responsibility he could scarcely think of now, a richness to savor if he survived, a delicate secret that could change the lives of almost everyone he knew.

But Leleth had shown him something else, too. She had given him a vision of Ineluki, with Sorrow in his hands. And all Ineluki's malice was bent upon . . .

*The tower!* The peril of the present hour suddenly rushed back. *I must take Bright-Nail there. I have been wasting time!*

Simon turned to look again at Eahlstan's stone face. He bowed to the League's founder as to a liege-lord, relishing the strangeness of it all, then turned his back on the statue-flanked throne and walked quickly across the stone tiles.

The tapestries in the standing room were gone, and the stairway to the privy was exposed. Simon scrambled up the stairs and out through the privy's window-slit, nervous excitement struggling with terror inside him. The bailey might be full of armed men, but they had forgotten about Simon the Ghost Boy, who knew the Hayholt's every nook and cranny. No, not just Simon the Ghost-Boy—Sir Seoman, Bearer of Great Secrets!

The cold wind hit him like a battering ram, almost toppling him from the ledge. The wind threw snow almost sideways, stinging his eyes and face so that Simon could scarcely see. He held on to the window-slit, squinting. The wall outside the window was a pace wide. Ten cubits below, armored men were shouting and metal clashed against metal. Who was fighting? Were those giants that he heard roaring, or was that only the storm? Simon thought he could make out huge white shapes thrashing in the murk, but he dared not look too long or too closely at what waited for him if he tumbled from the wall.

He turned his eyes upward. Green Angel Tower loomed overhead, thrusting out from the muddle of the Hayholt's roofs like the trunk of a white tree, the lord of an ancient forest. Black clouds clung to its head; lightning split the sky.

Simon let himself down from the ledge, then inched forward along the wall on his hands and knees. His fingers rapidly grew numb, and he cursed the luck that had lost his gloves. He clung to the icy stone and tried to keep low so the incessant winds would not pluck him loose.

*Usires on the Tree! This wall was never so long before!*

He might have been on a bridge above the pits of Hell. Screams of pain and rage, as well as less definable sounds, drifted up from the murk, some of them loud enough to make him flinch and almost lose his grip. The cold was terrible, and the wind kept shoving, shoving. He kept his eyes on the wall's narrow top until it ended. An emptiness as long as he was tall yawned before the wall's edge and the turret that surrounded Green Angel Tower's fourth floor. Simon crouched beside this gap, braced against the buffeting wind as he tried to nerve himself to jump. A surge of air shoved him hard enough to make him lean forward until he was almost lying down atop the wall.

*There it is,* he told himself. *You've done it a hundred times.*

*But not in a blizzard,* another part of him pointed out. *Not with armed men down below who would chop you to pieces before you even knew whether you'd survived the fall.*

He grimaced against the sleet and tucked his hands underneath his arms to bring some blood back into his fingers.

*You carry the secrets of the League,* he told himself. *Morgenes trusted you.* It was a reminder, an incantation. He touched Bright-Nail to make sure it was still secure in his belt—its quiet song rose to his touch like the back of a stroked cat—then carefully lifted himself to stand hunched at the corner of the wall. After teetering precariously for long moments, waiting for the wind to slacken just a little, he said a brief prayer and leaped.

The wind caught him in midair and shoved him to the side. He fell short of his landing. For a moment he was slipping away into empty space, but his clawing hand caught in one of the crenellations and he jerked to a halt, dangling. As the wind tugged at him the tower and sky seemed to twist above his head, as though any moment all of creation would go topside-down. He felt the stone sliding from beneath his damp fingers and quickly pushed his other hand into the gap as well, but it was scant help. His legs and feet dangled over nothingness, and his grip was giving way.

Simon tried to ignore the fierce pain that raced through his already aching joints. He might have been tied to the wheel all over again, stretched to the breaking point—but this time there was a way out of the torment. If he let go, it would be over in a moment, and there would be peace.

But he had seen too much, suffered too much, to settle for oblivion.

Straining until agony shot through him, he pulled himself a little higher. When his arms had bent as far as he could make them, one hand scrabbled free, searching for a firmer handhold. His fingertips at last found a crevice between stones; he hauled himself upward again, an involuntary shout of pain forcing its way out through his clenched teeth. The stone was slippery, and for a moment

he almost fell back, but with a last jerk he pulled his upper body into the crenellation and slithered ahead, his legs
still protruding.

A raven, sheltering beneath the tower's overhang,
stared at him, its yellow eyes blank. He pulled himself a
little farther forward and the raven danced away, then
stopped with its head tipped to one side, watching.

Simon dragged himself toward the tower window,
thinking only of getting out of the icy wind. His arms and
shoulders throbbed, his face felt seared by the bitter cold.
As he caught at the sill, he suddenly felt something seize
him from head to foot, a burning tingle that ran up and
down his skin, maddening as biting ants. The raven
leaped into the sky in a flapping blur of black feathers,
caromed once again the powerful wind, then flew upward
out of sight.

The stinging grew stronger and his limbs twitched
helplessly. Something began squeezing the air from his
chest. Simon knew that he had leaped directly into a trap,
a trap set just to catch and kill overeager scullions.

*Mooncalf,* he thought. *Once a mooncalf . . .*

He half-crawled, half-fell through the tower window
and onto the stairway. The agonizing pressure abruptly
ceased. Simon lay on the cold stones, shivering violently,
and struggled to catch his breath. His head throbbed, especially the dragon-scar on his cheek. His stomach
seemed to be trying to crawl up his throat.

Something shook the tower then, a deep pealing like
some monstrous bell, a sound that rattled in Simon's
bones and aching skull, unlike anything he had ever
heard. For a long moment the world turned inside-out.

Simon huddled on the stairs, trembling. *That wasn't the
tower's bells!* he thought when the echoes had died and
his shattered thoughts had coalesced. *They rang every
day, all my life. What was it? What's happening to everything!?*

A little more of the chill wore away, and blood rushed
back to the places it had fled. More than just his cheek
was throbbing. Simon ran his fingers across his forehead.
There was the beginning of a lump above his right eye;

even touching it lightly made him suck in his breath. He decided he must have struck his head on something as he flung himself through the window and onto the stairs.

*It could have been worse,* he told himself. *I could have hit my head when I was jumping to the battlement. I'd be dead now. But instead I'm in the tower—the tower where Bright-Nail needs to ... wants to ...*

Bright-Nail!

He reached down in a panic, but he had not lost the sword: it was still caught against his hip, tangled in his belt. At some point it had rubbed against him and cut him—two small snakes of dried blood coiled on his left forearm—but not badly. And he still had it. That was the important thing.

And the sword was quietly singing to him. He felt rather than heard it, a seductive pull that fought past the pain in his head and battered body.

It wanted to go up.

*Now? Should I just climb? Merciful Aedon, it's so hard to think!*

He raised himself and crawled to the side of the stairwell, then propped his back against the smooth wall as he tried to rub the knots from his muscles. When all his limbs seemed to bend again in more or less the way they should, Simon grabbed at the wall and pulled himself to his feet. Immediately, the world began to tip and spin, but he braced himself, hands pressed flat against the tracery of reliefs that covered the stone, and after some moments he could stand unaided.

He paused, listening to the wind moaning outside the tower walls and the faint din of battle. One additional sound gradually became louder. Footsteps were echoing up the stairwell.

Simon looked around helplessly. There was nowhere to hide. He drew Bright-Nail and felt it throb in his hand, filling him with a heady warmth like a swallow of the trolls.' Hunt-wine. For a brief moment, he considered standing bravely with the sword in his hand, waiting to meet whoever was mounting the stairs, but he knew that was terrible foolishness. It could be anyone—soldiers,

Norris, even the king or Pryrates. Simon had the lives of others to think about, a Great Sword that must be brought to the final battle; these were responsibilities that could not be ignored. He turned and went lightly up the steps, holding Bright-Nail leveled before him so the blade would not scrape against something and give him away. Someone had already been on these stairs today: torches burned in the wall-sconces, filling the places between windows with jittering yellow light.

The stairs wound upward, and within a score of steps he came upon a thick wooden door set into the inner wall. Relief swept through him: he could hide in the room behind it, and if he was careful, peer out through the slot set high in the door to see who climbed behind him. The discovery had come not a moment too soon. Despite his haste, the trailing footfalls had not grown any fainter, and as he paused to fumble with the doorlatch they seemed to become quite loud.

The door pivoted inward. Simon peered into the shadows beyond, then stepped through. The floor seemed to sag beneath his feet as he turned and eased the door closed. He stepped away so the edge of the door could swing past without hitting him, and his back foot came down on nothing.

Simon made a sound of startled terror and grabbed at the inside door handle. The door swung into the room, tipping him even farther backward as he stabbed with his foot for something to stand on. Panic-sweat made his grip on the door handle treacherous. The torchlight leaking in through the doorway showed a floor that extended only a cubit past the door jamb and then fell away in rotted splinters. He could see nothing below but darkness.

He had barely regained his balance, pulling himself back onto the fragment of flooring with one hand, when the great and terrible bell rang a second time. For an instant the world fell away around him and the room with the missing floor filled with light and leaping flames. The sword, which he had held tightly even while dangling over nothingness, tumbled from his grip and fell. A moment later the flames were gone and Simon was tottering on the edge of floor. Bright-Nail—precious, precious thing, the hope of all the world—had disappeared into the shadows below.

The footfalls, which had stopped for long moments, started again. Simon pushed the door closed and huddled with his back against it, on a narrow strip of wood over empty blackness. He heard the footsteps pass his hiding place and move away up the stairwell—but he no longer cared who shared the tower with him. Bright-Nail was lost.

They were so high. The walls of the stairwell seemed to lean inward, closing on her like a swallowing throat. Miriamele swayed. If that ear-shattering bell rang a fourth time, she would surely lose her balance and fall. The plummet down the battering stairs would be unending.

"We are almost there," whispered Binabik.

"I know." She could feel *something* waiting for them just a short distance above: the very air trembled. "I don't know if I can go there. . . ."

The troll took her hand. "I am also frightened." She could scarcely hear him over the shrilling of the wind. "But your uncle is being there, and Camaris has now carried the sword up to that place. Pyrates is there, too."

"And my father."

Binabik nodded.

Miriamele took a deep breath and looked up to where a thin gleam of scarlet leaked past the bend of the stairwell. Death and even worse was waiting there. She knew she must go, but she also knew with terrible clarity that the moment she took her next step the world she had known would begin to end.

She ran her hands across her sweaty face.

"I'm ready."

Smoky light throbbed where the stairs opened into the chamber above. Thunder growled outside. Miriamele squeezed Binabik's arm, then patted at her belt, touching

the dagger she had taken from the cold, unmoving hand
of one of Isorn's men. She took another arrow from her
pack and fitted it loosely on the string of her bow.
Pryrates had been hurt once—even if she could not kill
him, perhaps she could provide a crucial distraction.

They stepped up into the bloody glow.

Tiamak's thin legs were the first thing she saw. The
Wrannaman lay unmoving against the wall with his robe
rucked up around his knees. She choked back a cry and
swallowed hard, then mounted higher; her face lifted into
the streaming wind.

Dark clouds knotted the sky beyond the high windows,
ragged edges agleam with the Conqueror Star's feverish
light. Flecks of snow swirled like ashes beneath the
chamber ceiling where the great bells hung. The sense of
waiting, of a world in suspension, was very strong.
Miriamele struggled for breath.

She heard Binabik make a small noise beside her.
Camaris knelt on the floor beneath the green-skinned
bells, his shoulders shaking, black Thorn held upright before him like a holy Tree. A few paces away stood
Pryrates, scarlet robes rippling in the powerful wind. But
neither of these held her attention.

"Father?" It came out as little more than a whisper.

The king's head lifted, but the motion seemed to take a
long time. His pale face was skeletally gaunt, his eyes
deep-sunken, gleaming like shuttered lamps. He stared at
her, and she felt herself falling into shards. She wanted to
weep, to laugh, to rush to him and help to make him well
again. Another part of her, trapped and screaming, wanted
to see this twisted thing that pretended to be him—that
*could not* be the man who had raised her—obliterated,
sent down into darkness where it could not trouble her
with either love or terror.

"Father?!" This time her voice carried.

Pryrates cocked his head toward her; a look of annoyance hurried across his shiny face. "See? They pay no
heed, Highness," he told the king. "They will always go
where they do not belong. No wonder your reign has burdened you so."

Elias shrugged his shoulders in anger or impatience. His face was slack. "Send her away."

"Father, wait!" she cried, and took a step forward. "God help us, don't do this! I have crossed the world to speak to you! Don't do this!"

Pryrates held up his hands and said something she could not hear. Abruptly she was seized all over by some invisible thing that clung and burned, then she and Binabik were thrown back against the chamber wall. Her pack fell from her shoulder and tumbled onto the floor, spilling its contents. The bow flew from her hand and spun away out of reach. She fought, but the clinging force gave only enough to allow her a few slow, twitching movements. She could not move forward. Binabik struggled beside her, but with no more success. They were helpless.

"Send her *away*," Elias repeated, more angrily this time, his eyes looking at anything but her.

"No, Majesty," the priest urged, "let her stay. Let her *watch*. Of all the people in the world, it is your brother," he gestured to something Miriamele could not see, "—who is unfortunately beyond appreciating it now—and your treacherous daughter who forced you onto this path." He chortled. "But they did not know that the solution you found would make you even greater than before."

"Is she in pain?" the king asked brusquely. "She is no longer my daughter—but I will not see you torture her."

"No pain, Highness," he said. "She and the troll will merely be . . . an audience."

"Very well." The king at last met her eyes, squinting as though she were a mile distant. "If you had only listened," he said coldly, "if you had only obeyed me . . ."

Pryrates put a hand on Elias' shoulder. "All was for the best."

*Too late.* The emptiness and desperation Miriamele had been fighting broke free and spread through her like black blood. Her father was lost to her, and she was dead to him. All the risks, the suffering, had been for nothing. Her misery grew until she thought it would stop her heart.

A fork of lightning split the sky beyond the window. Thunder made the bells hum.

"*For . . . love.*" She forced her jaws to work against the alchemist's prisoning spell. Each faint word echoed in her own ears, as though she stood at the bottom of a deep well. She told him, but it was too late, too late. "You . . . I . . . did these things . . . for love."

"*Silence!*" the king hissed. His face was a rawboned mask of fury. "Love! Does it remain after worms have gnawed the bones? I do not know that word."

Elias slowly turned back to Camaris. The old knight had not moved from his spot on the floor, but now, as though some power in the king's attention compelled him, he crawled a few steps closer, Thorn scraping across the stone tiles before him.

The king's voice became curiously gentle. "I am not surprised to see that the black sword chose you, Camaris. I was told that you had returned to the living. I knew that if those tales were true, Thorn would find you. Now we will act together to protect your beloved John's kingdom."

Miriamele's eyes widened in horror as a figure that had been blocked from her sight by Camaris now became visible. Josua lay crumpled just a little to one side of her father, arms and legs splayed. The prince's face was turned away, but his shirt and cloak were sodden crimson around his neck, and blood had pooled beneath him. Miriamele's eyes filled with blurring tears.

"It is time, Majesty," said Pyrates.

The king extended Sorrow like a gray tongue until it nearly touched the old knight. Although Camaris was visibly struggling with himself, he began to lift Thorn to meet the shadowy blade in the king's hand.

Fighting against the same force that bound Miriamele, Binabik gave a muffled shout of warning, but still Thorn rose in the old man's trembling hands.

"God, forgive me," Camaris cried wretchedly. "It is a sinful world . . . and I have failed You again."

The two swords met with a quiet click that cut through the room. The noise of the storm diminished, and for a moment the only thing audible was Camaris' moan of anguish.

A point of blackness began to pulse where the tips of the two blades crossed, as though the world had been ripped open and some fundamental emptiness was beginning to leak through. Even through the bonds of the alchemist's spell, Miriamele could feel the air in the high chamber suddenly grow hard and brittle. The chill deepened. Traceries of ice began to form in the arches of the windows and along the walls, spreading like wildfire. Within moments the chamber was furred with a thin surface of ice crystals that shimmered in a thousand strange colors. Icicles were growing on the great bells, translucent fangs that gleamed with the light of the red star.

Pryrates lifted his arms triumphantly. Glinting flakes clung to his robe. "It has begun."

The somber cluster of bells at the ceiling did not move, but the bone-shaking sound of a greater bell rang out once more. Powdery ice fluttered as the tower trembled like a slender tree caught in storm winds.

※

Simon tugged at the handle and cursed quietly. This lower door was wedged shut—there would be no easy entry into the room beneath the missing floor—and now he heard footsteps coming up the stairwell again.

His joints still hurt fiercely, but he scrambled back up the stairs to the other door as quickly as he could, then stepped inside, taking care this time to stand at the very edge of the flooring, which had held his weight before. He was forced to move far to the side of the door as it closed. As the footfalls passed outside, he carefully made his way along the strip of wood to look through the door slit, but by the time he could reach it he glimpsed only a small dark shape vanishing up the stairwell, lurching strangely. He waited a score of heartbeats, listening, then crept outside and took a torch from the nearest bracket.

To his vast relief, Simon saw by the torch's light that there was indeed a bottom to the chamber below, and

though parts of that lower floor had rotted through as
well, it was mostly intact. Bright-Nail lay gleaming in a
pile of discarded furniture. Seeing it lying there like a
piece of splendid jewelry thrown onto a midden heap, Simon felt a violent pang. He must get it back. Bright-Nail
must go to the tower. Even from a distance, he could feel
its yearning.

A faint thread of the blade's song coiled through his
thoughts as he found what seemed the most stable spot on
the floor below, gripped the butt of the torch between his
teeth, then slid his legs over the edge of the strip inside
the doorway. He let himself down to the full extension of
his arms, then dropped, his heart fluttering as he landed.
The wood creaked loudly and sagged a little, but held. Simon took a step toward Bright-Nail, but his foot sank as
though into muddy ground. He hurriedly pulled it back to
see that a section of the floor a little larger than his boot
sole had crumpled and fallen in.

Simon got down onto his hands and knees. He made
his way across the treacherous surface with slow caution,
taking more than a few splinters as he probed before him.
The cry of the wind outside was muffled. The torch
burned hot beside his cheek; its quavering flame threw
his shadow up on the wall, a hunched thing like a beast.

He stretched out his hand. Nearer . . . nearer . . . there!
His fingers closed around Bright-Nail's hilt, and instantly
he could feel its song intensify, vibrating through him,
making him feel welcome . . . and more. Its need became
his need.

*Up,* he thought suddenly. The word seemed a glowing
thing before his mind's eye. *It's time to go up.*

But that was easier said than accomplished. He sat back
on his haunches, wincing as the floor creaked, and removed the torch from his teeth. He lifted it and looked
around. This room was wider than the one above; the half
of the ceiling that had not been the wood floor of the upper chamber was a slab of pale stone, seemingly without
support. The walls were bare except for a faint scrawl of
carvings, overlaid with dust and soot. There was nothing
to afford any holds for climbing, and even if he jumped,

he could not reach the bit of flooring that edged the doorway above.

Simon pondered for a moment. The sword's pull was a
shadow behind his thoughts, an urgency like a quiet but
steady drumbeat. He slid Bright-Nail into his belt, reluctantly releasing the hilt, then resettled the torch handle in
his jaws. He crawled back across the floor toward the
door he had tried from the stairs, but it was just as impassable from the inside: either damp weather or shifting
timbers kept it firmly closed no matter how he pulled. He
sighed, then crept back to the middle of the room.

Moving with extreme care, he dragged bits of broken
furniture across the floor, setting each piece carefully on
or beside the last, until he had made a shoulder-high pile
near the sealed doorway. As he was sliding the scarred
surface of a discarded table into place at the top of the
heap, he again heard someone mounting the steps.

It was hard to tell, but this time there seemed to be
more than one set of feet. He crouched in silence, steadying the tabletop with his hand, and listened to the footfalls move past the door beside him, then, after a few
dragging moments, echo softly past the door above. He
held his breath, wondering which of his many enemies
might be climbing the tower, knowing that he would discover the answer all too soon. Bright-Nail tugged at his
thoughts. It was hard to sit still.

When the noises had faded, Simon prodded at the pile
until he was certain it was steady. He had tried to point all
the jagged edges and snapped legs downward in case he
fell, but he knew that if he did, he and the spiky pieces of
broken chairs, stools, and heavy tables would probably
break through the floor together and tumble down into yet
a lower room. He did not think much of his chances if
that happened.

Simon climbed the pile as gently as he could, laying
his body flat across the tabletop until he could draw his
legs up behind him. The flame of the torch he held in his
teeth sizzled the ends of his hair. He clambered to his feet
and felt the unsteady mass rock gently beneath him. Balancing carefully, he removed the torch and held it up,

looking for the sturdiest spot on the edge of flooring overhead.

He was moving toward the edge of the teetering pile when the bell rang for a third time.

Even as the thunderous peal grabbed the entire tower and shook it, and the pile of wood fell away beneath him, Simon let go of the torch and leaped. One piece of the flooring overhead broke loose in his hand, but the other held. Panting, he grasped another section with his free hand and struggled to pull himself up, even as gusts of purple fire chased themselves across the walls and everything shifted and blurred. His arms, already tired, trembled. He pulled himself higher, reaching out a hand to grab at the doorsill, then lifted his leg until it was on the strip of floor. The echo of the bell faded, although he felt it still in his teeth and the bones of his skull. The lights flickered and died, but for a faint glow beneath him. He could smell smoke rising from the torch that now lay among the shards of the piled furniture.

Grunting with the strain, Simon dragged himself the rest of the way onto the safety of the narrow band of wood. As he lay gasping for air, he saw flames beginning to lick up from the floor below.

He scrabbled to one side as cautiously as haste would permit, pulled the door open, then sprawled forth onto the stairs. He tugged the door shut, leaving a few orphaned tendrils of smoke to float and dissipate, and waited for his hands to stop shaking quite so violently.

He pulled the sword from his belt. Bright-Nail was his once more. He was still alive, still free. Hope remained.

As he began to climb he felt the blade's song rise inside him, a chant of joy, of approaching fulfillment. He felt his own heart speed as it sang. Things would be set right.

The sword was warm in his grip. It seemed a part of his arm, of his body, a new organ of sense as alert and attuned as the nose of a hunting hound or the ears of a bat.

*Upward. It is time.*

The pain in his head and limbs flowed away, to be

filled with the ever-rising triumph of Bright-Nail, clutched firmly in his hand, safe from all harm.

*It is time at last. Things will be set right. It is time.*

The sword's urging grew stronger. He found it hard to think of anything but putting one foot before the next, carrying himself up toward the top of the tower, to the place where Bright-Nail longed to go. Knotted, red-shot clouds showed in the windows he passed, scarred by the occasional jagged flicker of lightning, but the noise of the storm seemed curiously muffled. Far louder now, at least in his thoughts, was the song of the sword.

*It's finally going to end,* he thought. He could feel that, Bright-Nail's promise. The sword would bring a halt to all the confusions and dissatisfactions that had plagued him for so long; when it joined its brothers, everything would change. All that unhappiness would end.

There was no one else on the steps now. No one moved but Simon, and he could feel that everyone, everything, waited for him. All the world hung on the fulcrum of Green Angel Tower, and he would be the one to shift that balance. It was a wild, heady feeling. The sword pulled him on, singing to him, filling him with imprecise but powerful intimations of glory and release at every upward step.

*I am Simon,* he thought, and could almost hear trumpets flare and echo. *I have done mighty deeds—slain a dragon! Won a battle! Now, I bring the Great Sword.*

As he mounted up, the stairs shimmered before and behind, a downward-flowing river of ivory. The pale stone of the stairway wall seemed to glow, as if it reflected the light that burned within him. The sky-blue carvings were as heartbreakingly lovely as flowers strewn before the feet of a conqueror. Completion was ahead. An end to pain awaited him.

The bell tolled a fourth time, even more powerfully than before.

Simon staggered, shaken like a rat in a dog's teeth as the echoes boomed and resounded down the stairwell. A blast of freezing air rolled past him, blurring the carvings on the wall with a milky skin of ice. He almost dropped the sword again as he lifted his hands to his head and cried out. Stumbling, he grabbed at the frame of one of the tower's windows for support.

As he stood, shivering and moaning, the sky outside changed. The broad smear of clouds vanished, and for a long moment the full blackness of the sky opened before him, dotted with tiny, cold stars, as though Green Angel Tower had torn free of its moorings and now floated above the storm. He stared, teeth clenched against the bell's fading echoes. After three heartbeats the black sky clotted with gray and red and the tower was surrounded by storm once more.

Something tugged at his thoughts, fighting against Bright-Nail's unslackening pull.

*This . . . is . . . wrong.* The joy that he had shared, the feeling that he would somehow make things right, ebbed away. *Something bad is happening—something very bad!*

But he was already moving again, mounting the stairs toward the dim glow. He was not the master of his own body.

He struggled. His limbs felt distant, numb. He slowed himself, then managed to stop, shuddering in the freezing wind that blew down the stairwell. Tiny whiskers of ice hung from the walls, and his breath clouded about his head, but he could feel an even greater coldness lurking somewhere above him—a coldness that somehow *thought.*

He fought for a long time on the stairs, struggling to regain control of his own arms and legs—a struggle against nothing visible that went unobserved except by the cold, inhuman presence. He could feel its hungry attention as the sweat beading on his skin froze and fell tinkling onto the steps. Steam rose from his overheated body, and where the warmth left, deadening chill crept in.

The cold took Simon at last, filling him. It moved him like a puppet on a stick. He jerked and began to stagger upward once more, screaming silently from the prison of his skull.

He stepped up out of the stairwell and into the vaporous bellchamber; the ice-blanketed walls glimmered and sparkled. Storm clouds surrounded the high windows, and light and shadow moved sluggishly, as though the cold gripped them, too.

Miriamele and Binabik stood beside the door, writhing slowly, caught somehow like flies struggling in amber. His eyes widened as he saw them and his heart thudded painfully behind his ribs, but he could not call out or even stop his feet from carrying him forward. Miriamele opened her mouth and made a muffled noise. Tears filled his eyes, and for a moment her pale face held him like a lamp in a dark room—but the thing that gripped him would not be denied. It swept him past his friends like a river current, tugging him toward the cluster of pillars at the center of the chamber.

Beneath the frost-furred bells three figures waited, one kneeling. The part of Bright-Nail that had entangled itself with him danced and leaped ... but the still-Simon part quailed as Elias turned toward him with a face like a dead man's. The mottled gray sword in his two fists lay against black Thorn, and where they touched there was nullity, an emptiness that hurt Simon's mind.

Shivering, Camaris turned to Simon, his hair and brows powdery with ice. The old man's eyes stared in abject misery.

"My fault ..." he whispered through chattering teeth.

Pryrates had watched Simon's lurching entrance. Now the priest nodded, smiling tightly. "I knew you were in the tower somewhere, kitchen boy—you and the last of the swords."

Simon felt himself drawn closer to the place where Thorn and Sorrow met. Through Bright-Nail, whose song coursed inside him, he could feel the music of the other two swords as well: the dancing throb of life that was within all of them grew stronger as the moment of their joining approached. Simon felt it like the speeding current of a river's narrows, but he could also feel that there was a barrier that somehow kept the blades apart. Although two of them were touching, and only a few cubits stood between them and the third, they all remained as widely separated as they had ever been.

But what was different now, what Simon felt deeply and wordlessly in his mind's inmost, was that soon there would be a great change. Some mighty universal wheel lay loose on its axle, ready to turn, and when it did all the barriers would fall, all the walls would vanish. The swords sang, waiting.

Before he knew it, he was stepping forward. Bright-Nail clicked against the other two blades. The shock of contact traveled not just through Simon, but through the room as well. The black emptiness where the swords met deepened, a hole into which the entire world might fall and perish. The light changed all around: the star-glow seeping in through the windows deepened, turning the chamber bloody, and then the dreadful bell tolled a fifth time.

Simon trembled and cried out as the tower shook and the energies of the swords, still pent but fighting now for release, traveled through him. His heart stuttered, hesitated, and almost stopped. His vision blurred and darkened, then gradually came back. He was inextricably caught in something that burned like fire, that dragged like a lodestone. He tried desperately to pull away, but a supreme effort only made him sway gently, caught on Bright-Nail's hilt like a fish dying on a hook. The bell's echoes died out.

Even through the music of the swords, Simon could sense the chill presence he had felt on the stairs growing stronger, vast and weighty as a mountain, cold as the gaps between stars. It was closer now, but at the same time it hovered just beyond some incomprehensible wall.

Elias, who seemed almost unmoved by the exuberating power of the swords, raked Simon with mad green eyes. "I do not know this one, Pryrates," he murmured, "—although there is something familiar about him. But it does not matter. All the bargains have been kept."

"Indeed." The priest moved past, so close that his robe touched Simon's arm. A buried part of Simon shrieked with disgust and fury, but no sound passed his quivering lips: he was now little more than something that held Bright-Nail. The sword's vaulting spirit, connected now to its brothers, uncaring of human struggles and human hatreds, waited only for whatever would happen next, eager as a dog expecting to be fed.

"All bargains are kept," Pryrates rasped as he took a place beside the king's shoulder, "and all is now set in motion. Soon Utuk'ku the Eldest will have harnessed the Pool of Three Depths. Then we will have completed the Fifth House, and all will change." He looked at Simon and his eyes glittered. "This one you do not know is Morgenes' kitchen-whelp, Highness." Pryrates grinned. "This *is* satisfying. I saw what you did to Inch, boy. Very thorough work. You saved me some tiresome effort."

Simon felt a powerful rage bubbling up inside him. In the red light the priest's smug face seemed to hang bodilessly, and for a moment Simon could see nothing else. He struggled to move his limbs, to pull Bright-Nail away from its brothers so he could smash out the murderer's life, but he was helpless. The flame of anger blazed without release, so hot that Simon felt sure it would scorch him to ashes from within.

The tower rocked again to the thunderous voice of the bell. Simon stared, even as the floor shook before him and his ears popped, but the bronze bells at the center of the chamber did not move. Instead, a ghostly shape appeared, a bell of sorts, but long and cylindrical. For a moment, as the phantom bell vibrated, Simon saw flames sheeting again outside the windows, the sky gone endlessly black.

When the noise had died, Pryrates lifted his hands. "She has conquered. It is time."

The king lowered his head. "God help me, I have waited long."

"Your waiting is over." The priest crossed his arms before his face, then lowered them. "Utuk'ku has captured the Pool of Three Depths. The swords are here, waiting only for the Words of Unmaking to release that which binds them, then the force that was prisoned within them will sing free and bring you everything that you have desired."

"Immortality?" asked Elias, shy as a child.

"Immortality. A life that outlasts the stars. You sought your dead wife, Highness, but you found something far greater."

"Do not . . . do not speak of her."

"Rejoice, Elias, do not grieve!" Pryrates brought his palms together and lightning scratched across the sky outside the tall windows. "You feared you would have no heir when your disobedient daughter ran away—but you yourself will be your own inheritor. You will never die!"

Elias lifted his head, his eyes shut as though he basked in a warming sun. His mouth trembled.

*"Never die,"* he said.

"You have gained powerful friends, and in this hour they will pay you back for all your suffering." Pryrates stepped away from the king and thrust his red-sleeved arm toward the ceiling. "I invoke the First House!"

The great invisible bell sounded again, crashing like a hammer in a god's smithy. Flames ran through the bellchamber, capering across the icy walls. "On Thisterborg, among the ancient stones," Pryrates intoned, "one of the Red Hand is waiting. For his master and you, he uses the power of that place and opens a crack into the between-places. He unfolds the first of the *A-Genay'asu'e* and brings forth the First House."

Simon sensed the cold, dreadful something that waited growing stronger. It was all around Green Angel Tower, drawing nearer, like a hunting beast coming stealthily through the darkness toward a campfire.

"At Wentmouth," Pryrates cried, "on the cliffs above the endless ocean where the Hayefur once burned for travelers from the lost West, the Second House is now built. The Storm King's servant is there, and a far greater flame lifts to the skies."

*"Do . . . not . . ."* Binabik, held by Pryrates' magics, struggled to move forward from the walls. His voice seemed to come from a great distance. "Do . . . not. . . !"

The priest flicked a gesture toward him and the troll was silenced, squirming helplessly.

Again the bell rang, and the power of it seemed to pulse on and on, reverberating. For a moment Simon heard voices rising outside, screams of pain and terror in the language of the Sithi. Red lights flickered in the icicles hanging from the bell-chamber's vaulted ceiling.

"Above Hasu Vale, beside the ancient Wailing Stone, where the Eldest before the Eldest once danced beneath stars that have burned out—the Third House is built. The Storm King's servant lifts another flame to the skies."

Elias suddenly took a wobbly step. Sorrow's blade dipped as he bent, although it still touched the other two swords. "Pryrates," he gasped, "something . . . something is burning . . . inside me!"

"*Father!*" Miriamele's voice was faint, but her face was contorted with terror.

"Because it is time, Majesty," the alchemist said. "You are changing. Your mortality must be scorched away by clean flame." He pointed at the princess. "Look, Elias! Do you see what your weakness does to you? Do you see what the sham of love would bring you? She would make you into an old man, sobbing for your meals, pissing in your bed!"

The king straightened up and turned his back on Miriamele. "I will not be held down," he gritted. Every word seemed an effort. "I will . . . take . . . what was promised."

Simon saw that the priest was smiling, though sweat trickled down his egg-smooth brow. "You will have it." He lifted his arms once more. Simon strained until he thought veins would burst in his temples, but could not pull free from the crossed swords. "In your brother's stronghold, Elias," Pryrates said, "in what was the very heart of his treachery—at Naglimund we build the Fourth House!"

Simon again saw the unfamiliar black sky framed in the window. At the bottom of the sill, the Hayholt had become a forest of pale, graceful towers. Flames ran among them. The strange sight did not vanish. The Hayholt was gone, replaced by . . . Asu'a? Simon heard shrieking Sithi voices echoing, and the roar of flames.

"And now the Fifth House!" cried Pryrates.

The tolling of the phantom bell this time brought back

Simon's view of storm clouds and whirling snow. The high-pitched anguish of the Sithi gave way to the dulled shouts of mortals.

"In the Pool of Three Depths, Utuk'ku gives way to the last of the Storm King's servitors, and beneath us the fifth and final House is created." Pryrates spread his arms, palms down, and the whole tower trembled. A kind of sucking pull reached down the length of Bright-Nail, through Simon's arm, tugging at his heart and even his thoughts as though it sought to draw them out whole. Across from him, Camaris bared his teeth in an agonized grimace, Thorn quivering in his fist.

A fountain of icy blue light sprang up through the floor of the bellchamber, roaring and crackling as it passed through the blackness where the swords touched. Diminished and distorted by that passage, it continued up past Simon's face and spattered the glinting ceiling with blue sparks. Simon felt his body convulsing as tremendous energies flowed around him and through him. Inside his battered thoughts the swords thrilled exultantly, their spirits released. He tried to open his mouth and scream, but his jaws were locked tight, teeth grinding. The coruscating blue light filled his eyes.

"And now the three Great Swords have found their way to this place, beneath the Conqueror Star. Sorrow, defender of Asu'a, scourge of the living; Thorn, star-blade, banner of the dying Imperium; Bright-Nail, last iron from the vanished West."

As Pryrates called each name, the great bell rang. The tower and all around it seemed to shift with each sounding, the delicate towers and flames giving way to the squat, snow-covered roofs of the Hayholt, then appearing once more with the next reverberating clang.

Caught in the grip of terrible forces, Simon felt himself burning from within. He hated. Smoldering clouds of rage rose up inside him, hatred at being tricked, at seeing his friends murdered, at the terrible devastation that Pryrates and Elias had caused. He wanted to swing the sword in a deadly arc, to smash everything in sight, to kill those who had made him so horribly unhappy. He could not shriek—he could not even move except to twitch help-lessly. The rage, ordinary escape blocked, seemed to pour out through his sword arm instead. Bright-Nail became a blur, something not quite real, as though part of it had gone away. Thorn was a dark smear in Camaris' hands. The old man's eyes had rolled up in his head.

Simon felt his monstrous anger and despair break free. The blackness where the swords met widened, an unend-ing emptiness, a gate into Unbeing, and Simon's hate poured into it. The void began to crawl up Sorrow's length toward Elias.

"We harness the great fear." Pryrates moved to a spot behind the king, who now seemed as trapped and helpless as the other two swordbearers. The priest spread his arms wide, so that for a moment Elias seemed to have another pair of hands. "In every land, the fear has spread. The kilpa make the seas boil. The ghants crawl through the streets of the southern cities. The beasts of legend stalk the snows of the north. The fear is *everywhere*.

"We harness the great fear. In every land, brother is turned against brother. Plague and famine and the scourge of war turn people into raging demons.

"All the strength of fright and fury is ours, funneled through the pattern of the Five Houses." Suddenly Pryrates laughed. "You are all such small minds! Even your terrors are small ones. You feared to see your armies defeated? You will see more than that. You will see Time itself roll backward in its rut."

King Elias jerked and twitched as the blackness crawled up the blade toward him, but he seemed unable to release Sorrow. "God help me, Pryrates!" A convulsive shudder ran through him, a tremor of such power that he should have fallen to the floor. The nightdark void touched his hands. "Aaaah! God help me, I am burning up! My soul is on fire!"

"Surely you did not think it would be easy?" Pryrates was grinning. Sweat sheeted down his forehead. "It will get worse, you fool."

"I do not wish immortality!" Elias screamed. "Ah, God, God, God! Release me! I am burning away!" His voice was distorted, as though some inconceivable thing had invaded his lungs and chest.

"What you wish is not important," Pryrates spat back. "You will have your immortality—but it may not be all you had hoped."

Elias writhed. His shrieks were wordless now.

Pryrates extended his hands until they hovered on either side of Sorrow's hilt, only inches from Elias' own fingers. "It is time for the Words of Unmaking," he said.

The bell thundered, and once more Green Angel Tower was surrounded by the tragic delicacy of burning Asu'a. The stars in that black sky were cold and tiny as snowflakes. The tower seemed to shake like an agonized living thing.

"I have prepared the way!" Pryrates called. "I have crafted the vessel. Now, in this place, *let Time turn backward!* Roll back the centuries to the moment before Ineluki was banished to the realms beyond death. As I speak the Words of Unmaking, let him return! *Let him return!*" He lapsed into a bellowing chant in a language harsh as shattering stone, as cracking ice. The blackness spread out over Elias and for a moment the king vanished utterly, as though he had been pushed through the wall of reality. Then he seemed to absorb the blackness, or it flowed into him; he reappeared, thrashing and shrieking incoherently.

*Elysia, Mother of Mercy! They've won! They've won!* Simon's head seemed full of storm winds and flame, but his heart was black ice.

Once more the bell caroled, and this time the very air of the chamber seemed to grow solid and glassy, bending Simon's gaze as though he looked through a mirrored tunnel. There seemed no up or down. Outside, the stars began to smear across the sky in long white threads, tangling like wormholes in sod. Even as his life bled from him and out of Bright-Nail in searing waves, he felt the world turning inside out.

The bellchamber grew dark. Distorted shadows loomed and shifted across the icy chamber, then the walls seemed to open and fall away. Blackness flowed through, bringing with it a deeper chill, a freezing, ultimate cold.

Elias' agonized screams had become a choking near-silence. He and Pryrates were now the only things visible. The priest's hands flickered with yellow light; his face gleamed. All the warmth of the world was leaking away.

The king began to change.

Elias' silhouette bent and shifted, growing monstrously, even though his own contorted form was somehow still visible in the center of the darkness.

The deadening chill was inside Simon, too, seeping in where the flames of his fury had burned away his hope. His life was being drawn out of him, sucked clean like marrow from a bone.

The cold, cold thing that had waited so long was coming.

"Yes, you will live forever, Elias," intoned Pryrates. "But it will be as a flitting shadow within your own body, a shadow dwarfed by Ineluki's bright flame. You see, even with the wheel of Time turned backward in its track and all the doors opened to Ineluki once more, his spirit must have an earthly home."

The sounds of the storm outside had ceased, or could no longer penetrate through the strange forces that clutched the bellchamber. The fountain of blue light flowing upward from the Pool had narrowed to a silent stream that vanished into the blackness of the swords' joining and did not reemerge. When Pryrates had finished, there was no sound in the dark room but the rapid chuffing of the king's breath. Scarlet flames kindled in the depths of Elias' eyes, then his head rocked back as though his neck had snapped. Vaporous red light leaked from his mouth.

Simon watched in horror; through the swords he could feel the way being opened, just as Pryrates had said. Something too horrible to exist was forcing its way through into the world. The king's body jerked like a child's doll dangling on a string. Smoldering light seemed to spring forth from him everywhere, as though the very fabric of his body was fraying apart, revealing some burning thing beneath.

Somewhere Miriamele was screaming; her small, lost voice seemed to come from the other end of the universe.

The bellchamber was gone. All around, angles as strange as if reflected in broken mirrors, stood Asu'a's needle towers. They burned as the king's body burned, crumbled as Time itself was crumbling. Five centuries were sliding away into the frozen black void. Nothing would be left but ashes and stone and Ineluki's utter triumph.

"Come to us, Storm King!" shouted Pryrates. "I have made the way. The Words of Unmaking release the power of the swords, and Time turns withershins. History is undone! We shall write it anew!"

Elias writhed, and writhing grew larger, as though whatever filled him was too large for any mortal form and stretched him almost to the point of bursting. A suggestion of antlers flickered on the king's brow, and his eyes were pits of shifting, molten scarlet. His outline wavered, a moving tide of shadow that made it impossible to discern his true shape. The king's arms parted. One hand still held the elusive blur of nothingness that had been Sorrow; the other hand extended and the fingers spread, black as charred sticks. Emberlight played in the creases.

The thing paused, flickering and shifting. It seemed saggingly weary, like a butterfly newly emerged from a cocoon.

Pryrates took a step back and averted his face. "I have . . . I have done what you asked, mighty one." His smug grin was gone: the priest had willingly opened the door, but what had entered shocked even him. He took a deep breath and appeared to find some core of strength. His face again became feral. "The hour is come—but it is not your hour, it is *mine*. How could I trust one who hated every living thing to keep its bargain? I knew that once you had no need of me, your promises would be wind in darkness." He spread his wide-sleeved arms. "Mortal I may be, but I am no fool. You gave me the Words of Changing, thinking them a toy that would keep me childishly amused as I did your bidding. But I have learned, too. Those Words will become your cage, and then you will be *my* servant. All creation will bend to you—but you will bow to *me!*"

The unstable thing at the room's center eddied like blown smoke, but its black, scarlet-streaming heart remained solid. Pryrates began to chant loudly in something only recognizable as language because of the empty spaces between noises. The alchemist seemed to change, reeling in the red-shot darkness that surrounded the king like a fog; his limbs curled and snapped in a ghastly, serpentine way, then he faded into a coiling shadow, a wide rope of blackness that drifted around the place where the king or whatever had devoured him now stood. The shadowy coils tightened around the smoldering heart. The world seemed to bend farther inward, distorting the two shapes until only flame and steam and darkness pulsed at the center of the bellchamber.

The whole of creation seemed to collapse in on this place, on this moment. Simon felt his own terror surge out, crackling through his arms, through Bright-Nail and into the midst of the clotted dark.

The blackness bulged. Tiny arcs of lightning flickered about the room. Somewhere outside, Simon knew, the Asu'a of five centuries before was burning, its inhabitants dying at the hands of Fingil's long-dead army. And what of everyone else? Was all Simon knew gone, borne away by Time's circling wheel?

The lightnings jittered about the chamber. Something pulsed at the center, a storm of fire and thunderheads that suddenly gaped, filling the room with blinding light. Pryrates, his real form restored, staggered backward out of the beating radiance, which promptly collapsed back into shadow. For a moment the priest raised his arms triumphantly over his head, then he teetered and dropped to his knees. A vaguely manlike form coalesced out of the darkness and stood over him, a scarlet suggestion of a face fluttering atop its misshapen head.

Pryrates shuddered and wept. "Forgive me! Forgive my arrogance, my foolishness! Oh, please, Master, forgive me!" He crawled toward the thing, banging his forehead against the almost invisible floor. "I can still do you great service! Remember what you promised me, Lord—that if I served you well I would be first among mortals."

The thing retained its grip on shifting Sorrow, but extended its other blackened hand until it touched the alchemist. The fingers cupped his smooth wet head. A voice more powerful than the bell, as ragged and deadly as the hiss of freezing wind, scraped through the darkness. Despite everything else that had happened, Simon's eyes filled with frightened tears at the sound of it.

*"YES. YOU WILL BE FIRST."*

Jets of steam lifted from beneath the king's fingers. Pryrates shrieked and threw up his arms, grabbing at the hand, but the king did not move and Pryrates could not free himself. Runnels of flame sped down the alchemist's robe. Above him, the king's face was an indistinct lump of darkness, but eyes and ragged mouth blazed scarlet. The priest's scream was a sound no human throat should have loosed. Vapors enveloped him, but Simon saw his threshing arms steaming, cracking, shriveling into waggling things like tree limbs. After a long moment, the priest, all bones and burning tatters, fell to the floor and twitched like a smashed cricket. The jerking movements slowed, then stopped.

The thing that had been Elias slumped, head down, so that nothing could be seen of it but shadow. Still, Simon could feel it drinking the energies that raced through Bright-Nail, Thorn, and Sorrow, regaining the strength to control its stolen body. Pryrates had hurt it, somehow, but Simon could sense that it would be only the work of moments before it recovered. He felt a tiny flutter of hope, and tried to let go of his sword hilt, but it was as much a part of him as his arm. There was no escape.

As though it sensed his attempt to break free, the black thing looked up at him, and even as his heart stumbled and almost failed, he could glean its implacable thought. It had smashed Time itself to return. Even the mortal priest, no matter what powers he had wielded, would not have been allowed to close the door again—what possible chance could Simon have?

In this moment of horror, Simon suddenly felt the shock of the dragon blood that had once scorched his flesh and changed him. He stared at the unsteady black shape that had been Elias, the ruined husk and its fiery occupant, and felt an answering stab of pain where the dragon's black essence had scarred him. Through the pulsing unlight that moved between Bright-Nail and Sorrow, Simon felt not only the all-consuming hatred that had been the blood of the Storm King's deathly exile, but also Ineluki's terrible, mad loneliness.

*He loved his people,* Simon thought. *He gave his life for them but did not die.*

Staring helplessly across the short distance between them, watching as the thing regathered its strength, Simon remembered the vision Leleth had shown him of Ineluki beside the great pool. Such shattering unhappiness had been in that face, but the determination had been a mirror of Eahlstan's as he had sat in his chair and waited for the terrible worm he knew he must meet, the dragon that he knew would slay him. They were somehow the same, Ineluki and Eahlstan, doing what must be done, though life itself was the price. And Simon was no different.

*Sorrow.* His thoughts flittered and died like moths in a flame, but he clung to this one. *Ineluki named his sword Sorrow. Why did she show me that?*

Something was moving at the edge of his vision. Binabik and Miriamele, freed by Pryrates' death, reeled a few steps forward. Miriamele fell to her knees. Binabik staggered closer, head held low as though he walked into a powerful wind.

"You will destroy this world," the troll gasped. Although his mouth was stretched wide, his words seemed quiet as the whir of velvety wings. "You have lost your belonging, Ineluki. There will be nothing for your governing. *You do not belong here!*"

The clot of darkness turned to look at him, then raised a flickering hand. Simon, seeing Binabik quail before the destroying touch, felt his fear and hatred rise anew. He fought against that surge of loathing, although he did no¹ know why.

*Hatred kept him alive in the dark places. Five centu ries, burning in emptiness. Hatred is all he has. And I have hated, too. I have felt like him. We are the same.*

Simon struggled to keep the image of the living Ineluki's suffering face before him. That was the truth beneath this horrible, burning thing. No creature in all the cosmos deserved what had happened to the Storm King.

"I'm sorry," he whispered to the face in his memory. "You should not have suffered so."

The surge of energy from Bright-Nail suddenly grew less. The thing that held Sorrow turned back to him, and waves of terror broke over Simon again. His heart was being crushed.

"No," he gasped, and groped inside himself for a solid place to stand and live. "I will ... fear you, but I ... *will not hate you.*"

There came a still instant that seemed like years. Then Sir Camaris rose slowly from his knees and stood, swaying. In his hands, Thorn still throbbed with blackness, but Simon felt the drain of its forces weaken, as though what he himself felt had somehow run down through the point of connection into Camaris as well.

"Forgiven ..." the old knight croaked. "*Yes.* Let all be ..."

There was a wavering at the center of the darkness that was the Storm King. For a moment, the scarlet light grew less, then died. A glowing red haze leaked free, agitated as a swarm of bees. In the center of the shadows, wreathed in smoke, the pale visage of King Elias shimmered into existence, his face contorted in pain. Wisps of smoke curled from his hair. Flames darted on his cape and shirt.

"*Father!*" Miriamele's entire being seemed in her cry.

The king turned his eyes to her. "*Ah, God, Miriamele,*" he breathed. His voice was not entirely human. "*He has waited too long for this. He will not let me go. I was a fool, and now ... I am .., repaid. I am sorry ... daughter.*" He convulsed, and for a moment his eyes blazed red, though his knotted features still remained. "*He is too strong ... his hate is too strong. He will ... not ... let me ... go. ...*"

His head began to sag. Emberlight bloomed in the cavern of his mouth.

Miriamele shouted wordlessly and lifted her arms. Simon felt rather than saw some fleeting thing snap past him.

A feathered white shaft sprouted from Elias' breast.

For a heartbeat the king's eyes were his own once more, and his gaze locked with Miriamele's. Then his features twisted. A roar louder than thunder tore from the king's gaping mouth and Elias toppled backward into shadow. The roar became an echoing, impossibly loud shriek that seemed to have no ending.

For a fleeting instant Simon felt an impossibly cold *something* scrabbling at the place where the dragon's blood had entered his heart, seeking to find refuge in him if its other host was denied to it. The thing's hunger was all-swallowing and desperate.

*No. You do not belong here.* Simon's thought echoed Binabik's words.

The clawing thing fell away, shrieking soundlessly.

Flames climbed up and outward where the king had stood, mushrooming beneath the roof of the bellchamber. A terrible cold blackness was at the center of them, but as Simon watched in shattered awe, it began to fragment into darting shadows. The world tipped again, and the tower shuddered. Bright-Nail throbbed in his grip, then dissolved in a whirl of black; a moment later, he was holding only dust. He lifted his trembling hand near his face to stare at the sifting powder, then stopped, astonished.

He could move again!

A chunk of stone from the ceiling overhead crashed down beside him, spattering him with sharp fragments. Simon took a reeling step. The chamber was afire, as though the stones themselves were burning. One of the blackened bells tumbled from the cluster at the ceiling and crashed to the floor, smashing a crater in the stone tiles. Shadowy figures moved around him, their motions distorted by the walls of flame.

A voice was calling his name, but he stood at the center of fiery chaos and saw no direction in which to turn. The swirling sky appeared in a jagged opening above his head as more stone fell. Something struck him.

# 33

# Hidden from the Stars

✻

Tiamak stood awkwardly, waiting. The duke listened patiently to the two Thrithings-men, then nodded and replied; they turned and walked through the melting snow toward their horses, leaving the duke and the Wrannaman alone beside the fire.

When Isgrimnur looked up and saw his visitor, he did his best to smile. "Tiamak, what are you doing standing there? Aedon's Mercy, man, sit down. Warm yourself." The duke tried to beckon, but his arm sling prevented it.

Tiamak limped over and sat down on the log. For a moment he held his hands before the flames without speaking, then said: "I am so sorry about Isorn."

Isgrimnur turned his red-rimmed eyes away and stared across the foggy headland toward the Kynslagh. It was a long time before he spoke. "I do not know how I will tell my Gutrun. She will be heartbroken."

The silence stretched. Tiamak waited, unsure whether he should say more. He knew Isgrimnur far better than he had known the duke's tall son, whom he had met only once, in Likimeya's tent.

"He was not the only one to die," Isgrimnur said at last. He rubbed at his nose. "And there are the living to be taken care of." He picked up a stick and tossed it into the fire, then blinked at it with an intent fury. Tears glinted on his eyelashes. The silence grew again, swelling to almost frightening proportions before Isgrimnur broke it. "Ah, Tiamak, why wasn't it me? His life was ahead. I am old. My life is over."

The Wrannaman shook his head. He knew there was no answer to that question. No one could plumb the reasoning of They Who Watch and Shape. No one.

The duke dragged his sleeve across his eyes, then cleared his throat. "Enough. Time for mourning will come." He turned back to Tiamak, and the Wrannaman for the first time saw the truth of Isgrimnur's words: the duke *was* old, a man long past his prime. Only his great vitality had masked it, and now, as though the struts had been kicked from beneath him, he sagged. Tiamak felt anger that such a good man should suffer.

*But everyone has suffered,* he told himself. *Now is the time to gather strength, to try to understand and to decide what comes next.*

"Tell me what happened, Tiamak." The duke forced himself to sit upright, restoring a semblance of self-discipline he clearly needed. "Tell me what you saw."

"Surely I have little to say that you . . ." the Wrannaman began.

"Just tell me." Isgrimnur shifted his broken arm to a more comfortable position. "We have a while before Strangyeard can come and join us, but I imagine you have spoken to him already."

Tiamak nodded. "When I was putting salve on his wounds. Everyone has stories to tell, and none of them pleasant to hear." He composed himself for a moment, then began. "I traveled with the Sithi for what seemed a long time before we found Josua. . . ."


"So you believe Josua was dead already?" The calmness of the duke's deep voice was belied by the unhappy nervousness of his free hand, which passed in and out of his beard, tugging and plucking. His beard looked thinner and shabbier, as though he had pulled at it too often in recent days.

Tiamak nodded sadly. "He was struck very hard on the neck by the king's sword. There was a terrible noise when it hit, a snapping, and then the blood. . . ." The small man shuddered. "He could not have survived it."

Isgrimnur brooded for a moment, then shook his head.

"Ah, well. I thank Usires Aedon in His mercy that at least Josua did not suffer. An unhappy man, though I loved him. An unhappy ending." He looked up at a shout in the distance, then turned his gaze back to the Wrannaman. "And you were then knocked senseless yourself."

"I remember nothing after I heard the bell again . . . until I awakened. I was still in the place where the bells hung, but I did not know it at first. All I could see was that I was surrounded by a whirlpool of fire and smoke and strange shadows.

"I tried to climb to my feet, but my head was spinning and my legs would not work properly. Someone caught at my arm and dragged at me until I could rise. At first I thought I had gone mad, because no one was there. Then I looked down and saw that it was Binabik who had helped me.

" 'Hurry,' he told me, 'this place is falling into pieces.' He pulled at me again—I was dazed and did not entirely understand him. Smoke was everywhere and the floor was pitching beneath my feet with loud grinding noises. As I stood wavering, another shape appeared. It was Miriamele, and she was dragging a body across the floor with great effort. It took me a moment to see through the dust and ashes that it was the young man Simon.

" 'I killed him,' Miriamele was saying over and over. Tears were streaming down her face. I did not understand why she thought she had killed Simon when I could see his fingers moving, his chest rising and falling. Binabik hastened to help her and they pulled Simon across the floor toward the stairwell. I followed them. A moment later the tower shook again and a great chunk of stone fell down and shattered on the spot where I had stood." Tiamak reached down and pointed at the cloth wrapped around his leg. "A piece flew free and cut me, but not badly." He straightened up.

"Miriamele wanted to go back for Josua, but the floor was shaking powerfully now, and more pieces of the ceiling and walls were crumbling. Binabik was doubtful, and they began to argue. My wits were coming back. I told them that the king had broken Josua's neck, that I had seen it happen. Miriamele was hard to understand—she seemed to be half-asleep, despite the tears—but she had begun to say something about Camaris when one of the bells broke loose and smashed down through the floor. We could hear it clang as it struck on something below. Smoke was everywhere. I was coughing, and my eyes were as wet as Miriamele's. I did not much care at the moment, but I felt sure that we would be burned or smashed to death, that I would never know what had happened to cause all this.

"Binabik grabbed Miriamele's arm, pointing to the ceiling, shouting that there was no time. Simon would be difficult enough to carry. She fought him for a moment, but her heart was not in it. The three of us picked Simon up as best we could—he was limp; it made him very difficult to carry—and we scuttled into the stairwell.

"The smoke was not so thick down below the first turn. The fire seemed to burn only in the bellchamber, although I heard Binabik say something that made it sound as if the whole tower had been in flames just instants before. But even if it was easier to breathe, I was still certain we would not survive to reach the ground: the tower was pitching like a tree in a strong wind. I have heard that in days long past one or two of the southernmost islands of Firannos Bay disappeared because the earth shook so hard that the sea swallowed them. If that is true, their last moments must have felt like this. We could barely keep on our feet in the narrow stairwell. Several times I was thrown against one of the walls, and we were lucky we only dropped poor Simon twice. Stone was shivering down and dust was everywhere, choking me as thoroughly as the smoke had."

Tiamak paused and pressed his fingers against his temples. His head hurt. Remembering the desperate flight down the stairs made it ache almost as badly as it had then.

"We had gone down a little farther—it was fearfully difficult to make our way, and the very steps seemed to be breaking apart beneath our feet—when a figure appeared out of the dust below us. It was smeared with ash and

grime and blood, and its eyes stared. At first I thought it
some horrible demon that Pryrates had summoned, but
Miriamele cried 'Cadrach!', and I recognized him. I was
astonished, of course—I had no idea how he of all people
had appeared in this place. I could hardly hear him above
the groaning and rumbling of the tower, but he said: 'I
waited for you,' to no one in particular, then turned and
led us down the stairs. I was angry and frightened, and I
could not help wondering why he did not offer to help
carry Simon, who was a terrible load for a young woman,
a troll, and a small man like me to bear. Simon was now
beginning to move a little more, mumbling to himself and
struggling weakly. It made him even more difficult to
carry.

"Then there was a time I can hardly remember. We
went as fast as we could, but there seemed little chance
we would escape before the tower collapsed completely.
We were still very high up, maybe ten times a man's
height. As we passed one of the windows, I saw the tower's spire hanging crookedly, as if the whole tower bowed
from the waist. You notice strange things at such times, I
suppose, and I saw that the bronze angel at the spire's tip
had its arms extended as though it was poised to fly away.
Suddenly the whole spire shivered, broke loose, and fell
down out of sight.

"There were cracks in the walls of the stairwell wide
enough to put your arm into, Isgrimnur. Through some of
them I could see gray sky.

"Then the tower shook again, so strongly that we fell
down on the stairs. It kept shaking; it was almost impossible to regain our feet, but we did at last. When we had
scrambled down a few more paces, the twisting of the
staircase suddenly opened onto nothing. The side of the
tower wall had gone, fallen away outward: I could see it
lying in great shards, spread out on the snow beneath,
white on white. A great chunk of the staircase had gone
with it, so that there was a gap many paces across, and
beneath lay a fall of twenty cubits onto darkness and broken stone."

Tiamak paused for a moment. "What happened next is

strange. Had I stayed in my swamp, I would not believe this tale from someone else. But I have seen things that have changed what I believe is possible."

Isgrimnur nodded somberly. "As have I. Go on, man."

"We were stopped at the gap, staring hopelessly at the bits of rubble working loose from the ragged edge and tumbling down into shadows."

" 'So here it ends,' Miriamele said. I must say that she did not sound particularly upset. She was fey, Isgrimnur. She had worked as hard as any of us to stay alive, but she seemed to do it only to help the rest of us.

" 'It is not over . . .' Cadrach said. The monk sank to his knees beside the edge of the pit and spread his hands flat over the nothingness. The tower was quivering itself apart, and it seemed to me that the man was praying—although I admit I could think of nothing better to do at that point. As he did, he twisted his face like a man lifting a heavy load. At last he looked over his shoulder to Miriamele. 'Now cross,' he said. His voice was strained.

" 'Cross?' She stared at him. There was anger on her face, strong anger. 'What final trick of yours is this?'

" 'You once said . . . only trust me again . . . when stars shone at midday,' the monk said softly. Every word was an effort. I could barely hear him, and I could not understand what he intended or what he was talking about. 'You saw them,' he said. 'They were there.'

"She looked at him for what seemed like a dreadfully long time as the tower trembled. Then she gently set Simon's shoulders down and took a step toward the pit. I reached out to pull her back, but Binabik stopped me. He had a strange look on his face. So did she, for that matter. So did Cadrach.

"Miriamele closed her eyes, then stepped out from the edge. I was certain that she would fall down and be killed, and I may have shouted something, but she walked out onto the solid air as though the stone steps were still there. Isgrimnur, there was nothing beneath her feet!"

"I believe you," the duke grunted. "I have been told Cadrach was once a mighty man."

"She opened her eyes and did not look down, but

turned to Binabik and me and beckoned us to bring Simon. For the first time, there was something lively in her face again, but it was not happiness. We wrestled Simon down—he was groaning by then, awakening—and she reached up and took his feet, then began to back away over the nothingness. I could not believe what she was doing—what *I* was about to do! I slitted my eyes so I could see only Miriamele moving carefully downward, and followed her. Binabik was beside me, holding Simon's other shoulder. He looked between his feet, but then looked up again very quickly. Even a mountain-troll has some limits, it seems.

"It took us a long time. There were still things like steps beneath us; we could not see them, and we had no idea how far to either side they extended, so we went very carefully. The tower was making deep moaning noises now, as though its roots were being plucked from the ground. If I live a thousand years, Isgrimnur, I will never forget walking across nothingness and trying to stay on my feet as everything pitched and tipped! He Who Always Steps on Sand was truly with us. Truly.

"At last we reached a place where there was real stone. As I stepped onto it and let out my breath, I looked back. Cadrach was on the far side still. His face was gray as ashes and his sides were heaving. He looked like a drowning man before he sinks the last time. What strength did it take him to do what he had done? Nearly all, it seemed.

"Miriamele turned and called to him to cross, but he only lifted his hand and sat back. He could barely speak. 'Go on,' he said. 'You are not safe yet. That was all I had.' He smiled—smiled, Isgrimnur!—and said: 'I am not the man I was.'

"The princess cursed him and cursed him, but more rock was tumbling free, and Binabik and I shouted that there was nothing to be done, that if Cadrach could not, he could not. Miriamele looked down at Simon, then back at the monk. At last she said something I could not hear, then reached down for Simon's feet. As we hurried down the stairwell, I looked back and saw Cadrach sitting beside the broken edge, and the light from the gray sky shone on him through the broken wall. His eyes were closed. He might have been praying, or just waiting.

"We went down another flight, and then Simon was fighting to be let free. We set him down, since we could not carry him against his will—he is quite strong!—but neither could we wait to see if his wits were about him. Binabik pulled at his wrist, talking to him all the while, and he stumbled along with us.

"Dust was so thick from crumbling stone that I could barely breathe, and now there was fire, too, a blaze which had burned away one of the inner doors and was filling the stairwell with smoke. Beyond the windows we could see other pieces of the tower's upper stories topple past. Simon pointed to one of the windows and shouted we must go there. We thought he was addled, but he grabbed Miriamele and dragged her toward it.

"He was not addled, or at least in this he was not, for outside the window was a porch of stone—perhaps it has some drylander name—and beyond it the edge of a wall. It was still a long drop to the ground, but the wall was not far away, only a little farther than I am tall. But the tower was shaking itself to pieces, and we almost fell from the porch. More pieces were dropping. Simon suddenly bent down and grabbed at Binabik, said something to him— then flung him through the air! I was astonished! The troll landed on the edge of the wall, slipped a little on the snow, but held his balance. Miriamele went next, jumping without help; Binabik kept her from sliding off when she landed. Then Simon urged me, and I held my breath and jumped. I *would* have fallen if the other two had not been waiting, because the stone porch had begun to tip downward as I went, and I almost did not leap far enough.

"Now Simon stood, trying to find his balance, and Miriamele was screaming at him to hurry, hurry, and Binabik was shouting, too. Simon leaped and landed, and as he did, most of the porch dropped away, crashing into the snow beneath. We all three caught at him and pulled him to safety before he toppled off the wall.

"A few moments later the entire tower collapsed in on

itself with a noise like nothing I have ever heard, louder than any thunderstorm ... but you heard it. You know. Pieces of stone bigger than this tent smashed past us, but none hit the wall. Most of the tower fell inward, and a cloud of dust and snow and streaming smoke rose up as high as the tower had reached, then spread out across the castle grounds."

Tiamak took a deep breath. "We stood for a long time staring. It was as though I watched a god die. I learned later what Miriamele and the others had seen in the towertop, and that must have been stranger still. When we could think of moving again, Simon led us down through the throne room, past that astounding chair of bones, and out to meet you and the rest. I thanked my Wran deities that the fighting was all but over—I could not have lifted a hand if a Norn had put a knife to my neck."

He sat for a while, shaking his head.

Isgrimnur cleared his throat. "So nothing could have survived, then. Even if Josua or Camaris lived until the end, they would have been crushed."

"We will never know from what remains in that rubble," Tiamak said. "I cannot think we could recognize ..." He remembered Isorn. "Oh, Isgrimnur, please, please forgive me. I forgot."

Isgrimnur shook his head. "The doors to the antechamber came open a short while before the end—I suppose Pyrates' dying put an end to his deviltry, his magical wall or whatever it was. Some of the soldiers nearby pulled out those of the fallen they could before the tower began to collapse. I, at least, have my son's body." He looked down, struggling for composure, then sighed. "Thank you, Tiamak. I am sorry to make you remember."

Tiamak laughed shakily. "I have not been able to stop talking about it. We are all of us in this camp babbling away at each other like children, and have been since the tower fell, since ... since everything happened."

The duke stood, slowly and painfully. "I see Strangyeard coming. The others will meet us. Will you come along, Tiamak? These are important matters, and I would like you to be with us when we talk. We need your wisdom."

The Wrannaman gently bowed his head. "Of course, Isgrimnur. Of course."

⚜

Simon wandered through the rubble of the Inner Bailey. The melting snow had shrunk away to reveal patches of dead grass, and here and there a freshet of new plant life which the sorcerous winter had not destroyed. The different hues of green and brown were soothing to his eyes. He had seen enough of black, ice-white, and blood-red to last him several lifetimes.

He only wished that everything followed such ordinary patterns of renewal. It was a short two days since the tower had fallen and the Storm King had been vanquished, a time when he and his friends should have been rejoicing over their victory, yet here he was, wandering and brooding.

He had slept through the night and the first day after their escape, a thick, bone-weary slumber. Binabik had come to him the second night, telling him stories, explaining, commiserating, then finally sitting with him in silence until Simon fell asleep once more. Others had visited him throughout the morning of this second day, friends and acquaintances reaching out, proving to themselves that he lived, just as the sight of these visitors showed Simon that the world still made a kind of sense.

But Miriamele had not come.

When the unclouded sun had begun to slide down past noon, he had nerved himself to go and see her. Binabik had assured him the night before that she lived and was not badly hurt, so he did not fear for her health, but the troll's reassurances had only made his other unhappiness stronger. If she was well, why had she not come to him or sent a message?

He had found her at her tent, in conversation with Aditu, who earlier that morning had been one of his own visitors. Miriamele had greeted him in a friendly enough fashion, and had exclaimed sorrowfully over his various wounds, as he had over hers, but when he expressed his sadness over the deaths of her uncle and father, she had suddenly grown cold and remote.

Simon wanted to believe it was no more than the justifiable bitterness of someone who had lived through a terrible time and had lost her family—not to mention her own unhappy role in her father's death—but he could not fool himself that there was nothing more to her reaction than that. She had been reacting to him, too, as though something about Simon still made her dreadfully uncomfortable. It made him miserable to see that distance in her eyes after all they had been through together, but he had also felt fury, wondering why he should be treated as though it had been his cruelty to her that had marred their trip into Erkynland, instead of the other way around. Although he had struggled to hide this anger, things had only grown chillier between them, and at last he had excused himself and gone out into the wind.

Into the wind and up the hill he had gone, to wander now through the slushy grounds of the abandoned Hayholt.

Simon paused, staring at the great pile of spread rubble that had once been Green Angel Tower. Small figures moved in the ruins, Erchester-folk scavenging for anything worth saving, either to trade for food or as a keepsake of what was already a fabled event.

It was strange, Simon reflected. He had gone as deep into the earth as anyone could, and had climbed equally as high, but he had not changed very much. He was a little stronger, perhaps, but he guessed that was a strength mostly caused by the inflexibility of scarred places; other than that, he was much the same. A kitchen boy, Pyrates had called him. The priest had been right. Despite his knighthood, despite all else that had happened, there would always be the heart of a scullion inside him.

Something caught his eye and he bent forward. A green hand lay at the bottom of the gulley beside his feet, fingers protruding from the mud in a frozen gesture of release. Simon leaned forward and scraped away some of the soggy clay, exposing an arm, then finally a bronze face.

It was the angel of the towertop, fallen to the earth. He poured a handful of puddle water over the high-boned face, clearing the eyes. They were open, but no life was in them. It was a tumbled statue, nothing more.

Simon stood up and wiped his hands on his breeches. Let someone else drag it from the muck and take it home. Let it sit in the corner of someone's cottage and whisper to them beguiling stories of the depths and heights.

But as he trudged away across the commons yard, turning his back on the wreckage of the tower, the angel's voice—Leleth's voice—came back to him.

*"These truths are too strong,"* she had said, *"the myths and lies around them too great. You must see them and you must understand for yourself. But this has been your story."*

And she had showed him important things indeed. The proof of that, at least in part, lay scattered over a thousand cubits of ground behind him. But there had been more, something that had teased at the edge of his understanding, but which time and circumstance had kept him from pondering. Now the curious thread of memory came back to him, and would not be denied. He had come closest to seeing it in the throne room. . . .

His footsteps echoed across the tiles. There was no other sound. This was a place no one had yet come to scavenge—the mute specter of the Dragonbone Chair was enough to raise fearful hackles in the best of times, and these had not been the best of times.

The afternoon light, warmer than the last time he had been here, spilled down from the windows and gave a little color to the strew of fading banners, although the malachite kings were still cloaked in their own black stone shadows. Simon remembered a void of spreading nothingness and hesitated, his heart pounding, but he swallowed his momentary fear and stepped forward. That blackness was gone. That king was dead.

In full daylight the great throne looked less daunting

than he remembered it. The great toothy mouth still menaced, but some vitality it had once had seemed gone. There was nothing in the eye sockets but cobwebs. Even the massive cage of wired bones sagged in places, and it was clear that some were missing, although none lay around the chair. Simon had a dim recollection of seeing yellowed bones somewhere else, but pushed it away: something different had caught his attention.

Eahlstan Fiskerne. He stood before the stone statue and examined it, trying to find the thing that would scratch the itching spot in his memory. When he had seen the martyr-king's face in his Dream Road vision, there had been something familiar about it. In the throne room before, on his way to the tower, he had thought the resemblance was to the statue he had looked at so often. But now he knew there was something else familiar about the face. It was much like another, one he had also seen many times—in Jiriki's mirror, in reflecting ponds, in the shiny surface of a shield. Eahlstan looked much like Simon.

He lifted his hand and stared at the golden ring, remembering. The Fisher King's people had gone into exile, and Prester John had later come to claim the killing of the dragon and with it the throne of Erkynland. Morgenes had entrusted him with the ring that told that secret.

*"This is your story,"* the angel had said. Who else to entrust with the knowledge and record of Eahlstan's house than ... Eahlstan's heir?

As he stood before the statue, the sudden, certain knowledge splashed him like cold water, raising goosebumps of fear and wonder.

Much of the afternoon slid by as Simon paced back and forth across the empty throne room, lost in thought. He was staring at Eahlstan's statue again when he heard a noise in the doorway behind him. He turned to see Duke Isgrimnur and a few others filing into the chamber.

The duke looked him over carefully. "Ah. So you know, do you?"

The young man said nothing, but his face was full of conflicting emotions. Isgrimnur observed Simon carefully, wondering how this could be the same person as the stripling brought to him on the plains south of Naglimund a year before, draped like a sack across the saddle of a riderless horse.

He had been tall even then, although surely not this tall, and the thick reddish beard had been only soft boy-whiskers—but there was more to the change. Simon had developed an air of calm, a stillness that might have been either strength or unconcern. Isgrimnur worried more than a little about what the boy might have become: what had happened to Simon seemed to have changed that stripling of a year ago beyond reclaiming, almost beyond recognizing. His childhood had been burned away, and now only manhood remained.

"I think I have realized some things, yes," Simon said at last. He carefully smoothed all expression from his face. "But I do not think they matter very much—even to me."

Isgrimnur made a noncommittal sound. "Well. We have been looking for you."

"Here I am."

As the group moved forward, Simon nodded toward the duke, then greeted Tiamak, Strangyeard, Jiriki, and Aditu. As Simon said a few quiet words to the Sithi, Isgrimnur saw for the first time how like them the young man had become, at least at this moment—reserved, careful, slow to speak. The duke shook his head. Who would ever have imagined such a thing?

"Are you well, Simon?" asked Strangyeard.

The youth shrugged and offered a half-smile. "My wounds are healing." He turned to Isgrimnur. "Jeremias brought me your message. I would have come to your tent, you know, but Jeremias insisted you would come to me when you were ready." He looked around the small company, his face closed and careful. "It looks like you're ready now, but you've come a long way up from camp to find me. Do you have more questions to ask?"

"Among other things." The duke watched the others

seat themselves on the stone floor and made a face. Simon
smiled with good-natured mockery and motioned to the
Dragonbone Chair. Isgrimnur shook his head, shuddering.

"Very well, then." Simon collected a stack of fallen banners and put them down on the step below the throne dais.

With only one good arm, Isgrimnur took a little time to
lower himself to the makeshift seat, but he was determined
to do it without leaning on anyone. "I am glad to see you
up and around, Simon," he said when he could talk without breathing hard. "You did not look well this morning."

The young man nodded and eased down beside him.
He moved slowly, too, nursing many hurts, but Isgrimnur
knew he would heal soon. The duke could not help feeling a sharp twinge of envy. "Where are Binabik and
Miriamele?" asked Simon.

"Binabik will be here soon," Strangyeard offered.
"And . . . and Miriamele . . ."

The youth's calm evaporated. "She's still here, isn't
she? She hasn't run off, or been hurt?"

Tiamak waved his hand. "No, Simon. She is in camp
and healing, just as you. But she . . ." He turned to
Isgrimnur, seeking help.

"But there are things to be discussed without
Miriamele here," the duke said bluntly. "That is all."

Simon absorbed this. "Very well. *I* have questions."

Isgrimnur nodded. "Ask them." He had been expecting
this since he saw Simon standing in mute absorption before the statue of Eahlstan.

"Binabik said yesterday that bringing the swords was a
trick, a 'false messenger'—that Pyrates and the Storm
King wanted them all the time." Simon pushed at one of
the sodden banners with the heel of his boot. "They
needed them so they could turn back time to before
Ineluki's last spell, before all the wards and prayers and
whatnot had been laid on the Hayholt."

"All of us outside saw the castle change," the duke said
slowly, caught off balance by Simon's question. He had
been certain the youth would want to ask about his newly-
discovered history. "Even as we fought against the Norns,
the Hayholt just . . . melted away. There were strange tow-

ers everywhere, and fires burning. I thought I saw . . . ghosts, I suppose they were—ghosts of Sithi and Rimmersmen in ancient costume. They were at war, right in the midst of our own battle. What else could it have been?" The clean afternoon light flooding in through the high windows suddenly made it all seem unreal to Isgrimnur. Just days ago, the world had been gripped by sorcerous madness and deadly winter storms. Now a bird twittered outside.

Simon shook his head. "I believe that. I was *there*. It was worse inside. But why did they need us to bring the swords? Bright-Nail was less than a league away from Pryrates for two years. And surely, if they had really tried, they could have taken Thorn, either when we were coming back from Yiqanuc or when it was lying on a stone slab in Leavetaking House up on Sesuad'ra. It doesn't make sense."

Jiriki spoke up. "Yes, this is perhaps the hardest matter of all to understand, Seoman. I can explain some of it. As we were struggling with Utuk'ku at the Pool of Three Depths, much of her thought was revealed to us. She did not shield herself, but rather used that strength in her fight to capture and use the Pool. She believed there was little at that point we could do even if we understood the truth." His slow hand-spread seemed a gesture of regret. "She was correct."

"You held her off a long while," Simon pointed out. "And at a great price, from what I heard. Who knows what might have happened if the Storm King hadn't been forced to wait?"

Jiriki smiled thinly. "Of all of who fought beside the Pool, Likimeya understood the most in the short time we touched Utuk'ku's thoughts. My mother is recovering very slowly from the battle with her ancestor, but she has confirmed much that the rest of us suspected.

"The swords were almost living things. That will come as no surprise to anyone who bore one of them. A large part of their might was, as Binabik of Mintahoq suspected, the unwordly forces bound by the Words of Making. But almost as much of their power was in the effect those Words had. Somehow, the swords had life. They were not creatures like us—they had nothing in them that humans or even Sithi can fully understand—yet they lived. This was what made them greater than any other weapons, but it was also what made them difficult for anyone to rule or control. They could be called—their hunger to be together and to release their energies would eventually draw them to the tower—but they could not be compelled. Part of the terrible magic the Storm King needed for his plan to succeed, perhaps the most important part, was that the swords must come to the summoning themselves at the proper time. They must choose their own bearers."

Isgrimnur watched Simon think carefully before speaking. "But Binabik also told me that the night Miriamele and I left Josua's camp, the Norns tried to kill Camaris. But the sword had already chosen him—chosen him a long time ago! So why would they want him dead?"

"I may have the beginning of the answer to that," Strangyeard spoke up. He was still nearly as diffident as when Isgrimnur had first met him years before, but a little boldness had begun to show through in recent days. "When we fled Naglimund, the Norns who pursued us behaved very strangely. Sir Deornoth was the first to realize that they were ... oh!" The archivist looked up, startled.

A gray shape had rushed into the throne room. It bounded up onto the steps before the dais, knocking Simon onto his side. The young man laughed, tangling his fingers in the wolf's hackles, trying to keep the probing muzzle and long tongue from his face.

"She is full of gladness to see you, Simon!" Binabik called. He was just coming through the doorway, trotting in a futile effort to keep pace with Qantaqa. "She has been waiting long to bring you greeting. I was keeping her away before, while your wounds were new-bandaged." The troll hurried forward, distractedly greeting the rest of the company as he wrestled Qantaqa to the stone floor beside the dais. She yielded, then stretched out between Binabik and Simon, huge and content. "You will be pleased for knowing I have found Homefinder this afternoon," the troll told the young man. "She wandered away from the fighting and was roaming in the depths of the Kynswood."

"Homefinder." Simon said the name slowly. "Thank you, Binabik. Thank you."

"I will take you for seeing her later."

When all had settled in once more, Strangyeard continued. "Sir Deornoth was the first to see that they were not so much chasing us as ... herding us. They drove us out in fright, but they did not kill us when they surely could have. And they only became desperate to stop us when we turned toward the innermost depths of Aldheorte."

"Toward Jao é-Tinukai'i," said Aditu softly.

". . . And they also killed Amerasu when she had begun to see Ineluki's plan." Simon pondered. "But I still do not see why they tried to kill Camaris."

Jiriki spoke. "They were content when you had the sword, Seoman, although I am sure it made Utuk'ku unhappy when Ingen Jegger brought her the news that Dawn Children accompanied you. Still, she and Ineluki must have thought it doubtful we would so quickly grasp what they planned—and as it turned out, they were correct. Only First Grandmother perceived the lineaments of their plot. They removed her and sowed much other confusion beside. For those who dwelled in Stormspike, the Zida'ya were then little threat. They must have felt sure that when the time came, the black sword would select you or the Rimmersman Sludig or someone else to be its bearer. Josua would come for Bright-Nail—his father's sword, after all—and the final rituals could take place."

"But Camaris came back," said Simon. "I suppose they didn't suspect that might happen. Still, he had carried Thorn for decades. It only makes sense the sword would choose him again. Why should they fear him?"

Strangyeard cleared his throat. "Sir Camaris, may God rest his troubled soul—" the priest quickly sketched the Tree, "—confessed to me what he could not tell others. That confession must go with me to my grave." Strangyeard shook his head. "Ransomer preserve him! But the reason he confessed to me at all was that Aditu and Geloë wished to know whether he had traveled to Jao ... whether he had met Amerasu. He had."

"He told Prince Josua his secret, I am sure," muttered

Isgrimnur. Remembering that night, and Josua's terrible expression, he wondered again at what mere words could have made the prince look as he had. "But Josua is dead, too, God rest him. We will never know."

"But even though Father Strangyeard swears that it had nothing to do with our battles here," Jiriki said, "it seems that Utuk'ku and her ally did not know that. Nakkiga's queen knew that Amerasu had met Camaris—perhaps she somehow gleaned the knowledge from First Grandmother herself during their tests of will. Having Camaris suddenly and unexpectedly appear on the scene, perhaps with some special wisdom Amerasu might have given him, and also with his long experience of one of the Great Swords . . ." Jiriki shook his head. "We cannot know, but it seems they decided it was too much of a risk. They must have thought that with Camaris dead, the sword would find a new bearer, one less likely to complicate their scheme. After all, Thorn was not a loyal creature like Binabik's wolf."

Simon leaned back and stared at nothing. "So all our hopes, our quest for the swords, were a trap. And we walked into it like children." He scowled. Isgrimnur knew that it was himself he berated.

"It was a damnably clever trap," the duke offered. "One that must have been a-building for a long time. And in the end they failed."

"Are we sure?" Simon turned to Jiriki. "Do we *know* they've failed?"

"Isgrimnur has told how the Hikeda'ya fled when the tower fell—those that still lived. I am not sorry that he did not pursue them, for they are few now, and our kind give birth infrequently. Many died at Naglimund, and many here. The fact that they fled instead of fighting to the death tells much: they are broken."

"Even after Utuk'ku wrested control of the Pool from us," Aditu said, "we fought her still. And when Ineluki began to cross over, we felt it." The long pause was eloquent. "It was *terrible*. But we also felt it when his mortal body—King Elias' body—died. Ineluki had abandoned the nowhere-place which had been his refuge, and risked final dissolution to enter back into the world. He risked, and he lost. There is surely nothing left of him."

Simon raised an eyebrow. "And Utuk'ku?"

"She lives, but her power is destroyed. She, too, gambled much, and it was through her magics that Ineluki's being could be fixed in the tower during the moment when Time was turned withershins. The failure blasted her." Aditu fixed him with her amber eyes. "I saw her, Seoman, saw her in my thoughts as clearly as if she stood before me. The fires of Stormspike have gone dark and the halls are empty. She is all but alone, her silver mask shattered."

"You mean you saw her? Saw her face?"

Aditu inclined her head. "Horror of her own antiquity made her hide her features long ago—but to you, Seoman Snowlock, she would seem nothing but an old woman. Her features are lined and sagging, her skin mottled. Utuk'ku Seyt-Hamakha is the Eldest, but her wisdom was corrupted by selfishness and vanity ages ago. She was ashamed that the years had caught up with her. And now even the terror and strength she wielded is gone."

"So the power of *Sturmrspeik* and the White Foxes is finished," Isgrimnur said. "We have suffered many losses, but we could have lost far more, Simon—lost everything. We have much to thank you and Binabik for."

"And Miriamele," Simon said quietly.

"And Miriamele, of course."

The young man looked at the gathering, then turned back to the duke. "There's more brings you here, I know. You answered my questions. What are yours?"

Isgrimnur couldn't help noticing how Simon's confidence had grown. He was still courteous, but his voice suggested that he deferred to no one. Which was as it should be. But there was an undercurrent of anger which made Isgrimnur hesitate before speaking. "Jiriki has been talking to me about you, about your ... heritage. I was astonished, I must say, but I can only believe him, since it fits with everything else we've learned—about John, about the Sithi, everything. I thought we would be bringing you the news, but something in your face told me you had already discovered it."

Simon's lips quirked in an odd half-smile. "I did."

"So you know that you are of the blood of Eahlstan Fiskerne," Isgrimnur forged on, "last king of Erkynland in the centuries before Prester John."

"And the founder of the Scroll League," Binabik added.

"And the one who *truly* killed the dragon," Simon said dryly. "What of it?" Despite his calm, something intense and powerful moved beneath the surface. Isgrimnur was puzzled.

Before Isgrimnur could say anything more, Jiriki spoke. "I am sorry I could not tell you earlier what I knew, Seoman, my friend. I feared it could only burden and confuse you, or perhaps lead you to take dangerous risks."

"I understand," Simon said, but he did not sound pleased. "How did you know?"

"Eahlstan Fiskerne was the first mortal king after the fall of Asu'a to reach out to the Zida'ya." The sun was setting outside, and the sky beyond the windows was turning dark. A brisk wind coursed through the throne room and ruffled some of the banners on the floor. Jiriki's white hair fluttered. "He knew us, and some of our folk came at times to meet with him in the caverns below the Hayholt—in the ruins of our home. He feared that what we Zida'ya knew would be lost forever, and even that we might turn against humankind entirely after the destruction that Fingil had wrought. He was not far wrong. There has been little love for mortals among my folk. There was also little love for immortals among Eahlstan's own kind. But as the years of his reign passed, small steps were taken, small confidences exchanged, and a delicate trust began to build. We who were involved kept it a secret." Jiriki smiled. "I say 'we,' but I myself was only the message-bearer, running errands for First Grandmother, who could not let her continuing interest in mortals be widely known, even within her own family."

"I was always jealous of you, Willow-Switch," said Aditu, laughing. "So young, and yet with such important tasks!"

Jiriki smiled. "In any case, whatever might have been if Eahlstan had lived and his line had continued did not come to pass. The fire-worm Shurakai came, and in killing it, Eahlstan was himself killed. Whether his eventual successor John knew something of Eahlstan's secret dealings with us and feared we would expose John's lie that he was the dragon-slayer or there was some other reason for his enmity toward us, I do not know. But John set out to drive us from the last of our hiding places. He did not find them all, and never came near to discovering Jao é-Tinukai'i, but he did us great harm. Almost all our contact with mortals ended during John's life."

Simon folded his hands. "I am sorry for the things my people have done. And I am glad to know my ancestor was such a man."

"Eahlstan's folk scattered before the wrath of the dragon. Eventually they settled into their exile, I am told," Jiriki said. "And when John came and conquered, all hope of regaining the Hayholt was gone. So they nursed their secret and went on, a fishing folk living close to the waters as they had been in the days of Eahlstan Fiskerne's ancestors. But Eahlstan's ring they kept in the royal family, and passed it down from parent to child. One of Eahlstan's great-grandchildren, a scholar like his forebear, studied the old Sithi runes from one of Eahlstan's treasured scrolls, then had the motto that was the family's pride—and Prester John's secret shame—inscribed upon the ring. That was what Morgenes held in trust for you, Seoman: your past."

"And I'm certain he would have told me some day." Simon had listened to Jiriki's tale with poorly-hidden tension. Isgrimnur stared, looking for the cracks in Simon's nature that he half-expected, but feared, to see. "But what has it to do with anything now? All the royal blood in the world did not make me less of a dupe for Pryrates and the Storm King. It's a pretty tale, no more. Half the noble houses in Nabban must have Imperators in their history. What of it?" His jaw was set belligerently.

Several of the company turned to Isgrimnur. The duke moved uncomfortably on the step. "Erkynland needs a ruler," he said at last. "The Dragonbone Chair is empty."

Simon's mouth opened, then closed, then opened again.

*"And. . . ?"* he said at last. He stared at Isgrimnur distrustfully. "Miriamele is in good health and has only a few wounds. In fact, she is just the same as she ever was,"—the bitterness in his voice was plain—"so surely she will soon be able to rule."

"It is not her health that concerns us," said the duke gruffly. Somewhere, this conversation had gone wrong. Simon was acting like one awakened from his rightful sleep by a group of misbehaving children. "It is—damn it, it's her father!"

"But Elias is dead. She killed him herself. With the White Arrow of the Sithi." Simon turned to Jiriki. "Come to think of it, since that arrow certainly saved my life, I suppose we have evened our debt."

The Sitha did not respond. The immortal's face was, as usual, unrevealing, but something in his posture suggested he was troubled.

"The people have suffered so under Elias that they may not trust Miriamele," Isgrimnur said. "It's foolish, I know, but there it is. If Josua had lived, they might have welcomed him with open arms. The barons know the prince resisted Elias ever since he began to go bad, that he suffered terribly and fought his way back from exile. But Josua is dead."

"Miriamele did all those things, too!" Simon cried angrily. "This is nonsense!"

"We know, Simon," said Tiamak. "I traveled with her a long way. Many of us know of her bravery."

"Yes, I know it, too," Isgrimnur growled, his own irritation flaring. "But what is true does not matter here. She fled Naglimund before the siege started and she did not reach Sesuad'ra until after Fengbald had been defeated. Then she vanished again, and wound up in the Hayholt with her father at the very ending." He grimaced. "And there are tales, doubtless spread by that whoreson Aspitis Preves, that she was his doxy while he served Pryrates. Rumors are flying."

"But some of those things are true of me, too. Am *I* a traitor?"

"Miriamele is not a traitor, God knows—and *I* know."

Isgrimnur glared at him. "But after what her father has done, she may not be trusted. The people want someone on the throne they can trust."

"Madness!" Simon slapped his hands against his thighs, then turned to the Sithi. He seemed ready to burst. "What do you two think of this?" he demanded.

"We do not concern ourselves in these kind of mortal affairs," Jiriki said a little stiffly.

"You are our friend, Seoman," Aditu added. "Whatever we can do for you to help you in this time, we will. However, we also have only respect for Miriamele, though we know her but little."

Simon turned to the troll. "Binabik?"

The little man shrugged. "I cannot say. Isgrimnur and the rest of you must be making decisions to settle it yourselves. You and Miriamele are both my friends. If you are wishing advice later, Simon, we will take Qantaqa off for walking and we will speak."

"Speak about what? People telling lies about Miriamele?"

Isgrimnur cleared his throat. "He means he will talk to you about accepting the crown of Erkynland."

Simon turned back to stare at the duke. This time, for all his newfound maturity, the young man could not hide any of his feelings. "You are . . . you are offering *me* the throne?" he asked derisively, incredulously. "This *is* madness! Me? A kitchen boy!"

Isgrimnur could not help smiling. "You are much more than a kitchen boy. Your deeds are already filling up songs and stories everywhere between here and Nabban. Wait until the Battle in the Tower is added to the tally."

"Aedon preserve me," Simon said in disgust.

"But there are more important things." The duke grew serious. "You are well-liked and well-known. Not only did you battle a dragon, you fought bravely for Sesuad'ra and Josua, and people remember that. And now we can tell them that you have the blood of Saint Eahlstan Fiskerne, one of the most beloved men ever to hold a throne. In fact, it if weren't true, I would be tempted to make it up."

"But it doesn't mean *anything!*" Simon exploded.
"Don't you think I've thought about it? I've been doing
nothing *but* thinking since the moment I realized. I am a
scullion who was taught by a very wise, very kind man.
I have been lucky in my friends. I have been caught up in
terrible things, I did what I had to, and I lived through it.
None of that has anything to do with who my great-great-
however-many-greats-grandfather was!"

Isgrimnur waited a few moments after Simon finished,
letting some of the youth's anger pass. "But don't you
see," the duke said gently, "it doesn't matter whether it
changes anything or not. As I said, I don't think it really
matters much if it's *true* or not. Dror's red mallet, Simon,
Prester John's story was a myth—a lie! I've had to struggle with that discovery myself in the last few days. But
does it make him any less a king? People need to believe
something whether you want them to or not. If you don't
give them things to believe, they will make things up.

"Right now they are frightened of the future. Most of
the world we know is in a shambles, Simon. And the survivors are wary of Miriamele because of who she is and
because of uncertainty about what she's done—and because she's a young woman, to speak bluntly. The barons
want a man, someone strong but not too strong, and they
want no civil wars over a reigning queen's choice of hus-
bands." Isgrimnur reached out to touch Simon's arm, but
decided against it and drew his hand back. "Listen to me.
The people who followed Josua love you, Simon, almost
as much as they loved the prince. More in some ways,
perhaps. You know and I know that what blood flows in
you makes no difference—it's all red. But your people
need to believe in something, and they are cold and hurting and homeless."

Simon stared at him. Isgrimnur could not help feeling
the force of the young man's rage. He had grown indeed.
He would be a formidable man—no, he was so already.

"And for such tricks you would have me betray
Miriamele?" Simon demanded.

"Not betray," Isgrimnur said. "I will give you a few
days to think about it, then I will go and put it to her my-

self. We will bury our dead tomorrow, and the people will see us all together. That will be enough for now." The duke shook his head. "I'm not going to lie to her, Simon—that's not my way—but I wanted you to have a chance to hear me first." He suddenly felt immensely sorry for the young man.

*He probably thought he would have a chance to lick his wounds in peace—and he's got plenty of them. We all do.*

"Think about it, Simon. We need you—all of us. It will be hard enough for me to pull my own dukedom together, not to mention what will happen to young Varellan, orphaned in Nabban, and whoever still remains in Hernystir. We need at least the appearance of the High King's Ward again, and someone the people trust sitting on the throne at the Hayholt."

He rose from the low stair, trying not to show how much his back hurt, bowed stiffly to Simon—which in itself was an odd sensation—and stumped away across the throne room, leaving the rest of the circle in silence. He could feel Simon's eyes on his back.

*God help me,* Isgrimnur thought as he emerged into the twilight. *I need a rest. A long rest.*

❧

He looked up from the fire at the sound of footsteps. "Binabik?"

She moved forward into the light. Despite the cool spring night and the patches of still unmelted snow, her feet were bare. Her cloak fluttered in the breeze that swept down the hillside from the Hayholt.

"I couldn't sleep," she said.

For a moment Simon hesitated. He had not expected anyone, least of all her. After the day-long memorial for Josua, Camaris, Isorn, and the other dead, Binabik had gone off to spend the evening with Strangyeard and Tiamak, leaving Simon alone to sit before his tent and think. Her arrival seemed a thing he might have dreamed while staring into the campfire.

"Miriamele." He clambered awkwardly to his feet.

"Princess. Sit down, please." He gestured to a stone near the fire.

She sat, drawing her cloak close around her. "Are you well?" she asked at last.

"I'm ..." He paused. "I don't know. Things are strange."

She nodded. "It's hard to believe it's finished. It's hard to believe they're all gone forever."

He moved uncomfortably, not certain if she spoke of friends or enemies. "There are still lots of things to be done. People are scattered, the world has been turned upside-down...." Simon waved his hand vaguely. "There's lots to do."

Miriamele leaned forward, stretching her hands toward the fire. Simon watched the light play across her delicate features and felt his heart clutch hopelessly. All the royal blood in the world might run in his veins, rivers of it, but it did not matter if she did not care for him. During all of today's rites for the fallen, she had not once met his eyes. Even their friendship seemed to have faded.

*It would serve her right if I let them force me to take the throne.* He turned away to stare at the flames, feeling low and mean-spirited. *But it is hers by right.* She was Prester John's granddaughter. What difference did it make that some ancestor of Simon's had been king two centuries ago?

"I killed him, Simon," she said abruptly. "I traveled all that way to speak to him, to try to let him know I understood ... but instead I killed him." There was devastation in her words. "Killed him!"

Simon searched frantically for something to say. "You saved us all, Miriamele."

"He was a good man, Simon. Loud and short-tempered, perhaps, but he was ... before my mother ..." She blinked her eyes rapidly. "My own father!"

"You had no other choice." Simon ached to see her in such pain. "There was nothing else you could have done, Miri. You saved us."

"He knew me at the end. May God help me, Simon, I think he wanted me to do it. I looked at him ... and he was so unhappy. He was in so much pain!" She rubbed at her face with her cloak. "I will not cry," she said harshly. "I am so weary of crying!"

The wind grew stronger, sighing through the grass.

"And sweet Uncle Josua!" she said, more quietly now, but with a core of urgency. "Gone, like everyone else. Gone. All my family gone. And poor, tormented Camaris. Ah, God. What kind of a world is this?" Her shoulders were heaving. Simon reached out and awkwardly took her hand. She did not try to pull away, as he felt sure she would. Instead, they sat in silence except for the crackling of the fire. "And C–Cadrach, too," she murmured at last. "Oh, Merciful Elysia, in some ways he is the worst. He wanted only to die, but he waited for me ... for us. He stayed, despite all that had happened, despite all the terrible things I said to him." She lowered her head, staring at the ground. Her voice was painfully raw. "In his way, he loved me. That was cruel of him, wasn't it?"

Simon shook his head. There was nothing to say.

She suddenly turned to him, eyes wide. "Let's go away! We can take the horses and be half a dozen leagues from here by morning. I don't want to be a queen!" She squeezed his hand. "Oh, please don't leave me!"

"Go away? Where? And why would I leave you?" Simon felt his heart speed. It was hard to think, hard to believe he had truly understood her. "Miriamele, what are you talking about?"

"Curse you, Simon! Are you really as foolish as people used to think you were?" She now grasped his hand in both of hers; tears gleamed on her cheeks. "I don't care if you were a kitchen boy. I don't care that your father was a fisherman. I only want you, Simon. Oh, do you think I'm an idiot? I *am* an idiot, I suppose." Her laugh had a touch of wildness to it. She let go of his hand for a moment to wipe at her eyes again. "I've been brooding about this ever since the tower fell. I can't stand it! Uncle Isgrimnur and the others, they're going to make me take the throne, I know they will. And I'll go back to being the old Miriamele again, except this time it will be a thousand, thousand times worse! It will be a prison. And then I'll have to marry some other Fengbald—just because he's dead doesn't mean there aren't a hundred more just like him—and I'll never have another adventure, or be free, or do what I want to . . . and you'll go away, Simon! I'll lose you! The only one I really care about."

He stood, then pulled her up from the stone so he could put his arms around her. They were both shaking, and for a little time all he could do was grapple her to him and hang on, as though the wind might sweep her away.

"I've loved you so long, Miriamele." He could not keep his voice steady.

"You frighten me. You don't know how you frighten me." Her voice was muffled against his chest. "I don't know what you see when you look at me. But please don't go away," she said urgently. "Whatever happens, don't go away."

"I won't." He leaned back so he could see her. Her eyes were bright, fresh tears trembling on the lower lashes. His own eyes were blurring as well. He laughed; his voice cracked. "I won't leave you. I promised I wouldn't, don't you remember?"

"Sir Seoman. My Simon. You are my love." She sucked in her breath. "How did it happen?"

He leaned forward, pressing his mouth against hers, and as they clung to each other the starry sky seemed to spin around the place where they stood. Simon's hands moved beneath her cloak and he ran his fingers down the long muscles of her back. Miriamele shuddered and pulled him closer, rubbing her damp face against his neck.

Feeling the length of her pressed against him filled Simon with a kind of drunken, joyous madness. With his arms still locked around her, he took a few staggering steps toward the tent. He tasted the salt of her tears and covered her eyes and cheeks and lips with kisses as her hair swirled around him and stuck to his damp face.

Inside the tent, hidden from the prying stars, they wrapped themselves tightly around each other, clutching, drowning together. The wind plucked at the tent cloth, the only sound beside the rustle of clothes and the urgent hiss of their breathing.

For a moment the wind tugged the tent door open. In

the thin starlight, her skin was pale as ivory, so smooth and warm beneath his fingers that he could not imagine ever wanting to touch anything else. His hand slid across the curve of her breast and ran down her hip. He felt something catch inside him, something almost like terror, but sweet, so sweet. She held his face between her hands and drank his breath, murmuring wordlessly all the while, gasping quietly as his mouth moved down her neck and onto the delicate arch of her collarbone.

He pulled her closer, wanting to devour her, wanting to be devoured. His eyes overspilled with tears.

"I've loved you so long," he whispered.

Simon awakened slowly. He felt heavy, his body warm and boneless. Miriamele's head nestled in the hollow of his shoulder, her hair pressed softly against his cheek and neck. Her slender limbs were wrapped around him, one arm splayed across his chest, the fingers tickling beneath his chin.

He pulled her nearer. She murmured sleepily and rubbed her head against him.

The tent flap rustled. A silhouette, a slightly darker spot against the night sky, appeared in the gap.

"Simon?" someone whispered.

Heart pounding, suddenly ashamed for the princess, Simon tried to sit up. Miriamele made an unhappy sound as he slid her arm lower.

"Binabik?" he asked. "Is that you?"

The dark shape pushed in, letting the flap fall shut behind.

"Quiet. I am about to light a candle. Say nothing."

There was a muted clinking as flint met steel, then a tiny glow sprang up in the grass near the tent door. A moment later a flame bobbed at the end of a wick and soft candlelight filled the tent. Miriamele made a groggy noise of protest and buried her face deeper in Simon's neck. He gaped in astonishment.

Josua's thin face hovered above the candle.

"The grave cannot hold me," said the prince, smiling.

# 34

# Leavetaking

✦

**Simon's heart thumped.**

"Prince Josua. . . ?"

"Quietly, lad." Josua leaned forward. His eyes widened for a moment as he saw the head pillowed on Simon's chest, but then his smile returned. "Ah. Bless you both. Make her marry you, Simon—not that it will take much coaxing, I think. She will make a splendid queen with you to help her."

Simon shook his head in amazement. "But . . . but you . . . surely . . ." He stopped and took a breath. "You're dead—or everyone thinks you are!"

Josua seated himself, holding the candle low so that the gleam was mostly shielded by his body. "I should be."

"Tiamak saw your neck broken!" Simon whispered. "And no one could have gotten out of that place after we did."

"Tiamak saw me *struck*," Josua corrected him. "My neck should indeed have been broken—as it is, it still hurts fiercely. But I had my hand up." He extended his left arm and the tattered sleeve pulled back. Elias' manacle still hung on the swollen wrist, the metal flattened and scarred. "My brother and Pryrates forgot the gift they had given me. There is some poetry in that—or perhaps God wished to send a message about the value of suffering." The prince's sleeve rustled back into place. "I could barely use the hand for two days after I awoke, but the feeling is coming back now."

Miriamele stirred and opened her eyes. For a moment

they widened in dread, then she sat up, clutching the blanket to her breast. "Uncle Josua!"

Smiling crookedly, he lifted his finger to his lips. She pulled the top part of the blanket around her—leaving most of Simon exposed to the cold air—and threw her arms around him, weeping. Josua, too, seemed almost overcome. After a few moments Miriamele pulled away, then looked down at her bare shoulders and colored. She hurriedly lay back on the bedroll again and pulled the blanket up to her chin. Simon took back his half of it with gratitude.

"How can you be alive?" she said, laughing and dabbing at her eyes with the blanket's edge.

Josua explained again, showing her the dented manacle.

"But how did you escape?" Simon was anxious now for the story to continue. "The tower fell!"

The prince's head moved from side to side. Shadows flittered on the tent wall. "That is one thing I cannot know for certain, but my guess is that Camaris picked me up and carried me down in the first moments. I have come close to many campfires in the past nights, and heard many things. It sounds as though the confusion and smoke and flames were such that he could have gone down the stairwell ahead of you. We first came into the tower from beneath, through the tunnels; I believe he went out that way as well. All I know for certain is that I woke up beneath the stars, alone on the beach beside the Kynslagh. But who except Camaris would have had the strength to carry me so far?"

"If he went down before us, then Cadrach must have seen." Miriamele fell silent, pondering this.

"It's a miracle," Simon breathed. "But why have you told no one? And what did you mean when you said Miriamele would be queen? Won't you. . . ?"

"You do not understand," the prince said quietly. There was a strange edge of merriment in his voice. "I am dead. I wish to stay that way."

"What?"

"Just as I said. Simon, Miriamele, I was never meant to

rule. It was agony for me, but I saw no other course but to try to push Elias from the throne. Now God has opened a door for me, a door that I believed forever shut. To die or to take the crown were my only choices. Now, I have been given another."

Simon was stunned. For a long while he said nothing. Miriamele was silent, too. Josua watched them, a smile playing across his mouth.

"It is shocking, I know." The prince turned to his niece. "But you will be a far better ruler than I ever would—as will Simon."

"But you are John's true heir," Simon protested, "even more than Miriamele! And I'm just a kitchen boy you knighted! They say I'm a descendant of Saint Eahlstan, but that means nothing to me. It doesn't make me fit to rule Erkynland or anything else."

"I heard that tale, Simon. Isgrimnur and the others keep secrets poorly, if they ever meant to keep your heritage secret." Josua laughed quietly. "And I was not at all surprised to hear that you are of Eahlstan Fiskerne's blood. But as to whether that makes you more or less fit than me, Simon—you do not know all, even so. I am no more John's heir than you are."

"What do you mean?" Simon moved slightly so that Miriamele's head found a more comfortable position on his breast. She was not looking at Josua now, but up at Simon, her brow furrowed with worry or deep thought.

"Just as I said," the prince replied. "I am not John's son. Camaris was my father."

Simon sucked in his breath. "Camaris. . . ?"

Now Miriamele did look at the prince, as startled as Simon. "What are you talking about?"

"John was old when he married my mother, Efiathe of Hernysadharc," Josua said. "A measure of the distance in their years is that he felt no qualms about giving her a new name, Ebekah, as though she were a child." He frowned. "What happened after that is not particularly surprising. It is one of the commonest and oldest stories in the world, although I do not doubt she loved the king and he loved her. But Camaris was her special protector, a young man, as great and fabled a hero as John. What began as a deep respect and admiration between them grew into something more.

"Elias was John's child, but I was not. When my mother died birthing me, Camaris went mad. What could he think but that his sin had sentenced his beloved, who was also the wife of his closest friend, to death?" The prince shook his head. "His agony was such that he gave away everything he had, as one who knows he will die—and he must have felt he was dying, since every breath, every moment, was so full of pain and terrible shame. At last he took the horn Ti-tuno and went in search of the Sithi, perhaps to expiate the sin of participating in John's persecution of them, or perhaps, like Elias, he hoped the wise immortals could help him reach his beloved beyond death. Whatever the aim of his pilgrimage, Amerasu brought him secretly to Jao é-Tinukai'i, for reasons of her own. I have not discovered all that happened: my father was so distraught when he told me it was hard to make sense of everything.

"In any case, Amerasu met with him and took the horn back, perhaps to keep it for him, perhaps because it had belonged to her lost sons. Exactly what passed between them is still a mystery to me, but apparently whatever she told him was no comfort. My father left the forest deeps, still grieving. Soon after, when his despair finally outweighed even his terror of the sin of self-slaughter, he cast himself over the side of a ship into the Bay of Firannos. He survived somehow—he is fearfully strong, you know; that trait his blood certainly did not pass on to me!—but his wits were shadowed. He wandered through the southland, begging, living in the wilderness, subsisting on the charities of others, until he found his way at last to that Kwanitupul inn. In a way, I suppose, he knew peace for that time, despite the harshness of his life and his own poor wits. Then, after two score years, Isgrimnur found him, and soon peace was taken from him again. He awakened with the old horror still fresh in his mind, and the knowledge he had tried to murder himself added to it."

"Mother of Mercy!" Miriamele said feelingly. "That unhappy man!"

It was hard for Simon to encompass the breadth of the old knight's suffering. "Where is he now?"

Josua shook his head. "I do not know. Wandering once more, perhaps. I pray he did not try to drown himself again. My poor father! I hope that the demons that plague him are weaker now, although I doubt it. I will find him, and I will try to help him toward some kind of peace."

"So that's what you're going to do?" Simon asked. "Look for Camaris?"

Miriamele looked at the prince sharply. "What about Vorzheva?"

Josua nodded and smiled. "I will search for my father, but only after my wife and children are safe. There is much to be done, and it will be almost impossible for me to do any of it here in Erkynland where I am known." He laughed quietly. "You see, I am imitating Duke Isgrimnur and letting my beard grow to better my disguise." The prince rubbed his chin. "So tonight I ride south. Soon old Count Streáwe will have a late-night visitor. He owes me a favor . . . of which I will remind him. If anyone can spirit Vorzheva and the two children out of the Nabbanai court, it will be Perdruin's devious master. And he will enjoy the sport of it more than any payment I could ever make him. He loves secrets."

"The dead prince's wife and heirs disappearing." Simon could not resist a smile of his own. "That will make for a few stories and songs!"

"So it will. And I'm sure I will hear them and laugh." He reached over and squeezed Simon's arm, then leaned farther to embrace Miriamele, who clung to him for a long moment. "Now it is time for me to go. Vinyafod is waiting. It will be dawn soon."

Dreamlike as the conversation was, as the whole night had been, Simon was suddenly unwilling to let Josua go. "But if you find Camaris, and if you have Vorzheva with you, what then?"

The prince paused. "The southland will need at least one more Scrollbearer besides Tiamak, I believe—if the

League will have me. And I can think of nothing I would like better than to put all the cares of battle and judgment behind me to read and think. Perhaps Streáwe can help me purchase *Pelippa's Bowl,* and I will be the landlord of a quiet inn at Kwanitupul. An inn where friends will always be welcome."

"So you are truly going?" asked Miriamele.

"Truly. I have been given the gift of freedom—a gift I had never expected to receive. I would be ungrateful indeed to turn my back on it." He stood up. "It was very strange to hear my funeral rites spoken at the Hayholt today. Everyone should have such a chance while they still live—it gives one much to think about." He smiled. "Let me have a few hours' start at least, but then tell Isgrimnur, and whatever others can be trusted, that I live. They will be wondering about the disappearance of Vinyafod in any case. But do tell Isgrimnur soon. It pains me greatly to think of my old friend mourning for me: the loss of his son is burden enough. I hope he will understand what I do."

Josua moved toward the tent flap. "And you two, your adventures are only beginning, I think—although I hope those to come are happier." He blew out the candle and the tent was dark again. "Just as I would be a fool not to take what I have been given, Simon, you will be a fool indeed if you do not marry my niece—and Miriamele, you will be a fool if you do not take him. The two of you have much work to do, and many things to set right, but you are young and strong, and you have been given a schooling like none the world has ever seen. May God bless you both, and good luck. I will be watching you. You will both be in my prayers."

The tent flap lifted. Stars glimmered above Josua's shoulder, then all was dark again.

Simon settled back, his head whirling. Josua alive! Camaris the prince's father! And he, Simon, with a princess lying beside him. The world was unimaginably strange.

"So?" Miriamele asked suddenly.

"What?" He held his breath, worried by the tone of her voice.

"You heard my uncle," she said. "Are you going to marry me? And what's this about the blood of Eahlstan? Have you been hiding something from me all this time to pay me back for my serving-girl disguise?"

He exhaled. "I only found out myself yesterday."

After a long silence, she said: "You haven't answered my other question." She took his face and pulled it near hers, running her finger along the sensitive ridge of his scar. "You said you would never leave me, Simon. Now are you going to do what Josua told you to do?"

For answer, he laughed helplessly and kissed her. Her arms curled around his neck.

❦

They had gathered on the grassy hillside beneath the Nearulagh Gate. The great portal lay in ruins; birds fluttered above the stones, quarreling shrilly. Beyond the rubble the setting sun glinted from the wet roofs of the Hayholt. The Conqueror Star made a faint red smear in the northernmost corner of the darkening heavens.

Simon and Miriamele stood arm in arm, surrounded by friends and allies. The Sithi had come to say farewell.

"Jiriki." Simon gently disengaged himself from Miriamele and stepped forward. "I meant what I said before, although I said it in childish bad temper. Your arrow is gone, burned away when the Storm King vanished. Any debt between us is gone, too. You have saved my life enough times."

The Sitha smiled. "We will start afresh, then."

"I wish you didn't have to go."

"My mother and the others will recover more quickly in their homes." Jiriki gazed at the banners of his people ranged along the hillside, their bright clothes. "Look on that. I hope you will remember. The Dawn Children may never be gathered again in one place."

Miriamele stared down at the waiting Sithi and their

bold, impatient horses. "It is beautiful," she said. "Beautiful."

Jiriki smiled at her, then turned back to Simon. "So it is time for my folk to go back to Jao é-Tinukai'i, but you and I will see each other before long. Do you remember I told you once that it took no magical wisdom to say we would meet again? I will say it once more, Seoman Snowlock. The story is not ended."

"All the same, I will miss you—we will miss you."

"It may be that things will be better in days to come between my folk and yours, Seoman. But it will not happen swiftly. We are an old people, slow to change, and most mortals still fear us—not without reason after what the Hikeda'ya have done. Still, I cannot but hope that something has indeed changed forever. We Dawn Children, our day is past, but perhaps now we will not simply disappear. Perhaps when we are gone there will be something of us left behind beside our ruins and a few old stories." He clasped Simon's hand and then drew him forward until they embraced.

Aditu followed her brother, light-footed and smiling. "Of course you will come to see us, Seoman. And we will come to you, too. You and I have many a game of shent yet to play. I fear to see what clever new strategies you will have learned."

Simon laughed. "I'm sure you fear my shent-playing the way you fear deep snow and high walls—not at all."

She kissed him, then went to Miriamele and kissed her too. "Be kind and patient with each other," the Sitha said, eyes bright. "Your days will be long together. Remember these moments always, but do not ignore the sad times, either. Memory is the greatest of gifts."

Many others, some who would stay to help in the rebuilding of Erchester and the Hayholt and remain for the coronation, others soon to return to their own cities and people, clustered around. The Sithi gravely and sweetly exchanged farewells with them all.

Duke Isgrimnur pulled himself away from the crowd surrounding the immortals. "I'll be here yet a while, Simon, Miriamele—even after Gutrun's ship comes from

Nabban. But we'll have to leave for Elvritshalla before summer begins." He shook his head. "There will be an ungodly lot of work to do there. My people have suffered too much."

"We couldn't hope to begin here without you, Uncle Isgrimnur," said Miriamele. "Stay as long as you can, and we will send with you whatever may help you."

The duke lifted her in his broad arms and hugged her. "I am so happy for you, Miriamele, my dear one. I felt like such a damnable traitor."

She smacked at his arm until he put her down. "You were trying to do what was best for everyone—or what you thought was best. But you should have come to me in any case, you foolish man. I would happily have stepped aside for Simon, or you, or even Qantaqa." She laughed and spun in a circle, dress flaring. "But now I am happy, Uncle. Now I can *work*. We will put things to rights."

Isgrimnur nodded, a melancholy smile nestling in his beard. "I know you will, bless you," he whispered.

There was a piercing shout of trumpets and a rumble from the crowd. The Sithi were mounting. Simon turned and lifted his hand. Miriamele pushed in beneath his arm, pressing against him. Jiriki, at the head of the company, stood in his stirrups and raised his arm, then the trumpets called again and the Sithi rode. Light from the dying sun gleaming on their armor, they picked up speed; within moments they were only a bright cloud moving along the hillside toward the east. Snatches of their song hung in the wind behind them. Simon felt his heart leap in his chest, full of joy and sadness both, and knew the sight would live with him forever.

After a long and reverent quiet, the gathering at last began splitting apart. Simon and his companions started to wander down toward Erchester. A great bonfire had been lit in Battle Square, and already the streets, so long deserted, were full of people. Miriamele dropped behind to walk with Isgrimnur, slowing her pace to his. Simon felt a touch on his hand and looked down. Binabik was there, Qantaqa moving beside him like a gray shadow.

"I wondered where you were," said Simon.

"My farewells to the Sithi-folk were being said this morning, so Qantaqa and I were at walking along the Kynswood. Some squirrels that were living there have now come to a sad end, but Qantaqa is feeling very cheerful." The troll grinned. "Ah, Simon-friend, I was thinking of old Doctor Morgenes, and of the prideful feeling that he would have if he saw what is happening here."

"He saved us all, didn't he?"

"Certain it is that his planning gave us the only chance we had. We were being tricked by Pryrates and the Storm King, but had we not been alerted, Elias' ravagings would have been worse. Also, the swords would have been finding other bearers, and no fighting back would have happened in the tower. No, Morgenes could not be knowing all, but he did what no other could have done."

"He tried to tell me. He tried to warn us all about false messengers." Simon looked down Main Row at the hurrying figures and the flicker of firelight. "Do you remember the dream I had at Geloë's house? I know that was him. That he was . . . watching."

"I do not know what happens after we are dying," Binabik said. "But I am thinking you are right. Somehow, Morgenes was watching for you. You were being like a family for him, even more than his Scroll League."

"I will always miss him."

They walked along for a while without speaking. A trio of children ran past, one of them trailing a strip of colorful cloth which the others, laughing and shrieking, tried to catch.

"I must go soon myself," said Binabik. "My people in Yiqanuc are waiting, wondering no doubt what has happened here. And, being most important, Sisqinanamook is there, also waiting. Like you and your Miriamele, she and I have a tale that is long. It is time that we were married before the Herder and Huntress and all the folk of Mintahoq." He laughed. "Despite everything, I am thinking her parents will still have a small sadness when they see I have survived."

"Soon? You're going soon?"

The troll nodded. "I must. But as Jiriki said to you, we will have many more meetings, you and I."

Qantaqa looked at them for a moment, then trotted ahead, sniffing the ground. Simon kept his eyes forward, staring toward the bonfire as though he had never seen such a thing. "I don't want to lose you, Binabik. You're my best friend in the world."

The troll reached up and took his hand. "All the more reason that we should not be long parted. You will come to Yiqanuc when you can—surely there is being a need for the first *Utku* embassy ever to the trolls!—and Sisqi and I will come to see you." He nodded his head solemnly. "You are my dearest friend also, Simon. Always we will be in each others' hearts."

They walked on toward the bonfire, hand in hand.

✺

Rachel the Dragon wandered through Erchester, her hair bedraggled, her clothes tattered and soiled. All around, people ran laughing through the streets, singing, cheering, playing frivolous games as though the city were not falling apart around them. Rachel could not understand it.

For days she had hidden in her underground sanctuary, even after the terrible tremblings and shiftings had stopped. She had been convinced that the world had ended over her head, and felt no urge to leave her well-stocked cell to see demons and sorcerous spirits celebrating in the ruins of her beloved Hayholt. But at last curiosity and a certain resolve had gotten the better of her. Rachel was not the kind of woman to take even the end of the world without fighting back. Let them put her to their fiendish tortures. Blessed Rhiap had suffered, hadn't she? Who was Rachel to hesitate before the example of the saints?

Her first blinking, molelike view of the castle seemed to confirm her worst fears. As she made her way through the hallways, through the ruins of what had been her home and her greatest pride, her heart withered in her breast. She cursed the people or creatures who had done this, cursed them in a way that would have made Father Dreosan turn pale and hurry away. Wrath moved through her like a tide of fire.

But when she had finally emerged into the almost-deserted Inner Bailey, it was to discover one puzzlement after another. Green Angel Tower lay in a shambles of stone, and the destruction and fire-scorchings of recent battle were everywhere, but the few folk she encountered wandering through the desolation claimed that Elias was dead and that everything was to be made right again.

On the tongues of these, and of many others she met as she went down into Erchester, were the names of Miriamele, the king's daughter, and someone called Snowlock. These two, it was said—he a great hero of battles in the east, a dragon-slayer and warrior—had thrown down the High King. Soon they would be married. All would soon be made right. That was the refrain on every tongue: all would be made right.

Rachel had snorted to herself—only those who had never had the responsibilities she had would think this a task that could take less than years—but she could not help feeling curiosity and a faint flickering of hope. Perhaps better days were coming. The folk she met said Pryrates had died, too, burned to death somehow in the great tower. So a measure of justice had been done at least. Rachel's losses had finally been avenged, however tardily.

And perhaps, she had thought, Guthwulf could be saved and brought up again from darkness. He deserved a happier fate than to wander forever while the world aboveground returned to something like order.

Kind folk in Erchester had fed her from their own meager stores and given her a place to sleep. And all evening she had heard the stories of Princess Miriamele and the hero Snowlock, the warrior princeling with the dragon-scar. Perhaps, she had considered, when things were calm again she would offer her services to the new rulers. Surely a young woman like Miriamele, if she had been brought up at all well, would understand the need for order. Rachel did not think that her heart would ever entirely be in her work again, but felt sure she had something to offer. She was old, but there might still be use for her.

Rachel the Dragon looked up. While her thoughts had been meandering, her feet had led her down to the fringes of Battle Square, where a bonfire had been lit. As much as possible had been made of scant provisions, and a feast of sorts had been laid in the middle of the square. The remnants of Erchester's citizenry milled about, shouting, singing, dancing around the fire. The clamor was almost deafening. Rachel accepted a piece of dried fruit from a young woman, then wandered over to a shadowy corner to eat it. She sat down against the wall of a shop and watched the carryings-on.

A young man passed her, and his eye caught hers for a moment. He was thin and his face was sad. Rachel squinted. Something about him was familiar.

He seemed to have the same thought, for he wheeled and walked back toward her. "Rachel?" he asked. "Aren't you Rachel, the Mistress of Chambermaids?"

She looked at him, but could summon no name. Her head was full of the noise of people on the roofs shouting down to friends in the square. "I am," she said. "I was."

He stepped forward suddenly, frightening her a little, and put his arms around her. "Don't you remember me?" he asked. "I'm Jeremias! The chandler's boy! You helped me escape from the castle."

"Jeremias," she said, patting his back softly. So he had lived. That was a good thing. She was happy. "Of course."

He stepped back and looked at her. "Have you been here all along? No one has seen you in Erchester."

She shook her head, a little surprised. Why should anyone have been looking for her? "I had a room . . . a place I found. Under the castle." She raised her hands, unable to explain everything that had happened. "I hid. Then I came out."

Grinning, Jeremias grabbed her hand. "Come with me. There are people who will want to see you."

Protesting, although she did not quite know why— surely there was nothing better an old woman like her had to do—Rachel allowed herself to be led through the swirling crowds, right across Battle Square. With Jeremias tugging at her until she wanted to ask him to let go, they passed so close to the bonfire that she could feel its heat down into her cold bones. Within moments they had pushed through another knot of people and approached a line of armored soldiers who held them back with crossed pikes until Jeremias whispered something in the captain's ear. The sentries then let them through. Rachel had just enough strength to wonder what Jeremias had said, but too little breath to ask.

They stopped abruptly and Jeremias stepped past her toward a young woman sitting in the nearest of two tall chairs. As he spoke to her, the woman turned her gaze toward Rachel and her lips curled in a slow smile. The Mistress of Chambermaids stared at her in fascination. Surely that was Miriamele, the king's daughter—but she looked so much older! And she was beautiful, her fair hair curving around her face, shimmering in the fireglow. She looked every inch a queen.

Rachel felt a kind of gratitude sweep over her. Perhaps there would be some kind of order to life after all, at least a little. But what concern could Miriamele, this radiant creature as exalted as an angel, have with an old servant?

Miriamele turned and said something to the man sitting back in the shadows of the chair beside hers. Rachel saw him start, then clamber to his feet.

*Merciful Rhiap,* she thought. *He's so tall! This must be that Snowlock, that one they all speak of. Someone said his other name, what was it?*

". . . Seoman . . ." she said aloud, staring at his face. The beard, the scar, the streak of white in his hair—for a moment he was just a young man. Then she knew.

"*Rachel!*" In a few long steps he was before her. He stared down at her for a moment, his lips trembling, then a wide grin broke across his face. "Rachel!" he said again.

"Simon. . . ?" she murmured. The world had ceased to make any kind of sense. "You're . . . *alive?*"

He bent down and grabbed her, squeezing hard. He lifted her high in the air so that her feet wiggled above the ground. "Yes!" he laughed. "I'm alive! God knows how, but I'm alive! Oh, Rachel, you could never imagine what has happened, never, never, never!"

He put her down but took both her hands in his. She wanted to pull them free because tears were streaming down her cheeks. Could this be? Or had she finally gone mad? But there he was, red hair, idiot grin, big as life— bigger than life!

"Are *you* . . . Snowlock?"

"I am, I suppose!" He laughed again. "I am." He let go for a moment, then draped an arm around her. "There is so much to tell you—but we have time now, nothing but time." He lifted his head, shouting: "Quick! This is Rachel! Bring her wine, bring her food, get her a chair!"

"But what has happened?" She craned her neck to look up at him, impossibly tall, impossibly alive, but Simon for all that. "How can this be?"

"Sit," he said. "I will tell you all. And then we can begin the grand task."

She shook her head, dazed. "Grand task?"

"You were Mistress of Chambermaids . . . but you were always more. You were like a mother to me, but I was too young and stupid to see it. Now you shall have the honor you deserve, Rachel. And if you want it, you shall be the mistress of the entire Hayholt. Heaven knows, we need you. An army of servants will attend you, troops of builders, companies of chambermaids, legions of gardeners." He laughed, a man's loud laugh. "We will fight a war against the ruin we have made, and we will build the castle again. We will make our home a beautiful place once more!" He gave her a squeeze and steered her toward where Miriamele and Jeremias waited, smiling. "You will be Rachel the Dragon, General of the Hayholt!"

Tears trickled down her cheeks. *"Mooncalf,"* she said.

# Afterword

🐾

**Tiamak pushed** with his toe at the lilypad. The part of the moat in the shadow of the wall was quiet but for the hum of insects and the splashing of Tiamak's own feet dangling in the water.

He was watching a water beetle when he heard footsteps behind him.

"Tiamak!" Father Strangyeard sat down awkwardly beside him, but kept his sandaled feet out of the moat. "I heard you had arrived. How good it is to see you."

The Wrannaman turned and clasped the archivist's hand. "And you, dear friend," he said. "It is astonishing to see the changes here."

"A great deal can happen in a year," Strangyeard laughed. "And people have been hard at work. But what is *your* news since your last message?"

Tiamak smiled. "Much. I found the remnants of my townsmen, scattered mainly through other villages across the Wran. Many of them will come back to Village Grove, I think, now that the ghants have retreated to the deep swamp." His smile dwindled. "And my sister still does not believe half of what I tell her."

"Can you blame her?" asked Strangyeard gently. "I can scarcely believe the things I saw myself."

"No, I do not blame her." Tiamak's smile returned. "And I have finally finished *Sovran Remedys of the Wranna Healers*."

"Tiamak, my friend!" Strangyeard was honestly delighted. "But that is wonderful! I am hungry for it! Is there a chance I can read it soon?"

"Very soon. I brought it with me. Simon and Miriamele said they would have copies made here. Four writing-priests, just to work on my book!" He shook his head. "Who would ever have dreamed?"

"Wonderful," Strangyeard said again. His smile was mysterious. "Come, should we not head back? I think it is almost time."

Tiamak nodded and reluctantly pulled his feet from the water. The lily pad floated back into place.

"I have heard that this will be more than a memorial," the Wrannaman said as they gazed at the incomplete shell of stone, littered with the boards and covering cloths of absent workers, that rose where Green Angel Tower had stood. "That there will be archives as well." He turned suddenly to look at his friend. "Ah. I suspect you know more about those four writing-priests than you told me."

Strangyeard nodded and blushed. "That is *my* news," he said proudly. "I helped draw the plans. It will be magnificent, Tiamak. A place of learning where nothing will be lost or hidden. And I will have many assistants to help me." He smiled and stared across the grounds. Two slow-moving figures made their way through the building site and passed through the recently completed doorway into the shadowed interior. "Most likely my eye will be so bad by the time the thing is finished—if God has not yet called me, that is—that I won't be able to see it. But that does not worry me. I see it already." He tapped his head and his gentle smile grew wider. "Here. And it is wonderful, my friend, wonderful."

Tiamak took the priest's arm. They made their way across the grounds of the Inner Bailey.

"As I said, it is astonishing to see the changes." The marsh man looked up at the castle's hodgepodge of roofs, almost all patched now, gleaming in the late afternoon sun. Higher up, a scaffolding had been erected over the dome of the chapel. A few workmen moved across it, tying things down for the night. Tiamak's gaze roved to the far side of the Inner Bailey wall and he paused. "Hjeldin's Tower—it has no windows in it any more. They were red, were they not?"

"Pryrates' tower . . . and storehouse." Strangyeard sketched the Tree on his breast. "Yes. Fire will be put to it, I expect, then it will be leveled to the ground. It has been sealed a long time, but no one is in much of a hurry to go inside, and Simon—King Seoman, I suppose I should say, although that still sounds faintly strange to me—wants the entrance to the catacombs beneath sealed as well." The archivist shook his head. "You know I think knowledge is precious, Tiamak. But I have not objected to any part of that plan."

The Wrannaman nodded. "I understand. But let us talk of more pleasant things."

"Yes." Strangyeard smiled again. "Speaking of such, I have come by a fascinating object—part of the castellain's account book from the time of Sulis the Apostate. Someone found it when they were cleaning up the Chancelry. There are some astonishing things in it, Tiamak—just astonishing! I think we just have time to stop by my chamber and get it on our way to the dining hall."

"Let us go then, by all means," Tiamak said, grinning, but as he fell in beside the archivist, he turned for a last look at Hjeldin's Tower and its empty windows.

☷

"You see," Isgrimnur said softly. "They have covered it with fine stone, just as Miriamele said."

Gutrun wiped at her face with the scarf. "Read it to me."

The duke squinted down at the slab set into the floor. The place was open to the sky, but the light was fading fast. *"Isorn, son of Isgrimnur and Gutrun, Duke and Duchess of Elvritshalla. Bravest of men, beloved of God and all who knew him."* He straightened up, determined not to cry. He would be strong for his lost child. "Bless you, son," he whispered.

"He must be so lonely," Gutrun said, her voice quavering. "So cold in the ground."

"Hush." Isgrimnur put his arm around her. "Isorn is not here, you know that. He is in a better place. He would laugh to see us fret so." He tried to make his words firm. It did no good to question, to worry. "God has rewarded him."

"Of course." Gutrun sniffed. "But, Isgrimnur, I still miss him so!"

He felt his eyes misting and cursed quietly, then hastily made the Tree sign. "I miss him, too, wife. Of course. But we have our others to think of, and Elvritshalla—not to mention two godchildren down in Kwanitupul."

"Godchildren I cannot even brag about!" she said indignantly, then laughed and shook her head.

They stood a while longer, until the light had vanished and the stone slab had fallen into shadow. Then they went out again into the evening.

They sat in the dining hall, filling the chairs around John's Great Table. All the wall sconces held torches, and candles were set about the table as well, so that the long room was full of light.

Miriamele rose, her blue gown whispering in the sudden silence. The circlet on her brow caught the torchlight.

"Welcome, all." Her voice was soft but strong. "This house is yours and always will be. Come to us whenever you wish, stay as long as you like."

"But be sure and be here at least once a year," Simon said, and raised his cup.

Tiamak laughed. "It is a long journey for some of us, Simon," he said. "But we will always do our best."

Beside him, Isgrimnur thumped his goblet on the table. He had been making healthy inroads into the supply of beer and wine. "He's right, Simon. And speaking of long journeys, I don't see little Binabik."

Simon stood up and put his arm around Miriamele's shoulder, pausing for a moment to pull her close and brush the top of her head with a kiss. "Binabik and Sisqi have sent a bird with a message." He smiled. "They are performing the Rite of Quickening—Sludig knows what I'm talking about, since it almost got us all killed—and then traveling with their folk down-mountain to Blue Mud Lake. After that, they will come to visit us here." Simon's grin widened. "Then, next year, Sludig and I will be off to visit them in high Mintahoq!"

Sludig nodded his head vigorously as various jests were made. "The trolls invited me," he said proudly. "First what-do-they-call-it—'Croohok'—they have ever asked." He raised his cup. "To Binabik and Sisqi! Long life and many children!"

The toast was echoed.

"Do you really think you will slip off on such an adventure without me?" asked Miriamele, eyeing her husband. "Leave me home to do all the work?"

"Good luck trying to outrun Miri," Isgrimnur chortled. "There's a woman who's already traveled more of the world than you have!"

Gutrun elbowed him. "Let them speak."

Isgrimnur turned and kissed her cheek. "Of course."

"Then we will go together," Simon said grandly. "We will make it a royal progress."

Miriamele gave him a sour glance, then turned to Rachel the Dragon, who had paused in the hall's far doorway to quietly berate a serving lad. Rachel's eyebrows had shot up at Simon's offhand remark. Now she and Miriamele shared a look of disgusted amusement.

"Do you have any idea what sort of trouble that will be?" Miriamele demanded. "To take the whole court into the mountains to Yiqanuc?"

Simon looked around the hall at the amused faces of the guests. He ran his fingers through his red beard and grinned. "I am not quite civilized yet, but they are doing their best." Miriamele poked his ribs, then leaned against him again. He lifted his goblet high. "It is so good to see you all. Another toast! To the Prince's Company! Would that Josua were here to see it—but I know he will be honored, wherever he is!" The rest of the companions laughed, all now privy to the secret.

Tiamak stood. "As a matter of fact, I bring word from ... an absent friend. He sends his great love, and wishes you to know that he, his wife, and their children are well." The announcement was greeted with shouts of approval.

Isgrimnur rose abruptly, teetering a little. "And let us not forget to drink to all the others who also fought and fell that we could be here," he cried. "All of them." His voice shook a little. "God preserve their souls. May we never forget them!"

"Amen!" cried many others. When the cheers fell away, there was a long moment of silence.

"Now drink up," Miriamele ordered. "But keep your wits. Sangfugol has promised to play us a new song."

"And Jeremias will sing it. He has been practicing." The harper looked around. "I don't know where he has gotten to. It is annoying to have the singer unprepared."

"You mean some singers are prepared?" Isgrimnur laughed, then made a face of mock fear as Sangfugol waved a heel of bread at him threateningly.

"When your ears are other than stone, Duke Isgrimnur," Sangfugol replied with a certain frostiness, "then you can make jokes."

The hall had fallen back into merriment and general conversation when Jeremias appeared at Simon's shoulder and whispered something in his ear.

"Good," said Simon. "I am glad he came. But you, Jeremias, what are you doing, scuttling around like a servant? They are expecting you to sing later. Sit down here. Miri will pour you some wine." He got up and forced a protesting Jeremias into his chair, then walked toward the door.

In the entrance hall, a somber man with a dark horsetail of hair awaited him, still wearing traveling clothes and a cloak.

"Count Eolair." Simon went forward to clasp the Hernystirman's hand. "I hoped you would come. How was your journey?"

Eolair looked at him keenly, studying him as though they had never met before. He bent his knee. "Well enough, King Seoman. The roads are still not good, and it is a long trip, but there is little fear of bandits anymore. It does me good to get away from Hernysadharc. But you know of rebuilding."

"It is Simon, please. And Queen Inahwen? How is she?"

Eolair nodded, half-smiling. "She sends her greetings. But we will play those tunes later, I suppose, when Queen Miriamele and others can hear them—in the throne room, where these things must be done." He looked up suddenly. "Speaking of throne rooms, was that not the Dragonbone Chair I saw in the courtyard outside? With ivy growing upon it?"

Simon laughed. "Out for everyone to see. Fear not—a little wind and a little damp won't hurt those bones. They are stronger than rock. And neither Miri nor I could bear to sit in the thing."

"Some children were playing on it." Eolair shook his head in wonderment. "That was something I never thought to see."

"To the castle children, it's only something to climb on. Although they were a little worried at first." He extended a hand. "Come, let me take you in and give you something to drink and to eat."

Eolair hesitated. "Perhaps I would be better off finding a bed. It was a long ride today."

Now it was Simon's turn to look at Eolair carefully. "Forgive me if I am speaking out of turn," he said, "but I have known something for a long time that you should know too. I would have waited until we had spoken more, you and I, but perhaps it would be best to tell you now." He took a breath. "I met Maegwin before she died. Did you know? But the strange thing was that we were really leagues apart."

"I know something of it," said the Count of Nad Mullach. "Jiriki was with us. He tried to explain. It was difficult to understand what he meant."

"There will be much to talk about later, but here is the

one thing you must know." Simon's voice dropped. "She was herself at the last, and the only thing she regretted leaving was you, Count Eolair. She loved you. But by giving up her life she saved me and freed me to go to the tower. We might none of us be here today—Erkynland, Hernystir, everything else, all might be under cold shadows—were it not for her."

Eolair was silent for a while, his face expressionless. "Thank you," he said at last. A little of his brittleness seemed to have gone.

Simon gently took his arm. "Now come, please. Come and join us. Up the corridor you have a room full of friends, Eolair—some of them you don't even know yet!"

He led the count toward the dining hall. Firelight and the sound of laughing voices reached out to welcome them.

# Appendix

✦

# PEOPLE

## ERKYNLANDERS

Barnabas—Hayholt chapel sexton
Deornoth, Sir—of Hewenshire, Josua's knight
Eahlferend—Simon's fisherman father
Eahlstan Fiskerne—"Fisher King," founder of League of Scroll
Ebekah, also known as Efiathe of Hernysadharc—Queen of Erkynland, John's wife, mother of Elias and Josua
Elias—High King, John's oldest son, Josua's brother
Fengbald—Earl of Falshire, High King's Hand
Freobeorn—Freosel's father, a blacksmith of Falshire
Freosel—Falshireman, constable of New Gadrinsett
Guthwulf—Earl of Utanyeat
Heanwig—old drunkard in Stanshire
Helfgrim—Lord Mayor of Gadrinsett (former)

Inch—foundry master
Isaak—Fengbald's page
Jack Mundwode—mythical forest bandit
Jeremias—former chandler's apprentice, Simon's friend
John—King John Presbyter, High King, also known as "Prester John"
Judith—Hayholt Mistress of Kitchens
Leleth—Geloë's companion, once Miriamele's handmaid
Maefwaru—a Fire Dancer
Miriamele—Princess, Elias' daughter
Morgenes, Doctor—Scrollbearer, Simon's friend and mentor
Old Bent Legs—forge worker in Hayholt
Osgal—one of Mundwode's mythical band
Rachel—Hayholt Mistress of Chambermaids, also known as "The Dragon"
Roelstan—escaped Fire Dancer
Sangfugol—Josua's harper
Sceldwine—captain of the prisoned Erkynguardsmen
Shem Horsegroom—Hayholt groom
Simon—castle scullion (named "Seoman" at birth)
Stanhelm—forge worker
Strangyeard, Father—Scrollbearer, priest, Josua's archivist
Towser—King John's jester (original name "Cruinh")
Ulca—girl on Sesuad'ra, called "Curly Hair"
Welma—girl on Sesuad'ra, called "Thin One"
Wiclaf—former First Hammerman killed by Fire Dancers
Zebediah—a Hayholt scullion, called "Fat Zebediah"

## HERNYSTIRI

Airgad Oakheart—famous Hernystiri hero
Arnoran—minstrel
Bagba—cattle god
Brynioch of the Skies—sky god
Bulychlinn—fisherman in old story who caught a demon in his nets

Cadrach-ec-Crannhyr—monk of indeterminate Order, also known as "Padreic"

Caihwye—young mother

Craobhan—called "Old," adviser to Hernystiri royal house

Croich, House—a Hernystiri clan

Cuamh Earthdog—earth god

Deanagha of the Brown Eyes—Hernystiri goddess, daughter of Rhynn

Diawen—scryer

Earb, House—a Hernystiri clan

Eoin-ec-Cluias—legendary Hernystiri harper

Eolair—Count of Nad Mullach

Feurgha—Hernystiri woman, captive of Fengbald

Frethis of Cuihmne—Hernystiri scholar

Gullaighn—escaped Fire Dancer

Gwynna—Eolair's cousin and castellaine

Gwythinn—Maegwin's brother, Lluth's son

Hern—founder of Hernystir

Inahwen—Lluth's third wife

Lach, House—a Hernystiri clan

Lluth—King, father of Maegwin and Gwythinn

Llythinn—King, Lluth's father, uncle of John's wife Ebekah

Maegwin—Princess, daughter of Lluth

Mathan—goddess of household, wife of Murhagh One-Arm

Mircha—rain goddess, wife of Brynioch

Murhagh One-Arm—war god, husband of Mathan

Penemhwye—Maegwin's mother, Lluth's first wife

Rhynn of the Cauldron—a god

Siadreth—Caihwye's infant son

Sinnach—prince of Hernystir, also known as "The Red Fox"

Tethtain—former master of the Hayholt, "Holly King"

## RIMMERSMEN

Dror—storm god
Dypnir—one of Ule's band
Einskaldir—Isgrimnur's man, killed in forest
Elvrit—first Osten Ard king of Rimmersmen
Fingil Bloodfist—first human master of Hayholt, "Bloody King"
Frekke Grayhair—Isgrimnur's man, killed at Naglimund
Gutrun—Duchess, Isgrimnur's wife
Hengfisk—Hoderundian priest, Elias' cupbearer
Hjeldin—Fingil's son, "Mad King"
Ikferdig—third Hayholt ruler, "Burned King"
Isgrimnur—Duke of Elvritshalla, Gutrun's husband
Isorn—son of Isgrimnur and Gutrun
Jarnauga—Scrollbearer, killed at Naglimund
Nisse—(Nisses) author of *Du Svardenvyrd*
Skali—Thane of Kaldskryke, called "Sharp-nose"
Sludig—Isgrimnur's man
Trestolt—Jarnauga's father
Ule Frekkeson—leader of renegade band of Rimmersmen, son of Frekke

## NABBANAI

Aspitis Preves—Earl of Drina and Eadne
Benigaris—Duke of Nabban, son of Leobardis and Nessalanta
Benidrivis—first duke under John, father of Camaris and Leobardis
Brindalles—Seriddan's brother
Camaris-sá-Vinitta, Sir—John's greatest knight, also known as "Camaris Benidrivis"
Dinivan—Scrollbearer, secretary to Lector Ranessin, killed in Sancellan Aedonitis
Domitis—bishop of Saint Sutrin's cathedral in Erchester
Eneppa—Metessan kitchen woman, once called "Fuiri"
Elysia—mother of Usires Aedon, called "Mother of God"

Fluiren, Sir—knight of Sulian House, member of John's Great Table

Gavanaxes—knight of Honsa Claves (Clavean House) for whom Camaris was squire

Hylissa—Miriamele's mother, Elias' wife, killed in Thrithings

Lavennin, Saint—patron saint of Spenit Island

Leobardis—Duke of Nabban, killed at Naglimund

Metessan House—Nabbanai noble house, blue crane emblem

Munshazou—Pryrates' Naraxi serving woman

Nessalanta—Dowager Duchess, mother of Benigaris

Nuanni (Nuannis)—ancient Nabbanai sea god

Pasevalles—Brindalles' young son

Pelippa, Saint—called "Pelippa of the Island"

Plesinnen Myrmenis—ancient scholar

Pryrates—priest, alchemist, wizard, Elias' counselor

Ranessin—Lector of Mother Church, killed at Sancellan Aedonitis

Rhiappa, Saint—called "Rhiap" in Erkynland

Seriddan, Baron—Lord of Metessa, also known as "Seriddan Metessis"

Sulis, Lord—Nabbanai nobleman, former master of Hayholt, "Heron King," also known as "The Apostate"

Thures—Aspitis' young page

Usires Aedon—Aedonite religion's Son of God

Varellan—youngest son of Leobardis and Nessalanta, Benigaris' brother

Velligis—Lector of Mother Church

Xannasavin—Nabbanai court astrologer

Yistrin, Saint—saint linked to Simon's birth-day

## SITHI

Aditu (no-Sa'onserei)—daughter of Likimeya and Shima'onari; Jiriki's sister

Amerasu y-Senditu no'e-Sa'onserei—mother of Ineluki, killed at Jao é-Tinukai'i, called "First Grandmother," also known as "Amerasu Ship-Born"

Benayha (of Kementari)—famed Sithi poet and warrior
Briseyu Dawnfeather—Likimeya's mother, wife of Hakatri
Cheka'iso—called "Amber-Locks," member of Sithi clan
Chiya—member of Sithi clan, once resident of Asu'a
Contemplation House—Sithi clan
Drukhi—son of Utuk'ku and Ekimeniso, husband of Nenais'u
Gathering House—Sithi clan
Hakatri—Amerasu's son, vanished into West
Ineluki—Amerasu's son, killed at Asu'a, now Storm King
Initri—husband of Jenjiyana
Jenjiyana—wife of Initri, mother of Nenais'u, called "the Nightingale"
Jiriki (i-Sa'onserei)—son of Likimeya and Shima'onari, brother of Aditu
Kendhraja'aro—uncle of Jiriki and Aditu
Kira'athu—Sitha healer
Kuroyi—called "the tall horseman," master of High Anvi'janya, leader of Sithi clan
Likimeya (y-Briseyu no'e-Sa'onserei)—mother of Jiriki and Aditu, called "Likimeya Moon-Eyes"
Mezumiiru—mistress of moon in Sithi legend
Senditu—mother of Amerasu
Shi'iki—father of Amerasu
Shima'onari—father of Aditu and Jiriki, killed at Jao é-Tinukai'i
Vindaomeyo—famed arrow-maker of Tumet'ai, called "the Fletcher"
Year-Dancing House—Sithi clan
Yizashi Grayspear—leader of Sithi clan
Zinjadu—of Kementari, called "Lore-Mistress"


# QANUC

Binabik (Binbiniqegabenik)—Scrollbearer, Singing Man of Qanuc, Simon's friend
Chukku—legendary troll hero
Kikkasut—legendary king of birds

Nimsuk—Qanuc herder, one of Sisqi's troop
Nunuuika—the Huntress
Ookequk—Scrollbearer, Binabik's master
Qinkipa (of the Snows)—snow and cold goddess
Sedda—moon goddess
Sisqi (Sisqinanamook)—daughter of Herder and Huntress, Binabik's betrothed
Snenneq—herd-chief of Lower Chugik
Uammannaq—the Herder

## THRITHINGS-FOLK

Fikolmij—Vorzheva's father, March-thane of Clan Mehrdon
Hotvig—High Thrithings randwarder, Josua's man
Lezhdraka—Thrithings-man, mercenary chieftain
Ozhbern—High Thrithings-man
Ulgart—a mercenary captain from the Meadow Thrithing
Vorzheva—Josua's wife, daughter of Fikolmij

## PERDRUINESE

Charystra—landlady of *Pelippa's Bowl*
Lenti—Streáwe's servant, called "Avi Stetto"
Streáwe, Count—master of Perdruin
Tallistro, Sir—famous knight of John's Great Table
Xorastra—Scrollbearer, first owner of *Pelippa's Bowl*

## WRANNAMEN

Buayeg—owner of "the spirit-hut" (Wrannaman fable)
He Who Always Steps on Sand—god
He Who Bends the Trees—wind god
Inihe Red-Flower—woman in Tiamak's song
Nuobdig—Husband of the Fire Sister in Wrannaman legend
Rimihe—Tiamak's sister

She Who Birthed Mankind—goddess
She Who Waits to Take All Back—death goddess
Shoaneg Swift-Rowing—man in Tiamak's song
They Who Breathe Darkness—gods
They Who Watch and Shape—gods
Tiamak—Scrollbearer, herbalist
Tugumak—Tiamak's father
Twiyah—Tiamak's sister
Younger Mogahib—man of Tiamak's village

## NORNS

Akhenabi—spokesman at Naglimund
"Born-Beneath-Tzaaihta's-Stone"—one of Utuk'ku's Talons
"Called-by-the-Voices"—one of Utuk'ku's Talons
Ekimeniso Blackstaff—husband of Utuk'ku, father of Drukhi
Mezhumeyru—Norn version of "Mezumiiru"
Utuk'ku Seyt-Hamakha—Norn Queen, Mistress of Nakkiga
"Vein-of-Silverfire"—one of Utuk'ku's Talons

## OTHERS

Derra—a half-Thrithings child
Deornoth—a half-Thrithings child
Gan Itai—Niskie of *Eadne Cloud*
Geloë—a wise woman, called "Valada Geloë"
Imai-an—a dwarrow
Ingen Jegger—Black Rimmersman, huntsman of Utuk'ku, killed at Jao éTinukai'i
Injar—Niskie clan living on Risa Island
Nin Reisu—Niskie of *Emettin's Jewel*
Ruyan Vé—patriarch of Tinukeda'ya, called "The Navigator"
Sho-vennae—a dwarrow

Veng'a Sutekh—called "Duke of the Black Wind," one of the Red Hand

Yis-fidri—a dwarrow, Yis-hadra's husband, master of the Pattern Hall

Yis-hadra—a dwarrow, Yis-fidri's wife, mistress of the Pattern Hall

## PLACES

*Anvi'janya*—place of Kuroyi's dwelling, also known as "Hidden" or "High" Anvi'janya

*Ballacym*—walled town on outskirts of Hernysadharc territory

*Bradach Tor*—high peak in Grianspog Mountains

*Bregshame*—small town on ·River Road between Stanshire and Falshire

*Cathyn Dair, by Silversea*—Hernystiri town from Miriamele's song

*Cavern of Rending*—where Talons of Utuk'ku are trained

*Chamul Lagoon*—a place in Kwanitupul

*Chasu Yarinna*—town built around keep, just northeast of Onestrine Pass in Nabban

*Elvritshalla*—Isgrimnur's ducal seat in Rimmersgard

*Falshire*—wool-harvesting city in Erkynland, devastated by Fengbald

*Fiadhcoille*—forest southeast of Nad Mullach, also known as "Stagwood"

*Fire Garden*—tiled open space on Sesuad'ra

*Frasilis Valley*—valley east of Onestrine Pass (other side of pass from Commeis Valley)

*Garwynswold*—small town on River Road between Stanshire and Falshire

*Gratuvask*—Rimmersgard river, runs past Elvritshalla

*Grenamman*—island in Bay of Firannos

*Hall of Five Staircases*—chamber in Asu'a where Briseyu died

*Harcha*—island in Bay of Firannos

*Hasu Vale*—valley in Erkynland

*Hekhasór*—former Sithi territory, called "Hekhasór of the Black Earth"

*House of Waters*—Sithi building on Sesuad'ra

*Khandia*—a lost and fabled land

*Kiga'rasku*—waterfall beneath Stormspike, called "the Tearfall"

*Leavetaking House*—Sithi building on Sesuad'ra, later center of Josua's exile court (Sithi name: "Sesu-d'asu")

*M'yin Azoshai*—Sithi name for Hern's Hill, location of Hernysadharc

*Maa'sha*—hilly former territory of Sithi

*Mezutu'a*—the Silverhome, abandoned Sithi and dwarrow city beneath Grianspog

*Mount Den Haloi*—mountain from Book of the Aedon where God created world

*Naraxi*—island in Bay of Firannos

*Observatory, The*—domed Sithi building on Sesuad'ra

*Onestrine Pass*—pass between two Nabbanai valleys, site of many battles

*Peat Barge Quay*—dock in Kwanitupul

*Peja'ura*—former forested home of Sithi, called "cedar-mantled"

*Pulley Road*—road in Stanshire

*Risa*—island in Bay of Firannos

*Shisae'ron*—broad meadow valley, once Sithi territory

*Si'injan'dre Cave*—place of Drukhi's confinement after Nenais'u's death

*Soakwood Road*—a major thoroughfare of Stanshire

*Spenit*—island in Bay of Firranos

*Taig Road*—road leading through Hernysadharc, also known as "Tethtain's Way"

*Venyha Do'sae*—original home of Sithi, Norns, Tinukeda'ya, called "The Garden"

*Vinitta*—island in Bay of Firannos

*Wealdhelm*—range of hills in Erkynland

*Ya Mologi*—("Cradle Hill") highest point in Wran, legendary creation spot

*Yakh Huyeru*—("Hall of Trembling") cavern beneath Stormspike

*Yasirá*—Sithi sacred meeting place

# CREATURES

*Bukken*—Rimmersgard name for diggers, also called "Boghanik" by trolls

*Cat*—a gray (in this case) and undistinguished quadruped

*Diggers*—small, manlike subterranean creatures

*Ghants*—chitinous Wran-dwelling creature

*Giants*—large, shaggy, manlike creatures

*Drochnathair*—Hernystiri name for dragon Hidohebhi, slain by Ineluki and Hakatri

*Homefinder*—Simon's mare

*Hunën*—Rimmersgard name for giants

*Igjarjuk*—ice-dragon of Urmsheim

*Kilpa*—manlike marine creatures

*Niku'a*—Ingen Jegger's chief hound, bred in kennels of Stormspike

*Oruks*—fabulous water monsters

*Qantaqa*—Binabik's wolf companion, mount, and friend

*Shurakai*—fire-drake slain beneath Hayholt whose bones make up the Dragonbone Chair

*Vildalix*—Deornoth's horse

*Vinyafod*—Josua's horse

*Water-wights*—fabulous water monsters

# THINGS

*A-Genay'asu*—("Houses of Traveling Beyond") places of mystical power and significance

*Aedontide*—holy time celebrating birth of Usires Aedon

*"Badulf and the Straying Heifer"*—a song Simon tries to sing to Miriamele

*Battle of Clodu Lake*—battle John fought against Thrithings-men, also known as "Battle of the Lakelands"

*"Bishop's Wagon, The"*—a Jack Mundwode song

*Boar and Spears*—emblem of Guthwulf of Utanyeat

*Breathing Harp, The*—Master Witness in Stormspike

*Bright-Nail*—sword of Prester John, formerly called "Minneyar," containing nail from the Holy Tree and finger-bone of Saint Eahlstan

*"By Greenwade's Shore"*—song sung at Bonfire Night on Sesuad'ra

*Cellian*—Camaris' horn, made from dragon Hidohebhi's tooth. (Original name: "Ti-tuno")

*Citril*—root for chewing, grown in south

*Cockindrill*—Northern word for "crocodile"

*Conqueror Star*—a comet, ominous star

*Day of Weighing-Out*—Aedonite day of final judgment

*Door of the Ransomer*—seal of confession

*Du Svardenvyrd*—near-mythical prophetic book by Nisses

*Falcon, The*—Nabbanai constellation

*Fifty Families*—Nabbanai noble houses

*Floating Castle, The*—famous monument on Warinsten

*Frayja's Fire*—Erkynlandish winter flower

*Gardenborn, The*—all who came from Venyha Do'sae

*Good Peasant*—character from the proverbs of the Book of Aedon

*Gray Coast*—part of the shent board

*Gray-cap*—mushroom

*Great Swords*—Bright-Nail, Sorrow, and Thorn

*Great Table*—John's assembly of knights and heroes

*Green Column, The*—Master Witness in Jhiná T'seneí

*Hare, The*—Erkynlandish constellation name

*Harrow's Eve*—Octander 30, day before "Soul's Day"

*Hesitancy, a*—Norn spell

*High King's Ward*—protection of High King over countries of Osten Ard

*Hunt-wine*—Qanuc liquor

*Indreju*—Jiriki's witchwood sword

*Juya'ha*—Sithi art: pictures made of woven cords

*Kei-vishaa*—Substance used by Gardenborn to make enemies drowsy and weak

*Kingfisher, The*—Nabbanai constellation

*Kvalnir*—Isgrimnur's sword

*Lobster, The*—Nabbanai constellation

*Mansa Nictalis*—Night ceremony of Mother Church

*Market Hall*—a domed building in central Kwanitupul

*Mist Lamp*—a Witness, brought out of Tumet'ai by Amerasu

*Mixis the Wolf*—Nabbanai constellation

*Mockfoil*—a flowering herb

*Muster of Anitulles*—Imperatorial battle-muster from Golden Age of Nabban

*Navigator's Trust*—Niskie pledge to protect their ships at all cost

*Night Heart*—Sitha star-name

*Ocean Indefinite and Eternal*—Niskie term for ocean crossed by Gardenborn

*Oldest Tree*—Witchwood tree growing in Asu'a

*One Who Fled, The*—Aedonite euphemism for the Devil

*Pact of Sesuad'ra*—agreement of Sithi and Norn to part

*Pool of Three Depths, The*—Master Witness in Asu'a

*Prise'a*—"Ever-fresh," a favorite flower of Sithi

*Quickweed*—Wran herb

*Rabbit-nose*—mushroom

*Red knifebill*—Wran bird

*Rhao iye-Sama'an*—the Master Witness at Sesuad'ra, called the "Earth-Drake's Eye"

*Rhynn's Cauldron*—Hernystiri battle-summoner

*Rite of Quickening*—Qanuc Spring ceremony

*Saint Granis' Day*—a holy day

*Saint Rhiappa's*—a cathedral in Kwanitupul

*Sand Beetle, The*—Wran name for constellation

*Serpent, The*—Nabbanai constellation

*Shadow-mastery*—Norn magics

*Shard, The*—Master Witness in Mezutu'a

*Shent*—a Sithi game of socializing and strategy

*Snatch-the-feather*—Wran gambling game

*Sorrow*—Elias' sword, a gift from Ineluki the Storm King

*Speakfire, The*—Master Witness in Hikehikayo

*Spinning Wheel*—Erkynlandish name for constellation

*Sugar-bulb*—Wran tree

*Tarbox, The*—inn at Falshire

*Tethtain's Axe*—sunk in the heart of a beech tree in famous Hernystiri tale

*Thorn*—black star-sword of Camaris

*Ti-tuno*—Camaris' horn, made from dragon's tooth, also known as "Cellian"

*Tree, The*—(or "Holy Tree," or "Execution Tree") symbol of Usires Aedon's execution

*Twistgrass*—Wran plant

*Uncharted, The*—subject of Niskie oath

*Wailing Stone*—dolmen above Hasu Vale

*Wedge and Beetle, The*—Stanshire inn

*Wind Festival*—Wrannaman celebration

*Winged Beetle, The*—Nabbanai constellation

*Winged dolphin*—emblem of Streáwe of Perdruin

*Wintercap*—Erkynlandish winter flower

*"Woman from Nabban"*—one of Sangfugol's songs

*"Wormglass"*—Hernystiri name for certain old mirrors

*Yellow Tinker*—Wran plant

*Yrmansol*—tree of Erkynlandish Maia-day celebration

*Yuvenis' Throne*—Nabbanai constellation


*Knuckle Bones*—Binabik's auguring tools.
   Patterns include:
   Wingless Bird
   Fish-Spear
   The Shadowed Path
   Torch at the Cave-Mouth
   Balking Ram
   Clouds in the Pass
   The Black Crevice
   Unwrapped Dart
   Circle of Stones
   Mountains Dancing

# WORDS AND PHRASES

## QANUC

Henimaatuq! Ea kup!—"Beloved friend! You're here!"

Inij koku na siqqasa min taq—"When we meet again, that will be a good day."

Iq ta randayhet suk biqahuc—"Winter is not being the time for naked swimming."

Mindunob inik yat—"My home will be your tomb."

Nenit, henimaatuya—"Come on, friends."

Nihut—"Attack"

Shummuk—"Wait"

Ummu Bok—"Well done!" (roughly)

## SITHI

A y'ei g'eisu! Yas'a pripurna jo-shoi!—"You cowardly ones! The waves would not carry you!"

A-Genay'asu—"Houses of Traveling Beyond"

Hikeda'ya—"Cloud Children": Norns

Hikka Staja—"Arrow Bearer"

Hikka Ti-tuno—"Bearer of Ti-tuno"

M'yon rashí—(Sithi) "Breakers of Things"

Sinya'a du-n'sha é-d'treyesa inro—"May you find the light that shines above the bow"

Sudhoda'ya—"Sunset Children": Mortals

Sumy'asu—"Fifth House"

Tinukeda'ya—"Ocean Children": Niskies and dwarrows

Venyha s'ahn!—"By the Garden!"

Zida'ya—"Dawn Children": Sithi

## NABBANAI

á prenteiz—"Take him!" or "At him!"

Duos preterate!—"God preserve"

Duos Simpetis—"Merciful God"

Em Wulstes Duos—"By God's will"
Matra sá Duos—"Mother of God"
Otillenaes—"Tools"
Soria—"Sister"
Ulimor Camaris? Veveis?—"Lord Camaris? You live?"

## HERNYSTIRI

Goirach cilagh!—"Foolish (or mad) girl!"
Moiheneg—"between" or "empty place" (a neutral ground)
Smearech fleann—"dangerous book"

## RIMMERSPAKK

Vad es . . . Uf nammen Hott, vad es . . . ?—"What? In the name of God, what?"

## OTHER

Azha she'she t'chakó, urun she'she bhabekró . . . Mudhul samat'ai. Jabbak s'era memekeza sanayha-z'á . . . Ninyek she'she, hamut 'tke agrazh'a s'era yé . . ."— (Norn song) means Something Very Unpleasant
Shu'do-tkzayha!—(Norn) "mortals" (var. of Sithi "Sudhoda'ya")
S'h'rosa—(Dwarrow) Vein of stone

# A GUIDE TO PRONUNCIATION

## ERKYNLANDISH

Erkynlandish names are divided into two types, Old Erkynlandish (O.E.) and Warinstenner. Those names which are based on types from Prester John's native island of Warinsten (mostly the names of castle servants or John's immediate family) have been represented as variants on Biblical names (Elias—Elijah, Ebekah—Rebecca, etc.) Old Erkynlandish names should be pronounced like modern English, except as follows:

*a*—always *ah,* as in "father"
*ae*—*ay* of "say"
*c*—k as in "keen"
*e*—*ai* as in "air," except at the end of names, when it is also sounded, but with an *eh* or *uh* sound, i.e., Hruse—"Rooz-uh"
*ea*—sounds as *a* in "mark," except at beginning of word or name, where it has the same value as *ae*
*g*—always hard *g,* as in "glad"
*h*—hard *h* of "help"
*i*—short *i* of "in"
*j*—hard *j* of "jaw"
*o*—long but soft *o,* as in "orb"
*u*—*oo* sound of "wood," never *yoo* as in "music"

## HERNYSTIRI

The Hernystiri names and words can be pronounced in largely the same way as the O.E., with a few exceptions:
*th*—always the *th* in "other," never as in "thing"
*ch*—a guttural, as in Scottish "loch"
*y*—pronounce *yr* like "beer," *ye* like "spy"
*h*—unvoiced except at beginning of word or after *t* or *c*
*e*—*ay* as in "ray"
*ll*—same as single *l:* Lluth—Luth

## RIMMERSPAKK

Names and words in Rimmerspakk differ from O.E. pronunciation in the following:

*j*—pronounced *y:* Jarnauga—Yarnauga; Hjeldin—Hyeldin *(H* nearly silent here)
  *ei*—long *i* as in "crime"
  *ë*—*ee*, as in "sweet"
  *ö*—*oo*, as in "coop"
  *au*—*ow*, as in "cow"

## NABBANAI

The Nabbanai language holds basically to the rules of a romance language, i.e., the vowels are pronounced "ah-eh-ih-oh-ooh," the consonants are all sounded, etc. There are some exceptions.

*i*—most names take emphasis on second to last syllable: Ben-i-GAR-is. When this syllable has an *i*, it is sounded long (Ardrivis: Ar-DRY-vis) unless it comes before a double consonant (Antippa: An-TIHP-pa)

*es*—at end of name, *es* is sounded long: Gelles—Gelleez

*y*—is pronounced as a long *i*, as in "mild"

## QANUC

Troll-language is considerably different than the other human languages. There are three hard "k" sounds, signified by: *c*, *q*, and *k*. The only difference intelligible to most non-Qanuc is a slight clucking sound on the *q*, but it is not to be encouraged in beginners. For our purposes, all three will sound with the *k* of "keep." Also, the Qanuc *u* is pronounced *uh*, as in "bug." Other interpretations are up to the reader, but he or she will not go far wrong pronouncing phonetically.

## SITHI

Even more than the language of Yiqanuc, the language of the Zida'ya is virtually unpronounceable by untrained tongues, and so is easiest rendered phonetically, since the chance of any of us being judged by experts is slight (but not nonexistent, as Binabik learned). These rules may be applied, however.

*i*—when the first vowel, pronounced *ih,* as in "clip." When later in word, especially at end, pronounced *ee,* as in "fleet": Jiriki—Jih-REE-kee

*ai*—pronounced like long *i,* as in "time"

' (apostrophe)—represents a clicking sound, and should be not voiced by mortal readers.

## EXCEPTIONAL NAMES

*Geloë*—Her origins are unknown, and so is the source of her name. It is pronounced "Juh-LO-ee" or "Juh-LOY." Both are correct.

*Ingen Jegger*—He is a Black Rimmersman, and the "J" in Jegger is sounded, just as in "jump."

*Miriamele*—Although born in the Erkynlandish court, hers is a Nabbanai name that developed a strange pronunciation—perhaps due to some family influence or confusion of her dual heritage—and sounds as "Mih-ree-uh-MEL."

*Vorzheva*—A Thrithings-woman, her name is pronounced "Vor-SHAY-va," with the *zh* sounding harshly, like the Hungarian *zs*.